THE
SHADOW
MATRIX

A Novel of Darkover

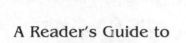

A Reader's Guide to
DARKOVER

THE FOUNDING

A "lost ship" of Terran origin, in the pre-Empire colonizing days, lands on a planet with a dim red star, later to be called Darkover.
DARKOVER LANDFALL

THE AGES OF CHAOS

1,000 years after the original landfall settlement, society has returned to the feudal level. The Darkovans, their Terran technology renounced or forgotten, have turned instead to free-wheeling, out-of-control matrix technology, psi powers and terrible psi weapons. The populace lives under the domination of the Towers and a tyrannical breeding program to staff the Towers with unnaturally powerful, inbred gifts of *laran*.
STORMQUEEN!
HAWKMISTRESS!

THE HUNDRED KINGDOMS

An age of war and strife retaining many of the decimating and disastrous effects of the Ages of Chaos. The lands which are later to become the Seven Domains are divided by continuous border conflicts into a multitude of small, belligerent kingdoms, named for convenience "The Hundred Kingdoms." The close of this era is heralded by the adoption of the Compact, instituted by Varzil the Good. A landmark and turning point in the history of Darkover, the Compact bans all distance weapons, making it a matter of honor that one who seeks to kill must himself face equal risk of death.

TWO TO CONQUER
THE HEIRS OF HAMMERFELL

THE RENUNCIATES

During the Ages of Chaos and the time of the Hundred Kingdoms, there were two orders of women who set themselves apart from the patriarchal nature of Darkovan feudal society: the priestesses of Avarra, and the warriors of the Sisterhood of the Sword. Eventually these two independent groups merged to form the powerful and legally chartered Order of Renunciates or Free Amazons, a guild of women bound only by oath as a sisterhood of mutual responsibility. Their primary allegiance is to each other rather than to family, clan, caste or any man save a temporary employer. Alone among Darkovan women, they are exempt from the usual legal restrictions and protections. Their reason for existence is to provide the women of Darkover an alternative to their socially restrictive lives.

THE SHATTERED CHAIN
THENDARA HOUSE
CITY OF SORCERY

AGAINST THE TERRANS
—THE FIRST AGE (Recontact)

After the Hastur Wars, the Hundred Kingdoms are consolidated into the Seven Domains, and ruled by a hereditary aristocracy of seven families, called the Comyn, allegedly descended from the legendary Hastur, Lord of Light. It is during this era that the Terran Empire, really a form of confederacy, rediscovers Darkover, which they know as the fourth planet of the Cottman star system. The fact that Darkover is a lost colony of the Empire is not easily or readily acknowledged by Darkovans and their Comyn overlords.

REDISCOVERY *(with Mercedes Lackey)*
THE SPELL SWORD
THE FORBIDDEN TOWER
STAR OF DANGER
WINDS OF DARKOVER

AGAINST THE TERRANS
—THE SECOND AGE (After the Comyn)

With the initial shock of recontact beginning to wear off, and the Terran spaceport a permanent establishment on the outskirts of the city of Thendara, the younger and less traditional elements of Darkovan society begin the first real exchange of knowledge with the Terrans—learning Terran science and technology and teaching Darkovan matrix technology in turn. Eventually Regis Hastur, the young Comyn lord most active in these exchanges, becomes Regent in a provisional government allied to the Terrans. Darkover is once again reunited with its founding Empire.

THE BLOODY SUN
HERITAGE OF HASTUR
THE PLANET SAVERS
SHARRA'S EXILE
WORLD WRECKERS
EXILE'S SONG

THE DARKOVER ANTHOLOGIES

These volumes of stories, edited by Marion Zimmer Bradley, strive to "fill in the blanks" of Darkovan history and elaborate on the eras, tales and characters which have captured readers' imaginations.

THE KEEPER'S PRICE
SWORD OF CHAOS
FREE AMAZONS OF DARKOVER
THE OTHER SIDE OF THE MIRROR
RED SUN OF DARKOVER
FOUR MOONS OF DARKOVER
DOMAINS OF DARKOVER
RENUNCIATES OF DARKOVER
LERONI OF DARKOVER
TOWERS OF DARKOVER
MARION ZIMMER BRADLEY'S DARKOVER
SNOWS OF DARKOVER

THE
SHADOW
MATRIX

A Novel of Darkover

MARION ZIMMER
BRADLEY

DAW BOOKS, INC.

DONALD A. WOLLHEIM, FOUNDER

375 Hudson Street, New York, NY 10014

ELIZABETH R. WOLLHEIM
SHEILA E. GILBERT
PUBLISHERS

First Printing, September 1997

DAW TRADEMARK REGISTERED
U.S. PAT. OFF. AND FOREIGN COUNTRIES
—MARCA REGISTRADA
HECHO EN U.S.A.

PRINTED IN THE U.S.A.

To Susan Rich
who read all the drafts and asked for more

THE
SHADOW
MATRIX

A Novel of Darkover

PROLOGUE

"Tell me again why we came out here to visit Priscilla Elhalyn," Dyan Ardais muttered as he went down the staircase ahead of Mikhail. "And why we agreed to attend this . . . thing?"

Mikhail Lanart-Hastur looked at his companion, at his dark hair and fair complexion in the flickering light of lampions and started to reply. A flash of lightning illuminated the worn carpet beneath his feet as a boom of thunder rattled the walls of Elhalyn Castle. There was a rush of rain against the panes of the windows.

"We were a little drunk at the time," he finally said, when the noise abated. "And there were all those girls in Thendara, making themselves pretty for us."

"Well, we aren't drunk now, and going to a seance is not my idea of a good time!"

"How do you know? How many seances have you been to?"

"None! I think talking to dead people, or trying to, is a perverse idea."

Mikhail laughed softly. Young Dyan Ardais, whose paxman he was, was a rather nervous man of eighteen. "What? Are you afraid that medium of Priscilla's will conjure up your father?"

"Gods! I hadn't even thought of that! I never knew him when he was alive, and I don't want to make his acquaintance now!"

Mikhail had had several days to regret the impulse that had brought them to the decaying pile that was Elhalyn Castle. He knew he was old enough not to do such things, and that Dyan was his responsibility, his charge. If only they had not both been so bored, and ripe for mischief. Well, there was no help for it. They were the guests of Priscilla Elhalyn, the sister of Derik Elhalyn, the last king of Darkover, and they could hardly get on their horses and ride off into the storm.

"Most likely it will be a total failure, Dyan, and they will not bring the ghost of Derik Elhalyn down from the overworld. Or her father, or my grandmother Alanna Elhalyn either. Although I wouldn't mind seeing her. She died a long time ago, and I have always been a little curious about her. I'll bet we won't even have a good tale to tell when we get back."

"That would be fine with me." Dyan sounded less fretful, calmed by Mikhail's good humor. "So far it has been a pretty dreary time, hasn't it—unless you count meeting those retainers of hers. I never knew that anyone gave houseroom to bone-readers and mediums before."

"The Elhalyn have always been rather eccentric."

"What you mean is that Priscilla is only slightly less crazy than her mad brother, don't you? That Burl fellow gives me the creeps, and I am sure it is his doing that we have to attend this ghost-calling."

Mikhail laughed again, but he shared Dyan's opinion of the bone-reader. It was an activity that was found in the marketplaces of any of the cities of Darkover, but not one normally encountered in the home of a *comynara*. Still, he knew that trying to see into the future was a perfectly human desire, and he suspected that Burl merely possessed a small talent, a *laran* not unlike the Aldaran Gift of foreseeing.

The other of Priscilla's confidants, the woman Ysaba, was, in his opinion, the stranger of the two. Mikhail had seen bone-readers and other diviners before, but a medium was beyond his experience. He sensed she had *laran*, but it was not of a kind he had ever encountered before, and he suspected the woman had never trained in any Tower. He wished he could ask her outright, but that would have been very impolite.

The two young men walked through a dusty corridor, and were met by Duncan MacLeod, who was in charge of the stables but did duty as *coridom* as well. He was a grizzled fellow, his face weathered, and his eyes sharp with suspicion. Still, the stables were in good repair—better than the castle itself, which had been let go to ruin under Priscilla's careless stewardship. Priscilla's staff was old, and few in number. There were no young maids to keep up the rooms, and no lads learning to manage the stables, which was puzzling as well. Elhalyn Castle was nearly empty of people, with a hollow quality that was unnerving.

In fact, it was the most peculiar household Mikhail had ever seen. Priscilla had lived there, alone except for her children and her few servants, for the years since the Sharra Rebellion, and the unfortunate events which had left so many members of the Comyn either dead or insane. She seemed perfectly happy in her solitude, a little vague at times, but not obviously mad as her brother had been. The Elhalyns were often unbalanced, he knew.

Mikhail had a good many questions that he could not ask without appearing rude, not the least of which was the parentage of Priscilla's five children. There was Alain, who was nearly fifteen, Vincent at thirteen, and Emun ten, as well as two daughters, Miralys and Valenta, shy girls of nine and eight. Priscilla had never married, and whatever lovers she had taken over the years remained unnamed and unknown. Since the Elhalyn women had *comynara* status, they had a freedom of choice not permitted to most females, but he still found the whole thing rather unsettling. He had never thought of himself as stuffy, but he nonetheless found himself unsettled by her irregular style of living.

Duncan led them through a narrow passage which connected the main portion of the castle to the narrow dungeon that was the remnant of a much earlier time in Darkovan history, when the land-holding families waged terrible wars with one another. It smelled of age, of old stones and the bones of the earth beneath it, and he tried to shake off the feeling of oppression it gave him.

At last Duncan opened a heavily timbered door, and a gust of cold air billowed out. Just then there was another shock of thunder, and the roof of the passage trembled, shedding a fine rain of rotted wood and flakes of whitewash down onto the sleeves of his tunic. Dyan made a disgusted noise and ran nervous fingers through his hair, then brushed the litter away.

They followed Duncan into a round room that would have been almost cozy if it had not been quite so chilly. There was a small fireplace, and it was lit, giving off the smell of balsam logs, though it was not enough to warm the room. The walls were stone, and they were damp with moisture. Mikhail could see patches of mold on their faces, and the pleasant scent of the logs barely concealed their musty odor. A few sputtering candles were set on a small table in the center of the room, making eerie shadows on the walls and the decaying tapestries that were hanging there.

Mikhail tried to imagine the room during the past, with long dead Elhalyn sheltering there, under seige from their foes. But the room was too shabby, too cold, and too dreary for any romantic notions. The place was just a relic of another time, and one that he was glad was gone.

Priscilla and her medium, Ysaba, entered the room, interrupting his reverie. The little Elhalyn woman seemed more excited than Mikhail had seen her before, her golden eyes gleaming in the flickering light. There was an air of anticipation about her; she seemed to be expecting something wonderful to occur. Her hair was the color of apricots, and her skin seemed nearly golden in the light. No one would ever have called her a beauty, but she seemed quite pretty in her undisguised eagerness.

"Please, sit at the table," she invited, gesturing gracefully.

Mindful of his manners, Mikhail held a chair for her, and saw that Dyan was performing the same office for the medium, his distaste for the task apparent. They took the remaining seats, and he wondered where Burl, the bone-reader was.

The table had been polished recently, and it shone in the golden light, the smell of beeswax rising pleasantly beneath his forearms. Mikhail turned his attention to a large globe of quartz sitting in the middle of it. It had a faint bluish cast, but it was not the intense blue of a matrix crystal. Out of the corner of his eye he saw Duncan throw something into the fireplace, and there was a brief flare as it began to burn. A thick, flowery scent began to fill the room, something similar to the incenses his sister Liriel used, but heavier and not as pleasant. It made his eyes prickle, and his fingers started to feel rather numb.

Ysaba gazed into the globe, her pale eyes vacant. She was a plain woman, with the very fair coloring of the Dry Towns, and he was not sure of her age. There was thunder, and a flash of lightning shone through the high, narrow windows, blinding him for a second. The wind gusted against the walls of the ancient dungeon, but the structure barely trembled under the fury of the storm.

The chamber was silent, except for the crackle of the fire, and the sobbing of the wind outside. Mikhail felt a draft along the floor, from the door behind him, and wriggled his toes in his boots. He hoped this was not going to take very long. The somewhat shabby room he and Dyan were sharing was at least warm, and he wanted to return to it, and go to bed!

"Join hands, please," Priscilla said, interrupting his thoughts.

Dyan gave a litle start, then reluctantly slipped his hand into Mikhail's right one. He extended his free hand reluctantly, and Ysaba clasped it. Mikhail felt Priscilla take his left hand, and put her other into that of the medium. It was surprisingly warm and soft.

"You must not break the circle," the medium said quietly.

Why did I let you talk me into agreeing to this, Mik?

We could hardly deny Priscilla's request, could we?

If either of us had any spine, we certainly would have!

Mikhail could sense the younger man almost squirming with discomfort. Although he was mildly uneasy, he did not share Dyan's emotions, for his ever-lively curiosity was now fully engaged. This was going to make a wonderful tale to tell!

There was a moaning sound, and after a moment Mikhail realized it was not the wind, but the medium. It was a very strange noise, something he could hardly believe was coming from a human body. The thick, acrid odor from the fireplace seemed to increase, and he had a sudden urge to sneeze. Mikhail wriggled his nose and managed to stifle the reflex.

The globe in the center of the table began to darken, as if it were filled with smoke. A shape started to form, and Mikhail felt the hairs on the nape of his neck stir with awe. Part of his mind was sure it was some peculiar sort of *laran*. But another portion of it was filled with the memory of ghost-tales he had heard as a child.

The shape thickened, and something pale and wispy seemed to seep out of the quartz. It was a long, convoluted, ropy object, and after a moment of hovering in the air, it bent toward the medium. Mikhail could hear Dyan's breathing, noisy and harsh, and glanced at him. The younger man had his eyes firmly closed, his hand quivering in Mikhail's grasp. Even with the stifling incense, he could smell the scent of sweat—his own and Dyan's. He gave his friend what he hoped was a reassuring squeeze just as the specter touched Ysaba's chest.

There was silence for a moment, and then a voice emerged from the medium's throat. "Who are these strangers?" It was a rather feeble tenor, reedy and unpleasant.

Mikhail felt Dyan's hand twitch in his grasp. *What sort of ghost doesn't know who we are?*

Derik—if it is he—never met us.

Oh. I suppose. His mental tone was unconvinced, and Mikhail agreed, but was willing to wait upon events. Now that he had gotten over his initial fear, the entire event was becoming interesting. How was Ysaba producing that voice, he wondered.

"Brother, may I present *Dom* Mikhail Hastur, son of Javanne Hastur and grandson of Alanna Elhalyn, and *Dom* Dyan Ardais, son of Dyan-Gabriel Ardais." She sounded like a proper hostess, not someone speaking to a specter, and Mikhail found himself admiring her air of calm.

"Why are they here? What do they want from me?" There was a whining tone in the words that set Mikhail's teeth on edge.

"They came to see me, which was very kind of them, for we have very little company at Elhalyn Castle. Were it not for the children and Ysaba and Burl, I would be very lonely."

"They are spies!"

"Nonsense! They are only young men!" Priscilla looked more animated as she answered than she had since they arrived, as if she enjoyed arguing with her dead brother. "They have played with the children and ridden over the estate, and made themselves at home."

"Send them away. They disturb me!"

"Derik, I am weary of my loneliness," she responded petulantly. "It is so pleasant to have someone to talk to."

"Send them away! They want to injure me."

"Derik—how could they hurt you?"

While this exchange continued, Mikhail took a long look at Ysaba in the flickering light. He watched her throat, trying to see if the muscles moved when Derik spoke, and found that they did not. Where the devil was the sound coming from? Were they really listening to a ghost?

Then, above the medium's head, Mikhail saw something move in the air. It was a wispy motion, like a curl of smoke, and he could just barely make out the features of a man. The room felt colder, and as he watched, the wisp thickened, becoming opaque, so that the wall behind Ysaba was no longer visible.

"Dyan Ardais was no friend to me," the thing said. "They are all my enemies, sister, all of them. You are my only friend. And I have something to tell you!" There was a conspiratorial quality in the words, and Mikhail sensed something in them that seemed both promising and unpleasant.

"But, Derik—you must tell me. I have been waiting for months!"

"There is a plot against me. It is not these men, but . . . others. And these boys will tell everything . . . all will be ruined! They will try to stop us from. . . ." The voice trailed off into silence.

Priscilla considered the words for a moment, peering at Mikhail and Dyan with her gray eyes. Her brows knitted into a frown for a moment, then she relaxed. "Mikhail, promise Derik you will never speak of this to anyone." She seemed used to her brother's fears, and sounded as if she were humoring a cranky child. At the same time there was a husky quality in her tone that seemed very unsisterly to his ears.

Mikhail considered. He had always taken giving his word very seriously, and he did not want to swear a binding oath if he did not intend to keep it. He realized that if he mentioned this incident to anyone, he would be thought as mad as Derik. No one knew that he and Dyan had come to Elhalyn Castle, so it would not be difficult. And he was curious enough about what the ghost might say to make the promise. "I swear I will never speak of this to anyone."

Beside him, Dyan shifted in his chair. "I swear I will never mention anything to anyone." There was a vehemence in his voice, and Mikhail knew he meant it. *I am going to forget this ever happened as fast as I can!*

"You see?" Priscilla asked, looking pleased.

"Oaths can be broken."

"Why should they? They bear you no malice, dear brother."

There was a lengthy silence, and the smoky figure above the medium swirled in the air, shifting and changing subtly. The effect was dazzling. Then, without any warning, the shape rushed at them, trailing long streams of vapor. Mikhail felt a mist brush across his brow, and he shrank back, his heart pounding against his ribs. Beside him, Dyan gave a yelp of pure terror, and clamped his hand so hard he nearly broke Mikhail's fingers.

It was over quickly, and the mist withdrew, but Mikhail found he was gasping for air, and that in spite of the cold of the chamber, he was drenched with sweat. Beneath the table, his legs were trembling.

"Their hearts seem good enough," the spirit admitted grudgingly.

"Of course their hearts are good. They are very nice boys."

In spite of his terror, Mikhail nearly laughed at being called a boy. Priscilla was perhaps eleven years his elder, but she acted like a crone most of the time. He sucked in his cheeks and swallowed the chuckle that threatened to burst from his mouth. He had always had a tendency to laugh when he was frightened or alarmed, and his mother had sometimes said he would likely laugh on his way to the gallows.

Slowly, his fear dissipated, and with it, the urge to giggle. Mikhail swallowed in a dry throat, wishing for a glass of wine. If all the ghost could do was surround him with mist, there really was nothing to be afraid of. And it was a shame he had given his word never to speak of the incident, because it would make such a good tale.

Mikhail was lost in his own thoughts, so he almost missed Derik's next words. "The Guardian wants you. It is time!"

"At last!" Priscilla looked delighted, even in the poor light of the fire. Her thin face was alight with pleasure, and she looked more like a girl than a woman with five children. But there was also something unhealthy about her reaction, and Mikhail lowered his eyes quickly. Guardian? What was that? "Soon we will be together again, brother," she whispered just loud enough for Mikhail to hear.

Despite his intense curiosity, he decided he did not want to know any more than he did already. Be together? Was Priscilla planning to die? It did not sound like it. Then he shrugged, to ease his tension and banish his own sense of embarrassment. He had stumbled into something that was none of his business, and the sooner he was out of it, the better.

The shimmering shape above the medium began to fall apart, and then the globe on the table clouded up again. Ysaba's hands opened, releasing her grip on the others, and she slumped forward, onto the table. She banged her head against the shining surface with an audible thump, and he winced with empathy.

Duncan, who had remained in the shadows until now, stepped forward. He had a glass of wine in one hand, and he lifted the woman up by her shoulder, and held it against her lips. Then his eyes met Mikhail's, and there was an expression of shame and loathing in them. The mouth of the medium opened a little, and some wine trickled into it, though more dripped down her chin.

From the corner of his eye, Mikhail could see Dyan wipe the hand which Ysaba had held against his trousers. His young face was twisted with distaste, and Mikhail felt a stab of guilt. He never should have brought his friend to Elhalyn Castle.

Mik, I feel filthy! I never want to go through anything like this again! Let's leave at first light—please! This is a terrible place!

I think you are right. But I wonder what this "Guardian" is?

I don't care if it is Aldones himself—I just want to get away from here!

Mikhail silently agreed with Dyan's sentiment. The following morning, in spite of the rain, they rode back to Thendara. They did not speak of the strange event, as if by silent agreement, then or afterward. But, from time to time, Mikhail thought about it, and wondered if he had really heard the voice of the ghost of Derik Elhalyn, and asked himself who the Guardian might be.

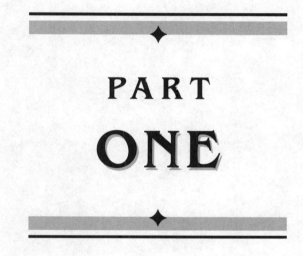

PART

ONE

1

Mikhail Lanart-Hastur rode along the banks of the River Valeron enjoying the fine autumn day. The breeze ruffled the golden hair on his brow, and his blue eyes mirrored the color of the water. The air was crisp, and the trees along the banks were clothed in golds and russets which reminded him of a certain pair of penetrating eyes that belonged to his cousin Marguerida Alton. Of course, he realized, almost everything reminded him of her, and in fact it was difficult not to think of her instead of focusing on the task before him.

He was returning to the Elhalyn lands he had visited briefly four years before. Then he had been the paxman of Dyan Ardais and the nominal heir of Regis Hastur—as indeed he still was. Now he had been appointed Regent to the Elhalyn Domain, charged with the responsibility of testing the sons of Priscilla Elhalyn to determine if any of them was mentally stable enough to take on the largely ceremonial but important task of being king.

Mikhail remembered his previous encounter with Priscilla, which had ended in a seance, and shook his head a little. He wondered if Burl, the bone-reader, and Ysaba, the medium, were still her companions. He knew the Elhalyns had left the castle shortly after he and Dyan had been there, and had removed to Halyn House. That was where he was going, accompanied by two Guardsmen, Daryll and Mathias. He should have had a larger entourage—his new and unwanted position demanded it. Priscilla had wished that Mikhail should come alone, but as eager as his uncle was to restore the Elhalyn kingship, that was out of the question. Regis had sent the Guardsmen, and Mikhail was glad of their company.

Whenever Mikhail thought about the meeting in the Crystal Chamber in Comyn Castle just before Midsummer, his spirits sank. He had gone over and over the events, trying to unravel them. First his Uncle Regis had announced that he was disbanding the Telepathic Council, which had helped govern Darkover for more than twenty years, and was restoring the traditional Comyn Council. Then, without warning or consultation, he had appointed Mikhail as Regent to Elhalyn, and Mikhail had accepted the position out of his sense of duty. He had not had time to think it over, to weigh the merits or consider the ramifications. He really had had no choice but to accept.

The anger that had simmered within him for months stirred in his belly. Mikhail had never had reason to be angry with his uncle until now, and he hated feeling this way. But he could not avoid the realization that Regis had manipulated him into a position he did not want, for reasons he refused to explain. Only his own deep sense of duty had made him submit, grinding his teeth with frustration. There was something going on that he was unable to understand. His only comfort was that he was not alone in his feeling—no one, except perhaps Danilo Syrtis-Ardais, knew what Regis Hastur was up to at present.

Mikhail knew his uncle to be a clever and canny man, a man who had managed to guide Darkover through a terrible period in her long and bloody history. He had always trusted Regis, but now this trust was besieged by his own emotions, and doubts as well. He had analyzed the problem as well as he was able, and found within it enough contradictions to give him concern. He had even permitted himself to wonder if Regis Hastur knew what he was doing—only briefly before he choked off the thought and banished it to the back of his mind.

Mikhail thought about his most recent interview with Regis, just before he had set out. His uncle had seemed tired and distracted, and he had felt very uncomfortable asking for Regis' time and attention. The Elhalyn Regency was a small matter compared with restoring the Council, the problem of the contested heirship of the Alton Domain, or the possibility of the Aldarans returning to Comyn society.

The Hastur charm, of which Regis had an unusual amount, was absent. Mikhail had asked the questions he wished—felt he needed— to have answered, and had gotten less than satisfactory replies. His uncle had not offered any hints as to what he wished to accomplish, and, in retrospect, Mikhail realized he had not been very supportive or even attentive. "You will handle it well, Mikhail. I am sure of that. We will talk further when you return for Midwinter. Take your time over the testing of the lads. There is no urgency."

The encounter had left Mikhail with the feeling that what he had been told to do was not very important—and worse, that he was not either. He had ended up feeling exiled, the way he had after Regis' son Danilo had been born, unwanted and something of a bother. Intellectually he was sure this was not the case—then or now—but he was honest enough with himself to admit that his feelings were more than a little injured.

The problem, as he saw it, was that Regis seemed to be trying to turn back the clock, claiming that the restoration of the Elhalyn kingship was necessary, as was the Comyn Council. At the same time, Regis insisted that these moves were not reactionary, but were in the best interests of the future. It sounded plausible until Mikhail examined it carefully.

He did not think for a moment that Regis did not have some plan, some scheme, in mind. The only piece of real information he managed to pry out of his uncle was Regis' conviction that Darkover must become truly united—that the Aldarans must become part of the Comyn Council—and soon, too.

Since the Aldarans were mistrusted by the other Domains, Regis was having a very hard time convincing the other members of the Comyn Council to agree to what little of his plan he revealed. Mikhail's own parents were opposed to the idea, as were Lady Marilla Aillard and her son Dyan Ardais. *Dom* Francisco Ridenow seemed to change his mind every other day, and only Lew Alton supported the idea completely.

Mikhail did not have the reservations about the Aldarans that his parents did. He had visited them years before, quite unknown to his mother and father. He was acquainted with old *Dom* Damon, his son Robert, the heir, and Robert's twin, Hermes Aldaran, who had recently taken over the position of Darkover's representative to the Terran Senate from Lew Alton. And he knew Gisela Aldaran, their sister, who had been a charming young woman at the time. He had liked them, and knew perfectly well that they did not have horns and tails.

But prejudice against the family was old and ran deep. Darkovans had very long memories, especially in matters of treachery, and the Aldarans had betrayed the Council years before. It was all very well for Regis to say that bygones should be forgotten, that it was time to heal old wounds. He had clearly not anticipated the steadfast resistance he encountered to his propositions.

Mikhail was not sure even his uncle could manage to smooth things out, for all his powers of persuasion. The more he pressed, the more he was opposed, particularly by Mikhail's mother, Javanne Hastur. In a great many ways, his mother's behavior since the meeting in the Crystal Chamber had been even more distressing than Regis'. She had always been a headstrong woman, but the announcement of his Regency had provoked in her some single-minded fury that he could not understand. She was no longer the mother he knew, but a cold and distant stranger. There had been a few moments when he had even allowed himself to wonder if she were completely sane. Her mother had been an Elhalyn, after all, and they were known for their instability. He did not entertain this terrible idea for any length of time because, since Regis Hastur was her brother, he might find himself doubting his uncle for the same reasons. That thought was too much to bear.

The wind blew a scatter of leaves across the trail, their color exactly the red of Marguerida's hair. Mikhail decided he would rather moon over his beloved than try to untangle more troubling matters.

Their parting at Arilinn Tower five days before had been hard, even though they had both tried to put a brave face on it. She had retreated into the particular remoteness he now knew she hid behind when she was upset. They had not spoken of their love, for that would have been too painful. Instead, they had talked of unimportant matters, using the inconsequential to conceal the feelings that threatened to overcome them both.

Mikhail and Marguerida had gone to Arilinn just after Midsummer, Marguerida to begin her studies of matrix science, and Mikhail to learn what he needed to know to test the Elhalyn boys for *laran,* which had turned out to be more complicated than he had imagined. It was a little ironic, he thought, that Marguerida was trying to learn matrix science, when, in one sense, the crystals themselves were anathema to her. Her first weeks there had brought on another siege of threshold sickness, from the proximity of the matrix relays in the Tower. That, at least, was the only explanation anyone could offer.

Much to the displeasure of *Mestra* Camilla MacRoss, who was in charge of the beginning students at Arilinn, Marguerida had been allowed to live in one of the several small houses that were kept for visitors, guests, and the families of those who had come to the Tower for healing, instead of sleeping in the communal dormitories with the others. It was an unheard of arrangement, and it had made things even more difficult for Marguerida. *Mestra* MacRoss did not like any of her charges getting special treatment, unless she herself granted them.

He smiled a little at the memory, for he knew Mestra Camilla from his own days at Arilinn, years before. She had been old then, and was now ancient. No one, not even Jeff Kerwin, the Keeper at Arilinn, dared suggest to her that she might consider retiring from her position. She was very set in her ways and very strict, which was hardly surprising, since those in her command were almost always youngsters, adolescents coming into their *laran,* full of vitality, mischief and often powers which were not completely under control.

From the outset, the two women had not hit it off. *Mestra* Camilla was very able at dealing with teenagers, but Marguerida was an adult, and not a particularly malleable one. Or rather, Mikhail reflected, his independent, self-directed cousin was quite disciplined and even obedient in her own way, which was decidedly not to the liking of the older woman. She asked too many questions, the ingrained habit of a decade of academic training. She always wanted to know *why* things were done in a certain way, even though he knew she had tried to restrain her lively curiosity. "Why" was not a word of which Camilla MacRoss approved.

The other students at Arilinn had not improved the situation. They were all intent on demonstrating their abilities, eager to quit their student status and move on to becoming mechanics or technicians, or even Keepers. Taking their tone from both Camilla, and from Loren MacAndrews, the oldest of the students, they treated Marguerida as an interloper. They resented her age, her experience, and the speed with which she learned. And the fact that she was an Alton, and heiress to the Alton Domain, did not sit well. The Alton Gift of forced rapport was a thing both prized and feared, and for it to be possessed by a woman who had spent most of her life off Darkover made everyone a little uneasy. They were uncertain that she would behave properly—that she would use her Gift ethically.

Marguerida, who was stubborn to the bone, had responded with her quiet pride and fierce determination. Ill as she was, she had refused to ask for special treatment. Jeff had been forced to intervene. This had made things even worse between Marguerida and Camilla, for it smacked of preferential treatment, since Jeff was kin. They had retreated into careful formality, which merely concealed their mutual hostility rather than lessening it.

Mikhail had been glad that he was there, although it had been difficult for both of them, to be so near and have to treat one another with cold formality. The love they had declared to one another before Midsummer was unchanged, but circumstances prevented them from doing more than taking occasional walks together in one of the several gardens at Arilinn, or riding out on nice afternoons. They talked about everything from what Marguerida perceived as ridiculous customs to the nature of deities on Darkover and other worlds. He had always yearned to travel the stars, and hearing about the planets she had visited was both wonderful and miserable. He envied her her travels and her education, yet he cherished every moment spent in her fascinating company. At least his sister Liriel was still at Arilinn, and she was a true friend to Marguerida. But Mikhail knew he would be missed, and was quietly glad of it.

Mikhail thought about Marguerida's stepmother, Diotima Ridenow-Alton, who was very ill with something no one could quite understand, neither Terran medics nor Darkovan healers. It seemed to be a form of cancer, but it had not responded to any treatment. They had tried for weeks to halt the deterioration of her now frail body. Then, after much argument, the decision had been reached to put her into stasis, until some new method could be discovered. It was, at best, a stopgap measure.

His beloved had been more than distraught, for she loved Diotima, the only mother she had ever really known. Between trying to live close to the powerful matrix screens, the recurrence of the threshold illness, and deep sorrow about her stepmother, she had alternated between being frantic with worry or depressed. While Marguerida had done her best to pretend she was in good spirits and even laughed at his jokes, underneath it all, he knew she was suffering. Only her fierce pride kept her from losing control—that and her obstinacy.

The rush of water over the stones made him think of her laughter that was all too rare these days, and the brisk touch of the breeze against his skin of Marguerida's sharp tongue. He laughed aloud. The sound made his big bay, Charger, snort in response and prick his ears. Behind him, Mikhail could hear the pleasant jingle of the bridles of the two Guardsmen, and he sensed they were wondering what caused his amusement. It was too complicated to explain, even to men he knew as well as he did Daryll and Mathias. Besides, he was not going to admit that he was turning into a lovesick romantic when, at age twenty-eight, he should be well over such silly behavior. Next thing he knew he would be writing poetry!

It had been a long time since he had had the company of members of the Guard, and he was slightly uncomfortable about it. As a child, running free in Comyn Castle, there was always a Guardsman nearby. He had seen them as men to give him piggyback rides or tell him stories. He had not known then that there was good reason for their vigilance, that assassins were about in the streets of Thendara, that they were murdering children in their cradles.

But, after the World Wreckers had been defeated, and Regis Hastur, his uncle, had found Lady Linnea and had their first child, he had been somewhat freed of their presence. Not entirely, for he was still the official heir to Hastur. He had been fourteen when Danilo Hastur was born, old enough to go first to Arilinn for some training, then into the Cadet Guards for two years. It had not really registered at the time that it indicated a change in his status, that he was no longer quite the favored child he had been a few years earlier. It was not until he became paxman to young Dyan Ardais that he had ceased to have members of the Guard in close proximity all the time, as befitted his status as an adult. He had formed strong friendships during his time in the Guard, and these had persisted, so that the men riding behind him were companions and fellows at arms more than watchdogs.

All he wanted to do, he realized, was reach Halyn House as quickly as possible, test the boys, find a suitable candidate for the kingship, and get free of the Regency. He did not want to think what his life would be like if this did not come to pass. He stroked the strong neck of the big bay with his free hand and found himself remembering the last time he had traveled this way.

Whose idea had it been, to ride off and visit the reclusive Priscilla Elhalyn—his or Dyan's? Mikhail could not remember. All he was certain of was that it had been about four years ago, and they had both been ripe for adventure. They had just gotten on their horses and ridden off to the west on a lark, neither of them thinking very clearly. That the reclusive Priscilla might not welcome them with open arms did not occur to them until they were almost there, and neither of them could easily back down without appearing a fool.

After three days of steady riding, they had come to Elhalyn Castle unannounced. Priscilla Elhalyn had not appeared very perturbed by the intrusion. After all, Mikhail was the grandson of Alanna Elhalyn, who had been the sister of Priscilla's own father, Stefan. A visit from a cousin was always acceptable, her attitude implied. Indeed, in her rather vague and disordered way, she behaved almost as if she had expected them. She was a small woman, with eyes clouded like gray agates, surrounded by her children and few servants, pleasant enough, but hardly the adventure he had been hoping to have.

Elhalyn Castle itself was a modest pile—not as large or impressive as Ardais—but well-built and strong. One of the servants said it dated back to the Ages of Chaos, when the Compact had finally ended the wars which had plagued the planet for so long. Studying the stonework, Mikhail had suspected the building was not that old. Still, with the muddle that passed for history from that time, he knew that anything was possible.

So much had been lost during those troubled times, so many records, and so much knowledge. Some of the knowledge was better off lost, he knew, for they had used matrices in ways that were unthinkable to his mind. There had been *clingfire,* a stuff that adhered to the skin and burned to the bone, which was a terrifying idea. And that was not the worst. Mikhail could hardly imagine it, and was glad for Darkover that those terrible times were far in the past.

Not that recent times had been uneventful, of course. The Sharra Rebellion had wracked the world shortly after his birth, and the World Wreckers had tried to destroy the entire ecology of Darkover a few years later. But, for nearly the last two decades, things on Darkover had been quiet. There was no real need of the protection of Guardsmen, except that as Elhalyn Regent he had a certain status, and it was customary.

Elhalyn Castle had been in a shocking state of disrepair, and Mikhail wondered why. The climate of Darkover was unforgiving. The winters were brutal, and all the houses he knew were well-maintained, just to ensure the basic health of the residents during the coldest months of the year. Drafty corridors and doors that creaked on their hinges were a new and rather unpleasant experience. Dyan had some pungent comments to make on the subject, but Mikhail put it down to the well-known eccentricity of the Elhalyns.

Mikhail had studied Priscilla's five children for any hint of the documented instability of the Elhalyn line, but they had seemed healthy and normal, despite the oddity of their home. They were unused to strangers, and rather shy, but after a day, they seemed to accept the two men well enough. The two girls, the youngest of the children, Miralys and Valenta, stopped hiding behind their mother's skirts, and the boys—Alain, Vincent, and Emun—asked questions about horses, Thendara, the Terranan, and other matters of curiosity. The boys had admired Valient, the sire of his present horse, and Dyan's spirited mare Roslinda, remarked on the clothing they wore, and generally behaved like other youngsters he had known.

It had been rather tedious, until the night of the seance. He could still remember the cold touch of whatever had spoken and shuddered. He was, in retrospect, very glad that the ghost of Derik—if it had been he—had extracted his oath never to speak of the incident. Doing so would have cast serious doubts on his own sanity, he was sure.

But when he made that promise, he had never expected to return to the Elhalyn lands, nor to see Priscilla and her children again. Certainly he had not anticipated becoming Regent for the Elhalyn Domain, with orders from Regis Hastur to find one among the three sons of Priscilla to reclaim the long vacant throne of the kings of Darkover.

There had been several times since that tumultuous meeting in the Crystal Chamber when Mikhail had wished to refuse the Regency. That choice would have perhaps restored his relationship with his parents, as well as relieving him of an unwanted burden. But his sense of duty was too strong. He could not bring himself to speak the words. If only he had not been trained to rule!

For that matter, if only his parents were not so stubborn and mistrustful of him, of Lew Alton, and Marguerida. There was no good thinking about it! He had been trained to be a dutiful heir to Regis Hastur, to rule, and then it had all been snatched away from him. All he could do was his best at the task ahead of him, even if it did feel as if he had been shuffled off. Any *leronis* could have tested the boys, and he knew it. But Regis had insisted that Mikhail do it, and would settle for no one else.

The longer he thought about it, the more certain Mikhail was that he was missing critical pieces of information. He had not been shuffled off, no matter how he felt about it. He was part of the plan—an unwilling pawn in one of Regis' games. It was infuriating! He felt trapped, both by his loyalties and by his uncle's manipulations. He was not free to pursue his own ambitions, and he resented it more than he had realized until this moment.

It was all very dispiriting. There was little comfort in the realization that no one, so far as Mikhail knew, was entirely happy with the things that Regis proposed. He felt a brief empathy for his young cousin, Dani Hastur, who should by now have been proclaimed heir. All he had managed to get out of anyone was a cryptic remark from Lady Linnea. "Regis is not certain of Dani yet." If Mikhail felt exiled and trapped at the same time, how must Danilo Hastur feel?

Everything Regis had proposed, even the inclusion of the Aldarans in the Comyn Council, was very logical. But Darkovans, Mikhail knew, were not a very logical people. They were passionate, and when their emotions were in full cry, as it seemed his mother's were at present, they did not listen to anything but their hearts. And, he decided, Regis did not seem to grasp this.

Mikhail wondered what secrets his uncle was keeping, thinking a little guiltily of his own. He had never spoken of the seance, and he had never revealed his two visits to the Aldaran family. These were small things, and Regis had told him once that half of statecraft was having information and knowing when to use it and when not to.

Mikhail dismissed his conflicted thoughts with a shrug. All this speculation was giving him a headache. He knew that Regis had changed in some manner, and all he could do was live with it. He could not quite put a name to the difference, but now he thought about it, there was also something almost hasty in his actions, as if he had some secret timetable he must keep to.

Enough! It was too beautiful a day for such thoughts. He could now see the looming bulk of Elhalyn Castle against the horizon, and was relieved that Priscilla had left the place. Halyn House was the old dower residence ten miles closer to the sea and he only hoped it was in a better state than the moldering castle, which even from a distance looked run-down and depressing.

But even if it wasn't any better kept, he believed he could put up with it so long as he knew it was not going to be forever, that long before he entered his dotage he would be free of either the Regency or the possibility of taking Regis' place once and for all.

Odd. Once he had wanted that—had longed for the thankless job that Regis had done so ably for two decades. That was long before he met Marguerida. He let out a soft chuckle that made Charger prick his ears. Mikhail let himself remember the lists he had made as a youngster, of things he intended to do when he took the throne. They had been, he suspected, both idealistic and extremely foolish.

The wind shifted a little, and the smell of the Sea of Dalereuth wafted toward him. It was a sharp scent, full of salt and something he could not put a name to. Marguerida would know, for she had grown up on an oceanic world after she left Darkover at the age of five. Even with the impressions of Thetis he had gotten from her mind over the months, Mikhail had no real sense of what it was like to live beside a rolling ocean, full of odd creatures shaped like stars, or the leaping sea-mammals she called *delfins*.

Sometimes, he knew, she longed for Thetis, for its warmth, and Mikhail wondered if she would ever be completely happy on Darkover. He hoped she would, because he could not be happy without her, and if she left, he could not bear it. And after her training in the Tower was complete, she would be free to do just that—leave Darkover. It was not a happy thought. If she chose to depart, it would create havoc and likely ruin whatever plans Regis was hatching.

A strange croak from overhead made him look up, letting go of his morbid thoughts. There was a large bird, some sort of crow, but a type he had never seen before. It was shining black, with patches of white feathers across the edges of the wings. It looked at him with a suspicious red eye, cried again, and circled above him three times. He flinched a little, for the bird looked dangerous with its large talons and sharp beak.

Mikhail watched the bird wheeling in the air, enjoying the perfection of its flight. He followed it until it vanished, then urged his horse ahead. It was still several miles to Halyn House, and if he wanted to arrive before dusk, he needed to hurry.

As he rode, Mikhail experienced a slight frisson of uneasiness that had been lurking in the back of his mind for miles. Then he silently cursed himself for a superstitious fool. That sea crow had been no omen, no portent of doom. He was just out of sorts from being given a task he did not wish for and did not want.

He began to sing, his voice lifting in a rather naughty ditty he had learned from Marguerida, a student drinking song from her days at University. It was quite wicked, and he could hear the Guardsmen chuckling behind him, a cheerful noise that so lightened his heart that he nearly forgot his cares as he rode toward Halyn House.

2

It was such a beautiful day, Margaret Alton reflected, that it was a shame it was being ruined by her headache. Sitting on a low bench in the fragrance garden at Arilinn, she tried to use the methods she had learned during her four months in the Tower to alleviate the pain. But although she had mastered the technique, her headache stubbornly refused to stop pounding in her skull.

She flinched as the intensity of the pain seemed to increase, until it felt as if someone were stabbing stilettos into her brow, just above the eyes. She could feel the pulse of her blood, hot in her veins, and she suddenly realized this was no ordinary headache.

No, Margaret decided, this was something entirely different from the dreadful sensation she got in her head when she remained too long within the Tower. It had never occurred to her that being near large collections of matrices would be almost impossible for her—even though the sight of a personal starstone made her queasy. And nothing had prepared her for the environment of Arilinn Tower—for the enormous energies confined behind the stone walls. Worse, no one else had realized what the great screens were doing to her until she fell violently ill.

Her first experience had been a harrowing one, with an episode of threshold sickness almost as terrible as the one she had suffered at Castle Ardais the previous summer. Whenever she looked at the building, and remembered those first days in the student dormitory, she shuddered. She could have died, she knew.

Fortunately she had not, and the problem had a fairly simple solution. Outside the actual Tower, away from the energies of the matrices, her illness abated. She now lived in a little cottage outside the walls. She loved it, for here she was free of the constant chatter of her fellow students, and their hostility as well. It was the first time she had ever lived alone, and the sense of separateness, of privacy, soothed something within her she had not even known was painful. She only entered the Tower for lessons now. And those were devoted at present not so much to studying her own *laran,* as to learning various meditative techniques that would permit her to be in the proximity of the large number of matrix stones that were housed in Arilinn or any Tower.

The Tower was nothing like she had imagined before she came there. Margaret had assumed the place would be a single building, like those she had glimpsed on her two visits to the overworld a few months earlier. Instead, it was a small but bustling community, with the Tower at its center. There were weavers who made robes especially for the inhabitants, farmers growing grain, skilled copyists who worked in the archives, trying to preserve those records of the past which still existed, and many other craftspeople.

Margaret discovered that the reason it could take a lifetime to learn matrix science was that one could not take in very much at a time. It was not like music or history, where a student could sit down, read a dozen texts, attend several seminars and then lay claim to some expertise. Old Jeff Kerwin had been at it for longer than she had been alive, and he was still learning things.

There were several houses of the sort she now lived in. They were only a few years old, constructed to house the families of people who had brought their loved ones to Arilinn for healing, an innovation brought about by her Uncle Jeff. Her father, Lew Alton, stayed in another one, during his frequent trips from Thendara to see how Dio's treatment was progressing. He would have stayed there all the time, but Jeff had put a stop to that, saying that Lew's presence was disruptive.

It was quite true, since Lew tended to become angry or agitated— demanding solutions when no one was quite sure yet what the nature of the problem was. All they knew was that for some reason Dio's cells were disintegrating, despite all attempts to halt the progress of her strange disease.

Now Diotima Ridenow rested in the center of a room, the walls gleaming with huge crystals, looking like some sleeping princess from a fairy tale. Margaret had managed to visit her a few times, but the presence of so many matrix stones in a small space had been impossible to endure for very long. She felt guilty about that and angry at herself, even though she knew it was silly. Margaret was sure, somewhere in her mind, that if she were only strong enough, she could get over her profound aversion to the matrices, and be able to sit with Dio.

It had driven her wild not to be able to do something for her beloved stepmother. She was, after all, her father's child, and the need to be active, not helpless, was enormous. After several weeks of frustration which interfered with the study of her Gift, she hit upon the idea of using her precious recording equipment as a means of being present.

Using the two recorders she possessed, her own and Ivor Davidson's, she began to make recordings of all the songs she remembered from her childhood on Thetis, the many she had learned or relearned since returning to Darkover, and anything else that took her fancy. Just the act of singing made her feel less helpless, less frustrated. She was not, she knew, a great singer, just a very thoroughly trained musician. Margaret lacked that quality that distinguished the artist from the amateur, but she did not think it would matter to her stepmother.

When she had filled up a disk—about twenty-six hours of singing, with occasional stories that seemed to go with the music—she had ventured into the chamber, set up Ivor's player, and started it running. Margaret did not give a damn that she was violating half a dozen Terran rules about technology restrictions on planets like Darkover, or that the equipment actually belonged to the University, and she should have returned it. True, she had not informed the music department that she would not be returning to University in the foreseeable future, and they likely assumed she was diligently continuing the survey of Darkovan music which had brought her to the planet five months earlier. She knew that was hairsplitting. She was fairly certain she would never leave Darkover, and she was not going to transmit her work to her department, to let some other person muck about with it.

The batteries that ran the device were good for six months of continuous use, and she decided that if she had to, she would get her mother's brother, Captain Rafe Scott, to find some means to get her more if she needed them. He worked at Terran HQ in Thendara, and she was fairly certain he could obtain the things even if he could not requisition them. Margaret knew she should be disgusted with herself for even thinking such things, but it was for Dio, and that seemed more important than anything else.

So the glittering chamber was filled with song, from dawn till dawn. Margaret did not know if it did any good, if Dio could even hear her voice, her song, but it made her feel better, knowing that her stepmother was not entirely cut off from human contact.

Sometimes, after spending the day with Dio, Lew would come to Margaret, looking strained but calm. He told her several times that the songs were wonderful, that even if it was not helping Dio, it made *him* feel good to hear her voice. And others, technicians and students at Arilinn, who usually held themselves aloof from her, had sought her out to say they found themselves listening to the music, stopping in to sit with Diotima's comatose body, when they entered the chamber to monitor the woman. It was the warmest contact she had with those in the Tower, and the only one free of suspicion or resentment.

She had come expecting to find an environment like that at University, and instead discovered that Arilinn was a hotbed of competition. Those with high levels of *laran* tended to lord it over those with less, including Regis' two daughters, who had come to begin training at the same time she had. Several of the women had the ambition to become Keepers, which was understandable, since there were not many things which women could do on Darkover other than marry or become Renunciates, if they wanted authority of any sort. A few of the men nourished the same goal, even though male Keepers were still a rarity.

Margaret had been hurt and puzzled by the rather hostile welcome she had received. It had taken her quite some time to realize that she had in great measure exactly what many of the youngsters yearned for. Margaret knew they would have been shocked to discover, and disbelieving if she told them, that she would have cheerfully given them the Alton Gift, and what she had of the Aldaran Gift of foreseeing, if such a thing had been possible. She had never wanted *laran,* and she still did not. It was something to which she had had to resign herself, and it gave her little pleasure, even though she had made some progress.

Margaret rubbed her forehead with her right hand, trying to erase the pain in her skull. Her left hand, gloved in layers of spider silk, rested on her lap. Restlessly, she flexed the fingers of her gloved hand, sensing the lines of power etched into her skin, trying not to remember how she had gotten them while wresting a keystone from a Tower of Mirrors in the overworld. The months since she had battled the long dead Keeper, Ashara Alton, for her life, and her soul, had blurred the memories a little, but they were still vivid enough that when she thought about it, she grew chilled and frightened.

The mitten of silk helped. She had begun by using any glove that came to hand, until, in Thendara just before Midsummer, she had found that a silk glove worked better than a leather one. But only for a short time. After three or four days, the silk itself began to deteriorate, as if the lines on her flesh were fraying the fibers.

Liriel Lanart-Hastur, her cousin and perhaps her best friend, had suggested soon after she arrived at Arilinn that perhaps the gloves needed to be more than one layer thick. Neither of them had much skill with a needle and thread—they agreed that sewing was an intolerable bore—but Liriel had been persistent. She had experimented until she found that four layers of silk would withstand the constant outflow of energy from Margaret's shadow matrix. Her efforts had produced a clumsily sewn object that was bulky and uncomfortable to wear, covering the palm and going over the wrist bone, but leaving the fingers free.

Then Liriel had sent a pattern from Margaret's hand to a master glover in Thendara, with detailed instructions. A tenday later, four pairs of mitts had arrived, the seams so finely graded, despite the several layers, that they were quite comfortable to wear. The glover now sent a new batch every few weeks, and had started adding embellishments, so that, in addition to her plain ones, Margaret now had gloves with fine embroidery around the cuff, and one pair that was encrusted with tiny pearls below the knuckles. She wore gloves on both hands most of the time, since this attracted less attention than only using one.

The breeze shifted, ruffling Margaret's fine hair, and making it tickle her throbbing brow. She shifted on the stone bench, which was cool against her legs despite the fineness of the day, and chewed her lower lip. There was something about this particular headache, something she should know, that she could not quite make herself grasp.

Then, in a flash, Margaret realized that this was the sort of headache she had had the day that Ivor died so suddenly. She was cursed with just enough of the Aldaran Gift of foretelling that she got hints of things to come—not enough to be useful, only terrifying and infuriating.

She felt sick. Margaret's first thought was of Dio, that something terrible was about to happen. What if, somehow, the stasis stopped, or if it was not enough to keep her stepmother alive? She could not stand that. Dio had to live, to get better!

In her alarm, Margaret rose from the bench, and turned to go into the main body of Arilinn Tower. She took three steps, then stopped. Rushing into the stasis chamber in her current state was stupid. She would only make herself sick. Or make Dio worse.

Where was Liriel? Her cousin had been a technician at Tramontana Tower when Margaret came to Darkover, but she had settled at Arilinn to be near Margaret while she began her arduous studies of matrix science and the Alton Gift. Margaret had not wanted to come to Arilinn at all, but would have preferred to go to Neskaya where Istvana Ridenow was Keeper, and study with her. She still was not sure how she had let herself be persuaded to come to Arilinn—her kinsman, Jeff Kerwin, known also as Lord Damon Ridenow, had convinced her that a few months there would be worthwhile, and she had been so exhausted from her adventures that she had agreed. Dio was being treated there, and that had settled the matter.

When she had arrived on Darkover, she had never imagined the vast number of relatives she would discover here. After years of being the only child of Lew Alton, she was now, she felt, up to her hips in cousins and uncles—several of whom were either in residence at Arilinn, or frequent visitors. Ariel, Liriel's twin, was there, with her husband Piedro and their injured son Domenic, and their four other sons. She had become quite friendly with those children, particularly little Donal, whom she had inadvertantly sent into the overworld. He was a lively scamp, bored by being cooped up with his very anxious parents, and she had begun to teach him the rudiments of the Terran language, even though she knew that this would displease both the boy's mother and her aunt. It was a secret, and thus far Donal had managed to keep it, which gave her a good opinion of him. Donal never made her feel like a freak, but instead seemed to think she was an interesting person for someone so old. Lady Javanne came frequently to see Ariel, but she was most often in Thendara, intriguing and trying to persuade Regis Hastur of this or that.

Liriel! One thing she had managed to learn in her months at Arilinn was not to shout mentally, which was a problem most young telepaths encountered. With the Alton Gift of forced rapport, she had rather a lot of mental voice, and finding the discipline to control it had been one of her few triumphs to date.

Yes, Marguerida.

I am having one of those headaches that I get when I have premonitions. Is Dio all right?

I monitored her half an hour ago, and she was quite as usual. I stayed to listen all the way though that Thetan voyage song—the rhythm is almost hypnotic.

You didn't hear all of it—only the portion I know, which is the part that the folk on our island owned. And the rhythm is the movement of the waves, so of course it is hypnotic. Are you sure she is well?

As sure as I can be.

Then something else is wrong—or is going to be wrong soon. Dammit! Why do I have to have these stupid scraps of foreknowledge? You would think that I would either have nothing, or a clear, concise lump of stuff that I could deal with.

That would certainly make it easier, Marguerida. Like so much else, the ideal is very far from the reality. When did it start?

About half an hour ago. I thought it was just one of my usual headaches from being around matrices—only I haven't been around the Tower much this afternoon. I worked with Jeff this morning, had my second breakfast, and was just going to go over to the scriptorium to see how the work is progressing on those records that Haydn Lindir found, when, bang, my brain was being attacked by skewers. So I sat down in the fragrance garden, thinking that I just needed to get some sun and relax, and it got worse and worse.

I see. Well, for the moment, I cannot find anything amiss.

It might not have anything to do with Arilinn, I suppose. I mean, Mikhail could have fallen down a cliff and broken his neck.

Stop that right this minute! I will put up with that sort of thing from my sister, since she has such a vivid imagination, and no self-control whatever! I expect better of you!

Yes, Liriel. Margaret's response was almost meek. She accepted criticism from her cousin as she did from no one else, not even her father.

There, that is better. If anything had happened to my brother, you would know it, and there would be no uncertainty whatever.

You are probably right. I do wish that my father and yours were not being such stubborn idiots.

Wish yourself to the moon and it will be easier, chiya. *They are men, after all, and men always insist on being right, even when they are quite wrong. The person I feel most sorry for is Uncle Regis, caught in between the two of them, and the members of the Cortes who have to listen to their argument.*

Do you think they will ever straighten things out between them—at least to the point where Dom *Gabriel will let me . . .*

Well, if you gave up the Alton Domain to Father, he might see his way clear to stop behaving like a dolt, but I think he is almost enjoying trying to best your father at something. I believe he has stopped thinking of you or Mik or anyone except himself and his injured dignity.

I'd do it in a second except the Old Man would not like it, and he has enough on his plate, worrying about Dio. Why do things have to be so complicated?

If I knew the answer to that, I would be the wisest woman on Darkover, and several other planets as well, Marguerida. Have you eaten?

Oh, yes. I still don't believe how much I manage to eat without gaining an ounce. Even though I know perfectly well that laran is powered by body energy, it goes contrary to everything I know about diet!

I confess a little envy at your figure, Marguerida. And, I have observed, your shadow matrix radiates continuously. It is a very interesting phenomenon—from a technical point of view. It is also why your gloves wear out in a tenday or so.

I know, and I wish someone could think of a better way for me to manage than to always have to wear these things. I feel very outre. Even wearing two, so I don't draw attention to the left hand, still makes me self-conscious!

Oh, I don't know. Maeve Landyn was saying the other day that your mitts are rather fetching, particularly since Master Esteban has started adding bits of embroidery.

I feel like a freak, and I hate it.

I know you do, chiya, *and you should not. Now, go get some tea or something. Or get Dorilys from the stables and go for a ride. That always makes you feel better.*

All right, but it won't be the same without Mikhail.

Margaret knew that Liriel was right, that she needed some exercise. And the little pewter-colored mare that Mikhail had given her, as a way of making her stay at Arilinn less unpalatable, was a delight. She had fallen in love with the horse the first time she had seen her, running in the front paddock at Armida, months before. She was a spirited filly, with dark mane and tail, almost silvery hooves, and a coat like polished metal.

Learning matrix technology was exhausting, and the rides were revitalizing. The fresh air and sunshine never failed to restore her innate humor, and Margaret knew she had been neglecting herself the past few days.

But since Mikhail had gone, in a parting that was difficult for both of them, she had barely gone out to the stables to visit her horse. She knew that Dorilys would be taken care of by the grooms, that she would be exercised and curried and fed. But the little mare reminded her of Mikhail, and her heart was not really in it as she left her house, having changed into her riding skirt and put leather gloves on over silken ones, and walked toward the stable.

The headache had abated a little, but it was still sufficiently present to be noticeable, like distant thunder which is more felt than heard. Margaret yawned, trying to relax her jaw, and entered the shadowed interior of the barn. It smelled of clean straw, spattered water, and manure—a combination she found pleasant and somehow comforting. One of the grooms saw her and met her with a big grin.

"*Domna!* Dorilys is going to be pleased to see you. You haven't been absent for this long since you were sick."

"You should be scolding me for neglecting my pretty girl, Martin."

"Why, *domna,* I would never do such a thing. It isn't my place, and I am sure you have been busy at your studies up at the Tower."

Margaret gave up. She was never, she suspected, going to be completely comfortable with being deferred to, treated as if she were someone special. She had spent too many years being Ivor Davidson's assistant, taking charge of luggage and travel itineraries, dealing with petty bureaucrats and customs agents with larcenous hearts, or coping with academic rivalry and jealousy, to turn into a *comynara* overnight. No matter how she was treated, she still felt she was only Margaret Alton, Fellow of the University, not Marguerida Alton, heiress to a Darkovan Domain, a noble in almost any Terran hierarchy she could think of.

It was a little disheartening, knowing that with the best intentions in the world, she was probably never going to be able to behave in a manner that would please her formidable aunt Javanne Lanart-Hastur, or other matrons of her generation. She remained too independent, too headstrong, and lacked either the will or the capacity to defer to males or pretend to be stupid and meek. Within the confines of Darkovan society, she was an outsider and seemed likely to remain so, no matter how hard she tried.

Since she could not change her character, however, Margaret decided that she would just have to make the best of things, and go for a nice ride on a fine autumn day. It was almost fifty degrees, and the wind was only a cool draft, smelling of leaves being burned for potash, and the drifting scent of bread from the Arilinn bakery.

Martin brought Dorilys, saddled and almost dancing, across the cobblestones to the mounting block. Behind him another groom had a comfortable cob, and she realized with a start that Martin intended to accompany her. It would do no good to ask him not to—she was a female, and females, unless they were Renunciates, did not go for horseback rides alone. He would not understand, and, worse, he would be hurt. She knew that she was altogether too sensitive, and that she could be manipulated by Martin or any other servant, so she shrugged, stepped onto the mounting block, and threw her leg over into the saddle.

Dorilys threw her head back, and half-reared, expressing her delight at having Margaret around. The little filly did not seem to mind the grooms riding her, but she always made it clear who her preferred rider was. She began to dance around, impatient to be out and about. Slapping the reins lightly against the satiny neck of the horse, Margaret started out of the stableyard, with Martin following her.

Arilinn Tower stood on a plain that ran down to the river, so there was a great deal of flat ground. Much of it was covered with trees—similar to maples, elms, quickbeam, and other hardwoods—not the conifers so typical of the lands farther north. But there were several open areas which afforded a good ride.

There were fields around the little town near the Tower, but they were empty now, the harvest over. The stands of trees around the fields were ablaze with autumn color: red, orange, russet, and gold. The soft breeze brought the smell of leaves and fallow earth to her face, accompanied by the pleasant scent of burning foliage. There was a small enclave of charcoal makers nearby, and she knew they were busy at their work.

Margaret had discovered, much to her own surprise, that the quiet rhythm of the agricultural year was very soothing. She loved to escape from the confines of the Tower, to be away from the tremendous energy of the place, and ride among the fields. She had watched the farmers tend those fields, then seen them bring in the grain. She had been to the mill along the River Valeron where the grain was ground for flour. A little to the west of the mill there was a lumber operation, and beyond it a settlement of dyers who used the waters of the great river in their work.

She let Dorilys move into a moderate trot, longing to give her her head and run, but aware that Martin's cob would be left eating dust if she did. Margaret fell into the steady rhythm of the horse, and slowly the persistent headache began to fade. The ruddy sun warmed her face slightly; she had become accustomed to the relative cold of Darkover.

After about twenty minutes, they reached the banks of the river. It was running softly, the water gurgling between the rocks along the shore. There were stands of bulrushes, dried now, rustling in the breeze and making a pleasant sound that was almost musical.

She turned west, her heart brimming, thinking of Mikhail riding somewhere ahead of her, beyond the horizon. What was he seeing, she wondered, and what was he thinking. Margaret slowed to a walk, for the banks of the river were irregular and not the best place for a horse. Martin rode silently behind her, the steady sound of his cob's hooves a reassuring note in the music she felt was all around her. It seemed a vast symphony to her trained ears and mind, and for the first time she wondered why that form did not seem to be present on Darkover. Darkovans sang at the drop of a hat, and very well indeed, but as far as she had been able to discover, they had never gotten around to creating large orchestral works. She made a mental note to ask Master Everard when she was back in Thendara.

The thought of the old Guildmaster brought back the memory of Ivor Davidson, her mentor and friend, who had died soon after their arrival on Darkover. She missed him, but her first grief had lessened, and she could now recall him without great pain. If Ivor had not died, she would never have ended up in the Kilghards with only Rafaella n'ha Liriel, her Renunciate guide and friend, when she began to have her first bout of threshold sickness. How would Ivor have managed, she wondered? She had never been sick during all the years they journeyed around the Federation together, collecting and studying indigenous music, unless one counted the occasional cold. For all the excellence of their technology, Terrans had never managed to conquer the common cold, and she didn't think they ever would.

The tension in her body was easing as she idly watched trees and running water, allowing her mind to wander where it would. What a good idea Liriel had had, suggesting a ride. How clever she was. As was so often the case when she thought of her cousin, Margaret smiled. Liriel and her brother Mikhail almost made up for having to endure the rest of the Alton clan—Aunt Javanne and Uncle Gabriel, their older sons, Gabe and Rafael, and Liriel's twin, Ariel. Almost. Ariel still made Margaret cringe, with her constant fussing and worrying. The woman was halfway through her pregnancy now, with a sixth child conceived about the time Margaret had arrived on Darkover, the daughter she had longed for.

The smile faded. Every time she thought about that yet unborn child, Margaret got a terrible sinking feeling in her stomach, a sense of danger. That girl was going to be trouble. What a terrible thing to think about a child not yet born! It was the sort of premonition that made her curse the fact that she had some of the Aldaran Gift of foretelling, and hope, against all her feelings, that she was totally wrong.

Then, in between one breath and the next, Margaret experienced a bleakness, a sharp pang of loss. She jerked the reins in her surprise, and Dorilys whinnied in complaint. She drew to a halt, and Martin rode up beside her, looking concerned.

"What is it, *domna?*"

"I don't know. I felt as if a shadow had crossed the sun. I think we should go back now." She sighed. It was such a beautiful day, and she had been enjoying herself. She did not want to go back to Arilinn. More than anything, she wanted to ride west, to follow Mikhail, to let the Domain and her studies go hang. But dutifully she reined the horse around, and they headed back in the direction of the Tower, just visible above the trees.

The stableyard seemed just as they had left it, and nothing appeared amiss. Margaret dismounted, gave the reins to Martin, and patted Dorilys quickly but perfunctorily on the neck. "Another day, my pretty. Another day we will have a good run." The horse nickered in response, and looked at her with great dark eyes, as if she understood every word.

Then she hurried to the Tower, her heart pounding a little. Her booted feet sped over the paved walkway, and she passed the bakery and the scriptorium where she had planned to spend the afternoon. She did not pause at her little house, because the closer she got to the Tower, the greater was her sense of urgency.

Something had happened, something bad, and her mind began to manufacture all sorts of things. Dio had gotten out of stasis, or Ariel had gone into premature labor, or Mikhail had . . . No! Margaret slackened her pace a little and forced herself to stop theorizing! She was an academic, not a hysterical female who went off the deep end! She was a Fellow of the University, dammit!

Liriel?

Yes, Marguerida. There was something sad and guarded in the answer.

What's happened?

Domenic . . .

Oh, no! Margaret came to a complete halt on the walkway. She felt her body turn to ice, to stone. *But he was getting better!* That was not entirely true. Her own quick actions had saved the boy's life immediately after his accident, but his neck had been broken, and he would never be able to use his arms or legs again. The Healers had done their best—and she now knew that their best was, in some ways, as good as any offered by Terran medical technology—but the real damage was irreparable. *How?*

He choked. It happened so quickly that no one could do anything.

Margaret felt her anger rise, and held it back with a great effort. Poor Ariel! If the child had been taken to a Terran medical center, she knew, they would have put a breathing tube in his throat, because the greatest danger with a neck broken in the third cervical vertebra was what had just happened. She had not known that when he had been injured, but in the ensuing months she had made it her business to discover as much as she was able about such injuries, so that she could do as much as she could to prevent the very death she had foreseen at Armida months before. If only Ariel had not been so stubbornly insistent on keeping the child at Arilinn.

Now it was too late, and the boy was gone. She felt tears begin to trickle down her cheeks, and the vast grief for Ivor that she thought was past returned in full force. But Ivor had been old, had lived a long and meaningful life. Domenic had been a child of nine; he had hardly started to live!

Despite the reasons her rational mind offered her, Margaret still felt that if she had just been more persuasive in her arguments, more insistent, this tragedy might have been avoided. If only, she thought, she had not had the premonition at Armida, or managed to conceal it better, if Ariel had not gone off half-cocked, taking a clumsy carriage out in the start of a summer storm. If, if . . . it was all hindsight, and she knew it.

She felt sad, but even more she felt guilty, as if somehow the death of the little boy were her fault. Margaret felt as if she were some sort of jinx. Ivor had died, and Dio was dying! She shook herself all over and scolded herself for being a morbid idiot. It was no one's fault— but she wanted someone to blame, and the best candidate was always herself. It was not even Ariel's fault. She suspected, however, that her cousin was in much the same state as she was, looking for a scapegoat.

How is Ariel taking it?

Quite well, under the circumstances. But I would not let her see you right now.

No, that would be pushing my luck. I'll go back to my house for the present.

Margaret turned back on the pathway, and retraced her steps toward the little house that had been her home for four months. It was made of stone, the inner walls paneled in polished wood. There were five rooms: two bedrooms, a parlor, dining room, and kitchen. It was cozy and civilized, and she liked that, after years of enduring sometimes primitive conditions with Ivor.

When she entered, she could hear her servant, Katrin, a soft-spoken woman in her fifties, rattling around the kitchen, banging pots and pans. A nice smell floated in the air—rabbithorn stew, she thought. Margaret's appetite was gone, but she knew it would return. Sometimes her need for food seemed like the only constant in her daily life.

The tears had continued, and now her nose was starting to get stuffy. She found a handkerchief, a large square of linen embroidered with pretty flowers, and mopped her eyes and blew her nose. Then she sat down in a large chair beside the small fireplace in the parlor and let herself grieve silently, her chest heaving with sobs, and tears obliterating sight. She did not want Katrin to hear her, to try to comfort her. She wanted to let herself release all the sorrow that seemed to fill her slender body.

The light in the room began to fade, as the bloody sun sank below the horizon. The handkerchief was now a sodden, disgusting rag, and she didn't seem to have the strength to get up and find another. Her face hurt from crying, and her nose was red from repeated blowings. There was a wire around her chest, cutting into her breasts, and the pleasant smell of horse on her riding skirt was nauseating to her.

Margaret wanted to stop crying, to stop feeling sad, or sorry for herself. She should be thinking of Ariel, of Piedro Alar, Ariel's patient and long-suffering husband, of the little boy she had hardly known before he was injured. All she could think of was Dio, and Ivor.

Then the tears began to slacken, and she stared to feel restless and useless, sitting there in the growing dusk. She wanted to be comforted, but there was no comfort. Except the music. That never died, or went away to remote places, or said unkind things. *My, what a morbid mood I am in,* she thought, finding something quite comforting in feeling wretched. With a great effort, she stood up, went into the bedroom, and fetched her little harp from where it stood in the corner of the room. She found another hanky, too, because she suspected she was not really finished with her crying.

Returning to the living room, she removed the cloth case from her instrument and started tuning it. Margaret realized she hadn't taken it out in a couple of weeks, that she had neglected her music in the press of her studies at the Tower. She hadn't recorded any new music for Dio in almost a month! Not that her sleeping beauty of a stepmother was going to complain, but if she *could* hear the music, she must be getting tired of it by now.

Margaret warmed up with a few simple scales, readjusted the tuning, and started to play randomly. The cascade of notes was sweet to her ears. After several minutes she found herself picking out one of her favorite pieces, Montaine's *Third Etude*. It had originally been intended for the piano, and she had adapted it to the harp as part of her honors program at the University. It was complex enough to engage her attention, but sufficiently familiar to offer her no real challenge.

Still, after two playings, she started to do some variations, as if the exercise demanded it. Margaret noticed what she was doing in a distant, abstract way, noting that she had just turned one of the themes on its head in a way she had never done before. It was just the sort of play that went on in Ivor and Ida Davidson's house in the evenings. They always had several students living in the large house just outside the confines of the Music School. She did not think of the house often, for when she remembered University, she almost always thought of the dormitories where she had spent her first rather miserable year, before Ivor had heard her singing in the library and helped her find something that gave her life a direction and meaning. It brought back a simpler time, a happier time for her, when there had been no complications, no death, no uncertainties about her life.

As she played, Margaret found herself remembering Ivor's funeral in Thendara, and how many of the members of the Musicians Guild, who had never even met him, had carried his coffin to the graveyard and offered their songs. She had sung that day, but now her voice seemed stilled, as if her grief could not be vocalized. Ivor was old and Domenic had been young. That was the difference.

Her fingers played across the strings, and she found the dirge she had sung for Ivor that day emerge from the harp. It was a fine piece of music, twenty-eighth century Centauri. It was a sad thing, but there was a feeling in it of hope that began to ease her pain a bit.

Barely aware of what she was doing, Margaret stopped playing the dirge and began to pluck another tune from her harp. After several minutes, she realized that she did not know the piece at all, that she was making it up as she went along, thinking of the little boy taken untimely, of all the things he would never experience. It was a strong song, a piece that moved her even as she was creating it. And it was her own, not borrowed from another! Her mind, so well disciplined for years, observed the composition and found it good. Margaret rarely created original work, and she allowed herself to rejoice in the music that flowed from her fingers, uncritically for once. It had, she noticed, something of the sound of the river as she had ridden beside it a few hours before, something of the rushes waving in the breeze, and the call of some songbird she had heard without really noticing.

Margaret was so deep in the music that she did not hear the front door open, and was unaware she had a visitor until she came to a halt and heard the soft sound of a throat clearing behind her. She turned abruptly to find Lew Alton standing in the entrance to the parlor, a light cloak draped over his arm. He wore a rather shabby riding tunic, and his silvered hair was tousled.

"Father! How long have you been standing here?" She searched his face, suddenly tense, trying to discern his mood as she had when she was a child. Then Margaret realized that she no longer had to do that, that this Lew Alton was quite a different man from the one she remembered. He no longer drank himself into despair, nor raged like a beast. But the habits were long-standing, and it was hard to completely trust the man she had begun to know in the past few months.

"I have no idea. I was so entranced by your music that I lost track of time. What is it?" Lew smiled slowly, as if the movement was strange, new to him, and his eyes gleamed with interest.

"I don't know—I just made it up."

"Well, I certainly hope you can remember it, for it is quite splendid."

"Oh, yes. I was scoring it as I went along."

"You make it sound so simple," Lew said, setting his cloak aside. "I am always rather awed that you can remember so much music, but you never told me you could compose." He sat down across for her, searching her tear-stained face.

"I don't, much. Not like Jheffy Chang, or Amethyst."

"Who?"

"People I knew at University. Jheffy composed all the time, and he and Am used to have a kind of ongoing contest when I lived at Ivor's house. It was terrific, because they were completely unself-conscious about it. Music, new music, just seemed to leak out of their bodies, all the time. I never had that ability, which is a good thing, because if I had, I would never have ended up becoming Ivor's assistant."

"Why not?"

"Father, you don't ask a racehorse to pull a plow, do you? Or expect a drayhorse to run a race?"

"Are you calling yourself a plowhorse, daughter?" He sounded stern, yet playful at the same time.

"Musically, yes, I am. I am good enough to imitate others, to interpret, but I am not particularly original or creative. Or, at least, I wasn't when I was studying at University. And I don't really regret it a bit, because the demands of being an original composer are enormous. Jheffy was something of a prodigy, and he was very vain and had the social skills of a marmot. Am was better, because she came from a long line of musicians, and her family hadn't spoiled her as

Jheffy's did him. Not that she was a pleasant person—she wasn't one bit—but she didn't have to prove herself the best every second of the day."

"I am sorry that my work in the Federation Senate prevented me from watching you learn your music, *chiya*. It sounds much more interesting than I ever imagined. I feel that I have missed so much of your life. I was not there when you had your first love, or . . ."

"But, you were, Father! Mikhail is my first love. And there will never be another, no matter what happens." She blushed. "Did I say that I was glad to see you?"

"No, but I knew it from the way your face lit up when you realized I was here. It is very heartening to see that look in your eyes. I cannot imagine why I didn't mind missing it for so many years."

"Well, if I had seen you before, after I went to University, my eyes would not have sparkled, but glared. And there are still a few times when I remember how impossible you were on Thetis, when you refused to tell me my history and were hoping I would grow out of my mental block, the overshadowing that *she* did to me, that I still want to box your ears and call you names!"

"And quite rightly. I am sure I deserve any number of ear boxings, and I am pleased that you have chosen to forgo the experience."

"Have you come to see Dio?"

"Of course. But when I arrived, I found out that young Domenic had just died and decided that seeing you was more immediate. I confess I hardly expected to find you playing your harp by the fire."

"Well, I was crying earlier, and feeling as if everything were my fault. But I remembered something Aunt Javanne told me about you, about how you always assumed you were the author of anything that went wrong, and how I was very much like you—too much sensibility for my own good, or something like that. So it was as natural as breathing to turn to music."

Thyra was like that, about music. I never thought I would have anything to remember about her that was good. He quirked an eyebrow at her. "Why?"

"Because music is something that I have always been able to trust. It never gets angry at you, or runs away, or dies. It only is. Maybe if you are a composer, it is different. Now that I think about it, there was something about Jheffy that seemed a little desperate at times, as if he were afraid he would wake up one morning and discover the music had left for Aldebaran with another composer. But if you are mostly a performer, it is very dependable and trustworthy. Not to mention comforting. I can say things by playing music that I never can say in words."

"I see. There is a great deal more to this music business than I ever imagined." He nodded, then smiled slightly. "How are you?"

"Sad, of course, but a little angry, too."

"Angry?"

"Well, Domenic did not have to die, did he? I mean, if he could have received the services of a Terran medical facility, he wouldn't have choked to death. I have a lot of respect for matrix science now, but I still think that putting total dependence on it is just as stupid as believing that technology is the answer to everything. There needs to be some compromise, some middle ground, and it seems to me that no one is even trying to work it out."

"If you study human history, I think you will find that people are so emotionally invested in doing things in their customary manner that they prefer to resist change, even when it is in their own interest."

"I know that, but I still don't like it!"

"Of course you don't, daughter. And, yes, Domenic might have lived. But the healers were unable to mend the injury, so he would have been entirely helpless for the rest of his years. Even Terran nano-technology might not have been able to reverse things. I don't know, and the matter is out of our hands now."

"I know, but that doesn't make it any easier to accept. And I am concerned about Ariel, too, even though I do not like her. She is still a few months away from birthing, and I have learned enough here in Arilinn to realize that the impact of her distress on the mind of her daughter is likely to be terrible." *Is this why the glimpse I saw of Alanna Alar in my vision is of such an angry woman? Maybe it is my fault, because I foresaw that Domenic would never reach adulthood, and then he got hurt when the carriage overturned and—*

"Marguerida—you cannot change the past, and you cannot prevent the future."

"No, but that won't stop me wanting to!" She set the harp aside and began to pleat the bottom of her tunic with nervous fingers. After a minute of silence, she said hoarsely, "I hate it here."

"You mean Arilinn? Or Darkover?"

"Arilinn. I love Darkover, although I find some of its customs pointless. I went riding earlier, and because I am a woman, one of the grooms insisted on coming with me, which meant that I could not gallop across the fields like a fiend, which was what I wanted to do. But I am not at ease here, despite all the efforts of Jeff and Liriel and some of the others to make me comfortable. I cannot sit in a Tower

circle because being in a room with lots of matrices is still impossible
for me. And several of the students seem to regard me as some sort of
monster. They stare at this," she said, holding up her left hand, "and
try to see through the silk. They do not like to work with me, and one
of the older healers, Berana, has outright refused to have anything to
do with me. The word 'abomination' floats across her mind like an oil
slick. Ugh! She makes me feel as if I were dirty or something."

"I see. Why haven't you said anything sooner?"

"Well, as long as Mikhail was here learning how to test for *laran,* it
was not so bad. It wasn't good, but I could look forward to taking rides
with him, to talking to him about . . . well, anything. And I didn't
want to whine and complain. I kept thinking it would get easier when I
learned more, but instead it has become harder every day. My sensitivity to the crystals has, if anything, increased. I have to spend a great
deal of energy just keeping myself together, because my impulse is to
blast the damn things to flinders."

"I wouldn't worry about that," Lew answered calmly. At the same
time, he shifted in his chair as if uneasy.

"Oh, wouldn't you?" she snarled. "I do, because I have some idea
of what I am able to do. This thing," Margaret went on, shaking her
fist at her father, "is not like any matrix that has ever existed before,
because it is not from anything in the material world. I've spent a lot
of sleepless nights talking with Jeff, and with Hiram d'Asturien, who
knows more about the history of matrix science than anyone else alive,
trying to figure out what is going on. What I have, Father, is a portion
of the overworld engraved on my flesh. Not only that, it was once the
keystone of the Keep of Ashara Alton, who was the most powerful
leronis who ever lived, even taking into account the natural exaggeration that is bound to accrue to historical figures. I suspect that if I lost
my temper, I could blast Arilinn off the face of the world. I wouldn't
be surprised, even, if that is not what might have happened at Hali
centuries ago."

"I see you have given this a great deal of consideration, *chiya.* And
I must say you have shown a great deal of patience and endurance.
Much more than I was capable of at your age." He sighed.

"Maybe," she said hesitantly. Then she took a deep breath and
plunged ahead, determined to tell him what she must while she still
had the courage. "Father, I just don't know if I can stay here much
longer. Javanne is going to show up, looking daggers at me for just
existing, and Ariel is likely going to get hysterical if she even catches a
glimpse of me, since she still blames me for Domenic's accident. And
it is just killing me. I feel as if I have a chest full of broken glass most

of the time. I thought, a few months ago, that I had come home, but now I am starting to doubt it. I feel as estranged at Arilinn as I did before I came back to Darkover."

"You should have been an actress, Marguerida, because I never suspected how unhappy you were here."

"Well, there is no help for it, since I don't really want to be a wild telepath. I don't want to be any sort of telepath at all, frankly. I'd give anything to undo the past. Well, maybe not anything. I would not give up Mikhail, or you. But it is not enough. I need some peace, some quiet!"

"You wanted to go to Neskaya, and study with Istvana Ridenow, before you were persuaded to come to Arilinn. Do you still wish that?"

"If I must be in a Tower, I would rather be with Istvana than anyone. She never makes me feel as if I have two heads and a tail!"

"Good. I think I can manage that much, daughter. It is the least I can do for you."

Margaret stared at Lew, too astonished to speak for a second. Her heart gave a leap of delight, of release. Then she steeled herself, afraid that she would be disappointed. It could not be this easy! "Can you, really?"

Lew looked at her solemnly, but with just the hint of a twinkle in his eyes. "I am not without influence, you know."

Margaret laughed and then found herself crying again. The sobs rose in her chest, swelled up into her throat, and broke out of her mouth in spite of her efforts to silence them. She bent over, holding herself, hugging her arms around her, wailing her grief and loss. It was a dreadful noise, and she was ashamed of it, but she could not stop, and Lew made no effort to halt it. Instead, he just sat and waited, as if he understood how needful it was.

It was completely dark by the time she finally managed to stop weeping, and her face felt sore. She mopped her cheeks for the hundredth time, blew her nose, and sank back against the chair, exhausted. And, to her disgust and surprise, hungry. The smell of dinner wafted through the room, and Katrin appeared in the doorway, a white dab of flour on her short nose. She looked at Lew, grinned a little, and only said, "I had better set another place."

Margaret chuckled softly. "One good thing about Darkover—meals always seem to appear on time, and frequently."

"Yes, they do. Now go wash your face." He grinned suddenly. "I used to tell you that on Thetis, didn't I? Your face always seemed to be dirty."

"Yes, Father, you did, and it was. Thank you very much."

"For what?"

"Just thank you." And then she retreated quickly, for the tears were threatening to begin again. She could not speak all the words that were brimming in her heart, her love for this man, this father she had so lately discovered. There would, she hoped, be time to say them, but not with a dirty face and an empty stomach. It would have to keep.

3

Halyn House was so well concealed within a grove of tall trees that Mikhail and his Guardsmen almost rode by without realizing they had reached their goal. Only a thin stream of smoke above the trees indicated human habitation, and Daryll's keen eyes spotted it. At twenty-three, he was the younger of Mikhail's two companions, and by far the more lively minded, always ready with a jest and not in the least intimidated by Mikhail's position. Mathias, the other Guardsman, was nearly forty, and of a slow and sober disposition. Mikhail had known him since he was a child, for he was from the Alton Domain. He knew he could trust them both completely, and was reassured by their presence, since the feeling of unease he had had along the road seemed to be getting stronger the closer they came to their journey's end.

They found their way through the trees with difficulty, for there were many fallen branches on the little path, wood that should have been collected and set to dry for the coming winter. As they finally emerged into the stableyard, Mikhail frowned, filled with quiet despair. Duncan, the old man Mikhail remembered from his previous visit, crept from the shadows of a rather dilapidated building, alerted by the sound of their steeds. The sour smell of rotting hay was everywhere. Shakes were missing from the roof, so the stables must be leaking, and other evidence of disrepair was apparent. One trough was tilted on its side, and the other had a green and scummy look, as if the water had been standing in it for several days.

Mikhail could now see the roof and upper story of Halyn House itself, though a large hedge prevented him from seeing the rest, and he was more than a little shocked. The upper windows were empty of glass, boarded over in some places, but left open in others. Tiles were missing from the peaked roof, and one chimney sagged and looked as if it might fall over at any moment.

Duncan simply stared at the three, as if they were some type of apparition. The man had aged a great deal in four years, and looked as if he had lost weight as well. His clothing was worn, his boots so thin at the toes that one stocking was visible. The old man's hair was filthy, matted against his skull, and his teeth were rotting.

Before Mikhail could speak, the wind shifted, and a smell of sulfur blew into his nostrils. It was a hot, acrid scent, and it came from somewhere beyond the house itself. It took him a minute to identify the odor. He had not known there was a hot spring in the area until now.

"Hello, Duncan. How are you keeping these days?" he began, speaking with more cheer than he felt.

"Welcome, *vai dom*. I'm as well as I can be." Then he hesitated, looked at the ground, and shuffled his feet anxiously. "Are you expected?" He cackled eerily. "Last time you wasn't."

"Yes, I am." What if Priscilla had changed her mind, and had not bothered to tell anyone? What if he had learned how to test for *laran* and made this journey for nothing? Regis Hastur had assured him just a few days earlier that things were fine, but something could have happened, he supposed. No, he would have been told.

"*Mestra* Emelda did not inform me," Duncan muttered, his humor evaporating as he rubbed his gnarled hands together. "There is no place prepared for all these horses. There is no feed."

Mikhail ignored the man's inhospitable words and dismounted. He was tired and hungry, and his temper was starting to fray. The smell of the stables disturbed him, and the sense of wrongness about the place plucked at his nerves. He had no idea what was going on, but he was determined to get to the bottom of things immediately.

"Who is *Mestra* Emelda?" He had never heard of this woman, but the tone of Duncan's voice made him uneasy.

"*Mestra* Emelda," the old man repeated, as if it explained everything.

Daryll dismounted and took Charger's reins, since it was clear that

Duncan had no intention of doing anything but stand there and look bewildered. "I'll see to the horses, *Dom* Mikhail. We have enough feed for tonight—though from the smell of the place, there isn't a scrap of clean hay to be had. Whew!" He curled his nose a little and grimaced in distaste. "Tomorrow I can ride over to that village we passed about five miles back, and have some sent over."

"Tomorrow?" Duncan looked at the Guardsman suspiciously. "Surely you are not staying! She won't like that a bit."

"Of course my men are staying," Mikhail snapped, exasperated.

"No, they won't," the old fellow growled, now looking almost hostile.

The feeling of unease which had plagued him the closer he got to Halyn House burst into a sudden moment of fear. He stamped it down roughly and studied Duncan more closely. The man he remembered had been crochety, but never rude. And he had been neat in his person, and intelligent as well. This fellow seemed to be another person entirely—a sullen and rather stupid man. His eyes seemed glazed now that Mikhail was near enough to see them.

Mathias was off his steed and walking toward the stables, his broad shoulders stiff, as if he expected the worst. He disappeared beneath the shadowed door of the barn, and Mikhail heard a curse. A moment later he emerged, his sober and normally tranquil face red with rage. "That's no way to treat good stock!" he thundered, and looked ready to knock Duncan down.

Mathias had grown up with the horses for which the Alton Domain was famed, and had a passion for the animals that most men reserved for women. The expression on his normally pleasant face was outraged. The situation in the stables must be worse than Mikhail had assumed.

"What do you mean, Mathias?"

"I only took a glance, but it was enough! Some of the animals are standing in ditches up to their hocks, and the stalls are filthy. I never saw anything like it."

"I don't have time to take care of those animals," sniveled Duncan, looking a little ashamed. "It's all I can do to just keep the wood chopped for the fire, and . . ."

"It's going to take a lot to muck out those stables," Mathias interrupted, "and the roof needs repair. This place is a disgrace!"

Mikhail agreed with him, and hoped that the house itself was in better shape. He had spent enough time at Armida to know the ins and outs of good management, and was rather surprised to realize how much he had learned without knowing it. He had mucked out stalls, curried his horses, sat up all night with foaling mares, broken his own steeds, and dealt with cases of colic and other equine troubles. But the stables at Armida were very well run—*Dom* Gabriel Alton would not have permitted anything else—and the horses were well-treated. It made him sick to think of the poor animals within this stable.

It was still an hour to dusk, and he felt an enormous reluctance to go into Halyn House now. It was a strange sensation, a kind of prickling of his skin, a chilliness that had nothing to do with the cooling of the air. Instead, he turned to Daryll and Mathias, nodding. "Let's see what we can do to make the place livable before dark."

Daryll and the other Guardsman exchanged a look. It was one thing for Mikhail to do chores while they were on the road, and quite another now, the look suggested. And under ordinary circumstances, they would not have been reduced to stablehands either, for there were always grooms around, and boys learning their craft. It was clear they were uneasy about the situation, trying to balance Mikhail's dignity with the need to make some order.

He did not wait for them to agree, but marched into the dank and gloomy building. Mikhail was glad his belly was fairly empty, for the stink was enough to make his gorge rise. He went to the nearest stall, slipped alongside the miserable horse there, and took the hackamore from its hook along the wall. He slipped it over the horse's head and carefully backed the animal out.

The beast was too dispirited to offer any resistance. There were sores on its legs. It had not been farried in a long time, so the hooves were grown out, and the poor thing was cowhocked. The skin hung along its ribs, and the animal was listless, too weak to show any spirit. He recognized the horse as one that Vincent had ridden four years before, a fine animal that deserved good treatment. Mikhail turned it around slowly, then led it out of the stable and into the yard. He looped the lead over a rail, and gave the horse a pat on the neck. It looked at him with enormous dark eyes, then shifted uncomfortably from hoof to hoof, as if its legs were painful.

"Can either of you clip his feet? I never quite got the knack of it."

Mathias grunted, went to his own horse, and took a leather bag off the back. In a few moments, he had a sickle-shaped knife in his callused hand. "I always carry this—you never know when you will need it." Then he bent down and took the nearest hoof and started to slice off the excess cartilage.

Daryll had followed Mikhail's example, and brought out another animal, a nice little colt. In a few minutes, they had gotten all the

horses out of the stable, and Mathias was cutting off the overgrown
hooves with a vengeance. He swore softly as he worked, gentling the
horses, though they were all too feeble to give him much trouble.
There were six animals in all, none of them in any better shape than
the first. Duncan just stood and watched, his dull eyes following their
movements.

Mikhail and Daryll found rakes and shovels, and started to clear
out the worst of the mess. The smell of ammonia was overpowering.
The rotten hay was full of worms, mostly earthworms, but there were
some parasites as well. And they disturbed several families of rats,
who ran squeaking into the shadows.

It was backbreaking labor, foul and stinking, but Mikhail found it
helped him shake the sense of rage and powerlessness that had arisen
in him. There were stalls that had not been used in years, and in these
the earthen floor had not been worn into troughs by the restless movement of overgrown hooves. Indeed, they were fairly clean, and only
needed a fast raking to set them to rights. Daryll climbed into the loft
and found a bale of hay that had not yet mildewed, then spread it
around sparingly.

"I don't blame ol' Mathy for bein' in a fury, one bit. Those are
decent horses, and it isn't right to treat 'em so badly," the Guardsman
said. Then he glanced up, toward the ceiling. "The rain will come in if
we don't see to it."

"I know. I've never seen anything like this. What a shambles!"

"I'll go for fresh hay at first light, and see if I can find a workman
who can fix the roof. That is . . ." he paused, ordering his thoughts,
"if we are going to remain. Are we?"

"We don't seem very welcome, do we?"

"Not if that old geezer is anything to judge by, we aren't. Look!
Here's some horse salve! Just the thing for those sores."

"Good. We need to get the trough clean, for I don't think fouled
water will do them any good. I suppose that old Duncan has been
watering them with a bucket, for while they look half starved, they
don't appear to be dehydrated. Take the salve to Mathias, will you,
while I look around and see if there is any feed. Those animals look
like they haven't been fed in a week."

"We've got enough oats on the mules for tonight, *Dom* Mikhail.
For ours and these poor, starved beasties. It goes right to my heart to
see them. When I took that palfrey out of her stall, I swear she said
'Thank you' and would have fallen on my neck with gratitude, if she
had arms instead of legs."

Mikhail grinned at the Guardsman's words, and felt his tension abate. Daryll was imaginative, although he tried to hide it. A good man. Both of them, he reflected, were fine men. The situation was not what he had expected. When he had visited Elhalyn Castle four years before, the household had been somewhat ramshackle, but the stables had been in decent order, and if the linens on the bed were worn, at least they were clean and decent. The unease which had almost vanished while he labored returned, and his smile faded. If the condition of the stable was any measure, then Halyn House was likely to be dreadful.

"When you go to the village, see if you can find a lad or two to help with the horses. I suspect that there is no staff—though I am damned if I can figure out why! When I visited four years ago, at the castle, there were not many servants, and Duncan was doing the duties of the *coridom,* even though that was not his job."

"Why?"

"The *coridom* was not in his right mind—a bit past his work—but *Domna* Elhalyn did not seem to notice. Or care. She is . . . eccentric."

"Daft sounds like a better word, if you don't mind my plain speaking. Not notice!" Daryll looked outraged, his cheeks reddening a little, and his blue eyes sparkling. "That there Duncan seems a ninny, too— past his work or just dimwitted."

"I know. And he wasn't like that four years ago. He was quite capable, and managed things well enough."

"You'll set things to right, *dom.*"

"I rejoice in your confidence, and only wish I shared it."

Daryll chuckled. "I never mucked out a stall with a lord before, so I think if you will do that, you will get things in order before the cat can polish her ear."

Mikhail experienced a wave of emotion from the Guardsman, a feeling of near devotion, of immediate loyalty that would become unswerving in time. Until that moment, he had not realized that he had been evaluated, observed, and judged, probably by both of his companions. He had never really considered before that those who followed his orders and did his bidding might have strong opinions. Or, rather, he had known it, but never felt it. Mathias had served under his father, while *Dom* Gabriel was still in charge of the Guard, and likely measured him against the Old Man. He wondered if he had measured up yet. Would he ever? Rather to his surprise, he found he wanted to command the kind of loyalty his father and his uncle did.

He glanced down at his hands. There was a blister starting on his forefinger, and his palms hurt from the unaccustomed labor. He was warm, sweaty, and he stank almost as much as the barn. His shoulder ached, and his thighs as well. If he had had his wish, he would have sat down and refused to move for an hour.

But Mikhail knew he could not put off going to the house any longer, however much he might long to. He trudged out of the dimness of the barn, then stopped and washed his hands under a pipe that ran from the wall, and should have run all the way to the still scummy trough. A piece of wood that supported it had broken and lay on the ground, and from the look of the dirt around it, had been broken for several weeks. Mikhail shook his head.

Then he spotted some rot in the wood around the pipe, where it came from the wall of the barn, and made a mental note to get it repaired. He splashed some water over his sweating face, wiped his sleeve across it, and hoped that there was a working bath in Halyn House. Then he turned and headed for the hedge which surrounded the structure.

There was an opening in it, and he passed beneath the thick barrier, to find himself standing in a rather unkempt garden. The foliage he recognized as the tops of carrots, onions, and other vegetables that grew below ground. There was a net that had once protected berries, but it was broken, and from the look of it, the birds had been feasting.

Mikhail shook his head, then heard the sound of a crow again. He looked up, and found a large bird watching him from a tree beside the house. It was a very handsome beast, perhaps the same one he had seen earlier, and the white on the edges of its wings gleamed redly in the last light of the day. It looked at him with intelligent eyes, shifted from claw to claw as if doing a little dance, then opened its beak. It flew down to the hedge, settling lightly on the topmost branches, and flared its wings, so the feathers gleamed in what remained of the light. The sun was just below the horizon, and the sky was an ominous color, thick clouds billowing, red, and purple.

He found himself fascinated by the odd behavior of the bird. Mikhail looked at it, unable to tear his eyes away for a moment, and felt as if it were trying to tell him something. Then the crow made a slow, croaking sound, like a door that needed oiling, and clacked its beak several times. The whole thing gave him the shivers, so eerie was the movement and the sound. Mikhail swallowed hard, shook the feeling away, and hurried toward the door of the house.

The door opened into the kitchen. Inside was an elderly man who jumped at the sound of Mikhail's boots on the wooden floor of the room. He was stirring a pot on a raised stone hearth, and spun around with a long-handled wooden spoon in one trembling hand. His eyes widened at the sight of a stranger.

Mikhail had not expected to come in by the back door, though the kitchen garden should have suggested he would. He glanced around the room quickly. It had high ceilings, two good-sized fireplaces for roasting, a long table in the middle, now covered with an odd collection of cooking vessels and serving pieces, and worn wooden floors. There was a pump on one side of the room, above a wooden sink which was piled with dishes. Beside it there was a rack with more dishes stacked into it. He gave a sigh of relief. At least the kitchen was cleaner than the stables.

"What are you doing here?" The old man took in Mikhail's sweat-stained traveling clothes and the muck still clinging to his boots. He didn't appear quite so bewildered as Duncan had, for his eyes were alert.

"I am Mikhail Hastur, and I am seeking *Domna* Priscilla Elhalyn."

"The more fool you," the fellow muttered quite rudely, and turned his back.

Mikhail hesitated. For the first time in his life, the name Hastur had evoked no expectable reaction. He was aware that servants took their tone from their masters and mistresses. It was most peculiar. The behavior of Duncan and the cook was hostile, and if he had not been so tired, he would have been offended. He had never before encountered such rudeness, and his strong sense of unease increased.

He realized he was piqued, partly because he had never before been in any situation where the name Hastur did not provoke immediate respect, and sometimes slavish obsequiousness. He relaxed a little, and made a mental note to be sure to tell Marguerida about it the next time they spoke; she would be sure find the whole thing amusing. Anyone else would be outraged—his mother or Uncle Regis—but his beloved would see the humor in it.

Usually, just the thought of Marguerida made him feel wonderful. But now it did not, and he wondered why. Something must have happened, in just the last few hours, he realized. It would have to keep. Later, when he had eaten and bathed, he would contact her. Now he needed to find Priscilla.

"You planning to stay to supper?" the cook asked in a sullen voice.

"Yes. There will be me, and my two Guardsmen as well."

The cook cackled. "That will put her High and Mightiness in a fine temper—three for dinner! I hope you ain't very hungry, because there won't be much for that many."

The pot smelled of boiled fowl and onions, and although it was hardly Mikhail's favorite meal, his empty belly was growling with hunger now. "We have been cleaning out the stables, so our appetites are very healthy."

"Cleaning the . . . a Hastur mucking out stalls!" The cook turned around again, peering at him. "Now, there is something I never thought to hear. It won't do you any good you know, for the *mestra* won't let another chicken into the pot. Very thrifty, she is."

The cook clearly did not mean Priscilla, but the other woman, Emelda, whom Duncan had mentioned. Thrifty? The Elhalyn Domain was wealthy, and there was no need for stinginess. She must be the housekeeper. He had had enough encounters with such persons over the years to know that they could be very bossy, petty tyrants. And, remembering how vague Priscilla had been on his previous visit, it would not surprise him to discover her in the thrall of a determined servant. Still, he was perturbed. There were children here with, he assumed, normal appetites, and he shuddered at the thought of them not having enough to eat.

Mikhail shrugged. He wasn't going to find out anything standing there. He was surprised by his sudden reluctance to move, to leave the kitchen. His mind felt muzzy, as if he had drunk a great deal of wine. It must be the effect of all that exercise in the stables.

He walked slowly out of the kitchen and into a dark corridor that smelled of must and mildew. After fifteen paces it opened into a dining room, a sad little room with a collection of chairs that seemed to be from several sources around a long table that had not been waxed in years. One end was thick with dust, but the other showed signs of recent use, the dull surface of the wood scuffed and smeared with grease. The wood was cracked in several places, the fine veneer split. The room was depressing, and all thoughts of a capable if bossy housekeeper vanished in the gloom.

It was chilly, and when he looked at the fireplace on one wall, he saw that there was a small brazier set on the firedogs, with no ash around it. That thing would barely produce enough heat to warm a mouse, and it must make the room very smoky. Curious, he went over and bent under the mantelpiece, peering up into the chimney. Utter darkness met his eyes, and he realized that the chimney was completely blocked with cinder. One more thing to have repaired.

Mikhail stepped back, glanced at the tattered tapestries along the walls, and felt a sense of helplessness and despair rise in his mind. Unlike his father, or his brother Gabe, he had never had the charge of a household. Comyn Castle, where he had spent his youth, was efficiently run by an army of servants; Armida and Castle Ardais as well.

He knew that food had to be transported from farms to kitchens, that wood had to be cut and dried for burning, that linens were gotten from the markets in Thendara, but he had no idea how to maintain a chimney! Or what to do about mildewing passages. It seemed an enormous task, and one, in his present state of hunger and weariness, that seemed quite beyond him. Then he told himself that he was the Elhalyn Regent, and could order things to be done. But if Duncan or the nameless cook were anything to judge by, he was not certain his orders would be heard, let alone obeyed.

His body still felt gripped by a strange lethargy, and it took all his determination to leave the chilly dining room and continue into the rest of the house. Mikhail went though a living room or parlor, and saw an embroidery frame beside the fireplace, suggesting that either Priscilla or one of her daughters had been doing some fancy work. It was an ordinary thing, but the most reassuring sight since his arrival.

He ventured into the foyer, a once beautiful chamber, now shabby and decayed. There were large slabs of stone set into the floor, but some were cracked, and a few had shifted out of their places, so they rose unevenly above the level of the floor. A long window on one side of the front door had been covered with several pieces of lumber, pegged in poorly, and he could feel the movement of air between the boards. The slight smell of sulfur from the hot spring drifted in, and he wrinkled his nose.

The house was very quiet. He looked toward the stairs, trying to hear some movement from the upper floor. There were five youngsters in this place, yet it seemed too silent. Armida, in his adolescence, had rung with heavy footfalls, young voices, and doors banged open and closed. Javanne had often complained she never had a quiet moment, and said that if she had known how noisy children were, she might not have borne so many. Right at that moment, Mikhail would have been pleased to hear the heavy footfalls of young men, the way he and his brothers had shaken the stairs at Armida. There was something very wrong about the quiet of this house, but he could not really put his finger on it.

A soft rustle of cloth made him look into the shadows beside the staircase, and after a moment, a woman emerged. She was skinny, almost scrawny, and had very dark hair, nearly black, curling around her narrow face. There was something strange about the actual color—a greenish tint that puzzled him—but in the poor light, it might be his eyes playing tricks on him. However, the color of her gown was no trick of light. It was that particular red which he knew was reserved for the most formal gowns of Keepers.

For a moment they stood staring at one another. Then the woman spoke haughtily. "What are you doing here?"

"I am Mikhail Hastur, and I have come to see to the children. Where is *Domna* Priscilla."

"See to the children! They don't need seeing to." She gazed at Mikhail with her gray eyes, and he felt such a rush of giddiness that he had to turn away.

"Who are you?" he snarled, finally regaining his wits. How dare this female look directly at him! What was going on?

"I am Emelda, and you have come a long way for nothing. You must leave immediately."

Before he could answer, Priscilla came out of the corridor behind the stairs. Her eyes seemed empty, and her apricot hair had faded to gray. He remembered her as a rather plump woman, but now she seemed thin, almost gaunt. "I heard voices." She saw Mikhail and stopped moving, looking at him as if he had appeared out of the air. "Oh. It's you. You came here with your friend Dyan, didn't you. Well, not here—you came to Elhalyn Castle. But I remember you." She seemed very pleased with herself at this. "What are you doing here now?"

"Regis Hastur has appointed me Elhalyn Regent, *domna*, as I believe you have been told."

"Oh, that. Yes, I believe I received some message about that. It does not explain your presence here. I did not invite you, did I?" Priscilla looked puzzled, then a little worried, as if she had remembered something unpleasant. Her eyes shifted uneasily toward Emelda.

Mikhail's mind felt filled with nasty insects, buzzing wildly. "As Regent, I must see to the well-being of your children, as well as test the boys," he managed to say. "I have arrived with two of my men, and . . ."

"You brought people with you!" This was Emelda, and she looked angry. "We cannot have that."

Mikhail reached the end of his patience. "Be quiet, whoever you are. This is none of your concern!" *No damn housekeeper is going to tell me what to do! And what is she doing, dressed in the color of a Keeper?*

The dark-tressed woman drew herself up. "I am Emelda Aldaran, and it is very much my concern. Why, without my guidance—"

"*Domna* Elhalyn," he thundered, startled by the roar in his voice, "what is going on?"

Priscilla glanced from one to the other, as if she were trapped between two hungry beasts. Her pale eyes glittered in the faint light in the foyer, and her hands began to tremble. "I don't know what you mean," she answered feebly.

"I mean that you are living in this tumble-down house with broken windows, that your servants are uncivil, and that your stables are a disgrace!"

"If you do not like it, leave," smirked Emelda. "You are not wanted here, or needed."

Once again Mikhail had the sensation of his energy being sucked out of his mind, and he turned a suspicious look on the strange female. She had *laran*, no doubt, and claimed Aldaran lineage—probably some *nedestra* child, though she seemed rather too old to be a daughter of either Robert or Herm Aldaran. It did not matter, and she might be lying. What did matter, he decided, trying to pierce the fog in his mind, was that she had some hold over Priscilla, and was running Halyn House to suit herself. He had the urge to throttle her, and almost immediately felt weak and giddy.

What in Zandru's hell was she? Mikhail had never encountered anyone quite like Emelda. He gritted his teeth and concentrated on Priscilla, blocking the other woman from his mind with as much force as he could bring to bear. As soon as he did, the sense of weakness left, and if he had not been a trained telepath, he would have thought he had imagined the entire sensation.

"My place is here, until one of the lads can be found suitable to claim the throne—that might take a year or more. And I have no intention of living in a rackety house during the coming winter. How could you have let the children live in such a mess?" He felt outrage, for the children he remembered from his previous visit.

"They do not mind," Priscilla replied, as if that answered everything.

"*Domna*," Emelda whispered, "he must not be allowed to interfere when the Guardian calls you. You must make him go away now."

"Emelda is right. I have changed my mind. I never should have let Regis Hastur persuade me . . ." She spoke with more assurance than before, but the words came in a monotone, without inflection, as if she were a puppet.

"It is no longer in your hands, *domna*. The Comyn Council has approved of my appointment as Regent, and I am here to stay." This was not precisely true, since the Council remained embroiled in its own problems, and for the most part, the meetings had been shouting matches between *Dom* Gabriel and Regis, or Lew and *Dom* Gabriel. But the Council had not disapproved either. The Elhalyn Domain was the least of their concerns, and Mikhail's seat on the Council had been voted on and passed, over his own father's very vocal objections.

At that moment, Mikhail would have gladly handed his place over to either of his brothers without a bit of regret. He could just see Gabe confronting Emelda—the image was very funny and somehow heartening. Knowing Gabe's explosive temper, he would have tossed the woman out the front door by now. Odd—he had never found the thought of his eldest brother so pleasing before.

"How dare you speak to me like that!" Emelda was bristling now.

"I will speak to you as I wish. Now, get out of here and let me speak to the *domna* alone."

"Really, Mikhail," Priscilla intervened, "you have no idea what you are doing. Just because you are Regent does not mean you can come in here and take charge. I always have Emelda by my side—I must, for she is my guide."

This mild resistence from Priscilla was unexpected. He considered for a moment. As far as he knew, his powers as Regent were unlimited, certainly where the well-being of the children was concerned. He was less sure of how much authority he had over Priscilla herself, but he decided to bluff now. Let Regis sort it out later, if he overstepped himself. He was going to do this job, and do it well, and no petty tyrant was going to stop him. If he must, he would behave like his bull-headed brother Gabe.

"I am taking charge, *domna*. I am going to see that this house is repaired, for the winter which is coming, and that the children are well cared for. You may do what you wish, of course, and your companion as well. I have no interest in your activities."

"But why? We will not be here for long."

Mikhail looked at Priscilla again. "Oh? And where are you intending to go? Back to Elhalyn Castle, perhaps?"

"Oh, no. We are going away soon." Her eyes were furtive now, and the expression on her face was secretive and pleased at the same time. If she had been a cat, there would have been cream on her whiskers, he thought. "You needn't bother about the children. The Guardian will see to them soon."

"Guardian? . . . *What* Guardian, *domna?*"

He was certain it had something to do with the seance he had attended four years before, where Derik Elhalyn, or something pretending to be his ghost, had told Priscilla about some "Guardian." It had given him the shivers then, and it did so now. "What happened to Ysaba? Is she here, too?" He had not liked the woman, but she had seemed harmless enough.

There was a silence in the drafty foyer, broken by the sound of boots approaching from the living room. Mikhail watched Priscilla look at her companion, and something passed between them, something that was dark and terrible. "She is gone," Priscilla said very softly, as Daryll came into the entry.

"We got the horses settled and fed, *Dom* Mikhail," the young Guardsman said. He made a half-bow to both women, and raised his pale eyebrows at the sight of Emelda's garment. A leronis? *Here?*

Mikhail caught the thought, and from the stiffening of Emelda's back, he suspected she had heard it as well. "Very good. You had better get some of the remaining food from our packs, because the cook seems to think there won't be enough to go around." He was very glad of Daryll's presence, of the Guardsman's trained vigilance, as well as his earthy common sense. After just ten minutes with the two women, his mind felt bruised.

"You cannot expect us to feed your men!" Emelda shrilled the words. "This is intolerable. I will not have it."

"Silence! If you say another word, I will stuff a rag in your mouth. You are not the mistress here!"

"But she speaks for me," Priscilla muttered, looking very confused and distressed.

"Then you are a greater fool than I imagined," Mikhail answered, no longer even pretending to be polite.

Emelda turned on her heel and marched out of the room, her red robe fluttering around her ankles. Priscilla followed her, calling anxiously and begging the other woman to forgive her.

"What was all that?" Daryll was curious, his eyes alight with interest.

"I don't know. I only wish I did."

"Who's the one in the red dress?"

"She says she is Emelda Aldaran, and she might be, for all I know. All I can be certain of is that she seems to have *Domna* Elhalyn in her thrall, and I am just not sure how to displace her." He sighed. "And I am quite certain she has no real right to the robe she is wearing either."

Before he could continue, Mikhail heard a slight creaking at the top of the stairs. He looked up and found several pairs of eyes observing him from above. As his eyes adjusted to the gloom, he could make out the faces of the two girls, Miralys and Valenta, and their brothers, Vincent and Emun. They all looked worried—anxious and poorly fed—and he found himself furious. He had seen children of peasants who looked better nourished!

Valenta slipped down the stairs, peeking over the railing from time to time, as if she were afraid of something. The boys and Miralys followed her, stepping very quietly. As soon as the youngest girl reached the uneven floor of the foyer, she rushed toward Mikhail. Then she put her hand in his, and looked up at him in such silent beseechment that he was nearly moved to tears. She knelt and leaned trustingly against his leg. "I knew you would return," she whispered.

4

Mikhail swallowed his growing fatigue, as well as his sense of outrage, and explored the upper story of Halyn House, where the children were housed with two old nurses, Becca and Wena. He was furious at the disrepair, at broken windows and piles of shabby clothing and linens everywhere. The girls, he found, shared one bedroom, and the boys another, which left three chambers unoccupied. The old women slept in the nursery, a small room beside the girls' bedroom, and it was cleaner than the rest, as if they took better care of themselves than of their charges.

Much to his surprise and pleasure, Mikhail discovered that there was a fine and working bathing chamber. It almost made up for the wreck of a bedroom he finally picked from those on the second floor. The bed hangings were rotten, and the mattress had not been restuffed in years. The ticking had several holes in it, and he fervently hoped that no mice had taken up residence.

With the girls trailing him silently, he started looking for bedding. None of the children had spoken after Valenta's whispered remark, and the boys had vanished into their own room. He was too tired and too angry to try to worm anything out of them. There would be time enough for that later. Right now he wanted clean sheets and blankets.

He opened doors, and finally found a cupboard stuffed full of bedding. The linens he discovered were so thin he could see through them, and the blankets could have stood a washing, but they were more stale from long storage than dirty. He barely noticed how peculiar it was to be managing chores he had always left to servants, but he was remotely aware that his mind seemed none too clear. It was all he could do to manage simple tasks, and he wondered if he might be coming down with some ailment or other.

Daryll and Mathias brought in all the luggage, and made no complaint at being asked to do maid service. Becca and Wena, looking not much changed from when he had last seen them, were no help at all. They appeared a little thinner, which was not surprising in light of what the cook had said, and rather dim-witted. When he asked them where he might find some towels, they just squawked like a pair of hens, and retreated into the nursery, muttering about their lack of responsibility for the chaos around them.

Mikhail tried to ignore his increasing revulsion as he looked around. But when he came into the room where the three lads shared a noisome bed, he could not. He discovered Alain Elhalyn sitting in a chair, staring into space. He was in his bedclothes, a shabby robe with foodstains on the breast, and the smell of old sweat on it. It was thin, like everything else, and poorly mended in several places. The oldest boy did not seem to know or care who Mikhail was.

"Is Alain ill?" Mikhail asked Vincent, who seemed the healthiest of the bunch. He was a handsome boy, with the prominent features of the Elhalyn line, and an air of assurance that set him apart from his siblings.

Vincent shrugged. "Ill? Maybe. Emelda says he is feeble-minded." He appeared indifferent, and not at all like the boy Mikhail remembered. "He just sits there, and Becca comes in and takes him to the toilet." The answer disturbed him.

"He was not feeble-minded four years ago, Vincent!" The simmering rage at the neglect he saw everywhere in Halyn House was more than Mikhail could stand. "He had already been through his threshold sickness, and was a fine lad."

"Was he? I can't seem to remember. It doesn't matter, does it? I'm the one you want." Vincent grinned, and there was something in his eyes that Mikhail mistrusted immediately. It was gone before he could measure the look, but Mikhail had a sinking feeling in his belly that had nothing to do with an empty stomach. He was starting to believe that the place was cursed, but he suspected the curse had a human form, and that its name was Emelda.

Who was she, and what had she done to the children? They were no longer the cheerful, noisy brats he remembered, but more like mice, except for Vincent who swaggered and bristled at every turn. He had the impulse to put them onto horses the following morning and drag them away from this dreadful house. But Alain did not look as if he could endure a ride of a mile, let alone the long journey to Thendara, and Emun was not in much better shape. The youngest boy looked haunted, started at noises, and kept peering anxiously over his stooped shoulder. And in the shape the horses were, they would falter in a day.

Was there a carriage? He did not remember one in the stable. Anything would do—a wain, a haycart! He wanted to leave Halyn House immediately! Even without the children.

As soon as he had this thought, Mikhail realized he sensed a whispering in his mind. He was stunned! Could that woman be influencing him? It was subtle enough that he had almost missed it, but it was also clear that Emelda was up to some mischief. It was fortunate, he decided, that she was an Aldaran—if she had not been lying—and not an Alton. That she might have a measure of the Alton Gift of forced rapport was frightening.

How was he going to get her out of the house? Mikhail had never laid hands on a woman in his life, no matter how great the temptation, and he wasn't sure he could. His Guardsmen would drag her off, if he ordered it, he assumed. But she was a woman! How could he bear the humiliation of handing that scrawny bit of trouble over to two big men? Surely there was a better solution. All he needed to do was think of it, but his mind seemed fuddled and tired. Tomorrow, after a good night's sleep would be time enough. Emelda was none of his concern—the children were.

Still, he could not let go of the problem. What would his father do? It was a peculiar question to ask himself, considering his rather hostile relationship with *Dom* Gabriel. But the Old Man was a nononsense sort of fellow, and Mikhail—for perhaps the first time—wished he was more like him. Gabriel lacked sensitivity, of which Mikhail felt he had too much, and rolled over opposition without any hesitations. Just the thought of *Dom* Gabriel was strengthening, and he needed every ounce of energy he could muster.

He was not going to resolve the problem standing in the middle of the hall. For a moment he wondered what he was doing there. What had he been seeking? Oh, yes. Towels.

He was aware that he had just forgotten something, but he could not drag it back into his mind, no matter how hard he tried. All he wanted was a long bath and some clean clothing. That, at least, he had in his baggage. He would feel more himself after a bath. He grabbed his things and went into the steaming chamber. It was the cleanest place he had seen in Halyn House, and that made him feel less helpless.

Lowering himself into the hot water, Mikhail relaxed. He felt an impulse to sink down into the water, to let the water cover his head, to float away into. . . . He shot up, spouting water from his lips, his lungs straining for air. Why had he done that?

Puzzlement gave way to cleansing anger. His mind cleared. Then doubt dispelled the momentary clarity. Mikhail suddenly felt powerless, ill-equipped, to deal with the children. Agreeing to be Regent for the Elhalyn children had been a great mistake. He should have insisted that one of his brothers undertake the task. He was going to need help, the aid of someone more experienced and better trained. He would have to get in touch with Regis and—

Mikhail cringed. He had not even been here a day, and already he had failed. He just was not up to the challenge, was he? Doubt gnawed at him, as it had when he was an adolescent, after Danilo Hastur had been born, and Mikhail's position had altered. *If I had been good enough, Regis would never have needed a son.*

He tried to shake away his sense of his own unworthiness, but the feeling persisted that he was not nearly the man he imagined himself to be. He was fit only to be paxman to Dyan Ardais or some other lord of the Domains. But Regis had given him a task, and he must try to accomplish it, no matter how he felt, and he must do it alone!

His first duty was to these children. That meant he must get the house in order, and see to their health. Mikhail could not even attempt to test the boys in their present state of malnutrition and filth. He wasn't even sure he had really learned enough at Arilinn to do it right.

Mikhail began to scrub himself with a dried gourd, and make a list of things to do. Fix the windows, clear the chimneys, repair the roofs, and get the laundry done. In the morning he would send Daryll to the village to get workmen. He would hire some maids to clean, some men to fix things. These, at least, were tasks he felt able to manage—even though he realized, with mild amusement, that he really had no idea of how the laundry at Armida functioned. And he would wager that Marguerida would know such things, not because she was female, but because she had lived on other worlds, and had likely, being the observant woman that she was, taken note of it. She had probably hung around recording the songs the laundresses sang, or what the black-smith chorused while he forged the horseshoes.

He was so involved in thinking of Marguerida that he hardly noticed he was rubbing just one place almost raw. When he did, Mikhail frowned. He stopped, rinsed his arm, and finished his bath much more rapidly than he normally did. He wound himself in a threadbare towel, and made a mental note to send for new linens as soon as possible. Then he got into his clothes and hastily left the room.

In the hall, he could sense he was being watched. Mikhail turned and looked up and down the corridor. He felt muzzy from the warmth of the bath, and he tried to make himself alert. The hall seemed empty, but after listening carefully he heard the faint rustle of cloth from the door of the girls' bedroom, and realized that Miralys and Valenta were likely watching him. Relief coursed along his veins, and he realized he had been half expecting someone to pounce out of the shadows with a knife. He was spooked, for certain, and he had better get hold of himself immediately.

After a moment, Miralys came out of her room, trying very hard to appear casual. "Do you feel better now?" she asked softly.

"Yes, much better."

She was a beautiful child, in spite of her soiled garments and unwashed hair. Her skin was almost translucent, with an alabaster complexion that other women tried to accomplish with baths of milk, and her eyes were a pale gray that was almost silver. He suspected that when washed, her hair would be red, but now it appeared to be a dirty brown. She had a blossom of a mouth, and a dainty nose, and resembled, Mikhail thought, some princess out of one of Liriel's fairybooks.

"I am glad for you. You looked so funny, trying to sort out the linens."

"Well, I have never made a bed before, actually. Why are there no servants, except for your nurses and old Duncan?"

"*She* won't permit it, and most of the folk in the village are afraid to come here."

"Why?"

"I am not allowed to say." Her eyes were wide now, fully dilated, as if she longed to speak but was unable to. *Help me!*

The silent cry was heartrending, but before he could answer her, Miralys turned and ran back to her room, banging the door closed behind her. He could hear her sobs, and then the voice of one of the nurses, hushing her. Mikhail started to reach for the doorknob, then drew back. He had no business in the room of a young girl.

Instead, he went back to his own room, found his comb, and tried to bring some order to his damp hair. The mirror above the dresser was black with dust, and he looked around for something to wipe it with. He found a rag, cleaned off the mirror, then gave the dresser top a lick and a promise, missing the good clean smell of wax and polish that the rooms should have had. Then he looked at himself, clean-shaven, his dark blond hair already curling across his brow. If they ever managed to overcome the opposition of his parents, Mikhail decided, he and Marguerida were going to have a brood of curly-mopped urchins, for certain. This thought, so new and odd, made him laugh, and his blue eyes crinkled. It felt good to laugh, but it made him miss her even more, for laughter had become their custom, almost a second language between them.

What will we name them? he wondered, as he walked out of the bedroom and started down the stairs. There were already a great many Gabriels and Rafaels in the family, but he would not object to a son called Lewis, even though his sister Ariel had already used it for one of hers. And Yllana, perhaps, after Marguerida's Aldaran grandmother. That would offend Javanne, his mother, of course.

Mikhail walked into the living room before he had quite finished his list of names, knowing that he would tell Marguerida about them at the first opportunity, and that she would be amused. He found Priscilla Elhalyn sitting at the embroidery frame, one hand holding a needle above the linen, staring into the fire. She started a little, stabbed the needle into the material, and folded her hands into her lap demurely.

"Good evening, *domna.*"

"Is it evening?" She looked around, for the room was rather dim now. The fireplace had been lit, but none of the candles in the sconces. "I had not noticed. No wonder I was having trouble seeing my stitches."

Mikhail took a long stick of wood from one of several on the mantelpiece, set it aflame, and started to light the candles. "This should make it easier to see."

"I suppose. But it is so wasteful."

"Wasteful?"

"Candles are very expensive."

"*Domna,* you are a great lady, of a great Domain. There is absolutely no reason to live in the dark." *Unless someone has told you to.*

It occurred to Mikhail that all those boarded-up windows made the rooms in the house almost as dark at midday as at night. He wondered if the disrepair was not deliberate, to keep Priscilla and her children in the shadows. It was a fleeting thought, and gone almost before he had time to consider it.

"Perhaps—but none of that matters. I won't need any candles soon." She sounded sleepy, dreamy, and more passive than he remembered her.

"Tell me, *domna,* how long has Emelda been with you? She interests me."

"Really? I am glad, for she is a wonderful woman. I don't know what I would have done without her. Let me see—it is so hard to remember. She came here at the Midsummer before this one, I believe. Yes, that's right. And then Ysaba . . . went away. She was here for several months, then she left, and came back after this Midsummer."

"I see." It had been, he suspected, during the absence of the odd woman that Priscilla had agreed to let her children be tested for *laran.* She seemed to him a most suggestable female, not precisely weak, just easily led by stronger personalities. Certainly Ysaba had been able to influence her, and now Emelda.

There was something about the medium, some hesitation in Priscilla's voice, that aroused his curiosity. He had not liked Ysaba, with all her spooky airs, but he sensed that she had not departed willingly, and wondered if she could be found. He had some questions he would very much like to put to her.

Emelda wafted into the room then, trailing her red draperies as well as a faint smell of some incense. She ignored Mikhail and went directly to Priscilla, bending over the frame, and began to comment on the progress of the work. In a moment, she was finding fault with the stitchery. "This will not do! You must unpluck this whole flower, for it is badly done."

"Yes," Priscilla answered calmly, her eyes rather vague. "*Dom* Mikhail found me trying to work in the dark—silly me. He kindly lit the tapers for me."

"*Domna,* listen to me. The light is bad for your eyes. You must try harder, to learn to work in the dark." This was whispered, but Mikhail could hear it well enough.

"I will have some glaziers come and replace the glass in the windows," he announced, "and then you will be able to see without the expense of candles." The scene was becoming more surreal by the second.

You will do no such thing! The sudden intrusion of her thoughts startled him.

Out! Get out of my mind! I am the master here! The vigor of his response pleased him, releasing some of the tension that had possessed him just a moment before.

You are going to ruin everything!

Mestra *Mischief, nothing would please me better!*

Daryll and Mathias came into the room at that moment, and Emelda looked at them angrily. When they entered, Mikhail immediately noticed that his mind felt clearer, as if whatever mental cloud the woman projected was subject to the number of people present. What in Zandru's hell was she? No *leronis,* for sure, no matter what she was wearing. And how was he going to get her out of the house?

Priscilla stiffened then. "I cannot have these men in my house," she said. "My daughters are . . ."

"Much safer with them than without," Mikhail interrupted. "Not only will my men remain, *domna,* but I intend to see that there are maids and menservants as quickly as possible. This house needs care, and I intend to see that it is tended to, as well as your children. If you do not care about them, I do."

Priscilla Elhalyn's somewhat prominent eyes bulged, as if she was straining in some inner conflict. "Take Vincent, and begone. He is the one you want—I understand that. The others must accompany me when I leave."

"That is not now yours to command, *domna.*" Leave? What did she mean? The attraction of doing just as she suggested was enormous, for he had thought that Vincent was the likeliest candidate to take the Elhalyn throne, and release him from the troublesome position of Regent. But he could not forget the silent cry for help of Miralys. He was damned if he was going to abandon the children just because it would be simpler.

More, Mikhail was aware that he was being subtly manipulated toward departure, and the more he felt it, the stronger was his determination to remain until he had done what he came to do. *No cursed hedge-witch is going to push me around!*

To his surprise, Emelda seemed to flinch and shrink a little at his thought. Then she plucked at Priscilla's sleeve, murmuring something to her, and the two women left the living room, just as four of the children came in.

Alain was missing, which Mikhail did not find surprising. From the condition of the oldest son, Mikhail rather doubted he could have made it down the stairs unassisted. He had been too tired and self-involved to do more than make a cursory examination of any of the children, to note their shabby clothing and general appearance of neglect, and then to make mental notes of things that needed to be done. He felt a small pang of guilt for taking a bath and finding clean clothing, instead of immediately starting to set things to rights. Then he chided himself for thinking he was some sort of wizard, who, with a wave of his hands, could restore the disorder that had built up over years of neglect. He was just a man, and, in many matters domestic, a very ignorant one at that. But he was determined to do his best, even if it meant upsetting Priscilla and her strange companion.

Mikhail approved of what he saw as the other children presented themselves. It was clear that they had all made an effort to tidy themselves for the occasion. Hair had been brushed and combed, hands and faces washed. They still looked more like beggars than the children of a Domain, but Mikhail was pleased. "A house takes its tone from the master," was the saying in the hills, and he felt there was truth in that more than he ever had before.

Emun studied the two Guardsmen, now wearing their uniforms instead of their traveling garb; his young eyes were wide with admiration. Mikhail realized that by now, under other circumstances, both boys, as well as Alain, would have been in the Cadets. It would probably be the best thing for them, to get out of this gloomy house and away from mediums and shadows. But the one condition that Priscilla had made was that her children were not to be removed from her, under any circumstances.

Mikhail thought he might be able to overset this stricture, on the grounds of unfitness, but it would demand going to the Cortes Court, which was currently embroiled in the dispute of *Dom* Gabriel concerning the Alton Domain, as well as the possibility of the Aldarans returning to the Comyn Council. The judges of the Cortes were, by all accounts, tearing out their collective hair, addressing things for which they had few or no precedents. It would also mean returning to Thendara without the children, and he suspected that would put them at risk. He had never wanted to be two places at once so much as he did at that moment—three, if he counted his desire to be at Arilinn with Marguerida.

What a dilemma! He had to make sure the children were well, if only to get one of the boys onto the throne. To do that, he had to stay in this madhouse. Otherwise, he would end up being a puppet king himself, with his young cousin Danilo pulling the strings. He was fond enough of Danilo, but Mikhail knew he had no desire to be put in such a situation. It would be hard for him, and probably even harder for Danilo.

Doubt gnawed at him, ruining his appetite. He could sense the eyes of the youngsters, watching him, anxious and expectant. Only

Vincent seemed confident, and Mikhail again found himself uneasy about the middle son. Perhaps he was only preening to conceal his own uncertainty, but there was something peculiar about Vincent, something he could not quite name. He just didn't know enough about young men, despite having been one once, to feel secure in any judgment.

Regis should not have sent him here on his own, he decided. He should have arrived with tutors, a swordmaster, and a couple of dames for the girls. Why hadn't he? His uncle was a canny man, and he rarely did anything carelessly. What if Regis was just trying to get him out of the way?

All the emotions of displacement he had experienced when he was fourteen flooded back. It was an unwelcome and unpleasant knot of emotions, and Mikhail tried to quell it, but it continued to nag at him all through the miserable meal of overboiled fowl and soggy grain that followed. It was a very silent meal, except for occasional questions from Vincent. The girls ate as if they were starving, and Emun wolfed down his portion of chicken and looked to see if there was more. Halfway through the meal, one of the old nursemaids appeared, went into the kitchen, and returned carrying a tray which he assumed was for Alain.

When Mikhail could drag his mind away from his own worries, he felt furious. He had always been taught that children were precious, and the way these four and Alain had been treated outraged him beyond words. He tried to engage them in some sort of conversation, but the girls remained mute, and Emun answered with monosyllables. Vincent was happy to expand on anything, as if the sound of his own voice was reassuring, but he actually had very little to say that was worth the hearing.

As soon as the meager meal had been consumed, Mikhail was glad to rise from the dull-surfaced board. He bade the children good night, and watched them troop quietly out of the room. Then he turned to his men. "Daryll, I think that you can bed down in the living room, by the fire, and Mathias can take the first watch." He knew it was pointless to suggest that neither of them needed to sleep on the floor outside his door—they would not have listened. He was in their charge, and they were determined to take care of him, expecially here.

"Very good, *dom*. And I will set out at first light for that village, and see what I can do about getting some workmen."

"See if you can hire a laundry woman, and some maids, as well. I have seen sties that were cleaner than this house."

"I will do my best, of course. Strange house, isn't it?"

"Quite." He understood what Daryll was not saying perfectly well, but he did not want to encourage the man to criticize Lady Elhalyn openly.

Mikhail left them, went upstairs, and stood for a moment, listening. It was very quiet in the hall, too quiet. There was something unnatural about the silence, and more, disturbing. But it would have to keep until tomorrow.

He entered his bedroom, and immediately felt a sense of wrongness. Mikhail could not put his finger on what he sensed. Then he noticed just a hint of fragrance, a lingering whiff of incense. He was certain that Emelda had been in his room, though for what purpose he could not imagine.

Mikhail felt exhausted and livid at the same time. He began to search, suspecting some mischief, and sorted first through his garments. Particles of dust fell from the folds of the cloth, although he could not be certain if they had been put there or were merely the settling of house dust. It did not seem to him that his clothing should have gotten flecked with dust so quickly. So he shook his clothing out fiercely, using the activity as an outlet for his simmering rage.

Then he unmade the bed, for what remained of the scent was strongest near it. Mikhail pulled off the blankets, then the sheets. In the flickering light from the small fireplace, dust motes danced in the air. It was not drawing very well, and he thought the chimney was probably half full of ancient clinkers. He should have told Daryll to ask for a sweep to come, if such a person existed in the nearest village. He needed to find some paper and start writing these things down, unless he expected Daryll or Mathias to ride over to the village every other day.

Mikhail yanked the pillows out of their cases, his nose prickling at the faint smell of must. He had spent twenty minutes making that bed, and he was undoing it in five, much to his displeasure.

Something fell out and plopped onto the bare mattress. It was only a small sewn bag, of the sort that country folk used for simples and poultices. The maids at Armida often put little sacks of lavender in the pillows, to aid in sleep. From the faint scent he noticed, this was most assuredly not lavender, nor balsam either. Mikhail had no idea what was in it—Liriel was the one who knew about herbs and plants. A pity she was not here.

But something about the innocent-appearing object made his skin crawl. He reached for it carefully, and picked it up. For a moment he dangled the thing by its tiny strings, resisting the urge to lift it to his nose. For no rational reason, he was sure that would be a bad choice.

Then he started to toss it into the fireplace. He stopped just as the strings were about to leave his fingers, an abrupt movement. If it were some noxious stuff, the fire would send it into the air. Why did he think it was poison? Why did he assume it had some hostile intent?

Mikhail flogged his brains wearily. He had never been presented with quite this sort of problem before—how to dispose of some unknown thing that might be dangerous. If the window had not been boarded up, he would have dropped it outside, and dealt with it in the morning. He did not possess that peculiar *laran* which allowed one to know about things by the feel of them, and had never wished for that talent until that moment.

How did one deal with such things? If burning was not an option, then what? Drowning or burial, he decided slowly, his mind feeling as if it were full of glue. He was not a superstitious yokel, but he was reluctant to just to let the object be. If it was harmless, which he doubted, it did not matter what he did, but if it was dangerous, then he had to handle it with care.

Finally he left the room with the bag held at arm's length, went to the privy, and dropped it down the hole. Then he took the bucket that stood beside the seat and emptied it into the channel. Mikhail pumped the bucket half full again, and left it for the next person who used the privy.

As soon as he had disposed of the little bag, Mikhail felt less stupid and tired. He was not sure that this was not an illusion, but he decided that it was better to be cautious than otherwise. He went back to his room and met Mathias coming up the stair, carrying a chair from the dining room in one hand, and a blanket in the other. They glanced at one another, their eyes almost meeting. He could sense that Mathias, usually the steadiest of men, was disturbed at something. Mikhail would have asked him what the matter was, but from the closed expression on the face of the Guardsman, he decided that when Mathias wanted to tell him, he would. He had too much respect for his men to start prying now.

When he entered the bedroom again, it felt perfectly ordinary, and Mikhail decided he had handled the matter well. It was a small thing, but it gave him enormous reassurance in his weariness. He tugged the bedclothes back into place, and took off his boots. For a few minutes, he just sat by the fireplace, wriggling his toes, and luxuriating in the pleasure of it.

He longed for bed, for sleep. But he would not rest until he had reached Marguerida, felt her mind in his, heard her mental laughter. Sleep could wait for a few more minutes. Mikhail took his matrix stone out from beneath his tunic, carefully removed it from its silken pouch, and looked into it. The fire reflected on the facets of the stone as he breathed slowly and deeply, drawing himself into a trance. As he did, the weariness seemed to fade away, and while he did not want to jump up and dance a jig, neither was he almost too tired to sit up.

Mikhail focused, and the room seemed to fade away. *Marguerida?*

He sought her presence, his awareness of her unique energy, and felt her answer. It seemed to be a small and distant reply, much weaker than usual. *Mikhail? Is that you?*

Yes, beloved.

Are you all right? You seem a little . . . hazy.

Mikhail hesitated. Part of him wanted to tell her all the strange things he had discovered when he reached Halyn House, but another portion of his mind resisted. He would look like a proper fool, wouldn't he, complaining about broken windows and stopped-up chimneys. And for all he knew, that little bag he had just disposed of was some harmless thing.

I am quite tired. Halyn House is a mess, and I spent my first hour here cleaning out the stables.

You cleaned out the stables? I don't understand, Mik.

Domna *Priscilla has a very small staff.*

Oh. Well, I am glad to know you have arrived safely. I've been worried, picturing you falling down cliffs and other foolish things.

She did indeed seem subdued from the energetic woman he knew. Perhaps she was getting weary of him. Or perhaps she had decided she did not want to wait for their impossible situation to sort itself out and was considering another course. *I am sorry to hear you have had a bad day.*

Oh, Mik! I am a total idiot. She paused for what felt like a long time. *I don't know how to tell you this, except just to say it. Domenic died this afternoon.*

I see. And you are blaming yourself again, very likely. He felt the pain of loss in his chest, the sorrow and the grief, but it was remote. Later, when he was less tired, he knew it would hit him harder. But now he was too pleased to feel Marguerida to allow this pain to reach him completely.

Only a little. In between crying my eyes out and talking to my father about how much I hate it at Arilinn now that you are gone.

Really? Mikhail felt heartened.

Yes, of course. I mean, you know I never wanted to come to a Tower to begin with, and only did it because I had no other choices. And I didn't want to come to Arilinn either—the only thing that made it acceptable was that you were here training too. And, of course, Dio is here. Since you left, things have become much more uncomfortable for me—the others, you know—and if it were not for Liriel . . . no matter.

Are they plaguing you again? Damn them.

Some. But I told the Old Man everything, and I think he is going to try and persuade Uncle Jeff that it is time I go up to Neskaya and study with Istvana. It would be easier to travel now than later in the year, and, truthfully I think if I don't get away from Arilinn soon, I am going to go quietly mad. Or maybe noisily!

That would be tragic.

Well, it wouldn't be a very long trip—going crazy, I mean. Getting to Neskaya will be, but maybe I can hire Rafaella to come with me. I would love to see her again. I miss her so much. Are you sure nothing is wrong? You seem so foggy.

I am only tired, my love. And missing you.

Well, go to sleep, then. I am glad to hear your voice, however distantly, but if you are herding small children, you will need your strength.

Indeed, I will. They are none of them that small, Marguerida. The youngest of the children is twelve, I believe. Valenta. A very pretty little girl, though it is her sister, Miralys who is going to be the beauty.

Are you trying to make me jealous?

No. Are you?

Just a little. But not of a child! I was never jealous before, that I can remember, so I can't be sure. I know you have resisted the charms of an entire panting generation of comely lasses, Mik, but I still worry. I mean, it would solve so many problems if you married one of the Elhalyn daughters, even though you are almost old enough to be. . . .

Precisely. I am just old enough to have fathered them, which makes any alliance scandalous. Though, frankly, the idea of bedding Priscilla Elhalyn is repugnant.

Good!

Wicked woman!

How old is she?

Priscilla? About thirty-eight, though she looks older.

A hag! I am delighted to hear it!

Not quite that, but she seemed to be working toward hagdom. Marguerida—you are the only woman in the world for me!

Oh, Mik. I love you so much, and I miss you. If I were not so sad about little Domenic, I would be dancing around the room with joy.

I will tell you something that came into my mind today—the names of our children. I have never, in my entire life, considered that.

Me either. What names did you pick?

I decided there were enough Gabriels and Rafaels in the family, but I thought Lewis would be a good name for a son, and perhaps Yllana for a daughter.

I would never have thought of Yllana, but she was my grandmother. Wouldn't that choice make Aunt Javanne furious.

My thought exactly!

I think, though, that I would wish to name my first daughter Diotima.

Why didn't I think of that? He knew that the reason he did not think of that name was because he could not bear the thought of Marguerida's mother not being alive.

It doesn't matter. But it was a nice thing to think—Mik, would you mind terribly, if we have a son, if we called him Domenic? Mikhail was then swept with a powerful sense of sorrow and rightness, at the same time. And he had a feeling that perhaps *that* Domenic, if he ever came into the world, would live long enough to fulfill a real destiny, instead of dying young, or being murdered, as had Domenic Lanart-Alton, after whom the Alars had named their son. Third time was a charm, they said. And he chided himself a little for being superstitious and silly with exhaustion.

No, Marguerida. I think that would be wonderful!

I'm glad. I was afraid you would not like the idea.

Actually, it is perfect, and fitting. You seem to have some instinct for choosing well, my dearest.

You only say that because I picked you to love! He had a sense of her easy laughter. *You are falling asleep on me! Go to bed! Good night, my Mikhail, my beloved! Sleep well.*

Good night, Marguerida. Peace to you.

5

Two days later, Margaret and Lew Alton set out from Arilinn. The morning was overcast and there was a chill in the air that had not been there before. Dorilys was unusually frisky, as if the brisk autumn breeze excited her. Lew was astride a big black with a white star on his brow, an older horse which seemed to find the mare's antics annoying, since he kept snorting at her.

Margaret was glad to shake the dust of Arilinn from her skirts, although parting from Liriel had been sad. She did not know when she would see her cousin again—certainly not for months—and she found she was going to miss her a great deal. But that was her only regret, and if she never set eyes on *Mestra* MacRoss again, or some of the others at the Tower, she would be content.

Domenic's death had disturbed her more than she could have anticipated. She had somehow managed to avoid Ariel before her departure, even though she wanted to offer her heartfelt condolences. Liriel, coping with the main brunt of Ariel's grief, had assured her it would create more anguish for her sister to see Margaret. While she packed her things, she wept, her emotions veering wildly from anger to sorrow. How, she wondered, did anyone take the risk of having children, when such terrible things could happen to them? It was not a question which had occurred to her previously, and it perturbed her until she realized that what she was really wondering was whether she could ever take such a risk herself.

For all her talk with Mikhail about naming a yet unborn child Domenic, the entire notion of bearing children frightened her. Not just the idea of becoming pregnant, but the consummation, the sheer physicality that must precede it, almost revolted her. She knew that while she was now free of the overshadowing that Ashara Alton had placed on her while she was a child, she still shrank from the thought of sex. It terrified her, even when she imagined Mikhail as her partner. She could mentally get to the undressing part, but after that Margaret found that she got chilly all over, and her throat closed up, so she could barely breathe.

She had never even kissed a man until she pressed her lips to Mikhail's, with the entire city of Thendara laid out beneath them. It had been wonderful and terrifying. Maybe it was for the best that *Dom* Gabriel and Lady Javanne were so utterly opposed to any marriage between them, since she suspected that she would balk at the last minute. Her entire adult knowledge of that came from what she had seen in vid-drams, and it did not look very appealing. It was so *physical!* Damn Ashara for leaving her crippled like this! That thought was so silly that she chuckled, and the sound caused Dorilys to prick her ears and neigh in comment.

I have lived too much in my mind, I suppose, and not enough in my body. If only the cure for it were not so . . . animalistic. And awkward! I don't know how anyone manages it, but it seems they must, or else the species would have died out long ago. I wish I could ask someone—but Liriel is as virginal as I am. It is something I might have been able to talk to Dio about . . . but . . . and I would die before I asked Father. Both of us would be very embarrassed. Maybe Lady Linnea . . . no, I couldn't! Or even—God help me—Javanne!

Still, the farther they got from the huge complex of matrix screens, the more relaxed she felt. It was as if some great pressure in her skull had gone away. Now, if she could just get her heart to behave, could cease longing for Mik and being repelled by the idea at the same time, perhaps she could feel peaceful as well as relaxed.

After so many years of keeping herself apart from other people, of living a life of music without any real friends except Ivor and Ida Davidson, she found that she genuinely enjoyed the increasing intimacy she had with Liriel. It was a shame she had made no other friends at Arilinn, unless she counted Haydn Lindir, the archivist. He reminded her a little of Ivor—a pleasant, fussy old scholar with a vast store of knowledge. And, likely, Neskaya would be different, but not any better.

Margaret was looking forward to returning to Thendara for a few days. She wanted to visit Master Everard in Music Street, and see Aaron and Manuella MacEwan in Threadneedle Street. She wanted to see the headstone she had ordered for Ivor's grave, which was now finished and put into place. She missed her late mentor very much, and the death of Domenic Alar had opened a wound she thought had been healed. Margaret could remember seeing the dead when she was just a child, at the end of the Sharra Rebellion, but she had been so young, and she had not grieved for those people. This was different, it was personal, and she had no recent experience to prepare her for the swings of mood and the deep emotions that battered her.

Margaret was going to need some warmer clothing, for Neskaya was miles farther north, on the knees of the mountains. It was not, she had been informed, as cold as Nevarsin, the City of Snows, where the *cristoforos* had their monastery, but was likely very cold for her taste. She must remember to visit the glover as well. She tried not to think about the Tower at Neskaya, though, because she was afraid she would encounter the same silent resentment she had met at Arilinn. Someday she would know enough to never have to enter a Tower again, but not yet. She was still too raw, too dangerous, to be out on her own. She knew she could leave Darkover, that no one could restrain her; she also knew this was not the proper course to follow, much as she might long to.

Margaret forced herself to stop chasing her demons. She wanted to look on the bright side, and so she began to think of Rafaella n'ha Liriel, her friend and former guide. She hoped the Renunciate would be in Thendara, and not off guiding traders or doing other business. Rafaella had been her first real friend on Darkover, and she treasured the woman. Besides, she was curious about how the budding romance between the guide and Margaret's uncle, Rafe Scott, was faring. She had sniffed it out while the two women had been in the Kilghards, and thought it amusing that if Rafaella chose to make Captain Scott her freemate, she would then, if in name only, be Margaret's aunt. This was a relationship she rather fancied, unlike the blood kinship she had with Javanne Hastur, Mikhail's mother.

Fortunately, she and Lew had managed to escape Arilinn before Javanne arrived. She was coming to take her grandson's body for burial. They might meet upon the road, but Margaret hoped that they would not, for while Javanne was much too proud and dignified to say anything, just being around her made Margaret feel stuck full of pins.

It would have been more proper to remain at Arilinn, to have accompanied the coffin back, but once Jeff Kerwin had been persuaded that she would be better served by studying with Istvana Ridenow, Margaret was too afraid he'd change his mind to chance staying longer.

There had been some opposition to the idea of her leaving Arilinn after only a few months. It was still the most important Tower on Darkover, at least in reputation, and there was a degree of pride in being there. Those who had lived and worked at Arilinn for most of their adult lives regarded the other Towers as provincial, lacking in tone and character. And Istvana had, Margaret had discovered, a certain reputation for innovation that the older folk, like *Mestra* Camilla MacRoss, looked at askance. There was, it seemed, some small rivalry between the two Towers. To leave Arilinn after such a brief time smacked of subtle insult, and voices had been raised. She had not been privy to these discussions, but Lew had, and he had favored her with a rather biting commentary on the entire scene.

She felt torn, as usual. Margaret wanted to avoid Javanne more than anything, but she felt like a coward because of it. Things had been so much less complicated before she arrived on Darkover, and she longed for the simplicity of her previous life. She might as well have asked for the moons, she decided, and tried to put it out of her mind.

Margaret did not succeed. She found her mind running back to her own failings, and to the hostility of the younger students at Arilinn. She had studied, and she had studied hard, but she realized she had not enjoyed the experience, as she had enjoyed her time at University. Part of it was the attitude of the other students, which she felt keenly. The rest of it was her own resentment at being sent back to school, and to study something so alien as telepathy. She realized that if she had studied it as a youngster, it would have been less difficult than it was now, but there was no help for that. Besides, Margaret was fairly certain that if she had tried to confront the shade of Ashara Alton in her teens, she would not have lived to tell the tale.

No matter how often she was told that she had nothing to fear from the long dead Keeper, that Ashara had been completely undone during her battle in the overworld, Margaret still had the certainty that she was not entirely finished with her ancestor. It was not just the presence of the network of lines on her flesh, but something more. It lacked the clarity of a foretelling, and she was relieved that she had not had any visions of the haunting little woman. As far as Margaret was concerned, if she never had another bout with the Aldaran Gift, it would be just fine. Telepathy she could deal with—barely—but the ability to see into the future was just too terrible to be borne.

Of the three experiences she had had with the Aldaran Gift, it was the second which disturbed her the most. This had been about the child which Ariel Alar carried in her swelling womb—the girl they would call Alanna. There was something about the child swimming in Ariel's womb that she found disturbing. She had had the vision immediately after Domenic's accident. Margaret discovered she wanted very much to dismiss it as some stressful imagining. But she did not believe that, and she was too honest to pretend that she did.

As for the last vision, the sight of Hali Tower as it had existed in the past, it did not bother her at all. She knew it worried Jeff and her father, but she could not help that. Not all visions came true, or happened as they were foreseen. Liriel had explained that, much to Margaret's relief. All she knew was that she had no great foreboding when she thought of Hali, as she did when she considered the yet unborn baby. She had already had more adventures, Margaret reflected, than most people had in three lifetimes; if she could arrange it, she was not going to have any more.

Margaret chuckled, and Lew looked at her. "Might I share the joke?"

"I was just thinking that I don't want any more adventures in my life!"

Lew Alton roared with laughter, and it warmed her to hear it. His horse, however, took umbrage, and reared its head, jingling the rings on the bridle, and snorting. "Good luck," he said, when he finally managed to stop his merriment. "I hope you have a very boring life, daughter, but I doubt that you will. There is, it seems to me, something about us which attracts trouble."

"Humph! I'd expect something like that from Aunt Javanne, but not from you!"

"Your aunt is a canny woman, despite her character flaws, Marguerida. She often called me storm crow,' and she was not far off the mark."

"She always manages to make me feel like a bug." Margaret paused. "One she'd like to squash."

"Oh, certainly. Javanne is a strong woman, a determined woman. She has always been that way. She likes to arrange things to suit herself. But I suspect she rather envies you."

"What?"

"She would never, never admit it, of course. But, *chiya,* think. You have been educated, have traveled between the stars, have seen other races—things she can hardly imagine. Javanne has lived in a small circuit—raising children at Armida, visiting Thendara to bully Regis, managing the lives of her young, without, you will notice, a great deal of success. It is not just Mikhail who escaped her thrall. He is only the most obvious. Liriel has chosen her own path which, in truth, is just as limited as Javanne's, but somewhat more varied. Gabe and Rafael are still unmarried, despite her efforts to the contrary. And Regis is not nearly as compliant as she wishes him to be. Not to mention the wear and tear of being married to *Dom* Gabriel."

"I guess I had not thought about it like that. But why didn't she let Mikhail leave Darkover? I've never really understood that. I mean, after Danilo Hastur was born, when Regis didn't need Mik any longer, why did she oppose his leaving?"

"I suspect that she would not allow him what she could not have herself. Javanne is a classic egotist, daughter. It is not a lovely thing, but since I suffer from something of the same affliction, I can pardon her faults more than you can. You are still very young, and very judgmental."

"Classic? That is not a thing I would ever call you—or her, for that matter!"

"No, but I am certainly an egotist. If I had not been, I would never have endured." He chuckled. "I never thought of myself in that way when I was young, of course, because one doesn't. If the young could have even an inkling of their inate self-centeredness, they would make a great many fewer mistakes."

"I suppose that makes me an egotist, too." What a discouraging realization. Margaret flinched, since she thought of herself as fairly generous and helpful, not like her more gifted classmates at University, or even Ivor, who had been truly self-absorbed about his music.

"Yes and no. You are a great deal more mature than I was at your age, I believe. The result of your exposure to other cultures, one assumes. I think that seeing how others live is always humbling. And you lack my besetting sin—foolish pride. So many things in my life would have been different but for my pride, my refusal to ask for help, and my insistence on doing things my own way."

"Well, if you end up surrounded by real talents, as I did in Ivor's house, you can't get stuck-up. You have no idea how humbling it is to be a fine second fiddle in a house full of musical geniuses! Not that they lorded over me, because Ivor and Ida did not permit it. But I knew that I was never going to be a real creator, the way Jheffy was. Still, being a Fellow of the University was a good thing, and I was extremely proud of it. I still am, and sometimes I wish I could just go back there and pick up where I left off."

"Why?"

"Father, research is very satisfying. There are no personalities to cope with—well, academic jealousies, of course—but you can bury yourself in the archives and just learn. There are some Scholars at University who spend their lifetimes learning—writing about their discoveries or giving lectures." She sighed, wondering if she could ever convey the joy she felt in being an academic. "A well-documented paper is a wonderful thing. It is real, something you can hold in your mind. An intellectual artifact. It does not matter what world you came from, or what your sex is, or how old you are. There is something very . . . pure about it."

"You are very wary of emotional entanglements, aren't you?"

"I have not had very good luck with them. I loved Ivor a great deal, as I would have loved you, I suppose, if we had known one another better. He died much sooner than he should have. I wish you could have known him."

"The glimpse I had of him while you were trying to find Donal Alar in the overworld made me quite envious, *chiya*. Part of me rejoices that you had so fine a foster father, and the rest of me regrets that I missed all that time with you."

"Yes, he was a good parent, if a wee bit absent-minded. But, you see, as much as I loved Ivor and he probably loved me, there were no deep emotions. I mean, not like the feelings I have about you or Dio. We were both, I suppose, the servants of music—priest and priestess. We never discussed anything intimate, the way Mik and I or Liriel and I do sometimes. We were attached, but it was more from circumstance than anything else. He had had so many students—fifty-three years of young musicians—and he had loved them all, in a nice, impersonal way. And his wife, Ida, loved us as well. She was supportive and comforting, and all of us felt as safe in that house as we would anywhere in the galaxy, but it was not . . . really warm. Well, now I think about it, Ida is a very warm woman, but I never let myself get too close to her. She and Ivor never had any children of their own, only those of other people. I don't know if she missed it or not. I think, though, if she missed anything, it was giving up her own career in favor of Ivor's. I know she was a budding synthiclavierist when they met. And, from her occasional performances, she was extremely good, almost brilliant. But instead of being a famous player, she became a clavier tutor, and dozens of well-known musicians have studied with her. To have studied with Ida Davidson is considered a great honor in musical circles."

"Do you think she regretted having a private rather than a public career?"

"I asked her once, and she said that being a famous musician is very wearing, and not all it is cracked up to be."

"She sounds like a fine person, and I am deeply grateful to her for fostering you so well. Your manners, when you left Thetis, were in a sorry state, and, truthfully, I despaired a little. But, when I watched you at Arilinn, it struck me that you are every inch a lady."

Margaret felt herself redden to the roots of her hair. "A lady? Me? *Domna* Marilla—she's a lady! Or Linnea. I am just a hoyden who happens to be the heiress to a Domain—quite a different thing! They know what to do, what to say in any circumstance."

"And Javanne?" Lew asked, his voice brimming with amusement.

"Well, certainly my aunt is a proper lady—but she is of a different sort than Linnea or Marilla. She knows what to say, but she does not always do it!"

"In other words, she is more like you than like *Domna* Marilla."

"Oh, my! I suppose she it—and how much she would loathe the comparison!" She paused and thought for a moment. "I think I would say that both of us are somewhat cold."

"How odd."

"Why?"

"Because I think I would have said that you and Javanne are very passionate people, not cold at all. But, you were speaking of your wariness—I wish you would go on, if it is not too uncomfortable for you to speak of it."

Passionate? Margaret had to take a minute to consider that. It was a new thought, and not an entirely comfortable one. She knew she was deeply passionate about music, and now about the planet of her birth. But those had a certain quality of abstraction, of distance about them. She loved Mikhail—there was no question of that—but she was not sure she felt passionately about him. She was passionate *toward* him, which was a very different thing than her feelings about Darkover or music. It was too new an idea, and too knotty a problem to sort out now, so she set it aside, a little reluctantly.

Margaret sorted through a muddle of thoughts and feelings, most of them freighted with more emotion than she was ready to address. "Until I came to Darkover," she began slowly, "I don't think I ever felt the real warmth of human contact, except a few times with Dio. This was mostly because Ashara kept telling me to keep myself apart, whispering in my brain like a piece of bad music, until I just stopped trying. I got very good at keeping my distance, so maybe a part of my personality is suited to remoteness. Sometimes it is very hard to tell where Margaret Alton starts, and where Ashara leaves off. She must have been a very bitter woman, and I wonder if I will ever know the reason for it. She is so enigmatic, so present and so far away at the same time." Margaret gave a sigh. "And then I have to go and take a fancy to the one man on Darkover that I cannot have. So, yes, I am wary. I have good reason."

"Don't be defensive. I was not criticizing you. I know that nothing in your history would lead you to trust others, and I am aware of my own part in that. As for Mikhail, we shall have to see. Don't give up hope yet."

"Hope will break my heart, Father." Margaret was ashamed of the anger and bitterness in her voice, and gave Dorilys a quick jab in the sides with her heels. The little mare responded by lengthening her stride, and Margaret rode ahead, making further conversation impossible.

When Margaret and Lew arrived at Comyn Castle just before nightfall, they were greeted by servants. The horses were taken to the stables, and they went to the Alton suite in silence. It was not an uncomfortable thing, the way it had been between them when she was a child and Lew Alton had shunned her, just a respectful quiet where both of them kept their thoughts to themselves.

But Lew was called away almost before he had time to get out of his riding boots, and she was relieved to be totally alone. Margaret bathed, put on fresh garments, and asked her maid, Piedra, to bring her a tray of supper. She knew she really should go find Lady Linnea and be properly social, but she was too tired and too sad to want company.

Instead, after she had eaten, Margaret got out her recorder and listened to the notes she had made four months before, on the trail with Rafaella. She had added to it while she was at Arilinn, for she had discovered an entire body of songs that were sung only in Towers, written by Keepers and monitors and technicians, that no one had ever bothered to mention to her. The music was beautiful, closer to ancient plain chant than most Darkovan songs, and there was a quality of isolation in it that drew her. Margaret could almost picture long-dead Keepers whiling away cold nights over their rylls and guitars, creating the pieces to comfort themselves.

It was the first chance she had really had to concentrate on her work in a long time, and she was deep in thought, writing a few lines for what she hoped would someday be a monograph, when Lew finally returned. Part of her mind was completely absorbed, and while aware of his presence, she did not stop until she had her thoughts down. Then she started a little, and felt a little guilty. She turned off her machine and bit her lower lip anxiously.

"What are you up to," he asked cheerfully.

"I was just trying to organize my notes. Between trying to learn how to control my telepathy and the headaches I got from being around all those matrices, I haven't had the energy until now. I can't tell you how relieved I am to be away from the Tower, and I do not look forward to going to Neskaya, even though I will be with Istvana Ridenow."

"You seemed very far away when I came in. Tell me, *chiya*, do you miss it?"

"University? Yes, I do. I have spent a third of my life there. It has become a habit with me. I miss the discourse, the intense curiosity of other scholars, the opportunity for contrasts."

"Contrasts?"

"Well, all information at University gets analyzed through the parameters of comparison and interrelationship. Darkover has some pretty interesting variations on the human norm, and I don't have anyone to discuss them with! Oh, Mikhail always tries to understand what I am talking about—he is very curious about the places I've been—but he often doesn't see what is so fascinating to me. He accepts Darkovan customs as the norm of *how human beings behave,* instead of being merely one point along a broad spectrum of behavior."

"I understand completely! When I first went to the Senate, I was constantly shocked by the wide variety of human behavioral "norms." And, for a Darkovan, I was fairly sophistocated. Some of the things I encountered seemed so strange, and I could not for the life of me figure out why some people did the things they did. But, I got used to it, after a couple of months of getting glared at for passing a Medinite on the left in the hall, instead of staying to the right. After some years acceptance of variation became second nature to me—now I have more trouble with the unyielding nature of my fellow Comyn than ever!" He smiled wryly. "This telefax came for you while I was away."

Margaret held out her hand for the thin sheet. She took it and saw that the sender's code was that of the University. Maybe they were revoking her fellowship. She tore it open and read through the script rapidly.

Then she grinned and looked up at her father. "It is from Ida

Davidson. She thinks she can get passage to Darkover soon, to claim Ivor's body. There is some problem with travel permits."

"I am not surprised." Lew sounded almost angry.

"Why?"

"The Expansionists in the lower house are trying to prevent travel to Protectorate worlds, as a way to force them to become member worlds. They have tried to get two bills passed since I left the Senate to limit or exclude trade from worlds which are not willing to open their doors to Expansionist policies. The Senate has managed to defeat both of them, but it was a close thing."

"But that's crazy."

Lew shook his head. "I spent a lot of time while I was in the Senate studying the history of governments—without, I confess, the benefit of your scholarly training. Tell me—do they still use Kostemeyer's text on the life of empires at University?"

Margaret held back her sense of surprise. Somehow she had never thought of her father as a person who would have read the hoary central text of the Socio-Historists. It had been written two hundred years before, by a Centauri, and while it had been superseded by more recent works, it was still a classic. "Yes, and it is required, too. It is part of the core reading for History of Civilization, which everyone has to take—much to the annoyance of the engineering and technical students, who seem to think that history is something that happens to other people." Margaret realized that she was still thinking of Lew as the man he had been when she was very young, not the informed and intelligent Senator from Darkover. Of course, when she had left for University, they had never had discussions like this one. How wonderful to discover this man, this father she had been denied as a girl, and to find out that he was so interesting!

"Do you remember what he says about the cycles—what does he call them?"

"The tides, Father."

"Yes, that's it. Now I remember—'To ignore the ebb and neep of the tidal flow of all forms of governance is the folly of empires.' Rather grand, isn't it? He had a lovely way with the language. In my opinion, just now, the Terran Federation is in the beginning of an ebb, which is characterized by both oppression and various sorts of decadence."

"Decadence? I don't understand."

"When a culture runs out of ideas, it becomes decadent. And, in my opinion, the Federation is rapidly running out of both ideas and sense!" His face reddened a little along his cheekbones, and his eyes glittered with passion. "Instead of recognizing that each world is a unique and wonderful place, they have started to believe that imposing Terran technology and behavior on the member worlds is the road to control. What they do not appear to understand is that rather than gain control, they will only cause rebellion!"

"Why?"

"Because the Federation cannot know what's best for everyone, and particularly not for Darkover and other Protectorate worlds! There is this perception that Protectorate worlds are taking resources from the Federation and giving back nothing in return."

"Was that one of the reasons you gave up your seat in the Senate?"

"You mean did I see it coming?"

"Yes."

"Perhaps. I noticed that the bureaucracy was becoming more complex, which is always a signal of oppression, in my understanding of history. There has been a proliferation of permits, taxes, and laws concerning the movement of goods and people. It has grown slowly, beginning just about the time you left for University, and at first it did not appear to be anything malignant. By the time Dio got ill, however, I could see the handwriting on the wall, and I knew that I could no longer function in the increasingly hostile environment of the Senate. The travel tax alone has been raised three times in the past nine years."

"I know. Don't forget, I made all the arrangements when Ivor and I went from world to world."

"Of course you did. I just didn't think of that."

"What I noticed was that our funding kept dwindling. When I began traveling with Ivor, we could go second class, but on the last two trips we had to go third because there were almost no travel funds. And I couldn't understand it. My fellowship grant was being eaten up with new taxes, and the stipend was less each year. They will probably revoke my grant eventually . . . if I don't go back. And I don't suppose I will, ever." She felt more despondent than she would have thought possible.

"But, Marguerida, you don't need the grant. You are the heir to the Alton Domain, and you will never. . . ."

"I earned that grant, Father! I worked for it. It isn't a great deal of money, of course, but it was mine. I don't want some damned Expansionist taking it away from me!"

He sighed. "I know it is important to you, but . . ."

"Father, I cannot submit papers to the University if I am no longer a Fellow. I could not complete Ivor's work, or do any of my own. That would be intolerable."

"You really loved it, didn't you?"

Margaret knitted her fingers together. "It was not exactly that I loved it, but it was totally mine. I was not a Fellow because of you or even because of Ivor. It was not something I could inherit. I had to work very hard to create an original piece of scholarship that earned me my fellowship, and while it is a rather obscure thesis that few people will ever dig out of the archives, it was completely original. I don't want to lose that. It isn't logical—I just don't!"

"There is something more to this than your fellowship, isn't there?"

"I am never going to be a 'good' Darkovan woman, Father. I am never going to be willing to submit meekly to men like *Dom* Gabriel, who imagine they know what is best for me. If you had sent me back here when I was an adolescent, I might have learned to be another sort of person. Now, it is too late. I am too used to being able to do what I like, regardless of my gender, and I resent the restrictions of having to have a chaperone or a groom and all the rest of it. The only reason I put up with it is because it would reflect badly on you if I behaved as I normally would on University."

"I didn't realize how much you chafed under Darkover's rein," Lew said slowly.

"There is nothing anyone can do about it. Oh, certainly sometimes I think about giving up my claim to the Domain, getting on the first ship I can find, and shaking the dust of Darkover from my skirts. Do you know, when I came here, I was very happy. Things *smelled* right and *sounded* right for the first time in my adult life. I had been longing for Darkover without even knowing it. That was before I really understood that I was only a pawn in a local game of chess, that I am Marguerida Alton, not just plain Margaret."

She took a deep breath and plunged ahead, releasing the tension that had preyed on her for months. "I am an heiress." The words tasted foul in her mouth. "I am a thing to be used for your purposes or Regis', to thwart *Dom* Gabriel or someone else. I am not free to marry as I wish, to pursue my own ends. I am not a person, but only an object." She tried to keep the bitterness from showing in her vocal tone, but she could not help it.

"I think you are mistaken in that."

"What would you do if I decided to become a Renunciate?"

He stared at her, astonished. "Anything in my power to stop you."

"Exactly!"

"But you love Mikhail, and you want to marry him, don't you?"

"And that is supposed to be enough? Marriage? Shall I wear a shackle on my arm until I die in childbed or just get old and doddering?"

He ran the fingers of his single hand through his hair, tumbling the tresses across his furrowed brow. "Well, I *do* wish to see you settled down, and—"

"And let my mind be blunted by counting linens, arranging meals and directing the servants! I do love Mikhail, but I do not think that being married to him, even if you can arrange that miracle, will ever satisfy me completely. I am too used to *thinking*, to studying and learning." She stood up from behind the desk. "We are never going to be able to see eye to eye on this, Father. I will do my best to be a dutiful daughter, but I cannot promise to enjoy it." She sighed and looked slyly at her father. "Now, is there anything you can do to make it easier for Ida Davidson to travel to Darkover? I must send her the disks I've done, and a better guide to the language than I had when I arrived. I want her to feel as comfortable here as possible, and if she can get the basic language down before she lands, that will help enormously. I am sure Uncle Rafe Scott can help me—he enjoys making himself useful, and I have no hesitation in taking advantage of it." She grinned at her father.

Lew looked bemused. "Termagant," he said affectionately.

"By all accounts, I come by it very honestly. Thyra was my mother."

"And you have never reminded me more of her than in this moment. Give me the telefax. I'll go over to Terran HQ tomorrow and see what I can do. Don't expect much."

"Thank you."

"I can see that you care a great deal about *Mestra* Davidson."

"I do."

"Then I will do everything in my power to bring her to Darkover." He sighed softly. "I know it is hard for you, *chiya*. And I think you are doing a fine job of bending as much as you are able. I found the demands of our world burdensome, and railed against them. And I suppose I have forgotten how difficult it is to be a woman here—how restricted you are. I would change the world for you, if I could."

"Would you, really?"

He grinned. "In a flash! But since I cannot, we must just do the best we can together. Perhaps between us we can make a difference."

"Well, it is nice to know that you would upset the social order to make me happy—even if you can't do it!"

"I think I have been trying to do just that for my entire life—not very successfully, I admit. That is why I am not trusted, and why you are not as well."

"Like father, like daughter?"

"Precisely!"

"I never thought of myself as any sort of rebel, Father."

"Neither did I, but it seems we are fated to be revolutionaries, whether we wish to or not. You are the future, *chiya,* and I think that it will be a very good one, if we can just manage to get through the present—which, as always, is difficult."

You are the future. Margaret let herself sink into that thought, and felt a sense of calm descend over her. Perhaps she was not as much of a pawn as she imagined. She smiled at Lew, and he smiled back, as if he knew her thoughts without any words.

The next morning there was a light dusting of snow on the streets of Thendara as Margaret, carrying her small harp, set out from Comyn Castle. She had sneaked out, knowing that custom demanded she take a Guardsman with her, or at least her maid. She needed to be alone, so she ignored her position, slipped down the stablecourt stairs, and darted out a back door of the castle without being seen. It gave her a delicious sense of pleasure, to escape, and she was ready to revel in the freedom of it.

Margaret drew in a long breath of the brisk air. There was not much wind, and her cloak was warm around her. Thendara smelled completely different in the first snow: fresher, somehow. She listened to the crunch of it under her boots, the calls of street merchants, or mothers scolding children, and ignored the occasional looks she got as she entered the fringe of the Terran Sector. She knew she should not really be out alone, but after her conversation with Lew the previous night, she felt rebellious and downright contrary.

She reached the gate of the little graveyard where Terrans were interred and picked her way among the headstones until she found Ivor's. She had ordered it when he died, and it had been put into place while she was at Arilinn. The stonemason had done a fine job. Ivor's name was carved in Terran characters, without any errors.

The other graves were covered with leaves or pine needles, untended and a little forlorn. But Ivor's had been raked clear of debris. She saw a bunch of autumn flowers resting against the headstone, gathered into a bundle, their petals now blighted with frost and wondered if Master Everard or someone else from the Musicians Guild had put them there.

For several minutes she just stood and looked at the stone, thinking about Ivor and all the things which had happened to her since he died. Then she removed the cloth cover from the harp, tuned the strings in the cold, dry air, and began to play. Her mitted fingers warmed up, and her voice as well.

Margaret plucked the strings, and after several pieces she started into the work she had composed for Domenic. She had refined it a little, but it was essentially as it had come from her fingers days before. When she was done, she stopped and looked down at the stone. It wanted words, but she had not found any yet. Perhaps she would, someday, if she was fortunate. She let the silence of the graveyard fill her up for a minute, then asked, "Well, what do you think, Ivor?"

Only the breeze answered her, but she felt that her teacher would have approved.

6

Margaret Alton and Rafaella n'ha Liriel set out for Neskaya six days later, in the company of several other Renunciates and a Dry Town merchant. There were horses and mules, bundles of baggage, cook-pots, blankets, tents and enough grain, it seemed to her, to feed an entire herd of animals. It was utterly chaotic, or appeared to be. No one cared very much that she had *laran,* was the heiress to a Domain or a Fellow of the University. These things were of no importance on the road, and after enduring the funeral of little Domenic, and the tensions of the Comyn Castle, she felt a great sense of relief.

After Margaret had demonstrated that she could be trusted to saddle her own horse, to follow the steed ahead of her on a narrow trail, to keep her head if something went wrong, she found herself accepted. Doing simple tasks, like setting up a tent or laying the wood for a fire, were wonderfully restorative to her battered spirit. Daniella n'ha Yllana, the trail boss, stopped treating her like a soft city girl after the second day, and actually praised her on the third. She warmed to that, as always.

The first day they passed by the ruins of Hali Tower, and Margaret did not have any visions of the place as it had looked before its destruction, as she had when she had seen it before Midsummer. It was just a tumble of blackened blocks of stone. Still, it brought back memories of the journey from Armida to Thendara, when she and Mikhail had ridden together and talked about so many things. It made her miss him poignantly, but not to the point of misery. She was just glad to be going to Neskaya.

By the fourth day, they had left the plains and climbed into the Kilghards, with the Hellers looming up behind. It was much colder now, and the wind blew off the mountains, snaking into the folds of her cloak and making her shiver. Snow fell, adding to what was already on the ground, and the track became slippery and treacherous. If this is autumn, she thought, it must be hell in full winter. By the end of the day she was exhausted and chilled to the bone, very glad to dismount Dorilys, and start setting up the camp.

Daniella observed the sky with an astute weather-eye and conferred with Rafaella and some of the other Renunciates, clearly worried. Margaret was almost too tired to care, but the little ripples of unease from the minds of the Renunciates penetrated her weariness, adding anxiety to her exhaustion.

While she and Rafaella wrestled with setting up the tent, she asked, "Is there a problem?"

Rafaella shrugged. Her short, curly hair was tucked under a knitted cap of green wool, and her cheeks were rosy from the cold. "We could get a storm tonight. Can't you smell it?"

Margaret tugged the floor cloth into place and staked down one corner, then sniffed the air. "No, I don't notice any difference. All I know is that it is cold as mischief, and my fingers are stiff."

Rafaella gave her a fond look. "I keep forgetting that you are still new to Darkover. This is nothing, really. By Midwinter, the trail will be nearly buried."

At the word Midwinter, Margaret felt a sharp jab, as if someone had pricked her skull. She straightened abruptly, and her back muscles spasmed. The alarm she felt was terrible. "Buried? But, I must return to Thendara then. My mentor's wife is coming to Darkover, and I really need to see her!" That was something which had been settled, with great expense in telefaxes and guarantees for passage by the Alton Domain, to Margaret's relief. She wanted to see Ida again, to make that link with her former life, with a kind of sorry desperation that made her feel both shamed and pleased.

The Renunciate nodded and smiled grimly. "Don't worry, Marguerida. It is not an impossible thing, merely a difficult one. It will be a hard journey, but I am sure you will be able to go back to Thendara when you must."

"Do you know, I sincerely wish that the occasional flyer was permitted."

"Humph. A flyer—only the Aldarans have those, and one or two of the Towers, and they are not likely to give you the loan of theirs. And you would miss all this wonderful scenery!" Rafaella gestured broadly at the jagged mountains, her eyes twinkling merrily. "Not to mention the good company."

"Well, I am glad of the company, certainly. But I confess I would prefer to arrive more than to travel." She made a face. "I will stop complaining as soon as we get some supper. I am ravenous." She smiled at her friend, and they finished setting their tent up in record time. Margaret dragged the bedrolls into the tent and got them arranged.

By the time she was finished, she was a little warmer and in better spirits. A large bowl of trail stew—dried meats and vegetables to which hot water only needed to be added—and a slab of bread purchased in the last village they had passed completed the job of restoring her. She dunked the bread into the rich mixture and chewed it, feeling her body warm and the tension in her jaw vanish.

For the first time since they left Thendara, a guard was posted. Rafaella and one of the other Renunciates took the first watch, and Margaret lay awake in her bedding, in spite of her exhaustion, until her friend came into the tent. She could sense the anxiety in the camp, and knew it was something more than just the weather. Weather did not demand a guard.

"What is worrying Daniella?" she asked Rafaella as the other woman crawled under her covers.

"There is a chance of catamounts, Marguerida. Our horses and mules would make a fine meal. We noticed some droppings, back down the trail a mile or two. Don't worry!"

"Oh. Why did I ever leave University!" Margaret felt herself shiver all over, not with cold, but with fear. She was sure there was something more bothering Rafaella, and almost wished she were not so ethical. Her training had progressed enough that she could have snatched the information from the mind of her friend without any effort at all. Only her own strong sense of honor prevented her.

Slightly chagrined, she remembered how she had worried about having her own privacy invaded the previous summer when she had finally realized that she was a telepath in a world where telepathy was a feature of the culture. She had been afraid that people would just poke about in her mind whenever they wished, not realizing that the opposite was a greater danger, and a more likely event. Of the several sorts of *laran* common on Darkover—the empathy of the Ridenows, the future seeing of the Aldarans, the catalyst telepathy of the Ardais—none held a greater peril than the forced rapport of the Altons. In the wrong mind, it was capable of ruthlessly crushing all but the strongest barriers, extracting information, or overwhelming another person. She understood now why the Altons were looked upon with some suspicion, and treated warily.

Rafaella chuckled in the darkness between them. "I don't know, but I am glad you did. Life with you has been very interesting, and I have missed you while you were at Arilinn. Did you like it?" Margaret had been too tired the previous evening for more than a sleepy good night. She had not even asked Rafaella about Rafe Scott, although she was very curious as to the progress of this odd love match. She had never been very interested in such things before, but now she discovered that she was. It must be because she wanted to be with Mikhail— silly of her.

"No, not really. I mean, I enjoyed mucking about in the old records in the scriptorium, and it was a relief to learn ways to focus my *laran*. But the building itself gave me a constant headache, and some of the other people there were not very glad of my presence. I hope the folk at Neskaya will be less hostile to me."

"I think they will be. Arilinn, being the principal Tower of Darkover, is very . . . self-important. Neskaya is cozy by comparison. At least, when I visited my sister during the time she was there, it seemed very nice. I think it is Istvana Ridenow's influence, because she is a woman who likes peace and quiet and wishes everyone around her to be at ease."

"I hope so, for another month or three of having people look at me as if I were a bug, and an ugly one at that, would be very unpleasant." She flexed her left hand, feeling the presence of the lines of energy over her skin. "I had to struggle to keep my temper a lot of the time."

Rafaella was snuggling into her bedding. "I have seen you get angry a few times, but I never thought of you as having a hot temper. Do you?"

"Oh, yes. It is pretty fierce, when I let it go, so I try not to. And the last place I wanted to get furious was at Arilinn. I felt as if I had been permitted to stay there on approval, which is very uncomfortable to start with. I haven't felt that self-conscious since my first year at University."

"That is all behind you now, Marguerida. And in a couple of days you will be at Neskaya. Good night."

"Sleep well, my friend."

Margaret listened to the faint noises of the camp for a few minutes. She could hear the horses stamping and snorting, and the faint rush of the wind, cold and penetrating, though not fierce. The crackle of the fire was audible, in the quiet of the encampment, and the steady snoring of the Dry Town trader in the next tent made a rhythmic buzz. When she slipped into sleep without really knowing it, the noises of the camp transformed into dreams.

A scream woke her. Margaret sat up abruptly, sending her blankets tumbling off her chest. The horses were bugling with alarm, and she heard shouts outside the tent. She was on her feet before she could think about it, her thick stockings crunching into the thin layer of snow outside the tent opening, chilling her toes instantly.

The small fire did not afford much illumination, but in the near darkness she could see several figures. Daniella and one of the other Renunciates had their weapons out, and were fighting with five muffled men, their faces invisible beneath thick scarves. Margaret felt her throat close in panic. Then she heard the scream of a mule, and her mind went to Dorilys. She heard more than saw Rafaella stagger out of the tent and rush toward her compatriots.

Margaret, knowing she was no use in a knife fight, ran toward the hobbled animals. If anything happened to the horses, they would have a hard time reaching the next village. But her thoughts were for her beloved mare more than anything else, and she felt the hot rush of adrenaline in her blood as she slipped and slithered across the icy snow.

There were more muffled men, trying to untie the hobbles. One had Dorilys' hackamore in his gloved hand, but the little mare was doing her best to escape. She backed, reared slightly, then twisted her fine head around and sank her teeth into the man's shoulder. Margaret was surprised because she had never seen a horse do that before.

He roared with pain and punched the horse's shoulder with a fist. At the same moment, there was another sound behind her, the bubbling wail of someone injured, and all her panic vanished. All Margaret could think of was her horse, her gift from Mikhail, and all the rage she had swallowed during her time at Arilinn boiled up into her throat. As she charged the robber, she could feel her left hand heat up beneath the silken mitt, as if the lines on it were alive.

Margaret grabbed the man, pulling at his rough jacket. He turned, raised a hand, and slammed her across the face, sending her careening backward into the snow. Then he stood over her, his muffler displaced to reveal a leering face with yellowed teeth and gleaming eyes. The shock of falling made her see stars briefly, superimposed on the terrible visage of the bandit, and then her fury cascaded. She could smell the silk mitt burning off her hand as he reached down to seize her throat.

Margaret swung her left hand and felt it contact his face. There was a tingle as skin met skin, like a small electrical shock. Then the bandit spasmed violently, releasing his grip on her clothing. His arms went out and his legs splayed, and he arched backward, shrieking. The acrid stench of emptying bowel and bladder mingled with the scent of singed flesh, as the robber flopped over in the snow, dead.

Alerted by his cries, two other bandits who had been at the horses charged at her, thrusting their short knives forward in a threatening manner. Margaret staggered to her icy feet, and lifted her now bare hand. The lines of her shadow matrix flared, casting a blue light on the snow, and one of the robbers hesitated. He looked at the now dead man, at her hand, and took a step back, but his companion was not so cautious.

"Giley! That's a *leronis!*"

"They bleed, too—she just killed my brother!" Then he swept at her, extending the knife arm toward her belly.

Margaret side-stepped the way she had been taught in her martial arts classes at University, and nearly slipped on an icy patch. But she caught the leading arm in her right hand, gripping the wrist just as the unarmed combat instructor had told her, years before, and flipped the bandit over. There was the popping sound of breaking bones, and she winced. It was a sickening noise, and she had to force herself not to retch. All those boring sessions in the gym had paid off, but they had not prepared her for the reality.

There were terrible sounds behind her, where the Renunciates were outnumbered. The clang of weapons striking each other, and the shouts and screams made Margaret turn and look. She could not see clearly in the flickering light of the fire who was friend and who was foe. They were just shapes moving around, struggling and fighting.

Margaret felt helpless for a second. She had never learned knife fighting, just the sort of defensive maneuvers she had used on the bandit. Then she picked out Rafaella's slender form near the fire, struggling to keep a tall robber from stabbing her. And that brought the fury back instantly. She started forward, stepping over the dead body of the first attacker, not sure what she was going to do.

Her throat seemed thick, heavy with energy, and she tried to swallow. But her mouth was very dry, and she did not succeed. Behind her, she heard the rapid footfalls of the man who had not attacked her moving away as quickly as he could. She licked her lips and took another hesitant step toward the melee.

"STOP!" The word came from her heavy throat, startling her. Her forehead throbbed, as if her skull might burst apart at any second, and her eyes felt blurry.

Then her vision cleared, and Margaret saw that there was no movement before her. It looked as if everyone had turned to stone. The horses nickered uneasily, and one of the mules brayed, but everything else was silent. Part of her mind was stunned, but the rest noticed that her command had not affected the horses or the mules.

Dazed by this turn of events, Margaret stared stupidly at the tableau. Then she managed to swallow, and realized that she had once again used the Voice, that peculiar aspect of the Alton Gift which allowed her to command the minds of others. It did not always occur in the Alton line, but it seemed that her training as a musician had strengthened the innate talent.

She should have felt relief. Instead Margaret realized that she still had no idea how to undo her command. Her studies at Arilinn had not dealt with the Voice, although she and Liriel had discussed it a few times, and tried to discover ways to discipline it. No one at Arilinn was interested in anything except her telepathic capacities of enforced rapport, so that she would not inadvertantly invade the minds of others. She had used the Voice once before, again without intention, when young Donal had awakened her from sleep, and it had taken the combined efforts of her father, Jeff Kerwin, Mikhail, and Liriel to remedy the problem.

Margaret did not give a fig for the bandits—if they froze to death, it was no more than they deserved. But Rafaella and the rest of the Renunciates, as well as the trader, were another matter altogether. She had to think of some way to release them, and soon. Standing about in the cold was going to kill all of them if she didn't think of something quickly.

Her feet were turning to ice under her, and she was starting to shiver. Margaret strode back into the camp, toward the fire. She tossed a brand into it, and the embers flared. At the same time, she tried to think of what to do.

When she had commanded that rascal Donal, she had said "Get out," and he had vacated his small, young body, and gone into the overworld. But here she had only said "Stop", so it seemed likely that she had not sent anyone away to that dreadful place where she had found the Tower of Mirrors, and defeated the shade of Ashara Alton months before. This, Margaret decided, was good. Now, if she could only think what to do.

She touched Rafaella's extended arm lightly, and found her friend was cool, but not yet cold. Like Margaret, she was not wearing her boots, and she would soon grow chill. Certainly her toes would get frostbitten if she stood there too much longer. Then she tried to move the arm, and discovered that it was not stiff, but it was resistant. Margaret shook her friend by the shoulder. "Wake up, Rafi!"

There was no response, and Rafaella still stood, staring at her opponent, her face grim and purposeful. Margaret frowned. Perhaps she had to use the Voice to undo her handiwork. But how? She did not know how to summon the command voice—it only seemed to function when she was frightened or upset, not when she needed it. What a useless thing!

Why hadn't all those clever folks at Arilinn instructed her how to utilize the Voice? Or how not to! All her resentment at the hostility she had endured began to boil up again, fresh and vital. Had there been anything in the ancient records she had read that might help?

As Margaret racked her brains, she felt the blue lines that lay across her left hand begin to warm. She looked down. They were like crackles of electricity across her skin, not painful but disturbing. For just a second she wondered if she could arouse the sleepers by touching them with her matrixed hand. Then she remembered how the robber had died, and decided she did not know enough about her matrix to risk that. No one did, which was the heart of the problem.

She stamped her feet, trying to keep the chill from distracting her. The cold was penetrating her clothing, and she wished she had her cloak on. She did not want to take the time to fetch it. She wanted an answer, and she wanted it now! She might experiment on the bandits, of course. It would serve the bastards right if she fried them! She enjoyed that thought for a second, then dismissed it almost reluctantly. *I am not that bloodthirsty—or am I?*

What had happened before, to provoke the Voice? She tried to remember the few moments before she had shouted. Her throat had felt thick with power. Could she do that deliberately?

Margaret focused her mind, as they had shown her at Arilinn, and thought only of her throat. Much to her surprise, she felt the muscles tighten, and the lines around her hand felt different. How? She tried to analyze the sensation, for the lines were, if anything, cooler than a moment before, not hotter, as she had expected. But her throat was warm, nearly hot, as if she had an unswallowed coal just below her larynx.

"Wake up, Rafaella!" Margaret spoke the words without much hope.

"What?" The Renunciate blinked, stared at the knife in her callused hand, then looked around the camp.

Margaret was too busy feeling relieved to speak. Then she hurried over to the closest of the rest of the Renunciates, and told her to wake up as well. The woman did, groaning as blood began to course down her arm. She had been wounded by a knife, though the man who had injured her was dead at her feet.

"Quick, Rafaella—Samantha has been hurt!" Margaret left the bleeding woman, and went swiftly toward Daniella and Andrea, who were croached in defensive stances, facing three bandits. She was terrified that she would lose the Voice, so she needed to hurry and wake up all her companions. She moved rapidly from one to another, hardly aware that she was shivering all over. The trader, Rakiel, was the last, and he looked at her, dazed.

"What in Zandru's hells is going on?" Daniella bellowed these words, staring at the still immobile bandits, her cheeks red with fury. Her eyes almost sparkled in the firelight.

Margaret stood in silence as the trader rose to his feet. She was too tired to explain anything, suddenly empty of rage or fear or any emotion whatever. Daniella was glaring at her, bristling. There was a question in her eyes, and cold suspicion. And all Margaret had the strength to do was lift her hands into the cold air, and shrug slightly. Then, realizing that her oddly marked left hand was now bare, she tucked it behind her back, out of sight.

A great emptiness rose in her breast, and she swayed back and forth. Distantly, Margaret was aware of movement around her. She knew that the Renunciates were dispatching the bandits with complete efficiency, and that somehow it was her fault that they were helpless to defend themselves. She did not want to think about it, but she found herself doing just that, in spite of her efforts.

Rafaella was bandaging Samantha's arm. There was nothing left for her to do. Margaret turned and stumbled back into the tent and collapsed on her bedding, still trembling. She looked down at her hand, where a few minute before blue lines had danced over the skin, and hated herself. She wanted to cut off her hand, to just hack it off, and let the blood drain from her body.

At Arilinn, they had warned her of this. She knew, intellectually, that she was having a reaction to using her *laran,* a kind of instant depression. When working in a circle, in a safe environment, this reaction did not occur. But she could not work in a circle! All she could do was fry bandits without intention. She felt her self-hatred like a physical object, a thing she wished to be free of. And it all centered on the shadow matrix.

If only she had not wrested the keystone from Ashara's Tower in the overworld. If only Mikhail had not urged her to pull it out, had not wrapped phantom arms around her waist and lent his weight to her struggle. This was all his fault!

The utter foolishness of that thought began to restore her spirits, as thinking of Mikhail always did, even when she wanted to box his ears for being particularly obstinate and Darkovan. If she had not taken the keystone, then the Tower would have continued to exist, and she would likely have died. She was alive, and while she was not entirely glad of it, she decided it was better to be alive, even despairing, than dead.

Rafaella stuck her head through the tent opening. "Get those wet stockings off. You are going to catch your death!" She pushed into the tent and started to remove her own, reaching for a dry pair that had been part of her pillow.

Dry socks. The idea seemed ludicrous. How could she be thinking about her stockings when she had just been responsible for the deaths of numerous men, even if they were brigands. What did it matter if she got pneumonia and died? It would be better for everyone—well, not for her father or Mikhail. The Old Man would be devastated, and he would never forgive himself, since she would not have been on the way to Neskaya except for his influence.

Margaret reached to her pillow clumsily, and pulled out dry socks and another silken mitt. In the dim light of the tent, this one looked green, and the one on her right was blue. She really ought to make them match, but she did not have the strength. Instead, she tugged off her sodden stockings, pulled on fresh ones, and wiggled her toes against the warm fabric. Then she drew the mitt over her left hand.

Her bottom was cold, from falling into the snow, and she realized that she needed to change clothes. But she felt too tired to move, and just watched Rafaella. Then the Renunciate pulled on her boots and stood up. "I am going to go help haul the bodies," she announced, and left.

Haul the bodies. The phrase seemed to bounce around in Margaret's skull, a cold stone of pain and terror. Two of those bodies were men she had killed. One she had burned alive! And there was no way to change that fact. She was going to have to live with it. But she would never tell anyone what she had done. It had been too simple, too quick and alarmingly easy. And if she had not managed to rouse the Renunciates, she would have killed them as well.

Grim-lipped, she removed her damp skirt, put on another, and then sat and listened to the activity beyond the walls of her tent. She could hear the slushing sound of bodies being dragged across the thin crust of snow, the voices of the women and the trader. Then she heard a slight wooshing noise, and suddenly the interior of the tent seemed very bright. They were burning the bodies. The smell of scorching flesh and garments drifted on the breeze, foul and vile.

Margaret slipped under the covers, shivering. She was hungry, ravenous, but she knew that she would spew up anything she ate right then. She bent her arm and pillowed her head against it, staring into the flashing light from the bandit pyre through the fabric of the tent. *If I learn nothing else, I am going to find a way to control the Voice! To hell with this abomination in my hand, and the Alton Gift. But I will never use the Voice again without knowing what I am doing! Never, I swear it!* Weak with horror, hunger and cold, Margaret tossed for a time, then slipped into a fitful sleep.

Two afternoons later, they arrived in the town of Neskaya. The sun of Darkover was setting, coloring the heavy clouds a bloody pink, and the town itself was already quiet. They passed houses with candlelight flickering through the few windows, and saw people hurrying on various errands.

Margaret stared up at Neskaya Tower, its white stones limned a rosy color by the lowering sun. Even at this distance, she could sense the presence of matrix relays behind the stones. She had never thought she would be glad to see any Tower, but since their encounter with the bandits, her companions, except Rafaella, had been edgy around her, wary. She had refused to explain anything, stubbornly retreating into silence, and that had not helped the situation. She did not want to admit that she had the command voice, for while the Renunciates had known she was the heiress to the Alton Domain, and that she was going to the Tower, they knew nothing more about her.

There was a spacious inn, and the company headed for it. Margaret drew her weary horse aside. "I think I had better go right to the Tower, Rafaella."

Her friend sighed. "Yes, you should. But I will take you. It only looks easy to get to. The streets wind around like noodles, and you could easily get lost." She dismounted, unhitched one of the mules from the train, and got back on her horse.

They rode away without bidding farewell to anyone, and Margaret could sense the relief in her former trailmates. She did not blame them a bit. Even though they had been born into a telepathic society, and accepted *laran* as a natural thing, they could not view what had happened on the trail without uneasiness. But it was a sad thing, for she liked the strong, independent women and had been on the way to making friends with some of them before they had encountered the bandits.

Margaret was grateful that the terrible events on the trail had not changed Rafaella's feelings toward her. She could sense that her first Darkovan friend still cared for her, still trusted and liked her. And she knew that Rafaella had refused to tell her sisters anything, for she had heard her saying that it was Marguerida's business, not theirs, in her fiercest voice. The loyalty of this woman eased the bleakness that had clung to her for the past two days, touched her tenderly. She wished that Rafi could remain with her in Neskaya, then decided that would not be fair. She was not some family retainer, but a free woman, with her own life to pursue.

Margaret sensed her own bitterness. Rafaella could do as she pleased, could enter into a freemate relationship with Rafe Scott if she wished. But she—Margaret—could not. She could not marry whom she wished, or live as she chose. She was the heiress to the Alton Domain, a telepath with an unusual focus of power, and her life was *not* her own, so long as she remained on Darkover. And, in her heart, she knew that she could never leave the planet, that she could not return to University, or anywhere else. She was too dangerous, and even if she learned to control her strange matrix, she would still be a very dangerous person. More, if the Terrans ever got even a sniff of what she could do, untrained as she was, they would lock her up in some laboratory and pick her to pieces. She sighed deeply, decided that she was working herself into a really wretched mood, and tried to think of something pleasant. When she could not, she just looked around, trying to conjure up some curiosity about this new place.

The streets were narrow, even narrower than those in Thendara, as if the folk there crowded together for warmth and companionship, against the mountains above them, and the snows. The shop signs were not hung out from the buildings, as they were in Thendara, but were set against the faces of the structures, and she guessed that the wind here was more fierce and would have pulled them away. She saw a luthier's sign on one house, and a weaver's shuttle carved on another. Rafaella led the way, guiding the mule which had Margaret's baggage on it, and she brought up the rear.

But at last the way widened, and Margaret moved her horse ahead, so she could ride beside her friend. "I am sorry about all this," she began, uncomfortably.

"Sorry for saving my life? Really, Marguerida, for a smart woman, you can be a real idiot sometimes."

"Guilty as charged."

They both laughed, and the tension that had existed between them for two days vanished. "You did what you needed to, and so did we. Believe me, killing those bandits was not a thing we wanted to do. It was hard, but it was also needful."

"Rafaella, I killed a man—broke his neck, I think. And I burned another alive. I never killed anyone before, and never thought I would. It makes me feel all hollow inside. And the only reason I did not awaken the rest of the robbers was that I was terrified they would attack us again. So I'm responsible for killing them, too, even though it was your swords that did the actual. . . ."

"Marguerida, stop berating yourself. You did what you had to do, to protect yourself and the rest of us, and we are all grateful, if a little disturbed."

"I keep smelling their bodies burning."

"So do I! We were all disgusted, for to kill a man when he cannot defend himself is against everything we believe in. Daniella went off and puked for half an hour, after we got the pyre burning. But you will be safe and sound in the Tower in very soon, and you can forget all about this."

"Rafi—I don't think I will ever be able to forget what happened, if I live to be a hundred."

Rafaella sighed deeply. "No, you probably won't. None of us will, even if, someday, one of us makes a song of it." Then her familiar laugh rang out. "But, Marguerida, it was . . . spectacular! I mean, I have had more than a few adventures on the trail, but nothing so remarkable. I can't help it. Seeing you . . ."

"What?"

The Renunciate seemed embarrassed now. "Before you spoke—I just caught a glimpse, since I was busy trying to stay alive. I saw you with the horses, and I watched you—well, kept getting peeks—flame that fellow. You shone! You were covered in blue light for just a moment, and it was . . . magnificent! Even with all the horror, I never saw anything so remarkable in my life!"

Margaret was stunned. "Did the others . . . ?"

"They got a few impressions, yes. And they were not as thrilled as I was, to be sure. But they won't gossip about it because they don't want to be thought mad."

"No wonder they kept looking at me as if I had two heads."

"I know. They tried not to, but they are human, Marguerida. As are you."

"I'm not so sure anymore."

"Marguerida—you saved our lives. Be content with that."

It was dark when they finally reached the walls of Neskaya Tower, but there was a groom waiting near the entrance, to take Margaret's horse and unload her mule. She dismounted, and Rafaella did as well. They looked at each other in silence for a moment.

"I shall miss you, Marguerida."

"And I you. I wish you could stay here."

Rafaella shook her head. "This is not my place, but I will arrange to return and escort you back to Thendara. I am sure the time will pass quickly."

"I hope so." She felt forlorn and lost.

"There, there, Marguerida. Don't look so sad." Rafaella curved her arms around Margaret's shoulders, embracing her gently, and kissing her cheek. "You are going to break my heart, *chiya!*"

Tears trickled down Margaret's cheeks, and she kept swallowing noisy sobs. Her friend stroked her hair and let her cry until she managed to stop. "You be careful now! I don't want anything to happen to you!"

Rafaella nodded, then grinned. "I don't want anything to happen to me either! Farewell, for now." Then she gave Margaret another quick kiss on the cheek, and got on her horse. As she rode away, Margaret could sense Rafaella's emotions, and knew that the parting was as painful for her friend as it was for her. It reminded her of her leavetaking from Liriel, and she wished she could just stop saying good-bye to people she cared about. At the same time, it was heartening to know that Rafaella would miss her, that she was cared for and even loved. The ache in her heart abated, and she was almost glad.

After Rafaella had vanished from view, Margaret stood in the courtyard, getting herself calmed. It was not until she noticed that her feet were cold that she finally and reluctantly entered the Tower, and found Istvana Ridenow waiting for her, smiling and so clearly glad to see her that her heart felt warm.

"Breda!" Istvana used the form meaning something between sister and kinswoman, and it was so heartfelt that Margaret almost began to cry again. "How lovely that you are here at last."

"Hello, Istvana. If I had known how cold it was going to be up here, I might have stayed at Arilinn. . . . Well, no, I wouldn't, even then."

"It was difficult for you, wasn't it?" The little *leronis,* who barely came up to Margaret's shoulder, gave her a gentle pat on the arm. "I was afraid it might be."

"Yes, it was hard." She felt an enormous relief to be able to admit it to her stepmother's kinswoman, for she liked and trusted the petite empath enormously. "I expected to be in something like my first year at University, but instead it was . . . hostile. I tried to fit in, but I could feel some of the people resenting me all the time. I did make a few friends, but not with the Tower folk. The Archivist, Hiram, and Benjamin in the scriptorium were friendly enough, because they realized I was a scholar. And while Mikhail was still there, it was not so bad. But after he left, and Domenic died, poor boy, it was intolerable. I felt like I was being stabbed at every second, and I hated the feeling of the matrices around me. And I don't know that I will be any more comfortable here than I was there, because the energy of the relays does things to my body that I don't even want to think about, let alone describe to you."

Istvana chuckled and led Margaret into the lowest floor of the Tower. They entered a large room, clearly a common room for the inhabitants of Neskaya, set about with comfortable couches and chairs. There was a guitar standing in one corner. She saw a mug left on a small table, and an empty plate. It was, she decided, untidy, but in a pleasant way. Cozy—that was the word. Rafaella had used it, and she was right. The rug on the floor was worn and a bit dusty, and—though she knew she was on another world—the whole scene reminded her of the living room at Ivor Davidson's house.

"I appreciate your tact, Marguerida, and I know you are trying to spare my feelings, but I am a much tougher old bird than you might think. Don't forget, I trained at Arilinn myself, so I know how it can be."

"You mean it wasn't me?" She felt amazed.

"It was you, to be sure, because you are very powerful, but it was not personal."

"Now I am totally confused."

"We are not angels, *chiya.* We are still subject to envy, fear, suspicion, and all the other unlovely flaws of humankind. And what I remember from my youth at Arilinn was that many of us, the younger ones, were always vying for praise and power, snapping at each other like marls fighting over some tidbit. I have tried to prevent such things here, because it disrupts the work, not to mention rubbing me quite the wrong way. But every time a new candidate arrives, a kind of wary examination occurs. They all look at the new one and think, 'Is this one stronger than I am?' To tell you the honest truth, it sometimes astonishes me not that a circle works as well as it does, but that it can function at all! Each time is something of a miracle, because I know how great the struggle is to set aside the ego and submit to the needs of the group—particularly if you have no love for any one of the members of a circle."

"I wish someone had explained this to me at Arilinn—it might have made things easier."

Istvana shook her head, causing her small red veil to tremble against her faded yellow hair. "It does no good to explain such things to an adolescent—we are all so self-absorbed at that age—and the training itself usually eases the situation. Working with someone every day, trusting them, rubs the self away, at least enough to create a circle, and once one has worked in a circle, and found the satisfaction of it, it becomes second nature, I suppose. One thing that your appearance on Darkover has done is cause us to reexamine our methods a little, and that is good."

"Were you very self-centered when you went to Arilinn?" Margaret was close to Istvana, because the woman had nursed her through her first and most dramatic bout of threshold sickness, intimate with her in something of the same way she had been with her late mentor, Ivor Davidson. But, for all of that, she knew almost nothing of Istvana's history or past.

"Absolutely. I was a skinny, spotty little thing with a very high opinion of herself one day, and just another telepath the next. The shock was enormous, and I didn't like it, because I am very proud, you see. And headstrong. I think my parents were quite relieved to have me gone from home, because I was always into some wickedness or another." She chuckled at the memory.

Margaret had a hard time imagining this assured and self-contained woman as a teenager. "I see. Well, I am glad to be here and not there, truly."

"Are you hungry?"

To her surprise, Margaret found that she was. She had lost her appetite after the bandit attack and had only eaten because she knew she must. Food had tasted flat and stale, and she had eaten mechanically and without pleasure. "Yes, I am."

"Good. I expect that after several days of trail food you will enjoy sitting at a table, too."

"Yes, I will. But I'd like to bathe first, and get out of these clothes. I do not mind the smell of horses, but I am pretty stinky, and I do not think anyone should have to endure that at dinner."

Istvana showed her to a room on the next floor, a sleeping room, where her baggage had already been left, and told her where the bathroom was. Then she left Margaret alone for the first time in days, and she felt a great relief, despite the humming sense of the relays above her.

As she unpacked her clothing, Margaret noticed that for some reason the presence of the large matrices nearby was not as disturbing as it had been at Arilinn. Puzzled, she stopped and looked around. Was there some sort of damper in the room?

Then she noticed that the walls and ceiling of the room were hung with great swathes of silk, concealing the stones. It made the entire chamber look like a vid-dram harem, and she chuckled. It was not the thin silk of the sort that her mitts were made of, but a thicker textile, dyed the color of *kiriseth* liquor. She had been too distracted by her parting from Rafaella and listening to Istvana's small revelations to pay attention to this chamber. It was a very nice room, and someone had gone to a great deal of effort and expense to make it comfortable for her. Even the quilt on the bed had a silken covering.

Tears welled up in her eyes again, at the sense of being cared for. Great, racking sobs rose in her throat, and she let herself weep until she had nothing left except a sense of exhaustion. She caught a glimpse of herself in a small mirror on one wall, and saw a red-eyed, puffy-nosed stranger. Her hair had escaped from its clasp behind her neck, and her short bangs curled against her brow.

Margaret stuck out her tongue at the woman in the mirror, gathered her cleanest garments, and headed for the bathing room. She was safe now, or as safe as she could be, and the smell of something roasting rising from the lower floor spurred her into action. Everything would be all right, she told herself. It *had* to be.

7

Margaret descended the staircase from the second floor to the first, feeling refreshed from a long, hot soak in the tub, and warm for the first time in several days. The smell of roasted meat made her mouth water, and she tried to swallow, but her throat seemed constricted. Her winter chemise was drawn close beneath the dark green wool tunic and it felt more like a noose than the soft textile it was. Below her waist, three petticoats and a heavy skirt moved against her ankles on the narrow stairs, causing her to proceed with care.

She was tense at the prospect of meeting new people, and even though she knew the reason, it did not seem to help. Margaret had tried all her life to get beyond her innate shyness, her anxiety at meeting new people. But each time she did, it was the same—dry mouth, perspiration, and just a hint of headache. She was wary, not only of strangers, but of those she already knew. It was an uncomfortable feeling and since she was in the company of telepaths, one that would be difficult to conceal. At least when she was at the University, no one could sense her emotions.

The common room of Neskaya Tower seemed crowded at first glance, then sorted itself out into seven people, including Istvana Ridenow. Most had the red hair that so often appeared in those with *laran*, but one woman had golden tresses, tightly braided down her back, and there was a man with dark locks above eyes like blue ice. The company was clearly waiting for her, and Margaret took a deep breath.

Istvana stood up, her red robe shifting across her slender body. "Marguerida! You look much better now. Come and meet my people." My people. There was no mistaking the pride in her voice at the mention of her colleagues, and Margaret could also feel her emotions. They were friendly, cheerful, and so welcoming that some of her fears began to fade.

More, it was a complete contrast to her first day at Arilinn. There she had been greeted by a dozen adolescents, steel-eyed and suspicious, and *Mestra* Camilla. There had been no sense of welcome, no overt friendliness. She had been with Regis' two daughters, Cassandra and Lina, who came to the Tower with her, and all of them were met with the same stiff silence. They had been introduced perfunctorily, and then sat down at a long table for a silent meal. Surrounded by youngsters, who in age might almost have been her own children, with Camilla the only other adult in the room, Margaret had ended up feeling more lonely and estranged than she could have imagined possible. She had wanted to stand up and walk out of the room, and had had to force herself to remain in her chair, and pass plates of food down the long board.

"I feel better, thank you." After another quick glance, she discovered that there were no real youngsters in the room. With no hard-eyed adolescents judging her, her belly's tension uncoiled. It was not that she disliked the young, for she had become quite close to Donal Alar, and his older brother Damon during her stay at Arilinn. But she found they intimidated her more than a little.

"José, will you get Marguerida some wine? Now, let me see. I shall begin with our youngest, I think." Istvana flashed a brilliant smile, as if some society hostess determined to make her party go well. "Marguerida, this is Bernice Storn, who has only been with us a year."

A small woman with hair like fire and dark brown eyes rose and made a little bow. She looked to be about seventeen, and she reminded Margaret of someone else. It was the way her facial bones were set, and after a moment she realized that Bernice resembled Regis Hastur's consort, Lady Linnea. "Welcome to Neskaya," the girl said in a soft voice, just above a whisper.

"I am very glad to be here," Margaret answered, reflecting that the girl seemed quite timid, almost mouselike. The man Istvana had called José handed her a small glass full of golden wine, and gave her a quick grin.

"I am José Reyes. Istvana has been on pins and needles awaiting your arrival, so I am glad you have finally gotten here." He was as tall as Margaret, and very handsome, with his dark hair. But his pale eyes were disturbing, even as they gazed past her face, to avoid direct contact. She could sense his curiosity about her, but nothing else.

"Thank you for the wine."

"Pins and needles—nonsense!" Istvana sounded faintly indignant. "I hope I am better disciplined than that."

One of the women laughed. "If you had been less so, you would have driven all of us quite mad. I am Caitlin Leynier, one of the technicians here, and your kinswoman at one remove or another"

"Leynier? I do seem to recall that name from the mists of the Alton past—which I confess still confounds me, although I have tried valiantly to memorize the family tree. It is nice to meet a relation." She liked Caitlin immediately. There was something about her that was clear and pure, like spring water.

"Well, it is six or seven generations back, and hardly counts now. I am sure you have already found that you are connected to more people than you ever imagined possible, for Istvana has told us that you spent most of your life off Darkover, dashing from planet to planet. Is that true?"

"One does not dash—I only wish that were possible. Travel on the Big Ships is cramped, uncomfortable, and extremely boring—so that you are very glad to make landing and almost kiss the ground when you get to where you are going."

"I see." Caitlin flashed a generous grin, and her green eyes twinkled. "I had quite another impression from reading a book of my brother's. It all sounded very exciting to me. When I was young, of course." Since she appeared to be no older than Margaret, she decided the comment was meant ironically.

Istvana took Margaret's arm in a firm but gentle hold, and drew her away from Caitlin, much to her regret. Then she was introduced in rapid fashion to Baird Beltran, a man about Istvana's age, Moira di Asturien, a pretty woman about thirty, Hedwig Hart, the woman with the wonderful golden hair, and finally to Merita Rannir, who peered at her nearsightedly. Each welcomed her in a friendly fashion, and she could sense the general air of acceptance, so different from her entrance into Arilinn. Her unease lessened as she sipped the wine and answered questions, so that by the time they left the comfortable common room and moved into a dining chamber which lay a few paces away, she was almost relaxed.

There was a long table, covered with a white cloth, with chairs along the sides, and one at the end, clearly for Istvana. It was set with the pretty blue-and-white china which Margaret knew came from the kilns of Marilla Aillard, the mother of Dyan Ardais, and clear glass goblets from the Dry Towns. There were platters of roasted fowl and cooked meats, bowls of vegetables and grains, and others full of preserved fruits.

Everyone took a chair, and Istvana indicated to Margaret that she should sit at her right. José Reyes took the chair beside Margaret and reached with a graceful hand for a bowl of roots that looked like mashed potatoes. Before he could grasp it, Caitlin, who was sitting on his other side, slapped his hand playfully.

"None of that! He is quite greedy about that dish, and if he serves himself first, there will be none left for the rest of us," she informed Margaret, leaning forward to peer around José.

"And who gorges on the featherberry pie whenever she gets the chance?" José did not appear in the least deflated by Caitlin's words, and Margaret could not help but contrast this meal with those she had endured at Arilinn, when she could bring herself to eat with the others within the Tower.

There was a fairly strict heirarchy at Arilinn, a kind of formality that seemed utterly absent here. Meals were taken separately, and while she had remained in the Tower itself, she had always eaten with the youngest people. The technicians took their meals at one hour, and the mechanics at another. Mikhail had been placed with the monitors, which pleased him not at all. She had been deeply grateful that her sensitivity to matrix screens was so great that she could not endure to continue living there, and after she had moved into her little house, she had eaten most of her meals there.

Neskaya was another situation entirely. Food was passed, jokes were made, and everyone ate as if it might be their last meal for some time to come. They were a boisterous bunch, except Merita, who ate in silence, a little remote from the rest. More than that, they seemed to be a curious group of people, not just Caitlin, but José, Baird, and Hedwig all wanting to know about everything from the Big Ships to the size of the harvest in the south. It was as if, Margaret thought, this was a different Darkover from the one she had entered a few months before.

The meal was finished at last, and she was longing for her bed.

Most of the company left, to begin their nightly labors at the screens above, but Caitlin remained at the table. "So, how do you like us thus far?"

"Very much. I was expecting to sit with the other students—except there is only Bernice Storn, it seems. Unless there are others I have not met yet."

"There are a few, either upstairs minding the relays or sleeping. Conal is abed with the fever—he's a technician, too. You will meet everyone eventually. But we are a small Tower compared to Arilinn, a circle plus eight or nine more. And we all know how Arilinn is, so we wanted to make you feel as welcome as we could. Is Camilla MacRoss still looking down her nose at everyone?"

Margaret laughed. "She is, I'm afraid. The rest of the students seemed almost frightened of her, and I suppose it would have been tactful if I had pretended to be as well. But I know her sort—the university was rife with such."

"What do you mean—her sort? Here, have a little more wine."

"I don't know if I should, Caitlin. I don't want to be put to bed with my boots on my first night here. Oh, well, just a little won't hurt." Margaret was relaxed for the first time in months, feeling that here she was almost safe, that she would not be criticized or made to think she was doing something wrong. She sipped at her glass. "There are people, I think, who find something they can do . . . um, say juggle. And they learn to juggle quite well, perhaps even become champion jugglers. And then, for no reason I can understand, they stop learning, and pretend that juggling makes them superior to everyone, and particularly to acrobats and wire walkers and equestrians and animal tamers." Listening to herself, she wondered if the wine was a good idea. She was as close to drunk as she ever became. But it was so nice to be able to talk without fear of censure that she could only hope she was not making a fool of herself.

Caitlin nodded. " 'That dog only knows one trick,' we say in the mountains. That is Camilla, for certain."

"Are you from the mountains, then?"

"Yes, from the foothills of the Hellers. My family has been there for centuries, grubbing out a living with the sheep and goats and a few crops. I was glad to leave home, though I miss them sometimes. When I arrived at Arilinn to begin training, I thought I had fallen into Paradise. The Plain of Arilinn is very beautiful, particularly in summer. I had two dresses, one with many patches, and one with only a few, and my boots were almost worn through. Some of the others looked at me

as if I were a spook, because while the Leynier name is old and respected, I did not come from the branch of the family that was
wealthy. But my *laran* was enough to win me some respect, and as
soon as I could, I left Arilinn and came here."

"Why Neskaya?"

"My mother is a connection of Istvana's."

"I see. Tell me, if you will, how you came into possession of that
book you mentioned? The one your brother had?"

"You mean, why am I not semiliterate like so many other females?"

"I would not have been so blunt about it, but yes."

"The Aldarans are not as reluctant to learn new tricks as the rest
of the Domains, which is one reason they have been exiled from the
Comyn Council for generations. My father's sister married into the
Aldarans, and when she was widowed, she came back to us, and she
taught me to read and write, and a great deal more. Not that we had a
lot of books, poor as we were. But I learned everything I could, being
a very curious person."

"I was starting to think that everyone on Darkover was incurious,
except . . ."

"Except?"

"Well, my cousin Mikhail Hastur is very interested in things that
his father says are entirely unnecessary."

"I see. Is he as handsome as they say?"

Margaret felt her cheeks redden at the question. "He is not a
burden to the eyes," she responded quietly.

Caitlin chuckled. "Tell me, why do you wear those mitts? Is there
some new fashion in Thendara, or are you cold? Istvana told us that
you had lived on a very warm world for a long time—it sounds interesting, and rather fantastic to me. She said you lived beside an ocean
for years and years." There was an undertone of disbelief in Caitlin's
voice, and a little envy as well.

"That is true, I did. Sometimes I dream about it, although it has
been over ten years since I stood on the shores of the Sea of Wines
and watched the flower boats come in at the rising of the morning
star. All the folk of the outer islands, wreathed in garlands, come
padding in, singing and chanting. The wind smells of blossoms and
wine, which is how the sea got its name, of course. They make the first
catch of *ferdiwa*, the spring fish, wrap them in kelp, and build great
firepits on the shore. There is nothing like that wonderful smell. The
fish is roasted until the flesh is white and flakes from the bones. It
tastes almost sweet . . . as sweet as summer peaches. And everyone

eats and drinks until they cannot budge, except the dancers, who seem to be able to keep from getting drunk somehow."

Caitlin's eyes were bright with interest, and Margaret hoped she had forgotten about the mitts. She was grateful to Istvana for not telling her folk about her peculiar matrix, because it still made her squirm to think about it. "And was the sea warm enough to swim in?"

"Oh, yes. Everyone who lives on Thetis is within easy distance of the sea, or one of the rivers, if they live on the Big Island, and everyone swims."

"How strange. We have a sea on Darkover, but I never heard of anyone getting into it on purpose. It is much too cold."

Margaret's thoughts went to Mikhail, living very near the Sea of Dalereuth, and wondered if he had gone to look at it. If he had, he had made no mention of it in their infrequent contacts. As she thought of him, a shiver of unease traced itself along her nerves. He had been so odd the last few times—vague and preoccupied with the "Elhellions," as he had called them a few times. "No, from what I have heard about the Sea of Dalereuth, I don't imagine anyone swims in it voluntarily."

"But you haven't explained the mitts, Marguerida. You don't mind me calling you that—we are cousins, after all—do you?"

"No, I do not mind. When I was small, I was called Marja, but I feel rather too grown-up for that now. And I have become very, very weary of *domna* this and *domna* that, particularly at Arilinn, where everyone seemed to be obsessed with their lineage. I used to want to grind my teeth sometimes, when someone would get offended that I didn't know their ancestors for seven generations back, as if who their grandfather was made them . . . somehow special."

Caitlin was quiet for a moment, looking thoughtful. "I see. Do you know, until this very moment, I never thought about how much time is spent discussing who married whom, or the names of their children, and their histories. I take it that such matters are not subjects of conversations to the Terranan?"

Margaret laughed, relieved that she had once more deflected Caitlin's lively mind from the matter of her fingerless gloves. "There are worlds where asking a man who his mother was could get you killed, Caitlin. And others where you and I could not converse at all, because either we were of different orders of society, or because we were not connected properly. You have no idea of the diversity. I found a bit of verse, something that predates Terranan space travel, which makes it about four thousand years old. Let me see. Ah, yes.

"There are nine and forty ways
Of constructing tribal lays,
And every single one of them is right.

"At least, that is how I remember it. I think what the author meant is that each tribe thinks their way is the only way, and that this is not true, since it leads to wars and feuds."

"You must find us terribly ignorant and backward."

"No, Caitlin, I don't. Infuriating, yes. And often puzzling, because I don't understand why the Darkovans do some things and not others. But I understand the pride of our people, and sometimes I want to take my uncle, *Dom* Gabriel, by his broad shoulders and shake some sense into him. He is not a stupid man, but right now he is behaving in a rather stupid way."

"You mean his taking the matter of the Alton Domain to the Cortes?"

"Yes, I do. I know that he thinks he is doing the right thing, but it is pretty hard on my father, and none too pleasant for me. He wants me to be declared his ward."

"Uh-huh. Even up here, we have heard about that. Istvana says that once *Dom* Gabriel gets an idea in his head, nothing short of a bolt from Aldones will cause him to change his mind. This is a very unpleasant subject for you, I am sure. So tell me about the mitts. They are quite fetching, and I have never seen anything quite like them. All those layers of colored silk!"

Margaret was torn between confiding in this woman, and pushing away from the table and running away to her room. After a moment, she reached for the wine carafe, tipped a bit more into her glass, and looked at Caitlin, lifting the glass vessel and gesturing. Caitlin nodded, and Margaret poured some wine into her glass.

"I don't know how much Istvana has told you about me, so please stop me if I repeat what you already know. When I arrived on Darkover, I had no notion of *laran*, Gifts, or any of the rest of it, and, frankly, I could have gone my entire life without finding out. But, before I left Darkover, when I was about six, I was overshadowed by Ashara Alton, and she blocked my channels. I don't know why she did that, but she seems to have imagined I was some sort of threat to her. And according to Gareth Ridenow at Arilinn, my channels are not completely open yet. There does not seem to be any precedent for me. He said he couldn't decide if I was a monster or a miracle."

Caitlin laughed at this. "I can hear him saying just that. A good man, Gareth."

"Anyhow, it was killing me—being overshadowed and blocked. I really do not understand the ins and outs of it, and probably I never will, although I have done as much research in the Arilinn scriptorium as I was able, and learned a great deal. So, with Istvana's help, I went into the overworld—which I will not talk to you about!" Margaret shuddered all over and felt her brows draw together in a frown. "It still gives me the occasional nightmare. But during the experience, I touched a matrix which was the keystone of Ashara's overworld abode, and when I came to my senses, I had a pattern on my left hand which is, as near as anyone can tell, the facets of that matrix stone. I keep it covered, because otherwise I am . . . or it is, dangerous."

Caitlin was listening intently. "Is that why Istvana had your chamber swathed in a Domain's ransom of wintersilk? We all wondered about it, and she wouldn't say a word, except perhaps to Merita, who never, never gossips."

"Yes. The energy from matrixes runs along my nerves like cold fire, and just being in this room is a little uncomfortable. If I learned nothing else at Arilinn, I did find out how to endure that. If I had my way, I would never enter a Tower again, but until I learn more about how to control my *laran,* I am stuck, I suppose—unless I can figure out a way to study someplace other than a Tower."

"Thank you for telling me about it. I had no idea I was being so nosy when I asked. Your eyes are getting glazed. Go to bed!"

"I am sleepy, but it was good to talk to someone about it. I am a private person, and I keep myself apart, even when I long to be close to other people. I have to struggle to trust others, even when they mean well."

"I will not betray your trust, Marguerida."

Despite her weariness, when Margaret got to her room, she felt restless. After getting into her thick nightgown and brushing her hair, she still did not feel ready to sleep, and after pacing back and forth for a few minutes, she realized that she was missing Mikhail, that she wanted to speak to him, to feel the touch of his mind.

She stripped away the mitt on her left hand, focused her mind as she had learned, and breathed deeply. For a while nothing happened. Margaret began to wonder if the silken hangings of her room were preventing her from reaching her beloved. Just when she was about to give up, however, she felt the familiar energy, faint and almost feeble, brush the edges of her mind.

Mikhail!

Marguerida? Where are you?

I arrived at Neskaya earlier today, and I am sitting in a bower of silk, like some princess in a fairy tale. There is probably a pea under the mattress, to test me.

What are you talking about? Mikhail sounded distracted, and almost angry.

Nothing of importance, dearest. How are things with your young charges?

Exhausting. I don't think I've had a whole night's sleep since I got here. And Priscilla and her friend . . . are very odd.

Her friend? Who is that?

What? I have a splitting headache, Marguerida.

You sound very strange, Mik. Are you all right?

Yes. No. I am just tired beyond belief.

Then good night, sweet Mikhail.

Good night, my Marguerida.

She sat in the chair for several minutes, going over the conversation. Margaret was more than a little uneasy, but she tried to dismiss it. Something was wrong, she was certain, for Mikhail was never short with her. Who was this friend of Priscilla Elhalyn's, and why had he refused to tell her about it? Was he in some danger, and wanted to spare her worry? Didn't the bonehead realize that she worried more when she did not know what was going on? Of course not! Males could be so idiotic sometimes. And likely it was nothing at all—just his weariness and her own.

Then doubt began to flourish in her weary brain. There was someone else, and Mikhail was afraid to tell her. There was probably some girl there who had taken his fancy, some woman of good family to whom no one would object, who would not disturb the precious balance of power between the Domains if Mikhail married her. Regis Hastur or Lady Linnea had probably sent someone off to Halyn House for just that purpose.

Her mouth tasted like iron as she pulled the mitt back over the lines on her hand. She firmed her lips, swallowing the despair that rose in her throat, and got into the bed. The mattress was soft beneath her tired muscles, and it smelled of balsam and cleanness. She rested her head on the pillow, and let the tears come.

I am not going to break my heart over this, Margaret told herself fiercely, as she fell into an uneasy slumber.

8

Mikhail ground his teeth in frustration and tried not to notice how very weary he was. After several weeks in residence in Halyn House, he was no closer to testing the boys, and all of his limited energy was devoted to trying to get the place into good enough repair for the coming winter. Already it was much colder, though the first heavy snows had yet to come. The wind from the sea gusted around the old place, crept in through windows he had tried to repair, under doors that no longer hung straight in their frames, and rattled the roof tiles.

He had just finished another infuriating and futile interview with Priscilla Elhalyn, and his head felt full of mites, all cheerfully gnawing at his mind. He had tried again to persuade her to either move back to Elhalyn Castle, or to take the children away to Thendara. She had looked at him with her usual vague expression, a slight smile playing across her lips. "But we *are* going away, all of us except Vincent," she had said.

"Where are you going?" Mikhail had asked that question so many times now that he had lost count.

"Away to a place where we will be happy," she replied, as she had before. Then she had turned and gone down the corridor to the dark, little room where she spent most of her days and all of her nights, leaving him feeling infuriated and helpless. As she reached the dimness in the shadow of the stairs, she turned back, smiling sweetly. "If you would only take Vincent and be gone, it would be better, you know. He is the one you want, and the only one you will have. The others are coming with me, when I go."

"Go where?" He shouted at her, venting some of his frustration. She had said this sort of thing several times before, hinting in a portentous way that never failed to annoy him. Just once he wanted to get a straight answer out of the *domna.*

"That is no concern of yours, and I do not think you should be here when we leave. I think . . . it might be fatal. And that would be very sad. Just take Vincent, and return to Regis Hastur."

With these words, she vanished, and he stood in the hall, clenching his fists. It took all the discipline had not to follow her, seize her by the arm, and shake her until he got some sensible answers. He had never laid hands on a woman before, and had never wanted to, even when his own sisters were being their most annoying, so he was rather shocked by the violence of his feelings.

Mikhail shook his head, trying desperately to clear his thoughts. The house seemed to loom over him, and even though the windows in the front had been reglazed, it was still a dark place, gloomy and forlorn. As for Vincent, he was a sadistic bully to his brother and sisters and seemed to take real pleasure in tormenting the girls whenever he had the opportunity.

Darkover had survived incompetent Elhalyns in the past—too many of them by Mikhail's lights. That was not a good reason to put another bad apple on the throne. He felt they should either eliminate the largely ceremonial position, or put someone in it who was both sane and able. Vincent seemed fairly intelligent, and there was nothing overtly insane about him, but his character concerned Mikhail. As eager as he was to be rid of the Regency, he was too honorable and responsible to take the easy way out, particularly since this solution was just what Priscilla proposed.

Mikhail compared Vincent to his own brothers for a moment, and realized that their characters were already well-formed by the age of fifteen. Gabe was already bossy and certain of himself, and Rafael was a natural compromiser. They had both changed a little but not greatly, and he doubted Vincent would improve very much with age.

The real problem, he thought, was that he no longer trusted his own judgment. He lacked any objectivity. He was prejudiced against Vincent, not so much because the lad was headstrong, but because he was cruel. Even without testing, Mikhail knew that Alain would never be able to take the throne. The thought of the oldest boy sitting in his bedroom day after day, being spoon-fed by either Becca or Wena made him feel ill. And the training he had received at Arilinn had yet to be put to use. Alain was simply untestable, and so was Emun. The youngest son was full of terrors, jumping at the slightest sound, and nothing Mikhail had tried to do to help him had had the least effect.

In his own mind he knew that of the five children, the two girls seemed the strongest and most able, both in mind and character. Of course, in his present distracted state, he hardly dared to believe this. They both regarded him more in the light of a savior from some fate they refused to reveal, but he was certain it had something to do with Priscilla's plans. They repeatedly begged him to take them away from Halyn House, and he might have done so, had he not felt that leaving the misbegotten place would have been an admission of failure, a defeat of his supposed Regency.

Mikhail had managed to contact Regis Hastur twice since his arrival, once to inform him that he had reached Halyn House, and another time to tell him that the place was a wreck. Neither time had he hinted that he was having difficulties, that he felt out of his depth. And Regis had barely had the time to listen to him, just assuring him that he was certain Mikhail could manage such a simple task as testing the children, and finding a new ceremonial ruler.

After this second brief contact, Mikhail had determined he would not bother his uncle again, no matter what. He pushed down his sense of having been dismissed, where it mingled with his doubts of his own competence, his general feeling of unworthiness, and his growing despondency. This was his problem, and he was going to solve it, alone and unaided! At times he considered just taking the children and leaving, though he was still unclear if he had the authority to do that. And who could he ask, without revealing that he was, as Marguerida had put it so vividly about another subject, up to his waist in snakes.

Mikhail did not even have the comfort of frequent contact with his beloved for he found that whenever he tried to speak to her, he talked of trivial things, mischief that Vincent had gotten into, or how pretty the girls were. He sensed that if he told her the truth, her respect for him would be damaged, that he would appear a feeble fellow, unworthy of her love. And reaching anyone from Halyn House telepathically seemed oddly difficult. It almost felt as if there were a telepathic damper on the place, though he had looked from attic to basement and found nothing to suggest that this was the case.

It all seemed to come back to the enigmatic Emelda, and he could not think of any way to deal with that problem. This was Priscilla

Elhalyn's home, and if she wanted to keep a household *leronis,* as had the Elhalyn and other Domains in the past, there was no reason he could think of to deny her. He was becoming more and more certain that Emelda was nothing of what she pretended, neither Aldaran nor an actual *leronis.* The Towers kept records of those gifted with *laran,* and it was rare for anyone to elude them. A few slipped by in each generation, but they were usually folk with small gifts, people like Burl, the bone-reader.

He tried to question Emelda whenever he had the opportunity, but she was both wary and hostile. Mikhail realized she was powerful, but he lacked the kind of training he would need to measure her potency. He despaired of dealing with some wild telepath, there, alone and with only his moderate talents to support him.

And he rarely had the leisure to interrogate the odd woman, or Priscilla, during one of her infrequent appearances. He had never suspected that running a household or looking after children was so demanding, and his respect for his mother increased daily. Just the struggle to get provisions for the coming winter was enormous. Added to that, the necessary repairs took up most of his time. There were calluses on his hands, and he had smashed a fingernail trying to hammer a peg into a window frame. And, as exhausting as his days were, his nights were worse. They were hellish, for all the children experienced nightmares, and he kept having to get up and tend them. The two old women, Wena and Becca, did not stir at the screams, and left both the lads and the girls to themselves.

His men, Daryll and Mathias, were exhausted as well, doing double duties as grooms and draymen, and even as laundresses and maids. They took turns sleeping outside his door, but their sleep, too, was disturbed by terrible dreams which left them weary and anxious. His expectation that people from the village could be hired to help had not become a reality. A few came grudgingly to work during the day, but none would remain through the night. And soon even these refused to come to Halyn House, insisting that it was an evil place. That he secretly agreed with them did not improve his disposition. Mikhail was certain that the presence of Emelda was the likely cause of the reluctance of the villagers to enter Halyn House, but his weary brain could find no solution to the problem. From a few remarks he had overheard, he realized that the villagers thought she was an actual *leronis,* not, as he believed, a fraudulent one, and were terrified of her.

The worst part of it was that Mikhail knew he was having a hard time thinking clearly. His brain seemed stuffed with Dry Town cotton or perhaps the gluey, overcooked porridge that was served at breakfast. If he could just find a decent cook to replace the old fellow who lurked in the kitchens, scowling and refusing to take any orders!

He felt frustrated that he had accomplished nothing, and the feeling of helplessness grew greater each day. Mikhail tried to fight it, to feel that he was getting the house into better repair, that the children had better food. But he knew that this was not his job, that he was not there to fix windows, but to find out if any of the boys could take the Elhalyn throne.

If only he could concentrate! He tried very hard, but he kept getting distracted by basic tasks, like keeping the kitchen full of nourishing food. He even thought of sending one of the Guardsmen to Thendara, to bring back more people. But where would he put them? Halyn House was still in such disrepair that it could not hold very many more than already lived in it. Even when it was new, it had not been intended to house more than the old lady and a few servants. And he *should* be able to manage a few children on his own!

He tried to cheer himself up by counting the things he had managed to accomplish. The chimney in the dining room was unclogged at last, so the room was slightly more pleasant in the evenings. Glass was sent for and set into some of the windows. The quality of the food improved slightly, though the cooking of it remained unpalatable. He had gotten a woman in the village to sew up some clothing for the children, so they no longer looked like ragamuffins. The horses were well taken care of. Not much for several weeks in residence, but something.

Despair ate at him. He could not stand to be in the house another minute! Mikhail looked through the new windows and saw that it was a pleasant day. Perhaps some exercise would clear his mind. He grabbed his sword, strapped it on, and went out through the kitchen, ignoring the grumbling cook, who was scaling some fish that had arrived that morning from the village.

The clouds were few and small, and there was a good wind off the sea. It smelled of brine, a salty scent that seemed to blow away his exhaustion a little. He recognized another smell. There was snow on the way, and soon. He glanced to the north and saw dark clouds along the horizon. Yes, winter was on its way. Mikhail held back a shudder. The idea of wintering in this miserable house was almost more than he could bear.

Mikhail walked toward the hedge that separated the back of the house from the stables. He heard the rough voice of a crow, and glanced around. He spotted the flash of white along the wing edges that he now recognized as a sea crow, and he was certain, the very bird which had greeted him the day he arrived. There were a good many crows in residence at Halyn House, but only the one sea bird. The others were the ordinary variety, all black, and somewhat smaller than this animal. He had gotten used to the soft caws with which the flock announced the dawn, the thump of their feet on the roof over his bedroom, and rather enjoyed the gossipy exchanges he heard every morning. It was, he thought, about the only normal, pleasant thing at Halyn House.

The sea crow was another matter, for it ignored everyone except Mikhail, and watched him closely whenever he was out of doors. There was something a little disquieting about the intensity of this avian interest, and Mikhail could not decide if the bird was friend or foe. He found it perched in the hedge, almost invisible among the dark greens, a place the crow seemed to favor. He waved, just to be polite, and pushed through the opening in the hedge.

Mikhail walked into the now clean stableyard, where Daryll and Mathias had set up a small quintain, a man-shaped dummy on a series of ropes and pulleys, so that it would move. They had weighted the feet with wooden blocks, and some broken horseshoes, and it was not a bad job. He watched it swing in the wind for a moment, admiring the cleverness of his men. The two Guardsmen spent a little time every day, either practicing on the dummy, or sparring with each other, and Mikhail realized he should have joined them much sooner. It would be good for him.

There was no one in the stableyard at the moment. Even old Duncan seemed to be absent. He could hear the horses in the now clean and repaired stable, snorting and stamping in their stalls. He shrugged and drew his weapon, approaching the dummy and feeling slightly foolish.

Mikhail warmed up with a few feints and parries, enjoying the sensation of muscles pulling and pushing. He shifted the sword from hand to hand, as his master had taught him when he was about Emun's age. He really should get Vincent and Emun out here and start them training. Few men, he knew, could fight as well with either hand, but his old master, Amday, had been insistent that if he could learn the trick, he should. Mikhail had hated it at first, feeling clumsy with his left side, but after a time his muscles had learned, and soon he had become comfortable with it.

After his muscles were limber, he began a concentrated attack on the dummy. Each blow he landed made the straw-stuffed object shift on its ropes. The wind gusted and added to the motion, so he had to dance around on the somewhat uneven footing of the yard. He landed a glancing blow, and the dummy, caught in a gust, shot toward him instead of retreating.

Mikhail only managed to step aside at the last second. The dummy swung past him, ruffling his hair. He could hear the ropes creak and strain as the dummy reached their limit and began to move back toward its post. Something wet under his left foot caused him slip, and before he knew it, he was on the stones, his legs splayed in a split that nearly tore his groin muscles. At the same time, the dummy swung back, coming right at his head.

Mikhail threw himself down, ignoring the protest of his hamstrings, and the straw thing passed over his head by no more than a finger's width. He could feel the heaviness of the wooden blocks ruffle his hair. Maybe it was not such a clever thing, after all. He scrambled to his feet, breathing shallowly, and moved out of the orbit of the object. The wind seemed to drag the air out of his lungs; dust rose around him, so his eyes stung with grit, and his vision blurred.

As Mikhail rubbed his eyes, trying to clear them, he heard a creaking noise. The ropes holding the quintain strained in the wind. Mikhail spun around in the sudden whirlwind, trying to move out of the orbit of the noise, but it seemed to be everywhere, and he lost any sense of direction, his mind blunted. He felt more than heard a rush of movement in the air, of something coming at him, and twisted around, trying to step out of the way.

There was another noise, a raucous, rough caw, and he jumped at the sound. He heard the flap of wings above his head, and looked up. There was a flash of black and white. The wind dropped, and Mikhail blinked his eyes clear of dirt. A moment later, the sea crow landed on the dummy's head and deposited a large green dropping on it. The dummy went still, as if the minor weight of the crow were sufficient to stop its movements.

The crow regarded him with hot, red eyes, as if trying to convey some important information. Mikhail looked at the bird, then made a deep bow. "Thank you, Lord Crow. I think you might have saved me from serious injury."

He felt his neck prickle then, and looked around. The stableyard was still deserted, but he was sure someone was watching him. He looked back toward the house, and saw, for only a moment, the white circle of a face in one of the windows on the second floor. Then it was gone, and he was not even sure he had seen it. And there was no way to guess who it was.

The crow spoke again, and Mikhail turned back. He slipped his sword into its sheath and groaned. His thighs were burning with pain, and his left shoulder hurt like the devil. He noticed he had scraped the palm of one hand when he slipped, and he wiped it on his tunic.

Mikhail's heart slowed to its normal, steady beat, and his breathing deepened. He had been terrified when the dummy came at him, but too busy to notice it. Now he felt the fear course along his blood like poison dregs, and he started to shake all over.

The sea crow lifted its great wings, the white feathers on the edges flashing in the pale sunlight. It gave a small hop, flapped, and lighted on Mikhail's shoulder so hard he nearly staggered. The bird was heavier than it looked. He could smell the odor of fish as the crow dug its huge talons into the cloth of his tunic.

Close up, the bird seemed enormous. Mikhail was aware of the sharp beak, capable of taking out an eye, very close to his face. But, despite this, he was not alarmed. Instead he felt curious for the first time in days, as if his mind at last had cleared.

The animal shifted from claw to claw, and Mikhail extended his left arm. He had handled hawks all his life, but never anything like this. It moved down the length of his arm until it stood just above his wrist. Then it opened its yellow beak and wiggled its tongue, a comical gesture that would have made him laugh if he had not been quite so awed. There was an air about this crow that demanded respect, and he did not feel his bow a few minutes before was at all foolish.

Was it the same crow he had seen twice his first day at Halyn House? He had heard its rough caw several times since then, but had been too tired and too busy to notice. Did it have some purpose? It certainly was not behaving like any crow Mikhail had ever seen before—or any other bird, for that matter.

There were individuals, he knew, who had a *laran* that allowed them to communicate with animals, but he had never shown the slightest hint of it. He could sense something of its energy—very distantly—and the intelligence that lurked in the small brain. But beyond that it was only a very handsome bird, and nothing else.

The crow gave a squawk that almost sounded like a word, and Mikhail nearly jumped. Gisela Aldaran had owned a raven, he remembered, that had been trained to mimic words, and he wondered if the crow had the same ability.

"What?" It seemed polite to speak, if only that much. The crow repeated the sound, and it resonated in Mikhail's ears. *"Go?* Are you telling me to leave? I would, in a flash, if I had any choice in the matter, believe me!"

The bird stared at him with its penetrating eyes, then seemed to shrug and launched itself from his arm. It flopped down on the stones of the yard for a moment, then took off for the trees. Mikhail stood and watched its flight, wondering what to do. In the end, he waved to the bird and went back to the house.

The clarity of mind Mikhail had achieved in the stableyard persisted through a hot bath and a change of clothes. It was still with him when he went down to eat dinner with the children and his Guardsmen. As had become the custom, Priscilla and her shadow were absent, eating their food in the little room at the back of the first floor where they spent most of their time.

"I saw you in the yard," Mira said. She smiled, and two dimples appeared in her now fuller face. She was such a pretty child, though she was still anxious. And her sister, Val, often looked hunted, as did Emun.

"Was that you looking down from the window upstairs? Did you see me almost bested by a dummy?" Mikhail spoke with forced cheer. It had not been the girls' room window, for that was on the other side of the house, where he had seen the white face.

She shook her head. "No, I was in the linen room with Wena. Since you fixed the window in there, it is quite pleasant. And I only saw you for a minute, because Wena wanted me to fold sheets with her." She groaned comically and stretched out her arms. "It is hard to keep them from getting on the floor. You were dashing about changing the sword from hand to hand."

"Are you a two-handed fighter then, *Dom* Mikhail?" Vincent almost bellowed the words, for he seemed to have no concept of speaking moderately. Mikhail had suggested several times that he might speak more quietly, but Vincent continued to shout, to the extent that Mikhail wondered if he were not somewhat deaf.

"Yes, I am, Vincent."

"When are you going to teach me? Have you ever killed a man?"

"The purpose of swordsmanship is not so much to be able to kill, Vincent, as to be able not to. We have not had a war on Darkover in a long time, and I hope we never will again. We keep up the practice of sword fighting because we want to be able to defend ourselves if the need arises." His earlier idea of starting to train Vincent and Emun in basic swordsmanship was less appealing now. Vincent was just a little too bloodthirsty to be trusted, and Emun too frail.

"So you haven't killed anyone?" The boy looked disappointed. "If I knew how, I would. There's a big crow that lives in the trees that I'd like to kill right now. When are you going to start teaching me? I can't very well be king if I can't manage a sword, can I?"

Mikhail picked up a plate of overbaked rolls and took one while he thought. The more he saw of Vincent, the less Mikhail could envision him being even a puppet ruler. He was too headstrong, too arrogant, and too cruel. And he was almost a year older than Danilo Hastur, who would follow Regis. In Mikhail's estimation, Danilo and Vincent were incompatible—a problem he had not even thought of when he had taken on his onerous task. The Hastur boy was not forceful, and so far had shown nothing of Regis' talent for bringing people together. Vincent would bully Danilo into tatters, as likely as not.

He tried to tell himself it was not part of his assignment to decide which of Priscilla's three sons would be best suited to become king, only to find one who was sane enough to sit on the throne. But he felt a deep longing to choose someone with actual qualities of leadership, not just a warm body. Of course, Regis might not have intended that he find such a person—his uncle had been uninformative on the subject—and might have assumed that any Elhalyn, so long as he was not overtly unstable, would suffice. That the real power would remain in Hastur hands was a given, but the more he thought about it, the less Mikhail liked it.

With sudden clarity he realized that if Darkover must have a king, it should be a real job, not a makeshift traditional position to satisfy people like his father. And it should be done by an able person, not a manipulable weakling. Otherwise, why have a king at all?

Looking around the table, he had a sinking feeling. Even without testing for *laran* and other qualities, he realized that the only male present who was sane enough and sound enough to do that job was himself, and the way things had been going, he was not that certain of his own mind these days. It gave him a feeling of quiet desperation, that he would be trapped into becoming the Elhalyn king, into being a dummy on a throne which had no real power, only empty respect. He must not leap to any conclusions! If Vincent was unfit, there was still Emun to hope for. And who knew what they would be like once they were away from Priscilla? They might both be better, calmer lads. Then again, they might be worse. The excellent appetite he had worked up at the quintain faded away.

His own sense of duty kept getting in his way! Mechanically, Mikhail took some overcooked roots onto his plate and raged silently. He loved his cousin, Danilo Hastur, but he understood the character of the young man well enough to realize that it was not as strong as his own. Mikhail could not take the Elhalyn throne without doing damage to his cousin's rather tenuous self-esteem. He knew that he would end up trying to run things, and that Dani would resent it. And he cared enormously, he discovered, about Danilo Hastur. It would not be good for Dani, and more, it would not be good for Darkover, to have the balance of authority tilted so badly.

"When are you going to teach me to use a sword?" Vincent yelled, interrupting Mikhail's thoughts. His face was red, as it often was when he did not get his way, and his eyes seemed to swell in his skull. Mikhail could see the girls flinching, although they should be used to the racket by now.

"As soon as you learn to moderate the tone of your voice while you are in the house," he snapped.

Vincent opened his mouth, then appeared to think better of it. He settled for glaring at Mikhail, then pinched Val on the arm so hard she squeaked.

Mikhail was on his feet before he quite knew what he was doing. He swept around the table, grabbed Vincent by his collar, and hauled him out of his chair. The lad was almost as big as he was, and he resisted. But he was so surprised that all he could manage was a flail of flabby arms, and a weak buffet along Mikhail's shoulder.

"Go to your room!"

"I won't! You have no right . . ."

Mikhail did not wait to hear more. He grabbed Vincent by the shoulder and the back of his belt and frog-marched him to the door. Then he shoved him out of the dining room, and closed the door behind him. He could hear Vincent yelling on the other side, screaming with rage, almost incoherent. "How dare you! You can't treat a king like that!"

Mikhail waited to see if Vincent would try to come back, but after a minute of shouting, he heard the heavy sound of enraged adolescent footfalls storming away. He turned around and discovered that the remaining children, as well as his Guardsmen, were looking at him with unfeigned amazement. Emun was almost trembling, his pale cheeks totally colorless, and his eyes very wide.

"I dislike having my meals disrupted with argument," he said. "It upsets my digestion." It was more than that, of course. Mikhail had terrible memories of dinners at Armida, with his parents either shouting at each other, or sitting in a cold, congealing silence that was bad enough almost to ruin a normal adolescent appetite. When he had gone to live at Castle Ardais, he had been relieved to discover that Lady Marilla Aillard, Dyan Ardais' mother, never permitted disputes at the table. It had led to many a tedious evening, but Mikhail preferred that to argument.

"You should not have done that," Miralys said quietly.

Mikhail returned to his chair, and looked at her with interest. The girls kept very quiet most of the time, as if they were trying to hide themselves from something. Val seemed to be the more energetic of the two, for she had a constant twinkle of merriment in her eyes, and Mira the more confident. But the tone of her voice was not at all confident. She sounded frightened, and he knew she was more afraid of her brother than he had realized. Why? It was more than just bullying, but he could not put his finger on it.

He thought about *Dom* Gabriel and Lady Javanne, then about Regis and Lady Linnea, who were, in many ways, more his real parents than his biological ones were. All of them had been strict, and *Dom* Gabriel had a tendency to roar when he was thwarted. But Mikhail had never felt really afraid of any of them, and, as far as he could tell, neither his brothers nor his sisters were genuinely frightened of *Dom* Gabriel. No one enjoyed his frequent bursts of ill-humor, but if his father had suddenly ceased to express them, Mikhail would have thought him ill.

"Why is that, Mira?"

She did not answer, but pursed her lips and bent her head over her supper. Val looked around the table, shrugged, and replied, "He will take it out on us. He always does."

A finger of unease seemed to run along Mikhail's nape. "What do you mean?"

Valenta looked at him as if he had lost his wits. "My brother *likes* to hurt people." She said this in a cold, uninflected voice, as if she were stating a known fact, and could not quite understand why he was asking the question.

Mikhail ignored the sinking feeling in his belly, and a sour taste filled his mouth. She was absolutely right; he had known it for weeks. But he had refused to believe it, had kept trying to convince himself that he was misjudging Vincent somehow. And with a great sense of regret, Mikhail realized that he had been avoiding paying real attention to these children, that he had let himself become absorbed in the problems of setting the rackety house in some order because he did not feel up to the challenge of understanding these strange creatures. He knew that Vincent was cruel, and that the younger children were afraid of him. He just didn't want to face it. Why the devil had Regis given him this job—he wasn't up to it!

"That is going to stop." Mikhail barely believed what he said, but he wanted to reassure the children. *Of course—I am going to watch Vincent every second of the day and night! What a dreadful joke.*

Val shook her head, sending black curls swirling around her cat-like face. "You can't stop Vincent. No one can."

"Why not?"

"Because if he can't get you with his hands, he'll give you the headache or the grippe."

"I see." Mikhail picked up his goblet and took a swig of local cider, sweet and dry at the same time. He did see, for the first time since he arrived, that Vincent had been let run wild, that if he had been sent to a Tower for training as soon as he showed signs of *laran,* he might not do the things he did. He really had to sit down and do the testing he had come to do, and soon.

This was Priscilla's fault, for refusing to let her children be trained, but it was too late to start blaming. They could have gone to Dalereuth, the closest Tower, almost on the sea for which it was named, if she had not let them come to Arilinn. If anyone was to blame, it was Regis himself, for letting things go for so many years.

It all came back to *laran,* didn't it? Before he had encountered Marguerida Alton, Mikhail had never really given a thought to what a double-edged blade the ability to read minds could be. He had grown up in a telepathic community, where the trait was both anticipated and desired, and because, as his beloved often reminded him, he was inside Darkovan culture, he never saw that there was any liability in it.

Laran was so much a part of Darkovan culture that he rarely thought about it, until Marguerida had pointed out rather angrily that it affected everything. Her position was that it was overvalued, to the point of obsession. And until his sister Ariel had revealed her enormous pain and self-hatred for her own lack of *laran,* he had not realized how painful it was for those who did not possess the gift.

During his time at Arilinn, while Marguerida began her own training, Mikhail had found himself forced to examine many things he took quite for granted. The scholarly mind of his beloved was something he had never encountered before, either in man or woman. She was able to argue—and even seemed to revel in dispute—any position, clearly and incisively. This, she informed him, was called sophistry, and was frowned on in academic circles. But during several of their afternoon walks, or their pleasant rides in the meadows and fields around the Tower, she had cheerfully dissected Darkovan culture. It seemed to release something vital in her, for her eyes always sparkled like yellow agates, and he knew she missed her academic life at University more than she ever admitted.

Sometimes she took the position that *laran* was a good thing, and other times that it was not. Marguerida would make reference to other cultures she knew about, where people bred for strength or intelligence or skin color. Mikhail was fascinated, filled with longing to visit other worlds. But what had come out of these discussions was a greater understanding on his part that Darkover was not as simple as he had always imagined it to be. She was always fair, but she also always followed her arguments to their logical conclusions, some of which were not very appealing.

One of the matters they had often talked about was the problem of the untrained or wild telepath. This was very much on her mind, because she had been just that for some time. She had never suspected, for instance, that she had the ability to use her voice to command people, until she had inadvertently sent young Donal Alar into the overworld. Marguerida still got the shivers, he knew, when she remembered that, and thought of all the times she could have injured someone.

The only conclusion that had come out of these talks was that, since *laran* on Darkover was a fact of life, the Towers were necessary. Since he knew how much she loathed the very existence of the great relays, that the stones themselves sent her into anguish, he knew this was a difficult admission.

But until that moment, Mikhail had never considered that Vincent was misusing his untrained *laran* on his siblings because he himself would not have done so. He had been stupid, assuming that this pack of wild children functioned with the same rules he did. He began to wonder if Priscilla Elhayln was more than merely eccentric, because he could not imagine any other explanation for her bizarre behavior.

"I think it is time Vincent learns he cannot do just as he pleases," Mikhail said quietly.

"But he can!" Emun blurted out the words, then looked as if he wished he had bitten his tongue.

"Go on."

The boy looked helplessly at his sisters. No one spoke for several minutes, and the only sound in the room was the crackling of the fireplace and the noise of spoons and knives hitting plates and bowls. Daryll and Mathias continued to eat, appearing deaf, though Mikhail knew that Mathias would speak to him later. The older Guardsman was gruff, but he was also wise, and during the weeks, Mikhail had come to depend on his opinions and observations.

Finally Miralys spoke. "It does not matter what he does to us, because we are all going away, and he is going to be king. We all know that. And, truthfully, it cannot be too soon."

"Going away? Where are you going?"

"We are not allowed to talk about it." Val mumbled the words, looking as if she wanted to say more, but was afraid to.

For the first time in his life, Mikhail Hastur wished he had the Alton Gift of forced rapport. He was shocked at himself. He had never wanted to invade the thoughts of another. The very idea told him that he was totally out of his depth, that he needed help, experienced help. He had a wild telepath on his hands—two, if he counted the enigmatic Emelda.

As he tried to think what to do, he felt his mind begin to cloud. It was a subtle thing, a feeling of passivity and weakness, but he noticed it almost at once. Anger surged in his blood, and he felt himself tremble with rage.

A moment later he heard a faint shriek from the back of the house, and outside the dining room window, the hoarse caw of a crow. Then his mind was clear again.

"Look! It has begun to snow!" Valenta pointed toward the window as she spoke, sounding relieved to find something to say that was innocuous and safe.

"So it has," he answered, clinging to the clarity of his mind stubbornly. *I have to get some help, and quickly. But from whom? I don't really know the folk at Dalereuth, and it is such a small Tower. Besides, if it is snowing here, they are already up to their knees in the stuff. Why didn't I understand sooner? And why won't I ask Regis? I can't. Who, then? What a dunce I am!* Liriel! *Of course!*

9

By the time he got to his room, Mikhail was feeling the strains of his recent exercise—and the fatigue, too. His hamstrings were aching, and he had the start of a serious headache. All he wanted was his bed and unbroken sleep for a change. There was something he had intended to do, but for the life of him, he couldn't think what it was.

He undressed, automatically checked the room for mischief, and settled into the bed. It smelled slightly musty, and he found himself longing for the clean scent of the sheets at Armida. Mikhail had come to hate Halyn House over the days, and focused his ill-feeling on it, rather than hating Emelda or Priscilla. He would rather be almost anywhere else. No, that was not true. He wanted to be at Neskaya, with Marguerida, even though he knew that winter had already arrived there. His cousin had complained of it during their most recent late evening communication. When was that? He couldn't remember when he had last spoken to her.

The thought of Neskaya seemed to enlarge in his mind, filling him with longing. Mikhail wanted to abandon the house, the Elhalyn children, everything. He wished he were an ordinary man, or that Marguerida were an ordinary woman, and that their destinies were of no importance to Darkover. Of course, if that were the case, he would not be huddling under the blankets in a house that remained drafty even after all the repairs he had had done. No ordinary man would have been saddled with this unmanageable task.

Mikhail Hastur sighed softly, snuggled down against the pillow, and let his eyelids close. He wanted so much to talk to Marguerida, but he didn't have the energy to concentrate, to take out his matrix stone and send his thoughts to her. All he wanted was sleep. If only he could remember. . . .

In a few moments, he was sound asleep, dreaming of Marguerida Alton. They were walking through a summery field, their hands linked. He could smell the flowers and the dry earth beneath their feet. She turned her face toward him, lifting her lips for a kiss. Mikhail brought his mouth down to hers and . . .

A scream yanked him from sleep like a faceful of ice water. It was a terrible sound, a wail of terror bubbling from a throat. Mikhail got gooseflesh just listening, even though he knew it was one of the children having a nightmare.

Still muzzy with sleep, he shoved his feet into fur-lined slippers and put on a thick robe. Mikhail pushed his fingers through his hair, yanking a tangle so hard it hurt. He glimpsed himself in the shadowed glass and grimaced. For a moment he stared at his reflexion. He was haggard and gaunt with weight loss. There were dark circles under his eyes, and he looked haunted. When had he lost so much weight?

Mathias was sitting up outside the door, rubbing his eyes. With a quick glance, Mikhail realized that his man did not appear a great deal better than himself. The older Guardsman had lost weight also, and the hair on his head looked brittle and dry in the light of the lampions. Why hadn't he noticed that earlier?

He stifled another sigh and trudged down the long corridor toward the sound of the screaming. Either Emun or Alain was having a bad dream. He was not sure which. Vincent never seemed to have nightmares. Mikhail stopped abruptly at this idea. It was important, but the thought wriggled out of his focus and faded before he could examine it.

He could hear the sound of one of the old nurses coming from her bed, complaining as usual. They had not done that when he first came, but had just let the children scream and cry. Only at Mikhail's insistence had they grudgingly begun to come during these all too frequent scenes. When he had asked them why they did not attend to the youngsters, Becca had peered at him with eyes that were clouded with the start of cataracts and announced, "They have to grow out of it—pampering won't help!"

At the time he had thought that an odd answer, and since the two ancient women had been Priscilla's nurses years before, he had wondered if they had ignored her in the same manner when she was a girl. That would certainly explain Priscilla's peculiarities. Having had the attention of loving and concerned servants all his own childhood, Mikhail was hard pressed to imagine the neglect he suspected.

He heard muttering, and knew it must be Becca. Wena was almost always silent, while Becca never seemed to stop talking. Both were really past their work, and should have been given retirement long since. With the refusal of the villagers to stay at Halyn House, though, he was glad of their presence, as little help as they actually were.

They claimed to have been nurses to Alanna Elhalyn, who had been dead for over half a century. Mikhail guessed they were almost eighty, though neither of them would admit it. And they possessed all the irritating habits of old retainers—treating everyone as if they were quite young and a little slow, insisting that they knew best, and refusing to change their ways.

His admiration for his mother, Javanne Hastur, increased as he had tried to cope with this unlikely bunch of youngsters. He had taken a spare moment to write her to that effect, and shipped the letter off with a messenger, but he had received no reply. She was either still sulking up at Armida, feeling betrayed by both her brother Regis and by Mikhail himself, or already in Thendara, fomenting intrigue. Sternly, he set his thoughts aside and followed the howling sound which he recognized all too well now.

Emun was sitting in the middle of his bed, clutching the bed-clothes, his head thrown back, a thin, terrible noise emanating from his slender neck. He was a skinny boy, all knees and elbows and eyes too large in a narrow face. The pale reddish hair, tangled and matted now, from thrashing in the bed, looked dirty, and he had bitten his lower lip until it bled. There were deep circles under his blue eyes, and Mikhail knew he had torn the palms of his hands with his short fingernails.

Emun was showing signs of threshold sickness, but he had not yet begun to manifest the actual disease. This had puzzled Mikhail more than a little, when he had the energy to think. The onset of *laran* was usually accompanied by this illness, sometimes violently and sometimes otherwise. In Mikhail's case, it had been a fairly mild event, but he remembered how sick Marguerida had been the previous summer at Ardais Castle, and, despite what he had learned at Arilinn, he remained doubtful of his ability to deal with it.

Tonight, his mind almost clear for a change, he found himself wondering why it had not either arrived in full force, or remained in abeyance. Mikhail had been told at Arilinn, and knew from his own experience, that when it began, it came all at once. Emun's apparent false starts were puzzling, and while he was grateful that he was not having to deal with the full-blown problem, he was worried that when it arrived, he would not really be capable of handling it.

It was, he felt, as if something was preventing Emun from coming into whatever *laran* he would possess as an adult, if these nightmares did not kill him first. That was impossible, of course, unless either Priscilla or Emelda were interfering with the lad's channels in some manner. To Mikhail, such an action was unthinkable, but he knew that Ashara Alton had overshadowed not only Marguerida, but numerous other women during the centuries since her death. So, while he might find the idea horrifying, clearly there were people who were not governed by his own ethics.

Liriel would know the answer to many of his questions. *Liriel!* That was what he had been trying to remember when he went to bed! As a matrix technician, she was superb, though her innate modesty prevented her from realizing her potential. And she could test the girls, he realized, which was something it would be quite inappropriate for him to do. They were young enough to be his daughters, and that put them out of bounds for him. Now, if he could just keep a thought in his head long enough to do something!

As soon as Mikhail formed this idea, he felt the familiar sense of mental exhaustion, passivity, and despair. He struggled with it, the subtle feeling of loss, unworthiness and fear that gnawed at him during every waking hour. He had no time for his own concerns now.

Mikhail sat down on the edge of Emun's bed and took one small shaking hand in his own. The other boys were asleep in the big bed, or pretending to be. Emun's night terrors were so frequent an occurrence that his screams rarely roused them.

He studied the child. The pupils of the boy's eyes were pinpricks in the flickering light of a bedside candle, and he stared at Mikhail without recognition. Tears streaked his cheeks, and he was clammy with sweat. Becca, grumbling audibly, shuffled into the room. She grunted and put a small log on the little fire that was banked in the hearth. Then she set a pot on it, and began to heat some water for tea.

"Emun, what is it?"

The boy did not answer immediately. He looked at the corners of the room, into the deep shadows, and seemed to be expecting something to jump out at him. His hand clamped on Mikhail's, as if holding on for his life. Finally, Emun's eyes dilated toward normalcy, and his thin shoulders relaxed. "I don't know. Something bad was in here."

Mikhail waited. All the younger children were convinced the house had ghosts. He had learned a little of the history of Halyn House since his arrival, that it had been built for the mother of some Elhalyn who could not abide her daughter-in-law, four generations before. One of the workmen from the village had said that the long dead woman still walked, and swore he had seen her. By all accounts, Maeve Elhalyn had been a determined woman, one who brooked very little opposition, the terror of her children and grandchildren. It might be her ghost, he thought, or that of the handmaid she had purportedly murdered in a fit of fury. The place was so isolated that Maeve could have slain a bevy of servants without anyone's being the wiser.

Sometimes he had the feeling that the place really was haunted, as Armida was, though all the Alton spooks seemed to be benign. He had seen things drifting through the corridors a couple of times that made the flesh on his arms go bumpy, and heard some moans that were not the product of childish mischief. He was not overly imaginative, so he tried to find logical explanations, such as the house settling, or the wind coming in oddly. But he could not deny that the Halyn House was an eerie place, with the smell of sulfur from the springs coming when the wind blew from the north, and all the shadows.

"Was it a dream or something else?" Mikhail asked the question very quietly. He reached behind Emun and plumped the pillows, then leaned the boy back against them. Becca came over with a cracked mug full of sweet smelling tea, and set it on the table by the bed. The old woman tugged the covers straight, giving Mikhail a glance that suggested he was not competent for such, then tucked them around Emun's shallow chest, clucking under her breath. The stink of tooth-rot wafted from her mouth, and Mikhail tried to ignore it.

"There was something in the room—a spook—and it was trying to get me," Emun replied. He took the mug off the nightstand and drank a large mouthful, then coughed as it went down the wrong way.

Mikhail patted the lad on his thin shoulders. When Emun managed to catch his breath, he asked, "Why would a spook try to get you, Emun?"

"It was angry," the boy answered, as if this explained everything.

"I see. Angry at you, or just angry."

Emun considered the question and settled more comfortably into the pillows. He seemed to be relaxing, and Mikhail was grateful. There had been several nights recently when nothing had calmed him except powerful herbs, which left him dull and stupid the next day. "It felt like it was trying to eat me up,' he finally said.

"Eat you?" This was new, and Mikhail was alarmed.

"Like a banshee."

"Emun, banshees don't come this far from the mountains."

"I know that, Mik!" He went from being a terrified boy to being a normal adolescent in a flash, and tried to grin feebly. "I said 'like' a banshee!"

"Yes, you did. But since you have never seen a banshee, I don't know how you can make a comparison."

"Well, I can. Vincent told me all about them."

"And how many banshees has Vincent met?"

Emun laughed at this. "None, of course. I don't know anyone who has ever seen one, unless you have."

"No, I have not, for which I am sincerely glad. My father saw one, when he was high up in the Hellers years ago, and from his description, it is a thing I am happy to have forgone."

Emun smiled wanly at Mikhail's words. "Maybe it was the ghost of a banshee." He looked now like a very ordinary lad, not the completely terrified boy he had been a few minutes before.

Mikhail reflected for a moment on the strangeness of this conversation, but all he was really concerned about was calming Emun and getting back to sleep. No, there was something he had to do first. Why couldn't he remember what it was? "That is a pretty scary idea—and I don't think you came up with it yourself. Did Vincent tell you that banshees had ghosts?"

"Yes," Emun admitted reluctantly. "He said nothing could stop the ghost of one."

"I have never heard of anything like that! And I believe I would have. Now put the dream out of your mind, young man. Just finish your tea, and go back to sleep."

"I muh tend to these cuts, first, *Dom* Mikhail," Becca interjected. "They be bad, and I dun' want young Emun to take a inflammation. Yur the apple of my eye, Emun, and dun't you furget it." She pinched his thin cheek in her bony fingers, and Emun looked as if he would have liked to have throttled her for treating him like a baby.

"Yes, of course," Mikhail answered, looking away to spare Emun the embarrassment of having a witness. He could sense that the lad was feeling stronger from his anger at the old nurse, and that this was restoring what little vigor the boy possessed. It was as much as he could hope for. "I will leave you to it."

Mikhail left the boy's room quickly, glad that this nightmare had not given the boy fits. He was going to have to do something about Vincent Elhalyn, but he was not sure what. The logical thing would be to send him to Arilinn, if it was not too late for that already. He frowned at the idea of bullying Vincent encountering *Mestra* Camilla MacRoss. But Priscilla, while she had urged him to take Vincent and go, was absolutely adamant that he should not enter a Tower for training. It was almost as if she were afraid that something would be discovered about the lad, or that something would happen to him. And, as with her other strictures, she offered no reasonable explanation. Indeed, he should have gone there, or to another Tower, as soon as he showed his *laran*.

Val had warned him just a few hours before that Vincent would find a way to get revenge for being sent from the dining room, and he had not taken her seriously. He was a fool, and a failure. He couldn't even manage to discipline an adolescent! What good was he? How could he have ever imagined he was fit to rule!

As he trudged wearily back toward his room, Mikhail decided he simply must get some help, and right away. It gave him a hollow feeling of failure, that he could not manage the simple task of testing the Elhalyn children and discovering which of them would make a suitable king without the aid of others. Then he remembered something Lew Alton had told him, one day while they walked together in the day garden at Arilinn. The two of them had spent a lot of time together there, and they had become close in a way Mikhail had never been intimate with his own father. How annoyed *Dom* Gabriel Alton would have been if he had known, and how betrayed he would have felt.

"It is a wise man who knows his own limitations," Lew had said. Then he had added with a certain dryness, "It has taken me several decades to understand that."

That memory reassured him, and the sense of failure faded. He wished he could talk to Lew again, because he was sure the older man would offer him wise counsel. Where was he? In Thendara, likely, or at Arilinn visiting Diotima. Mikhail paused, hesitant as he was so frequently these days. He couldn't bring himself to run to Lew Alton or anyone else with his problems. There had to be another way.

The back of his neck itched then, and he reached up to scratch it. After a second, Mikhail realized it was not physical itch, but a mental one. Liriel! The image of his sister danced in and out of his consciousness, like a shimmering veil. It was as if just the thought of her caused his mind to scatter like leaves in the wind.

Grimly, he concentrated, making the picture of his sister stronger in his mind. He thought of her full-fleshed body, soft and yet quite strong. Mikhail remembered the way her garments always smelled of mountain balsam mixed with one of her incenses—a sharp, refreshing scent. He felt his hands curl into fists as he passed Mathias sitting in the hall. The Guardsman gave him a look, lifted an eyebrow in curiosity.

"How's the lad?"

"As well as he can be with being frightened all the time."

"I am glad. He is a good boy, you know, when he isn't shivering in his bedclothes."

"Yes, I do know, and it goes to my heart that he is so plagued. I tell you, Mathias, this place is . . ."

"Cursed, my lord?"

"I was going to say unhealthy, but cursed will serve."

"Are we going to remain here?"

"I don't really know." Again, he felt possessed by indecision.

"We will be snowbound in a couple of weeks, you know." Mathias spoke the words with his usual ponderousness, as if trying to convey some vital information without quite saying it.

"Yes, I know." *And I don't know if I can survive an entire winter in this house.*

Mikhail opened the door to his room, and went inside. He stood before the fading fire for a time, his hands clasped behind his back in an unconscious imitation of Regis. Now he felt less unsure of himself, and his sense of resolution increased as he waited. He would contact Liriel, who had much more experience in these matters, and ask her advice. Mikhail found his mouth drawing into a slow smile. He had never asked Liriel for anything before, but somehow he knew she would be very pleased.

He added a few pieces of wood to the fire, sat down, and drew his matrix stone from beneath his nightrobe. His fingers fumbled at the drawstrings of the silken pouch, and he nearly dropped it. He sensed a mental pressure, just a hint of something, so vague and subtle he could hardly believe it was real. Mikhail ignored it, focusing all his thoughts and energy on just getting the jewel into his palms.

As Mikhail stared into the faceted depths of his matrix, he found himself thinking not of his sister, but of Marguerida. He glanced at his rumpled bed and frowned. The covers should be tossed with love. He wondered if it was ever going to be possible to marry the woman he loved so deeply, longed for with every breath.

It was a delightful distraction, to think of Marguerida, but he suspected that he would regret it later. The important thing now was to reach Liriel. Slowly, with enormous concentration, he forced his mind to empty of any thought except the need to contact his sister.

Liriel!

What! It is the middle of the night! You seem to be calling from the wrong end of a well, bredu.

He found his mouth trying to widen into a grin. The tense muscles of his face felt taut and unwilling to move in this now foreign manner. Liriel was a deep sleeper and a slow awakener. He could sense her grumpiness, and discovered that it had a quality of refreshment, for it was a simple emotion, without any secret meanings. *Forgive me, Liri.*

What do you want?

He hesitated, unsure again. *Help. Advice.*

From me? You never asked my advice except on the best diet for ferrets in my whole life. Mik, are you well?

Not really. There is something going on here that is beyond my abilities, and I truly need you. Can you come to Halyn House?

Come to . . . are you gaddy? No. I suppose not. You have never asked for my help before, so it must be very serious. Why me?

That cuts to the heart of it, Liri.

Is it something to do with the children? Marguerida told me you call them the Elhellions. Are they obnoxious?

I wish they were. I could bear some healthy brattiness, but this . . . they are being frightened to death, Liri. Something terrible is going on in this house, and I . . .

What do you mean?

Mikhail considered his next thought, and felt a mild confusion that lasted only a moment, but left him chilled and anxious. *It is difficult to put into words.*

Mik, what just happened? You . . . faded for a second.

That is part of the problem. Priscilla has this woman here, Emelda, who dresses like a leronis *and . . .*

She does what?

Liri, if you keep on interrupting me, I will never be able to tell you anything!

Sorry, Mik. You know how I am when I am awakened suddenly.

Yes, I know. Anyhow, this woman seems to have some influence over Priscilla and the children, and I have no idea what to do about it. She has laran, *but more than that I cannot tell you. She says she is an Aldaran, but I rather doubt that.* He hesitated again. *I think she has been muddling my mind.*

Do you mean that you have been living in a house with another telepath, and you never thought to mention it to anyone? She sounded very put out.

I do. Every time I start to think about . . . I get so . . . Liri, help me!

By Zandru's hells! You sound enthralled!

I think you might be right. Will you come?

Just me? Shouldn't I bring . . . no, I see now. I understand, I believe.

Liri, bring a goodly carriage, and . . . damn, I am fading again.

I will come, bredillu! *I will set out as soon as I can!*

The contact vanished, and Mikhail sat there, savoring the term *"bredillu,"* "little brother." He was older than his sister by more than a year, but he really did feel like a younger man at that moment. The affection in the word touched him, warmed him, and reassured him. It would be good to have her there, to be able to speak to her, and get her wisdom. Odd. He had never thought of his sister as wise, but she was. And it was time he began to respect it!

10

Liriel arrived at Halyn House six days later, at the tag end of a small snowstorm. Even before she entered the house, Mikhail knew she was in a foul temper. This was unusual, because Liriel was remarkably steady in her moods, calm and cheerful, for the most part. He had almost forgotten how much she loathed journeys.

Mikhail could not really blame her, for traveling, even from Arilinn, across the relatively flat plain of Arilinn and down the River Valeron, was not pleasant at this time of year. Ever since he had sent for her, he had been plagued with second thoughts, rocked with doubts, and wished he had not done it. He had just gritted his teeth and hoped he had not brought her on a fool's errand.

"I have traveled more this year than I have in my entire life," the large woman informed him, as she descended from the covered carriage she had come in, "and I like it less with each journey. I swear that if there was a rock to be found, my driver managed to find it."

She was muffled in a cloak of heavy green wool, and she had a shawl draped over it, so she appeared almost shapeless in the dim light of late afternoon. Her usually pale cheeks were quite rosy from the cold. Mikhail found he was very glad to see her. He had not realized until this moment how much he missed his family, even his mother and father.

The driver overheard her, and flashed Mikhail a broad grin. The carriage she had traveled in was large and well-sprung, the windows glazed and curtained to keep out the cold. Behind it rode four men, two in Guardsmen's uniforms and the others in ordinary clothing. Where was he going to put everyone? Halyn House was not large, and the servants' quarters remained in a sorry state of disrepair. Still, he was sure that Daryll and Mathias would help him sort things out, and it was not important. What was important was that his sister had arrived, and he now had someone to confide in.

"I am glad to see you, too, Liri! Come in and have a hot bath. That will take the ache from your bones and restore your usual good humor." He offered her an arm to get up the slippery stairs into the house, and she took it, clamping a strong hand around his forearm in a grip which surprised him.

She leaned against him a little, then sniffed the air. "I had not quite realized how close to the Sea of Dalereuth this place stood. Funny sort of smell. Cousin Marguerida says that travel is broadening, but the last thing I need is broadening," Liriel continued as they entered the foyer of Halyn House. She gestured at her body with a wry smile. "The smell of the sea disturbs me, Mik, and I don't know why. I am sure Marguerida would like it, though. She often longs for her Thetis, and sighs for warm winds and soft seas, you know."

"Yes, I have heard her muse on it a few times. And she sings those songs. . . . Some of those she recorded for Diotima's stasis are really wonderful. Do you think Dio can hear her voice?" He ignored the tightness in his chest that the mere mention of Marguerida's name brought on, and tried to appear uninterested. More, he tried to put from his mind how difficult it had become to communicate with his beloved the past few weeks. It was maddening and frustrating for him to be too tired to reach her most nights, and when he did, he found her remote and preoccupied with some matter that she would not discuss. She spoke of Istvana Ridenow's rather unorthodox methods of training, and about her new friend, Caitlin Leynier and the others at Neskaya, but underneath he knew that something was worrying her. He had begun to ask her a few times, but his attention had wandered, or one of the children had awakened. It was as if some force were determined not to let him have any peace and quiet.

"Hear the songs? What an interesting idea." Liriel gave her brother a warm look. "But I am sure you and Marguerida have much to discuss, other than her singing." There was no innuendo in her words, just a sisterly affection that made his heart swell.

Mikhail let his shoulders drop a little. There was no fooling his sister. She knew how he felt about Marguerida, and how Marguerida felt about him, better than anyone except Lew Alton. But she was discreet, and he knew she would not tease him more than a bit. "There is always the weather."

Liriel chuckled as she unwound the shawl and draped it from a hook, then removed her cloak as well. "If the two of you spend a moment discussing the weather, then I am a *cristoforo.*" She glanced up at the darkened rafters, then at the walls, hung with motheaten tapestries, and shook her head. "This is not a comfortable house, is it?" Behind her, one of the men was bringing in the luggage.

Mikhail shook his head. "You should have seen it before I got the workers in to mend the window frames and clear the chimneys. Priscilla and her children seem accustomed to the climate, but they were camping out in five rooms when I arrived."

"But why?"

"Damned if I know. Priscilla will not tell me why she insists on living in this moldering barrack. Maybe you can make more sense of her pronouncements than I have been able to." He hesitated. If he told Liriel about the seance, he would break his oath, even if it had been given to a ghost. With all the doubts he had, he could not quite bring himself to do it. But he had not promised not to speak of what little he had learned from the villagers.

Mikhail cleared his throat. "I believe it has something to do with a local superstition, Liriel. There is a hot spring about a mile up the road, which the village folk claim has healing powers, and a guardian spirit. Priscilla seems to have some obsession about this Guardian— don't ask me what it is, though. I haven't been able to find out more than I just told you. I wanted to go and take a look at it, but, frankly, just keeping up with the children has left me little time for anything else. I don't know how women manage so well. My respect for our parents and their skills at householding have increased enormously."

"Yes, I know. Mother showed me your letter when she came from Armida last month. It was kindly written, but I do not think she appreciated it much. She wants your loyalty, not your admiration, I'm afraid—but you know Mother!"

Mikhail shook his head. "I cannot serve two masters, and having to choose between Regis and Mother was very difficult. But I am sworn to Regis, to Hastur, and that takes precedence over any other consideration."

"I know, brother, but she cannot see that. It is one of the differ-
ences, I believe, between males and females, that an oath can be more
important even than blood." She sighed deeply, then smiled slightly.
"Fortunately, she is deep into brooding over Ariel's pregnancy just
now, and has let everything else go for the present. Once the child is
born, you can expect her to start her intrigues once again. She is
determined to put forth Rafael as Elhalyn Regent when she goes to
Thendara. She is in residence at Arilinn now, since the weather will
make travel more difficult as the season progresses. She was quite
curious about my departure, since I can control Ariel better than
anyone, and when I said I was only going to Thendara, I do not think
she believed me. It is a terrible thing to lie to one's own mother." She
did not sound as if she thought it was really a terrible thing, and
Mikhail grinned. Liriel had always been subtly mischievous, and he
had forgotten what a delightful quality it was.

"Thank you! Though Rafael would be welcome to the Regency,
and never thank me for it, if he got it. I don't think Mother realizes
how determined Uncle Regis is to do things his own way. No matter.
How is Ariel?" Mikhail found he was not surprised that Javanne was
intent on getting him out of the Elhalyn Regency, and while it saddened him a little, he realized that she would not see what she was
doing as an act of disloyalty or betrayal. Javanne expected her children
to be loyal to her, but did not seem to know that it went both ways.

"She seems quieter than she was right after Domenic died. But she
is still very fragile and delicate. I tried to persuade Mother not to
bring her to Thendara for Midwinter, but she is convinced that she
must be in the city, and that Ariel needs her clucking and attention.
Still, the coming of a daughter, so longed for for all these years, has
done a great deal to help her cope with the loss, and she keeps herself
busy sewing gowns and blankets. You would be astonished at her industry. Not to mention the amount of embroidery she plans to burden
the child with."

"Ariel always did like to decorate any plain surface. Do you remember when she painted the walls of your room with vines and
flowers?"

Liriel chuckled. "I remember that Father had a fit over it, though it
was quite pretty."

Priscilla Elhalyn came down the corridor toward them. In the
shadows beside the staircase, her eyes appeared larger than they really
were, and the faded red hair and prominent Elhalyn nose made a
somewhat grotesque appearance. Her mouth was tight and withhold-
ing, as if it had forgotten how to smile. She wore a shapeless brown

wool robe whose hem was worn, and her head was covered with a rectangular veil secured at the brows with several hairpins. Beneath the veil, the butterfly clasp in her hair had caught the threads in several places, so it was pulled and even torn.

Priscilla paused and looked at Liriel. She did not appear very pleased with the new arrival, but she sniffed and extended one thin hand stiffly. "Welcome to Halyn House. I trust your journey was not too wearisome." Then she noticed the man with the baggage and frowned. At that moment, one of the two Guardsmen who had accompanied Liriel came in, stamping his feet. Priscilla looked at Mikhail, a small frown on her brow.

"Thank you, *Domna* Elhalyn. Other than the wind finding its way through every crack and crevice in the carriage, and howling a great deal, it was not unpleasant."

"I have not traveled father than ten miles from Halyn House in many years, and I do not intend to. I think one should stay nearby one's home. All this gallivanting around from place to place seems a foolish occupation for a sensible woman."

"Of course it is, but sometimes it is necessary. Mikhail cannot properly test your daughters for *laran,* you know, so he asked me to come and do it."

The front door opened before Priscilla could reply, and old Duncan entered, followed by the rest of Liriel's entourage. There was more baggage, and suddenly the entryway seemed quite crowded. The smell of wet wool and snow wafted up as an icy blast from outside chilled the already cold chamber even further.

Duncan sniffed, rubbed his rosy nose, and said, "I dunno know where we're to put all these folk, *domna.* And there ain't fodder for all these horses. Though the stables is ready." He gave Mikhail a grin, as if he were proud that the barn was now clean and in as good repair as could be managed with a shortage of workmen and not a great deal of materials. The roof no longer leaked, the grain room was dry, and the horses lived in rather more comfort than the people in the house.

The Guardsman who had come in first, whom Mikhail now recognized as Tomas MacErald, the youngest son of the current armsmaster in Thendara, nodded at him, then spoke. "We can bed down in the stables, if we must."

"No," Mikhail answered. "I think we can get the back rooms in the servants' quarters into shape—though they will not be a great deal warmer than the stables, truthfully. And do not be surprised if Daryll and Mathias fall upon your neck with glad cries, Tomas. They have been standing watch, and will be delighted to share the task. And if you have some good gossip from Thendara, as well, their cup will be overflowing."

Domna Elhalyn glared at everyone, then turned to Liriel, as if they were quite alone. "I don't know why you should test my daughters," Priscilla said. "It is not as if I will permit them to go off to a Tower and learn things they do not need to know. I never should have allowed Regis Hastur . . ." She stopped speaking abruptly.

Liriel gave her brother a sharp look. *My goodness—she is even more eccentric than you told me.*

I know, and it troubles me. I have tried to tell her several times that wild telepaths are dangerous, but she only says that everything will be taken care of by the Guardian. Who that might be, I can't imagine.

Another figure came into the corridor and approached them. Mikhail had to restrain himself from shivering. He looked at Emelda, and saw the feral expression that seemed a permanent one. Her eyes were greenish in the light of the foyer, but they had a burning intensity that was disturbing. Except for their brief exchange of thoughts on the day of his arrival, he had never been able to sense her mind, not even the slightest thought. She seemed a blank point in the room. She glanced at Liriel, at Mikhail, then back to the tall technician. "This is the Disrupter I warned you of, *vai domna.* We must be careful, or the Guardian will be displeased," she whispered to Priscilla. Then she looked startled at the men who had accompanied Liriel. "These should not be present! They must depart immediately!" Her hiss was like steam on a griddle.

"My sister is weary from her journey," Mikhail announced ignoring Emelda. "I will show her to her chambers. Duncan, will you show Tomas and the others where the old maids' room is, and help get things settled."

Tomas gave a little sigh. "I don't suppose there are any old maids in the room, nor young ones either," he muttered quietly, and his companions guffawed. Priscilla looked bewildered, and the expression on Emelda's face turned murderous.

Mikhail could not bear the tension a moment longer. He wanted to grind his teeth or shout, anything to relieve the rage that was boiling in his belly. He turned, grabbed Liriel's baggage from where it sat on the floor, and started up the stairs. After a moment, he heard his sister's footfalls behind him. *Mik, she is like a witch from some old tale.*

Who—Priscilla or Emelda? They both seem like crones to me, even though they are not much different in age than we are. I should have warned you, but, frankly, everything here is so strange that I didn't know where to begin. Priscilla won't even pick her clothing without consulting Emelda. She seems completely in her power. And the children . . . !

Who is she? There is something about her . . . I can't put my finger on it.

Emelda? Well, she claims kinship with the Aldarans, though she refuses to be specific. She could be some nedestra child, I suppose. But I can't read her at all, which is very disturbing.

Hmm. Aldaran. Now, what does that remind me of? My brains feel like cotton.

She seems to have that effect on me as well.

What? Do you mean . . . ?

I think she is influencing me, but I can't seem to do anything about it.

I see. That makes sense—you do not seem yourself, quite. Does Regis have any idea of the situation?

Frankly, no. I have only managed to communicate with him a couple of times, and he seemed preoccupied. I have not wanted to bother him with my own troubles. He gave me a task, and I intend to complete it! And he has enough on his plate, right now, what with Father being difficult, and the Comyn Council being at sixes and sevens. I . . . wasn't sure but what I was imagining things. It is so strange here, Liri!

Mik, you are an idiot. That woman reeks of laran, if laran had a scent, and she clearly has enthralled Priscilla to a great degree. You should have asked for help much sooner. And you should never have been sent out here on your own. I cannot think what Uncle Regis is doing!

Mikhail hesitated. He would not criticize Regis Hastur, even to his sister, no matter how he felt. Nothing could make him disloyal to his uncle. And, since his mother had behaved so badly to her brother at the Council meeting, he was even more determined to be a faithful vassal. But Regis had put him in an untenable situation—asked to do a job he could not complete to anyone's satisfaction, let alone his own. *It is my understanding that Priscilla was willing to let me become Regent for as long as it took to find which of her sons might be suitable to take the throne, but nothing more.*

And Regis agreed to that? Mik, that doesn't make any sense at all!

I know. It has been driving me crazy, when I can think at all. He backed me into a corner, at the Council meeting, and he would not explain why. I almost feel that he sent me here to get me out of the way, for some reason I do not understand. I have always trusted Regis, more than I trust anyone alive, until this. And I wanted to do a good job here, to prove that I was useful.

Useful? What for? I mean, Mik, you are a fine fellow. You don't need to prove anything!

Thank you, sister. But would you think so if we were not family?

What is this nonsense? You are as capable and intelligent a man as I have ever known.

It must be trying to keep my head above water here. I don't feel very capable, let alone intelligent! And the plain truth is I want to find a suitable Elhalyn to take the throne, so I can be free of the Regency! I don't want to end up having to take the Elhalyn throne and answer to Danilo Hastur for the rest of my life.

I see. I had not thought of it in that light, of course. So, tell me about Priscilla's sons.

There are three—Alain, Vincent, and Emun. I was doubtful of Alain before I came here, because I had met him several years ago, and he seemed a little unsteady to me. I was right. Alain is impossible, ruined, though not, I think, by his laran, *but by some other thing I have not discovered. But I had hopes of Vincent.*

And now you don't. And Emun?

He is a frightened child, and I don't know if that can be remedied. I don't want to tell you too much, because I need to know what you think.

She chuckled at this. *I can see that Marguerida has had a good influence on you.*

What do you mean by that?

Only that in the past you did not care much for objectivity, brother. She sniffed the air as they came to the top of the stairs. *You did not really prepare me for this forsaken place. No wonder the Elhalyn are so peculiar, living here.*

You should have seen it before I had repairs done! It was a fine house, once, you know. I can't think why Priscilla has let it go to rack and ruin, but she is convinced that she is leaving here soon, though where she plans to go remains a mystery. There are a great many plants that grow here that I've never seen anywhere else, and the breeze from the sea of Dalereuth is very invigorating. At least, it was when I arrived here. I had no idea how awful it was in winter.

Mikhail, stop avoiding what is eating at you! You are the most maddening of men sometimes.

Worse than Gabe?

Humph. In my experience, there is no one more maddening than our brother. But you are really trying my patience!

Sorry, Liri. I was not doing it deliberately. This place has demoralized me—more than I realized until this moment. When Regis asked me to be Regent before Midsummer. I wasn't very pleased, but I did not imagine it would be this difficult a job. I had no idea how the children had changed in the four or so years since I last saw them, and I certainly did not expect Vincent to turn out the way he has.

And how is that?

I don't quite know how to describe it, because I've never encountered anything like it before. Priscilla has never said anything about Vincent's father, but I have been going on the assumption that he was the same man as Alain's father. She will not name him under any circumstances, just says that they are her sons.

What! No wonder she will not come to Thendara and has been keeping herself cooped up here for these past twenty years. Why, she could have had a dozen lovers!

There aren't many opportunities for sexual license out here, Liri.

True enough. Has she said why she won't leave?

Something to do with this Guardian she keeps talking about, or, rather, refusing to talk about. I have asked and asked, but I just haven't gotten any good answers.

"Curiouser and curiouser."

This was one of Marguerida's favorite phrases, and the sound of it in Liriel's mind was a little disquieting. He took a deep breath and dropped one of the bags, so he could open the door to Liriel's room. "Exactly. This was the best I could do for you. I am at the other end of the hall, and the children's rooms are between us, so you will likely be awakened by nightmares."

"Now there's a pleasant prospect," she answered dryly. *Tell me what is bothering you about Vincent.*

Mikhail hesitated a moment. He had forgotten Liriel's habit of going directly to the heart of things, her impatience and the clarity of her mind. Too, she seemed different than he remembered her, more confident, even as he was less. *He seems to take delight in projecting his nastiest emotions all over the place, and he particularly bullies his younger brother Emun. I have caught him torturing small animals—he hung a cat from the rafters, and it would have died but that Daryll discovered it first. There is just something about him that is bone mean— something that wasn't present when I saw him before.*

Do you think he is the cause of the nightmares you spoke of?

Yes and no. He is the only child who sleeps soundly, but he is completely untrained, so I don't know how he could manage it. The night I contacted you, Emun had one where he was trying to get away from something banshee-like that he said was trying to eat him. Then he told me that Vincent had told him some tale of banshee ghosts being unstoppable—where do children get these notions? But I cannot be sure if Vin-

cent is merely feeding his brother and sisters' imaginations, or is actively up to some mischief.

I see. You seem to be of two minds about this. I've never known you to be so confused, Mik.

Damn right, Liri. I am at my wits end, or perhaps beyond that! I just don't know what to make of the situation, which is why I asked for your help. "This room faces away from the sea, so you won't have a lot of wind to bother you, and the bedding is clean—I made sure of that."

"That was very kind of you, brother. But after four days of racketing about in that carriage, I should be perfectly content with a straw mattress and a skimpy blanket. I have never been so glad to get out of a conveyance in my life—and the thought of the return journey is very disheartening." *And if I read Priscilla Elhalyn rightly, she will want me to depart on the morrow.* She paused, then turned toward the open door. "And who is this," she asked in a quite different tone of voice.

Bright eyes beneath a tumble of dark curls shone in the flickering light of the torches set along the hall. After a moment, an entire face emerged from its hiding place beside the door, and Valenta stepped out, looking both curious and shy. In the flickering light of the lampions, her high cheekbones and budlike mouth beneath a tiny and very unElhalyn nose, seemed something quite remarkable.

"Hello, Valenta. Sister, may I present Valenta Elhalyn. This is my sister, Liriel Lanart-Hastur."

Liriel bent down, her tall, full body leaning until she was nearly at eye level with the child. She extended her hand slowly, and Valenta reached her own to grasp it. Liriel looked down at the small hand, with its six fingers, and nodded as if something had finally made sense to her.

"You are named for the moon," Valenta said softly, her voice barely above a whisper.

"Yes, I am."

"It is a very pretty name."

"Thank you." *What an attractive girl, Mikhail. And I think I may know who her father was—no Ridenow, for certain. I think she may be half chieri.*

Chieri? No one has seen one in years! I always thought they were gone, or only a legend. But that makes sense, now that you say it. I hadn't even thought of that—my brains must be turning to mush!

What of the other daughter? Is she like in form? Is she as beautiful?

No. She is red-haired—more typical in appearance than Valenta. A very beautiful girl. If I had seen her when I was seventeen, I would have broken my heart over her. She quite casts Valenta into the shade—though

*this does not seem to be a problem between them, for they are quite
devoted to one another.*

"Mother is very upset that you came here," Valenta announced.
"Why is that? Are you going to take us away from her?" *I hope so—
because I hate this place.*

"No one is going to take you away from your mother." Liriel
sounded reassuring, but not as if she was certain she spoke the truth.
"I am sorry she is upset."

Valenta shrugged, with the indifference of the young. "Mother is
almost always upset about something, so I don't mind. But I wish you
would take me away from here. Soon. Before Midwinter comes."

"Why is that?"

Valenta's eyes filled with tears, and she shook her small head until
the curls danced around her brow. She began to tremble all over. "I
must not tell you," she whispered, biting her little lips. Then she
turned and bolted into the hall, and they could hear the patter of her
footsteps, hurrying away.

Liriel and Mikhail stared at a each other. Liriel was more startled
than he was at Valenta behavior. Her eyes goggled slightly and one of
her pale red eyebrows lifted. It was a comical enough expression to
bring a small bubble of merriment into his chest, a feeling of relief and
gladness for the solid presence of his unflappable sister. Liriel asked,
"Is this how she is, or is she being peculiar?"

The question, posed quite seriously, was too much and Mikhail
laughed heartily, while Liriel looked annoyed. "Around here, that was
fairly ordinary. Valenta is a good girl, quite intelligent, and the least
troubled of the bunch. In fact, she and her sister, Miralys, seem to be
very normal young women. If I were permitted to choose a woman
rather than a man for the throne, either of them might be fine. Until
now, I have never completely understood what Marguerida meant
when she rails against our customs.

"Really?" Liriel gave him a penetrating glance, and something like
a grin began to play across her mouth.

"Yes. I started out assuming that she was just being Terran, that
she was thinking of things as they are on other worlds, not that she
was actually being sensible. When she tells me that the best person for
the job should have it, regardless of sex, my brain feels as if it is
starting to fracture. And that is despite all the time I have spent with
Lady Marilla, watching her nurture her pottery industry from one kiln
to a dozen, and knowing full well that this was a rather remarkable
thing. At the same time, I realize, I just thought she was keeping busy,
not that she was doing something . . . real."

"At least you can recognize that, which is more than we can say for Father. He is raging, cursing Lew Alton and Marguerida, as if they were put on Darkover just to irritate him. His latest plan is to go to the Cortes and demand that Gabe be made the heir to the Alton Domain, and that they force Marguerida to marry him. Mother told him not to be a fool, and to let her handle it, which led to an argument you could hear all over Arilinn, even if you had no *laran*. Father has not consulted our brother, or he would know that Gabe has taken the measure of our cousin, and now would not have her if she were the last woman on Darkover. He is properly frightened of her—ever since she used the Voice to send Donal off into the overworld."

"How did he find out about that? I thought we had managed to keep it a secret. I did warn Gabe that Marguerida was no one to make angry, but I don't think I told him about the Voice, or the rest of our strange adventure." Mikhail paused, remembering the night at Armida when Donal had tried to scare Margaret Alton by dressing up in a sheet and making spooky noises. He had awakened her suddenly, even though the little boy knew better, and she had spoken without either thought or any awareness that her voice alone might have powers. The command voice was, like many other aspects of *laran*, impossible to predict. But Marguerida had it in full.

"Gabe is not stupid, even if he is not as clever as you are, and it finally penetrated his thick skull that Marguerida will never be the sort of woman he can manage to his own satisfaction."

"I can't imagine anyone managing her, not even me. No matter how hard she tries, she is always going to be very headstrong and independent."

"Of course you cannot!" Liriel gave a little snort of amusement. "She did not grow up here, and expecting her to behave according to our ways is ridiculous. At least you understand it. If only Father could be as realistic. I cannot imagine he will come to his senses. He resents Lew so much that he can hardly eat. And he wants to keep Armida, at whatever cost. It has become an obsession with him."

"If only he were not so stubborn!"

"If only the wind were not so chill. Now get out of here. I want to bathe and put on some fresh clothing. This robe is so foul it is ready to take on a life of its own. And with what little I have seen so far of Halyn House, it might just do that."

"Of course. The bathroom is two doors down the corridor on the left, and you will find it perhaps the most luxurious place in the entire house. But the towels are a little worn and thin. I sent for more from Thendara, but they have not yet arrived."

Liriel chuckled. "I'll wager you never gave a thought to towels in your life before you came here." Then her face became serious again. "There is something familiar about that Emelda creature—I just can't quite bring it to mind. I am sure I have seen her before." She sounded troubled as she spoke.

"Have you now? Interesting. I have not managed to find out anything about her, except she has been here with Priscilla and the children for about a year, and has a lot of influence that I mistrust. And I won't bet with you," he added. "I hate to lose."

He turned then and left the room. In the hall he discovered Miralys, looking curious, and Valenta as well. "What are you girls doing out here?"

"Waiting for you," Valenta informed him. "Tell us all about your sister!"

"Yes, do! Val says she is as tall as you, and very large." Miralys was a contrast to her younger sister, not only in her fairer coloring, but in her mannerisms. Where Valenta was pert and almost forward, Mira was serene and more retiring. She moved with complete if unconscious grace, and possessed a remarkable assurance. Mikhail had seen her stand up to Vincent, and she had even bloodied his nose on one occasion. This was remarkable, for Vincent was tall and strong, and Miralys at fourteen was not more than five foot three, and looked as fragile as a lily. But she was fast, and her hands were remarkably strong for her size.

"My sister Liriel is, indeed, large of body, but she cannot help that. She was always so, even when she was a child. She is younger than I am, by a year, and she has a twin, my sister Ariel. So, you see, my family is very like yours—I have two brothers and two sisters."

"Yes, yes. But what is she? She is not a *leronis,* is she?"

"No, she is not. Liriel is a technician. For the most part she lives at Tramontana Tower, but recently she has been at Arilinn instead, helping our cousin Marguerida Alton begin her studies, and also caring for our sister, who is not so strong."

"Why is she here?" Miralys demanded. "Mother says she has come to take us away from Halyn House, but Val says that isn't so!" *If someone doesn't get me out of here soon, Vincent will hurt me!*

Mikhail rocked at the thought that came from Miralys, for he sensed that the girl meant something which had not occurred to him until that moment. There was a sense of peril in her mind, as if she feared she would be ravished against her will. He was so stunned it was several moments before he answered. "She has come to test the two of you for *laran,* certainly."

"Oh. And if we have a lot of it, can we go away and become *leroni?*"

"Would you like that? It isn't easy, you know. You have to study a great many things.

"I would rather be on a moon than stay here another winter," Miralys interrupted him. She was quite calm as she spoke, but her mind was aflutter with unease, and there was definitely a sexual component to it, one he had missed due to his own scrupulousness. Mikhail had been very careful with the girls, aware that his presence in the house had a quality of impropriety that could be misinterpreted by gossips.

Mikhail cursed himself for a fool. He should have guessed that as isolated as the Elhalyn children were, Vincent would present a potential threat to any likely female, including his own sisters. Alain was not a problem, his complete inability to make any decision preventing him from doing harm to another, and Emun was still too young. But Vincent, the bully, was another matter altogether. He realized it was his own upbringing which had prevented him from even imagining such a thing, for as much as he loved his sisters, it had never, as far as he could recall, crossed his mind to find them in the least desirable. When Mikhail had been an adolescent, he thought them both a terrible nuisance, and it was not until the past few years that he had come to realize that Liriel was a fascinating person in her own right. But he still tended to dismiss them from his mind, which made his asking Liri for help all the more amazing.

Incest was not unknown in the long history of the Domains, and for that reason there were very strong strictures concerning the relations between the sexes. Mikhail had been trained not to think of his sisters as women, and, he discovered to his dismay, he still regarded them as little girls, as children, even Liriel, who was as adult as he was himself. He likewise did not look upon women of his mother's generation as desirable, because that was also considered inappropriate. Those partners he had chosen, and they were few, were always girls near his own age, but not closer to him in blood than cousin, and usually not even that.

But here, so far from the centers of Darkovan civilization, there were not a great many women from which to choose. The village which stood between Elhalyn Castle and Halyn House was small, supporting perhaps two hundred folk, most of whom worked the fields in summer, growing the hearty wheat that flourished there. Now the refusal of the local girls to work at Halyn House began to take on a sinister shape that had nothing to do with either Emelda or any ghosts.

It was one thing, he knew, for a member of the Comyn to father a *nedestro* child on a peasant girl with her compliance, and quite another if she was taken against her will. The young women around Armida had been accepting the favors of various Altons for generations—Gabe had at least one son that Mikhail knew of, and Rafael a daughter—but there was a tacit agreement between the two groups that such activity was conducted with respect for the woman involved. The children of such unions were provided for, and in some cases, even reared by the Domain family. *Dom* Gabriel had never, as far as he knew, strayed from his marriage to Javanne, and Mikhail was reasonably certain he did not have any unknown siblings. *Dom* Gabriel was unusual in his restraint.

Did Priscilla guess that Vincent was a threat to his sisters, and was that why she kept telling Mikhail to take him away? And if this was the case, why hadn't the foolish female sent Vincent to Thendara or Arilinn long since. Then he remembered the seance, and the tone of *Domna* Elhalyn's voice when she spoke to her brother's ghost. What if . . . It made him uncomfortable. He wrenched his mind away from these speculations, feeling uneasy and almost dirty. No, he must be wrong! Priscilla would never do something so unseemly.

He faced the two young women. Both of them had asked for his protection during the weeks he had been there, but he had failed to understand the source of their fear. Mikhail wanted to kick himself. That he had forgotten the cries for help almost as soon as he heard them did not make him feel any better.

Mikhail had a sick feeling in his belly. As Elhalyn Regent, he was sworn to protect these little girls, and he knew he was not doing a good job of it. He had kept trying to manage things in such a way as not to offend Priscilla Elhalyn, nor to go against her wishes not to be separated from her children. He was an idiot. He had to take the children away—and soon.

But what would Regis Hastur say? He had not told Mikhail to bring the youngsters to Thendara. On the contrary, he had been fairly insistent that Mikhail should do nothing to disturb Priscilla's arrangements, that he should abide by her wishes, and do nothing more than see that the children were well, and find an appropriate son to sit on the Elhalyn throne. He had, in short, tied Mikhail's hands. He had not mistaken the implication that he should not return to the city until he had tested the boys and found a candidate for the throne, nor the feeling that he had been manipulated by his uncle into a completely untenable position. The entire Regency was a sham, something Regis had cooked up to both distract Javanne and other reactionaries from his plan to rejoin the Aldaran Domain with others.

Mikhail was not given to displays of temper very often. But at that moment he wanted very much to explode, to release his feeling of ill-usage and vent a rage he had been ignoring for weeks. Only the watchful presence of the two girls prevented him from kicking the nearest wall, or picking up the chair that his Guardsmen sat in during the night and smashing it into kindling. He was forced to be satisfied with a mental *Damn you, Regis,* and let it go.

It was bad enough that some little hedge-witch had been meddling in his mind, but that he had been cleverly manipulated by his uncle as well seemed to be an enormous betrayal. The more so, since he could not really think of a good reason for Regis to have set him a task that was doomed from the onset. What was it going to prove, if he did succeed in finding a son to occupy the throne? That he was good and loyal and would do Regis' bidding? That needed no proof, and if his uncle doubted him, he should have found another way to show it.

How much authority did he *really* have, and why had he not asked that question of his uncle when he had the chance? Or had he, and been subtly put off? Could he go against Priscilla's wishes and remove the children from Halyn House?

The problem, Mikhail decided after a moment, was that he did not think of the position as one of power, just of obligation, a duty he wished to be relieved of as quickly as possible. He had come there because Regis told him to, not because he wished to, or, in truth, even sincerely cared whether another Elhalyn took the ceremonial throne of Darkover. He had never known an Elhalyn king, as Regis and *Dom* Gabriel and the rest of that generation had, and discovered, to his dismay, that he had virtually no emotional investment in the prospect—except to escape taking on the task himself.

He sighed deeply, trapped in troubled thoughts as Liriel emerged from her room and started down the corridor toward the bathroom. The two girls watched her wide-eyed with interest. She was garbed in a voluminous gray bedrobe, and she glanced at them as well, passed by them, and entered the steaming room with the enormous tub.

"She's quite grand, isn't she?" Miralys' comment brought him back to the present.

"Yes, she is. Grand is the perfect word to describe her. That's very clever of you, Mira."

The girl gave him a sparkling look, a flicker of pale lashes, and a smile that would light a room. Mikhail knew that look, for he had seen it many times before, in other girls, though none so young as this one, since he reached adulthood. The lass was halfway to fancying herself in love with him, he thought, his heart sinking. At the same time he was not surprised, for she had no other men to consider, unless one counted his guardsmen. Mathias was too old to be of interest to the girls, but Daryll was a handsome man. He was not a Hastur, however. Even here, he knew that made a difference.

Mikhail dismissed that matter for the moment. "You girls had better go make yourselves neat for supper. You don't want my sister to think you are hoydens, do you?" It was a feeble ploy, but the best he could think of on the spur of the moment.

And clearly Mira saw right through it, because she gave him another glance through lowered lashes. Val, watching this byplay, gave her sister a light punch on the shoulder. "Come on, Mira! I need help with my hair, and you know that Wena is all thumbs."

Mikhail watched them scurry down the corridor toward the room they shared. He felt depressed, but it soon passed away. With Liriel there to help him, he could perhaps accomplish what Regis had sent him to do. It was a faint hope, but more hope than he had experienced for days. Satisfied, he turned and went to put on a fresh tunic for dinner.

Mikhail stood in front of the fireplace in the dining room, warming his hands, his back to the table. It was still a cheerless room, but the one window had been repaired, so there was no longer a draft which chilled the feet when the wind blew from the west, and he himself had rubbed wax into the shabby table that ran down the center of the room. The memory of that task lightened his mood a little. He drew his hands in front of him, and looked at them. Since he had arrived, they had done things he never would have imagined doing and they were scuffed and a little callused. But he liked that, the feeling of being capable of turning his ten fingers to any job, whether it was rubbing wax into a table, or pounding pegs into a window frame. When he thought about all the work he had done, getting Halyn House in some order, he felt quietly pleased. The black mood that came and went from his mind finally left him altogether.

Mikhail leaned an elbow on the mantle, starting to relax, and studied a collection of small ornaments that stood along it. There were chervines carved from stone, and a fine herd of wooden horses, the grain of the wood cleverly used to give the impression of muscles or hide. He noticed there was dust around them and almost pulled out his handkerchief to wipe it away. He chuckled at himself, then shook his head in wonder. He was becoming quite domestic! First apologizing for the worn towels, and now this.

Mikhail turned away from the fireplace and watched old Duncan set out wooden trenchers and implements. He could hear the pleasant murmur of masculine voices from the kitchen, and hoped the presence of visitors might have inspired Ian, the cook, to a greater effort than usual. How clever of Liriel to have brought both manservants and Guardsmen. He felt less vulnerable, and his mind seemed sharper. Now, if he could just get a grip on his emotions. Swinging between despair and hope was exhausting.

He sniffed tentatively, then sighed. From the smells issuing from the nearby kitchens, Ian had made no special efforts on Liriel's behalf. It would probably be their usual fare: the same overcooked fowl and boiled grain, lacking any spices or herbs. Not that Liriel would mind, he knew. She ate with a good appetite, no matter what.

Mikhail would have liked a rabbithorn stew, with some dried fruits in it, or a ragout of chervine the way the cook at Armida made it. Failing that, he would have cheerfully eaten fish, for the river abounded in them, even at this time of year. But Ian had a gift for completely ruining any fish that arrived at Halyn House, as if he hated things which swam. He either fried them so hard they could be used for doorstops, or boiled them so much they lost both flavor and texture.

He thought longingly of the dining room at Armida, or the great one at Ardais, then forced those images away. They reminded him too much of Marguerida, for he could not think of those rooms without remembering the first meals he had eaten in her presence. She had a way of consuming fish that was both elegant and efficient. Well, she had grown up on an aqueous world, so she had probably had a great deal of practice.

There would be, he was certain, boiled leeks, swimming in a shiny bath of broth, and hard rolls that could be used as projectiles, if Halyn House ever came under attack. He wished he knew more about cooking, and laughed at himself. First linens and then cookpots—what a fine figure of a man he was cutting.

Liriel swept into the dining room, with Mira on one arm and Val on the other. She was laughing, and had clearly started to make friends with the girls. A moment later Emun appeared, holding Alain by the sleeve. The youngest boy's hair was damp from a recent washing, and it clung to his narrow forehead, making his thin face seem even more anxious. His large eyes darted toward the shadows in the corners of the room, as if he expected something to jump out at him.

Alain's presence pleased him, for it was a rare occasion that got
the oldest Elhalyn out of his soiled clothing and into a room other
than his bedroom. Behind the boys, Mikhail saw Daryll; he knew that
his young Guardsman had taken to spending much of his free time
with Alain, talking to him quietly or telling him outrageous stories. At
times, these tales had almost seemed to rouse Alan from his stupor.
When it began, Mikhail had thought that Daryll was merely bored,
and looking for some occupation other than sleeping or keeping watch
outside his door, mending broken walls or helping with the roof of the
barn. Now he knew that Daryll had a genuine affection for the poor
lad, and was pleased that he had gotten Alain to come down to supper.

Duncan was setting out platters of rolls when Vincent arrived,
booming in his strong voice and swaggering. He looked very handsome in the light of the candles set along the table and in sconces on
the walls, his blue eyes dancing. Vincent swept the room with an arrogant glance, then walked up to Liriel, every inch the lord of the
manor.

"I bid you welcome to Halyn House, *domna.* I am sorry I was not
here when you arrived—I had some business to attend to." He stood
very close to Liriel, much nearer than was polite.

Mikhail was shocked and more than a little annoyed, but Liriel just
looked at the young man calmly. "Thank you for your welcome," she
answered courteously.

"And how do you find your chamber?"

It was hardly a seemly question, but Liriel only smiled. "It is quite
unexceptional."

"I ask because I am sure you are accustomed to great luxury. We
have none of that at Halyn House, because, my mother says, it weak-
ens the will."

"Luxury? My room at Tramontana is comfortable, but I would
never call it luxurious."

Vincent appeared a little nonplussed at this reply. "I meant at
Armida or . . ."

"I'm afraid I rarely pay attention to such things. My, something
smells good. Traveling has given me an excellent appetite."

A coil of tension Mikhail had not realized he had in his chest
relaxed. He had made a good decision, asking Liriel for help. Her
manners were superb, and almost nothing rattled her. Not even an ill-
mannered boy trying to flirt with her. Odd that he had never noticed
before.

By this time, Emun had gotten Alain seated at one end of the table, and put a napkin on his lap. Mira tugged at Liriel's sleeve, but Vincent took her hand and drew her to a chair, helping her into it, then took the one beside her. It was a highbacked seat, old, in need of reglueing, and it creaked audibly under the weight of the technician. Mira grabbed the place on the other side of Liriel, even though she normally sat as far from Vincent as possible.

Mikhail revised his estimate of Miralys. She was just as fearful of her brother as the rest of her siblings, but she concealed it better. Now she seemed determined to shelter in the shadow of his sister, no matter what. There was a look on her face, determination combined with adoration, that made her beauty even greater. Clearly she had decided that Liriel was a valuable ally.

Mikhail watched Valenta and Emun take places across the table, and waited for the appearance of Priscilla Elhalyn. He always did this, though she rarely came to the evening meal. He hoped Liriel's arrival had sparked a proper regard for polite behavior. When she did show up, he always seated her before taking his place at the table.

As Duncan came out of the kitchen with a platter of sorry-looking boiled fowl, their legs disjointed and sagging, Emelda came in from the living room. She wore a blue dress he had not seen before, and her rather skimpy hair was pulled back and tidy for a change. Her protuberant eyes passed over him uneasily.

"*Domna* Priscilla is much too upset to join us," Emelda announced, "and has sent me in her stead." With that, she marched to the head of the table, to the chair Priscilla would have occupied, and sat down, looking smug. She set her hands beside her empty plate and smiled at everyone.

Mikhail frowned. Emelda's sudden change of garb roused his suspicions. She was up to something, for he had never seen her wear anything except the red of a Keeper since his arrival. There was something in her manner that disturbed him, a tension he had never seen in her previously. Perhaps Liriel's arrival had upset her. If so, he was sincerely glad of it.

Then he wondered if Priscilla was actually upset, or if she had been forced to remain in her noisome chamber. He had suspected for some time that Emelda was drugging her mistress with various evil concoctions that he smelled when he ventured into the rear of the house. Mikhail had not pursued his suspicions—Priscilla was not his charge, only the children were. Or had he refused to inquire further because Emelda was so clearly hostile, and vigilant toward her mistress? It was too late to wonder about the past. What was he going to do about the present?

Suddenly he remembered sitting in the garden at Arilinn with Marguerida, during her first days there. "I do wish there was a text-book—several would be better! Studying matrix science without any references is making me crazy! The records in the scriptorium are not my idea of useful, for where they are not obscure, they resort to vagueness!" Then she had smiled at him, and he had felt his heart leap.

Now, recalling these words, Mikhail found he wished he had a book of some sort which told him what he could do, as Regent, and what he could not. He had never before been in any situation where he did not know exactly where he stood in the scheme of things, and he found he did not like it at all. He had never understood so well as now the frustrations that Marguerida must have experienced, trying to learn the customs of Darkover without the sort of materials she was used to.

And just at that moment, a nice text of the ins and out of *laran* would have been very useful. If he possessed such a thing, he likely could have dealt with Emelda on his own, without running to his sister to bail him out of the situation. As glad as he was of her presence, Mikhail felt that she would not have had to make a long and weari-some journey if he had not failed at his assigned task.

Mikhail noticed again that his mind was less muddled, though his emotions remained conflicted. Why was Emelda present, and why was Priscilla absent? He somehow knew the answer almost as soon as he formed the question. Emelda could only influence people in small numbers, and the arrival of Liriel and four men had likely upset her control. She dared not allow Priscilla to be present, or be out of the room herself. Emelda had to be there, for her own purposes. But did she really imagine she could control Liriel, who was well trained and skillful?

Mikhail smothered an impulse to walk up to the head of the table, grab the tiny woman by the arm, and show her out of the room. It was bad enough that she was sitting in her mistress' place, when she was, technically, no more than a servant. But he found he was curious as to what she was up to. If she was going to try to corrupt Liriel's mind, as she had done his, she was in for a nasty surprise!

He found Emelda watching him closely, her dark eyes narrow with suspicion. Mikhail ignored her and took his seat, as if nothing was the matter. He shrugged, put all his troubles out of his mind, and passed the bowl of leeks, with a few carrots added tonight, in celebration, he assumed, of Liriel's presence.

"I trust you will not remain here long," Emelda announced, looking at Liriel much too directly to be polite, "since your presence is a disturbance, and you are not welcome. In fact, the *domna* wishes that both of you depart tomorrow, or the day after at the latest. All of you!" She glared at Daryll, who was sitting beside Alain, serving him a portion of boiled grain.

"What utter bosh," Vincent answered her, his large voice ringing around the room. "Just yesterday she told me she was looking forward to having someone new to talk to."

"She never said anything of the sort," Emelda answered, drawing her dark brows together.

"Emelda," Mikhail began, "I am Regent for the Elhalyn. For all practical purposes, this is my house, not yours, nor Priscilla's."

"Oh, that!" The soothsayer was almost sneering. "The *domna* has decided that she has changed her mind—there will be no Regency, and . . ."

"The hell you say," roared Vincent, his pale face reddening with rage. "You interfering old biddy—shut your face before I shut it for you!"

Liriel swallowed her mouthful. "I do not think that I can finish testing the girls in so brief a time, and I do not expect to leave in the next few days."

"No testing! I will not permit it," Emelda snarled.

"You do not have any say in the matter," Mikhail said quietly. He could sense a coldness in the room that had nothing to do with the temperature. Emelda was trying to influence him—a cold, creepy feeling in his brain. He felt a shiver and realized that the girls and Emun were silently terrified. Alain appeared unaffected by the tension in the room, chewing his grain with calm and slow deliberation, and staring off at the fireplace, his light eyes vacant.

The silence in the room seemed charged with energy. Mikhail glanced at Daryll, who was keeping an eye on Alain, and thought he was either a fine actor, or he could not comprehend the whole matter. The steadfast presence of the young Guardsman was immensely reassuring.

Liriel swept the board with a calm glance. Mikhail watched her, enjoying the sense of her authority, and also knowing that he had support at last. "Any untrained telepath is a danger, and it seems to me that this resistance to discovering the nature of the gifts of these children is quite foolish. I do not understand *Domna* Priscilla's behavior. I do not believe you have any right to speak for her."

Emelda drew her lips back in a snarl. "When the four moons conjoin at Midwinter, the Guardian will do any testing necessary and . . ." She stopped abruptly, realizing she had said more than she intended. A bead of sweat shone on her forehead, and she was quite pale, her shoulders stiff with barely concealed rage. He watched her bite her lip.

Miralys shivered and moved closer to Liriel. "Don't let the Guardian have me," she whimpered.

Mik, these children are terrified, except Vincent, who cannot feel anything but his egotism. What is this Guardian?

I have told you everything I know, sister.

"There, *chiya*, we won't let anything happen to you," she said aloud.

"It will eat us up," Emun announced suddenly, his thin face twisted with anguish. "No one can protect us."

"You stupid whiner," Vincent sneered at his younger brother. "There is nothing to fear—not from the moons or the Guardian."

Mikhail took a deep breath. "I think that we are getting ahead of ourselves here," he began with more certainty that he felt. "There is nothing harmful that can come from testing. Liriel will examine the girls, and I will do the same for you boys, and we will get things settled." He could sense something from Emelda, an energy he had never experienced before, as if his brain was on fire. Mercifully, it only lasted a moment.

Before he could analyze the sensation, Vincent interrupted his thoughts. "There is no need for testing—I am the only one who can take the throne, and I want it!"

Emelda glared at Vincent, then at Mikhail, half rising in her chair, then settling back. "The Guardian does not want to have any testing. It is very angry already—and it will kill you if you remain here. I insist that you and your sister leave immediately and . . . !"

"That's enough!" Mikhail was surprised by his own vehemence. "You forget your place, Emelda. We are not leaving until I say so."

Liriel, this situation is getting out of hand!

I am quite aware of that, brother. That female is doing her very best to overshadow both of us—I'm surprised she didn't try it sooner.

Maybe she did. I realize that I have had a great deal of trouble making decisions—I wonder if Alain's feebleness does not come from that. Whenever I started to get things moving, I lost my concentration.

What do you mean?

Even ordering workmen here to fix up the house was an enormous effort, as if I were dragging myself through mud. I've been here for months, but it wasn't until last week that I managed to think of asking for help with the girls—logically, I should have done that within a tenday.

Hmm. Yes. I feel it, too. It is as if something were sapping my strength, something very subtle and gossamer, and I think if I had been here alone, I would not have noticed it for quite some time. I think we must find this Guardian, whatever it is. It has the feeling of a trap-matrix, but yet it isn't. I've never encountered anything like it.

Emelda was watching them with large, dark eyes, and her small hands were curved like claws. "You have no idea what you are doing," she jeered. "You are going to die." Then she laughed, as if she enjoyed the prospect. "Your pitiful talents are no match for the Guardian."

"And yours are?" Liriel asked with deceptive calmness.

"I am a servant of the Great One. I can see the future, and I know what will happen."

"Then you are deluded. No one knows the future. The best we can get is glimpses, and those are always a matter of interpretation. Why, you did not even know that I would come here, until Mikhail told you." The contempt in Liriel's voice was acidic, and, to everyone's surprise, Emelda shrank back.

"I know you will die," muttered the little soothsayer.

"You know nothing of the sort. You only wish I would, so that you can continue in your nasty little game." Liriel's face underwent a sudden change, her expression going from bland to alert so quickly that Mikhail tensed in response. "I know who you are, Emelda, and I know what you are!" Liriel's voice was stern and strong, and she seemed to Mikhail like someone he had never known before.

"What?" The little soothsayer looked alarmed, her eyes growing wide. Fresh sweat glistened on her brow, and she drove her nails into her palms while she gnawed at her lower lip, looking like a stoat.

"You are a hedge-witch, and nothing more. *Stop that!*"

Mikhail had the momentary impression that a darkness was beginning to extrude from the top of Emelda's head, a churning of the air he had seen before, but forgotten about almost immediately. When Liriel spoke, the air stilled immediately. He would have thought he imagined it under any other circumstances.

How did you do that!

Ever since that terrible night at Armida, when she used the command voice, I've been practicing with Marguerida whenever I had the opportunity—helping her learn some control of it. No one else at Arilinn was very interested in it, but it seemed to me that focusing entirely on her shadow matrix was a mistake. Much to my surprise, I discovered that I could do the trick from time to time. He could feel her pleasure in accomplishing that, a sense of triumph.

But I thought it could not be learned.

I did, too, when I began. Marguerida is a trained singer, so it is no surprise she can use the Voice almost instinctively. But I now know it can be, to some degree, studied and developed by anyone with laran. *I'll never be very good at it, but I have actually made Mother be still a few times.*

Emelda had shrunk back in her chair, looking startled and angry. The children were watching her, fearful and anxious, but also curious. It was clear from their expressions that they felt no sorrow in seeing the soothsayer humiliated, but instead were quite relieved that someone could stop her.

Then the tiny woman seemed to gather herself, and she leaned forward again. She focused her eyes on Liriel, and Mikhail saw the churning begin again, the smoke from the fire giving it form and substance. It looked thicker than before, and seemed to have more energy. At the end of the table, Alain suddenly pitched forward into his plate, and began to convulse. At the same moment, Emun shuddered, and clapped his hands to his narrow head, howling with pain.

Mikhail acted without thought, grabbing his plate off the table, still burdened with the unappetizing boiled fowl. Mikhail disked the clumsy object out of his hand, the way he had skipped stones across the lake at Armida when he was young, spilling food onto the board. It wobbled, then skimmed over the top of Emelda's head, dripping grease on her hair, and sliding through the disturbance like a wooden blade.

There was a flash, like distant lightning, and the soothsayer collapsed. Her eyes were open, rolling back into her skull, and her mouth lolled, drooling, as the fat from the fowl dribbled down her cheeks. The small body was slack, the hands alone twitching.

"Well done!" caroled Valenta, banging on the table.

Mikhail stood up quickly and went to Alain, drawing him upright in his chair. He cradled the boy's head against his chest and checked his pulse. The seizure was over, and Alain's breathing seemed normal. Even his color was better than usual. Emun had stopped his desperate howling, too, and looked a little embarrassed at his outburst. Only Vincent seemed unmoved, continuing to shovel food into his mouth as if nothing unusual had occurred.

The sounds of the uproar seemed to have penetrated into the kitchen, for a moment later, Mathias, Tomas, and the rest of the men burst into the dining room, their hands on their hilts. They drew to a halt, took in the unconscious woman in Lady Elhalyn's chair, and seemed uncertain what to do. Mikhail was glad to see they were alert and ready to leap to his defense.

Now that things were calmer, he glanced around the room, leaning Alain back in his chair. He saw Liriel holding Mira against her generous bosom, stroking the girl's hair gently and speaking so softly he could not hear her words. Duncan was standing in the doorway from the kitchen, holding a tray of cooked grain in his hands, his eyes shocked. Then his old hands trembled, and the food fell to the floor.

Valenta patted Emun's hand, but her eyes were dancing still, full of delight and glee. Then she said, "You were wonderful, Mikhail! If I had known that a plate of chicken would do that, I would have thrown one at Emelda long ago."

"I am sure you would."

Alain stirred against him, lifting his head and looking disoriented. The oldest boy glanced down at the front of his tunic. "How did I get so messy? Mother will be angry. These are my best clothes. Daryll helped me pick them." He sounded bewildered and unfocused, and had the querulous voice of a much younger boy.

Mikhail patted Alain's shoulder, reflecting that the shabby tunic was ready for the ragbag, and had been even before it had gotten food all over it. He, who had never paid much attention to his own clothing, except to choose the appropriate garment for the occasion, felt an outrage at the young man's attire. Priscilla was unfit to see to these children. This was not a new realization, but one he had had several times previously and forgotten.

How had the soothsayer done it? he wondered. He was a trained telepath, an able one, though not in any way remarkable. Mikhail found himself feeling uneasy now, doubting his own abilities again, because he was certain he should have known what Emelda was doing and stopped it. It had been subtle, but that did not seem to him to be a decent excuse for not realizing the nature of his continued befuddlement. He had had to get his sister to intervene. What kind of man did that make him? He felt outraged at everyone, including himself.

But his mind felt clear, really clear, almost for the first time. Unfortunately, the clarity was mercilessly critical of his slowness to grasp the nature of his mental fog. Marguerida had told him he seemed different, but he had not paid her enough attention, had not listened as he might have. He had been so intent on proving himself capable, that he had not noticed that he was behaving oddly, was missing things, forgetting things. It was as if he had awakened from a terrible dream into a nightmare of failure. The relief he had felt a few minutes before at the clarity of his thoughts now turned to fury at his own stupidity.

Then, realizing the futility of such ruminations, he looked down at Alain again. The young man was staring into space, slack-jawed and vacant. The too brief awareness he had shown was gone, as if it had never existed. His rage at himself shifted and changed to fury at *Domna* Elhalyn. How could Priscilla have permitted . . . ?

Emelda stirred, and Mikhail stopped his musing. He was not sure quite what she was, except that she was some sort of telepath he had never encountered before. What he was certain of was that she was a danger to the children. He had made a terrible muddle of everything so far, but now he could redeem himself a little.

Get her stone—now! Liriel's command was abrupt. He moved without thinking, reaching the far end of the table in a few strides. He extended his hand, swallowing his disgust, and closed it around the thong that lay around the scrawny neck of the soothsayer.

Emelda's eyes snapped open, and she clawed at his hand, tearing his skin with her nails. One hand raked his cheek as he yanked the thong, and tore away the hidden stone. "How dare you!" she shrilled.

It took more effort than he imagined, and he was revolted. All his life he had been trained never to touch the matrix stone of another, or even to consider such an act. It went against everything he believed. But he held the thing, dangling from the broken string of leather, away from him.

Emelda tried to grab it, but Mikhail held the object out of her reach. The bag that held the stone was only a few layers thick, he saw, much thinner than was usual, and the stone was somewhat visible beneath the silk. It was not bright blue, as he had expected, but dull and clouded. He would sooner have touched an adder.

Mikhail saw Liriel's hand close around the thong, well above the dangling stone, and take it from him. Emelda was screaming now, abuse streaming from her lips like poison.

"Give it back, you bastards! You have no right to touch me—I will kill you! I will see you die slowly—filthy bastards." She tried to snatch the object away, but Liriel, so tall compared to the short woman, pulled it out of reach, almost teasingly.

What are we going to do? If we touch the stone, it will kill her, and if we don't . . .

Leave this to me, Liriel answered. Then she turned around and cast the skimpy pouch into the fire. It fell on the flames, and the silk burned away in a moment, while the stone itself nestled unharmed on a blazing log.

Emelda threw herself away from the table, and rushed to the hearth. She tried to reach for the stone, but Mikhail grabbed and held her. She was strong for all that she was so small, and she fought him like an animal, clawing and scratching and screaming. He expected her to collapse as her matrix stone glowed in the fireplace, but she disappointed him by remaining not only conscious, but ready to scratch his eyes out if she could only reach them.

Mikhail held Emelda firmly for a moment, then balled one hand into a fist and struck her pointed chin. It hurt his already bruised knuckles, and he loathed the pleasure he had as his fist made contact.

The soothsayer went slack. He had wanted to do just this for weeks, he realized, feeling ashamed of himself.

"She will be all right," Liriel informed him assuringly, "or as well as she ever was."

"But won't she be injured by the burning of her matrix?"

"The heat of the fire will not actually harm the stone, and she clearly is not going to go into shock from losing it. But the fire will clarify the stone."

"Clarify? What do you mean?" Mikhail had never heard the term, and wondered if his sister had taken leave of her wits.

"Trust me." *That thing is a piece of some old trap-matrix, and how this hedge-witch found it, I don't know. Recently, I've come across knowledge of some things better left alone. There is a cache of records at Arilinn no one has looked at in generations, and rightly so. I found it while I was helping Jeff try to discover what we might do for Diotima Ridenow. After Marguerida left Arilinn, I elected myself as researcher, and I discovered this fascinating old manuscript, so faded and worn it was almost impossible to read. And I learned something about trap-matrices no one has suspected or used for generations.*

You are an amazing woman, sister.

Yes, I am. "Pick her up, will you?"

"I'd rather not." He was stunned by his sister's calmness and assurance. She had changed, become more certain, since he had last seen her. She had never shown the least tendency to boastfulness, and had certainly not regarded herself as remarkable. Was it because of Marguerida, or something else? He wanted to know, needed to know, because it was exactly that sort of certainty he found he now lacked.

Abruptly, Priscilla Elhalyn appeared at the door of the dining room, her face quite pale and her hair disordered. "What is this? What have you done to Emelda?" Her eyes had a strange light in them, part fury and part terror.

"We have stopped her from terrorizing your children," Liriel answered. "What were you thinking of, to allow this creature to—"

"How dare you!" Priscilla drew herself up to her full height, which was still very much shorter than Liriel or Mikhail. An expression of dignity played across her face, one Mikhail had not seen there since his arrival. "You have no right to tell me anything, you stupid cow." Then she stepped over and picked up the shoulders of the soothsayer, kneeling and pulling the woman into her lap. "I want you out of here at first light—both of you. If you do not leave, I will turn the Guardian loose, and—"

"You will do nothing of the sort," Mikhail interrupted. He found himself completely disgusted with this odd woman. More, he was tired of being threatened. He had reached some limit he did not know he possessed. If he did not control himself, he was very likely to do violence, if only to release the sense of outrage he felt for the children.

Ever since he had knelt in the foyer of Armida, above the injured body of Domenic Alar, his feelings toward children had changed. He no longer regarded them as mucky annoyances, but as curious creatures who could be rather interesting. His nephew Donal, for instance, was as bright a lad as could be wished for.

He had never felt emotionally attached to children before, not even Danilo Hastur, who was probably the one he knew best. But since he arrived at Halyn House, and found himself faced with the Elhalyn children, he had grown more attached to them. It had not happened at once, but each day had brought him a sense of purpose, muted by Emelda's interference, but there nonetheless. Now it was present in full force, and he was very angry at the woman crouching on the floor. She was hugging the still form of Emelda against her as she should have held her children, and he wanted to put his hands around her throat and squeeze until the breath left her.

Priscilla glared up at him, almost as if she was aware of his rage. "I want you to get out of my house!" she shrieked.

"Be quiet, woman! You have allowed your children to be manipulated by that miserable creature. How could you?"

"You don't understand! You cannot understand. Emelda told me . . ."

"A great many foolish things, in all likelihood. Why have you let this little hedge-witch nearly destroy your children?"

"No, no—she was strengthening them for their change!"

Mik, it is useless to argue with her. She is not sane any longer—if she ever was. She seems to think that soon the children will be transformed into . . . well, angels is the best I can come up with. Some sort of immortal, as much as I can gather from what she is thinking.

Wonderful. What should I do?

Your responsibility is to these children. Alain is never going to be well again, but we might be able to salvage the rest. We must get them away from this dreadful place now!

What about Priscilla and Emelda? And, for that matter, this Guardian thing they keep talking about?

Burning Emelda's stone has neutralized her for the moment, though I suspect she is so far gone that she will return to her former habits as soon as she can.

Who is she? You seem to know her.

I do, though it took me a while to recognize her. She was a blonde when I knew her, and weighed about twenty pounds more. She came to Tramontana about three and a half years ago, wanting training, and the Keeper tested her. I don't know the details, but she was rejected.

But she is a capable telepath. I find it hard to believe that the leronis *let her leave.*

I am unclear about that part. She just vanished one night. As to what happened, we may never know.

Priscilla staggered to her feet, letting Emelda slip back to the floor. She was breathing shallowly, and her eyes were like great pools of ice. "I will not permit you to continue as Regent for my children! If you try to take them away—I know that you are going to try—I will unleash the Guardian, and nothing can stand up to it! It is more powerful than any mortal, and more loving." She pressed shaking hands to her modest bosom. "Now, children, come to your mother. We are going to go to my rooms until these people leave tomorrow."

Only Alain stirred at all, and he with great reluctance. He shifted in the chair, half rose, then looked confused. The rest of the youngsters hung back, seeking guidance.

"Be still, Alain," Vincent barked. "I feel as if I had just awakened from a terrible dream."

"*Domna* Priscilla," Mikhail began, determined to at least attempt to discover why she had done the things she had, "why did you agree to Regis' proposal to begin with?"

"Why, Emelda told me to. She said it would not make any difference one way or another. She was sure you would take Vincent and be gone within a tenday! If I had not let you come, then Regis Hastur, may his name be cursed, would have tried to force me to his will. She said he would do that, if I did not. She tried to make you go away, but you were stronger than she expected. And the time was growing short."

"Emelda did all this, not the Guardian thing?"

"Certainly not! It does not concern itself with such mundane matters." Priscilla looked offended at the idea. "It is a great being."

Mikhail, she is lost in some terrible delusion. There is nothing you can do to reach her now.

"*Domna,* the children are no longer yours to order," Mikhail said slowly. He knew, in his bones, that it was not going to be as simple as taking the children away from Halyn House. He wished he had the counsel of someone older and more experienced, but there were only himself and Liriel. Her coming had precipitated the crisis, for if he had not brought her, he would almost certainly have succumbed to the slow poisoning of his mind that Emelda had wrought. "I am going to have to take all of the children away, and you as well." He could not help the sorrow in his voice, the sadness he felt for this poor, crazed woman. "You are ill, and we must see that you are taken care of."

For a moment there was silence in the room. Then Priscilla drew herself up to her full height, cloaking herself in a dignity he had never seen her demonstrate before. "Tremble, little man, tremble. You will die, as all who oppose me perish."

Before he could think of any suitable answer, she swept from the room in a flutter of draperies, leaving Emelda on the floor as if the soothsayer were a discarded garment. "What in Zandru's hells do you think she meant?"

"She meant," Vincent answered, "that she is going to call the Guardian." He shuddered a little. "The only thing is, it is rather difficult to rouse, even during the summer when it is most active."

"Vincent, what is this Guardian?"

He shrugged. "I'm not sure. I've only seen it in trances, and the memory is very faint. It has nothing to do with me, only with the others." Vincent cast a contemptuous look at his brothers and sisters.

"What have you seen?" Liriel demanded.

"Something long and skinny that shines."

Miralys was shivering. "It crawls in your brain, doesn't it, Emun? That's what you told me."

"Mother told me never to talk about it," Emun whispered, looking more and more anxious. "I never should have told you that—it will come and get us now." Emun's fear was obvious, even to the bewildered Guardsmen, and Alain was sobbing noisily.

What do you think, Liri? Something like the Sharra Matrix—gods forbid!

No, it doesn't have that feel to it. But the children are not good witnesses. They have been terrified for years with this bogey, and I cannot tell how much of it is this Guardian and how much is Emelda's meddling. But I think that it might be a chieri.

Those are never hostile, are they?

No, as far as I know. Yet both of the girls have a great deal of chieri blood in them, if I am not mistaken. And from the impression I received from Priscilla, she thinks of the Guardian as a loving thing.

If it is loving, why has it been terrorizing the children?

I believe that is more Priscilla or Emelda's influence than anything else. Do the locals fear this Ghost at the Springs?

No, not that I know of. They seem to hold it in awe, but they are unwilling to discuss it very much.

Emelda began to move then, and Liriel bent down and hauled the little soothsayer up by the front of her gown. With a ruthlessness he had never suspected his sister of possessing, Mikhail watched her examine the other woman as if she were an insect. He could sense that she was monitoring Emelda not at all gently.

Liriel released Emelda and turned to Mikhail. "We will remain awake, I think, for the night."

"Yes, I agree. And keep the children here."

Emelda seemed shriveled now, and older than she had appeared a few hours before. Her thin shoulders were stooped, and her black eyes were dull and lusterless. "It will not do you any good," she muttered. "Asleep or awake, you will be dead before sunrise." Then she cast a longing look at the log where her jewel still rested in the fire. The flames were lower, as the log burned away, and the stone shone in the dancing light, clear and seeming quite innocuous.

By midnight the dining room was quiet, the children having settled as well as they could into their chairs, drawing them close to the fireplace. Mikhail had ordered Duncan to bring blankets from the bedrooms, and the youngsters were bundled up in them. All the children looked anxious, except Alain who did not really understand what was happening.

Val stood abruptly, and Mikhail started. But the youngest girl was only putting her blanket on the floor. She gave him a twinkling grin. He knew she was not nearly as cheerful as she looked, only a bit more resilient than the rest.

He picked up another small log and added it to the fire. The sound of embers falling onto the hearth seemed enormous in the stillness of the room. Outside, the wind had lessened to a breeze.

In his mind, Mikhail began to go over the preparations he had to make for leaving Halyn House in the morning. He knew he had to get the children away—and quickly—Guardian or no Guardian. He was glad of the men that Liriel had brought, for he suspected that removing Priscilla Elhalyn was going to be a cat-fight. But his primary concern was the well-being of the youngsters. He had to keep them safe, not for the kingdom, and not to release him from the Regency, but because they were unable to protect themselves.

It gave him a peculiar sensation, to feel this degree of devotion to a bunch of brats he had barely known two months before. They had grown on him, even Alain, who was so pathetic. He had never before experienced the quiet passion he felt for these odd children, and he began to wonder if he would feel that way about his own some day.

Parenting, he decided, was a great deal more complex than he had ever imagined.

They would need blankets, food, cloaks, and such warm clothing as the children possessed. He would take not only the horses which had drawn Liriel's carriage, but another team as well. He tried to remember if there was a harness in the stables for a team of four.

Suddenly, the light of the fire seemed to dim, casting dark shadows in the corners of the room. Alain jerked in his chair. The room seemed colder now, and there was a smell in the room, a faint minty scent that was pleasant.

WHO DISTURBS MY REST? Mikhail felt the question rattle his mind—a booming sort of voice that sounded like thunder.

No one, Liriel replied quickly. She threw Mikhail a brief look.

WHO CALLS ME FROM SLEEP? Mikhail had the sensation of being throughly examined in a moment, then discarded just as rapidly. The children, on the other hand, reacted as if they had been hit by a bolt of lightning.

Val shot up from her cocoon of blankets, and Mira pulled hers over her head, as if she could escape the voice by hiding. Vincent leaped to his feet, roaring and shaking his fist. "Get out of my mind!" he howled.

Then Alain began to convulse again, and Mikhail strode toward him. Emun whimpered a little, then stuffed his knuckles into his mouth and bit down hard.

By the time Mikhail reached Alain, the youngster's back was arched, and he was choking on his own saliva. The slender body was racked with convulsions, great waves of muscular tremors that raced along his arms and legs. He turned the young man to one side, feeling more powerless than he ever had before.

Vincent staggered to his feet, roaring, and then rammed his head into the wall. Daryll and Tomas rushed to him, grabbed his arms, and dragged him away from the wall as blood began to course down the high forehead. Vincent fought them with amazing strength, and managed to pull free of Daryll. He balled a fist and swung wildly at the Guardsman.

The sound of laughter rang out in the room, loud enough to be heard even above Vincent's fury and the screams of the younger children. It was Emelda, and the sound of it was like the shriek of the wind.

"Now you are going to die!" She sounded quite pleased with this prospect, and not the least afraid. Mikhail could have killed her himself.

WHO DISTURBS ME? The booming mental voice nearly knocked Mikhail off his knees.

I, Priscilla Elhalyn, your servant, have called you. Destroy these impudent intruders! So that I and my children can come to you as has been appointed.

I DO NOT DESTROY!

These are enemies, and they will prevent me from bringing the children!

I WANT NO CHILDREN! LEAVE ME IN PEACE, WOMAN. YOU HAVE PESTERED ME ENOUGH!

Now the Guardian sounded annoyed more than anything else. Vincent was still struggling to get free of the Guardsmen. The younger children were quiet now, too quiet.

But you promised that I could. . . .

DELUDED FEMALE. I PROMISED NOTHING. GO AWAY.

I must bring the children to you, so that they may . . .

SILENCE!

The dining room became very still then, and Vincent stopped struggling. The sound of the fire and the ragged breathing of the company were the only noises. Even Alain's seizure ceased, and he went slack and boneless in Mikhail's hands.

Then there was a single wail from the back of the house, a half scream that made the hairs on Mikhail's neck bristle and his body go cold with fear. It ended abruptly, in midcry, and he knew that Priscilla Elhalyn had died in that moment.

Emelda knew it, too, and her eyes went wide with panic. She tried to rise from the chair where she was bound, her clawlike hands scrabbling at the ropes they had used to bind her. "No, no. It isn't supposed to be like this! We were going to live forever! We were going to be gods!"

Liriel rose from beside Miralys, drawing herself up grandly. A fine sheen of moisture gleamed on her face, and her gown rested damply against her bosom. There were lines of weariness around her mouth, and her red hair had half escaped from the butterfly clasp, so she presented the appearance of having just risen from sleep. In spite of this, she was a dignified figure, strong and sure of herself, and Mikhail regarded her with awe.

"Only gods are gods, not human beings," she told Emelda.

Outside the window of the dining room, a rough caw sounded, as if the crow agreed.

13

The soft light of a winter morning crept through the windows of the dining room, rousing the sleepers who had remained there through the night. The fire was nearly out, and the sour smell of the stale food remaining on the table pervaded the chamber. There were other odors as well, for Alain had soiled himself during his seizures, and one of the girls had vomited. No one had the energy to cope with the mess.

Mikhail looked around, swallowing in a dry and foul mouth. His muscles ached, and the place where Emelda had scratched him itched furiously. He was filled with a profound sense of failure and shame. It took all his will to banish these emotions and order his weary mind to function. He knew that as tired as he was, if he gave in to his jangled feelings, he would make even more mistakes.

The Guardsmen seemed the least affected by the events of the previous night. They were waking up, with the exception of Daryll who had managed to remain alert and on watch until dawn, stretching their legs, yawning, grunting, and generally behaving as if the dining room of Halyn House were a barrack. Mikhail rallied himself enough to direct his mind to the tasks at hand.

"Get the horses fed, and prepare to leave in a few hours."

"What are we going to do about her?" This was Tomas, and he was pointing at the snoring figure of Emelda, still bound in her chair. She looked small and harmless.

"I haven't decided yet."

Valenta was sitting up in her bundle of blankets, watching Mikhail with red-rimmed eyes. "She killed Ysaba, you know. Pushed her down the stairs."

"What? You . . . you told me she went away."

"That's what we were supposed to say. They both killed her—my mother and Emelda—and buried her under the hedge. They thought no one knew, but I saw them. That's why the crows keep coming around. They can smell the—" Suddenly Valenta's small face crumpled into tears. "I liked Ysaba!" she whimpered.

"When did this happen?"

"This spring. They told everyone she had left suddenly, but I knew that she was dead in the garden." She began to sob in earnest, and Liriel, rubbing sleep from reddened eyes, reached out to comfort the younger Elhalyn girl.

Mikhail was stunned now. He did not doubt Val's tale, for it was all too consistent with the general madness of Halyn House. He was lucky, he realized, that he had not come to a similar fate, remembering the way his mind had clouded when he was at the quintain. It would have seemed an unfortunate accident, and no one would have suspected anything.

With or without her bit of crystal, Emelda was clearly a dangerous person. But for all practical purposes he was the law here and could dispose of her as he chose. Mikhail had never been in such a position before, and found he did not like it at all. The power of life and death did not rest easily on his shoulders, and he knew that he would never be suited to that responsibility.

Duncan, who had slept in the kitchen, appeared, his lined hands trembling. He seemed to have aged a decade during the night. But he drew himself up, and looked at Mikhail. "You take the children away, and I will take care of the *domna.*"

"The *domna* is dead, Duncan," Mikhail answered.

"I know that. It is the kindest thing for her. I will dig her a grave before the ground is too hard, and put her to rest. I put her on her first pony, and her father before her. I owe her . . ." His voice trailed off for a second. "She was not always so. Once she was a fine woman."

"But you cannot remain here, you and the nurses and Ian."

"Oh, we'll manage. We can always go to the village." He looked at the children, who were white-faced, and exhausted, and shook his head. "Take them away from here, *vai dom.*"

"I intend to." He hesitated for a moment, then asked, "Duncan, do you know what the Guardian is?"

The old retainer frowned. "It's the father of them girls, it is." He gestured one gnarled hand at Mira and Val. "I think it is, anyhows." He seemed reluctant to continue.

That explains a great deal, Mik. A chieri—*a very old one I suspect. The Ghost Wind must have . . .*

Yes, it does, Liriel. But how did she ever convince herself that it would make her immortal?

At the risk of seeming prejudiced, I will only say that she was Elhalyn to the bone, dear brother. And we will never know the entire story—a shame, really.

You are right. But at least part of mystery is solved, and now we can leave the poor old thing in peace and quiet.

The rest of the early morning was spent in preparing for the journey. Clothes were gathered, and blankets as well. They ate a hasty meal of unhoneyed and creamless porridge in silence. Afterward, the Guardsmen began loading the carriage. The children were tense with apprehension, even Vincent, and Mikhail was uncertain what he ought to say to them. They seemed to understand that their mother was gone, but there was no emotional reaction he could discover, unless it was relief. He would deal with it later, he decided.

It was a chaotic morning, after a frightening and tiring night, and his nerves were strung to the breaking point. Only Mikhail's great sense of responsibility kept him from snapping at the men, at Liriel, or from doing violence to Emelda. He had never wanted to injure another person; his seething rage startled him, and disturbed him more than a little.

What should I do about Emelda, Liri?

That's a good question, and one that I don't have a ready answer for. If we leave her here, she will likely find some further mischief to get into, and I don't fancy a trip back to Thendara with her.

Quite! And what should we do with that crystal of hers? I dislike the idea of leaving a trap-matrix just lying around. Even if the fire neutralized it, I suspect it could be used again.

Umm, yes. My brain feels full of lead this morning, brother. And my eyes itch! I think the starstone must be destroyed, first of all. A hammer on the anvil should be good enough.

But what will that do to Emelda?

Smash the stone! If she dies, she dies!

Liriel!

I lack the patience to worry about anyone except the children. I moni-

tored them last night and they appeared well enough, considering. But this morning Vincent is showing signs of a head injury—from banging his noggin against the wall, most likely—and there is nothing I can do about it! It could be a mild concussion, or something much more serious. And Alain . . . is gone.

Gone? He looks all right to me.

Oh, his body is fine, but I think when his mother died, he nearly died, too. His mind was very fragile to start with. I believe that it was destroyed when . . .

Mikhail was overwhelmed with a fresh rush of feeling. He felt the leaden weight of responsibility for the sudden death of Priscilla Elhalyn, for Alain's ruined mind. The sense of failure he had managed to repress during their morning's preparations returned, and he felt as if he were fighting with that part of himself that knew how worthless he truly was. He struggled to silence the voice of that other Mikhail, wondering how he was going to explain the death of Priscilla to Regis Hastur. If only he could banish his shadow self—but it refused to be dislodged. Mikhail felt trapped in a dark cave of fear and disgust at his own shortcomings.

The mire of misery within him lasted for several minutes. Then, summoning all his willpower, he pulled himself together, used the fire tongs to remove the shining crystal from where it sat among the ashes, and stomped out through the kitchen, toward the stables.

The sky was clear, but he could see thick clouds toward the north. Weatherwise as he was, he hoped the storm would hold off for the rest of the day, and perhaps into the next. The snow from the previous storm was marred by the boots of the men, churned and soiled; this evidence of people other than himself was immensely heartening. The air smelled clean after the smoky atmosphere of the house, and the cold of it chilled his face. He stopped and drew deep breaths, letting the cold air brace him. It felt good.

As he approached the hedge which separated the garden from the way to the stable, he saw the great sea crow regarding him with a bright eye. It lifted its wings, so the white of the edges flashed in the pale sunlight, then gave a deep caw.

"I wish I had been able to understand you," Mikhail told the bird, feeling mildly embarrassed to be speaking to it. The crow withdrew its wings and hunched them back against its body, so it appeared to shrug. It seemed to be saying, "You did the best you could."

It was such a human gesture that Mikhail laughed, the sound startling, in the stillness of the morning. It felt good to laugh, and the crow did not appear to mind. Then it flew away, and he continued on his way to the stables.

The stables smelled of manure and straw, and the warm scent of horses. He could hear the voices of the men nearby, and the welcoming neigh of Charger. It was all reassuringly ordinary. Things like ancient *chieri* and trap-matrices belonged to the night, not the day. His way was clear at last. And as curious as he was to discover more about the being that lived at the springs, Mikhail had no wish to disturb it further.

He was glad that he had the children to look after. It was almost miraculous that they had survived. He was grateful that they had come through that dreadful night alive. And once he broke the matrix dangling from his fingers, Emelda would be no more trouble.

He walked toward the anvil which stood at the far end of the stable. His horse nickered as he passed by, a disappointed noise. "I'll see to you soon, I promise," he told the big bay.

Mikhail placed the shining stone on the dark iron of the anvil, and picked up a medium hammer that was nearby. Even in the dimness of the stable it shone with its own light, clear evidence that while the fire might have cleansed it, it was still potent. He could smell the forge, where the horseshoes were made, a pleasant, ashy odor. He hefted the hammer, then paused. He was reluctant to complete his task. Choices were easy, he thought, but consequences were not. And hadn't he made a royal mess of things, without adding to it by possibly killing that miserable little woman who remained bound and gagged in the dining room.

It was not that he had never killed before, for he had hunted bandits in the hills above Ardais with young Dyan. But those were men, and dangerous ones at that. This was different, not because Emelda was a woman, though that feature bothered him more than a little. Mikhail had been taught to treat matrix stones with respect, and he had never considered destroying one before. Then he remembered what he knew of the Sharra Rebellion, and how that ancient matrix had nearly destroyed Darkover, and decisively brought his arm up, then down, hard.

The hammer struck the gleaming stone, and it shattered into several small shards. Mikhail smashed these into dust, feeling a rush of liberty, as if he were at last free of something which had held him in check. Then he swept the twinkling bits into the ashes of the forge, and stirred them in. As he put the hammer back on the wall, where it belonged, he felt released from his waking dream. He was once again Mikhail Hastur, and had duties to attend to.

Everything was ready by midmorning. Mikhail, mounted on Charger, turned back in his saddle for one last look at Halyn House. Already it looked sad and deserted, although Duncan and the rest of Priscilla Elhalyn's servants were still within. There was a faint wisp of smoke rising from the kitchen chimney. He was not sorry to be seeing the last of the place, but he wished that things could have turned out less tragically. Priscilla Elhalyn was dead, and Emelda, while she still breathed, was no longer any danger to anyone. Destroying the stone had left her witless, as mindless as poor young Alain Elhalyn seemed to be. He could only hope that the healers at Arilinn could do something for the boy. Mikhail had considered dragging the soothsayer back to Thendara, but the carriage was crammed already, and he did not really think his resources could be stretched any further. Good servant that he was, Duncan would probably look after her for as long as she remained alive. And Regis would certainly send people there, to attend to matters.

Mikhail turned back and signaled the driver to start out. At that moment he heard a rush of wings, and the great crow flew toward him, cawing noisily. "Have you come to say good-bye to us?" he called. He ignored the surprised looks from Tomas and Will, and the grin he got from Daryll and Mathias. They thought the bird was a fine jest.

Then the sea crow alighted on the top of the carriage, settling its great talons into a bundle of baggage. It moved its feet back and forth, as if seeking a firm purchase, muttering to itself in crow, lifting a wing. When it had arranged itself to its satisfaction, it gave Mikhail a serene look from its red eyes.

"I think it likes you, *dom*," Daryll announced, barely holding back a fit of laughter.

Mikhail sighed a little, then chuckled. "I am afraid you are right, and I hope you will enjoy cleaning the droppings off the baggage when we halt for the night, Daryll."

The irrepressible Guardsman grinned. "To be sure, my lord. Cleaning off bird dropping is one of my favorite jobs."

The weather held through the first day of the journey back, and they made decent time, in spite of conditions on the road and the slowness of the heavily loaded carriage. Liriel rode inside with the children, and Mikhail and the men accompanied them on horseback. The crow showed no inclination to abandon them either, but rode on the top of the carriage or flew ahead, seeming to inform them of various points of interest along the way.

They stopped for the night at an inn about fifteen miles from

Halyn House. It felt wonderful to get off the horse, to warm hands before a good fireplace, to smell roasting meat and the slightly yeasty scent of the landlord's brew which floated in the smoky air. Mikhail was glad of a tankard of the stuff, a dark, rich beer, for there had been nothing at Halyn House but some bad wine.

They fell to with good appetite. Mikhail watched with some astonishment as Miralys disjointed a roasted chicken with her dainty hands, consumed both breasts and one leg, then belched with satisfaction as she wiped her mouth on her now greasy napkin. Her pale skin gleamed in the flickering light from the fireplace, and two spots of soft pink glowed along her slender cheeks. Her sister was no less eager in her eating, and Emun, who usually picked at his food, consumed a goodly portion. Daryll, as he had done so often before, fed Alain soup, looking at the boy with sad eyes.

Vincent, normally a hearty trencherman, picked at his food and almost fell asleep in his chair. He had been quiet during the journey, unlike the blustering youth he had been a day before. The lad kept rubbing his brow along the left temple, as if he had a headache. His sudden biddability concerned Mikhail, and he almost wished for the return of the bragging lad who bellowed at everything. Mikhail hoped that Vincent was merely quiet from a headache, and not something more serious. If only they had a proper healer, for though both he and Liriel could do small things, neither of them had that particular gift. And there was no healer in the neighborhood.

Everyone retired early except Mikhail. Liriel took the girls with her, to her chamber, and Daryll carried Alain up the narrow stairs, with Emun and Vincent trailing behind him like ducks. Mathias looked at Mikhail, as he sat before the fireplace, his legs stretched out, and a tankard in his hand, started to speak, then shrugged. He took up a position at the door of the common room and settled himself to wait.

Mikhail sat and sipped his beer. He felt alone—alone and dismal. He wished there were someone he could talk to, but his sister was asleep, and she needed her rest. He did, too. His eyes itched with fatigue. But he could not rest. How was he going to explain to Regis the mess he had made of things?

The inn grew still, and the fire fluttered around the logs in the fireplace. He could hear the faint sighing of the wind outside. It might rise during the night and make the rest of the trip more difficult. He felt mildly blessed that this first day had been so reasonable. Finding something to feel hopeful about made him feel slightly less terrible, and he sipped at his beer.

He savored his weariness, letting the beer relax his aching muscles. He was keyed up still, too restless to sleep yet, though his body yearned for its release. Finally, he drew his matrix from around his throat, removed the silken coverings, and directed his mind toward the one person he thought might understand his turmoil.

Marguerida, beloved!

Mik, darling! How lovely! But I can barely make you out. These hangings that Istvana put in my room are fine for protecting me from too much matrix energy, but they play hell with telepathy. I'll go down to the parlor—just a moment.

She sounded cheerful and happy, as he had not heard her sound in all her time at Arilinn. Some coil of tension in his chest unwound. He had not even known it existed until it left his body.

Here I am again! How are things at Halyn House? Are the Elhellions still waking you up at night?

We left Halyn House this morning, chiya. *Priscilla Elhalyn is dead, and I am taking the children back to Thendara.*

What happened?

It is a long story, and a sad one. Mikhail began to tell her everything, not sparing himself. He could sense her presence, could almost picture her intense concentration as she listened. *So I failed to protect the children from . . . whatever the Guardian was, from their mother, or from that wretched Emelda. Alain Elhalyn is as close to witless as makes no difference, and both Liriel and I are worried about Vincent. I can only hope he has nothing more dangerous than a mild concussion. I made a complete mess of everything and . . .*

Mik, don't be such an ass!

The tart words were like a bucket of icy water poured into his mind, bracing and chilling at the same time. He was almost too stunned to reply. *What do you mean?*

I mean you did the best you could in an impossible situation, and the only thing you didn't do was get help sooner. And now, at least, I understand why you seemed so peculiar.

Peculiar?

Unfocused and sort of evasive. I was starting to imagine all sorts of foolish things.

Such as?

Well, Emelda was a woman. . . .

Marguerida, there is no one but you for me.

Good! Now stop blaming yourself. Let my father do that. He does enough to himself for all of us, and he has had a lot more practice!

I'll be sure to tell him that when I next encounter him. I am certain he will be delighted.

I've told him myself a few times, and so has Javanne! Listen, you are tired, and everything seems worse when you are exhausted. Get some sleep. You'll have several days on the road, and you need all your strength for that. You can beat yourself over the head some other time!

How practical you are, my beloved. I suppose you are right.

And it almost kills you to admit it!

I can't fool you for a moment, can I?

Mikhail Hastur, you are a wonderful man, even when you are behaving like a goose.

I haven't told you about the crow.

The what?

He had the satisfaction of surprising her, and it felt delightful. *When I arrived at Halyn House, there was a large sea crow that kept watching me. Every time I left the house, there it was—watching me like a hawk.*

Good trick—a crow acting like a falcon.

Hush, or I won't tell you the tale. There were quite a lot of crows at Halyn House of the ordinary variety. I got used to the sound of their feet on the roof every morning. But this one was different. It seemed to take a great interest in me, and, when I was tilting at the quintain, it saved my life, or at least kept the damn thing from knocking me into the next week. My men think the animal is a fine joke. When we left, the beast just climbed onto the top of the carriage and came along for the ride. It is the most peculiar thing.

We had sea crows on Thetis, and they were quite intelligent. Do you think the bird will go all the way to Thendara with you?

Yes—it seems to have adopted me.

Well, then, I will look forward to meeting it.

How are things going at Neskaya?

I think I am making some progress, yet it seems as if I learn something, and then it wiggles away from me. It is very frustrating, but even more so for Istvana, I suspect, though she never lets on. But I am glad to be here instead of at Arilinn. The people with Istvana are friendly, and they don't sneer at me when I make a mistake. . . . Now get to bed! We can talk another time. I love you, Mik.

I feel better for talking to you, but if you are going to order me about when . . . when we are wed . . .

I am, so you had better become accustomed to it. I am not the least impressed by all your titles, and I have a very forceful disposition! Like your mother!

I know, beloved, I know. Good night.

Mikhail put away his stone, then sat watching the fire, finishing the last of his beer. He savored the strength of Marguerida Alton as she had been in his mind, the power of her, and beneath it, the passion she held for him. What, he wondered, would it be like when he was finally able to feel that passion directly? He imagined her hands running over his naked back, and found himself instantly aroused, despite his exhaustion. Would he ever find out what it would feel like to love her freely? Mikhail was afraid to hope.

He mounted the stairs slowly, his thighs feeling the stiffness of riding all day. After undressing, Mikhail lay between the covers, smelling the clean linen, listening to the wind against the tiles of the roof. Just before sleep claimed him, he heard the rough and familiar sound of his crow, as if it were bidding him good night. Then he slipped into deep dreamless sleep.

The following morning, the sky had clouded over; by the time they set out, snow was falling. The children were restless now, and Liriel was becoming crabbier by the minute. Mikhail, who had never ridden in an aircar in his life, had a sudden longing for one, to carry him and the rest of the company back to Thendara in an hour instead of at least three or four more dreary days.

By midmorning, the snow was coming down steadily, though not very thickly. They were riding along the river, and the gurgle of the waters which were not yet frozen was a pleasant sound amidst the soft rustle of the snow. There was only a light breeze which chilled the cheeks and ruffled his hair, and he was grateful for that. He was weatherwise enough to be concerned.

The crow, which was still riding atop the carriage, lifted off the baggage suddenly and flapped through the air. It landed on Mikhail's shoulder with a thump. He felt the sharp talons dig into the wool of his cloak, and he smelled the slightly fishy odor of the bird. It shifted from foot to foot, then settled into place.

"Are you going to do this all the time now?" He was becoming less uneasy with the bird, but he suspected he would never be entirely comfortable with that beak close by. The sea crow was a formidable animal at a distance, and more so close up. It gave a rough caw which he took for a yes.

Mikhail was glad of this diversion, since wondering about the crow kept him from thinking about the children. He kept trying to think what he should have done differently, and finding no answer. It was a futile pursuit, and he knew it.

"Do you expect to be presented at court?" he asked the crow

quietly, and was answered by the soft trill, the nearest thing to a musical sound the animal could make. "I am going to cut quite a figure, if you insist on sitting on my shoulder all the time."

Then he had the feeling of something brushing his thoughts, just a light touch, like a feather across his brow. There were no words in it, just the sense of some communication that he had never experienced before. It felt calm, but strong.

Mikhail turned his head slowly to look at the crow, and found red eyes gazing at him intently. The huge beak was no more than a hand-span from his own nose, sharp and dangerous. But he felt no threat, just a sense of certainty, as if he were being reassured that everything was all right.

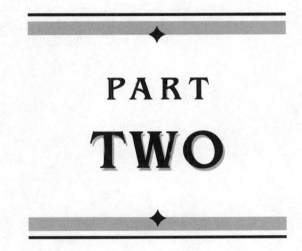

PART
TWO

14

They came to the gates of Thendara at dusk on the fifth day, in a wet snow that soaked the cloaks of the riders and made the horses shine with moisture. It took another hour and several detours to reach Comyn Castle, since the carriage could not travel on the narrower streets, but Mikhail sent Daryll and Mathias ahead to prepare for the arrival of five children, two of them ill.

As they passed taverns and cookshops, smelling of stews and roasted meats, full of the sound of voices, Mikhail asked himself why he had not contacted his uncle during the journey. After a few minutes of thought, he decided he was still deeply ashamed of his apparent failure at Halyn House. Nothing Marguerida or Liriel said made any difference to him on that subject.

When Mikhail Hastur rode into the Stable Court of Comyn Castle, with a sea crow riding on the pommel of his saddle, and a bleak mood dampening his spirits, he was not sure what to expect. But in the torchlight flickering on the swept stones of the courtyard, he saw not only grooms and servants waiting to care for them, but Regis himself, standing at the top of a low set of steps, his head uncovered in spite of the cold, his white hair shining in the ruddy light of the torches.

Danilo Syrtis-Ardais stood a few steps behind his master, alert as always, but with the hint of a smile gracing his mouth.

Mikhail dismounted, threw the reins to the closest groom, and climbed the steps to meet his uncle. Behind him he could hear the voices of the children, the two girls particularly, and Liriel hushing them as she climbed down from the carriage. When he reached Regis, he found himself tongue-tied. He had not felt this anxious in years.

But his uncle embraced him in a warm hug, his face so filled with obvious joy at their reunion, that Mikhail's fear's vanished. They stood in the chilly afternoon, not speaking, but only savoring the moment.

Then there was a flutter of dark wings, and the crow alighted on Mikhail's shoulder, giving Regis a red-eyed look that made the older man draw back quickly. "I promised I would present him at court, and he seems eager for the honor," Mikhail said, finding his tongue with relief. Regis' welcome was too genuine for him to continue feeling uneasy.

Regis laughed. "You always were the most unorthodox boy, Mikhail, and I see that you are still capable of surprising me. But I don't know what Lady Linnea is going to think of a crow in her dining room!"

"Oh, I don't think we'll have to worry about him. He prefers to remain outdoors and scrounge scraps from the kitchen. I hope you are not disappointed to see me return with all of the children, Uncle."

"I am never disappointed in you, Mikhail. And when you sent for Liriel, I rather anticipated that something was amiss. Come. Let's get inside." *I don't want to arouse any more gossip than I must.*

Of course, Uncle. And I am sorry I made such a mess of everything.

Nonsense! I pitchforked you into an impossible situation. In hindsight, I regret it. He smiled at Mikhail.

What do you know?

Only what Liriel has told me, which is a great deal. More to your credit than mine. Why didn't you ask for help sooner?

I couldn't.

Mikhail turned and looked toward his sister, who was coming up the stairs, holding the girls' hands tightly. She had not told him that she had contacted Regis, and he felt both relieved and somewhat betrayed. Her intention had been to protect him; still, he felt a little annoyed at sheltering behind her voluminous skirts, then angry at himself for being ungenerous.

Two servants were lifting Alain onto a stretcher, while Emun watched them with round eyes. He took his brother's limp hand and patted it, and Vincent stood beside him, quiet again, although he had

had several sudden bouts of fury during the journey. They had been at a loss as to what to do, for to have given the young man a sleeping draught might have been disastrous. He seemed to be able to answer questions, though he complained of headache, and started at noises and bright lights.

Emun, looking much older than his fourteen years, herded Vincent up the stairs, following the men with the stretcher. Mikhail reflected on what a good lad he was, to treat Vincent with such kindness after all the bullying he had endured.

They proceeded into the castle, a straggle of weary travelers. As they passed the door, the crow flew off with a caw, no doubt heading for the kitchens. Mikhail took off his damp cloak, shook it, and handed it to a servant who was close by. Then he stamped his cold feet and looked toward his uncle again.

Regis caught his glance, smiled, then shrugged. "I think that hot baths and clean clothing are the first orders of business."

Mikhail caught the guarded tone in his uncle's words, and studied him for a moment. There was something different about Regis, though he could not quite put a name to the change. He seemed much older, graver somehow. But he was too tired to untangle that puzzle now. "I think you are right."

At that moment, Valenta released her grip on Liriel's hand and approached the two men. She looked very hard at Regis, her dark eyes sparkling. "Are we going to live here now?" she demanded.

Regis leaned down, so that he was at eye level with the younger girl. His expression was mild, the way it had been with his own children, and with Mikhail. "Would you like that?"

"I don't know. It's nice and warm here. I haven't made up my mind yet."

"Do you know who I am?"

"Of course! With that white hair you must be Regis-Rafael Felix Alar Hastur y Elhalyn, and you are my cousin."

"You have the advantage of me, knowing all my names, which, truthfully, I rarely even think of."

"I am Valenta Felicia Stephanie Elhalyn. Now . . . where is that bath you mentioned?"

What a resilient young woman! Mikhail, is she always so . . . brash?

She has been since we left Halyn House. Even before that she demonstrated a lively mind. She and her sister are going to be remarkable—it's the boys who are the problem.

Yes. We will discuss it later.

"I am very pleased to have met you at last." He took Valenta's hand and bowed his head over it gracefully, considering his present posture, and then smiled at her. He stood up slowly, and looked at the other girl.

Miralys did not sparkle like her sister, but stood back a little, still clinging to Liriel's hand. The death of her mother had shaken her more than it had Valenta, and she had lost some of her calm assurance. Still, she looked Regis Hastur in the eye, swallowed hard, and made a small bob of a curtsy. There was great dignity in her stance, as if she were much older than her years. Mikhail experienced a rush of sadness that she had never had a real childhood. He knew what that was like, since he felt that he had not had one himself.

"This is Miralys, Regis," Liriel said. She looked down at the small girl. "I don't know all her names, for we haven't talked about that yet."

"What a pretty name, to be sure. Welcome to Comyn Castle."

"Thank you," Mira said very softly. "It seems very grand."

"Anything would seem grand after Halyn House," Val interjected, grinning. "Now, about that bath and some clean clothes."

"Of course. How rude of me to keep you waiting here." Regis gestured at a maid who was standing patiently at the back of the entryway. "Please show the young ladies to the Elhalyn Suite, and make them comfortable."

The maid, a woman in her twenties, came forward, took the two girls by the hands, and led them away. Valenta cast a cheerful look over her shoulder as they went, and Mikhail felt relieved that they, at least, appeared well enough. Miralys would recover in time, and Valenta was clearly ready for anything—even perhaps hoping for adventures. After the events at Halyn House, Comyn Castle would, he hoped, be blessedly dull.

Emun, who had been waiting silently in Liriel's shadow, still holding Vincent's hand, stepped forward. He looked even whiter than before, as if he were afraid of Regis. Vincent's face, by contrast, was empty of expression, and his cheeks were rosy. In the light of the room, Vincent looked every inch a manly figure, like the king he had planned to become. The glazed expression in his eyes, though, marred the effect somewhat.

Making a stiff bow, Emun stood before Regis Hastur, as if awaiting judgment, and expecting to be found wanting. His pale red hair, slack and brittle fell across his narrow brow. "I am Emun-Estavan Mikhail Elhalyn, and this is my brother Vincent-Regis Duvic Elhalyn y Elhalyn. I hope you will not be offended if he doesn't say anything—

he is not himself just now." The quaver in his voice was a near to a squeak.

Regis' face did not register any shock, but Mikhail knew he was startled by Vincent's name. He saw his uncle glance quickly at Danilo Ardais, then turn back. Mikhail himself was rattled by the name—Elhalyn y Elhalyn! If only he had managed to find out the full names of all the children earlier—why hadn't he asked? But they likely would not have told him. Even on his earlier visit, none of the children had mentioned their entire names, and he suspected that their mother had given them very strict instructions about it. But Derik had died long before Vincent had been conceived, so it was impossible that he was Vincent's father. Still, claiming Elhalyn y Elhalyn would make the lad's certainty that he would be the king more comprehensible. It was a shame that Priscilla had taken her secrets to the grave.

Regis glanced around, but none of the servants was standing close enough to hear Emun's quiet introduction. Who was Vincent's father, to make him claim such a name—unless he was some *nedestro* half brother of Priscilla's? And what would the Comyn Council make of it, if Regis ever let the knowledge be made public? He did not know if Vincent would ever be of sound mind again, or as sound as he had been, but it was clear that with such a scandalous heritage, he would never be acceptable as king. Mikhail could not decide if he felt more sorry or relieved. Certainly he was very sad about Vincent's present condition, but since he had given up any real hope that the young man could ever take the throne, even as a puppet to the Hasturs, he was slightly relieved that circumstances had conspired to make that impossible. It left him with only Emun as a suitable candidate, and the lad was so frail and thin that Mikhail was not certain he would live to adulthood.

Mikhail ignored the rush of despair that swelled in his chest. He was going to be stuck with a throne he did not want, and he might as well resign himself to the idea. The anger which had been absent during the trip stirred, and with it a deep resentment. Then a bleak mood began to darken his mind. Gods, he was tired! The only good he could see coming out of it was that some of the opposition to a potential match with Marguerida might vanish, since the Elhalyn throne had no real power, and therefore might not upset the balance between the Domains. But even that seemed dubious.

"I understand, and I have a healer waiting to see to Vincent, and to your other brother . . . Alain, is it?"

"Yes, *dom!*" Emun was trembling now, looking ready to cry.

Mikhail could not guess what was troubling the lad, nor why he appeared to be so terrified as he stood before Regis Hastur.

"You must be tired from the journey," Regis answered calmly.

"The carriage bumped a lot."

Liriel snorted. "Emun is being very tactful. I now know every rock between here and the coast intimately, having passed over them twice in a tenday. My bones will never forget them. Mikhail and the men had it easy."

Emun turned and looked over his slender shoulder at Liriel, giving her a look of enormous gratitude which lit his haggard young face and made him look like the child that he still was. She flashed Emun a brief conspiratorial grin, and Mikhail realized that his sister had a gift with these children that he had failed to notice before. Then Emun glanced toward Mikhail, as if seeking guidance for what he should do. He was clearly frightened, though Mikhail could not imagine why. There was nothing threatening about Regis Hastur, or even about Danilo Ardais, standing behind him.

I guess he isn't going to throw me into a dungeon, like Mother always said he would.

Emun's thought startled him, and he could tell that Regis had caught it as well. His uncle looked very perturbed, but before Mikhail had time to wonder what it meant, two manservants moved toward the boys, took them in hand, and bustled them out of the entry. When they were gone, everyone remaining breathed a sigh of relief.

Mikhail, what did he mean by that?

I am not sure, Uncle, but Priscilla had the children terrified, and she seemed to have the idea that you were going to snatch her children away and do terrible things to them.

I see. I wonder where she got that notion?

Mikhail had a good idea that Derik Elhalyn's ghost might be the perpetrator, remembering what it had said during the seance, but he was not ready to discuss it. Certainly not in the middle of the entryway, with servants all around. And he was just too tired to continue the matter at present. "Come on, Liri. In payment for my sins, you can have the first bath."

She chuckled. "That will be a good beginning, I believe, though the debt is rather larger than can be repaid in a day or a night."

"Oh, dear," Mikhail answered with a playfulness he did not really feel. "I think I am going to have to hear about this trip until I die."

"Longer than that," Liri replied cheerfully. "I intend to have an active life in the overworld."

Mikhail stared at her in horror for a moment, then realized she was teasing him as she had when they were young. She could not know that the very mention of the overworld turned his bowels to water, and that he hoped never to see another ghost as long as he lived.

"I do love family reunions," Regis announced, his blue eyes twinkling at his niece and nephew. "Now, off with the pair of you. You can squabble to your hearts' content until dinner, at which time I expect you to behave in a civilized manner."

"Will there be anyone besides you, Lady Linnea, and Dani?" Mikhail had a sudden feeling of unease, since Regis did not usually demand the best behavior when only the family was present. It was one of the things he liked best about meals at Comyn Castle, the informality and ease of conversation.

"We do have some visitors, yes."

"Are you going to tell us who, or make us sit on tenterhooks until supper?" Mikhail could feel his temper starting to rise, since he knew that Regis was being provocative, and deliberately so.

"Francisco Ridenow is here."

Mikhail was not surprised by the presence of the Ridenow representative to the Comyn Council, and had a brief moment of relief. But it was clear that he was not the only guest at Comyn Castle. "And?"

"A surprise, Mikhail."

He glared at his uncle for a second. "I have had enough surprises to last a lifetime," he snarled, finally allowing himself to vent his well-deserved spleen. Then he walked out of the entry, stamping up the stairs behind Liriel, not regretting his momentary fury. It was over quickly, for no one could stay angry at Regis very long. And, at least, he was back where he belonged, and his relief knew no bounds.

By the time he had soaked his aching bones, and donned a fresh tunic and trews, Mikhail was nearly restored to his normal good spirits. It was clear from Regis' welcome that he was not going to be punished or exiled. All his fears had come to nothing, and he was mildly annoyed with himself for being so foolish. He might even escape much criticism for the way he had handled the children and Priscilla.

Thus, he was whistling one of the songs Marguerida liked as he walked into the smaller dining room on the second level of the castle. The sound faded when he saw a woman standing with her back to him, with a familiar spine and red hair. Marguerida! No wonder Regis had been so mysterious! But how? He had spoken with her three nights before, and she had been at Neskaya.

Then the woman turned and faced him, and Mikhail realized it was not Marguerida Alton, but Gisela Aldaran. He had not remembered how alike they were in height and coloring, though this was hardly surprising. Marguerida was part Aldaran, after all. She smiled, and he noticed that her eyes were green, not golden, and that her teeth were somewhat more prominent than those of his beloved. But they could have passed for sisters to any unknowing eye. The hearty appetite which had accompanied him down the stairs vanished.

What the devil was she doing there? And what was Regis up to now? There was no doubt in Mikhail's mind that Gisela's presence was no accident, that it had a distinct purpose in Regis' schemes and plans for Darkover. And, knowing how his uncle's mind worked, he had a tingle of apprehension.

"Mikhail—how wonderful to see you again!" Her voice was deeper than Marguerida's, a throaty alto that sounded caressing, and his suspicions deepened. She had been a girl when last he saw her, and now she was clearly a woman.

"Gisela! This is a great surprise. Has Regis managed to get the Council to let the Aldarans breathe the sacred air of the Crystal Chamber, then? I have been away." *Damn Regis for springing her on me like this!*

"Not yet," she answered, as she moved smoothly across the floor to meet him. Gisela was wearing a green gown of finest wool, embroidered with roses all along the hem and cuffs. It fit her body closely, so that the shape of her fine figure was revealed almost immodestly. "But things are progressing to the satisfaction of almost everyone."

Mikhail bowed over her hand. "That is good to hear. We were all surprised when Regis proposed the return of the Aldaran Domain to the Council last summer—but my uncle never does the expected, does he? Who, might I ask, is not happy with the situation."

"I'm afraid that Lady Marilla is reluctant to agree, and your father is . . ."

"You need go no farther. My father seems to delight in being contrary. My mother has often commented to that effect, and she is a very wise woman."

Gisela smiled again. "Let us not talk of such matters. How are you?"

"Well enough, considering I have just ridden five days with a storm at my back, several small children crammed into a carriage too small for them, and a sister who would have liked to murder me many times over. And you?"

"Did you know I had married?"

Mikhail's chest loosened with relief. "No, I had not heard. We have not really had any contact for . . . what, almost six years? The only news of the Aldarans that has come to us was that your brother Hermes took Lew Alton's position in the Terran Senate. Who is your husband?" He looked around the dining room, but they were alone, except for a footman who was pouring wine at a sideboard.

"It was closer to seven years now, but I am glad you remember it as recent." Her voice was thick and honeyed, and she moved closer to him, eyeing him in a way he found alarming. He had seen that look on any number of faces of young women. He had never known exactly how to describe it before, but at that moment the word "predatory" leaped into his mind. He felt very much like a fat gander being stared at by a hungry fox. "I married Bertrand Leynier four years ago. And now I have two children."

"Two. How wonderful." Mikhail wished someone would arrive and rescue him from this uncomfortable conversation, but was relieved to know that she was not really husband hunting, just being overly friendly. "I do not know your husband—I have heard of him, I believe, but we have never met. I look forward to making his acquaintance." He managed to appear interested and polite, but his heart sank a little. Bertrand was a man of unsavory reputation, a minor landholder up in the Hellers, who was at least as old as *Dom* Gabriel and had already buried two wives. Surely the Aldarans could have done better for Gisela, even considering how they had been excluded from the mainstream of Darkovan society. A Terranan would have been better! Then he chided himself for being so uncharitable and provincial—a Terranan indeed!

Gisela shook her head, setting the fine curls that coiled around her forehead into movement. "You will not have that dubious pleasure, Mik. Bertrand had the good grace to fall and break his neck two years ago, much to my delight."

"I see you have not abandoned your habit of plain speaking," Mikhail replied with as much calmness as he could muster. A young widow of proven fertility, a woman near his own age, one he knew and had even enjoyed the company of at one time—though he had not thought anyone knew about that—was precisely the sort of person who would find favor in the eyes of many people. Except that she was Aldaran, of course.

Tired as his mind was, it examined the possibilities. He saw the fine hand of Regis Hastur in her presence, with the notion of healing the breach between the Aldarans with the rest of the Domains by marriage, of which he was likely the tool. Or perhaps he was wrong, and Regis intended that one of his brothers would suit Gisela. He spent a pleasant moment envisioning Gabe trying to cope with her quick mind, and decided that Rafael would make her a better husband. He, at least, was clever.

"Well, he was old, and he drank a great deal, and he had no conversation to speak of, and pretending otherwise will not change those facts. And I have never learned to be as ladylike as I might have been, having no mother to guide me."

Her smile, which had beguiled him a few years before, had lost its attraction, and her green eyes seemed calculating now. "Why are you in Thendara, then?"

"My son, Caleb, who has never been a hearty child, was in need of medical attention, and I brought him here. He is presently creating havoc at the Terran Hospital. You have no idea how exhausting children can be." Gisela sounded a little sharp, as if Caleb's infirmity was deliberate.

"Oh, yes, I do. I have just spent the past two months trying to manage the Elhalyn brood—the Elhellions they should be called—and not succeeding overmuch. If you think that young children are exhausting, just wait until they reach adolescence!"

"You terrify me." She did not appear at all frightened, but widened her smile and drew a little closer to him, as if seeking to return to their former intimacy. This had consisted of no more than some pleasant rides in the mountains, games of chess, and long conversations about everything from horse breeding to the state of Darkovan politics as they understood it at twenty-one and seventeen respectively. Which, he realized in retrospect, was not a great deal—mere youthful imagining.

Mercifully, Liriel came into the dining room at that moment, with Miralys and Valenta. The girls had been scrubbed, dressed, and turned out in good style. Even Val's wild mop of dark hair had been tamed a bit, and they were wearing long tunics of rose and gray respectively, with paler pink petticoats beneath them.

Mikhail was relieved to see her, and he turned to introduce his sister and the girls to Gisela Aldaran. "Liriel, this is an old friend of mine from my misspent youth, Gisela Aldaran. Gisela, my sister Liriel Lanart-Alton, and two of my charges, Miralys and Valenta Elhalyn."

The Aldaran woman flashed her brilliant smile and extended her hand in a rather condescending manner. "I am delighted to make your acquaintance," she drawled, ignoring the girls completely.

Since each of her hands was firmly entrapped by one of the children, Liriel was not forced to return the gesture. She nodded at Gisela calmly. "Well, this is certainly a delightful surprise. When did you arrive? How was the journey from Aldaran at this season?"

"Oh, we came in Father's flyer, right onto the tarmac at Thendara Spaceport. My father does not think that we should eschew the conveniences of Terranan technology just because a lot of old fuddy-duddies think it is un-Darkovan. It was a little exciting coming down from the mountains—the winds are so treacherous—but we arrived in one piece, and I, for one, am glad to skip a tedious journey on horseback."

"Since I have just spent several days in a poorly sprung carriage, I quite agree with you." *Mik, what the devil is she doing here? I never really thought to see an Aldaran standing around in the dining room. Was this what Regis was . . . ?*

I don't know, but I suspect the worst.

As well you should. Be careful.

I am always careful, sister, except when I am foolish.

I know, and that is precisely what worries me.

The footman came across the room with a tray of wineglasses, the golden contents gleaming in them, as Regis Hastur and his consort, Lady Linnea entered, followed by Francisco Ridenow and Danilo Syrtis-Ardais, Regis' paxman. A moment later they were followed by Gisela's father, Lord Damon Aldaran.

As glasses of wine were served, and *Dom* Damon greeted Mikhail with evident pleasure and enthusiasm, Mikhail was rather startled to see how much the man had aged since he had last seen him. He was no older than Regis, but looked ancient. His once red hair was streaked with gray, as was his beard, and there were wrinkles around his eyes that belonged to a much older man. The hand he thrust into Mikhail's was dry, and he squeezed the younger man's fingers hard, as if trying to prove his vigor.

Dom Damon was an older half brother of Beltran, who had been the heir to old Kermiac Aldaran before the Sharra Rebellion. But he was *nedestro,* and would never have come to be lord of the Domain had not Beltran died without issue, and Captain Rafe Scott had not refused the title. He had three legitimate children: Robert, his heir; Herm, who was now Darkover's Senator; and Gisela, the youngest. He had several other children, by various consorts and lovers, including a son, Raul, who was his horse master, and another, Renald, who piloted the flyer Gisela had spoken of. At least, this had been the case when Mikhail had visited them. For a moment, he had the impulse to ask *Dom* Damon about Emelda, but he quashed it. This was neither the time nor the place.

"You look none the worse for your adventures," *Dom* Aldaran boomed, and Mikhail realized that the man was probably losing his hearing.

"No, sir, none the worse. I am glad to see you." This was true, for Mikhail had always liked the man. He was intelligent, curious, and, for a Darkovan, very progressive. This would not win him friends on the Council, always assuming that Regis ever managed to get them to accept an Aldaran of any stripe on it. Robert, as Mikhail remembered him, was a sober man, rather dull, but more the sort of person who would fit into the Council.

Dom Damon clapped Mikhail on the shoulder, then reached for a glass of wine. He sipped a little, then he noticed the little girls, who were clinging to Liriel as if they feared they would be snatched away from her. He bent down and peered at them nearsightedly.

Just then young Danilo Hastur, Regis's son, came into the dining room, looking anxious at his tardiness. He looked around the room, and his eyes fell on Miralys. Mikhail heard his sharp intake of breath, and watched with amusement as the young man tugged his formal blue tunic straight and smoothed back his pale hair with a nervous hand.

Regis Hastur watched as well, and an expression came over his face, as if he were pleased with his son's reaction. Lady Linnea left his side then, came toward her son, smoothed his hair again quite needlessly, and led him over to meet the girls. She made introductions in a quiet voice, and Mira extended her free hand with her usual dignity while Valenta tried very hard not to giggle.

Mikhail gave her a stern look; she was still his charge, and he wanted her to behave well. Val twinkled at him, but sucked her cheeks in firmly, then lowered her eyes demurely, as if to say that this was all rather silly, but she would try to keep her countenance. What a marvel the child was, he thought. He only wished any of the boys showed half the intelligence of their sisters, and once more regretted that an Elhalyn queen would never be acceptable. It would be a good solution, but not one that he even wanted to try to convince anyone of.

The company sorted itself out and proceeded to the table. Mikhail found himself seated beside Gisela, with Francisco Ridenow on her other side, and braced himself for a long and trying meal. He watched young Dani hold a chair for each of the Elhalyn girls, showing his excellent manners even though he had eyes for no one in the room except Mira. He seated himself between them. Liriel, never uncomfortable, took a chair on the other side of Valenta, and gave Mikhail a small smile.

This could turn out more interesting than I expected.

Damn it, Liri—I don't want interesting!
Poor Mikhail!

He was unable to continue his mental conversation with his sister, for he realized Gisela had spoken to him. Mikhail summoned all his wits—they seemed at the moment few and scattered—brought his years of experience with husband-hunting females to the fore, and managed an answer. Then he favored his uncle with a look of censure, and had the pleasure of seeing Regis Hastur blush to the roots of his white hair, as if he had been caught at trickery.

The soup was served, followed by crispy fish, a rabbithorn forcemeat in a tender pastry, and several side dishes. Mikhail, his appetite returned, ate heartily, and Gisela, mildly rebuffed by his apparent indifference, turned her sensuous attentions toward Francisco Ridenow. By the time the dessert course was brought—honeycake with dried fruits—he was back in a good humor, and enjoying himself.

When, at the end of the meal, Liriel rose and took the Elhalyn girls away with her, he saw the stricken look on Dani Hastur's young face, as if the light had gone out of the room. Gisela made a move to reclaim his attention, but Lady Linnea intercepted her and drew her away. Mikhail sympathized with young Dani, and gave silent thanks to Linnea. He was too tired to deal with Gisela any longer. More importantly, he saw Regis Hastur nod, and he knew it was time for them to talk.

15

Regis kept a study on the same level as the smaller dining room. Mikhail followed him, with Danilo Syrtis-Ardais walking a pace behind, guarding the back of Regis Hastur as he had for more than two decades. Regis fully trusted no one except his paxman and his wife, and Mikhail had never been completely alone with his uncle in his life. He wondered if Regis ever chafed at being guarded all the time, and missed his solitude? Or whether his inseparable relationship with Danilo had forged them into merely two parts of the same whole.

Mikhail knew that this care with Regis' person dated back to the period when the World Wreckers had been busily assassinating many members of the Comyn, even going so far as to murder babies in their cradles. They had defeated these forces, but it had left a scar, a kind of paranoia that Mikhail did not quite understand, for he had been too young at the time to realize what was going on. But since he did not wish anything to happen to his uncle, he was glad of Danilo's quiet presence.

Seating himself behind a large desk, Regis looked at his nephew. The room was a spare one, where Mikhail had endured lectures on his duties and scoldings for his childish indiscretions. He did not doubt that his uncle had chosen this site for their discussion for the purpose of invoking these memories. Regis was not one to waste such an opportunity.

While Danilo poured them each a goblet of firewine, Mikhail leaned back in his chair and stretched out his long legs. He looked at the worn brown curtains that hung before the window, at the carpet whose pattern was almost indistinguishable now, and at the single decoration in the room, a portrait of Lady Linnea done some twenty years before. She had a few more wrinkles around her blue eyes these days, and her face had become heavier. She had been a very pretty girl, and now she was a grown woman, but the eyes of that young girl remained with her.

Mikhail forced himself to relax, refusing to begin the conversation. He had spent much of the journey planning what he would say to his uncle, scenarios that ranged from furious to cold, but now, faced with the actuality, they all vanished from his mind. He noticed Danilo observing him with barely concealed amusement, as if he knew it was a waiting game, and wanted to see who would be the first to speak. They smiled at one another as the paxman offered him a goblet.

After perhaps five minutes of silence, Regis, always a little restless, began to look uncomfortable. He fidgeted with his glass, shifted in the high-backed chair, and looked around the room, as if hoping to find some topic to begin with. "I am glad you are back," he said at last.

Mikhail found he was determined not to give an inch. "And I am glad to be here. After the trials of Halyn House, this seems like heaven to me."

"I did you an ill service, sending you there with so little support. But I did not really understand the situation—I still don't."

"Priscilla Elhalyn was hardly going to tell you she was in the power of a hedge-witch."

"Tell me about her—what was her name—Esmerelda?"

"Emelda, and she claimed to be an Aldaran. I almost asked *Dom* Damon if he knew of her, but good sense prevailed." From the look on his uncle's face, Mikhail was glad he had restrained his lively curiosity. "Liriel says that she came to Tramontana for training a few years back, and vanished under some sort of cloud. You would have to ask the Keeper there for the details." It was odd to hear his own voice, calm and almost severe, speaking these words. The anger which had burned in him for weeks had turned to ice, it seemed. He did not want to shout at Regis—well, only a little.

"I shall. I should have been told, but I try to leave the running of the Towers to the *leroni*. *Mestra* Natasha felt no need to inform me. It disturbs me greatly to think that there might be other untrained telepaths running around. *Laran* is rare, but not that rare, and it is now starting to pop up in the most unlikely places."

Mikhail nodded. "That is hardly surprising, considering how often men of the Domains share their favors with any comely female they can seduce."

"That is severe, Mikhail."

He gave a sharp snort. "If you want severe, discuss the topic with my cousin Marguerida. She will explain to you more than you ever wished to know about the evils of masculine . . . what does she call it . . . privilege! It has almost made me ashamed to be a man. But I warn you that you must be ready to lose the argument, since she is a fierce debater and takes no prisoners."

Danilo turned away, and Mikhail could see his shoulders shake with laughter. "That hardly strikes me as a suitable topic of conversation for you to be having with Marguerida," Regis answered, trying to look serious, but failing.

"We talk about everything, which is one of the many things I treasure about her, Uncle Regis. She is completely unafraid to tackle the most forbidden of subjects, to dissect them, sort out the parts, and come to her own conclusions. I think, had things been somewhat different, that my mother might have been the same, and that she dislikes Marguerida because they are alike rather than for any other reasons."

"Yes, Javanne was always clever." He fell silent, musing, and sipped at his wine. "Tell me more about Emelda," Regis said finally, unwilling to continue to talk about either his sister or Marguerida Alton.

"When I arrived, she was wearing the clothing of a *leronis*—well, as much as she could manage. The cloth was red by courtesy more than reality, and poorly dyed at that. This struck me as odd, since household *leroni* are no longer common. But everything about Priscilla's household was peculiar! It was a minor thing, and I had critical problems to think about—broken windows, chimneys that did not draw, stables that needed repair. I don't know if the children would have survived another winter in that place—but since the *domna* was planning that they should accompany her, I don't suppose she gave it any thought."

"Accompany her? Where was she going?" Regis leaned forward in his chair, and Mikhail realized that Liriel had not given his uncle any details.

"When Dyan Ardais and I went to Elhalyn Castle on a lark, about four years ago, she had, in addition to a few elderly servants and the children, a bone-thrower, and a medium from the Dry Towns in residence." Mikhail paused, considering the oath he had given to Priscilla. She was dead, as was Ysaba, and he was not sure how binding a promise given to a ghost might be. Still, it bothered him to speak of the event. "We even attended a seance where the shade of Derik Elhalyn may or may not have been present."

"You never told me!"

"Dyan and I were sworn to secrecy, and I am not a man who breaks his word! Besides, no one knew we had gone off to visit the Elhalyn, and I thought that if I mentioned the trip, I might get into trouble. Truthfully, I think both of us wanted to forget the entire thing. It was . . . unsettling."

"But you should have . . ."

"Uncle, I do not break my word." Mikhail was surprised by the steadiness of his voice, and rather startled at the undertone of danger in it.

"I see." Regis looked thoughtful—and also a little troubled.

"At the time, it seemed like the harmless eccentricity of a lonely woman. I just put it down to the general oddness of the Elhalyn line, since I do not really believe in ghosts—even the ones at Armida." He smiled at himself, realizing that he had just said something quite contradictory. "But on that occasion, there was mention made of something called the Guardian. I remember that I would think about it from time to time, and wonder what the devil it was. If I had been wiser, a great deal of tragedy could have been avoided. I probably should have told you about the seance before I departed—but I had given my word!"

"You seem to have learned the lesson of keeping your own council all too well, Mikhail."

"I had a good teacher," he snapped back, glaring at Regis.

"He has you there," Danilo commented.

"You are enjoying my discomfiture rather a lot," Regis retorted. Though he smiled at Danilo, his words barely concealed his mild outrage.

"I have so few opportunities," murmured the paxman.

This broke the tension, and all of them laughed. When they had stopped, Regis said, "Now, go on with your tale—and leave nothing out."

Mikhail took a deep breath and began. He talked until his mouth felt dry, documenting the peculiarities, and real dangers, of the prior months, and reliving the horror of the last night at Halyn House. When he was finished, his uncle and Danilo looked at one another, and something passed between them that he could not interpret. Regis looked sad and tired, and did not move, appearing to be lost in thought.

Then he asked, "This Emelda creature did not arouse your suspicions?"

"Yes and no. I kept finding myself mentally confused, and would think she might be the cause. Then I would somehow forget. It was really quite subtle, and there were days when I walked around in a fog, but I did not know it. Liriel says I was enthralled! What I do know is that if I had gone alone, without my Guardsmen, things would have turned out very differently. She had limitations, and the greater the number of people present, the less capable she was. I have never empathized with Marguerida's overshadowing so much as I do now. It is a monstrous thing to do to anyone." He hated to admit that the little woman had managed to bewilder him for weeks. The excellent meal he had just eaten lay like lead in his stomach.

"And you had no clear idea of what was happening?"

"None. Part of that was my own stubborness, however. I was determined to complete the task you had given me, even though I never wanted the Elhalyn Regency. I just kept trudging along, like a damn fool. Marguerida commented on my general fuzziness of mind a few times, and asked if I were ill, but she didn't manage to penetrate the fog I was in. It was a very humbling experience." There. He had made a clean breast of it. Why did he feel no relief? Why did he feel that he was being tested—and failing badly?

"What was it like?"

"That is rather hard to describe. If I had a doubt—and I discovered I had a great many—it swelled up in my mind like a wet cask. It was as if she had the talent to magnify all my fears into great monsters, so I tried to keep my attention on broken windows and other physical problems instead of anything else. Those, at least, were things I could fix."

Danilo cleared his throat, and both Regis and Mikhail looked at him. They had almost forgotten his presence, so quiet had he been. "That must have been painful for you, Mikhail. And it must have been very subtle, too, for you not to have been conscious of it." There was a strain in his voice, and Mikhail knew that Danilo was remembering his early encounters with the elder Dyan Ardais, who had coerced him with the Alton Gift when Danilo had been in the Cadets.

"I alternated between thinking I was losing my mind, believing I was imagining the entire thing, and feeling worthless." The tension had returned, and he wanted to break it, but he found he dared not.

"But why didn't you contact me?" Regis sounded angry and frustrated. "I still don't understand that!"

Mikhail looked directly at his uncle, narrowing his eyes and trying to control his anger. "Whenever I thought about you, I became filled with . . . self-loathing. I felt that if I asked for help, I would have failed you. It took all my strength to send for Liriel, and I do not believe there is another person on Darkover I could have asked. Not even Marguerida. The ill service you did me, Uncle, was not in appointing me Elhalyn Regent and sending me out there, but in failing to know the circumstances completely. I don't believe you had thought it all through." The bitterness in his tone was unmistakable, and Mikhail flinched inwardly. Who was he to be telling Regis Hastur such things? He must sound like a man trying to shift blame, when clearly it was he who had failed.

"That is what I told him," Danilo commented, then turned and poured himself a goblet of firewine.

Mikhail gaped at the paxman, relief seizing him. He could feel the rigidity of his shoulders, and saw that his free hand was clenched in his lap. He made himself shrug, forcing his muscles to relax. Perhaps things were not as bad as he imagined.

Regis frowned, then shrugged. "If I did not know you were both completely loyal to me, I would feel as if I were nursing vipers at my breast. But I am wise enough to realize I made a grave mistake, and grateful that it worked out as well as it did. Now tell me more about the children." The matter was closed, and Mikhail was left feeling more than a little frustrated. But at least he was not being lectured.

"There is not a great deal I can say. Alain, the eldest, is hopeless. Any chance he had for recovery from the neglect of his upbringing was ruined by the effect of the Guardian's intrusion. Vincent, too, was injured, although I do not know how badly. He was not a wonderful person to begin with, for his mother had filled his mind with all sorts of nonsense, and he imagined he would be the Elhalyn king and, I think, thought it was a more powerful position than it actually is. He was given to violence and cruelty before the incident, and while he has become more docile since, he had some fits on the road that frightened all of us. Poor Liriel. Trapped in a small carriage with a large adolescent trying to tear out the windows. I never suspected he was Elhalyn of Elhalyn, either, and I cannot imagine who his father was, if Emun is correct. The whole situation was . . . impossible." It took an effort to remain focused on reporting, and he could feel his weariness more with each passing moment.

"Yes, I know. The healers have examined both of them, and Vincent has suffered a trauma to his brain that cannot be mended. But what of the youngest, Emun Elhalyn?"

"I don't know. It would be some years before he could assume the duties of the throne. His *laran* is an unknown quantity, and I never did have a chance to actually test any of the boys. He seemed to be ready to manifest it, for he showed some symptoms of threshold sickness, but it never really began. I think that somehow either Emelda or Priscilla prevented it, and I can only imagine what sort of damage that might have done."

Regis looked as uncomfortable as Mikhail had ever seen him. He took a little more wine, felt it loosen his tongue further, and wondered if he ought to go on. When he was young, he had been so close to his uncle that Mikhail was surprised at how he felt—the sharp criticism that hovered at the tip of his tongue. He had a second's longing for that other time, for the innocence and trust that was their past together. But now he was a man, not a boy, and he had changed. More, Mikhail realized, his uncle had changed over the years as well. They were not strangers, but they were both different people than they had been.

"Priscilla was so caught up in her plans to become immortal, she barely seemed to know the children existed, except that she believed she had to take them with her when she went to join the Guardian. I can only guess at the workings of her mind. As for Emun, if he recovers from all he has gone through, being terrorized by Vincent, manipulated by the hedge-witch, and all the rest, then it might be possible to restore the throne. But I confess I rather doubt he will."

"Why?"

"It is a feeling, nothing more." Mikhail paused, trying to put into words the sense he had about the youngest boy. "I think you might have to wait another generation, Uncle, to see your plans come to fruition. And I believe your best prospect lies with the children of Miralys or Valenta, not with Emun. Since they are Elhalyn, and have *comynara* status, any children of theirs will have the best claim to the throne."

"You understand what this means?"

They had come to the crux of the matter at last, and Mikhail did not answer immediately. He could feel Danilo observing him with his usual care, the cool objectivity that the paxman seemed to bring to every situation. "If you mean do I understand that I am going to get stuck with being more than Elhalyn Regent, yes. But I will warn you that I am not going to take kindly to it."

"Why not? You are able, sane, and you were trained to rule."
Regis was more puzzled than angry.

"And that is the problem. Do you really think that I would be able
to be a figurehead, or answer to Dani for the next ten or twenty years?
The one thing I understand at last is that I cannot do that. Let one of
my brothers do the task. It is not for me, Uncle."

"You will do as you are told."

*Bredu, you raised him to be his own man! You cannot change that—
he is! How can you ask of him that he bow to Dani?*

*Damn it! I loathe it when you are right! What a sorry mess I have
made of things.*

Mikhail was too caught up in his own emotions to really register
what he was overhearing. No—not just his own feelings, but those of
the two men in the room. He felt slightly uneasy, being a party to such
an intimate moment between the two older men. And he was surprised to find Danilo championing him. Perhaps he had not failed
after all.

"We don't have to decide anything now, do we?" Mikhail asked
the question that rose in his mind. He had an inner sense that he had
to hold back events, for his own sake, but also for Regis'. Once again,
he had a sense that his uncle was moving too quickly, for reasons that
he did not understand. More, he had the strongest feeling that it was
his duty to slow events down. For the first time in his life, Mikhail felt
almost wise. It was a peculiar sensation, not entirely unpleasant, and
different from anything he could remember.

"No, you are right," Regis admitted grudgingly. "I suppose I am
feeling my mortality, feeling the pressure of time to order things . . .
which is rather foolish. And I do so hate feeling foolish!"

Danilo, in the middle of swallowing his wine, began to laugh, then
to cough. Regis rose and banged him between the shoulder blades,
looking a little concerned and perplexed at the same time. When
Danilo had recovered his breath, he looked at Regis and shook his
head. "No one can escape being foolish from time to time."

Regis made a comical face. "Oh. And I did so hope to be the
exception!"

This set Danilo off again, and Mikhail joined in the laughter,
aware that the moment had passed, that nothing of great importance
would be decided that night. It was an enormous relief.

He could feel the division within himself, between his loyalty to
Regis, to Hastur, and his desire to pursue his own ends. Since he was
part of the power structure, he knew he was supposed to put his own

needs second to those of the Domains. That was difficult, perhaps impossible, and he admitted it to himself.

Then he saw a troubled expression on his uncle's face. "What is it?"

Regis frowned. "I am trying to escape the feeling that if I had paid more attention, had even thought of Priscilla and her children, none of this might have happened. But if I had started to meddle in her affairs, then all the other Domains would have begun to wonder if I might not try to arrange theirs. I do feel guilty, I confess."

This was too much. The firewine had relaxed him just enough to throw caution to the winds. "I like that! You would not meddle in Priscilla Elhalyn's affairs, but you seem perfectly willing to do so in mine!"

Danilo looked as if he was going to lose control again. His normally pale face became rather red, and he seemed to be having trouble with his breathing. "He is right, you know," he finally managed to get out.

"No, I don't know. What do you mean?"

"Regis, old friend, you have been cheerfully meddling in Mikhail's life for years!"

Regis glanced toward Mikhail and quirked an eyebrow. "Have I, Mik? Come, tell me all my sins." He sounded neither angry nor upset, only interested and intensely curious.

Mikhail did not reply immediately, but he noticed that his uncle had not admitted any fault. He knew that Regis was unlikely to do so. Well, he had been invited to speak his mind, and he was not going to get another opportunity soon, if he knew Regis Hastur. But he decided to choose his words with a little care. "I am not an idiot, Uncle, and your 'surprise' of Gisela and her father was not lost on me."

His uncle's expression became neutral, as if he were trying to conceal his chagrin at being caught once again trying to arrange matters for his own purposes. "I thought you would be pleased to see her— you are old friends, are you not?"

Mikhail was not surprised that Regis knew this, but he was slightly chagrined. "Yes, we were friends. But I am not the same young man I was at twenty-one, and she is not the woman she was either. I have put up with all the pretty girls you and Linnea have thrown in my path since I was old enough to notice them, and I have been polite and courteous. But I don't have a yen for Gisela any longer—and the one I had years back was mild, to say the least."

"I am sure . . ."

"I am not your pawn, Regis, and I will not become one. I would like to point out, I am not the only unmarried son of Gabriel Lanart-Alton, although I suspect you have conveniently overlooked that. Your plan is clear as glass, to bring the Aldarans back to the Council by marrying me off to Gisela. It is even a logical idea. But I think that if you introduced this idea to other members of the Council, you would find a greater opposition than mine."

Regis looked startled, then thoughtful. "What do you mean?"

Mikhail took a bit more wine and tried to order his thoughts. "Last summer, when we were riding into Thendara, I had a very useful discussion with my cousin Marguerida about the balance of power in the Domains. I was trying to explain to her why my parents were so opposed to the idea of any marriage between us." He paused and nodded. "Marguerida clarifies things with her questions. The man who has her to wife will have a wise counselor."

"She was remarkable during that uproar in the Crystal Chamber," Danilo interrupted, "and I remember thinking much the same thing at the time." He grinned at the memory. "There you were, all screaming at each other, and she managed to bring everyone to a halt by telling us we were behaving like dolts instead of intelligent men. Clarifying is the exact word."

"Yes, yes, I know that you find her a paragon among women, Danilo! Perhaps the answer is for *you* to marry her!"

Regis found himself the focus of two pairs of astonished and angry eyes, and his face flushed.

"That would certainly be a solution," Danilo drawled, "but not one to which I would agree. She fears me, less than when we first met, but still she finds me less than comfortable. More, I fear her. Even were I inclined to marry—and I am not!" There was a quiet finality in his voice. "Please, Mikhail, continue. I am very interested in your thoughts, and Marguerida's, even if Regis is too impatient to listen to them."

"That puts me in my place," Regis complained. "This meeting is not going at all the way I planned."

Mikhail had never thought of Danilo Syrtis-Ardais as a potential ally, and certainly not where it concerned Regis. He felt surprised, and more than a little warmed, at the intervention of the paxman, and shot him a look of gratitude. "Yes, I know. I am sure you expected me to bow to your wishes, to say of course I would marry Gisela, for the good of Darkover. I know that I am not a private person, that I have certain duties and responsibilities, for as long as I remain your heir in name, and also am Elhalyn Regent."

"It was only an idea," Regis muttered, looked mild daggers at both of them. "I had hoped to make the Aldarans more acceptable in our usual way, with a proper marriage. In truth, I did not expect to have them show up on the doorstep as they did—I think that the *damisela* may have persuaded her father to advance things, for I did not plan to get them down to Thendara until Midsummer. I have been in very cautious negotiations for over a year now—quite difficult, for he is a hasty man at the best of times." Regis continued, "You are not the man I sent to Halyn House, Mikhail. I will have to become accustomed to that—give me time. Your experiences have changed you, and, truthfully, I don't quite know what to make of you just now." He made a wry face. "I don't suppose an appeal to your sense of duty would work? No, I thought not. Why is it my best-laid plans seem to come to mischief? It was such a nice solution, I thought."

"Well, I did not," Danilo snapped. "How could you imagine that Mik would take to Gisela when both Lady Linnea and I have told you that it will be Marguerida or no one? Are you going deaf, or do you only take the counsel of your own mind now?"

"You are very severe, my friend, and perhaps I deserve it. Please, go on, Mikhail, and I will try to hear your words." He smiled suddenly, and the expression was charming. "And Danilo will doubtless ring a peal over my head if I don't."

Mikhail was rather stunned by this sudden turn of events. He had never imagined that Danilo disagreed with anything Regis wanted, and it gave him an insight into the complexity of their lifelong friendship. Like many others, he tended to ignore Danilo Syrtis-Ardais, to forget that he was an extremely intelligent man, with a mind of his own. Danilo's skill at effacing himself was partially to blame, since he possessed a capacity for seeming almost invisible most of the time.

"I told Marguerida that much of the history of the Domains has been about preserving a balance of power, so that no one family was too much greater than another. And since the exile of the Aldaran Domain from our councils, this balance has become more difficult to maintain. The Aldaran Domain was very powerful when they were still in the picture, and has, in some ways, become more so since they have been gone. If we are to be Seven Domains once more, instead of the Six, we must strive to maintain a good balance among the families. Otherwise, we will fall into feuding, as we did during the Hundred Kingdoms and before, and we will be easy prey for the Terranan. And to propose that I wed Gisela Aldaran would provoke the other Domains enormously. Lady Marilla Aillard, for example, would be outraged, and my father would oppose any match of that sort, because he would see it as putting much too much power into these callused hands of mine." Indeed, his hands were as rough now as any farmer's.

"How did they get into that wretched condition, Mik? I have been meaning to ask you since you arrived." Danilo's question clearly stemmed from genuine curiosity, but Mikhail knew he wanted to give Regis some time to digest what he had said.

"Oh, if you muck out the stables, haul bales of straw into the barn, carry bags of grain into the kitchen, hammer nails with workmen, and do a dozen other chores, your hands will look like this, too."

"I had no idea that the conditions at Halyn House were so dreadful."

"I didn't mind, and it gave me a sympathy with the working men I might never have realized. Actually, Danilo, I almost came to enjoy it. It was a real thing, and it had a good result. Not that I have been idle all my life, but I have been kept from doing the dirty work most of the time. Except for occasionally fighting fires, I have had it easy. Shoveling manure gives you an entirely new perspective on things."

Both Regis and Danilo roared with laughter. "I never thought to hear such words," Regis said, when he was able to control his merriment. Then he grew thoughtful. "I suppose I should have made Dani my official heir long since, and regularized the situation, shouldn't I?"

Danilo and Regis exchanged a look which Mikhail could not interpret completely. There was something sad in the eyes of both. He wondered, as he had a few times previously, if there was something he did not know about Regis' son, some flaw that would make him unsuitable. He seemed a good enough boy, except for the constant look of anxiety around his eyes, and his preference for verse over any other pursuit.

"You are going to have to pay for your impetuousness at some point, Regis. You gave an oath, and if you break it, you will lose a great deal of the trust you have built up over the years." Danilo spoke gravely, slowly, as if aware that he was treading on some dangerous ground now.

"What do you mean," Mikhail asked, very puzzled.

Regis held out his empty glass, and did not respond until Danilo had replenished it. "I promised that you would be my heir, as you know, before I found my dear Linnea and had my own children."

"I know that."

"You do and you don't. The wording of it was rather tricky, and the interpretation even more so. The way it was done, as Danilo enjoys reminding me, was hasty and ill-thought, for it says that you will be my heir no matter what. This, at least, is how Javanne sees it, and a number of others as well. This is why I have not done anything—hoping the entire matter would go away. I do not want to be remembered as Regis Oathbreaker, Mikhail. When you snarled at me that you did not break your word, it made me feel perfectly disgusted with myself."

"I'm sorry, Uncle. I had no real idea. I never meant that to happen."

"No matter. I am stuck with leaving both you and my son in this ambiguous situation, which I hoped to resolve by making you the Elhalyn Regent. Javanne nearly took my head off—she saw right through my plots, as she always does." He sighed. "Danilo told me not to do it, but I did not listen."

"Well, that clears up some of my confusion, at least. I take it that unless I fall off a cliff and break my neck, or Dani does the same, you cannot untangle this mess?"

Regis nodded, looking sad. "I have not treated you well, Mikhail, have I?"

"Yes, and no. You have been a good uncle to me, a better father to me than my own, a teacher and a guide. But what you have done to your son disturbs me much more. No wonder he always looks at me so fretfully. I am surprised he has not wished me dead—well, he likely has."

"Well, perhaps he has, and doubtless felt dreadful about it afterward, since he is a very serious boy. Too serious, I fear."

"He did not look serious when he was staring at Miralys Elhalyn, Regis—he looked dumbstruck!" Danilo smiled to himself, which gave his face an expression of foxlike cunning.

"Yes, I noticed, and felt both relieved, since he has never shown the least interest in any girl, and incredibly old! Of course, Miralys is lovely, but I think her sister the real prize."

"When I was at Halyn House, Uncle, I found myself regretting that we cannot have an Elhalyn queen instead of a king, for the girls are by far the best of Priscilla's children."

"Now, there's a thought to set the Council on its ear!"

"Why have we never had a queen, if I might ask?"

"I don't know, lad. But it goes against all tradition, and I think I have done enough untraditional things during my time for me not to wish to do another."

"What do you mean?"

"Well, appointing Herm Aldaran to the Terran House eight years ago, for instance. And allowing him to remain as Senator when Lew Alton resigned, for another."

"That was not untraditional, Regis, it was simply high-handed!"

"What a sharp tongue you have tonight, Danilo. What would you have done?"

"Nothing different, but perhaps I would have moved with more subtlety," the paxman answered, not the least disturbed.

"There is a time for subtlety, and a time for boldness—the only problem is deciding which is which." He turned back to his nephew. "So, Mikhail, it is your opinion that a match between you and Gisela Aldaran would not only be unsuitable but would create more trouble than it is worth. Perhaps you are right. Have you any ideas to propose?"

Mikhail felt his face soften into a large smile. "I can only point out again that my brothers Gabe and Rafael are unmarried, and that, since they have no claim to the throne, are both more appropriate for such a marriage."

"You seem amused by the thought."

"Well, the idea of Gabe and Gisela is pretty funny, isn't it? Not that he wouldn't be a better husband than old Bertrand was. What was *Dom* Damon thinking of, handing her off to that old sot?"

"The pickings for suitable husbands for his daughter were rather slim, I suppose, but I agree that I would not have wanted my girls to be shackled to that old fellow. I am told he did it to keep her from galloping off with some Terranan or other. I would love to know the particulars! Only good manners prevents me from inquiring. It seems there were a lot of them around, up in the Hellers, more than I realized, and some of them were quite presentable." *I don't like it either. I have let things get out of hand! Damn!*

Mikhail glared at his uncle. "Do you think we will ever be able, on Darkover, to stop treating our females like children, and allow them to choose their own lives?"

Regis looked stunned. "No, I don't, so long as there is *laran,* and we value it. I hear the voice of Marguerida Alton in your words—she has had quite an influence on you, and not completely for the best, I believe."

Stung, Mikhail felt his face redden. "She is the finest woman I have ever known, and her influence on me has been to make me look at Darkover with new eyes, to more clearly see our strengths and our weaknesses."

Regis glared at his nephew for a moment, sincerely angry. Then his face relaxed, and a wry grin stole across his lips. "Damn, but you make me feel old!"

16

Margaret woke.

For a moment, she was not sure where she was. Then the faint moan of the wind against the stone walls of her room brought her fully awake. She listened to the gusts and smelled the odor of wet snow mingled with woodsmoke and the particular scent of the silken hangings around the ceiling of the chamber. She was at Neskaya Tower, and the storm that had battered the walls for two days was passing. Margaret realized how weatherwise she had become in so brief a time, and had a pleasant sense of accomplishment. Anticipating the weather was so much easier than mastering telepathy.

She had been dreaming again. She thought she had been dreaming about the dormitories at University, but now she realized it was another place with endless corridors. Looking for something again. She sighed and turned onto one side, snuggling beneath the covers.

What had she sought? If only she could remember!

It felt as if she had been looking for something all her life, running along dark corridors and past shadowed rooms. There had been a time when those night journeys had been full of terror. Now she knew the source of those memories, and they no longer frightened her. Or, she told herself truthfully, they did not scare her quite so badly.

Istvana Ridenow, who was now her teacher as well as her friend, said she would probably never be completely free of the shadow which Ashara Alton had cast over her for so many years. She had instructed Margaret in techniques that calmed her mind, and that had helped. Still, just the thought of that terrible woman, who had enthralled her when she was a child, was enough to set her shivering. Intellectually, she knew that Ashara was no more. She herself had destroyed what remained of the Keeper months before. Emotionally, she didn't quite believe it.

Margaret Alton smelled the balsam-scented sheets and blankets that covered her body, and that other odor, the strange smell of the great matrices, charged with energy, working above her. When she looked up, she could see the swathes of silk which hung from the ceiling, now casting huge shadows in the dimness of the room. Her little harp stood in one corner of the room, and there was a holo of Lew and Dio, but beyond that, there was nothing very personal in the chamber. She had been tempted by a few things in the marketplace, where she had gone with Caitlin Leynier, but she had only bought some shawls and a set of petticoats. They were not up to Aaron's quality, and she knew she was spoiled. She could have been packed and ready to depart from Neskaya in less than an hour. Why was she so reluctant to settle in?

Maybe it was because her life had been so peripatetic before she came to Darkover. Margaret knew this facile explanation was not the real reason she was not comfortable making Neskaya her home for the foreseeable future. In spite of Istvana's efforts, and the warm welcome she had received from the others at the Tower, she remained an unenthusiastic student.

Margaret was restless, despite her efforts to be otherwise. Something deep within her knew she was not going to remain at Neskaya very long. She could not define the feeling, but she had it in her bones. It lacked the power of a foretelling, but it was strong enough to trouble her. She had not discussed her feelings with Istvana, and had done her best to conceal them. But Caitlin had asked her several times what was bothering her, and she had been forced to make up excuses that left her feeling dishonest. It was not a logical feeling, and after years of depending on logic, she felt wary of trusting it.

After six months, she felt she had spent a lifetime on Darkover, and not a very quiet one at that. No, closer to seven, she realized, and her heart pounded a bit faster. Soon Rafaella would come back and take her away to Thendara for Midwinter. It had all been arranged. If the winter storms didn't mess things up for her, she would be seeing her father soon, and Mikhail as well. Sternly, she banished her fears from her mind. The thought of him was too painful to dwell upon.

Margaret lifted her gloved hand and slid it out from beneath the covers. She held it away from her, staring at its silhouette in the dimness. The matrix hidden beneath the silk marked a division in her life, one she had not yet become reconciled to. She was still Margaret Alton, Fellow of the University. But with each day, she became more this *other* person, this Marguerida Alton. Her marred hand seemed to represent all that she had lost and gained.

It had been bad enough to find herself suddenly a telepath, but the addition of the command voice was almost more than she could stand. She had worked on it with Liriel at Arilinn, and after her adventure in the hills, it had seemed wise to ask Istvana for additional help. She had not told the *leronis* about the bandits, but she had told her about sending little Donal into the overworld. Margaret knew that Istvana was aware she was holding something back, but the empath was too tactful to press her.

It had been a good choice, for Istvana, with her well-earned reputation for innovation, had devised several useful exercises that gave Margaret a better understanding of this part of her *laran*. If only the rest of it were so easily tamed!

She lowered her arm and tucked her hand back under the covers. The remnants of the dream intruded on her musing with a rush. She had been deliberately avoiding thinking about it for several minutes. She could feel the dream, simmering like a pot of water, right at the back of her mind, getting ready to come to the boil.

What had she been looking for? The dream had gotten hazy as she became more awake, but there was a disturbing *something* that lingered, like the odor of smoke in an empty house. She hadn't been looking for something, not really. No. It was more as if someone were calling to her.

At that thought, Margaret's mind immediately went to Mikhail Hastur. He was in Thendara now, and hardly likely to be up in the middle of the night trying to reach her. He had done that occasionally while he was at Halyn House, but since his return to the city, he had only contacted her during daylight hours. Of course, he might have been dreaming about her. It would not be the first time they had trysted in a dream. That was always so sweet, so tender, that she always woke up smiling.

Well, not always tender, she admitted, feeling her face heat in the darkness. He was, after all, a man, with the healthy sexual energy that she knew men possessed. She had caught the edges of a few dreams that were so passionate, so profoundly explicit, that Margaret felt ravished when she woke. It was thrilling, but it made her squirm at the same time. She still could not bring herself to think about the actuality—the hot, sweaty, moaning event that might someday await her. All the years of overshadowing had left her with a distaste for the physical, and she was not certain she would ever overcome it.

Margaret wrenched her mind away from those memories and tried to think of something else. Poor Mikhail! He felt so dreadful about how he had handled things with Priscilla Elhalyn and her children, even though Margaret had told him that he had done the best he could. He was, she decided, a little like her father, with an overlarge sense of responsibility, and a perfectionist as well. That thought made her smile in the darkness. *How ordinary I am, to fall in love with a fellow like my father. After all the trouble I had with Lew, you would think I would have jumped at the chance to choose an ordinary man like Rafael Lanart. Not Gabe, though. There is dull, and then there is maddening; Gabriel Lanart-Alton would have driven me over the edge in a tenday.*

Margaret did not like how much she missed Mikhail, how his absence was like a hole inside of her. It made her feel powerless and out of control whenever she let herself think about him, and she hated that. All the feelings she knew she should have learned as an adolescent—the healthy, natural lust, the feeling of being madly in love with some handsome boy—had been repressed by Ashara's interference. But she could not escape the longing for his laughter, the way his eyes crinkled and the pure sound of it. And Mikhail was the only person Margaret knew that she felt she could discuss anything with—even her father was not so accessible.

Reluctantly, Margaret drew her mind away from the image of Mikhail, and tried to focus on the dream still fluttering in her mind. She had had many dreams of this sort, lots of corridors and closed doors, shadow places. Sometimes she dreamed of the dormitories at University, but other times she walked a maze which resembled Comyn Castle. She had always thought she was looking for something, though what it could be she did not know.

This dream was different. She did not feel so much that she was seeking something as that something was seeking her. Calling her *name*. Was it just some dreamer, Mikhail or another, or was it something else entirely?

At the thought of her name, Margaret Alton, she had a sense that whatever it was was no dreamer at all. Whatever it was, it felt old. No, ancient was a better term. She shivered and huddled down under her blankets, drawing them tightly around her shoulders. The thought of something ancient calling to her brought up memories of a shining chamber and Ashara Alton. Hadn't she destroyed the last remnant of that old woman in the overworld?

Her palm burned beneath the soft glove, and Margaret could feel the throbbing along the lines of energy. It was not particularly painful, but it was powerful. *Nothing is ever entirely destroyed, is it?* she thought. *I don't want to have to go back into the overworld! Not now, not ever! What do you want from me! Whoever you are, why can't you leave me alone!*

She was trembling and breathing as hard as if she had been running kilometers, not lying in her bed. Margaret tried to still her rising hysteria. It had been weeks since she'd had an attack of the terrors, and she had thought she was over them. Ashara Alton was no more, and she could not hurt her again. Tears began to spill down her face as she struggled with her fears.

There was a light tap on the door, and Margaret jumped at the sound. "What is it?" she called, her voice high and childlike.

Istvana Ridenow opened the door and entered. "That was my question. My dear child, half the technicians in the Tower are having the cobwobblies. It is fortunate we were not doing anything very vital! What's wrong?"

"Damn the Alton Gift! I didn't mean to broadcast, and you would think with all this silk around me, I couldn't! I had a dream, not a bad dream, but a rather spooky one. The dream itself was just the same old thing I've been dreaming for years. I was in a place with a lot of halls and closed doors. I've always had those, but they seem to be more frequent recently."

"Yes, I know. You told me about one or two of them. How was this one different?"

"I felt as if someone were calling me, and that made me think of . . . of her! That was what panicked me."

"There, there, *chiya*. Ashara is gone, and she can't hurt you any longer."

"Tell that to my subconscious!" The anger charged along her blood, and some of the fear dissipated. Rage helped, but she hated being angry. It was all too reminiscent of Lew Alton's inexplicable furies when she was younger, even though she never smashed dishes or roared in the night. It made her feel stupid and helpless, in spite of its cleansing qualities.

Istvana did not answer. Instead she sat down on the chair on the other side of the room and closed her eyes. Margaret waited quietly, and the remaining terror faded away. She looked at the petite woman, blonde hair now faded to silver, and a smile began to play across her mouth. She was very like Dio in appearance, and she had some of the same quality of assurance that had never failed to calm her. But it hurt to look at her, because she did not know if she would ever see Dio alive and whole again. Sometimes the physical similarity between the two Ridenow women was almost painful, but not tonight.

"Yes. You are right. Something called you. I heard it, too, though I didn't pay much attention. I think I must have assumed it was Mikhail." Istvana spoke slowly, as if still deep in thought.

"Why?" Margaret felt her cheeks flame.

"*Chiya*, all of us are aware of . . . well, it is hard to ignore how much you two care for one another. It's very sweet, actually. I mean, ordinarily young love is rather like watching goats in spring, which is amusing but a little earthy. But your dream meetings with Mikhail are gentle and quite tender. Restrained, for the most part." She bent her head toward her chest for a moment, and Margaret knew that Istvana had caught the fringes of those other dreams, the ones that were close to pornographic.

"Oh, damn! I was afraid I was shouting lust all over the Tower."

Istvana lifted her head and laughed so hard her eyes began to tear. "I'm sorry, Marguerida. It is not kind of me to laugh," she said, when she had recovered her breath. "Outright lust would be easier to deal with, actually. But your longing is like an ache. Do you think your Uncle Gabriel will ever give in?"

"He is a very stubborn man."

"I've known mules with nicer dispositions," the *leronis* agreed dryly.

Dom Gabriel and Istvana had nearly come to blows over Marguerida months earlier, at Castle Ardais. She seemed to cause nothing but trouble, wherever she went. She wished she could run away, escape the whole, incredible mess. But there was almost three feet of snow around the Tower at the moment—they insisted this was a mild fall, and that it was sure to be an easy winter! The trails in the hills were already difficult and would soon be impossible. Besides, where would she go? To the moon?

That thought made Margaret chuckle slightly, and she felt better. "When my father came back to Darkover, I thought everything would get settled, but things still seem to be in a muddle, don't they? And I cannot seem to mend them, no matter how much time I spend thinking up solutions. I suppose it is like moving mountains—a nice metaphor, but easier said than done."

"Not a complete muddle, but . . . Let's get back to that calling. I think it is very important. I thought it was Mikhail, which is perhaps why I did not give it any attention until you became agitated, but now I recall it was not his voice I heard. It was a man, though, not a woman, so you can stop worrying about Ashara."

"Yes, you are right. It was a deep voice—basso profundo, not a light tenor like Mik's. It felt like the earth rumbling, almost. And no one I know has that sort of voice. Believe me, I know voices. Sometimes I wish I was back running around recording them and listening to old songs instead of trying to control my Gifts. I'm sorry. Everyone has been very patient with me, very understanding and all. But I still feel trapped." Margaret paused. "And when I have these dreams about halls and corridors and mazes, it is worse. I didn't realize that until I said it."

"Mazes? You mentioned that before—when you were recovering from the threshold sickness. I had forgotten it until now."

"So had I—and I was perfectly happy not to remember it! There are a lot of things I would be thrilled never to think about again!"

"Tell me about it again, please." Istvana settled back into the chair, drawing her garments around her more closely. It was chilly in the room, though not really cold, for the Tower was well heated. Margaret hauled a knitted shawl out of the drawer beside her bed and tossed it to the Keeper, then got out another for herself. She had about six now, soft wools, or wool combined with fine silk, in the green or russet colors she preferred, and sometimes she wore several at once.

Once she had drawn the shawl around her shoulders, and Istvana had done the same, Marguerida frowned. "The first time I went to Comyn Castle, I mean when Rafe Scott escorted me there, not when I was a little girl, I had this sense that I could see this labyrinth running through the place. I thought I was imagining it, but later I found out there is a kind of maze within the Castle. I guess it is a piece of Ashara's memory or something, because I haven't been able to find out very much about it. All I know is that I could find my way around Comyn Castle blindfolded if I needed to."

"Interesting. I have heard of it, but like you I haven't discovered much real information. Were you in that maze in this dream?"

"No, I wasn't. But wherever I was, it was similar. Did the architect of Comyn Castle build anything else?"

Istvana laughed again. "Architect? If there was one, his name is long gone. To my knowledge, the original Comyn Castle was built over a long period, two or three generations. Like most structures on

Darkover, it just grew and grew. And the building you are familiar with is a much more recent overlay."

"I had guessed as much. Who would know?"

"There might be some record of the history of the Castle in Nevarsin, Marguerida. The *cristoforos* have a lot of old texts."

"Moldering in the damp, no doubt," she said sourly.

"Now, now. The monks at Nevarsin take very good care of their books. Wait! Something is nagging at me here. My brain is full of stories tonight. Dancing stones. Something about dancing stones. Ah! Now I remember. It was something my old nursemaid told me, years and years ago, to keep me quiet when I was cranky. That is probably why I didn't recall it sooner. No one wants to remember a bad mood, do they? She told me about how the Altons raised Comyn Castle in one night by making the stones dance. That's nonsense, of course— the single night business. But she was quite definite that it was built by the Altons."

"You mean I may have some sort of . . . blood memory?"

"Well, it does seem far-fetched, when you put it like that."

Margaret nibbled on her lower lip and realized she was hungry. She felt as if she spent altogether too much time eating since she'd come to Darkover, but she knew her body was not yet accustomed to the rigors of the frigid climate or the physical taxation of telepathy. The sound of the wind outside made her yearn for the warmth of Thetis, and the smell of the ocean. Snow there was exotic, not commonplace. More, most of the planets she had visited with Ivor had been tropical or at least temporate. Darkover was, in her opinion, quite intemperate, weatherwise, and she wondered if she would ever adjust. She told her stomach to be quiet, because she could sense a question forming that was important. "What is memory?"

Istvana looked at her, her pale eyes a little confused. "Why, what we remember, of course."

"But, where does memory come from? I mean, it's part of our bodies, and therefore it is physiological. And if Terranan scientists are correct, then our cells 'remember' things—how to reproduce themselves, and how to repair themselves, too. Who knows what else they might be able to recall?" She hesitated, overwhelmed by the task of discussing DNA in *casta*. Even though they had been breeding for *laran* for centuries, the Darkovans did not seem to have ever developed a proper vocabulary for describing genetics." She paused, braced herself, and went on. "I suspect that the reason I can see the maze in Comyn Castle is some leftover from Ashara, or from one of the Keepers she overshadowed. That, at least, is an idea I can entertain without worrying about my sanity."

"You have grown enormously since I first met you at Castle Ardais, Marguerida. I never thought to hear you speak her name without a quiver in your voice."

"It is not easy, believe me!" She tried to conceal her intense pleasure in this praise, and her hunger for more. Marguerida thought she might be able to fill her belly to satiation, but her need for approval would remain for the rest of her life. "I still feel like a baby a lot of the time."

"We all do. I think we never outgrow our sense of not knowing, and that makes us feel childish. No matter how much we learn, there is always more. Tell me, other than hearing your name spoken by an unknown voice, do you remember anything more?"

"There was something else, something that was like a deep intonation. It almost sounded like a . . . a humming sound."

"A hum?"

Margaret frowned again and focused her mind on the fragment of sound, elusive and maddening. It was a word, she was sure of that. Her palm began to warm beneath the glove, the lines of energy pulsing. She could almost feel the word in her mouth, and she ran through sounds. Ah, bah, dah, fah, gah . . . "Hah!"

"Hah? You know what you heard?"

"No. The sound starts with a 'ha' noise. Like Hastur, but it wasn't that. Not 'haa' as in Hastur, but more like 'hah,' a longish sound. I think I would have remembered Hastur without any problem. The rest of the word is being very elusive."

Istvana sighed. "I hate it when my mind does that. Something is right there, on the tip of my tongue, and I can't . . ."

"Shh!" Margaret felt her face flame again. How rude, hushing the *leronis!* But something Istvana had just said . . . what was it? She tried to remember the precise words the *leronis* had used. The tip of the tongue! That was it! She ran her tongue against her upper teeth, wiggling it. What sounds were made with the tip of the tongue? "Lee."

"What?"

"The voice said . . . *Hali.* That's it!" A flush of relief flooded her tense shoulders.

"Hali? You mean the lake on the way to Thendara? Strange place. It always gives me the shivers."

"No, not the lake. I never told you about the trip from Armida to Thendara, did I?" She took in Istvana's rather blank expression. "I was riding with Uncle Jeff, and suddenly I pointed and asked if that tower I saw was Arilinn. He got the strangest expression and told me no, it wasn't, and that there was nothing there but the ruins of Hali Tower. It was real to my eye, at that moment, and I felt as though I could go up and knock on the door. In fact, I felt I almost *had* to. The feeling didn't last very long, and I almost forgot about it later. I mean, it wasn't anything like the compulsions that . . . Ashara put on me." Margaret shuddered all over. "I asked Jeff what would happen if I did enter it, and he said he didn't know, and then we started talking about time and space and a lot of other things."

Istvana looked rather puzzled. "Marguerida, there hasn't been a tower there for hundreds of years. There's only a ruin. It must have been a trick of the light. Lake Hali . . ."

"Mikhail saw it, too!"

"Did he? Or did he merely see the image in your mind? The power of suggestion is very strong between two . . ."

"He believed he saw the Hali Tower, and he also felt the same compulsion to go there I did. I remember thinking at the time that some day I would go back there and . . ."

"And what?"

"I don't know. When I saw it, and Jeff and I talked about time, he mentioned something called Time Search."

Now Istvana was openly concerned, and she did not try to conceal it. "Time Search! Marguerida, you are much too inexperienced to even consider such . . . I know that Damon Ridenow—the older one, not Jeff—did it once, but he was very skilled and had studied for years. Even so, it nearly killed him! Please, put this idea from your mind."

Margaret could sense the deep distress of the *leronis,* and she did not wish to cause her more. *How the hell do I put something out of my mind? No one can do that—the more you try not to think about it, the more it intrudes on your brain.* She shrugged and changed the subject. She knew Istvana well enough now that she was aware that it was useless to argue with her when she had decided something. Beneath all her empathy and kindness, she was a very determined woman. "I'm hungry."

Istvana looked relieved. "You are always hungry. I know that matrix work gives a healthy appetite, but you are the best trencherwoman I have ever seen. I don't know how you keep your figure. If I ate as often as you do, I would burst my seams. There's some soup in the kitchen. Come along."

Margaret got out of the bed and put on a thick overrobe, focusing her mind on the gentle rumble of her belly. She knew she was dissembling, and she did not like herself for it. She would not forget the dream, or the voice that called to her. But she could not do anything about it now, except push it down into the depths of her mind. After all—it was only a dream.

An hour later, after two bowls of thick soup and several slabs of bread slathered with butter and honey, Margaret felt replete and much less anxious. She left Istvana and returned to her room. As soon as she closed the door, she felt her hand begin to throb and an itching sensation started above her eyes. Over the past few months she had learned some control over her waking mind; recently, when someone tried to reach her through it, she got the itching. It was not pleasant, but at least it caught her attention.

Margaret sat down in the chair and leaned back, letting her careful control relax a little. After just a few seconds, the itching stopped, and she felt a familiar warmth steal into her body. Sometimes she could not immediately tell one mind from another, but Mikhail's was one she could always recognize instantly.

What are you doing up at this hour, Mik? The silk hangings in her room made it a little difficult to "hear" him, but she was too languid from her meal to move to another room in the Tower just now.

I wish I knew. Longing for you and feeling very frustrated I suppose.

Oh, Mik! Margaret knew that something was bothering him, something that had been fretting his mind since he returned to Thendara, and she wondered what it was. She remembered how he had never really told her what was going on at Halyn House until it was all over, and felt mildly troubled by this exclusion. She had thought she and Mikhail could talk about anything! But it was likely something to do with the Elhalyn children, and he probably did not think she was interested.

I just love it when you go all maidenly on me.

I know. It puffs up your male ego, doesn't it?

Don't be a cat! How are you?

Much the same. I keep learning and learning and finding out how little I know. And dreaming, too. Speaking of dreams, you really must stop yearning after me. People are beginning to talk!

Let them. Besides, I can't help it. I never wanted to be Romeo, but between my father and yours—

I know, I know. At least we aren't young and stupid, and we won't take poison or anything.

No, if I were going to use poison, it would not be on myself. But speaking of dreams, I had one a couple of nights ago.

Yes, I remember.

Not that one, you wicked woman. Occasionally I do dream about something other than you. And this one was peculiar, though at the time I didn't think about it very much. Since I came back to Thendara, there has been so much going on that a dream didn't have much priority. But I had it again tonight, oh, maybe two hours ago. Maybe it wasn't the same dream, but . . . there was this voice both times.

Deep, resonant, like the earth groaning?

Yes. How did you . . .

I heard it, too. I heard my name—or a version of it. Let me think here. Ah, yes, It called to "Margarethe."

Uh-huh. I heard "Mikhalangelo" in my dream, not Mikhail. The pronunciation was strange.

Well, you are one of the Lanart Angels. Did you hear anything else?

Just one word—Midwinter.

Midwinter? Margaret was surprised by this, and mildly disappointed, for she had expected Mikhail to tell her he had heard Hali. It was as if they had each been given parts of a puzzle, as if each of them had a piece, but had to join together to solve it. *Is there anything special about Midwinter? I don't know enough about Darkovan customs yet.*

It's a festival time, but the only thing I can think of that is special about the coming one is that the four moons of Darkover will all be visible—well, not really, since it tends to be even cloudier in winter than in summer—at the same time on Midwinter Eve.

How often do the moons appear at one time, Mik? Astronomy was a mystery to her, and Margaret knew it. She understood music, but thinking in three dimensions was beyond her.

Only a couple of times a generation, but it hasn't happened at Midwinter in hundreds of years. The street-corner fortunetellers are all abuzz with it, or I wouldn't have known at all. Priscilla Elhalyn was very fond of fortune tellers, and I suppose that made me more aware of the gossip than I would have been before. His mental voice had a grim quality now.

My poor Mik! If only . . .

If only Uncle Regis hadn't stuck me with the Regency.

Listen, Mik, we had similar dreams, but in mine I didn't hear a word about Midwinter.

What did you hear then?

Hali.

There was a sound in her mind, a kind of mental sigh. *I should have guessed, shouldn't I? We both knew when we saw the Tower that someday we were going there.*

Mik, no one is going to let us go running off into a ghost of a Tower, and you know it! You are just looking for any excuse to get away from the mess that . . . that your uncle put you in. She hated criticizing Regis Hastur, even slightly, but sometimes she could not help herself. And, at the same time, she sensed that Mikhail was disturbed about something else.

Of course I am! But that is neither here nor there. Do you really think we have any choice? Use your Aldaran Gift and tell me we don't do this thing, and I swear I'll never mention it again.

I don't know if I can, Mik. The Alton Gift is fairly straightforward. I can turn it off and on and either force rapport or not, as I choose. But the Aldaran Gift of foresight . . . that's a very different kettle of fish. It's random. I don't have much control over it yet. I can't just . . . access it like a computer or something.

No, I suppose not. I just remember how you saw Ariel's unborn daughter back at Armida the day that . . .

The day that Domenic had his accident. It is all right to say it. The grief of memory blossomed in her mind. *I was almost out of my mind, between Gabe's demanding that I marry him instantly and the rest. I've never had a vision that strong again, and frankly, I would be glad if I never did.*

I can understand that. I suppose it doesn't matter—but the dream had such urgency!

Suddenly Margaret did not want to talk about the dream any longer, and she changed the subject. *How are the Elhellions faring in Thendara?*

Alain and Vincent have been removed to Arilinn, where they are being looked after properly. I confess I am greatly relieved to be free of that particular responsibility. Emun seems to be fine—he has gained a few pounds and no longer looks like a ghost. I just wish I felt more confident of him. And the girls are wonderful. Young Dani has fallen completely in love with Miralys, and Lady Linnea is watching them as if they were a pair of breeding hawks. Valenta, on the other hand, regards me as the paragon of manly virtues. I must warn you, dearest, that she will likely be quite rude to you when you arrive here, seeing you as her rival.

It is a pity you cannot marry her, and keep me for a barragana.

Marguerida! What a shocking thing. I love it when you say unseemly things.

I know you do—which just encourages me! We must just wait, I suppose. I will be in Thendara soon.

Not soon enough for me! Good night.

Sleep well, Mikhail, with no more dreams to trouble you.

Mikhail vanished from her mind, leaving only the tenderness of his parting thought. She sat and savored it for a long time, knowing that it might be all she ever had of Mikhail Hastur. And if Neskaya did not become snowbound, she would be with him soon.

The room was cold now, and growing colder by the minute. Margaret noticed this and realized it was not that the temperature was falling, but that something was chilling her down to the bone. It was only a dream, and she did not have to think about it. But the sense of destiny gripped her in spite of her efforts to dislodge it.

"Hali at Midwinter," she whispered.

17

Winter arrived in Thendara on Mikhail's heels, and kept him confined in Comyn Castle for weeks. At first he had not minded, glad to be in a warm bedchamber, with good meals cooked and served at regular intervals, and the children seen to by people more skilled than himself. But after the dream he seemed to have shared with Marguerida, he became restless and irritable. What did it mean? And who had called to him?

Mikhail discovered that his recent experiences at Halyn House had left him with a powerful distaste for the supernatural, and at the same time, a great curiosity about it. The voice in the dream was all too reminiscent of the bellowing of the Guardian, roaring in his mind. He had a sinking feeling that he did not have a choice—something was going to happen whether he wanted it or not.

With time on his hands, Mikhail had consulted Yoris MacEvers, the archivist at Comyn Castle and had read as much as he could about Hali Tower before it was destroyed. It was a frustrating search, for so much had been lost during the centuries, and what there was seemed vague and not terribly useful. There might be more at Arilinn, but he did not feel he could ride off, even if the weather had allowed it, leaving Regis with a castle full of Aldarans and small children.

Everyone in the snow-bound castle was irritable, except the Elhalyn children, who were settling in nicely. And Mikhail knew the situation would not improve when his parents arrived. After several days of being on his best behavior, playing chess with Gisela and listening to *Dom* Damon's opinions on seemingly everything, he sank into a foul mood. Mikhail did not let it show, but it wore him down, to smile and smile, when he just wanted to be left alone.

The more time he spent with *Dom* Damon, the more Mikhail wondered at his uncle's wisdom in suggesting that the Aldarans should return to Darkovan society. It was obvious that the old fellow had some ideas that would infuriate his father and other conservatives, that he was ambitious for power, and frustrated by the long exile of his family. Unlike his son Robert, who had not yet arrived in Thendara, he seemed to lack patience.

It was clear, as well, that *Dom* Damon assumed that there would be a marriage between Mikhail and Gisela in the near future. Since his meeting with Regis, Mikhail had felt constrained to hold his tongue. He did not say that he would refuse such an alliance, since he knew that his uncle wanted to keep Damon happy. And there was no polite way he could tell Gisela to abandon any hopes she might hold. It was hard enough to endure her attentions as it was.

One evening, in his cups, *Dom* Damon had expressed his feelings about Regis, and they were not particularly respectful. Mikhail wondered if Regis knew how Lord Aldaran felt about him. Since very little that went on in Comyn Castle escaped his uncle's notice, he thought he must. He could only hope Regis was not bothered by it.

Gisela had brought both of her children with her on the trip to Thendara, and while the older boy languished in the Terran Medical Center, the younger one was at Comyn Castle. For several days, Mikhail had not seen the boy, but when he did, one afternoon, he found that little Rakhal was at the sticky stage of his development. How little Rakhal managed this fresh from his bath was a complete mystery to Mikhail. But with his new interest in parenting, Mikhail allowed the child to sit on his lap, pat his face, and discourse on such matters as appealed to his young mind.

He found that Gisela shrank away from Rakhal, and was impatient with him. It was obvious to him that she did not not like the child, or perhaps that she did not like children in general. Mikhail tried to be charitable, but his recent memories of Priscilla Elhalyn's neglect of her children, had made him acutely sensitive on this subject. He put Gisela's behavior down to an aversion for her dead husband, and bit his tongue when she pulled away from the grubby but sweet little boy.

For his own part, Mikhail spent as much time as he could with the youngest Elhalyns, who were now healthier and less anxious. One afternoon he took Emun and his sisters on a tour of Comyn Castle—they did not cover half of it before they were exhausted—and he was surprised at the questions they asked him. Some he could not answer, such as who had built the great, white pile. Others he could, and did. Emun remained nervous and strained, jumping at shadows and loud noises. Mikhail swallowed the despair that rose in his throat whenever he looked at the lad.

It was with great relief when he awoke to see just a hint of sun breaking through the clouds one morning. Mikhail pushed aside his blankets, dressed hastily, and headed for the stables without bothering with breakfast. A good ride would blow the cobwebs out of his mind, stretch his legs, and get him away from all the intrigues of the Castle.

As he strode out onto the snowy steps leading to the Stable Court, Mikhail drew a deep breath of clean air, and felt its crispness on his cheeks. Then he walked down the stairs and started across the cobbles.

Mikhail saw a figure, dressed for riding, standing on the cobblestones, and his heart sank. Gisela had clearly had the same thought as he, or perhaps anticipated his decision. She had her back to him, and he almost turned around and went back inside, to hide in the entry until she left. Instead, he bit back his irritation. It was too beautiful a morning to waste indoors. He sighed as a groom led a horse out of the stables for her, a little dun mare with white fetlocks. There was a sidesaddle perched on the horse's back, and as he approached, the groom helped her up into it.

Gisela settled herself into place, saw him, and gave him one of her sparkling glances. He had been pursued by women most of his life, but none, he decided, was more determined than this one. Mikhail's heart sank into his sturdy boots; there was no way to avoid accompanying her now.

He paused and studied her for a moment, trying to delay the inevitable. Gisela was wearing a heavy woolen garment of darkest green, and a small and impractical hat with a hawk's feather in it, rose kid gloves so thin they were almost a second skin, and riding boots in the blue favored in the Hellers and the Dry Towns. She made a very fetching picture, he admitted, but the blue boots clashed with the green of her riding clothes. And the gloves on her hands reminded him of Marguerida's, always clad in silken mitts, even when they caressed the strings of her harp. It made his blood run hot to think about those hands, and he forced himself to shut away the extremely erotic images.

"I see I am not the only one ready for a ride," she said, smiling at him. "Another day of listening to Rakhal prattle and I should have gone mad."

Mikhail quelled his rising annoyance, and only said, "Good morning, Gisela."

At that moment the morning sun touched her, gilding her form with radiance. She looked every inch a lady, commanding and sure of her place. She really was a most attractive woman, and he liked her, but she did not move his heart at all. That belonged to a pair of golden eyes, not green ones. Mikhail signaled the groom, and the man vanished into the darkness of the stables to saddle his big bay.

"Yes, it is a good morning! Just smell the air! There isn't a hint of snow in it for the moment!" She seemed very happy, more carefree than she had been recently. There was a confidence in her posture that had not been present before, and he had a mild frisson of unease.

"Then you will be able to go to the Medical Center and see how your son is faring, won't you?"

Gisela gazed down at him with utter incomprehension, as if he had just suggested that she ride naked through the streets of the city. Then she recovered herself slightly. "Uh, yes, of course. Not today, though. Tomorrow perhaps. We might go together?"

Before Mikhail could reply, there was a flutter of wings and the now familiar caw of his avian friend. The sea crow alighted on Mikhail's shoulder, and began to offer the noises that he thought of as birdly gossip. Mikhail had taken to keeping a window in his bedroom open a bit, and the crow had visited him there several times, always announcing himself with similar sounds. It made his room chilly, but Mikhail found he was actually fond of the crow, and flattered by its attention and devotion.

The bird shifted from foot to foot, fluttered its wings, and looked at him with great red eyes. Mikhail extended his arm carefully, and the crow scooted down until it stood on his wrist as a hawk might. "Have they been treating you well?" he asked the bird. He got a rough reply and decided that the crow found the pickings in Thendara to its taste.

"Aren't you afraid it will peck your eyes?" Gisela asked him, sounding a little uneasy.

"No, I am not." Mikhail could hear the impatience in his voice, and wished he had better control. More, Mikhail felt that he was in an intolerable situation, and he resented it deeply. By the time the groom finally brought out his horse, his good mood was gone, and he mounted with an angry jerk. The sea crow squawked in protest, flew away, circled, and returned to settle on the pommel once he was mounted.

"It is going to come with us?" Gisela asked. Her green eyes were a little wide, and her sultry voice was higher than usual.

"Oh, yes. It seems to like my company. I leave a window open in my room when the wind is not blowing too much, and it comes and tells me things. I do wish I spoke bird, for I am sure he knows all the secrets of Thendara by now." He turned his horse's head and started for the street.

Gisela drew abreast of him, eyeing the crow with distaste. "It does not seem a proper bird for a lord, or a future king," she commented dryly. Mikhail looked at her, feeling uneasy at her tone, and then they rode in silence for a time. The narrow streets of Thendara had been cleared of snow by householders and merchants, though there was a little ice in places. They rode through a pleasant bustle of activity, as shutters were flung open and merchandise brought out. He heard voices, gossiping and bargaining, a comforting racket, so different from the undercurrents at the Castle. A few people watched the riders curiously, and at least two waved, recognizing Mikhail.

"You do not seem very much like the man who came to us all those years ago, Mik."

"Don't I? In what way do you find me different?"

"You were never aloof with me then." She sounded as if she were deeply puzzled, and a little hurt.

"Forgive me if I have seemed distant, Giz. I have had a great deal on my mind recently."

"Oh, pooh! That is what people say when they do not wish to be honest. Don't you like me any longer?"

"Certainly I like you! What a silly thing to say!" It was true and untrue at the same time, he decided. He found Gisela Aldaran a charming companion, for she was quick-witted and frequently bawdy. But there were so many things he could not say, all lying thickly on his silent tongue, bitter and revolting.

Instead of concentrating on his feelings of ill-usage, he thought about her comment. Was he different? Mikhail did not feel himself to be so, but he knew that other people he was close to were different than they had been ten years before. Did he see them with new eyes, or were they actually changed? Marguerida insisted that Lew was quite an altered man from the one she had known as a child, and he felt the same way, to a lesser degree, about both Regis and Javanne.

Dom Gabriel, on the other hand, seemed the same as before, perhaps a little more crochety and given to temper.

But if he had changed, what had caused it? In one way Mikhail felt that his entire life had been fairly ordinary—unless he counted the events at Halyn House, or following Marguerida into the overworld on two occasions. Except for getting married, for the most part he had done what had been expected of him.

Marguerida said he had a curious mind, contrasting him to his father, whom she dismissed as having a closed one. Maybe that was it. He was interested in many things, from why the Terranan did things the way they did, to how Darkover might use technology without losing its singular identity. Perhaps it had been mucking out the Halyn House stables that had made him different. It had certainly given him a fresh respect for all the folk who labored in the fields and crofts, and enabled him to live a life of ease.

Gisela leaned out of the saddle and extended a hand as if to take his wrist. She had an expression on her face which he found too intimate. The crow took immediate exception to her movement, flaring its wings, and poking its sharp bill at her. The woman yelped and snatched her hand back, nearly overbalancing in the side-saddle. She regained her seat and glared at both the man and the bird. "Mik, that crow is a disgusting creature. They are birds of ill-omen, you know! Send it away!"

"I know the crows in the Hellers are thought to be such, but I am surprised to hear such silly superstitions from you. You have a good mind, and are educated. Besides, this is a sea crow, and that is quite a different matter." Mikhail had never been so grateful for a chaperon in his life. As long as they could keep discussing the bird, they would not be able to talk about more serious things. "This fine fellow greeted me when I arrived at Halyn House, probably saved me from a hard knock on the head at the quintain, and has chosen to accompany me far from its natural home. I am sure he must be the king of his kind, and that some upstart crow has now taken his position."

Almost as if it understood these words, the crow made a rough comment. He gave Mikhail a beady glare, as if to say, "I will deal with any interloper." It was serious and comical all at the same time, and Mikhail chuckled, his earlier mood restored.

They had ridden to the gate of the North Road now, and found it abustle with early morning traffic. There were many carts coming into the city with loads of straw, grain, root vegetables, and cages full of plump fowl. He spotted a Travelers wagon, gaily painted and accompanied by garishly dressed folk. There were pictures of puppets on its sides, and Mikhail grinned. It had been some time since he had seen one of the shows.

The Travelers were dressed in motley colors, their clothing torn to reveal underlayers, a very distinctive form of dress. They came to Thendara during the Midsummer and Midwinter Festivals, and the rest of the time they drove around the countryside, offering their entertainments in the smaller cities, and at places like Armida. His father did not approve of them, saying quite truthfully, that they were not respectable folk. But Mikhail found their little plays, which satirized lord and farmer with equal generosity, very amusing.

He had wondered about them a few times, since they were a relatively recent development. When he had been a lad, all entertainers were local folk, and then, when he had been eight or nine, if he remembered rightly, he had seen the first painted wagon, full of these cheerful people, arrive at Comyn Castle one summer day. It was soon after the World Wreckers, and they had been greeted—like all strangers—with suspicion. But they seemed harmless enough, and he really enjoyed their acrobatics, juggling, and the totally irreverent comedies they performed.

Mikhail wondered if Marguerida knew about the Travelers, and made a mental note to tell her about them. She would be very interested, as she seemed to be in all things. He was so deep in his thoughts that he nearly forgot about Gisela, who had been silent since the crow startled her. Mikhail noticed a train of heavily laden mules accompanied by some Dry Towners and a quartet of Renunciate guides, struggling to get through the jam of carts and animals that cluttered the road. Then he returned to the present, seeing a very familiar profile, a flutter of copper-colored curls under a knitted cap, a short, upturned nose, and a firm jaw.

"Rafaella n'ha Liriel!" He shouted across the noise of the throng, and she looked up, then smiled at him.

"*Dom* Mikhail!" She rode toward him, her smile increasing. "Well met! What a lovely surprise. I did not know you had come back to Thendara—but then I have been off in the west for the past month." She drew abreast of him, reined her horse to a halt, and patted its neck.

"It is wonderful to see you, Rafaella. How long has it been?"

"Oh, ages and ages. I have been more busy this season than I was in the last three years, dashing here and there with merchants, who all seem determined to come to Thendara or depart it at the same moment. My, what a handsome bird!" She chuckled. "I must say, you make a very odd appearance, with a crow on your pommel. Are you getting eccentric?"

Gisela cleared her throat in a very ladylike but determined way, and Mikhail felt his cheeks begin to warm with blush. He was so eager to see Rafaella that he had ignored her. "Not that, I trust, but I do seem to be forgetting my manners. Blame it on such a lovely morning! Much too lovely for formalities. Rafaella, this is the *Domna* Gisela Aldaran. Gisela, my friend, Rafaella n'ha Liriel."

"A pleasure, *domna.*" The Renunciate bobbed her head a little, but the expression on her face spoke volumes. He was very grateful that Marguerida's friend was so discreet, and gave her a little smile.

"The pleasure is mine," Gisela responded, not sounding at all pleased.

He could see the question in Rafaella's eyes. But he said nothing. Still, he felt very embarrassed, as if he had been caught doing something naughty, and he wished Gisela to one of the lesser of Zandru's hells. Why were things so complicated? Why hadn't Gisela remained indoors and let him ride in peace? Mikhail began to feel very put upon and aggrieved, but it was such a ridiculous feeling that after a second he let it go.

"Did Marguerida tell you about the bandits?" Rafaella asked, quite unaware of the strain between Gisela and Mikhail.

"Bandits?"

"Ah, she didn't." For a moment, Rafaella's face looked perturbed, then slightly embarrassed, for her pale cheeks reddened. "I expect she thought you would worry, though why anyone worries about things which have already happened has always been something of a mystery to me. Why bother thinking that you might have frozen to death in the storm, when the storm is passed, and you are not dead?"

"You are wise beyond your years, Rafaella. But—what bandits?"

"When we were on the way to Neskaya, our camp was attacked in the night by some scum that ought to have known better. They did manage to surprise us, and for a short time had the upper hand. But Marguerida . . . oh, blast! I have to catch up with my merchants. Besides, it is her tale, and I should not tell it without her leave. I will be in Thendara for a day or two before I leave again—you know where to find me." She put her heels into the horse's flanks and trotted away.

They picked their way through the traffic in silence, for the racket of voices, carts, and horses made conversation difficult. At last they left the noise behind, and the road, snow-packed blown to a hard, flat surface from all the feet and hooves that had trod it, lay empty before them.

"You seem to have some odd friends, Mik. First a crow, and now an Amazon! I was very embarrassed when you called out to her—what will people think?"

"I imagine they will think that I know her. It is nothing for you to be embarrassed about. You are becoming conventional, Giz. Rather like my mother," he added unkindly.

"I take it that she meant Marguerida Alton," Gisela began, ignoring his comments, her sensuous voice deep and a little dangerous. "Is it true about her, what I heard?"

"I cannot imagine, since I do not know what that might be." His voice was cold and formal, in unconscious imitation of Danilo Syrtis-Ardais who, when he chose, could cut one to the quick with only a few words.

"That she is deformed!"

Mikhail turned and looked at his companion with shock. "Deformed. Certainly not!" He knew the horror with which most Darkovans regarded any physical infirmity, but he expected better of Gisela.

"Then why does she conceal her hands, if she is not hiding some ugly malformation?"

"You have been listening to servants, Giz, and you know how they always get things wrong or exaggerate them." He was not about to talk about Marguerida's shadow matrix in the middle of the road, least of all with Gisela Aldaran.

"What is she hiding?"

Mikhail pursed his lips. "That is not a matter I feel free to discuss," he answered, drawing his horse's head apart from hers a little, trying to put some distance between them.

Gisela was having none of that. She reined her horse closer to him and demanded, "Do you care for her?"

"Again, that is not a topic for conversation."

"Then you do! I had heard some gossip, but I did not believe it. And, it is a pity that you will never be able to . . ."

"Gisela, stop, before you say something regrettable! This is no business of yours!"

"Oh, but it is, and you are a fool if you cannot realize it. Surely you cannot think you can marry her! She is the Alton heiress, and must marry lower than herself." There was a bitterness in her voice that stung him. "I understand these things, you see, for I have spent my whole life thinking about them."

"I said I did not want to talk about it, Giz!"

"No, Mikhail! There are breaches to be healed, and the best way to accomplish that is between you and me. Besides, I have already made up my mind to have you, and I always get my way. Always!"

"If you actually believe that, then you are a greater fool than I ever—" He stopped speaking before he said something irrevocable. *She sounds very much like Gabe,* he thought, finding a sudden glint of humor in the whole unpleasant situation. "Now stop behaving like a spoiled child and ruining a very nice ride."

Gisela turned her horse's head around abruptly, coming so close to Mikhail's horse that the crow flared its wings with alarm. She glared at him as she announced, "I have dreamed of having you since we first met, and I will have my way! More, I have the Aldaran Gift, and I have seen that I will marry a Hastur!" Despite the passion in her voice, Mikhail sensed an undertone of doubt.

Gisela gave her horse a brisk blow with her quirt, and the little mare started, then began to trot back toward the city gates. He was stunned at first, then very annoyed at not having gotten the last word. He felt chilled under his warm cloak.

Mikhail sat on his horse, knowing he should turn and follow her. But he was too angry. He reflected that she reminded him very much of Javanne when she was in a determined mood, and realized that he had not noticed that quality in her before.

Marry a Hastur? Not this Hastur, if he could help it! Besides, the Comyn Council would never agree. The future was not set in stone, but was something more fluid than he had ever imagined. He could have died at Halyn House, or broken his neck on the road, which would have put an end to all his futures. He spent a pleasant moment deciding which of his brothers might make the supreme sacrifice of taking Gisela to wife, and the start of a smile appeared on the corners of his mouth.

Calmer now, satisfied that he had handled Gisela as well as he could, Mikhail put his knees into Charger, and started up the North Road, toward the ruins of Hali, and beyond it, to Neskaya, where Marguerida was. If he followed his heart, he could be with her in five or six days of hard riding. But duty called, and after an hour, he reined in the big bay, and turned back toward Thendara.

18

Margaret Alton and Rafaella n'ha Liriel in the company of two Guardsmen entered Thendara just ahead of a small storm front. It had been at their backs for two days, threatening, but never actually reaching them. She was grateful for that, to all the many gods whose names she knew, even if she did not believe in every one of them. The Guardsmen said it was the mildest early winter they could recall, but as far as Margaret was concerned, it was sheer hell. Her fingers felt like icicles, and she was quite sure her feet would never be warm again.

The sight of the walls of Thendara heartened her. The trip had been mercifully uneventful—no bandits, no banshees, and only occasional blowing snow—but she was tired. Her bottom had, she was certain, developed calluses from hard riding, and her spine ached from tailbone to skull. But soon she would be at Comyn Castle, and if she had not gotten her days completely mixed, Ida Davidson would be arriving from University tomorrow or the day after. Fear that she might be delayed, that her dear friend might arrive and find no welcome, had troubled her chilly sleep since they left Neskaya.

The city was transformed to her eyes. The roofs were concealed with snow, and icicles hung along the edges of the houses. The streets

were open, though great mounds of frozen snow sat at corners, impeding the few carts that tried to move through them. But there was
something else, she decided, looking around alertly despite her weariness. What was it?

Then Margaret realized that there were long swags of greenery,
swathed in lengths of gold cloth, hung across the stone facades of the
houses and businesses, giving the city a celebratory air it lacked in
summer. Then, too, it seemed that the inhabitants of the city were
wearing clothing of brighter color than she remembered, as if they
were trying to counterbalance the gray and white of winter with boisterous hues.

They passed a market square, and she saw gaudily painted wagons,
five or six of them. They were unlike anything she had seen before on
Darkover. She could see that the sides of the wagons could be lowered
to become small stages, for one of them was being used for a small
performance. Her respect for Darkovans went up a notch at the sight
of a dozen people, enduring the chill of the day, watching the little
show with both interest, and clear familiarity. From time to time, one
of the audience shouted at the players, and was answered.

"Rafaella, what are these people doing?"

"What? Oh, you mean the Travelers? They are only allowed in
Thendara at Midsummer or Midwinter—the rest of the time they
keep to the countryside or the smaller cities. You missed them at
Midsummer because you were already at Arilinn. The Guilds don't
like them, so they keep them away."

"I don't understand. Why do the Guilds object—I assume you
mean the musicians and the actors—is there an Actors Guild? I never
thought about it before?"

"Oh, certainly. There is a Puppet Guild, one for dancers, and even
one for the costume makers." The Renunciate made a face, as if trying
to find a way to say something difficult.

Remy, one of the two Guardsmen that Regis had insisted accompany them, answered. "The musicians don't want the competition,
because some of the singers in the Travelers are just as good or better
than those in the Guild. But the real reason is that they are a bunch of
ruffians, and they sing what they like, or do plays that are . . ." he
made a face, "a bit ripe. They have a bit of fun at the expense of all
and sundry. Everyone likes to laugh at other folk. So they do plays
about fat merchants who cheat, or wives who beat their husbands, and
everyone laughs except the merchants or the husbands. Or they sing
songs that would make a *comynara* blush, begging your pardon, and
everyone has a chuckle."

"But I never heard of them before."

"There were always wandering entertainers, Marguerida, but it wasn't until about fifteen or twenty years ago that there were very many of them. I heard that Master Everard's son Erald spends some time with them, and that is the real reason he won't become Guild-master when Everard dies. They say he writes songs that mock the Comyn."

"I knew from Master Everard that he had written something that was banned, but not the reason." She looked at the wagons again, her scholarly curiosity aroused, and regretted that she would never again have the liberty to pursue her interests.

The other Guardsman, Helgar, a dour man of few words, added, "These players have no respect for anyone—they make fun of one and all. Even-handed of them, to be sure."

Remy grinned at his companions. "And one of their favorite targets is the Renunciates, which is why *Mestra* Rafaella does not really want to talk about them."

"Do they ever cause trouble—get people angry or anything?" Margaret had read about riots on a few planets which had been pro-voked by things as seemingly harmless as a song.

Rafaella shook her head, puzzled. "No. But their songs and japes do make the marketplaces buzz a bit."

As they rode down a narrow street, Margaret could see the roof of the castle rising above the rest of the city, and her heart felt lighter. Soon she would see her father and Mikhail, and she would be glad of that. And Ida Davidson, too. What would Ida make of Darkover?

When they entered the stableyard half an hour later, they found a large carriage blocking the way. It had six horses pulling it, and was heaped with boxes and cases on the top, so that it looked very unbal-anced. Swarms of grooms and servants surrounded the carriage, shouting and getting in each other's way. It was organized chaos, but no one appeared to mind. In fact, Margaret decided, they seemed to be actively enjoying it.

Margaret was too happy to be within reach of her goal to be an-noyed by this delay. She leaned back in her saddle, stretched her spine against it, and lifted her arms above her head. She felt the bones shift and move back into place all along her spine, with a few satisfying little pops.

As she lowered her arms, something struck her on the shoulder, nearly unseating her. As she regained her balance, Margaret was aware of something clutching her left shoulder, and she turned abruptly.

Red eyes and a fearsome beak confronted her, so close she could see the fine black feathers that began at the bill and ascended along a handsome head. It cawed softly, as if trying to tell her not to be afraid, while Dorilys snorted and stamped.

Margaret drew a sharp breath in the chilly air, and smelled an oily, fishy scent which brought a flood of images, of warm seas on Thetis, and a wind that was never cold. "Good day, my pretty," she said quietly. She had seen such birds on Thetis, and she found she was not afraid, just cautious.

So this was Mik's crow. Handsome fellow. It shifted from claw to claw, fluttering a little. At last she extended her left arm, and it scooted down until it perched on her wrist.

For a moment it did not move, and then it began to touch the glove, along the back of her hand with its beak. It did not peck, but instead moved the bill in graceful lines, tracing the shadow matrix hidden beneath leather and silk. Margaret held her breath, stunned, as her companions watched with great curiosity. Apparently satisfied, the crow raised its proud head and gave a sharp call.

At that moment, the door of the carriage opened, and Lady Javanne Hastur descended onto the cobbles. She turned, saw Margaret holding the crow on her arm, and her eyes grew enormous. "What are you doing with that bird?" she almost shouted. Then she advanced across the cobblestones, ignoring everything. "Shoo, shoo," she said, when she was a little closer, flapping her arm in a very silly way.

"Greetings, Aunt Javanne." Margaret could barely contain her laughter. Behind her she was aware that the men and Rafaella were in grave danger of disgracing themselves by giggling at Lady Javanne.

"Where did you get that animal!"

"It just landed on my shoulder, Aunt. And, if I am not mistaken, it is Mikhail's bird. There is no need to get . . . your feathers ruffled."

This was too much for young Remy, and he clapped a broad hand across his mouth and made a noise that might have been coughing if one did not listen too closely. The crow looked down at Lady Javanne, made a sound that was indecipherable, then lifted away in a flare of great wings, the white along the edges flashing in the torchlight of the stableyard.

"I might have known," Javanne muttered darkly. Then she turned and went back to the carriage without really acknowledging her niece. Piedro Alar was helping Ariel, out of the vehicle, and now Margaret could hear the voices of the children, eager to get out of confinement. A nurse, holding Kennard and little Lewis in her arms, managed to get down the steps of the carriage, and Donal and Damon Alar clambered out after her.

"Cousin Marguerida!" Donal, always irrepressible, trotted across to meet her, his young face alight with pleasure. The dark hair that set him apart from his brothers had fallen across his brow, and she thought he could have done with a haircut.

Margaret dismounted calmly. She stamped her feet, which seemed to have no circulation in them at present, and felt full of pins and needle. Then Donal reached her, and she bent down to him. A fierce hug encircled her shoulders, and with it the rather distinct smell of little boy, a warm, thick scent of healthy flesh and vigor. She returned the hug, then held him away from her. "I do believe you have grown an inch since summer, Donal. Have you been eating tall beans?"

"I never heard of those, but I would eat 'em if I could. I am almost as tall as Damon now, and wearing his old clothes. But I am going to get a new tunic for Midwinter. Father promised." *Mother is too busy with thinking of her new baby to notice my clothes, and that my toes are too long for my boots!*

Politely, Margaret ignored this thought. "How nice. Perhaps you would like to come with me, when I go to see the tailors in Threadneedle Street. If it is all right with your father."

"Oh, I am sure he would be glad to let you—he has a lot on his mind just now." In a lower voice he added, "I've been practicing my Terran with Great-Uncle Jeff, and he says I am getting the hang of it." He slipped his hand into hers trustingly, beaming at her. She had questioned the wisdom of her instruction a few times, but the little boy had been so bored at Arilinn, and, in truth, it had given her something to do besides study matrix science. He clearly thought she was a very fine person, for an adult, and she returned the sentiment. She found the lad intelligent and charming—perhaps too much so for his own good.

As far as Margaret was concerned, Donal and his brothers were the real future of Darkover, and she hoped that he would have the opportunity to learn to use his mind for the good of the planet. With an overanxious mother and a gloomy father, she was not at all certain that this would happen, and wished she could do something to help. But her own position was still too ambiguous, too complicated, for her to suggest that Donal might be well-served to be fostered by someone other than his parents, as was the common practice on Darkover. It was not her place, not yet.

Holding Donal's hand, she crossed the yard, stepping around servants wrestling with the luggage of the Hastur and Alar party. It struck her that she would like to foster this little lad herself, even though she was sure her aunt and the boy's mother would not like the idea at all. Ariel could barely stand to have any of her children out of her sight, and had become even more possessive since Domenic's fatal accident.

Rounding the obstruction of the carriage, Margaret saw that her father was standing on the steps leading from the stableyard. He was whistling under his breath, as he did when he was bored. In the flickering light of the torches, he looked tired but relaxed for a change.

Lew Alton saw her, and moved down the stairs, smiling his somewhat lopsided grin, his eyes crinkling. They reached one another in something of a rush, and just stood in silent greeting. Her heart felt gladdened by the sight of him, and if she was disappointed that Mikhail was not also present, it was only a small sorrow.

"Chiya!" He put his single hand on her shoulder and she could feel him squeeze his fingers into the cloth of her garment, putting into that gesture and the single word all the cherishing that she had longed for as a child. *You look wonderful, considering that you have just ridden such a long way. I am glad to see you.*

And I am glad to see you too, Father. If I do not sit on a horse for a tenday, I will be very happy. Dorilys is a splendid mount, but even the finest horse wears thin after a time. "Hullo, Old Man." She spoke to ease the rush of emotions that threatened to undo her. "You are looking well."

"Hullo, Uncle Lew," Donal piped up, grinning. "Cousin Marguerida is going to take me to see the tailors, so I can have a new tunic for Midwinter. I want a blue one!"

"Is she, indeed. Well, blue would suit you well enough, I suppose." He smiled at the little boy. "How was the journey, daughter?"

"Hasty and quite uneventful, thank you. No lost horseshoes, broken cinches, bandits, snow storms, or anything worth talking about."

"Let's get inside." Lew slipped his arm through Marguerida's, then offered his only hand to Donal, who took it, puffing up his small chest as if aware of the honor he was receiving. They climbed the stairs, allowing for Donal's shorter legs, in quiet harmony, and entered the vestibule that led into the castle itself.

Within, there was near chaos, for it seemed that Lady Marilla and Dyan Ardais had also just arrived, and there were servants and baggage all over the small chamber. Behind them, the Alar luggage was being brought in, with grumbles and shouts.

Margaret, suddenly conscious of her position as part of Darkovan society, left her father's side, and went to greet Lady Marilla Aillaird and *Dom* Dyan. It was the proper thing to do, and she was genuinely glad to see them. The little woman brightened when she saw her, left off harassing the servants, who were quite capable of ordering themselves, and embraced her in a scented clasp. "Neskaya seems to agree with you, and Isty has given me good reports of your progress."

"I am glad to hear that, for my own sense of the thing is that for every step forward I take, I take another two, or even three, to the rear. You are looking well. How is your expansion of the kilns faring? Everyone at the Tower enjoys the new dishes you sent. We eat off them every day, and I always think of you, and that first meal I ate at your table." She was babbling and she knew it, out of weariness and her own relief at having finally arrived.

Suddenly, Margaret sensed tension in the crowded entry and looked around, trying to determine its origin. All she saw was a fresh phalanx of servants hauling Lady Javanne's impressive pile of luggage, and Piedro Alar hovering over Ariel with his usual harried expression. Ariel was not, for once, looking daggers at her, and Javanne was too busy ordering the servants. It must be her imagination.

Pregnancy agreed with Mikhail's younger sister, for although she was near her term and ungainly, her color was good, and she had not gained too much weight. Even her usually dull hair had more luster. She said something to Piedro as Margaret watched, and they started to pick their way through the throng, toward the stairs which led to the floor above. This seemed a very sensible course to Margaret, and she decided to follow it.

Turning toward the staircase herself, Margaret drew off her riding gloves and tucked them into her belt. The blue silk mitts that she wore beneath them were a little travel-stained, and she curled her nose in resigned disgust. Then she loosened the clasp at the throat of her cloak, and breathed a sigh of relief.

She stepped around a trunk with the feathers of the Aillard Domain painted on its side and glanced up into the shadows of the stairs. Margaret had the momentary impression that there was a mirror on the staircase, and that she was being reflected in it. She had outgrown some of her lifelong terror of looking glasses during the past few months, but still found the sight of her own features a little disconcerting. Then, with a slight start, she realized it was not her own face, just one similar enough to resemble her in the shadow of the staircase.

And behind the figure of the woman who looked rather like her, Margaret saw Mikhail Hastur, an expression of rage distorting his handsome features. In an instant she knew that the tension she had felt must be his. He seemed to be trying to free himself from the grasp of the woman, for she had his hand clutched firmly in her own. He looked ready to commit murder. The expression on the face of the unknown woman was not pleasant either. Her heart sank. This was nothing like the meeting which she had spent most of the day imagining. Then she steeled herself to show no emotion, to keep herself remote and distant from everyone, as she had done all her life. For the first time, she was almost glad that Ashara's overshadowing had trained her to be aloof and reveal nothing of her feelings.

Lew, aware of her agitation despite her efforts to conceal it, moved across the room in her direction. He reached her side just as Mikhail and the woman got to the bottom of the stairs, and stood shoulder to shoulder with her. Mikhail dragged his hand away from the grasp of the stranger, his handsome face brightening as he glanced at Margaret. He looked harried, but there was no doubt that he was glad to see her.

Marguerida!

Mikhail—who is that woman! And why is she clinging to you like a limpet?

Later, my darling, later.

He did not greet her—or stop. Instead, he moved across the entry toward his mother and bowed deeply. Javanne did not respond at once, her sharp eyes sweeping the room with a quick glance, taking in all the unspoken tensions. They narrowed slightly when they fell on the unknown woman. Then she exhibited one of her more feral smiles. "Mikhail! How kind of you to come to greet me!" She extended one hand and swept the curls off his brow in a motherly caress that would have fooled anyone who did not know how things really stood between them.

Bravo, Javanne! She always knows how to make the best of a situation, when she sets her mind to it.

Lew's thought rang through Margaret's mind, and she found she agreed. She might not like her aunt, but she had to admit the woman had style and presence. Nothing put her out of countenance in public. It was, Margaret decided, a useful skill, and one she needed to cultivate. *Who is that woman clinging to Mik's arm like a Thetan bloodworm?*

That, I regret to say, is our cousin, Gisela Aldaran. She has been in residence for some time now, much to the displeasure of Lady Linnea, who fears she is harboring a cuckoo in her nest.

Aldaran? So that is what . . . I didn't . . . what happens if I tell the bitch to take her hands off Mik?

*Now, daughter! There is no need to come to a vulgar pulling of hair
. . . yet. You can see how little her attentions please him.*

I don't care! What the hell is going on?

*Let us just say that she nurses certain ambitions that will not be
fulfilled, shall we? Yes, I know you do not like it. You do not have to like
it, Marguerida. All you need do is endure it for the present.*

*Very well, Father, because you ask it. I will try not to embarrass you
with my bad manners. But I don't know if I can be polite to her.*

*Marguerida, you cannot embarrass me. And I do not expect you to be
polite, merely civil. Think of how Dio would handle the situation.*

*You mean I can look down my nose, as if something smelled bad, so
long as I pretend to be pleased.*

Precisely!

Even above the hubbub, Margaret could hear Mikhail's voice, continuing to talk to his mother, as if no one else was in the chamber. "I
passed Ariel on the stairs. She appears to be in fine fettle, considering
how advanced she is, and how ill she was this summer. Your vigilance
over her seems to have had a good result, Mother."

"Thank you, Mikhail. In truth, I am weary of the whole thing, and
will be very glad when the child is delivered. I am too old, I think, for
this."

"Old? Mother—do stop fishing for compliments!" There was a
gentleness in Mikhail's voice, a kind of soft teasing, and Javanne
smiled in answer, as if she enjoyed being the focus of attention, even
from her youngest son, the one she seemingly disliked and often dis-
trusted.

"I am not quite hagridden yet, am I?"

"Certainly not! Only a blind man would be unable to see that you
are a splendid figure of a woman, and will be for many years to come.
You do not look at all like a granny, you know." Mikhail seemed
almost to be flirting with his mother, though in a perfectly polite way.

"I am happy to hear it, I have started to feel as if I were ready to
dodder into the grave. You are looking well, son. And I enjoyed that
letter you sent me—oh, months ago—and have reread it a number of
times. Would that either of your brothers could understand the difficulties of parenting."

During this somewhat stilted but nonetheless sincere exchange of
pleasantries, Gisela Aldaran kept putting her hand on Mikhail's elbow
in a proprietary manner, and he kept removing it in an annoyed one.
Margaret observed this, her ill humor giving way to mild amusement.

Finally, unwilling to remain unnoticed any longer, the woman said, "Mikhail! Aren't you going to present me to your mother."

Her voice, as Margaret heard it, was sultry and suggestive, and her immediate dislike of the other woman hardened into something close to hatred. There was a long moment of silence, except for the continual chatter of the servants around them, while both Javanne and her son looked at Gisela as if she had just sprung from the tiled floor of the entry.

When neither of them spoke, she curled her hand back into the curve of Mikhail's arm, and said, "I am Gisela Aldaran," in a warm way.

"I am sure you are," Javanne answered abruptly, then grasped her wide skirts and swept past the startled Gisela, moving up the stairs with a grave dignity that was belied only by the two burning patches of redness on her high cheekbones.

Margaret observed this high-handedness with stunned admiration, swallowing a guffaw that threatened to escape from her throat. Beside her, Lew gave in to his lower self, and chuckled softly, bending his head down toward his chest to muffle the sound of it.

Javanne has always had a gift for using manners to her own advantage.

But why was she so . . . cutting, Father?

Think, Marguerida. If you are an impossible match for Mikhail, how much worse would be that limb of the Aldaran?

Father, I am never going to be able to understand Darkovan politics! I would have thought anyone other than me would be acceptable.

No, not anyone. And, reluctant as I am to deprive you of the pleasure of greeting Mikhail, I suggest we get out of this room and go to our suite.

There will be time enough to see him, won't there?

There will be, Marguerida, I promise.

An hour later, Margaret, bathed and dressed in a white wool gown with a pattern of black leaves around the hem and cuffs, emerged from her bedroom to meet her father. Despite the refreshment of the bath, she felt tired and cross. She had not anticipated a formal dinner on the evening of her arrival, and when Lew told her she must attend, she had bowed to his wishes with as much grace as she could muster.

The new gown helped a little, as did the soothing presence of Piedra, the maid who looked after her whenever she came to Comyn Castle. She had never seen the robe before, but had found it laid out for her when she returned from her soak. She sat patiently while Piedra brushed and combed her flyaway red hair into order, adding a pretty butterfly clasp that, like the robe, Margaret had never seen before.

"Have you been poking into the closets again, Piedra?" she had asked as the maid fussed over her hair.

"Yes and no. Your father ordered the dress when he knew you were returning. And those mitts to match, I believe, for they came from the glovers only yesterday. But, I confess, this hairpin is one I found when I was clearing out part of the Elhalyn Suite. It is much too old for either of those girls. They are very pretty, but still too young for such an ornament. I don't know who it belonged to, for it is very costly, with all that white metal, and those pearls. I saw that it matched your big pearl, so I thought it would not hurt to borrow it." The maid gave Margaret a sweet smile in the mirror.

"You take very good care of me, Piedra."

"I'm right pleased that you find my services worthy, *domna*. The head housekeeper wanted to send one of the waiting women who does for Lady Linnea sometimes, but I said to her that you did not like strangers about, and were used to me."

"Certainly not! Who else would leave me a fine lullaby on the pillow, so I sleep well?"

Slipping the butterfly clasp into place, Piedra patted the hair down, then reached forward and picked up the enormous black pearl which Lew Alton had given her on her first stay at Comyn Castle. It had belonged to her grandmother, Yllana Aldaran. It gave Margaret a feeling of connection with Yllana, whom she had never known, and a curious sense of security as well. She had died bringing Lew Alton's younger brother Marius into the world.

There was something very sad about that story. Tragic might be a better word. The Comyn Council had refused to recognize the marriage of Kennard Alton and Yllana, and she had only had *barragana* status, not that of wife. It had been cruel, and on the rare occasions when Lew was willing to discuss it, his voice had simmered with ancient rage.

She frowned. No matter how she teased Mikhail about it, she knew she would never agree to that position. It would be too humiliating, not only for her but for her father as well.

"Now what has put such a sad look on your face, *chiya?*"

"I was looking at my pearl, and thinking of Grandmother Yllana, and how sad her life was."

Lew chuckled, then shook his head. "My mother would laugh to hear you say that, because she and my father loved one another deeply, and she did not think of herself as having a terrible life. I wish you could have known her—hell, I wish I could have known her longer. I was so young when she died!"

"We don't seem to have a lot of luck with our mothers, you and I, do we?"

"Luck is not something that I pretend to understand, Marguerida. These days, though, I consider myself a very fortunate man, to have found you again and to know the woman you are becoming." Lew smiled a little over this, and Margaret basked in his unconcealed delight.

"Tell me about Gisela Aldaran."

"Must I?" He looked drolly discomforted. "Very well. She is, as you must have guessed, your cousin through several connections. She is twenty-four, a widow with two small children. And from what I have observed thus far, she is an intelligent if obnoxious young woman. Her older son is over at the Medical Center recovering from surgery, and the younger is here. Her father, *Dom* Damon Aldaran, is also in residence, and he and Regis have spent a good deal of time closeted in various rooms, trying to devise an agreement between them which will allow the Aldarans to return to the Council table. Myself, I don't have high hopes just now."

"And Gisela has set her cap for Mikhail?"

"Oh, she certainly has. And she has made no secret of it. She and Mikhail were friends when she was much younger—he visited them without anyone being the wiser—and there might have been a bit of flirting. I don't know."

"But why didn't he say anything before?" Margaret could hear the distress in her own voice, and knew it concealed a sense of betrayal. She had sensed that Mikhail was disturbed about something since his return to Thendara, yet she had never suspected this. She had thought they could say anything to one another, but it seemed she had been wrong in that. Her only comfort, and it was a cold one, was that he did not appear to fancy Gisela at all. Not that this would make any difference, if Regis decided that the best way to solve the problem of the Aldarans was to marry his nephew to the woman. She had been on Darkover long enough to know that this was a real possibility, and she wondered if Mikhail was obedient enough to accept it. It hurt, and she swallowed hard.

Lew grew thoughtful and quiet for a moment. "You have always regarded Mikhail's curiosity as an asset rather than a liability, have you not? Consider how things stood. He was reared to take Regis's place, then set aside, though never officially. So, here we have this intelligent young man with too much time on his hands, and no particular direction."

"He told me that being Dyan Ardais' paxman was not a very challenging task," she admitted.

Lew grunted in agreement. "I suspect that the most demanding thing he had to do was keep young Dyan from creating too many scandals—drinking too much and bedding where he oughtn't."

Margaret laughed in spite of herself. "Bedding where he oughtn't? Do you mean whoring or seducing?"

"Both! Don't distract me. We will have to go down to dinner very shortly, and I want to finish this. There is Mikhail, at loose ends, and there are the Aldarans, who have been excluded from Darkovan society for years and years. What would you have done?"

"I would have sneaked off and taken a look."

"Exactly! And that is what he did, and became friends with Herm and Robert Aldaran, Gisela's older brothers, just before Herm went to sit in the lower house of the Federation Parliament. And met Gisela. That is all there was to it."

"And now?"

"Now is quite a different matter, and will probably result in a great many cries of outrage. Gisela, for all her wit, does not seem to grasp the plain fact that no one would permit a marriage between her and Mikhail, for reasons of power."

"I am all too aware that everything on Darkover comes down to power, and none of it in the hands of the woman." She felt a little bitter, realizing that Gisela Aldaran was as much a pawn as she was, and that she could not do what she chose. And, as far as Margaret was concerned, Gisela could do what she wished, as long as she kept her hands off Mikhail Hastur.

"I know it isn't fair, *chiya*. It was not fair that I fell in love with Marjorie Scott, who, like my mother, was both Aldaran and Terranan. Now, let us ascend to the greater dining room and do the best we can."

"Yes, Father."

Lew gave her a sharp look. "I never mistrust you more than when you pretend to be obedient."

Margaret smiled at him. "That proves that you are a very wise man."

Lew Alton sighed, cast his eyes ceilingward, and then nodded. When he looked at her again, he seemed both grave and mischievous. "Women!"

"And what does that mean?"

"That females are both the greatest blessing and the greatest curse ever invented."

"Odd. I feel the same way about men—as well as thinking that we ought never have taught them to speak!"

Lew Alton's raucous laughter echoed as they walked into the hall. "They say, quite truthfully, that you cannot live with us, nor without us, and we cannot either."

19

Margaret had never been in the larger dining room of Comyn Castle before, so when she entered it with her father, she looked around with interest. It was a wide chamber, with a richly woven carpet sitting on a checkerboard of white and blue tiles. The walls were hung with tapestries depicting scenes from Darkover's past, including one of Hastur and Cassilda, the most popular subject in both song and art on the planet. This was the finest example she had ever seen. The weavers had used thousands of subtly dyed threads to depict the figures, and in the foreground she could see tiny flowers, no larger than her fingertip, dancing in the light that shone from the huge form of the legendary Hastur.

Her attention was drawn not to the enormous figure of Hastur, but instead to a group of musicians playing in one corner. Margaret had to resist the urge to go over and examine that part of the tapestry. She wanted to study the instruments up close, even though the hanging was up high enough that she knew she really would have needed a ladder.

Margaret sighed with regret, then she looked around the room itself. In the center of the chamber was a table that seemed to run for miles. She counted quickly, and found it was set only for thirty, but she was certain there were leaves stored somewhere to make it big enough for as many as a hundred. The chairs set around it were high-backed and carved with lots of curliques, and looked uncomfortable.

The height of the ceiling dwarfed everything, and Margaret looked up. To her surprise, there was a mural overhead, painted with figures of the four gods of Darkover, one in each quadrant. What an odd conceit, she thought, not really liking the image of Zandru in his wintry hell looming over her.

"Is this a state occasion?" she whispered to her father.

"Not quite. I believe that Regis wishes to create an aura of formality in order to subdue the raging sea of emotions." He swept his hand broadly around the room.

"I wish him luck. I can see that he wants to impress everyone, and show who is the master here." She gave a little sigh, feeling the ache in her legs, and was suddenly too tired to worry about Regis. "Is this like dinners you attended when you were Senator?"

"Yes. But at least the food will be better, and there will not be a lot of speeches to listen to."

"Did you hate it so much?"

"With Dio beside me, I did not mind, for she has a skill with people that I lack. She could endure the greatest bore in the universe without flinching—I am sure she did several times. It was only without her that it became unendurable."

"Well, I will try to be a satisfactory substitute, then." She had asked him about her stepmother's health, but nothing had changed. If only she could find some way to cure the woman, for Lew's sake, and her own. The desire to help burned in her, as fresh and hot as the day she had learned that Dio was dying. Then she realized that if she started to think about it, she was going to fall into despair, and that seemed rather pointless.

Seeking something to distract her, Margaret looked across the huge room. She saw Francisco Ridenow deep in discussion with Dyan Ardais. Javanne Hastur was talking to Lady Linnea, but from the expression on her face, she was not giving the conversation her full attention. Lady Marilla Aillard was watching Dyan with her frequent concerned expression, and beside her, Liriel Lanart stood calmly. They made quite a contrast since Liriel was as tall as she was round and Marilla was truly tiny.

She heard the clearing of a throat behind her and turned around. Mikhail Hastur, wearing a dark rose-colored tunic with silver braid, stood in the doorway. Each of his hands was held by a girl, and beside him stood a young man with a nervous expression. This must be Emun

Elhalyn and his sisters, though which of the girls was which Margaret
had no idea. Still, it was a great relief to see him with these children
instead of Gisela Aldaran.

Mikhail smiled at her, and she thought her heart would come right
out of her chest. Then he stepped forward, gave her a decent bow, and
looked up into her eyes as if he were a thirsty man who had just seen
the rivers of the world open at his feet. They stood staring at each
other, unaware that anyone else existed.

Then, with a visible start, Mikhail came back to the present and
remembered his duties. "Cousin Marguerida, may I present to you the
Damisela Miralys Elhalyn, and her sister Valenta, and their brother
Emun. Children, this is *Domna* Marguerida Alton."

Emun made a rather clumsy bow, and beads of sweat popped out
on his narrow brow. Miralys made a wonderful curtsy, as if she had
been doing it all her life, but Valenta just studied her, almost rudely,
before she bent her knees a fraction. Then the younger girl looked up
at Mikhail, who was still distracted, and nodded as if some mystery
had now been solved to her satisfaction.

Valenta released her grip on Mikhail's hand and stepped forward.
"I know all about you," she said quietly.

"Do you?" Margaret was not sure what to make of this. The young
girl's eyes held an expression that was disquieting, and she seemed to
be examining Margaret with great care. It was a much more intense
look than was considered polite on Darkover, but having stood up to a
thesis committee at University, she did not feel any urge to avoid the
dark eyes of the child. "That is interesting, because, quite truthfully, I
do not think I know all about myself."

Valenta grinned and her dark eyes danced with mischief. "You are
the one who is studying to be a *leronis* at Neskaya."

"It is true that I have been at Neskaya learning how to use my
laran, but I am not going to be a *leronis,* Valenta. If I am fortunate, I
might, in a few years, become a decent technician. But probably not."

"Why not?"

"I am rather old to be beginning to study matrices, Valenta, and
besides, being a *leronis* would not suit me at all." The idea of spending
the rest of her life surrounded by those eerie stones was intolerable,
but she did not say this.

"Well, I want you to tell me all about it, because I think it would
suit me perfectly. They are going to send me off to Arilinn next year,
and you were there this summer, weren't you? Will I like it?"

Before Margaret could frame a suitably tactful reply, Danilo Hastur entered the room, with Regis and his paxman close behind. Emun

Elhalyn brightened visibly when he saw young Dani, his solemn expression fading. But Dani had eyes only for Miralys, and she for him.

Mik, these youngsters are in love.

Yes, I know, and so does everyone else in the room. It would be a complete scandal before all these people if Dani were not a complete gentleman, and Mira a perfect little lady. I told you they were making sheep-eyes at each other.

You did, but until I saw it, I didn't realize how serious it was. Is that how we look to other people?

Oh, very likely, Marguerida. Damn, but I am glad to see you. And that gown is quite splendid! You look magnificent!

Why, thank you, kind sir! And where is your comely companion of earlier this afternoon.

Gisela will be here all too soon. I managed to escape her attentions by insisting that I had to escort the children. I have never hidden behind a woman's skirts in my life, and now I am cowering behind two little girls. Isn't that a fine jest?

No, not particularly. Shall I intervene on your behalf and tell the bitch to go to the coldest of Zandru's hells?

Much as I would enjoy that, I think not. Things are difficult enough without either of us displaying the usual family temperament. "Uncle Lew, you must be glad to have Marguerida back where you can keep an eye on her. Rafaella told me that she had a run-in with some bandits on the way to Neskaya. Do you know anything about that?"

"Marguerida did say she had encountered bandits on the journey to Neskaya, but thus far has not given me any details." He sounded amused rather than annoyed.

Margaret's heart sank. The last thing she wanted to do was discuss the matter of the brigands. She had sworn to herself that she would never mention the matter to anyone, and she was quietly furious at Rafi for letting the cat out of the bag. What could she say? She stood in silence, as her father and Mikhail looked at her expectantly.

Miralys had left Mikhail's side and was talking to Dani and Emun, seeming entirely in her element. Then there were voices in the corridor, and Margaret recognized Donal Alar's piping tones. But there were others as well, and there was no mistaking the dark and seductive voice of Gisela Aldaran.

Mikhail, looking like a man hunted by a pack of wolves, moved to Margaret's side quickly, all questions about bandits going out of his mind. She felt a sense of relief, and for a moment she was actually grateful that Gisela's presence had distracted him. "You don't mind, do you? A few more minutes' respite from our cousin would be a blessing."

"Another woman's skirts?" She slipped her hand into the bend of his elbow, even though she knew that the gesture would make Javanne angry. She was almost enjoying herself now. Her mood shifted, the depression fleeing, and what replaced it was a feeling of ease that she wished she could put in a box and keep forever. Margaret knew that part of it was the presence of her father, steady and certain. And she could endure anything so long as Mikhail was by her side.

Yes, but the only one I really want to—

Mikhail! Behind my skirts is one thing, but under them is quite another!

True, but can you blame me? You are the most beautiful woman in the world, perhaps in the entire universe. I have remembered our kiss on the terrace last summer so many times.

Stop! My face feels as if it is the color of a Keeper's robe!

Nonsense. You have just a hint of roses on your cheeks, nothing more, and no one would suspect that we were entertaining unspeakable thoughts for one another.

"Mikhail, I met your bird when I came into the stableyards—or rather he flew onto my shoulder and nearly knocked me off my horse. What a beautiful creature. We have some similar birds on Thetis—not quite so large, as I remember, but just as handsome. It made me a bit homesick."

"Beautiful, and a real nuisance. He seems to have decided that I belong to him, and no amount of discouragement does any good."

Donal Alar sped into the room just at that moment, followed with more dignity by his brother Damon, and his parents. Behind them came Gisela Aldaran with an older man who must be her father. There was another man as well, whose features were much like the father's, and she guessed he must be a son. She tightened her fingers on Mikhail's arm for a second, then drew her hand away.

They stood, shoulder to shoulder, their heights nearly equal, not touching but intimate all the same. It felt completely right, and when Lew Alton stepped beside her, Margaret experienced the sense of being protected that she had longed for all her life. She could face anything with her father and Mikhail beside her. So why was her heart beating rapidly, and her mouth so dry?

Gisela halted, glared at them with her vivid green eyes, then forced her mouth into a smile that held no warmth. "Hello, Mikhail," she began in her sultry voice, clearly intending to ignore Margaret. She moved toward him. Mikhail almost shrank back, then seemed to remember that he was a Hastur, and gave her a courteous nod.

Margaret studied the other woman, noticing the fine silk dress in a deep garnet color that fell in graceful folds around the leather slippers on her feet. The sleeves of the gown stopped above the elbow, so the smooth skin of her arms and soft hands were clearly visible. On one wrist she wore a thick bracelet of gold, set with red stones, and for an instant Margaret was surprised. Then she remembered that Gisela was a widow, not a maiden, and had children. Still, the thing on her arm looked nothing like the few *catenas* wristlets she had seen before. Perhaps it had been made off-world.

"Gisela, Robert, Lord Aldaran." Then Mikhail seemed at a loss how to continue. "Excuse me, but I have not had an opportunity to greet my sister Ariel. Uncle Lew, will you do the honors."

"Of course I will, Mikhail."

Faintheart!

True, my darling Marguerida, true. Now you see what a feckless fellow I really am. I would rather face a hundred bandits than Gisela right now. Besides, they are Lew's relations, not mine, so it is more proper.

I never heard such sophistry in my life, beloved!

If Lew Alton was nonplussed by Mikhail's abrupt departure, he did not show it. Margaret watched as Mikhail walked over to greet Ariel and Piedro, giving every appearance of a solicitious brother, and Lew smiled his grave smile. "*Dom* Damon, may I present my daughter, Marguerida Alton. Marguerida, *Dom* Damon Aldaran, and his son, Robert Aldaran, and his daughter, Gisela."

This clearly did not suit Gisela, and she stiffened, aware she had been subtly rebuffed. Her face froze, as she tried to find some way to recover. She moved her arm sharply, and the bracelet caught in the delicate silk of her dress, snagging the fabric and making her scowl.

"Lord Aldaran, Lord Robert, Lady Gisela," Margaret said formally, and made a decent curtsy.

Gisela had managed to release the bracelet from the cloth now, and she lifted her face with a feral smile. "So you are Marguerida Alton. We have heard so many stories about you." She stared at the mitted hands quite rudely.

"Stories? I cannot imagine why. My life has been quite unremarkable, overall." *Or at least until I came to Darkover,* she added silently.

Robert Aldaran gave his sister an unreadable look, and *Dom* Damon looked ready to spank his daughter. "You are too modest," the son began. "Even up in the Hellers news of your exploits have reached our ears."

Margaret decided, with an impulse that was unusual, that she liked this man. There was something sound about him, a kind of assurance that made her want to trust him. At the same time, she felt a little of her usual shyness stir. She could sense that her desire to like Robert triggered the old pattern of emotional distance which had plagued her for as long as she could remember. Damn Mikhail for abandoning her! At least her father was keeping close, and little Donal Alar was at her side, watching with alert eyes.

"Exploits? Do you mean when I slew the dragon, or when I traveled from Ardais to Thendara in a single night?" What were people saying about her? She felt herself shiver, even as her mouth spoke the satiric words.

Robert Aldaran chuckled and patted one thigh. "Ouch! You nearly pulled my leg out of the socket!"

"Did you kill a dragon, Cousin Marguerida?" Donal asked raptly. His eyes were wide with adoration, and he clearly imagined that she could do anything.

"No, Donal. There are no dragons on Darkover, but if there were, and I went to kill one, I would be sure to take you with me. I was just being very silly."

"Good. I wouldn't like to miss that."

"I was speaking," Robert continued, giving the little boy a friendly nod, "of your encounter with bandits between White Springs and Neskaya."

"Bandits!" Lord Aldaran, who had been standing none too patiently between his children, came to attention. "They get bolder every year. They steal horses and cattle, and anything else they can get their hands on. Something has to be done."

Robert nodded. "It is quite true that the number of gangs of thieves grows larger each year. Tell us about those you met and defeated."

Margaret had promised herself she would never talk about the terrible night, but there was no way she could think of to deny the event. And how the devil had Robert heard of it. It seemed that everyone had. She realized that most likely the merchant had told the tale in every inn on the rest of his journey, and the tale was probably all over the Hellers by now. So much for keeping it a secret.

She braced herself and began to speak. "You make it sound as if I were alone, which was not the case at all. There were four Renunciates, a Dry Town merchant, and myself, plus mules and horses. The bandits were somewhat greater in number, and they managed to surprise us in the middle of the night. I must say that it is a credit to the hardihood of Darkovans that they can even consider attacking in the cold—it had been snowing a little, and it was, to my mind, quite frigid. There were times I thought I should never be warm again.

"But my horse, Dorilys, alerted me. She woke me right up, and the next thing I knew, we were knee-deep in brigands. We managed to fight them off. Since I have no particular skill with swords, my contribution was to use what I have, which is the unarmed combat that I learned at University. I broke one man's neck—which was extremely unpleasant! And the worst part of it was that it was too easy."

Robert Aldaran gave her a curious look. He was a tall man, older than Margaret, with dark red hair, and a grave face that changed completely when he smiled. "But, *domna,* I heard there was more."

Margaret swallowed hard. She felt reluctant to offer the details, but it was clear that Robert was not going to be satisfied with anything less. And if she was correct in her assumption that the story was being told everywhere, she should make sure there were no exaggerations. If only her conscience were not so troubled. By Darkovan morés, she had not done anything very terrible.

"It was rather chaotic, with the Renunciates fighting and the bandits as well, and I did not quite know what to do. After I had succeeded in breaking the man's neck, I rather panicked, I suppose, because I just wanted it to stop! I just shouted 'Stop,' without really thinking, you see, as anyone might in the same circumstances." She found her mouth was dry, and felt her father pat her elbow, as if he knew how upset she was.

Margaret swallowed again, and tightened her grip on her father's arm. "I have the command voice, you see, and I am not quite accustomed to it." She stopped again, and looked down at Donal, who grinned up at her.

"That's right! Never, never wake Cousin Marguerida up from sleep—unless you want to end up—"

"Sleepwaking out the front door in the middle of the night," Lew finished the sentence. He gave Donal a look, and the lad subsided with an understanding twinkle in his eyes.

Robert and Gisela looked from father to daughter, and *Dom* Damon gazed at Margaret with interest. "What happened then," Lord Aldaran asked, his small eyes gleaming.

"Much to my surprise, everyone stopped! Which is to say they froze, as if they were statues in the snow. I was terrified because I could not think how to undo what I had done. But I did think of a way, and managed to get my companions back to normal. Not the bandits, however."

"You mean you left them to freeze to death?" Gisela asked, her voice rough with terror. There were goose bumps all along the smooth skin on her arms, and she shrank back. She looked at Marguerida, a light of fear in her eyes. "How could you?"

"What choice did I have?" Margaret did not believe herself. She sounded boastful, which was the last thing in the world she felt. "They outnumbered us, and one of the Renunciates was injured."

"Did you leave them in the snow, Cousin Marguerida?" piped Donal. "I would have liked to see that."

"The Renunciates dispatched them, and burned their bodies." She felt sick as she said it, and cowardly.

"Very good," Lord Aldaran announced, apparently not horrified in the least. "A better end than they deserved!"

Gisela was made of more fragile stuff, for she shivered all over, and shrank away, drifting toward Mikhail, who was still talking to Ariel. Margaret watched her, and noted that Mik did not seem to acknowledge Gisela's presence at his side.

Just as Robert Aldaran was about to ask her another penetrating question, the Lanarts entered the room. *Dom* Gabriel was frowning and Gabe looked very uncomfortable in his formal tunic, but Rafael smiled. Without listening to any further queries, Margaret left her father's sheltering side, and approached her uncle. "*Dom* Gabriel! Cousin Rafael! What a lovely surprise. I did not know you were here. And Cousin Gabe—how are you?"

Margaret slipped her hand into her uncle's arm, resting her hand lightly on his elbow. He gave her a puzzled look, as if surprised by being greeted warmly. "Well enough, well enough," he answered gruffly. "You are looking quite splendid."

She leaned her head a little closer to him, determined to make the best of the moment. She might not like her uncle, but he was safe, and would not make her feel miserable about her part in the death of brigands. "And you are looking as if you would rather be anywhere but here," she answered very quietly. "Is your leg hurting?" she almost whispered. Margaret knew that *Dom* Gabriel had been suffering from sciatica during the fall, and the way he favored one side told her he still was.

"A bit. Kind of you to ask." *Dom* Gabriel relaxed just a little. "You are a good girl, even if you are a bit headstrong and don't know how to behave. We arrived just an hour ago, with a storm coming up our backsides, and I barely had time to catch my breath. It isn't going to be much of a blow, but the wind was troublesome. Then Javanne insisted I come to dinner, though sitting down to supper with a pack of Aldarans is not my idea of digestible!"

Margaret laughed at this mild jest on her uncle's part. "No, not in the least digestible. Indeed, I think that *Dom* Damon would trouble a dragon's belly, don't you."

She was pleased when her uncle barked his rather loud laugh, making several people turn and look at him. "A shame," he said as quietly as his large voice would allow, "that they are extinct. I would like to hunt one, and better, I would like to see one eat . . . no matter. Go talk to Rafael, will you, and Gabe, since you seem determined to be pleasant. And don't think I don't know what you are up to—trying to turn me up sweet."

"Uncle Gabriel, I am sincerely glad to see you, no matter what you think. We see things very differently, but I know that you have the very finest intentions."

"All of which will likely come to ruin, what with Aldarans in Comyn Castle, and maybe on the Council, though I will oppose that with my last breath. At least you are behaving yourself. Who's that gal hanging on Mikhail's arm—I don't recognize her."

"That is Gisela Aldaran, Uncle."

His rather protuberant eyes bulged, and his face turned a dusky red. *"What!"*

"Yes. She seems to have decided that . . ."

"I don't care what she's decided—I won't have it!" He glared, as if the situation were Margaret's fault. Then his expression softened, and he looked at her with something approaching affection. "Just when I think things cannot get any worse—!"

Margaret patted his forearm with her free hand, because she really felt sorry for *Dom* Gabriel. "I know. But at least this is something that isn't my fault."

"It has been hard on you, hasn't it? I have made things hard for you. Sometimes, I feel as if I am the only man on Darkover who has not lost his wits completely!"

Margaret was surprised and touched by this expression of empathy, so unlike her uncle's usual behavior. He was still stubbornly opposed to Aldarans on the Comyn Council, to Lew sitting on it, or to any possible marriage between her and Mikhail, and likely to remain so. But he was a good man, a decent man, and she had to acknowledge that. She leaned over and gave him a quick peck on one rather rough cheek. *Dom* Gabriel started slightly at this affection, then brightened a bit.

"Now, why don't you go over and pry that woman off Mikhail's arm, and I will go make friendly conversation with Gabe and Rafael, and we will both do Lady Javanne proud, Uncle Gabriel."

"Very well." He sighed. "Ariel is likely going to tell me more about her pregnancy than I want to hear. I cannot tell you what a blessing it has been that she was at Arilinn and *not* at Armida these months. But you are right. Javanne is giving me one of her looks, and a scolding will follow if I don't do my duty." *Women! I am beset with women! May the Gods give me strength!* He cast his eyes up to the painted ceiling, gave Margaret's hand a perfunctory pat, and left her.

Rafael and Gabe Alton moved closer to her, both of them smiling. "Thank you for your kindness to the Old Man," Rafael began. "He's been like a baited bear for days, and the journey did not help a bit. And no matter how he pretends otherwise, he does like it when pretty women fuss over him."

"Don't we all. How are you, Marguerida?" Gabe, who was no longer interested in her as a potential wife, looked her up and down. "You seem thinner."

"I might be, but it is not nice of you to notice, Gabe. No matter how much I eat, I can't seem to put enough away to keep my weight up. Istvana says I eat enough for two people."

"Do you like Neskaya?" Rafael asked.

"Well enough, though I don't think I will ever be comfortable in any Tower. The people there are very friendly, and I have discovered another relative—Caitlin Leynier—who has become my friend. After Arilinn, it is heavenly. How are things at Armida?"

"We had a huge harvest," Gabe began, "and next spring we will have a bumper crop of foals. But we have had a lot of trouble with gangs of bandits this autumn. We fixed the roof, too—no more leaks in the Blue bedroom!" He grinned at her. Margaret remembered how she had been put into that room when she came to Armida the previous summer, and how Liriel had revealed that there was a leak in the ceiling, much to Javanne's displeasure.

"I am sure you are taking good care of Armida, Gabe. Is that little sister of my Dorilys going to foal? She looked like a fine mare when I saw her last summer, even though I did not have time to get to know her."

"She is, and she was covered by Black Bolt, so the result should be both beautiful and strong. I am hoping for a black, but Rafael hopes for a silver. We even have a small wager on it."

Margaret took a deep breath. "I cannot tell you how wonderful it is to talk of horses and harvests, instead of *laran,* and to be with my family! It is so good to see both of you!"

"Do you know, I feel very much the same, cousin, and I never thought I would say such a thing." Gabe, looking unusually thoughtful, nodded at her. "You made me look at myself a bit last summer, and I never had the chance to tell you that I was glad of it." His weathered cheeks reddened. Then he straightened a bit, drew up his broad shoulders, and went on. "I am a better man for you calling me a damn fool, Marguerida, and I think I am man enough to confess it."

Margaret exchanged a glance with Rafael, quite startled by this admission. The middle brother winked at her. "He is quite reformed, Marguerida, and even listens before he speaks these days. He is more like an angel everyday."

"I would not go that far," Gabe blustered.

Margaret stepped between her two cousins, touched both their arms lightly, and smiled from one to the other. "I think it is wonderful, whatever made you better behaved, Gabe. I am happy for you, and happier still that we can be friends."

"Look at Gisela Aldaran looking daggers at the Old Man," Gabe said. "Pretty woman, though nothing beside you, cousin."

"Got a bit of an overbite," Rafael offered.

"Set her cap for Mikhail, has she?"

"That does seem to be the way things stand." Margaret was amused by Gabe's clumsy remarks. And she was too tired now to contain any strong emotions. Her earlier anger had turned to ashes, and all she wanted to do was get through the meal and go to bed.

"She won't do at all. Father would never allow it, nor would the Council. Besides, we all know how the wind lies, don't we? Not to put you to blush, cousin. I know Mikhail, and once he sets his mind to something, he never wavers."

"She looks a bit like you, doesn't she?" Rafael asked the question and gave his brother a look, as if to tell him to change the subject.

"I suppose she does. In fact, when I saw her coming down the stairs earlier today, I thought for a second that I was seeing myself in a mirror. But her hair is a bit darker than mine, don't you think?"

Rafael gave her a nod, along with a thoughtful glance. "Yes. How was your journey to Thendara?"

"Quite uneventful, which is exactly how I like it! When we arrived, I saw some players that piqued my curiosity, and I am hoping to find out more about them while I am in the city. I am expecting a guest to arrive on the next ship, so when I go to fetch her, I think I will stop in that marketplace and take a look."

"You mean the Travelers? They came to Armida towards the end of summer, and performed a play, a magic show, and some acrobatics." Gabe smiled in memory. "It was quite a good thing, though the play was—nothing for the ladies! But the dancers were good."

"I think we are going to sit down to supper now. Let us hope we can get through the meal without Father and *Dom* Damon trying to stab one another with the butter knives," Rafael said. "Come on, Gabe. Let's get Marguerida seated and show some Alton family solidarity."

Margaret took a deep breath, steeled herself for the ordeal to come, and prayed to every god she knew of that the meal would pass quickly and without incident. Then she let the two brothers escort her, seating her beside her father on one side, and Gabe Alton on the other. He was not the dinner companion she would have chosen, for his mind was not very flexible, but he was safe. With all the cross-currents in the room, sitting between her cousin and her father seemed wonderful.

She sensed Mikhail looking at her across the table, where he was sitting between the two Elhalyn girls. He gave her a cheerful look.

I love you, Marguerida!

And I you—but if you make me blush, I will box your ears!

What sweet words!

He laughed, and the girls looked up at him, puzzled. Then Valenta glanced at Margaret, got a very amused look on her face, and joined in his laughter, as if he said something amusing. The moment passed, without anyone else being the wiser, and dinner was served.

20

Margaret set off the following morning wearing her warmest Darkovan clothing, but carrying her Terran documents in her pouch. She had considered for a few minutes getting back into her now hated Scholar's uniform to greet Ida Davidson when she arrived, but it was just too vile an idea. The thought of the cold synthetic against her skin and the smell of it in her nostrils was repellent. All the years she had been so proud to wear it seemed like a dream now, and she was determined never to put the thing on again. She was tired from the journey, and the dinner the previous evening had seem interminable. She had a headache—two of them actually. The first was from drinking a bit too much wine, but the second was a kind of shadow headache, caused by the presence of all the tensions at the table. After the quiet and harmony of Neskaya, Comyn Castle seemed noisy, both verbally and mentally.

She had been extremely glad to have Gabe Lanart-Alton as her primary dinner companion. His *laran* was minimal, and his interests commonplace. He assumed that since Margaret was the Alton heiress, she would wish to know everything that had happened since she had been at Armida. Margaret found herself interested, and amazed by the amount of work it took to maintain the place. Her respect for her cousin, and for her Uncle Gabriel increased appreciably, and she knew that either of them would have been surprised by it. He charitably forgive her vast ignorance of land management, and his dogged recitation formed a barrier between Margaret and the furies simmering along the board.

Margaret walked through the stable court toward the barracks where the Guardsmen lived. She reached the barricade that fronted the barracks, and a grizzled man in the green uniform of the City Guards saluted her smartly as she approached. He had black leather belts crossing his chest, and wore a sword on one hip. "May I help you, *domna?*"

"Yes, you can. I was wondering if Remy was on duty. I am going to the spaceport, and I would like an escort." She had gotten more used to not going everywhere by herself, though she was sure she would never be entirely accustomed to it.

"To be sure, *domna*. But Remy is not here. There was some trouble in the Horse Market and he went with the company to see to it. But I will find someone. Please, wait a moment."

He left her, and Margaret spent the time looking at the carvings on the entrance, and admiring the arrows and swords which adorned the white stone. Then the gatekeeper came back with a young man wearing a long cloak.

"This is Daryll MacGrath, Domna."

"Daryll? Are you one of the men who went with Mikhail to Halyn House?"

"I am, Lady." He gave her a bow, but his eyes were twinkling when he stood upright.

"I am Marguerida Alton."

He gave her a broad grin. "I thought you might be." Then he gestured, waving her ahead. "Where are we going, *domna?*"

"The spaceport. I am meeting a friend."

They left the barracks and started through the streets. A light snow had fallen, and there was a bitter wind that blew down the narrow ways between the buildings. Margaret decided her curiosity about the Travelers would have to wait for a better day. She was not sure of the exact arrival time of the ship, and she would rather wait there than be late.

The morning had advanced considerably by the time they came into the square where the John Reade Orphanage stood. She glanced briefly at the gray facade of the building, remembering the anguish of being abandoned in that austere place, and let it go. She never had to set foot in there again, and she tried not to think about other children, the offspring of Terran men and Darkovan women, who were still confined within its walls. They were fed and clothed and, she knew, turned into good Terrans, unless things had improved in twenty some odd years. She wondered briefly if it was still forbidden to speak Darkovan there, or if a more enlightened administration had changed that rule.

In a hundred strides, the bleak building was behind them, and she felt herself relax. Margaret had not even realized she was tense until the feeling was gone. A knot of anger lay in her belly, and a deep sense of loneliness rose in her throat when she saw the place. *Will I ever be really free of my childhood? Is anyone?*

When they approached the wall which separated the entrance to the port from the rest of Thendara, a number of Terran guards in their black uniforms came to attention, looking at them rather suspiciously. One came forward and blocked the way, scowling. In a loud voice, he told her to halt.

Margaret was surprised, and she looked at the man as she dug her documents out of her beltpouch. He seemed tense, as if expecting trouble. It puzzled her until she realized that dressed as she was, he had assumed she was a native.

Margaret held out her various documents, and the man ignored them completely. "State your business," he demanded in halting Trade-speech, his voice raised.

"I am meeting someone on the ship from Coronis." Margaret answered in Terran, and had the deep satisfaction of seeing the man's eyes dilate, and his mouth sag a little.

Then he recovered himself, looked her up and down, and shook his head. "No one is allowed in the spaceport without papers."

"I have papers, you dolt!"

"And just where did you steal them," he sneered.

"Steal? Of all the . . . what's your name?" She could feel herself start to get angry, and was disgusted at how much she wanted to vent all her tangled feelings on this total stranger. Margaret decided she was more out of sorts from the previous night than she had imagined, and reined herself in sharply.

"My name?"

"Yes, your name. I want to be sure I have it right, so I can tell my uncle, Captain Rafe Scott, precisely who it was who behaved like a ruffian. I believe the term is being 'put on report,' isn't it? Then it goes in your record forever, does it not?" Margaret knew very well how Terran bureaucracy worked, and that once something was in a file, it was nearly impossible to remove it, even if it was erroneous.

Another black-garbed man came hurrying forward. "What seems to be the problem?"

"This person seems bent on denying me entry to the spaceport, although my papers are in order, and I am meeting someone on the ship that I believe is landing even as we stand here, freezing our feet." There was a blazing light in the sky, and the sonic boom of a ship entering the atmosphere.

"Let me see," the second man said, holding out his hand. He scanned the documents quickly. "These seem fine." He held them out, and Margaret took them, and put them away.

"But, sir, she's a . . . a native!" the first man protested, his face white with rage. "We have our orders . . ."

"You have a lot to learn about Cottman Four, Ritter."

"How do you know she didn't steal them?"

"Be quiet, Ritter! You must excuse him, Miss Alton. He's only been here a week, and he doesn't know much."

"Of course, Lieutenant." She knew what the emblems on his tunic meant. "But I don't understand. Last summer there wasn't this sort of fuss." Margaret looked at the second man, and instead of meeting her eyes, he looked down at the stones beneath his feet.

"No, there wasn't, Miss. But some bigwigs think that . . . well, there was some sabotage in the spaceport on Ephebe Three a few weeks ago, and everyone has been put on alert."

Margaret gaped at him, shocked. She hardly believed him, since such events were rare. Then she forced herself to laugh casually. "I never thought to be mistaken for a saboteur, Lieutenant."

"Laugh if you like, but it is serious."

"I am sure it is, but I cannot help finding the entire situation amusing." Margaret savored the humor in the situation, and felt her earlier anger begin to dissipate. "Now—may I go? The ship will be down in a minute."

"Yes, you can. But your man here will have to wait. We can't let him into the port. Orders, you understand."

"I understand that the Federation is jumping at shadows." She turned. "Daryll, wait here for me, and I will be back soon," she told her Guardsman in *casta*.

"*Domna?*"

"It is all right. No harm will come to me in the spaceport, and the faster we get this done with, the sooner you can be back in your warm barracks!"

"Yes, *domna*. But, you watch yourself. You know how the Terranan are." His voice was dark with suspicion, as if he expected someone to harm her.

Margaret sighed. "I do, Daryll, indeed, I do."

She crossed beneath the arch which separated the city from the port, walked through two more checkpoints without incident, and then entered the building. Margaret went through several corridors, hating the dry heat of the air, and the stale smell of it, and finally reached the customs area. There was a long line on the other side of the barrier, and she stood on her tiptoes, hoping to spot Ida in the crowd.

And then, there she was, her slender body almost hidden behind a heavyworlder holding a case of some sort against his chest. She tried to wave, to get Ida's attention, but the little woman did not see her. Ida looked smaller than she remembered, smaller and older, too. Worn, that was the word she wanted. She jigged a little impatiently, and tried to school herself to tranquillity. But she was much too excited by Ida's arrival. Not precisely happy, since Ida would never have come to Darkover if Ivor had not died, but heartened. She had a deep sense of connection to this woman who had been her guide during most of her adult life.

The line snaked along slowly, the customs officers peering at papers, asking impertinent questions, poking through carry-ons, and putting the correct stamps in the proper places. At last Ida came to the head of line, saw her, gave Margaret a weary wave, and waited to be processed.

She came through the barrier, and Margaret swept her up in a firm hug that lifted the smaller woman's feet right off the floor. Then she planted a kiss on her cheek and received one in return. "You are, I think, the most beautiful sight I have seen in days," Ida murmured.

"Thank you! You look pretty wonderful to me, too! Come on. Let's get the rest of your luggage and get out of here. This way." Margaret took Ida's arm gently and led her down the maze of corridors until they reached the baggage area. They found Ida Davidson's case, and in a few minutes, they were out of the building, into the crisp air.

"My God! No wonder you are wearing wool. I had no idea it was so cold! I mean, yes, I knew that Cottman was a chilly place, but nothing prepared me for this, Maggie! Is it always like this?"

"This is actually a pretty pleasant day for this time of year. But I know what you mean, though. Come on. It is a goodly walk back to the Castle, and there is no ground transportation. Your all-weather cloak will keep you from freezing."

"If you say so," Ida answered doubtfully, shivering all over.

"I should have brought along a real cloak for you. I wasn't thinking, Ida. I'm sorry."

None of the guards tried to stop them as they walked through the open gate, but the man called Ritter gave Margaret a venomous look as they passed him. Margaret ignored him. All she could think of was getting Ida back to the Castle as quickly as possible. She cursed herself for not thinking to order a carriage.

Daryll was leaning against a wall, waiting, but he came to attention as soon as he saw Margaret. After a glance at Ida clutching the slithery cloth of the all-weather cloak around her, he swept his own off and drew it around Ida's shoulders in a single, graceful movement, as if it was the most natural thing in the world. Ida nearly jumped out of her skin at the quick motion, but then tugged the garment over her. "Thank you. I am past the age where I expect chivalry, but not so old I cannot enjoy some."

The Guardsman looked at her blankly, since Ida was speaking in Terran, not *casta.* But he seemed to understand that she was glad of the cloak, and grinned at the older woman.

"Will he be warm enough?" Ida asked Margaret in a worried way.

"Darryl will manage, I am sure. Give him your bags. The streets are rather slippery, and I don't want you to overbalance and fall. Here, take my arm."

"Very well," Ida answered, slightly grumpy. "I am not enfeebled, Maggie—not yet, anyhow."

"Of course you aren't, but if you broke your leg, you would end up in the Terran Medical Center, and I would hate to have your visit here ruined."

"Is this how you managed Ivor?" The asperity in her voice was a little muffled, as the small woman tried to manage with a cloak intended for a much taller person.

Margaret chuckled. "Oh, no. I never had to manage him, because he just dumped everything on me and assumed I could take care of it."

"Yes, he would have done that. He was a very single-minded man." She sounded near to tears, and Margaret could sense she was keeping her feelings in check by sheer will. "Did I tell you how much I appreciated the message you sent me when he died?"

"Yes, Ida."

"I am so tired that I can hardly think straight. After sitting on the ship for days, doing nothing but napping and trying to find a comfortable position, it does not seem reasonable. But I am weary to the bone, to the heart."

"I know, Ida, and I wish . . ."

"There is nothing you can do, child. Time is all that can heal me."

They moved slowly across the square, and Ida began looking around with mild interest as she leaned lightly on Margaret's arm. They passed by the orphanage, and the taverns and cookshops which clustered near the entrance of the port, and finally entered the narrow streets that led away from it. Ice crunched beneath their feet, and their breaths misted the air before them. The wind had died down a little, for which Margaret was grateful, both for Ida's sake and her own.

"Where are we going?" Ida asked after a while.

"See that great white pile up there, looming over the city? That is Comyn Castle, and that is where I am taking you."

"Oh. Somehow, when you said 'castle,' I thought you meant an inn or hostel, not a real castle." She panted a little, her warm breath making foggy billows in the air. "Why do you live in a castle?" Ida managed at last.

Margaret had not explained very much to Ida about her adventures since coming to Darkover, since the cost of telefaxes was enormous, and there was a great deal which she had not wished to expose to curious eyes. Although these communications were supposedly private, she had a dark suspicion that they were not really. She had informed Ida about Ivor's death, but had not said anything about being an heiress, having *laran,* or any number of other matters. Now she felt a little strange, guilty and tense for having said so little.

"Technically, I don't. I only stay at Comyn Castle when I am in Thendara. Right now I 'live' at Neskaya, which is a place north of here, where I am studying. I'd probably be there now, but the Midwinter Festival and your visit allowed me to leave for a time." How the devil was she supposed to explain the Towers of Darkover to Ida?

"Studying? Is this Neskaya a musical center?" Ida had a good ear, and it was clear she had listened to the language disks Margaret had sent months before, for her pronunciation of the word Neskaya was good.

Margaret laughed. "There is music everywhere on Darkover, Ida. I have collected enough material since I arrived to earn a full professorship, if I ever had the time and energy to get it organized. But since I do not expect to ever return to University—"

"You aren't coming back?"

"Not in any future I can foresee, Ida." The problem was, she thought, that she couldn't see any future at all. *So much for the Al-*

daran Gift. I wonder if Gisela has it. A pity I can't just ask the woman. But I could never do that.

"I see. I always imagined, and Ivor, too, that when he was retired, you would get his seat at University. We were really looking forward to that, I confess, because of all the students we had, you were the best real scholar. Not to mention a better musician than you ever gave yourself credit for. I think you were intimidated by Jeffy and some of the others into thinking you were not outstanding."

As always, Margaret warmed with praise, and shrank away at the same time. Then she tried to shake her mind free of old habits. "That is nice to hear, Ida. And I am sorry to disappoint you."

"Perhaps it is for the best."

"Why do you say that?" The street ahead of them looked fairly clear of ice, so Margaret released her grip on Ida, and the older woman gave her a little smile.

"Things have changed a great deal in the few months since you left. And not for the better either. There is talk of cutting off the funding, not just to the music department, but to all the arts, and some of the sciences as well. Those Expansionist Philistines insist that art is a luxury, not a necessity, and that public monies should be spent on important things, like more technologies and armaments. As if we needed more guns! We haven't had a war in generations! They are trying to suspend all the emeritus positions—say it's a waste of credits to support old geezers who are no longer making a contribution. And next term they are doubling the tuitions, and eliminating a great many of the scholarships as well. The Board of Regents is in an uproar, and it is perfectly dreadful." Ida's small face wrinkled with distress.

Margaret thought about the suspected sabotage on Ephebe, and some of the things Lew had told her, but decided not to say anything. "I see. My father suspected that things might go this way, so I am not really surprised, but I am saddened." She squeezed Ida's hand in her own. "We will be at the Castle soon, and then you can rest and have a lovely hot bath, and put all this nonsense out of your mind, Ida."

Ida began to shiver in spite of Daryll's cloak, and she fell silent, failing even to look at the shops that were open for business. Margaret was now glad she had said nothing about Ephebe, and bit her lower lip anxiously as she observed the older woman. Her breath came in little gasps, reminding Margaret all too much of how Ivor had been the day before he died so suddenly. She felt her heart clench with fear. What if she had brought Ida to Darkover, only to have her die like Ivor?

Then, to her astonishment, she had a flash, the sense of peering into another time, the way she had had on three previous occasions.

She "saw" Ida, now incredibly ancient, seated beside the huge fireplace at Armida, speaking quietly to a very pretty girl of about twelve years. She was wearing the oddest clothing—neither Darkovan nor Terran—and seemed perfectly at home. Margaret strained to hear any words in the vision, but the two were speaking almost in whispers, and all she caught was the pleasant crackle of the fire, and the sound of the wind outside.

Margaret was so surprised she nearly stumbled. The vision was gone almost as soon as it began. She would have doubted it earlier, but now she was ready to accept the image as something possible, if not immediately real. It might even happen. The experience left her light-headed, and she wished she had eaten a larger breakfast.

They reached the entrance to Comyn Castle which Rafe Scott had taken Margaret through in what seemed like another lifetime. The stairs leading to the entry had been swept clear of snow, and there were Guardsmen standing at the door. They bowed as they opened the door, and she felt Ida start a little.

"Maggie, dearest, are you someone important? I mean, I know you are the daughter of Senator Alton, but . . . " the older woman whispered as they entered the foyer. Daryll followed them carrying the bags, and a servant appeared immediately to take them from him.

"You could say that, Ida." Margaret's response was murmured, and she felt odd. She still was not used to thinking of herself as a person of importance.

Ida stood absolutely still for a second, taking in the tapestries and the paintings. Then, with trembling hands, she unhooked the cloak that Daryll had lent her and turned to give it to him. The hem was clotted with ice, for she was much shorter than the young Guardsman, and the white of the wool was stained in places, from being dragged over dirty cobbles.

Her little face registered distress as she saw the mess, and she looked up at the tall man. "Thank you for the loan of your garment—I hope you were not too cold—and I am sorry that I got it so dirty."

Daryll gave Margaret a look of inquiry, so she translated Ida's words. "Tell the *mestra* that it was an honor to be of service, and the day is quite clement for this time of year."

Margaret laughed, and Ida waited for her to stop. "What did he say? I have been listening to those disks you sent me, and I think I've learned some of the words, but I am so tired I can't follow him. And it sounds different when he speaks. What did he say?" She sounded tired and a bit querulous.

"Only that he was glad to lend you his cloak, and that the day is rather balmy for winter."

"Balmy! I shudder to think what he thinks is cold, then." Ida gave Daryll a piercing look, as if she suspected she was being made fun of.

"Come along. We have several miles of corridors to get through before we reach the suite. Well, that is a slight exaggeration. It will only seem like miles, but at least you will be warmer, Ida."

"Oh, yes, I feel more comfortable already." She tugged off the all-weather cloak that she had worn beneath Daryll's, and draped it over her arm. "Let's go. That hot bath you promised sounds like heaven."

The servant had preceded them, so by the time they reached the Alton Suite, the doors were open. Lew Alton was standing by the door, waiting. He was dressed in a dark brown tunic and matching trousers, and Margaret thought he looked very handsome in the pale light that streamed through the windows behind him.

"Ida, I would like you to meet my father, Senator Lewis Alton. Father, this is Ida Davidson, who was like a mother to me when I was at University."

Lew bowed, then offered Ida his single hand. "I am delighted to meet at last the person who took such good care of my little girl."

"A pleasure to meet you, Senator. Ivor and I did our best, but I think she would have turned out beautifully, no matter what." Ida smiled up at him as she shook his hand, her eyes twinkling. She was utterly relaxed now, and clearly not overly impressed. Why should she be? Ivor and Ida Davidson had fostered the sons and daughters of kings from planets where such arrangements still held sway, and treated them just as they did the rest of their charges. "Now, about that bath you promised. The stink of the ship seems to have gotten into my skin, and I want it gone. It has been a long time since I traveled, and I had forgotten how dreadful it was."

"You would think, wouldn't you, that with all the wonderful technology the Terran Federation holds, they could construct a ship that didn't smell like a cowbyre."

"A cowbyre, Senator, has a good, healthy smell. I know, for I was born on Doris, and we are famous for our cattle. If I ever smelled a barn that stank like those ships, I would think there was some sickness."

"Come on, Ida. I will show you to your room, and introduce you to my maid, Piedra. She probably has all your bags half unpacked by now, for she is very efficient."

"Thank you."

"And while you are bathing, I will order up some food—real food, not like that packaged stuff they offer on the ships. Would you like some soup, or something more substantial?"

"Oh, anything, so long as it is hot and filling." Ida seemed to sag a little, but her cheeks were rosy, and her eyes were bright. "If I never have to eat a nutrobar again, I will be quite content."

What the hell? Nutrobars are what they feed Imperial Marines!

I don't know, Father, but from what Ida has told me on the way, things are getting very odd in the Federation. I promise I'll tell you about it later.

Margaret shepherded Ida Davidson away, took her to a room adjoining her own on the west side of the Alton Suite, and gave her over to Piedra. The maid was waiting, and had already sorted out the small amount of baggage that Ida had brought. Fortunately, Piedra had a small command of Terran phrases which she had learned from Margaret, and she took the old woman neatly in hand.

Lew was waiting for her when she returned to the sitting room, stretched out in an armchair with his feet toward the fireplace. He had a steaming mug in his hand, and the sweet smell of herb tea rose from it. There was a pot of the stuff on a small table, and two more mugs, so she helped herself and sat down across from him.

"Did you know they had to cut funding to University?"

"Herm mentioned something of the sort. It was so minor compared to the other horse droppings the Expansionists are trying to get through that I didn't give it much thought."

"You didn't think it was important that they want to take away the pensions for professors emeritus? Or that they are cutting the scholarships?" She was outraged.

"Marguerida, there is a great deal more afoot than such small matters."

"It won't be a small matter to those it affects!" Margaret felt a passion for University that she knew she could never explain to her father, or to anyone who had not been there. "And, if they do that, what about the widows? Ida and Ivor gave their whole lives to taking care of their students, and if the pensions are revoked, how will she live? She is rather too old to go back to giving clavier lessons, I think."

"How old is she? With the LE treatments, it is hard to tell."

"Ivor was ninety-five, and Ida is two years younger, I think. She doesn't look old enough to be your grandmother, does she?"

"Not in the least. I would have guessed sixty, if I had been pressed." He paused, sipped, and sighed. "It is not just old professors, Marguerida, and their widows, who are being threatened. What the Expansionists propose is a complete overhaul of the economic basis of the Federation. At present, they are not able to realize their mad dream, but if there is another election, they might get a majority in the lower house, and then things would become very . . . unpleasant."

"But, Father, surely no one with any sense would support . . ."

"If you tell people it is in their own interest to do something, they will support it, even if it is a lie. Add to that the fact that the Expansionist Party is supported by the more rapacious elements of the Federation—those who have always believed that it was the purpose of all the planets to provide Terra with every luxury, even if it meant that people would starve for it, and you have the devil's own mess. These men have no religion except greed, and no more morals than a banshee. People have very short memories, and do not remember the World Wreckers. We here on Darkover remember, though, because they came so close to destroying us."

"Do you wish you were back in the Senate?"

"No, I don't. I would be taking out dueling licenses on a daily basis, in all likelihood, or drinking myself to death. I had the sense to know it was time to pass the torch to Hermes Aldaran, who is as wily as his name suggests."

"I hope you are right. Something happened at the spaceport that makes me very uneasy. They would not let me enter—I suppose I should have put on my uniform instead of wearing comfortable clothing—even though I had the proper papers. It was something about sabotage on Ephebe. And they wouldn't let my Guardsman accompany me into the port, because he was Darkovan, I guess. The man who stopped me accused me of stealing my papers. I've encountered that sort of treatment from native officials on a few planets, but Terran servicemen are not usually so rude, or paranoid either."

Lew nodded. "I knew about Ephebe, though I only heard a few days before you arrived, and it slipped my mind."

"What happened?"

"It is not clear, for I only had a brief account from Herm. He could not explain the whole matter, and had to use a rather shabby code we worked out just before I left. It seems that the locals were outraged at some new rule that was put upon them—you do know that Ephebe is owned almost completely by Transplanetary, don't you—and they took matters into their own hands, and managed to destroy most of the main spaceport. Transplanetary is demanding that troops be sent in to 'restore order,' and the Senate is dragging its collective feet."

"I don't understand. Why could he not tell you everything?"

Lew drank the last of his tea, made a terrible face, and set his mug aside. "It might have been construed as treasonous, if he had given

Regis and me the details. Because we are a Protected planet, rather than a member world."

"That makes a difference?"

"It certainly does. The Expansionists are deeply suspicious of Protectorates, and want nothing more than to bring them into member status, the better to seize their resources and dispatch them to Terra. Did you know that we made some tentative agreements after the World Wreckers to share some of our matrix science with the Federation. It was a mistake, and we realized it before it had gone too far. Regis did some very fancy footwork, as did I, and we managed to undo the damage. I was never so grateful for the Alton Gift as when I persuaded a few key people that the claims of matrix science were greatly exaggerated, and hardly worth notice. But afterward I was disgusted with myself, too, for using forced rapport, even in a good cause, reminded me altogether too much of Dyan-Gabriel Ardais's actions in the past." His head sank toward his chest, and he looked depressed. "The things I have done for Darkover!" he finished bitterly.

"Was that when information about Darkover was suppressed?"

Lew brightened a bit. "Yes. I managed to attach a small amendment to a trade bill, something so apparently unimportant that it was almost unnoticed, subtly altering the status of Protectorates in the Federation. By the time anyone realized what had happened, there was nothing they could do, other than rescind it, and there were other pressing matters that received attention instead. The Federation is starting to crack, Marguerida. It is too large to govern, and those who imagine they can run it are deluded. What is needed is not a return to the greedy policies of the past, but instead a whole new form of government, instead of the muddle we have now, a patchwork of agreements that no longer serve. Only the vision is lacking. The Terranan have expanded their horizons without enlarging their imaginations. I cannot do anything about that. All I can do is try to keep Darkover from being gobbled up by Transplanetary or some other corporation."

"I remember that Ida had a lot of trouble getting the papers to come here. Is that part of it?"

"Absolutely! The Expansionists want ships to carry goods, not people, and certainly not information about other worlds. That is how they hope to control the Federation, by limiting the exchange of knowledge. Their assault on University is only the first step. I do not believe they have a conscious plan. After being out of power for almost a generation, their majority in the Senate has made them a little drunk, I suppose. These are not thoughtful people, Marguerida. They are ambitious, and not evil by their own lights. And, I think, there is no one more dangerous than a man with power who does not realize he is capable of real evil."

They fell into one of the companionable silences that they had begun at Arilinn, when both were too tired to speak, and too sorrowful to wish to be alone. It was very pleasant, with the crackling of the fire, and the sound of the wind rising outside the castle. Margaret thought that her father had found some sort of peace at least, and she was glad for him. As for the Federation, it seemed more and more distant from her concerns, and she let herself think about other things, like Mikhail, and that peculiar dream they had shared a few weeks before.

Ida Davidson joined them, looking much refreshed, and wearing a strange garment of a sort Margaret had not seen before. At the same time, it seemed very familiar, and after a moment she realized it was similar to what she had seen Ida wearing in her flash of foresight. It consisted of a knitted tunic above voluminous wool trousers, not unlike the garments worn by Dry Town males, and over it, a striped coat in a variety of bright colors. Piedra had pinned a small veil over Ida's thin hair, which was too short to be braided or fastened up. The overall effect was both exotic and interesting.

Where, she wondered, had Ida gotten that getup? Margaret had seen Ida in her academic robes on important occasions, and wearing the usual clothes of Federation women not functioning in any official capacity—blouses, skirts, or dresses—but this was a totally different thing.

"Yes, I know. I look quite odd. I thought so when I stood before the mirror, and your maid had a great deal of trouble not giggling. But I had these things in a trunk, and I thought that since Cottman was such a cold place, my old Dorian things, which I haven't worn in a couple of decades, would be just the thing. Fortunately, I have not gained much weight, so they fit just fine. And I always loved this robe. Ivor said it made him think of Joseph, in the Bible, you know? The coat of many colors? And I am glad I brought them, because I never want to see those things I traveled in again!"

"You look wonderful, Ida. But tomorrow, weather permitting, we will go to my tailor in Threadneedle Street and get you something local." She gestured at her own garments. "Like these. We will probably have to take a small boy with us, my cousin Donal, who is eight and bright as brass. I promised him I would take him to get a new tunic, for Midwinter."

Lew had risen when Ida came in, and now he strode to the windows, watching and listening intently. "I think it will have to wait until the next day—it sounds like we are in for a bit of a blow tonight, and the streets will be terrible. And I think you should take a small carriage, unless you ride, *Mestra* Davidson."

"You must call me Ida, Senator. *Mestra* Davidson sounds very old, and I really don't want to feel old right now."

"Then you must call me Lew. Ah, here is food. I ordered some lentil soup, bread, honey, and mulled wine, as well as tea. I hope that meets with your approval."

"Lentil soup sounds perfect!"

There was a small round table at one side of the sitting room, where the servant set the tray down and began laying out the crockery. In a few minutes they were all seated around it, eating. Ida brought Margaret up to date on various scandals at University, and Margaret asked about people she knew there. Lew listened for the most part, and did not seem bored hearing about total strangers. Margaret knew he was studying Ida, and thought he liked the older woman.

It felt very good to have Ida there, good yet strange at the same time. She seemed to Margaret to be someone from another world, not the world of University, but just not Darkovar. When the meal was finished, and Ida announced that she wanted a nap, Margaret was mildly relieved, and guilty at the same time. She watched the small, gaily dressed figure leave the sitting room, then looked at her father.

"I know, Marguerida. It is sometimes hard to have guests, even the best loved ones. But I am glad to have the opportunity to meet her, and I think she will have a good time during her stay."

"I hope so. At least she has better linguistic skills than Ivor did, and will probably feel comfortable in *casta* soon enough. He would be like an idiot for weeks whenever we went to a new place, and then one morning he would wake up chattering like a jay. But during the time when he was speaking pidgin-whatever, I had to do all the translating, and it was exhausting."

"You really loved him, didn't you?" There was a note in his voice, a kind of sorrow, and perhaps a little envy as well.

"Yes, I did. And I miss him every day."

21

It was three mornings later when Margaret, Ida, and Donal Alar set off in a small carriage. Ida was wearing some clothes that Piedra had found for her, a blue tunic and matching skirt, with several petticoats, and over it, a fine woolen cloak of pale green. Her wispy gray hair was hidden under a knitted helmet she insisted was a Dorian cowherds cap, and while it was peculiar looking, it was properly modest by Darkovan standards, and warm as well. Ida seemed unperturbed that she might appear eccentric, which was a relief to Margaret.

As Margaret had anticipated, Ida had begun to use *casta* with a moderate fluency after she had gotten some rest. She asked the names of things without hesitation, quite unembarrassed by the present limitations of her vocabulary. She had a large array of nouns at her command, but her verb forms were still a bit inconsistent. Margaret knew she would treasure forever the expression on the face of Regis Hastur when Ida asked him the name of the wood that a chair was carved from, then informed him of its derivation from some old Terran tongue.

Donal was regaling Ida with a discussion of a hawk he had been training. He would begin in the Terran Margaret had managed to teach him while they were at Arilinn, then shift into *casta* when he ran out of vocabulary. Ida listened intently but Margaret was not sure how much she was learning about hawking. Years of listening to students had given Ida a great deal of experience with the young, and she noticed that occasionally the older woman would interrupt in order to tell Donal the Terran word. They were teaching each other!

Their first stop was not in Threadneedle Street, but in the small Terran cemetery where Ivor was buried. They reached it an hour after leaving Comyn Castle, for while it was a shorter journey on foot, the carriage had to take several detours in order to get through the narrow and icy streets.

The graveyard was silent, cloaked in snow, the headstones gleaming with ice in the pale sunlight. When they arrived at Ivor's resting place, they found the earth cleared of most of the snow, and the entire bed covered in evergreens. It made the other gravesites seem forlorn and neglected.

"How lovely. What a kindly thing to have done, Marguerida." Ida had fallen into using the Darkovan version of her name much of the time, though she still occasionally used the nickname Maggie. "Thank you."

"I did not do it, Ida. It must have been Master Everard, or someone from the Guild. I sent word to him that I was bringing you here today, and begged off visiting to another time. I hope you like the stone."

"I do. But why would the Guild people come out in the cold and . . ."

"Out of respect, I assume. When I was here a few months ago, there were fresh flowers, and the grave had been swept. This cemetery is only for Terrans, and maybe they thought that, as a fellow musician, it was their duty to look after it."

"That is very thoughtful," Ida mused, staring at the greenery.

Margaret shifted her feet on the cold ground, uncomfortable not with the cold but with a rush of feelings she could barely contain. "I wrote a dirge this autumn, just the music," she began, remembering how she had played it on her little harp when she came back to Thendara. At Neskaya, she had played it again, one evening, and found words to go with it, much to her surprise and pleasure. "The words came later. It's the first piece of composition I've done in ages."

"Did you? Can you sing it for me?" Ida seemed a little quiet, strained, her earlier good spirits gone.

"I can try. This is not the best place to sing."

Donal, who had stayed behind, talking to one of the Guardsmen who had ridden behind the carriage, now came trudging across the cemetery toward them. His little boots made crunching noises in the snow, and she remembered that he needed larger ones. He looked about with interest, clearly prepared to be amused.

After trying to think of a good excuse not to perform the piece, and wishing she had thought before she spoke, Margaret took several deep breaths, to warm up her vocal chords. Whyever had she mentioned her piece? She experienced a self-consciousness she had not had in years.

At last she began to sing, and became swept up in the melody and the words, so involved that she did not hear the rustle of cloth behind her. Her voice expanded as she sang, growing louder with each stanza, and the sound of the words drifted out over the grave and the nearby headstones, filling her once again with a sense of loss and peace at the same time. It had needed the words, she realized, and she had done a good job with them, and somehow found the right ones.

Ida was sobbing softly, and Margaret immediately felt terribly guilty. The sight of the grief on the face of the older woman tore her heart. What should she do? She could not move, could not bring herself to embrace the older woman. The ache in her own chest was almost too great to bear.

After several minutes, Ida dried her eyes with the edge of her cloak. "I hadn't cried, not a single tear, until now. Thank you, Margaret."

"What?"

"I couldn't. It was all unreal until now." Ida cleared her throat. "You seem to have attracted an audience," she managed, before another freshet of tears began.

Margaret looked around and discovered that Master Everard and several other people were standing a respectful distance away, waiting in the snow. There was a big man she recognized now as Rodrigo, who would succeed Everard as Guildmaster, and several others who had attended Ivor's funeral the previous spring. One of the women was openly weeping, and Margaret had the interesting sensation of being pleased by moving her, and at the same time, a slight sense of discomfort for so public a display of emotion. In her secret heart, she felt tears were a private thing.

Rodrigo looked at her, then shook his head. "It is regrettable that you position prevents you from becoming a member of the Guild, *domna.* You have a beautiful voice. And those words were splendid."

Master Everard nodded in agreement. "There is nothing to prevent her from being an unofficial . . ."

"A fine idea, Master," Rodrigo boomed.

Ida Davidson blinked fiercely, and Margaret could tell she was glad for the distraction from the members of the Guild. It gave her a chance to recover again. "That was beautiful, my dear, even if I only understood a tenth of it. Thank you. I hadn't really let him go, you see, until now. I kept expecting Ivor to arrive home, grumping about his stomach. Now I know he is really dead."

That was not for her master, but for Domenic. Or perhaps for both of them. I wish she could sing it for Mother—it might help her. But it would probably just upset her. I do wish Mother were more like Cousin Marguerida, and did not get so upset over every little thing. Then Donal looked up at Margaret. "This is the man who was listening to the stars sing, isn't it?" He spoke very quietly.

"Yes, Donal, it is."

"I remember you talking to him, when, you know . . ."

"What does he mean, Marguerida?"

"I will tell you later, Ida. Right now I had better introduce you to Master Everard and these others, before all of us freeze into statues."

"Of course." Ida stamped her feet. "He's really gone," she whispered. *And I cannot bring him home again. I was a fool to think it. There is no way in this cold to dig up the coffin, and it would be terrible to do so. And I can't go home without him. I am sure that Donal just said Ivor was listening to the stars sing—which would be just like him! Oh, how I miss him! That song she made is so tragic and yet so comforting. If only I could have understood all the words. . . .*

Margaret caught the thoughts as they flooded through Ida's mind and felt her face redden. She hadn't meant to overhear! Ida did not suspect that her former charge was a telepath. How was she going to explain things? It was too much right then. Her nerves were too raw, from Ida's grief and her own, to think of anything. Instead, Margaret turned and greeted the old music master, trying to ignore the several bobs, bows, and curtsies she received, and began to make proper introductions.

Ida Davidson had not spent all of her adult life in the circles of academia without learning precisely how to behave in a variety of circumstances. Her command of *casta* was not yet sufficient to be able to talk to Master Everard fluently, though she made a noble effort. Margaret watched her control her grief, and marveled. But the cold did not make for comfort, and after a short time, with promises of a future visit, they returned to the carriage and continued their journey.

The small brazier in the floor of the carriage had kept it relatively warm during their absence. When they settled back into their places, Ida said, "Marguerida, I think that it is going to be impossible to unearth Ivor's coffin for months. I hadn't really considered that aspect of things when I planned this trip."

"Nor had I. And you are right. The ground is totally frozen. And even if we could, I am not sure they would let you ship Ivor home. Things in the Federation are in such a tangle!"

"Damn!"

Margaret was surprised, because she had never heard Ida curse before. Donal watched their expressions, and reached out to give Ida a gentle pat on the hand. "I never asked you how long you were staying, Ida. I seem to have had my head in the clouds a lot lately."

"My return passage is booked for a month from now, but perhaps it can be changed. If the bureaucrats will permit it!"

"There, at least, I might be able to help. My uncle, Captain Rafe Scott, works at Terran HQ, and he seems to be very clever at fixing things."

"I don't want to go home without him." *I don't want to go back at all! Without Ivor, it isn't the same. And with all the funding cuts, I am likely to find myself out on the street. He isn't there—he is here! No, he isn't anywhere! Ivor—curse you for leaving me—again! He always seemed to be going away without me!*

Margaret ignored these thoughts as well as she was able. "You have come such a long way, and now to be frustrated—damn, indeed! But, you know, you will be welcome here for as long as you like. As far as I am concerned, you can stay here forever. We have lots of room, and, truthfully, I would love it. Do you really want to go back to University, with all the things that are happening?" She felt herself tremble just a little, wondering if she had any right to offer Ida a place on Darkover without asking her father or Regis Hastur first. Margaret also wondered how much of her generosity was based on that flash of vision, and how much on her genuine affection for the old woman. If only human things could be as clear as music!

"Not really. It just isn't the same without Ivor, and even though he was gone a great deal of the time, and I had charge of our students alone, I always knew he would come back. It is very sweet of you to offer me a home, too, Margaret. Why, I might even be able to complete his work here."

"Certainly, you could do that. Or you could just be a lady of leisure. The Alton Domain would welcome you." *You could stay here, by the fire at Armida, and teach that pretty girl. I wonder who she is? Alanna Alar, perhaps? Stop this immediately, Margaret Alton! You are meddling.*

"Well, I won't decide anything right now. But that is a very attractive offer, Maggie. Never to have to argue with some stupid bureaucrat again sounds wonderful. I thought I was going to lose my mind, a few times, trying to arrange to come to Darkover. The Federation seems to be losing its collective mind. My bags were searched four times!"

"Your bags! They never did that when I was traveling with Ivor."

Ida fell silent for several minutes, and Donal looked out the window of the carriage. Then the older woman nodded to herself. "No, likely not. The struggle I had with all the new regulations . . . I was furious, and I think it gave me something to keep myself busy. To keep my grief at bay." She sighed, dabbed a tear away, and straightened her shoulders. "Tell me, Margaret, how would I live, if I remained here?"

"Live?"

"Earn my bread, so to speak!"

Margaret laughed. "I am a very rich woman, in my own right, by Darkovan standards, and you would not have to do a thing except be your wonderful self. Or, you could do as you suggested, and continue to research Darkovan music. I have collected enough material to keep you busy for a decade, and I didn't even really scratch the surface. There are songs here that go back to Old Scotland, on Terra before they went into space, and also new ones that are interesting. As near as I can discover, no one has invented the symphonic form, but there is an enormous body of vocal music to be studied. I hardly scratched the surface. And the Musicians Guild would be delighted to help you and to share your knowledge, too. You would not be idle, unless you wanted to be."

"I am so used to fighting for funding, that I can't quite grasp the idea of not having to do it. More than that, I am beginning to realize that there is nothing to go back to, not really. The house belongs to University, and although I have life tenancy, I don't know if that will continue, with all the nonsense about cutting off pensions and such. I was not joking when I said I might end up on the street."

"I know you weren't, Ida. My father and I have been discussing it for the past few days. Even though he has retired from the Senate, he still keeps in touch with our current Senator, Herm Aldaran, and with some other people he knew. He thinks things are going to get worse before they get better."

"If they get better at all," Ida muttered bitterly.

It was almost midday when the carriage pulled into the intersection of Threadneedle and Shettle Streets, as close as they could get to Master Aaron MacEwan's shop. There was, mercifully, no wind to speak of, and the icy patches on the cobbles were few. The three of them walked down the street carefully, however, and finally arrived at their destination.

Manuella, Aaron MacEwan's wife, was solemnly folding a bolt of cloth at the great cutting table in the middle of the shop. Margaret remembered awakening on it the day Ivor died. Shivering, though not with cold, she felt that Ivor was everywhere today.

The tailor's wife brightened when she saw Margaret, and approached them with a smile and glad greetings. *"Vai domna!* How lovely to see you. Aaron will be back in a few minutes. He just stepped out to harass the embroiderers, even though I told him not to."

"Greetings, Manuella. May I present my teacher, Ida Davidson, and my young cousin, Donal Alar. He wants a blue tunic for the Midwinter Festival, and I need a fitting, I suppose, for whatever masterpiece Aaron has been working on for me. And I need to have things made for *Mestra* Davidson, who is staying with me now. Ida, this is Manuella MacEwan; though her husband is the master tailor, she is the one who runs the place."

The little woman beamed at this praise. "Of course! Welcome, *Mestra* Davidson." She then peered uncertainly at Ida, wondering if her words had been understood.

"Thank you for your welcome, *mestra."* She had the phrase down pat. Margaret could see Manuella relax at the answer. "I have been looking forward to coming here since Marguerida told me about your establishment." Ida used a word that actually meant something closer to "land-holding" and Manuella's eyes widened slightly, but the sense was clear enough. "I am wearing some things that were left in Comyn Castle, but they are somewhat too large, and I cannot sew a stitch." Her verb forms were not perfect, and she tended to use the infinitive rather than the gerund, but the meaning came across well enough. It did not seem to have occurred to Ida to ask one of the servants to alter the clothing she was lent. Like Margaret herself, she did not quite know how to behave with the maids and manservants.

"And why should you? Leave that to experts. Here, now. Nella! Where is that girl? Ah, there you are. Please take *Mestra* Davidson into the back and measure her. Then tell Doevid to go to the loft and bring down that bolt of dove gray wool, the green from Ardais, and . . ."

"Perhaps that mauve we just received," the girl broke in saucily. She was about fifteen, round and pert, a pretty young woman.

"Humph. Maybe, though I am not sure the color will suit *Mestra* Doevidson. That violet we have had since summer might be better."

"Yes, Manuella." Nella and Ida vanished behind the curtains at the back of the shop.

"Now, young man," Manuella began, "what sort of blue did you have in mind?"

"Do you have something very dark, like the sky after sunset, almost purple." He seemed to know exactly what he wanted, and Margaret was a little surprised. Both of his parents were very indecisive, and she could not imagine where he had learned to be so certain.

"Now, why do you want such a color?"

Donal looked up at Manuella, frowned for a moment, then shrugged. "I don't know—it just seems good or something."

The tailor's wife looked over at Margaret, as if to say that young boys wanting new tunics was a strange experience for her. Then she smiled at Donal again. "I believe we do have a short bolt in a color that you might like—it has been sitting in the loft for a long time, because no one really liked it."

"Maybe it was waiting for me," Donal announced, as if he expected such occurrences in his life.

Margaret had not realized how tense she had been until she began to relax in the calm atmosphere of the shop. Ida thought she had written the song for Ivor, but Donal had known it was for Domenic, and had been wonderfully discreet as well. She found herself wondering what sort of man this clever little boy was going to become, and wanting very much to see it.

Still, the incident had left her feeling conflicted and anxious. The smell of wool and silk and linen, mingled with dust and the scent of tea wafted around her. These odors made her think again of her first visit, and the pain of Ivor's death seemed fresh again. But the soothing atmosphere of the shop wore away the edges of her sorrow, muting it down to a bearable level. It was very restful, with nothing to trouble her immediately, no Domain lords and ladies arguing, no Gisela Aldaran clinging to Mikhail's arm.

Aaron stomped crossly into the shop, muttering under his breath, then stopped and smiled when he saw Margaret. He was a large man, black-haired and broad-shouldered, who looked more like a carter than a master tailor. Only the fluffs of fiber clinging to his sleeves gave any hint of his occupation. He made her a brief bow, glanced at Donal curiously, and said, "*Domna* Alton! What a pleasure to see you. Did you like the white gown your father ordered for you?"

"I love it, Aaron. It is very beautiful, and I received a great many compliments on it. The cut of the cloth is so wonderful, and I think that Lady Linnea and *Domna* Aillard were almost envious. No doubt they will want something of the sort for themselves."

"Well, if they envied that, when they see you at the Midwinter ball, their eyes will pop out of their heads."

"Aaron! What a thing to say," Manuella commented, throwing up her hands as if to say there was nothing she could do with her husband.

"Nonsense! You yourself said it is a remarkable bit of work, and I confess, *domna,* that I enjoyed the making of the gown more than I have anything in years. I was getting quite stale, making ordinary clothing for this one and that. Did you know that Rafaella came by and ordered a gown for the ball? I wondered at it, but she seems to think she will be attending."

"She did tell me, when we were returning from Neskaya, that she was going to be there with a friend." Margaret did not want to mention that the friend was her uncle, Rafe Scott, because she thought it was no one's business. She wished them the joy of their odd alliance, and only wished her own life could be as simple.

"I see. I confess I did not quite believe her. Renunciates do not often attend balls at the Castle," he finished, clearly feeling that people should know their places, and keep to them. "Now, let's get the gown out and see how it fits. You look to have lost a bit of weight, *domna*. And I shall warn you now that if you do not like the gown, I shall have to fall upon my scissors."

Donal, who had been listening to all of this with great interest, looked up at the tall tailor and said, "Why would you do that?"

"Because my heart would break," Aaron replied teasingly.

"Don't be foolish, Aaron," Margaret answered, before Donal could inquire further. "Everything you have made for me has been wonderful."

Manuella had left the main room, and now returned carrying something wrapped in a white sheet. She bore it across her arms, and moved as if holding something precious. She laid it on the cutting table and began to unfold the coverings.

Under the faint light from the street and the flickering illumination of the lampions, Margaret saw what at first appeared to be a mass of glittering gold on a bed of violet. Then Aaron leaned forward and picked it up, shook it out, and held it by the hanger.

Prepared as she was for something beautiful, Margaret still gasped with delight. The undergarment was a long column of violet silk, shining in the light, with a low neckline, though not at all immodest. Except for the sleeves, the underrobe was rather plain, almost severe, and she knew it would cling to the planes of her body like a second skin. After months of garments cut full, to conceal the body, she thought it might be rather outrageous, and, perversely, she liked the idea.

Margaret was a little surprised at her feelings of rebellion. Then, as she stared at the beautiful garment, she realized that Gisela Aldaran would be either shocked or envious, and that she was delighted by the prospect of one reaction or the other. *I never knew I was such a cat!*

The sleeves were large, gathered things, full at the shoulder and falling to midarm, where a wide ruffle cascaded down, ready to conceal the silken mitts she would wear. It was a form she had not seen on Darkover before. The edge of the ruffle and the hem were embroidered with golden silk, a pattern of tiny vines and small flowers.

The overtunic was made of a fine, sheer stuff, gold threads which shone like a sun even in the dim light of the room. It had no sleeves, so the purple of the undergown was visible along the arms, and then muted over the body. The neckline of the overtunic was high, and gathered into a small ruche which she knew would fall just beneath her square chin. It was very simple in its lines, but the overall feeling was one of opulence. Margaret fell in love with it immediately, then wondered if she was up to wearing such a dramatic gown.

"Aaron, this is magnificent! You have created a whole new style, and all the fine ladies of Thendara will be pounding at your door the morning after the ball, even if there is the mother of all snow storms."

"And that Gisela will be mad as fire," Donal added, looking pleased with himself. Margaret shot a quick look at the little boy—he did not miss much, did he?

Aaron ignored Donal, and looked both pleased and smug. "I am glad you find it good, *domna.* The glover has made some new mitts, of the same fine silk as the undergown, but a shade paler, and he promises that he will have them at the castle in good time. And the cobbler is working on the slippers even as we speak. Indeed, we must send to him, to make certain they do not pinch, for you will not want tight shoes to dance in."

"You seem to have thought of everything, as usual, Aaron. While he is here, I would like him to measure Donal for some new boots. Don't let me forget, please."

"Cousin Marguerida!" Donal seemed stunned.

"If you have grown taller, your feet must be longer."

"Thank you!" His face was red with blushing.

Aaron nodded at Margaret. "I want you to be as beautifully garbed as you are lovely. I don't get too many opportunities to dress fine ladies, but, as you say, once this is seen, I will be beleagered." He gave a deep sigh, but the twinkle in his dark eyes belied his apparent dismay.

Margaret had to laugh, at both Aaron's expression, and the slightly scandalized one on Manuella's face. "I know, Aaron. It is a terrible burden to be a genius. But someone has to do it."

"Please, my lady," Manuella protested, holding back a grin of her own. "Don't encourage him. He is difficult enough as it is."

"Difficult! I am the kindliest and most patient of men, wife. Now, please take her into the back and see to the fit. I think the underrobe will have to be taken in a bit. You really must eat more, Lady."

"If I ate any more, Aaron," she protested, "I would do nothing else." She heard him chuckle at this.

"I should be so fortunate," he rumbled at her back, and she could hear him pat his middle.

Margaret followed Manuella toward the back area as Ida came out from behind the curtains, trailed by Nella, who had a look on her face of barely suppressed merriment. Ida glanced at Margaret, well aware of the expression on the face of the girl, and gave a little shrug. *The language is very slippery, and I think I said something odd—no matter.* She did not seem at all discomforted by her gaffe, and Margaret sensed that she was actually having a very good time. She had a sudden spurt of delight, glad that Ida was there, that she was finding her way around in *casta,* but most of all that everything was going well.

The boy, Doevid, who had gone to the loft, came down the narrow stairs balancing several bolts as if they were matchsticks, and plopped them on the table. Margaret hesitated for a second, wondering if she should stay and translate for the older woman, then decided that Ida was perfectly capable of doing that herself, and that Donal was there to help.

In the back of the shop, it was quite warm. The smell of tea from the samovar that stood on a small table wafted up and made her mouth water. Margaret had not realized she was thirsty until now, but she knew that tea and fine silk did not mix, so she disrobed, except for her underwear and mitts, and let Manuella slip the violet undertunic onto her body inside out. The woman begin to pin along the seams, poking Margaret occasionally. She felt bony and uncomfortable, and wished she were not so skinny. It was as if the matrix on her skin consumed more energy than she could put into her body.

There should really be some way to regulate the matrix, she thought, trying not to fidget. *Everything is energy, or so the physicists say—so why are we entirely dependent on food as an energy source for matrix work? Because we are human beings,* she reflected rather ruefully, *not machines or angels.* She let her speculation lapse and wiggled her toes in her boots. The feel of the silk against her skin was very nice, and she started to think of nothing in particular, which was a vast relief.

When Manuella was satisfied with her adjustments, she slipped the overtunic on, again wrong side to, muttering under her breath. Her generous mouth was full of pins, so conversation was impossible, and Margaret did not want to talk anyhow. She was deep in the almost sensual enjoyment of the present moment. Here, there were no demands. Her shoulders drooped a little, and then she remembered that she had to stand up straight.

For an instant she was a little girl again, in a long line of small girls, hearing Matron tell them to keep their shoulders back, their hands folded in front of them, their feet together. She could almost smell the cold, dry air of the dormitory at the John Reade Orphanage. Then the feeling passed, and she was herself once more, adult and tired.

"You can come over to the glass, now, *domna*. You won't see the full effect until the gown is altered, but the colors are wonderful for you. Aaron thought the gold of the gauze was like your eyes."

Margaret moved carefully toward the mirror, and saw herself, pale-skinned and red-haired, reflected in the shining surface. The gown clung to her length like a sheath, and the small ruff beneath her chin was more becoming than she would have believed. "I look pretty fine, don't I?"

"Yes, you do. Of course, it helps that you have a good figure. Aaron nearly tears his hair out when someone comes in who is all curves and bulges, plump as a pigeon, and wants a fitted gown."

"No curves on me!"

"Now, now. There are a few, but just in the proper places."

"My chest is too flat!"

Manuella chuckled. "Be glad. The generous breasted sag after a few children. I will take it off now. Would you care for some tea?" Manuella began gently pulling the garments off over Margaret's head.

"Oh, thank you. My mouth feels so dry, and my throat . . . I was singing in the graveyard a while ago, and I think the cold air has made it sore."

Manuella made no comment, as if singing in the cemetery were a perfectly ordinary event, and put the gown back on its well padded hanger. While Margaret redressed, she poured tea into a thick mug, added two dollops of honey, and handed it to her. It was hot, but not scalding, and very sweet, but Margaret half emptied the container in her thirst. It slid down her throat smoothly, soothing her overworked vocal cords.

They went back into the front of the shop, and found that the cobbler had arrived, holding a bundle in his arms. Margaret realized that she would have to sit down for this part of the fitting, and brightened immediately. She sank onto a bench that sat beside the stair to the loft, and let the cobbler remove her boots, cupping her mug in her hands and feeling the warmth of the remaining tea seep into her palms.

Aaron and Ida were standing at the cutting table, and Ida was fingering the various fabrics, and chattering away to the big tailor, in a nice mixture of *casta* and Terran that did not seem to confuse the man at all. They made a funny picture, tall Aaron bending over tiny Ida, but they were getting along very well.

She looked around for Donal then, her heart speeding up for fear she had lost him. Margaret knew that no harm could come to him in Aaron's shop, but every time she looked at her charming little cousin, she remembered how she had inadvertently sent him into the overworld, and that he could have died there. Ah, there he was, in the shadow of the wide shelf that ran along the street, where goods were displayed in fine weather. There was someone with him, bent down to the level of the boy, in dark clothing, with his face turned away, so she could not recognize him.

Then she caught a glimpse of rufus-colored hair, and a quick, familiar gesture. "Ethan? Is that you?"

The cobbler had her feet in his hands, and was slipping something over her hose, but Margaret hardly noticed. "How do they feel?"

"Yes, *domna,* it is me. I was just talking to your cousin here, because he had a lot of questions." Ethan stood up, stepped from the shadows, and came to greet her, beaming. "He wanted to know about the Big Ships, and, oh, everything, just like I did when I met you."

"How do they feel?" repeated the cobbler, ignoring everything except his art.

Dutifully, Margaret wriggled her toes, and found the soft slippers did not pinch. She set her mug down on the bench, rose to her feet, and took a few steps. Ethan moved closer. He was still a skinny lad, but seemed to have grown a couple of inches in the months since she had last seen him. His face no longer had the hungry look of a frustrated boy. She remembered how she had gone to the letter writer in the Horse Market, as she was leaving with Rafaella for the Kilghards, and dictated an introduction to Captain Rafe Scott for him.

On impulse, she bent down and hugged him. She was pleased and surprised when he returned it. Indeed, his hug was fierce, hard and full of unspoken emotions. There was nothing complicated about these feeling, for they were clear and simple. Margaret wished everything were as easy as getting Ethan started on the way to the stars had been.

The cobbler was a single-minded fellow, if an artist, and tugged at her sleeve, demanding her attention. "They do not pinch, but the sole on the left one seems to poke me where it oughtn't. The arch is just a bit too low, I think." She rocked forward onto her toes, then back on her heels. "Yes, that's it."

"Very good. I wish all my customers noticed such things. They come in," he explained, "and take their shoes, then complain that they are not right, when they did not take the time to try them on."

"I learned a long time ago to pay attention to my feet, since an ill-fitting shoe will sour my disposition very quickly." She went back to the bench and let the cobbler peer at her feet, watching him take out a small ruler with arcane markings on it, measure something, then nod to himself. At last he was satisfied, removed the slippers, put them into a soft, cloth sack, and promised to have them delivered to Comyn Castle the following day. Before he could escape, she told him to measure Donal, and the lad grinned up at her.

Margaret sat on the bench, stocking-footed and too tired to put her footwear back on. Ethan sat down on one side of her while Donal was being measured. "You have grown, haven't you?" she asked.

"I have done that. Both my body, and my brain, which seems to expand more all the time. I am studying mathematics, as you said I must. It is very hard, but I love it. The Captain says I have a lot of talent for it. And, if the Terranan don't close the port, I will begin some engineering classes in the spring."

"Close the port?"

"HQ has more rumors than all of Darkover, and one is that they are going to close the port. The Captain says not to worry, so I don't. Well, not too much." The hero worship in his voice when he spoke Rafe Scott's title was unmistakable, and Margaret felt that she had done a good thing in sending Ethan to her uncle.

"It is as good as you hoped it would be, Ethan?"

He did not answer immediately, but looked thoughtful. "It is not anything like I imagined," he said at last, "not at all, but it is interesting. The mathematics are wonderful—I am doing calculus now, which the Captain says I need in order to understand spatial relationships."

"Calculus? I never got that far."

Ethan grinned. "Well, it truly strains my brain." Margaret could tell he was proud of his accomplishment, and knew that he probably had no one close who could understand what it meant.

"How does your family feel about all this?"

"They did not like it, at first, but Father said I had to do what was right for me. Mother tried to make me promise never to take ship, wanted me to sit around in HQ and write reports, but Father said not to be silly, that if I was offered the chance to travel, it was my fate to do it. She cried a lot, but then she stopped. Now she is trying to find me a girl, so I will change my mind or something. Mothers!" He said this last word with great feeling.

"How is Geremy?" She remembered his cousin, and how the two young men had led them to the house of Master Everard the day she had returned to Darkover. Only half a year had passed since that day, but so much had occurred that she felt she was an entirely different person—one she barely knew and did not entirely trust. It was a very disspiriting thought, and she set it away abruptly.

Ethan rolled his eyes toward the heavy beams in the ceiling very comically, and lifted his long hands with an expression of helplessness. "Geremy has fallen in love, and stands around mooning over Rachel MacIvan like a ninny. It is really disgusting! She has several others trailing after her, like a goose with a lot of goslings, for she is pretty enough, I guess. But vain, and really stupid."

"Have you told him that?" Margaret was amused, and she could tell that Donal, beside her, was taking it all in. It struck her that this must be a peculiar experience for her young cousin, that he had lived all of his short life in the shadow of his nervous parents, and that he had no real idea of how other boys behaved. He would be old enough to enter the Cadets in a couple of years, if Ariel Alar permitted it. Which she might not, being the person she was. At least she knew that Ethan was completely trustworthy, and that he would not lead Donal into mischief.

"No, I haven't. He would just be cross with me. I listen to his attempts at poetry, and his discussion of Rachel's hair, skin, the shape of her nose, and all of that, and pretend to be interested. I am too busy with my studies for girls, anyhow, so I do not see him often enough to be bored with it, but I do miss the old Geremy, Lady. We used to do everything together, and now we do nothing, for the Terranan discourage any visitors, and they no longer allow good lads to hang about the entrance to the port either."

"Yes, when I went to fetch *Mestra* Davidson, I noticed there were no boys about, but I thought it was just because of the cold."

"*Mestra* . . . is that woman the widow of your Professor Doevidson? She and Uncle Aaron have been yacking away like old friends, and I didn't really realize that she was a Terranan. Her accent is a bit strange, but I thought she was from up in the hills."

"Let me introduce you."

Margaret began to stand up, but Ethan restrained her lightly. Then he knelt on the floor and slipped her boots back onto her feet. His head was bent down as he said, "I never thanked you for what you did for me, *domna.*"

A little embarrassed, Margaret answered, "Of course you did, Ethan."

"Not enough. My family thinks I have lost my mind, that I will lose interest and come back to them. You were the first person who ever took me seriously, and that means more than you can imagine, *domna.*"

"She is good at listening, isn't she?" Donal piped up. He put a small hand around Margaret's wrist. "She's my favorite relative, even better than Mik."

"Why, thank you, Donal." Margaret was very touched, but she tried to hide it. The young man and the boy had made her feel their affection for her, and their complete trust as well. It was a strange sensation for her, and she wondered if, when she had children of her own, if ever, would they think of her so generously?

Then she stood up again, and took Ethan over to the cutting table. She waited until there was a break in the intense conversation between the tailor and Ida, then introduced them.

Ethan made a bow. "I only knew your husband for a day, *mestra,* but he was a good man, and I sorrow for your loss."

Ida looked at the young man. Margaret could tell she was translating his words in her mind. Then, her eyes filling with tears, she said, "Yes, he was." She blinked quickly, and gave Ethan a watery smile. "I am happy that you had a chance to know him, however briefly."

"The honor was mine, *mestra.*" Ethan's young voice, which had started to change into adult tones, was simple and sincere. What a good lad he was, and what a fine man he was going to become. She let her worries go for the present, knowing they would still be there, waiting for her, later, and smiled at both of them.

22

Mikhail Hastur stood before the mirror. It was the evening of the Midwinter Ball, and he was filled with apprehension. It had nothing to do with the many strong personalities resident in Comyn Castle, all bickering politely at one another. It was annoying, and, at times, infuriating, but it was not what troubled him. His belly clenched, and he felt as if the air around him were about to thicken, to curdle like cheese. Something was going to happen that night, and no matter how often he told himself that the dream he had shared with Marguerida was only that, he could not convince himself.

He studied his new tunic, twitched the hem down with an almost angry tug, and glared at himself. It was a deep blue, the color of *kiriseth* blossoms, and embroidered with that flower in gold. It felt stiff and itchy, though he knew that was only his imagination. His trousers were white, and his shoes were new, the leather dyed to match the tunic. The toes felt as if they were being pinched, but, again, he was sure that could not be. Was he right to have chosen the Hastur colors for this night, instead of the Elhalyn ones? It was too late to worry about it. He hated the outfit, he decided, and wished he were back in his comfortable riding boots, and his favorite old, shabby tunic.

In the next room, he could hear voices. His brothers were discussing something. He could hear Javanne's voice, too, sharp and curt. In the days since her arrival, Mikhail had walked a tightrope, trying to mend fences with her and his father, without betraying Regis at the same time. The strain had been enormous. He was formal and polite to both Marguerida and Gisela, and kept his distance from them both. Marguerida understood what he was doing, but Gisela kept trying to penetrate his armor. Fortunately, his mother and the two little girls had kept him very well chaperoned. Guarded was closer to the truth. He let himself grin, trying to ease the increasing tension in his muscles.

There was a knock on the door. "Come in."

Liriel poked her head in, then entered. He turned away from the mirror to look at her, and decided she looked absolutely magnificent. She was wearing a green gown that fell around her in graceful folds, concealing her size and weight. It was beautiful, and very plain, without any embellishment except a tiny line of gold thread around the hem, throat and cuffs. Her red hair was brushed until it shone, and she had swept it up over her ears, so there were swathes of bronze beside her cheeks. The butterfly clasp was almost hidden, but he could just see the tips of it peeking out.

"Are you ready, or do you want to admire yourself a bit longer?"

"Are you suggesting I am vain, Liri?"

"Not in the least, but you have been in here for half an hour, and I know it does not take you that long to dress. When I find you standing before the mirror, how can I help but think that you are admiring your fine figure?"

"Well, I wasn't. I hate this damn tunic—it seems gaudy, though I did not think so before. And I am not looking forward to an entire evening of dancing and making polite conversation with people I would cheerfully consign to the coldest of Zandru's hells."

"You mean dear Gisela?" There was no mistaking the irony in Liriel's voice, and he grinned.

"Gisela is a complete bother, and her father is worse. The only Aldaran I ever want to see again is Robert, who seems to have all the sense in the family. I wish Regis had never taken it into his head to invite them back to the Council. Let them stay up in the Hellers, plotting Aldones knows what. I've smiled until my face hurts."

"Poor Mik! Shall I protect you from her attentions?"

"There is no need. Valenta will do that—the little minx. She seems to positively enjoy driving Giz off. I think she knows that Gisela doesn't like children, which probably lends it savor. She is going to grow into a very interesting woman."

"If someone doesn't strangle her first," Liriel answered a little darkly. "Several times during the journey I was tempted myself."

Mikhail laughed in spite of his ill humor and a peculiar sense of unease for which he could find no explanation. "Yes, she can be maddening, but it is wonderful how much she has blossomed since leaving that dreadful house. I only wish Emun were as resilient." Although a good diet and untroubled rest had done a great deal to restore the boy, he was still very frail. Mikhail swallowed his persistent worry about Emun, and tried to think of more pleasant matters. He would stand up in a dance with Marguerida—that was something to look forward to.

"You really like the children, don't you?"

Liriel's question startled him out of his thoughts. "I do, though I never thought I would."

"You are going to make a fine father."

"If I ever get the chance—which at the moment seems very unlikely. I wouldn't marry Gisela for all the gold of Carthon, and it seems I cannot marry Marguerida. Should I wait for Valenta to grow up?"

"Mik! What a shocking thing to say. She could be your . . ."

"I know she could, but she isn't. She is half in love with me right now, as Mira was until she clapped her eyes on Dani, but it will not last. Besides, her present ambition is to become the Keeper of Arilinn Tower, and lord it over all the other telepaths on the planet. Come on. I hear Mother ordering up the troops, and I don't want to annoy her. I do that just by being alive."

A short time later, Javanne and *Dom* Gabriel led their family into the enormous ballroom of Comyn Castle. Mikhail was bringing up the rear, with the two Elhalyn girls and Emun, and he could hear the sound of music all the way down the corridor. The children were almost beside themselves with excitement, and he found their enthusiasm contagious. The persistent prick of unease at the back of his mind was fading, and he nearly forgot it.

There were two ballrooms in Comyn Castle, one on the lower floor which opened onto several terraces, and was used in summer, and this one which was reserved for winter occasions. It had a great set of high bay windows on the west wall, polished and gleaming. The lights of the spaceport could be seen, and the night was remarkably clear. Mikhail could see a few clouds scudding across the darkness of the sky. There would be a storm sweeping down from the Hellers soon, but probably not before morning.

The floor was tiled in the pattern of a great starburst, in the blue and silver of the Hasturs. It had been scrubbed until it shone, but not waxed. The musicians gallery was on the left wall, and on the right a long table set with sweets, small morsels of meat wrapped in pastry, and little white cakes, frosted in many colors. There was also wine there, and he found himself wanting a glass, not from thirst but for courage.

Mikhail swept the room with a quick glance, seeking one face among the throngs of people who had arrived before him. He saw Regis in deep conversation with Robert Aldaran, a serious expression on his face, and Lady Linnea nearby, with Gisela beside her. The look on Gisela's face was one of boredom and impatience, as if she wanted to get away from Linnea as quickly as possible, but was trapped by politeness. Danilo Syrtis-Ardais was in his usual location standing just an arm's length from Regis, staring off into space, and clearly trying not to overhear whatever was being said. He saw Regis frown and shake his head at Robert, and wondered what they were talking so solemnly about. A ball was no place to discuss anything important.

Just then Danilo gave him a sharp look, an unreadable glance. *Whatever happens, Mik—keep calm!*

That is not a very soothing thing to tell me.

No, it isn't. Regis is in a bit of a bind, but I think he has a way out of it.

Sometimes I wish my uncle were not so damned clever.

So do I, Mikhail, so do I. There was the sense of ironic humor in his thoughts, and Mikhail smiled to himself.

Many of the minor families of Darkover had come to Thendara, as had been the custom for years, to winter over in the less harsh weather there, and the room was almost full. Comyn Castle was crammed, and every house and hostel in Thendara was stuffed to bursting. Mikhail saw Rufus d'Asturien, and his pretty daughter Darissa, one of the many girls who had been paraded before him over the years. He had been in the Cadets with Rufus' son Emile, so he looked around and finally found him, hanging back against the wall below the musicians gallery, looking glum. Emile loathed dancing, and Mikhail was pleased and a little surprised to actually find him there.

He decided that it would be a good maneuver to introduce the Elhalyn girls to the d'Asturiens, if only to keep himself out of Gisela's orbit for another few minutes. But before he could accomplish this, young Danilo Hastur, looking very fine in a blue-and-silver tunic that was almost as overembroidered as Mikhail's own, arrived and took Miralys' hand, looking deep into her silvery eyes.

"I hope we can stand up in the *pafan* together, Mira," the boy said.

Mira smiled at him gaily. "Since I have been practicing it all week, I hope so, too. It would be a shame to waste all that instruction."

"Come on—let's go tell the musicians to play one. They are just fooling around right now, filling time, but I don't see any reason not to begin the dancing. That is what we are here for, after all." He took her hand tenderly, as if it might break, and drew her away.

Emun watched them over across the room, his eyes a little sad. "Is something wrong, Emun?" Mikhail asked.

"No, no. It is just that Dani is so . . . at ease. I wish I were."

"Oh, pooh," Val snapped. "He is just as sweaty-palmed as you are, Em."

"He doesn't look it!"

"Well, he is. Mira says his hand trembles like a bowl of redberry pudding whenever they touch, and is as wet as a fish."

These sharp words seemed to comfort Emun a little. Mikhail marveled once again at Valenta's ability to say things that would be cruel from anyone else, and have them sound perfectly reasonable. Emun gave a brief tug at the hem of his tunic, and straightened his thin shoulders.

Mikhail sensed rather than heard someone just behind him, and he turned to look. *Dom* Aldaran had just come into the doorway, wearing the great kilt his Domain occasionally displayed, draped around his ample middle, and over his shoulder. He had a sporran hanging from a thick belt, a white-and-black pouch made of fur, and had a sword dangling from his left hip. All in all, the appearance was rather more martial than seemed fitting for the holiday.

Dom Damon smiled at Mikhail, a baring of teeth that held very little real welcome, and nodded at the children who were on either side of him. He ran his pale eyes up and down Mikhail's form, and quirked a bushy eyebrow. "That is a fetching tunic, Mikhail, but I'll wager it will be itchy before the night is over."

"I think you are likely right," he agreed. The room was very warm already, and the more people who pressed into it, the hotter it would become.

"That's why I favor this—no needlework to catch on every little thing. Now, you, young woman, are a lovely sight. I think embroidery belongs on women, not men—and that dress is very becoming."

Valenta gave *Dom* Damon an unreadable look, as if she suspected he was trying to tease her, and made a nice curtsy. She was wearing a rose-colored silk gown, embroidered with silver. Her pale skin looked healthy, and it was clear that she was pleased with herself. "Thank you, *Dom* Damon." She managed to simper, while giving Mikhail an ironic glance.

Then Mikhail saw Marguerida and Lew Alton come in behind Lord Aldaran. He could just make out the shorter form of Ida Davidson beside her, but he barely noticed. His heart leaped in his chest. It was all he could do not to gasp, and he saw from the slight twinkle in her golden eyes, he knew his beloved was perfectly aware of the effect she was having, and enjoying every second of it.

Mikhail took in the line of the gown, so close to her slender body that it was nearly immodest, though the soft folds of the overgown did a reasonable job of concealing the fact. He took in the silken mitts on her hands, and the soft, violet slippers on her feet, and decided she had never been more beautiful.

Dom Damon, aware that he was no longer the center of attention, turned as well, looked at Marguerida and her father, and made a brief grunting sound that might have meant anything. Then he swiveled his head back to look at Mikhail, and there was no mistaking the slight glare in his eyes.

Mikhail ignored the older man, slipped past him, and bowed before his cousin. "You look wonderful, Marguerida. Dani and Mira have gone to tell the musicians to play a *pafan,* so perhaps we can stand up in it together."

Oh, dear. I will probably make a total fool of myself, Mik. I cannot dance at all well.

Nonsense. You are as graceful as a breeze, and you will have the best partner in all of Thendara, except Danilo Ardais. Here—this is the pattern, and all you need to do is memorize it, and listen to the music. That, I know, will be easy for you.

Ah, I see. Now, why didn't anyone ever show me dancing like that before? You've made it as clear as glass. Now, if Dom *Aldaran will just stop looking as if he wants to throttle me.*

To the devil with Damon Aldaran!

I could not agree more.

Calmly, she placed the fingers of her right hand in Mikhail's though he could feel the pulse of her blood beating in her body, then gave *Dom* Damon a look that made the older man turn away. Beside her, he could sense Lew trying very hard not to burst into laughter, while Ida Davidson looked at them with interest. He wondered how much Marguerida had told her, and if she knew there were telepaths in the room.

They make such a wonderful couple, so perfect together. Just as Ivor and I were, years ago. I don't quite understand what Maggie said, about there being some problem, because one would have to be a total fool not to know they were completely in love. This world is very confusing, and there is something . . . why can't I put my finger on it? Undercurrents, of course, but there are always those. Oh, dear . . . that must be Gisela Aldaran, looking ready to kill. I am very glad Maggie has told me of some of the people I'll meet here, and a little of their backgrounds. Ida's disordered thoughts gave Mikhail a moment's warning. By the time Gisela reached them, he was prepared for anything.

Or so he imagined, until Gisela Aldaran stopped and looked Marguerida over, as if she were a dairy animal which had somehow wandered into the castle. Her eyes raked Marquerida from head to toe, narrowing dangerously. Then she curled her lip and said in mildly accented Terran, "What a remarkable ensemble. I would never have the courage to appear in something so outré." Her voice was silky.

Mikhail was aware that Lew and Ida had both overheard this remark, and were ready to leap to Marquerida's defense. Before they could, she answered, "No, of course you wouldn't," in her calmest and most dignified voice, making it sound as if Gisela was not a very brave person.

Back off, bitch!

For a second Mikhail was shocked, for he had never suspected Marquerida of being so vehement. Then he realized that it was not her thought he had heard, that the tone was different. He glanced at Ida, for it was certainly a female, but it was not Ida either. Then he realized it was Valenta who had nearly shouted the thought, and he turned a curious look on the small girl.

Gisela, as well, was startled, and her cheeks flushed an unlovely red that did not suit her. She trembled a little, making the silver lace across her bosom move in her agitation. In a moment she had recovered herself, and glared at Valenta. In turn, the girl grinned shamelessly, her eyes alight with deliberate mischief.

As the musicians began to play the introduction to a familiar *pafan,* people started to form up in the long lines of the dance. Mikhail drew Marguerida away. He led her to a place halfway down the set, where he found himself buttressed on one side by young Dani and Mira Elhalyn, and on the other by Dyan Ardais and Darissa d'Asturien. He found he was holding his breath, and let it out. If Gisela's behavior was any indication, the evening would be very long, indeed.

Mikhail saw Robert Aldaran stroll over to his sister, and say something. Never in his life had Mikhail wanted to eavesdrop more than at that moment. But Robert took her arm and led her to the top of the set, and the first phrase of the music started the actual dance in motion. It was a slow work, with a small tambour keeping the steady beat, while fiols tossed the theme back and forth from one side of the small orchestra to the other.

The dancers faced each other across the lines, bowed or curtsied, then moved to the center to join hands and march four paces toward the gallery. Then there was a dip of knees, and another four paces, followed by a clasping of hands and a circling of each couple, which ended by placing the men on the opposite side of the line from where they had begun.

They rejoined in the center, and repeated the movements in the opposite direction, their backs now to the musicians. It was soothing and uncomplicated, as they changed sides again, weaving back and forth. The slowness of the rhythm was pleasant, and after a few times, he saw that Marquerida was actually beginning to enjoy herself.

See, I told you it was easy.

You were right. I still feel clumsy, but at least I am not embarrassing myself—or you.

No, I think you are magnificent—but I am a besotted idiot, and have absolutely no objectivity!

At last, the music ended, and the dance ceased. Mikhail placed Marguerida's hand lightly on his arm and led her to the refreshment table. "We both need some wine, I think."

"Oh, yes. I am really thirsty." She lifted a mitted hand and brushed a wisp of fine, curly red hair off her forehead. "And wishing Gisela Aldaran on the moon, too, though I shouldn't. Why can't she understand that . . ."

"She told me she had foreseen herself married to a Hastur, and knew it must be me."

"Oh. You mean she has the Aldaran Gift?"

"So she has hinted, but I think a very active imagination is more likely. She never showed a hint of it when I visited the Aldarans years ago."

"Tell me, Mik, are there any other females in your past that you have not told me about. Not that I am jealous, but I want to be prepared."

He picked up two glasses of wine and handed one to Marguerida. Then he looked around the room, at people chatting, as another dance was formed up. "I would say that there were a dozen women in this room right now who had been offered for my possible approval. Over there, the lady in the puce gown, that is Ysabet MacRoss, the great niece of Camilla MacRoss at Arilinn, who is very pleasant and extremely dull. She found me confusing, I believe. She's married to MacGowan now, and I think he suits her very well. And that lovely woman in pink is Darissa d'Asturien, now safely wed to one of her second cousins. She's always been something of a flirt. But there is no one for me except you."

"A pity that your parents do not see it that way. Oh, look. Here are Rafaella and Uncle Rafe. Do you know, I have never seen them together before, and hadn't realized what a handsome couple they make. And I have never seen him wear anything except his uniform."

Mikhail followed her gaze to the doorway, where Rafaella n'ha Liriel and Captain Rafe Scott had just entered. The sudden appearance of a Renunciate in the ballroom, unmistakable with her short-cut hair, caused a subtle stir. From the way her freckles stood out on her pale skin, Rafaella was not unaware of the raised eyebrows she was receiving. She gave Scott a sidelong glance, and Mikhail could see her swallow hard to gather her courage.

But he agreed that they made a good looking couple, both dressed in green, Rafaella in a pale, spring tone, with silver leaves everywhere, and Scott in a dark tunic with a modest amount of embroidery on it. And except for her clipped hair, there was nothing out of the ordinary about the woman. With her fiery tresses, she might have been mistaken for a daughter of the Domains.

"Poor Rafi! She looks as if she is going to faint from terror. I think she needs some wine, Mik." With these words, Marguerida took another glass off the table, and started across the room, skirting the dancers gracefully. Mikhail thought that Rafe Scott could also stand some refreshment, so he took a second glass, and followed her across the floor.

The relief on Rafaella's face, when she saw Marguerida approaching her, would have been comical under any other circumstances. Mikhail knew she was probably regretting coming, and decided he must try to put her at ease.

"You look lovely, Rafi!" Marguerida said, handing her the glass of wine.

"Do I? I feel very odd, for while I have attended any number of dances in my life, I have never been in quite such company before. Several of the ladies are looking at me as if I were a spook."

"Here, Scott, some courage in a glass!"

"I am forever in your debt, Mikhail. I had quite forgotten how beautiful this room was, for I haven't been in it in years. It looks as if the murals have been retouched, too. At least, I do not recall the colors being so bright." He took the offered wine and drained half the glass in one swallow. Then he smiled at his niece. "That is a wonderful gown, Marja—excuse me, Marquerida. I suspect you will set a new fashion in Thendara, and when you are an old woman with grandchildren, they will be wearing something like it at Neskaya or Dalereuth, and thinking it all the rage. Things here change so slowly." He seemed sad and slightly worried.

"Thank you, Uncle. I like it myself, though when I got dressed, I thought I was seeing someone else. This doesn't go with Margaret Alton, Fellow of University, nor with Marguerida, student at Neskaya."

"But it *is* perfect for the heiress of a Domain, *chiya.*"

"Maybe. But sometimes I think that that is a suit of clothing I will never fit into." She cleared her throat and changed the subject. "I saw young Ethan a few days ago, when I was at Aaron's shop, and he seems to find his studies at HQ very challenging."

Scott let out a brief groan. "That boy! He asks more questions than I can answer, and he makes me feel old. But I am glad you sent him to me, because he is going to be a fine spaceman, always assuming that—"

"What?" Mikhail interrupted sharply.

"I can't say, or at least I shouldn't." *Things at HQ are becoming less and less friendly, what with the Federation issuing new orders every hour on the hour, new forms and passes. It is a bureaucrat's erotic dream, but for the rest of us, it is a nightmare. Perhaps I am borrowing trouble—the interest on which is always ruinous—and it will all work itself out in a few months.*

That sounds pretty serious.

It is. The Federation does not like having protected planets that it cannot order about, and there are rumors that all the Protectorates will be changed soon. It is a ploy to force places like Darkover to give up their status and become full members, and they can do it, too.

How?

Quite simple, really. Stop trade, ruin the economy for a generation, and then come in and take over.

Does Regis know about this?

Not from me. Rafe Scott made a face, as if he had a bad taste in his mouth, and finished his glass of wine in a couple of gulps. *I am stuck in the middle, because of my double citizenship, and being half Darkovan, and my loyalties are pulling me in all directions. To inform Regis directly would be to break my oath to the Service, and not to would be breaking faith with Darkover. But as long as I remain in the Service . . .*

You sound as if you might not be there long.

I will stay in the Service as long as I am able, because it is useful to Darkover for me to be there. But if it comes to betraying the planet, I will resign. It would be a relief, actually.

Poor Uncle Rafe!

Captain Scott laughed at this, and Rafaella, who was aware that things were being discussed from which she was being excluded, gave him a shining glance. She did not appear to mind at all that she was the only non-telepath in the group. "Come on, old fellow. I came to dance, not to stand around."

Old fellow? Marguerida gave her uncle a look.

She tells me it's a term of affection, and I think it is, I am old, compared to her, and feeling older everyday.

Then get out while you can! Don't sacrifice yourself, Uncle.

The Service has been my life, chiya.

Well, then, it is about time you had another. Why, you and Rafi could go into business together, running a guide business or something.

Tours of scenic Darkover our specialty?

Exactly!

Scott chuckled softly, handed his empty glass to Mikhail, and led Rafaella toward the set that was forming up in the middle of the dance floor.

Valenta Elhalyn slipped in beside Mikhail, looked up at him with her gleaming eyes, and said, "Will you dance with me? I've been practicing for days and days, and I don't want to waste it. You do not mind, do you, Marguerida?"

"Of course not, Val." Then Mikhail looked at the two glasses in his hands, as if they had just then grown out of his fingers.

"No, I don't mind a bit, Valenta. One slow dance is about all I can manage at present. I think I will go over and stand by the windows, where it is cool—I feel a little flushed. Here, give me those! You look foolish, Mik."

Marguerida took the glasses from him, threading the stems between her fingers. A servant carrying a tray appeared immediately and almost snatched them out of her hands. Mikhail caught the scene out of the corner of his eye, and tried not to laugh. As adaptable as she was, he did not think Marguerida was ever going to become completely accustomed to servants.

Mikhail turned his attention away, and nearly ran into Gisela Aldaran. He managed to stop just short of knocking her down. She gave him a feral smile, as if aware that she had discomforted him. "Aren't you going to ask me to dance?"

"No, Giz, I am not!"

"What will people think, if you do not stand up with me?"

"I don't care a bit what people think, and if you keep flinging yourself in my way, they will take you for a hussy. Go away. You bore me." He was surprised at himself, for he knew he had not drunk enough wine to be so abrupt. But his temper was frayed, and he realized he had been longing to say those words for weeks.

Hussy! I like that, Mik! But I prefer bitch!

Valenta!

I'm only a little girl, and I can't help myself, can I?

You can, and you know it!

Yes, but I love the way your face gets when I am naughty!

And how is that?

You suck your cheeks in like you had a lemon in your mouth, and your eyeballs bulge.

You are a wicked girl, Val.

What can you expect from a crazy Elhalyn?

Mikhail could formulate no answer to this question. He moved around the stunned Gisela, and took his place in the dance. Liriel had tested Valenta, and said she was going to be a very powerful telepath indeed. Nonetheless, he was surprised by the strength of her mental voice, and also disquieted. She seemed to be coming into her *laran* almost too soon, and he felt a chill. Even with the best care in the world, a third of children did not survive threshold sickness.

The music took off and sent the worries from his head. It was a rather boisterous piece that demanded a lot of stamping and foot tapping, and was a favorite of his. He let himself became absorbed in the dance itself. Valenta hefted her skirts a bit, and matched his gestures, grinned at him impishly. Then it was over, and he was bowing over her tiny six-fingered hand.

"That was fun. Did I do well?"

"You are an excellent dancer, Valenta."

"I'm glad. You looked so worried, and now you seem happier."

"Do I?" His moods did seem to be shifting every five minutes, and he felt the stab of unease return again.

"Yes. Thank you very much. Now I am going to go find Danilo Ardais, and find out if he really is the best dancer on Darkover! You didn't see me, but I stood up with Francisco Ridenow, and he has no more idea than a cow how to dance."

Mikhail laughed in spite of himself. "Yes, but it doesn't do to say it."

"Oh, I didn't. I thanked him nicely and said I enjoyed myself. Oh, dear."

"What?"

"Gisela Aldaran is over talking to Marguerida, and she doesn't look happy. By the window."

Mikhail swiveled his head around so fast he almost put a crick in his neck. In the shadows of the long drapes he could just make out his beloved and Gisela, their heads bent toward one another, like conspirators. What he could see of their expressions was dismaying—antagonistic on Gisela's part, and remote on Marguerida's. He knew that face too well.

He moved across the room as quickly as he could, and came up just as Gisela said, "You cannot win, you know."

"I already have," he heard Marquerida answer, her usually pleasant voice chilly and distant, as if she were far away. She turned her head, looking out the window.

The sky was very dark above the lights shining from the port, and the few clouds had blown away. The stars gleamed above the city. The softer lights of lampions and torches in Thendara itself gave a warm glow to everything. It was very beautiful, and very calm.

Then Mikhail noticed that three of the moons stood in what seemed like a line, just above the horizon, their colors blending softly. Mormallor, the smallest and whitest, stood at one end, and mauve Idriel at the other, with Kyrrdis, blue and green, between them. He felt himself stiffen. The dream came back, vivid and immediate!

"You can't! They are going to announce the engagement tonight!" Gisela's voice, usually so silky, was almost shrill now.

"It does not matter," Marguerida replied, so calm she seemed made of stone. "You are deluded, Gisela. You have backed the wrong horse."

Gisela Aldaran stamped her foot and from the movement of her jaws, was clearly grinding her teeth. Mikhail hesitated, wanting to intervene, yet not wishing to get between them. He could feel the anger emanating from Gisela, and a serenity from Marguerida that surprised him. Her eyes seemed a little unfocused, as if entranced by some inner vision.

The blue light of Liriel, the fourth moon, rose above the horizon, just the smallest portion of it visible. And he felt something rumble along his bones, a sound like the earth moving. A voice like a crack of thunder roared in his mind, paralyzing his will.

"TO HALI! NOW!"

23

One moment Margaret was speaking to Gisela, listening to the sullen hissing of her voice, and the next she felt a vast weight press into her mind. It was horrible and terrifying, but part of her remained quite calm. She had an instant of disorientation, as if she were in two places at the same time. Whatever she had been about to say vanished. She struggled to pull away, but whatever it was, it was too strong. Then Margaret felt more than heard the the voice from her dream quake through her body, overwhelming all else. *TO HALI! NOW!*

She turned from the window, her hands shaking. The uncertainty she had endured since the dream was gone, replaced by an urgency that nearly overcame her. Her legs were trembling, and she felt as if there were a collar around her throat, pulling her away from the windows. It was not painful, just inexorable.

Margaret looked into Mikhail's eyes, and knew he felt it as well. She swallowed hard, took his hand, and said, "Come, my dearest. We have an appointment with destiny."

It was not until they had crossed half the great chamber that Margaret noticed no one else was moving. Musicians sat frozen above their instruments, in mid-movement. Regis Hastur's mouth was open, as if he had been cut off in the middle of a word.

She barely had time to take it in before the weight in her mind forced her to keep moving, clutching his hand. Margaret felt Mikhail resist her tug, looking around the room at the immobile figures. Finally, he shook his head, as if to clear it, and matched her strides across the room.

"Appointment with destiny? Did you have to be so melodramatic?" He sounded angry, and she could sense his reluctance, in spite of the irresistible compulsion of the repeated words in their minds.

Margaret smiled a little, despite the feeling that she might shatter at any moment. All she wanted was to get away from the dense pounding in her bones. There was no escape, but movement seemed to ease the pressure slightly. "Dio taught me never to waste a good exit line, Mik. Now, come on. We have to get away before they come to their senses!"

She could feel the separation within her mind. The portion which was in the grip of the voice was nearly mad with terror. This was the Marja part of her, the part which had been overshadowed. The other, Margaret, had no tool to use to help her younger self except her warped sense of humor. It was very strange, and she dared not analyze it. All she could do was accept each moment, and keep going. The other choice was madness, and she refused it.

"You aren't really suggesting that we rush off to Hali in the middle of the night in our dancing clothes, are you?" His anger was obvious now, but she knew it concealed terror. Hardly pausing for fear for her mind, she tried to understand. Fright seemed right, but Rage? Then she realized that the events at Halyn House must be ringing in his mind right now, with all the powerlessness he must have felt.

Unfortunately, Margaret did not have time to explain this to Mikhail—she must keep both of them in motion at any cost. "No. We need to change, then get to the stables as quickly as we can."

"But!"

"Keep going and stop arguing! I had another vision!" She raced down one flight of stairs, as fast as her skirts would let her, and heard the sound of his footsteps behind her.

"What was it?" He nearly knocked her down, his breath warm against her hair.

"Later, you idiot!"

"Yes . . . all right." They bolted down another flight, out of earshot of the ballroom.

They finally reached the corridor leading to the Alton Suite at one end, and the Lanart at the other, and parted. Margaret watched him go to his rooms, then hastily opened the door to her own. She was panting with exertion, her brow damp, and her head pounding. There was no one there, so she was forced to get out of her finery without help. In her haste, she tore the delicate fabric, her ears straining for sounds of pursuit. Surely someone was going to follow them soon. Her fingers twitched over the closings, and she was clumsy. "I'm going as fast as I can," she muttered at the booming voice in her head.

She put on thick hose, her riding clothes, and her scuffed and worn boots. Then she paused briefly, trying to think of what else to take. A knife seemed like a wise idea, so she grabbed the one she had used on the trail, and the little pouch with a flint in it, for starting fires. She tugged her cloak off its hook in the closet, and dashed into the hall.

Mikhail was just emerging from his own rooms, dressed in a plain brown tunic and trousers, with a green cloak looped over his arm. He looked taut, as if all his attention had narrowed to a single focus. It was painful to see, and she was very glad she was not an actual empath, because she suspected his emotions were as mixed as her own. He was not a man to be driven, she decided, and wondered how Regis could have believed he could be.

"I think whatever is moving us is keeping the others from coming," Mikhail muttered, his words a little slurred. "Come on—they won't keep still forever."

They charged down the stairs to the stableyard, bumping into one another in their haste, and each of them nearly falling at least twice. They were breathless by the time they reached the cobblestones.

She stumbled then, and shuddered all over. "What's wrong, Marguerida?" Mikhail asked.

"I think Ariel just went into labor," Margaret said, her heart beating faster.

"But she isn't due for at least another . . . tenday, is she?"

"I know. Ariel might not be ready, but the baby has other ideas. And be grateful, since that will distract everyone while we make our getaway!" Men, she thought, could be really stupid, even Mikhail. "I told you she would be born at Midwinter!"

"Yes, you did, and I will never doubt you again. Come on!"

There was no one but a sleepy lad in the stables, and he just looked at them stupidly while they got their horses. It was not his place to question members of the Domains. Mikhail went to the tackroom and grabbed their saddles. She fumbled on bits and bridles as he dragged them down the straw-strewn floor. It took all her will power not to start running from the stables, down the chilly street, and out of the city. At last, after what seemed an eternity, they were ready to leave.

As Margaret swung into the saddle, Dorilys danced beneath her, almost unseating her. She heard Charger bugle in the night. Then they were riding away, moving toward the arch above the stablecourt entrance.

There was a rush of air and a flutter of wings. From the corner of her eye, Margaret saw Mikhail's crow descend onto his shoulder, cawing raucously. It clung to him, then hopped down onto the pommel.

The sound of their hoofbeats on the cobblestones of the narrow street seemed to echo between the quiet buildings. Margaret wanted to urge Dorilys faster, to ease the weight inside her, but the stones were not meant for rapid movement. She had to let the horse choose her own pace, no matter what. She could not decide if she was afraid they would be caught now, or afraid they would not.

The city was moderately quiet here, but they could both hear distant sounds of celebration when they passed a few houses. When they rode through the little marketplace where Margaret had seen the Travelers' wagons, the space was alight with torches, and a good-sized audience was watching something being performed on the lowered side of a wain. She caught a glimpse of bright costumes in the flickering light, and heard a voice declaiming something.

The rapid sound of hoofbeats made some of the watchers turn to look at the sight of two riders racing through the marketplace. From the edge of her sight, she saw a few startled faces, and heard a shout of inquiry. Then they were heading for the gate to the old North Road.

The air was cold and crisp against her skin, making her shiver, though she was not sure if it was from excitement or the chill of the air. There was a faint smell of snow to come, but the sky remained dark and full of stars. Margaret looked up, for clear nights were a rarity. She gave Dorilys her head, and the little mare stretched out her neck and ran like the wind. Mikhail's horse, being longer legged, led them by a pace or two. The whole thing had the quality of a dream now, except for the steady pressure in her mind.

After perhaps an hour of hard riding, they drew their horses into a trot. Dorilys did not appear winded, but she had worked up a sweat. Margaret patted the smooth shoulder with her right hand, and heard a cheerful nicker in response. The horse seemed to find riding off into the night very exciting, and Margaret only wished she shared the feeling.

"I would give a lot to be in two places at once," Mikhail commented. His voice was a little hoarse, dry with riding, and she knew that his apparent ease was as much a pose as her own. They were being driven, and it was an enormous strain, one that could only be relieved by speaking of anything but that which compelled them ahead.

"You mean you actually want to be back in Comyn Castle right now?"

"Yes, and no. If you were right, and Ariel has gone into labor, in the middle of the ballroom, it is probably chaos. And perhaps no one has missed us yet. Are you certain she . . . ?"

"Yes, absolutely. I knew Alanna would be born tonight, as well as I know my own name. Even in the midst of *this*. I can sense your sister's pain. And I think I have learned one thing about the Aldaran part of my cursed Gift. I don't see everyone's future, only my own. So I know that Alanna Alar will be fine, because she and I are fated to know one another—even though at this moment I don't know if we are going to survive this madness. I know. That makes no sense. I can't tell you if Ariel will be all right, just Alanna." She did not add that the future she saw with Alanna in it was very troubled.

"That makes sense, as much as anything does right now. My head feels three sizes too big, and my jaw aches from clenching it. Tell me, what did you mean when you told Giz that she had backed the wrong horse—I confess that being compared to a stallion did not flatter me very much." In the near darkness, his voice was calm, as if the strain of the past few hours had left him too tired to be angry any longer.

Margaret laughed. "I was standing there, looking at the stars and thinking about nothing in particular, actually, when she came up and started in at me. Before I could get angry and step on her toes, I got another hint, a small flash. She doesn't know it yet, but she is going to marry Rafael, and be your sister-in-law, no matter what else happens. She was right—she is going to marry a Hastur—just not the one she expected. I suspect that *Dom* Damon tried to force Regis' hand, and make him promise to announce an engagement between her and you, but he was clever enough to find another solution."

"I see. So that was what Danilo meant." He gave a small sigh. "And will she be happy?"

"I have no idea. Nor do I give a damn!"

"Well, I did suggest to Regis that I was not the only unmarried member of the family, so it makes sense. Poor Rafael. What a woman to be saddled with!"

"I would not repine overmuch. Your brother is a steady man, and I think that what Gisela needs is someone who is immune to her fancies. She seems rather spoiled to me, being the only girl and the apple of her father's eye. Mik, we'd better start to move more quickly now. I am starting to feel hard-pressed again.

"You are right. Kind of whatever it is to give us a respite." With this ironic statement, they broke into a faster pace. The only sounds were the rhythm of the horses' hooves, and the sigh of the breeze in the empty fields. They passed through a dozing hamlet, then another, moving toward the moment they had both known awaited them when they saw the ghost of Hali Tower.

It was, Margaret decided, a peculiar sensation, compelled to be running towards she knew not what. It was different from the way she had felt when she was overshadowed by Ashara, similar and dissimilar at the same time. There was no sense of dread in her bones, no fear except a normal, human fear of the unknown. Something awaited her in the ruins of Hali Tower, something wonderful and terrible. But deep in her aching bones, she felt that whatever she was doing, it was the right thing for her.

Then she suddenly thought of her father, and all her serenity vanished. He would be frantic. What a foolish and thoughtless woman she was! What business did she have, running off in the middle of the night? She had no choice, but that did not ease her feeling of guilt. It was selfish of her, wasn't it?

Father! She sent the thought without much hope of reaching Lew Alton. It was hard to concentrate on horseback, and she was surprised when she felt an answering thought.

Marguerida! Are you all right?

Yes, I am fine, and Mikhail is fine. We are not trying to elope, really, though that is probably what people are imagining. The relief at his mental presence was enormous.

You were not even missed at first. Everyone was too busy seeing to Ariel—until she screamed, we were all standing about like statuary. I can only guess for how long. But Gisela noticed your absence, and raised the alarm. For a woman with a beautiful voice, she has a piercing shriek. And I am going to have a hell of a time thinking of a plausible explanation for your Ida. That is the least of my problems.

I am sorry, Father. We did not plan to dash off like this, really.

I know that, Marguerida. And at the moment, we have our hands full here. Whatever that was that called you and bewitched the rest of us played havoc with . . .

What! She could tell he was anxious about something that he was not telling her.

Several people were badly injured, Marguerida. I can only hope they can be healed. This is going to be a memorable night, if I survive it. Margaret realized he was not going to give her any details, and she could not decide whether she was relieved or annoyed. But she now knew Lew well enough to be aware that he was not going to budge, once he had made up his mind.

What about Gisela?

She is furious, of course. And Dom *Damon cannot quite decide if he is outraged or insulted. Don't think about them. Worry about the company of Guardsmen racing after you.*

Don't worry. They won't catch us.

How do you know?

I just do. Margaret was too tired to try and explain more.

Where are you going? Do you know that?

Hali Tower—and that is all that I know now. But, Father, I will be back. I know that, and I swear it.

How do you know you are coming back?

I just know. She kept her doubts out of her mind.

Hell and damnation! Very well—I suppose I will have to be satisfied with that. Godspeed, daughter, and come back as soon as you can. And take care of yourself. I could not bear to lose you, now, when I have just found you.

I know, dear Father. And I promise I will come back in one piece— you have my oath!

Then Lew Alton was gone, and Margaret urged her horse faster into the night.

By the time Margaret and Mikhail reached the ruins of Hali Tower, it was well past midnight, and the sky had begun to cloud up. The smell of snow was heavy on the wind, but none had fallen yet. In the light of the four moons, now close to midheaven, the eerie mists of the lake shone brightly. It was very quiet, except for the wind. The horses were weary, and even the bay hung its proud head as they drew to a halt.

They dismounted stiffly, and tugged their cloaks about them against the increasing cold. Margaret stroked Dorilys' side, feeling the heaving of her breath, and the sweat on the great muscles. "Good girl." She knew that she should tend the horse, walk her until she cooled down properly, but there was no time.

"Now what?" Mikhail sounded tired in the moonlight.

"I haven't a clue. I think we just have to wait." It was all she could do to keep on her feet now.

"Does all this seem as insane to you right now, as it does to me, Marguerida? I mean, here we are, out in the middle of the night, without food, obeying the gods know what. We have arrived at our destination, and all that is there is a pile of blackened stones—nothing like the Tower we saw last summer. I have never done anything so foolhardy in my life. I mean, what if nothing happens?"

Margaret was too tired to argue. She shrugged, put her arm around him, and rested her head on his shoulder. He smelled of horse and wine, plus the now familiar scent that sang Mikhail to her, which she would recognize anywhere in the galaxy. "Then nothing happens, and the Guardsmen find us, and we go back to Thendara and are a laughingstock for years to come. I can live with that—can't you?"

They stood in silence, holding each other lightly, neither speaking nor touching one another's minds. There was a deep content in the embrace, a sensation free of desire or longing. But for the growing cold, Margaret would have been happy to remain like that forever.

The sound of men and horses not very far away broke the spell. They could hear the jingle of bridles, the breathy snorts of exhausted steeds, and voices coming nearer. Margaret looked at Mikhail, and he met her eyes steadily, and they smiled. Then she kissed his lips softly, and felt his warm breath on her mouth.

NOW!

The mental command startled them, and Margaret glanced over Mikhail's shoulder. The white stones of Hali Tower stood gleaming in the gathered light of all the moons of Darkover. It shimmered for a moment, then solidified just as the Guardmen rode into sight.

"Look!"

Mikhail turned around, saw the Tower, and shivered. "This is it, I know it."

"Yes. Are you afraid, my dearest?"

"I am. But at the same time I feel it's right. Very strange."

They started moving toward the Tower as someone shouted behind them. There was a rumble of hooves, and Mikhail's horse screamed a challenge and charged the oncoming riders, making them scatter. Dorilys spun, reared, and lashed out at the air, just missing the closest Guardsman as they ran.

"By the Gods, what is that?"

"It's the Tower! How?"

"Get them—we can worry about the Tower later. They are going to get away!"

"Regis will have our heads if . . ."

"Damn Regis and damn Mikhail Hastur! Get them!"

Margaret stumbled and slid behind Mikhail, racing across the ground separating them from the shining building. There was an open door, and light spilled from it. Someone stood just inside; the shadow of a woman falling on the earth outside the Tower.

Mikhail grabbed her right hand, and pushed her ahead of him. Her outstretched arm reached into the light. Margaret met a subtle resistence, as if a veil stood there, invisible and adamant. She pressed, then hesitated. There was a flutter of dark wings over her head, and the great sea crow flew into the resistence she sensed, and into the yellow light beyond.

Margaret felt herself move through the veil, like stepping into honey. There was no sound for a moment—the wind was gone. The woman whose shadow she had seen backed up, her eyes wide, as Mikhail passed through beside her.

She turned and looked over her shoulder. Margaret could make out the shapes of horses and men, but she could no longer hear them. She could see Dorilys trying to pull away from an unfamiliar hand, and Charger stamping. She saw mouths move, and knew they were shouting at her, and then suddenly they were gone.

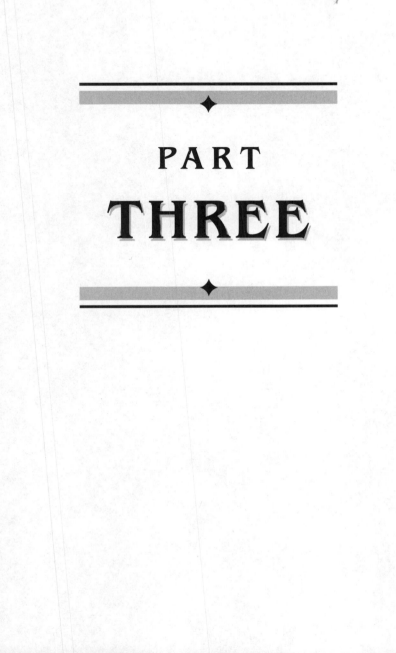

PART
THREE

24

Mikhail shook his head, trying to dispel the confusion and dizziness which nearly overwhelmed him. A glance at Marquerida showed him she was disoriented as well. What had they done? Were they mad? Then he realized that the great pressure in his mind, the dreadful compulsion, was gone. He was so weary after three hours of hard riding he could barely appreciate it.

He glanced around, first at the room they had entered, then at the woman who had opened the door. She had thin red hair, and eyes as golden as Marguerida's. She was robed in gray, and a shawl was looped haphazardly over her shoulders, as if she had grabbed the first thing to come to hand. Her age, he guessed, was somewhere between thirty and forty. She had an air of authority, but there was something *defeated* about her. Who was she? Mikhail studied her anxious eyes and restless hands. Her shoulders were hunched and tense.

The stone-walled entry chamber was bare of hangings. Even in the dim light, he could see that the mortar was black in many places, and there was a persistent smell that suggested smoke to him. Surely, there had been a fire here, although not recently.

There was another smell, too, but it was not the familiar ozone scent of matrix screens. It took him a moment to recognize it as the stink of burned flesh, and he swallowed hard. It almost seemed that the stones themselves retained the scent.

Beside him, Marguerida stood trembling. Somehow he could tell that it was not the sight of the burned stones which disturbed her, but Mikhail could not tell what it was. Her mind was closed, as if she were trying to make herself invisible. She was frightened, but of what?

Only the sea crow seemed unperturbed. It stood on a narrow shelf and gazed around with glowing red eyes. It made a rough comment, stretched its wings, then settled them back into place and started preening its feathers.

Mikhail took a few shallow breaths, smelling the sweaty, horsy odor on his body, and the sharp tang of adrenaline and wondered what to do. Lady Linnea had once told him that when in doubt, he should always behave with courtesy. Good advice. Mikhail felt an impulse to act, but while he had the will, he was nearly paralyzed with unease.

Finally his tongue found words. "Greetings, *domna.*" He made a bow. "I am . . ." his voice trailed off. Who was he now, in this place and time? If he was indeed in Hali Tower, then he and Marguerida were deep in the past and Mikhail Hastur was someone yet to be born. The complexity of it was too much for a moment.

Marguerida huddled beside him, drawing her cloak around her again, for the entry way was very chilly. "Well met, *domna,* I hope. Thank you for opening the door."

"I had no choice, did I?" The woman's voice was shrill, and the words grudging. Her eyes bulged with tension. "Welcome to Hali Tower. I am Amalie El Haliene, and I am Keeper here. Underkeeper, to be precise, but since I am the only *leronis* present, I do not think it is wrong to give myself the title I have so long deserved." She made a small gesture toward the ceiling with a six-fingered hand, and a bitter laugh escaped her narrowed lips.

At first her words made little sense. From the expression on Amalie's face, it was clear she expected them to know what she meant. But Mikhail could not concentrate properly. Something was wrong about the Tower, and he wanted to put his finger on it before he spoke again. Then somehow he knew that the Tower was, for all purposes, empty of any but themselves. It gave him a very strange sensation, for he had never been in a Tower that was not abustle with human thought. It was not the stillness of the building, but the mental silence that made his skin go rough with fear.

"I am Margarethe, and this is Mikhalangelo." *Mik, remember in the dream, those were the names we were called!*

He was so relieved to hear her voice in his mind that he almost did not understand her words. She had been gone for several minutes, frightened by something, but had aparently overcome her fears. If only he could do the same. *Were we? I didn't recall. And what are our family names? Dammit! If we claim to be . . .*

I know! This is rather more complicated . . . though I don't really know what I expected. The Hasturs and the Altons are going to be well-known families to her, so we'd better not say those names. She is afraid of us, and angry, too. And where is everyone?

Perhaps she will tell us, if we can calm her fears. What I want to know is when *the hell are we?*

I wish I knew, Mik.

"Why had you no choice, but to open the door *Domna* El Haliene?" Mikhail suspected that whatever had compelled them had likewise influenced her.

"That is an interesting question. Let's not stand about down here. There is a fire in my sitting room. Come along. You'd best keep your cloaks on, though. The Tower is . . . and leave that bird here. It reminds me of the sea, and my childhood, and brings me no cheer." She had her eyes focused on Mikhail, and she ignored Marguerida as completely as possible.

"As you wish, Lady. I cannot speak for the bird. He goes where he chooses."

Amalie sighed, a comfortingly human noise, and the rigidity of her posture seemed to unbend a little. "Oh, well. Everything else does as they please, so the crow can, too." *What is he, and why does that ill-omened bird come with him? Mikhalangelo? Surely it cannot be—for he is dead some twenty years in the dungeons of Storn. She had him killed, just as she had anyone else who opposed her.* The woman turned as these thoughts crossed her mind, as if too disspirited to conceal them. She walked ahead of them to the staircase, her slippered feet making a soft sound on the cold stone floor.

Mikhail gave Marguerida a look, knew she had overheard the *leronis'* thoughts as well, then shrugged, and followed. The frigid walls of the spiral staircase felt as if they were exhaling ice. There was a smell, too, of damp and must. And something more. *Pain,* he thought. The stones reeked of suffering. He felt his belly tighten with a new dread, and bit his lip as he climbed.

Mik!

What?

I think we are in the wrong place—at the right time, whatever that might be.

Are you having another vision?

Not exactly. It isn't clear, like a proper vision. But I think that whatever drew us here had no other available entryway. Hali is only a gateway, not our true destination. That is the best I can manage. A poor Gift, this Aldaran heritage. Mik, there is something very wrong here.

I have the same feeling. I know she was expecting someone, but I am not sure it was us. And she does not like you *one bit.*

No, she does not, and the feeling is mutual. I think I remind her of someone she hates, but I am so tired and unnerved that I cannot trust myself. I will jump at any shadow right now.

Jump away, dearest—right now all we have is our instincts.

They arrived at the landing, and Amalie showed them into a room on one side. It was a small chamber, with a fire burning in the grate, comfortable couches, and several highbacked chairs. Opposing walls were hung with tapestries, Hastur on one, and Cassilda on the other, so they faced one another across the room. They were unlike any versions of these historic people Mikhail had ever seen, less human and more mythic in some way he could not quite describe. And new as well, for he could see the faint outline of some other larger hanging that had been removed. There were dark lines, unmistakable marks of fire, on the walls here, darker than those on the lower floor, and the stench of old burning was stronger.

The spicy smell of mulled wine rose from a cauldron hung above the fire, but it did not conceal the older odors. The room was cool, as if the hearth could not even warm a chamber this small, and he was glad he was still wearing his cloak. His belly growled, and Mikhail realized he was hungry, that he had missed the feast, and all that had sustained him this evening were a few glasses of wine, and some meat-filled pastries, now several hours in his body's past. And centuries past as well.

"I cannot offer you much in the way of hospitality," Amalie El Haliene began. "I am alone here." Her tone was bitter, but there was fear in it as well. She took a heavy mug from a little table beside the fire, ladled some hot wine into it, and offered it to Mikhail. She started to sit down, then gave herself a little shake. Reluctantly, Amalie forced herself to take another mug up and fill it. She put it on a table beside Marguerida's chair, then backed away anxiously.

"Where is everyone—your monitors and technicians?"

"Gone, all gone." Her face was empty of expression. *Who are they? What do they want from me? These are not the ones I summoned—if I did. I must have been mad. . . . If only I were not alone here, and the others . . . I must not think on it!*

When she did not continue, Mikhail asked, "Gone where?"

Amalie stared at him vacantly for a moment, as if she could not completely grasp his question. She remained silent, and he could sense confusion in her mind, as if she were grappling with something too vast to understand. At last she burst out. "You must stop them! They cannot be allowed to destroy—".

"Stop who?"

"Hali Tower must not be ruined!" Her voice was harsh with hysteria now, but her face remained expressionless. It sounded as if she had said the words over and over in her mind, and was voicing them without any expectation of relief.

"Why should the Tower be ruined?" Mikhail demanded, the hairs on his nape bristling. The destruction of Hali Tower was a part of history, but it had not occurred to him that he might be present at the event.

Amalie gaped at him. "The warlords—Don't you know what you are doing here? Did you not come to aid me?" She was fixated on herself, and the Tower, and he knew she was unable to comprehend any other purpose for him and Marguerida.

"What warlords? And why should they want to destroy the Tower?" Mikhail knew that it was not this woman who had drawn them into the past, but he wondered if they had really been brought to help her. What if Hali Tower *were* saved? He held back a shudder as he imagined the impact of that possibility on the world that he knew.

Her eyes blazed, and her thin face twitched around them. "I see that you know nothing! You are useless to me!"

"Why don't you tell us, slowly, what you mean. Forgive our ignorance, *domna,* and begin at the beginning." Marguerida spoke quietly, her voice radiating calm. Mikhail felt himself ease at the sound of it, awash in a momentary serenity he wished could last forever.

Marguerida's efforts did not have the desired effect on Amalie El Haliene, however. Her golden eyes narrowed with pure hatred, her hands clenched. Her body was coiled with unspoken fury, so powerful an emotion that Mikhail felt nearly overwhelmed. It was an unreasonable response to Marguerida's question.

"What are you?" The voice that came from her mouth was pinched and frightened.

"I don't know what you mean, *domna,*" Mikhail answered helplessly.

"You are not what I expected, not at all."

"And what did you expect?"

"A warrior. There is nothing about you that . . ."

Mikhail shook his head. "I can use a sword well enough, but there are no warriors, as you know them, in my . . . my time." It felt odd to say that, considering Darkover's bloody past, but he knew it was true. They maintained the use of swords out of custom rather than need, to preserve the letter of the Compact. The late and unlamented Dyan-Gabriel Ardais had perhaps been the last of Darkover's real warriors. All the rest had preceded him to the grave before Mikhail was born.

"I see. What kind of shabby, dishonorable time do you come from, then?"

"I come from a time of peace, *Domna* El Haliene, not of war."

"Peace? There has not been such a thing in all the history of Darkover. The past is a vast killing field."

The past? Mik, she thinks we are from her past, not her future.

Yes, I see that. And I am not sure that telling her otherwise will be of any use. She seems to have her mind made up, that we are here to help her keep Hali Tower from destruction—instead of whatever that blasted voice wanted from us. I don't know why we are here, but the one thing I am certain of is that we are not here for that.

Agreed. More, she is doing a fair job of holding out. She knows something she does not want us to find out.

"I am sorry you are disappointed in me, *Domna* El Haliene. But I did not choose to arrive at your door, any more than you chose to open it."

"Yes. Perhaps I was mistaken. No, I cannot have been. It is not possible. I am never wrong. There must be some way for you to stop this disaster, to prevent *Dom* Padraic and *Dom* Kieran from tearing everything apart. Neither of them can be allowed to control Hali, to use me . . . as they plan!"

"And how is that?"

"Each wishes me to turn the power of the Tower against the other, of course. Are you stupid?" She sounded like a woman who had reached the limits of her own endurance.

"I am not stupid. I just don't know what you mean. Who are *Dom* Padraic and *Dom* Kieran?" Mikhail held back his annoyance with an effort, and told his growling stomach to shut up.

Amalie gave a sigh again. "*Dom* Padraic is my cousin, Padraic El Haliene, and he thinks that I will surrender the Tower to him because . . . because we are kin. He has already . . ." Her eyes widened with alarm, and she swallowed hard. "*Dom* Kieran is the King's Champion, Kieran Castamir." She paused, looked at him as if expecting the names to provoke some reaction.

She started to tell us something important, then changed her mind, Mik, I wonder what Padriac has already done? And there is something more—something that I can sense. It gives me the coldest feeling.

What?

Oh, God! Ashara! She was here, and not too long ago. I can feel her presence in this place. Why didn't I realize it sooner? Get me out of here!

Marguerida—stop it! Get hold of yourself right now! We must get more information, and if you get hysterical on me, we won't find out what we need to know.

Yes, Mik. I'll try. But it is so . . .

Mikhail sensed her trying to breathe more slowly, and watched her drain her mug of warm wine. When he sensed that she was back in control, he asked Amalie, "What happened to the Keeper here?"

"Him!" It was a sneer. "As soon as he realized that Varzil could not protect him, he left as if demons were after him." *Damn him, that feckless Karl Ridenow, taking what should have been my place! And damn Varzil for giving him the Keeper's position, and for dying. He is not dead yet, but he might as well be! Damn all men! They are weak, when they should be strong, and stupid when they believe they are clever. The Compact will not stand without Varzil. If Hali falls . . .*

Amalie seemed to realize then that her thoughts were audible, and two red blotches showed on her cheeks. She glared at both of them, a golden glare, and Marguerida matched it.

"Domna, this is all very interesting, but it does not provide us with an answer." Marguerida's voice was tense as she spoke, and Mikhail knew that the real or imagined presence of Ashara Alton was at the root of it.

"Don't you understand yet?" She directed this question to Mikhail, as if Marguerida were not there.

"No, *domna.* We do not. You have not told us anything of any use. Are your own wits disordered?" That paid her back for calling him stupid.

"Certainly not!" She spoke adamantly, but there was fear underlying her vehemence. It was nothing more than a mild flutter of apprehension, and she drew her attention from it quickly. Mikhail suddenly realized that she was terrified of losing her mind, and not far from it either.

Amalie cleared her throat, gave Marguerida a look of loathing, and began to speak. "Very well. I will try to be clear. Seventy years ago, Varzil Ridenow managed to force the kingdoms to make an agreement, and he destroyed, with his power, the great matrix screens. I am too young to remember how it was then, of course, but my father has told me of it. He was a mechanic at Arilinn then, a young man. It must have been wonderful!" Her thin face was alight with memory.

"*Clingfire* and *bonewater dust* were wonderful?" Marguerida demanded sharply. "I think not!"

"I will thank you to keep that unnatural creature silent. How can you stand her?"

"What do you mean?" *Keep still for a second, Marquerida. I know you want to shake her until her teeth rattle, but be patient.*

Yes, dearest, but it will not be easy. I would give a great deal to be able to explode!

"She reeks of the *laran* of the overworld. What manner of creature is she?"

"Margarethe is quite human, Amalie. Why should you think otherwise?"

"Human?" Amalie shuddered and looked into the fire. "I doubt that very much! She reminds me . . . never mind."

"All right. Now, you say that Varzil forced the kingdoms to stop fighting, and he destroyed the great matrix screens. That seems good."

"The Towers cannot exist without matrices. There were new ones found, smaller than before, but not without power. But it has not worked very well, for while men prattle of peace, they still prepare for war. True, they no longer send *clingfire* against one another, but they will again, and soon. Not all of it was destroyed, nor were all the great screens. There are hidden caches which even Varzil could not uncover."

"I see." Mikhail had always had the impression that once the Compact had been agreed upon, Darkover had become peaceful. But so many of the records had been lost through the centuries. He was not even certain of the precise date when Hali Tower had been totally destroyed. All he could do was hope that it was not *now,* not while they were there.

"This is not the only problem. Petty kingdoms vying for power are the least of it. Varzil made it possible for women, such as myself, to become Keepers, for he has discovered we are actually more capable than men. But he did not choose well." It was as if her tongue, guarded before, had finally loosened, and she dared not stop talking.

"Oh?"

"His favorite was a creature called Ashara Alton. She was Underkeeper at Neskaya, then Keeper after he left there, and came to Hali for a time. After he restored the Lake, he chose to retire, and she was installed here, at Hali, as Keeper. She was very powerful, even without the command of great screens. I came here when she had been Keeper for thirty years, and trained under her. But she is corrupt. There is something in her nature that is evil."

"Is?" Marguerida squeaked the word in spite of herself. "You mean she is still alive?" *I knew it! It was not my imagination! She is alive, in this time, and she is going to find me and kill me!* He could sense her terror, and knew that Amalie did too.

Amalie looked at her with grave suspicion. "Keep your tongue behind your teeth, foul witch! Are you in league with her? I should have known! The moment I heard your voice, I should have known."

"Ashara Alton was my foe," Marguerida said slowly.

"Was?" Amalie seemed puzzled for a moment by this. "So you claim, but I do not believe you, for you are too like her, that coldness, that icy way you have. You are her creature!"

Oh, God, Mik. What if she is right?

She is wrong. Istvana would know if you were other than what you are.

"You seem to fear Ashara more than you fear *Dom* Padriac and *Dom* Kieran."

"We drove her out of Hali—all of us here, plus half the *laranzu* in the world. It took that much, for she is one of Zandru's own. My brother died here, his blood spattered on the stones, and so did others! Many others. But she survived, and her powers were not undone. Now she sits in Thendara, like a spider, weaving her treachery, waiting to return to Hali. Oh, she pretends to be doing nothing more than advising on the building of the new Castle and on matters of state but she has the Hasturs in her thrall, and if Hali falls to either my cousin or the King's Champion, it makes no difference. She will reclaim her place either way."

Amalie's eyes were constricted, the pupils so tiny that they were almost invisible in the flickering light from the fireplace. She trembled as she envisioned these events, and it was clear that she had spent a great deal of time reliving them. Mikhail caught glimpses of dead bodies, bloated with rot, stinking of decay, but he could not guess if they were from the past or the future. Without doubt, poor, terrified Amalie had reason to fear madness.

"But if she wants the Tower, why are you so convinced that it will be destroyed?"

"Because if she cannot control it, she will allow no one else to have it! And Varzil cannot last too much longer. He has been hanging on for weeks, as if waiting for something, but he will perish soon, and then I will be truly lost. She will torture me, as she did others." The Keeper shuddered all over, and tears slipped down her thin cheeks.

He felt Marguerida stir beside him, her sense of terror slipping away slowly, and her resolve hardening. She flexed her left hand, like a cat preparing to claw at something. He rose to his feet. He felt caught between the two women—both so distraught he could not clearly read either of them. Amalie was certainly trying to conceal something, and Marguerida was on the edge of doing something desperate.

"I must see Varzil." As soon as he said this, he felt a sense of release and knew that finding Varzil was what he and Marguerida must do. He felt a tingling under his sternum, a warmth that spread out across his body, calming him.

"No!" Amalie was not looking at him, but at Marguerida. "That must not be!"

"If I am correct," Mikhail began reasonably, "then it was Varzil who called us through the years, to come to Hali now. I think, therefore, that he wishes to see us."

"It is a trick! *She* sent you here—you and that thing!"

"Where is Varzil! Tell me!" Marguerida's voice of command rang out against the cool stones of the Tower. It was not directed at him, but Mikhail felt himself cringe.

The effect on Amalie was even more remarkable, for she shrank into her chair, put her hands over her head, and screamed! "No, no—don't hurt me again!"

"No one is going to hurt you, *domna,"* he told the hysterical woman quietly.

Mik, what kind of Keeper was Ashara, that she should inspire such terror?

A very poor one, obviously.

She seems to be able to resist the Voice—as if she has had long practice in avoiding its influence, Mik.

Yes, she does. And we have to get to Varzil.

Why not just reach him telepathically? It should not be difficult, even if he is dying—if he is. That voice he used made my bones rattle, and it did not seem like the death-gasp of anyone.

I don't know. You notice we have not heard the voice since we arrived, which suggests to me that he is shielded in some manner—maybe to protect him from Ashara as well.

Don't mention that name! It makes me want to scream! How are we going to get Amalie to tell us. . . .

I can only think of one way, and you won't like it.

Mik, I have never forced rapport on anyone deliberately in my life! It is the thing I hate most about the Alton Gift—and fear as well.

I suppose we could hold her feet to the fire until she tells us.

That is not funny! Damn you, Mikhail Hastur! She is right to fear me, isn't she? I am a foul creature.

No, beloved, you are nothing of the sort. More to the point, you are nothing like your ancestor. You are not cruel or power hungry. But we must find Varzil, and I don't believe we have a lot of time.

And here I thought I was the logical one. Very well—but I loathe what I am about to do.

Mikhail watched Marguerida as she closed her golden eyes and began to breathe slowly and deeply. He could sense the energy in her tense body beginning to change, and even though her shadow-matrixed hand was shielded by the mitts, he could feel the power coursing along the hidden lines on her flesh.

Then, she opened her eyes and looked directly at Amalie, who was still sobbing into her hands. There was a gasp, and the woman lifted her head. Two pair of golden eyes met, and Amalie El Haliene tried to escape the gaze that pierced her consciousness.

Where is Varzil?

Please, please, do not hurt me. I must not tell you—you must not see him.

I will not hurt you.

You are her creature! Oh, Goddess—why am I so weak? If you obtain it, the world will never be whole!

Obtain what?

Mikhail was listening intently, lending Marguerida his silent support, as he had done before, knowing she needed it desperately. He could feel her self-loathing as she pressed Amalie for information. For someone who had had so little training, and had the Alton Gift, she was incredibly gentle. She was not probing Amalie's mind as she might have done, had she been a less ethical person, and was ignoring the fragments of memory that spun in the Keeper's struggling mind. There were bits of her past, emotions she was shamed by, experiences that were embarrassing, and he felt more than a little discomfort at seeing as much as he did.

Then he saw something gleaming, something huge and faceted, which could not be other than a starstone of remarkable size. It shone in his mind, glittering, drawing him into it for an instant. There was a slight mental tug, as if a part of him had been linked to that huge stone. His heart felt squeezed for an instant, and then the sensation was gone.

The woman slumped back in her chair, her head lolling back.

"Is she . . . ?"

"She just fainted from terror, Mik. She will be all right, or as well as she can be. She's been tortured like this for years. But I think it would be better if we left before she comes to. I *hate* this place, almost as much as she does."

"Does she?"

"Amalie wants to keep the Tower, but it will always be a place of torment for her."

"I see. And I think you are right. We have done all we can. But, what happened to the rest of the people here? I sensed something while you were . . . but it was gone too quickly.

"They were captured by one of those warlords, poor folk. She is genuinely distressed about that. Come on." Marguerida started for the door, and he followed her.

"Why didn't they catch Amalie?"

"She knows a few tricks, I discovered." The disgust in her voice made him want to weep, and he knew she hated herself for what she had just done. "Amalie learned how to make herself almost invisible telepathically—which probably saved her life while Ashara was Keeper here. What a tragedy."

There seemed nothing to say, so Mikhail went down the stairs behind her. He was tired, but part of him was very excited. He was going to meet Varzil the Good, perhaps the single greatest man in the history of his world—if he didn't slip on the stairs and break his neck! He made himself put one weary foot in front of the other until he reached the entryway.

25

When they reached the bottom of the stairs, the crow greeted them. Then it flew onto Mikhail's shoulder and rubbed its beak tenderly across the arch of his ear. He lifted a hand and stroked the shining feathers softly, as the crow shifted from foot to foot.

Marguerida had already left the Tower, and was standing in a little courtyard looking at the predawn twilight. The air was cold and crisp, but it did not feel like winter. He glanced at the sky. There were a few clouds, but it was fairly clear, and he could see the constellations he had memorized long ago. Astronomy, except for the movement of the moons, was not a science much practiced on Darkover, but his desire to travel to other worlds had made him curious, and he had learned the rise and set of the constellation called Aldones, which was below the horizon until the onset of spring. The constellation Zandru, centered on the baleful red star called Antares by the Terranan was visible at the beginning of winter. These, plus Avarra in fall, and Evanda in summer, were a calendar in the night.

He looked towards the eastern horizon, and saw the head and shoulders of Aldones, down to the bright, white star that depended from the belt. Yes, it was almost spring here. He could see Idriel rising, and knew that day would soon follow her.

He walked toward Marguerida, and found her breathing deeply, filling her lungs with air, as if drinking a rare vintage. "It doesn't even smell like Darkover, Mik." She had dark circles under her eyes, and her shoulders were drooping.

"What?" He sniffed. "Hmm. You are right. I wonder why?"

"Well, I never smelled this carrion scent before, as if there were a field of carcasses nearby. And there is another odor—ugh! Hot and cold at the same time. Come on—let's get away from here. I can feel Ashara in the very stones of this place, for she has walked here, even sat on that little bench. I can feel her everywhere in the Tower, as if she imprinted herself on the walls themselves."

"She seems to have had a talent for making stones do her bidding, doesn't she?"

Marguerida shuddered. "I wish we had brought our horses, even though I do not know if horses can travel in time. I hope Dorilys is all right."

"Don't worry. I am sure those Guardsmen have both Charger and Dorilys well in hand, and have probably taken them down to the inn near Hali. They are most likely in a warm barn, eating their heads off. And speaking of such, there should be some sort of stable here."

"I will ride a donkey to get away from here! We must hurry, Mik. I don't think Ashara knows about me yet, but she will soon." Her beautiful voice was thick with terror and exhaustion. Mikhail could only marvel quietly at her strength, knowing what entering Amalie's mind had cost her.

"Why do you think that?"

"She knew that I would exist, though I am not sure how. She was determined to destroy me before I destroyed her. None of that has happened yet. But I am starting to wonder if the reason she was waiting for me was that she had already encountered me here."

"That doesn't make any sense at all, Marguerida."

She gave him a weak smile and blinked away an unshed tear. "That is why they call it a paradox, my dearest."

They left the little courtyard, following a worn path and their noses. The distinctive odor of manure drew them to the stables, and they found, to their surprise and delight, several horses standing in the stalls, munching hay and stamping their hooves. Two were huge beasts, clearly bred for pulling carts or carriages, and one was an old mare, the whiskers around her muzzle white with years.

But there were three others, a roan gelding and two dun mares, which looked young and healthy. The roan poked its head out through the end of its stall and twitched its ears at the sight of strangers. Then there was a little rustling noise, and Mikhail saw a young man appear in the shadowy light of the barn. He was rubbing sleep from his eyes, and he had hay in his lank hair. His clothing was worn and filthy, and he stank, even at a distance of ten paces.

"Wha?" The man stared at them with vacant eyes, and rubbed his head in bewilderment.

"We need horses," Mikhail replied quietly.

The fellow gave a cackle that sent shivers up Mikhail's spine, a gruesome sound. "I ken no one was here, but me and them." He made a rude wave at the animals. "Bandits," he added, smacking his wide lips. "Ye be bandits."

"No, we are not thieves." Mikhail hated the idea of being a horse thief, even in these odd circumstances.

"Ye doan belong heres."

"Mik, I think he is a little slow." Marguerida had been standing in a deep shadow, but as she spoke, she stepped from it, and the man gaped at her. The hood of her cloak was down, revealing the windswept tangle of her abundant red hair, half of which had escaped from the amethyst-encrusted clasp she had worn at the ball.

The stableman stared at Marguerida for a moment, then gave a clumsy bow. "I never heard of no women bandits." Then he turned away, shaking his head as if he could not make heads or tails out of the situation. Mikhail watched him go, then unlatched the wooden catch that held the roan's stall door closed, and began to lead the gelding out of it.

He turned at a dragging sound, and found the man had returned, pulling two saddles behind him. One had a high cantle, and was clearly intended for battle, but the other was recognizably a woman's saddle, for riding sidewise.

"I am *not* going to ride in that thing—I would fall off in twenty paces!"

"No, of course not." Mikhail agreed with her, though he was sure that women did not ride astride in this time, or at least women of the Comyn never did. "You, there, bring another saddle for the lady—not a woman's but a man's."

The young man gaped at him, then let both saddles fall to the floor with a soft thump. Then he scratched his dirty head, his crotch, and just stood there clearly confused.

"Never mind. I'll find one myself, Mik. We have to get out of here as soon as possible! I can't stand this place!" She lunged through the barn, pushing a tangle of fine hair off her face with an impatient gesture. "I should cut the damn stuff off," he heard her mutter.

The gelding had taken his scent, and Mikhail began to saddle the animal, talking softly to it. It seemed to be a steady beast. He threw a worn blanket over the back, then lifted the saddle up. It was much heavier than those he was accustomed to, awkward and difficult to get into place.

Finally, Mikhail had the saddle on the horse's back, and he began to work the unfamiliar cinches and straps. He had just gotten them into place when he heard Marguerida return, lugging another high-cantled saddle behind her, cursing softly. She used a mixture of Darkovan, Terran, and some tongues he did not recognize, a muddle of abuse that was remarkable in its variety.

He left the roan, went to the stall where one of the dun mares waited, and opened the door. He led the animal out, then started to saddle it for Marguerida. She was strong, but she would never be able to raise the heavy thing alone. He watched her put the bit and bridle on the mare as he pulled the straps into position and tightened them.

Before they mounted, Mikhail tried to think of anything he should do before they left. He decided some extra blankets would be a good idea, and found a couple of horsy-smelling ones in the tack room. He was hungry, and the mulled wine had made him a bit muzzy. Still, he could not bring himself to go back into the tower and ask Amalie for food. He tied the blankets behind the cantle, and swung up into the saddle.

Marguerida was already on her horse, looking anxious and wan. "Which way?"

"Toward the Lake. Varzil is somewhere to the north of us—more I cannot guess. I can sense his presence, but he is hidden in some fashion."

"I know. He doesn't want Ashara to find him." The grim note in her voice as she spoke the hated name of her nemesis made the hairs on the nape of his neck bristle. "He is dying, but he is still more powerful than she is, powerful enough to conceal himself. And something else is distracting her. I am sure of that. And grateful." *If I could hide, I would. I feel as if I will be discovered at any moment.*

They set out from the Tower as the dawn turned into day. Mikhail noticed a stand of balsam trees, and another of some shrubs he had never seen before. How much had Darkover changed since the Ages of Chaos? How many plants and animals had been lost in the many devastating wars of the period?

After perhaps a mile's ride along the road that ran to the north of the Tower, toward where Armida would be, if it existed yet, they came to a small crater that glowed even in the pale daylight. It stank ferociously. He did not want to look into it, but he could not help himself.

The bottom of the crater was fused and twisted glass. Around it were the shattered remains of corpses and equipment. The distorted bones of the skeletons were burned black. From the scattering of leaves and debris over the bones, he knew it was not a very recent disaster—at least five years old and likely more. It was an appalling sight, and he was glad his belly was almost empty. As it was, a mouthful of bile mixed with wine choked up his throat, and he spat it out.

"If that is what *clingfire* does, then I cannot imagine how anyone brought themselves to use it," Marguerida said in a very soft voice.

"Neither can I. I have heard stories all my life, but I never realized how horrible it was. I thought they stopped using it when they formed the Compact."

"I sincerely hope we never see the actual stuff in action, Mik." She looked away, and they rode on. After a while, she said, "We have to think of a cover story, something plausible to say to anyone we encounter."

"I know. But I can't imagine what." He tried to get his thoughts in order. "Varzil called us Mikhalangelo and Margarethe. I wish we knew more than that, but the dream was not very clear, was it? Perhaps it is hard to talk through time." Mikhail felt his shoulders sag as he spoke.

"Amalie recognized our names, or believed she did. But she thought we had been killed. Damn. I would trade the whole Alton Domain for a glass of clear water, and a heel of bread just now. I cannot think straight on an empty stomach."

"We'll just try to avoid people—and as desolate as this countryside is, it should not be hard. I'm damned hungry, too! And thirsty. Don't talk about it—it just makes it worse!" Mikhail felt a slight itching, a maddening scrabble along the middle of his chest. He looked down, expecting to find some insect, then realized it was not an external sensation, but an internal one. He realized that it was part of the feeling he had had just before they left Hali Tower, drawing him in the direction of his goal. He paused and explored it, then said, "Take that little path up there."

Marguerida nodded meekly and reined her mare toward a thin track between some skeletal bushes. She was obviously completely exhausted, and he began to wonder how they were going to survive. All the things he should have thought of gnawed at his mind. But, beneath that, he felt a curious tranquillity, a sensation which seemed so strange that he almost doubted his sanity. Yet he could not shake the sense of his own destiny now—it had him firmly in its grasp, and there was no escaping it.

The sun had risen above the horizon, sending a red glow across the tortured earth. It was a dreary and barren landscape. Mikhail looked for familiar plants, and found only a few weeds struggling up from the blighted soil, sad, misshapen things going by stagnant pools. A scum lay on the surfaces of the small water holes, a pale blue stuff that looked as unhealthy as the growths beside them.

Mikhail found himself straining in the saddle, trying to find something familiar. Finally, he realized he was disturbed by how very quiet it was. The usual birdsong of early morning was absent, and the silence was eerie and as oppressive as the dreary landscape.

A light breeze lifted the edge of his cloak, bringing the scent of water. Mikhail swallowed, his thirst enormous. It was not a pleasant odor, but rank and foul. There was another pit on one side of the trail, another crater of glass, where some terrible explosion had occurred. There were no human skeletons to be seen. Instead he saw the corpses of some ducks, their feathers dry and falling into dust. They had not been burned, but he suspected that the water that shone in the shallow hole had poisoned them. The destruction made him heartsick and angry. How could his ancestors have done this to Darkover!

They were riding west now, with the sun at their backs; on the left, the strange waters of Lake Hali misted the air. They were pink and silver in the morning sun, a sight he would have thought beautiful had he not been so uneasy.

"Well, what do you think of all this, old fellow?" Mikhail addressed the question to the crow which was sitting on the saddle horn, trying to find a way to relieve the growing sense of despair filling his mind. The bird shifted from one foot to the other, and for once, made no reply. Instead it gave Mikhail a beady look with one red eye, an unreadable glance that did not ease his sense of displacement at all.

"Mikhail, how many people were there on Darkover during the time of Varzil?"

"Damned if I know. There are, by the best guesses of the Terranan, about twenty million now. Regis has always refused to run a census. I rather doubt that there were more than that in the past. Between low fertility and all these small wars, not to mention the larger ones before, I would guess that there were no more than seven or eight million, spread all over the continent, and pretty thinly at that. Why do you ask?"

"I want to know as much as I can, I suppose. Trying to predict the odds of meeting someone we ought to know, to keep my mind off my growling belly. I sometimes played card games, back at University, and I always won because I could keep track of them. I could have gone to Vainwal and become a gambler, if I enjoyed that sort of thing, I suppose."

"Now that is something I never knew about you. I don't really know much about you, do I, Marguerida?"

"No, I suppose not, but then I don't know you either, not really. You seem different than you were last summer, but we haven't had the time to talk much." She sighed.

"What do you mean—'someone we ought to know'?"

The wind shifted as he spoke, bringing the mist on Lake Hali toward them, drenched in moisture. His face felt almost wet, and he licked the mist off his lips despite his fear that it contained something poisonous. Had anyone ever drunk the waters of Hali, he wondered? He could not remember any tale of such an event. Still, the drops that fell on his tongue tasted just like any other water, and he was so parched that he was glad of it.

"From what I discovered in the records at Arilinn, this time was one where all the major families knew one another well—even more than today. They not only knew each other, but knew the geneologies back for a few generations. So I dare not tell anyone I am Margarethe Alton, for instance. It would be altogether too likely that the stranger would say, 'You can't be, because she is a short, fat woman in her fifties, and my second cousin once removed on my mother's side.' "

"I see what you mean. Well, we will just have to hope that we only meet traders and peasants, then."

"That is very optimistic of you," she growled. Then she looked shamefaced. "I did not mean to snap, but . . . you don't seem very worried."

"You are doing enough worrying for both of us, Marguerida." Suddenly he felt almost lighthearted. His earlier sense of certainty had deepened as they rode, as if they were approaching a goal he had always sought. And it was so strange a sensation that he did not dare to trust it, and could not have explained it in any case.

His beloved turned in her saddle, stuck out her tongue, and made a very rude noise. "I am not worrying, just trying to anticipate." She succeeded in looking outraged and dignified at the same time, and Mikhail had to grin at her. Happy or sad, she was wonderful. "How do you intend to explain the two of us running around unescorted? As I understand it, women were not in the habit of riding astride, or even going out in public much. They were kept inside, barefoot and pregnant, weren't they? We cannot pass for sister and brother, and we aren't married." She thrust her wrist out, to point out the absence of the *catenas* circlet which would have shown the status of a married women.

"A good point. You could be my *barragana* wench."

"True, I could. What a tale to tell our grandchildren. I can see myself, doddering and silver-haired, dandling some little lad on my arthritic knee, and telling him, 'Amos, when your grandfather and I took an all-expenses paid vacation in the Ages of Chaos, I pretended to be his mistress.' An amusing notion, but not very practical. And dangerous, too. We are nobodies here, Mik, but we have the appearance of somebodies—our height and coloring scream Comyn to the skies."

He was so busy chuckling at the mental picture of this imaginary Amos, that he hardly heard the rest of her words. Then, before he could answer, he heard the faint jingle of brass rings and the soft fall of hooves through the mist. The crow flared its wings, alerting him further.

Mikhail and Marguerida reined to a halt, tensing. The mist off the lake swirled across their eyes, making the twisted vegetation surrounding them seem even more sinister. The red light of the sun made bloody veils of the cloud. The sound of a single rider drew closer, and they both held their breaths.

All of Marguerida's concerns expanded in his mind, until Mikhail thought of one of his own. What if he had to kill someone—how might that change the past? What if he slew the ancestor of Regis and Javanne Hastur, and was never born at all?

The rider came through the mist, a portly man on a rather sorry looking old horse. He was wearing a russet shirt beneath a leather tunic, a felted hat with a single blue feather in it, and a shabby cloak, so ancient that its original color was unguessable. There was a heavy sword strapped across his back, a *claithmhor* of the sort he had seen in Aldaran Castle, the intricate basket hilt wet with mist.

The man yanked on the reins, looked very startled, and rubbed his eyes, as if suspecting he was seeing some specter. *"Dom* Mikhal Raven?" The reedy voice trembled as the man spoke. Then he peered at Marguerida, blinking several times, clearly disbelieving the evidence of his eyes. *"Domna* Margarethe of Windhaven? They said you were dead."

At least that solves the problem of our identities. Marguerida's thought was sharp and relieved at the same time.

Or gives us a new one. Maybe if we sit still, he will think we are a pair of ghosts and ride on.

The roan gelding snorted just then, and ruined any hope of passing for spirits. "No, not dead, so far." Mikhail's answer was muffled in the mist.

"But, how did you escape from the dungeons of Storn? It has been almost twenty years . . . and the ransom was never paid. And you have not aged a day." The man was becoming more and more agitated, his eyes bulging nervously.

"It is a long story," Marguerida answered. "One which we cannot tell, for in escaping we lost our memories, and nearly our minds. We barely know who we are."

Oddly enough this ridiculous explanation seemed to satisfy the stranger. "Do you remember me?"

Mikhail shook his head, pleased by Marguerida's quick thinking. "I confess I do not. Do you?" He glanced at his companion and saw she was tense. She shook her head.

"Well, I don't see why you should, since we only met twice, at the handfasting for Gabriella Leynier, and again at that funeral for *Dom* Estefan Aillard, where young Darien Ardais slew Melor Lanart. I am Robard MacDenis." He looked at Mikhail hopefully, as if expecting his name to jog the memory. "I was in the service of *Dom* Aran MacAran then. He's dead now, and his two sons with him." The reedy voice was filled with bitterness and regret.

"I am sorry to hear that, although I cannot remember *Dom* Aran at all." Mikhail could sense a growing confusion in the mind of Robard, confusion and fear as well.

"You still have that damn bird, I see. Or is it another?"

"No, it is the same bird."

"No one will believe me when I say I met Mikhal Raven, The Angel of the Serrais and Margarethe of the Golden Voice by the waters of Lake Hali." *They will think I have gone mad. Perhaps I have. There has been so much death, so much fighting and dying. All the Compact has done is stop the use of* bonewater dust, *and* clingfire . . . *and now Varzil has vanished, and no one believes it will survive him. It was a fine dream he had, but men are men, and they will kill one another for no better reason than that they can.*

Mikhail caught these thoughts as they crossed Robard's mind, felt the deep sorrow in them, the wounds to body and spirit that the turbulent times had wrought. He wished he could think of something to say, some way to tell the old fighter that the Compact did succeed, in the end. But he dared not.

How odd it felt to be thought to be this other man, this Mikhal Raven. There was no record of him in present day Darkover, nor of this Margarethe of Windhaven. He had never even heard of Windhaven, but suspected it might be somewhere in the Hellers. Amalie had said something about that Mikhal—that he had died in the dungeons of Storn. Still, he wished he knew the story of that man and that woman, if only to prevent himself from making too many mistakes.

Then he felt another tug at his heart, the link that had formed in the Tower. Varzil, if it was indeed he, was urging him along. They must get going. Mikhail knew that there was not a great deal of time left, though he could not guess how or why. He had to accept it as real, on faith. It was hard to do, wearing away at his feeble confidence, to go forward on a feeling alone.

Mik, we can't just leave him with any memory of us! It is dangerous for us, and for him, too. It wouldn't be fair! If he goes to some inn—are there inns now?—and gets tipsy and starts saying that he met us, the tale will get out, and people will begin to look for us. That, I think, is the last thing we need.

Yes, you are right. Go ahead—tell him to forget this meeting!

Me! You're right, of course. Damn the Voice, the Alton Gift, and Varzil along with it!

Marguerida closed her golden eyes for a moment, and Mikhail could feel the distaste in her for what she was about to do. Then she looked at Robard, took a sharp breath and said, "You will forget everything after you set out today. We are not here, and you never met us! You will go to your destination and remember only an uneventful ride beside the lake."

Robard MacDenis did not move. Then his face went slack, his eyes glazed, and he seemed to look right through them. He clucked to his horse, gave the ancient animal a gentle kick, and rode past them as if they did not exist.

Mikhail and Marguerida waited until the sound of horse and rider was lost in the mist. The expression on her face made him want to hug her, hold her, tell her she would never have to interfere again. He knew that using the Voice made her feel defiled and filthy, and there was nothing he could do about it. She had done no harm, but he knew that it made no difference to her.

He dared not attempt to comfort her either, for she was seething with rage, barely controlling her feelings. He knew her well enough to be sure she would snap and snarl at him if he tried. Mikhail sighed. She would have to work it out herself, but he pitied her for the pain she was suffering. He reined his roan forward, and they continued through the mist, moving steadily toward a goal he could not see, but only feel.

Mikhail urged his horse onward, and Marguerida copied his movements. The eerie silence grew as they rode, and neither of them had the energy to break it. It was a terrible feeling, an oppression from the earth itself, and all he could hope was that it would be better somewhere ahead.

26

It was close to midday when Mikhail finally turned his horse away from the shores of the Lake and headed north, following a thread of energy like a magnet that ran from his heart and drew him along. It was not as powerful as the calling had been, but he had a sense of urgency all the same.

Marguerida had barely spoken since their encounter with Robard MacDenis. He could not tell if she was too angry or simply too exhausted. By his own reckoning, they had been riding for nearly six hours, three of them racing from Hali, without a real rest.

They rode through a tract of land which was less devastated than that around the Tower. There were things growing, some familiar plants and trees, and here and there a bird gave call. A small animal darted across the trail before them. All he saw was a flash of brown fur and dark eyes, gone before he could even think of catching it. Mikhail had a great sense of relief. He had begun to believe the entire countryside was barren. The sight of the familiar plants—pale green shoots of wild millet and the blue flowers of flax—was immensely reassuring.

Mikhail could sense Marguerida's mood begin to lighten. There was a light breeze, smelling of damp earth and growing things, and the sun was warm on their backs. He could see some clouds coming in from the north, and knew it would probably rain by nightfall. They must find food and shelter by then. His belly had given up complaining, and although he was hungry, it was not uppermost in his mind. All he could really think about was reaching the destination he was sure awaited them.

"Do you have any idea where we are going, or are you just following your nose, Mik?"

"I have a sense where we are headed, Marguerida, but no more than that."

"Good. I hope that wherever it is, there is something to eat. Is it far?"

"I have no idea, and can't guess. Look, I am really sorry that you had to . . ."

"Don't apologize, Mik. It had to be done, and even though I hated it, I am glad that at least I have sufficient training now to control the command voice. If this had happened before I went to Neskaya, I could just as easily have killed both Amalie and that nice old man. Or left them witless. It just reminds me of how I was overshadowed. That bothers me most."

"I don't follow you."

"Don't you see that what the voice of command does, in a sense, is overshadow the other person temporarily. I mean, that is essentially what I did to little Donal last summer; I overshadowed his mind and sent him off to the overworld. There are, according to Istvana, several ways to cause overshadowing, but the Voice is the fastest, simplest, and most efficient." She fell silent for a minute. "The worst part, for me, is that it gets easier every time I do it. I can see how it could become so easy that I might be tempted to do it whether I needed to or not. Which, I suspect, is precisely what happened to *her*. She got accustomed to having her will obeyed, and then . . . addicted, perhaps? At least, when I was meddling with Amalie's mind back there, I sensed that when Ashara was still at Hali, she just ordered everyone around, without any sense of whether it was right or wrong. She lost something . . . I don't know what. And I almost think I need to know what, so I won't follow in her footsteps inadvertently."

"She was the first female Keeper, as far as we know, Marguerida. And, I think, she was the one who instituted the practice of Keepers remaining celibate. Maybe what she lost was any chance to be a woman, to love and have children."

"Oh, please!" Her voice was a little shrill, irritated and brusque. "You sound like Ariel!" Margaret quieted, thinking. "I will give her this—her timing was extraordinary," she added. She gave a sudden bark of laughter, very like Lew Alton's, but it lacked any real humor. "You could be right, though, that the struggle to become a Keeper made her ruthless. Why do you suspect . . . ?"

"Leonie Hastur, who was the last virginal Keeper at Arilinn, was, by all accounts I have heard, a very sad woman. There is a memoir at Armida, that Damon Ridenow wrote in his old age, that I read some of once. It is painful reading, because he felt a lot of guilt for doing what he did, and most of it was for how much Leonie, whom he adored, was damaged by the way we did things back then."

"I never knew he wrote anything except the journal I read while I was at Arilinn. That did not have much in it that was personal. Uncle Jeff let me have a look at it, and I found it interesting, but not very lively. I never guessed there was anything more. Jeff never mentioned it."

"No, he wouldn't. The text at Arilinn is public stuff, because it deals with Damon's discoveries about the nature of matrices—though I would give a lot to see what he would have made of yours, dearest. The memoir we have at Armida is quite different. I don't know why he wrote it, or for whom, other than himself. I found it quite by accident, in the library, stuck between a stud book from Kennard Alton's time and a Terran geography book that I suppose Andrew Carr left there. It had no printing on the spine or anything, just a plain volume of pages, with Damon's cramped hand in it. I read it, or most of it, and then I showed it to Liriel. She has it in her lair at Armida, with the rest of her treasures. When we return, ask her about it." As he spoke these words, Mikhail felt chilled. What if they never got back?

Mikhail knew she was thinking the same thing, but she only asked, "What did he say about Leonie Hastur?"

"Let me think. He felt that she was denied the opportunity to be all that she could have been, that she never had a choice about being anything except a *leronis,* because she started so very young. Even today we still have a tendency to think of *laran* first and people second, you know."

"All too well, Mik, all too well." There was a bitterness in her words that did not escape him. "I encountered it at Arilinn and I hated it. Sometimes it was as if the only thing that mattered about me was that I had the Alton Gift—as if nothing I had done or might do was important except that one thing. It made me feel like a footstool!"

In spite of the seriousness of her tone, he found himself laughing. He saw her frown, then joined in. "You are a very poor footstool, Marguerida. Why did you choose that particular piece of furniture?"

She thought for a moment. "Why, because a footstool has feet, but it does not walk, I suppose. It just remains in its place and lets people use it! It never tosses off someone with muddy boots, or smelly feet. And because it is an object, which is how I felt most of the mercifully brief time I was there. I was an object of curiosity and envy, and never, never was I a person with my own ideas or ambitions. That is probably overstating it by a lot, but that is how I felt."

"Hobbled?"

"Absolutely! My choices seemed limited to either remaining in a Tower for the rest of my life, or marrying and devoting my life to my offspring, in order to preserve the Alton Gift and whatever else I might have lurking in my genes. I started feeling I wasn't really human any longer, but just a vehicle for conveying *laran.*"

"And at Neskaya?"

"Istvana is a very subversive woman." Marguerida caught his look of surprise.

"Odd choice of words."

"I cannot think of any better description. She does not expect everyone to do exactly what she tells them, and she had some ideas of her own that would probably shock the people at Arilinn. I don't really have enough data to say more than that. I just know that Neskaya and Arilinn are worlds apart."

"Can you give me an example." He was fascinated, and glad for something other to concentrate on than the persistent worry at the back of his mind.

"Istvana encourages innovation and discussion. Can you imagine Camilla MacRoss asking her charges to talk to her about their studies?"

"No, I can't."

"There were a lot of discussions, like the ones I had when I was at University, about all sorts of things. There was one, I remember, that went on for three consecutive nights, between me, Caitlin Leynier, and Baird Beltran, about the ethics of telepathy. We never came to any conclusions, but we really thrashed out the problem. One night Beltran took the position that any form of mental exchange was a violation—he likes to tackle really extreme ideas—of privacy, even if both persons agreed to communicate! And it gave me a lot to think about, since the Alton Gift has a strong element of coercion in it."

"How could he defend that?" Mikhail was curious, but a little stunned. What sort of Tower was Istvana running up there, anyhow? He realized that, until he encountered Emelda, he had just assumed that the ethics of *laran* were quite simple and straightforward. He felt more than a little chagrined by his own innocence and naivete.

"By arguing that no one knows his own mind well enough to give informed consent to telepathy. He said that there is always a degree of coercion, either hidden or revealed, in it. And what was the most interesting element of the exchange was that part of it was spoken, but much of it was not. Caitlin and I agreed he had really made us examine all our ideas about *laran*."

Mikhail had a momentary stab of jealousy. He had never met the man, but he was envious that Baird had had this intriguing discussion with Marguerida, and that he had not. It did not matter, did it? They were together now, and that was what was important. So why did he feel so forlorn?

"I am sorry I missed it."

"I am too, because as we were talking, I kept thinking how nice it would be if you were there. Sometimes I get so frustrated by how close-minded so many Darkovans seem to be. And reactionary," she added darkly.

"We've had thousands of years to learn about *laran*, but we are still a little afraid of it, because we know how it can be misused. So we try to do the things that have worked in the past, and not get too fancy." He cleared his throat and went on. "We would like to think we are civilized, not the barbarians the Terranan assume us to be because we refuse to embrace their vaunted technology. We are, for the most part, polite, because a telepathic community could not survive without that." He gestured at the landscape. There was a crater about a hundred yards off the narrow trail, and it glowed faintly, even in the ruddy sunlight. "This is what can happen when we are not polite. The plain truth is that we are simply well-mannered, not civilized in the ideal sense. All human beings are wolves pretending to be nice doggies."

"That is a really depressing notion, Mik. And close to some things that people at University said, too. Maybe it is even true!"

"Yes, it is. I will be less gloomy when we reach our destination, or get some food into me, whichever comes first."

They rode on in weary silence for another half an hour, the thought of food occupying both their minds. Then Marguerida said, "Is that a house up ahead?"

"What?" He stood in the stirrups to get a better view. "It looks like a ruin." he answered, standing in the stirrups to get a better look.

"Damn!" She put all her disappointment into the word.

"Hush!" Mikhail peered ahead, his eyes starting to water. One second he saw a burned out structure, and the next he was sure there was smoke coming from an intact chimney. The thing seemed to shift even as he watched, back and forth.

He sniffed the air, but there was no smell of woodsmoke. Still, he kept seeing glimpses of a building with white stone walls. It was an illusion of some sort, though whether the ruin or the solid structure was the false image he could not guess.

Mikhail had heard of such things, matrix-generated veils which distorted light and shadow. He had heard of cloaks of illusion, although he had never seen one, and tended to regard them as legendary. The last thing he wanted was to tangle with some old trap-matrix. And in this here and now, these traps were not ancient, but were active and dangerous.

Then, in an instant, he was sure this was their final destination. The knowledge flowed through him like warm water, easing his fears. Still, Mikhail swallowed hard. It did not look very inviting.

He reined the roan off the trail and started riding toward the place. The closer they drew, the more the building appeared empty and deserted. He could see weeds growing from between blackened stones, broken walls, a collapsed chimney and a few smashed kitchen bowls, the pottery charred and dark.

Mikhail's belly was knotted, and his knuckles were white with tension. He could feel sweat trickling down his back, in spite of the coolness of the day. Had they been dragged across time to this? He felt caught between his own doubts and his sense of fate. It was like being pressed between two stones, and he wanted to break free of the weight. The only way was to go ahead.

They rode to the broken wall which had surrounded the building, now just a few stones high. When he looked over the wall, all Mikhail saw was an empty piece of earth, with debris on it. Then a mouse started from the weeds that grew at the base of the wall, darted through the foliage, and *vanished*. The feeling of desolation was enormous.

It was too quiet. The lack of sound was eerie. And it did not *feel* like an empty building, or like anything he had ever experienced before. Whatever it was, it lacked any sense of reality as he knew it, and he was very puzzled. Before he could decide what to do next, the crow flapped off the pommel of his saddle, and flew across the low stone wall and vanished just as the mouse had.

One second it was there, and the next it was gone, as if it had never existed. There was nothing to suggest that the bird had crossed the veil of a trap-matrix. Mikhail felt his heart race, and a chill sense of fear crept along his flesh.

When the crow reappeared a few moments later, flying across the low wall with its rough caw, he was immensely relieved, then furious at himself. He hated his fear, the closing of his throat, the bumps on his skin, and more the feeling of helplessness that came with it. Anger at his own weakness raced through his blood.

The bird landed on his shoulder, and turned its bill to his ear. Tenderly it began to nibble with the tip of it. Then it stopped and muttered something in its throat.

"I think the crow wants us to go over the wall." Mikhail's voice was tense, and his mouth parched. He felt the tugging at his heart, that peculiar link of energy he had had since leaving Hali Tower. It was no longer bearable, as it had been a few minutes before. Now it was a burning point in his chest, not painful, precisely, but not comfortable either. This was their destination. Why did he feel so reluctant to move?

He dismounted stiffly, his thigh muscles protesting a little. Then he stood beside the roan, breathing shallowly, fighting the fear that threatened to strangle him. Mikhail's knees were shaking, and he felt he could not move another step.

Marguerida dismounted and came to stand beside him. He could smell the faint scent of perfume that clung to her skin, mixed with the warm odor of horse and sweat and sunlight. Mikhail glanced at her, saw the tangle of her hair, half loosened from the ornate butterfly clasp, and smears of dirt where she had wiped her forehead. It was a very reassuring mixture, very real and ordinary. "Are we waiting for an engraved invitation?"

In spite of his tension, he smiled at the tart question. That was his Marguerida, his beloved! He knew she was not at all fearless, that the very name of Ashara Alton still had the capacity to make her tremble. But there she was, standing beside him, curious and ready, he suspected, to leap into the pits of Zandru if necessary.

"No. I am just being . . . I was going to say careful. That isn't it at all, Marguerida. I have this feeling that once I move, I will never be the same again, and I am not really sure . . ."

"Second thoughts?"

"And third and fourth as well. I am not afraid exactly. I can't explain it."

She slipped her right hand around his elbow and leaned closer to him. "There is a place on Zeepan called the Garden of Transformations, which is very famous. They say that if you enter it, you are never the same afterward. Pilgrims go there, but a lot of them never enter, because they become so scared of what they might become that they often turn back at the last minute. And those who do go in are never able to describe their experience."

"You seem to have a song or a story for every occasion. And you are right. That is how I feel this second. How did you know?"

She shrugged against his shoulder. "I minored in folklore," she murmured, as if that explained everything. He could feel her body tremble where it touched his. She took a shuddering breath. "Remember, no matter what happens, you will still be Mikhail Hastur, and I will still be Margaret Alton." *And I will always love you, no matter what!*

"Come on, then." Mikhail walked to the wall. It was low enough to step over with his long legs, and he did so. He seemed to be moving through glue, slowing down so much that every movement took hours and hours. He felt the resistance for what seemed an age, and then it was gone, and he was standing on the other side, gasping for air.

Marguerida was next to him a moment later, looking a little wild eyed from lack of breath. There was sweat on her forehead and she had bitten her lip. The blood welled out in a single red droplet. He watched as her hand rose to her face, wiped the moisture off her brow, and ran gloved fingers through tousled red curls. "Ugh! That was worse than coming through to Hali!"

Mikhail nodded and looked around. He was standing on a patch of well-tended grass, but it was not green. It was a strange rose shade, and small flowers danced on tender stalks. He knew that the only growth of that color was that which grew around the *rhu fead,* the chapel close to Hali Tower, and miles from this spot. He had never actually visited that sacred place, but he had heard enough descriptions to be more than puzzled.

Before him was neither the burned-out ruin nor the farmhouse he had glimpsed from a distance. Instead there was a low, round building made of white fieldstone and covered with slabs of turf. Vines grew from the earth, coiling up around the curving walls, and there was a smell of balsam and lavender in the air. A few conifers crowded around the building, their dark green branches casting deep shadows on the stones and the ground beneath them.

Mikhail glanced over his shoulder, looking for the horses, but there was nothing to see but a slight shimmer, hanging in the air like silver mist. The crow tweaked his ear again. "I sure hope you know what you are leading us into," he told the animal. All he got in answer was a flutter of wings.

They moved slowly toward the building, neither of them eager to enter. Marguerida had slipped her hand into his, and he felt the slight tremble of it in his clasp. He felt very small, as if he were a child, not an adult. There was a peculiar quality, a sense of illusion, but he could smell vegetation, the definitive scent of stone and moss, the pungent tang of turf. How could something be real and imaginary at the same time?

At least it does not have chicken legs.

What? Marguerida's sudden thought made no sense, but he could feel the undertone of humor in it.

In an old tale, there is a hut with fowl's legs, inhabited by a witch called Granny Yaga, who rides around in a mortar, and grinds naughty children with her pestle.

Now, there's a cheerful thought. Sometimes I wish your mind was less cluttered with interesting facts, dearest. Some of them are very disturbing!

I know. I can't seem to help it.

Mikhail could not see any windows in the dome-shaped building, and despite the pink grass they were walking on, he was certain this was not the *rhu fead.* He had the sense that his eyes were still being fooled. But it was where he had to be, and that eased his mind just a little. It was eerie, though, and he wished it were not.

They walked slowly around the structure, and finally found a narrow slit in the stones. A faint smell of smoke came out of it, and with it the odor of food. His mouth filled with saliva and Mikhail swallowed hard.

Should we knock or call out or something?

Knock on what? There is no door. The smell is driving me mad!

Me, too, Mik. I just hope there isn't a witch in there, stirring her cauldron, and expecting us for dinner—her dinner!

Don't be silly!

I'm sorry, Mik. I am just tired and scared, and when I get scared, my imagination goes wild.

Mikhail noticed how easily she admitted her fear, and wished he could do the same. At that moment he was not feeling either brave or manly, but he could hardly let himself know that, let alone Marquerida. He did let his own feelings echo hers for a breath or two. Then he thrust them down ruthlessly.

Mikhail forced himself to step into the narrow opening, expecting to find himself in darkness. Instead he entered a globe of radiance that nearly blinded him for a second. He felt Marguerida stumble against him and steadied her with his hand.

His eyes adjusted quickly to the brightness, and Mikhail saw a single room. There was a stone floor and bare walls. But they were not ordinary stones. They looked like glass, and a blue light gleamed from all around them. He could feel Marguerida trembling against his side.

Mik, I don't like this place! It is very like what that room . . . what her place in the old Tower looked like in my memory! It burns! My left hand feels as if it is on fire—except it is not painful.

I know. My whole body feels as if it is being pulled in several directions at once.

He gripped her arm and looked again. Now he could make out a long couch across the room from him. When he looked, it vanished and reappeared again in another place. The effect was dizzying. Everything was shifting, and he wanted to vomit. Instead, he closed his eyes firmly.

Through his eyelids, Mikhail could feel the light in the room alter. It was less bright, he decided. At last he opened his eyes and looked around. He was right—the light had dimmed.

His sense of disorientation left him. The couch no longer moved around the room, but remained in one place. Mikhail could see there was a fireplace on one wall, and someone standing beside it, bent over a cauldron. It was altogether too much like the stories which had been racing through Marguerida's mind for his liking, but he did not feel any sense of peril. He had to trust his instincts, and he found that this was more difficult than he had imagined possible.

But the pleasant smell of woodsmoke and cooking food started to ease his mind. He noticed a rickety table and some rather unsteady chairs at one side of the room, all set with crockery. Slowly, he let out his breath.

Something moved on the couch, and Mikhail shivered. He blinked a few times, and at last he saw a man lying there, draped in blankets. The slight rise and fall of breath was all that told him this was a living person and not a corpse.

Mikhail moved toward the couch, drawn to it before he could think. His boots made no sound as they crossed the shining stones. He realized that while he could smell the fire, he could not hear the crackle of flames, and that, except for the rough sound of his breath, the room was utterly silent. He barely had a thought for Marguerida, although he could sense her rising hysteria, and her struggle to overcome it.

He approached the covered figure and looked down into a face aged and worn. It had the features of a Ridenow, the pale hair and somewhat abbreviated nose. There were wrinkles on the parchment fine-skin, and the muscles sagged around the cheeks. The man seemed to be sleeping deeply, barely breathing.

Then the eyes slowly opened, and Mikhail found himself staring into a pair of pale blue orbs, clear as water. The wrinkled mouth twisted into a smile, showing large teeth and pink gums. "Well met, Mikhalangelo. Dear Margarethe—do not fear. This is not the place of your torment." The words broke the silence around them, and the crackle of burning wood was suddenly audible.

It was the voice which had called them through the centuries, but it did not seem as deep now. He looked at the ancient face, trying to memorize every feature. Was the man really there? Reflexively, he started to monitor the figure on the couch, and found that there was indeed a person there, not another illusion.

"Greetings, *dom.*"

"I would rise, but I cannot. It took what remaining strength I had to bring you here, and I was not certain I would accomplish . . . it." The voice faded into exhaustion.

Beside him, Marguerida tensed. He could sense her rapport touch the sick old man, though there were no words in it. All he had was the impression of energy moving past him, so fast he almost doubted his senses.

Marguerida shoved him aside abruptly, her brows drawn together in a frown. She knelt beside the couch, stripped the leather glove off her left hand, then placed her fingers around the throat of the man. It looked as if she might throttle him. Mikhail was stunned, and started to pull her away.

No, Mik! Not a word—I know what to do!

Reluctantly, Mikhail dropped his hand from her shoulder and stepped back. He could now see that her fingers were not actually touching the crepey skin along the throat of the man, and after a minute, he could tell that the energy had changed, that the man was breathing more easily, and the color in his face was better.

Marguerida removed her hand, her face so white that she appeared bloodless, and tried to get to her feet. Mikhail caught her before she fell to the stone floor. "That is not something I recommend on an empty stomach," she muttered, resting her head against his shoulder. She rubbed her forehead. "Actually, I don't think it would be much better with a full belly."

Such power! I did not guess.

The man on the couch looked up at them, and his eyes were almost bright. "I thank you, Margarethe—even if your methods are rather crude."

Marguerida lifted her head off Mikhail's shoulder and glared at the man. "I barely knew what I was doing," she muttered gruffly, looking pleased and irritated at the same time. Then she waggled the fingers of her hand, where they extended above the rather sweaty mitt, at him. "I haven't learned how to use this *thing* yet!"

"You do better than you think." He sighed. "There is little time left for me, and so much to do."

"Then you had better get about it," she snapped.

The man chuckled softly at her rebuke. "I am Varzil Ridenow, and I have brought you through time."

"We guessed as much. But why?"

Mikhail waited for an answer to his question, and watched Varzil pull one hand from beneath the blankets. An enormous ring glittered on his finger, the largest matrix he had ever seen on a human being. The light from it dazzled his eyes and he had to look away to keep from being blinded. "This is why."

"Your matrix?"

"Yes. I must give it to you before I die."

"You can't give me your matrix! It would kill you and me at the same time!"

"Really?" Varzil seemed amused. "As the keystone killed your companion?"

"That's different! What Marguerida has is . . . well, I don't know exactly what it is. Even though I was there, and helped her pull it out of the Tower of Mirrors. It is from the overworld, not from . . ." Mikhail wavered, letting the words fade.

Like the Sword of Aldones, the matrix ring of Varzil the Good was the stuff of legends. And the Sword had been just that, until Regis Hastur had wielded it against the Sharra Matrix. But Varzil's ring had vanished, and while there were several stories about what had happened to it, no one knew the truth.

Mikhail flogged his mind fruitlessly. There was too much to take in at once, and he sensed that he had no time for calm consideration. He could sense only urgency from the prostrate Varzil, urgency and need. He felt stirrings of resentment—this was even worse than Regis dumping the Regency on him without asking. This could kill him!

"Quite right." Varzil's words made him start. "It could, but it will not!"

The crow jumped off Mikhail's shoulder and flapped over to stand on the pillow above Varzil's head. Mikhail's head felt full of buzzing bees, rather angry ones, as he tried to make some sense out of the situation. "Why do you want to give me your matrix?" he finally managed to ask.

"Because it must not be left when I die—Ashara Alton would try to claim it, and if she succeeded, then she could return to Hali. It is her greatest ambition, and she must not do it!"

"Why not?" He decided he was not going to budge until he got some explanation which satisfied him.

"If Hali stands, then the world you know will never be."

"I think I see," Marguerida said quietly. "When I encountered her in my mind, the one thing she was determined to do was prevent me from destroying her—and if I never exist, then she has nothing to worry about. So, even though I have beaten her in the overworld, in this time, she could still—My head aches!" Her quiet calm vanished, as she tried to encompass the ideas racing through her mind. It was too much, and Mikhail realized she was going to faint.

He picked her up, swung her into his arms, and carried her to the table. Then he tucked her into a lopsided chair and forced her head between her knees. "Take deep breaths!" There was a muffled protest. "Don't argue with me! You, there, bring the *damisela* something to eat!"

Obediently, the crone shuffled across the room with a bowl of steaming stew and a slab of bread perched on the delicious smelling contents. Mikhail helped Marguerida sit upright, and watched her reach a trembling hand for the carved spoon that sat on the table. She filled the bowl of the spoon, drew it to her mouth, and crammed it between her lips. "Ouch! It's hot!"

The old woman put a pitcher on the table, and water slopped over the rim. Mikhail took it and poured two goblets. Then he lifted one and opened his mouth. It tasted sweet and fresh, and was the best water he had ever drunk. He drained the cup in a few gulps, hardly noticing that a little had slipped down the edges of his mouth. He wiped it with the edge of his sleeve, and turned back to face the man on the couch.

Varzil was watching him, the ancient eyes alert and clear. "Now, just how do you intend to accomplish this miracle of matrix science, Varzil?" The water seemed to have cleared his mind, but he was still brimming with fury at the ancient *tenerézu*.

The old man smiled slowly, as if savoring some secret jest. "First of all, you must be married."

27

At first, Mikhail did not believe he had heard right. He heard Marguerida choke behind him, then cough roughly. "Married?" What the devil was he talking about?

"You must be joined, become one, so that I may surrender my burden onto you."

"Burden?" Mikhail was getting angrier by the second. The old man was speaking in riddles!

"I think he means that he can't give you his ring until we are married, Mik." *Damn me for a silly woman! Who is going to marry us, out here in whenever, and why do I feel so bereft? I never wanted flowers and veils, fancy ceremonies. And the Old Man isn't here to . . . give me away—what a ridiculous custom, as if I were not my own person! Oh, hell! But maybe this is the only way—the only way we can have each other and to the devil with Comyn power struggles!*

Marguerida's thoughts ran across his mind like quicksilver. The emotions beneath them were conflicted and chaotic. Mikhail could sense joy, relief, fury, and a disappointment that made his heart ache.

"Margarethe is correct," Varzil answered quietly. "And I am sorry to ask it of you—this should be a joyous occasion, not something done of necessity."

"I still don't understand," Mikhail muttered. "And it is impossible for you to give me your ring—it would kill both of us."

Mikhail felt trapped in his own feelings. Anger and fear seemed to grip him while he struggled to silence them. He did not want the ring, and certainly he did not want to be manipulated into the plans of this stranger—even if he was the most powerful *laranzu* in history. It was too much to take in, and his mind balked abruptly.

Varzil smiled, the years falling from his face. "Time travel is impossible—what I propose is merely very difficult."

Mikhail felt the statement enter his mind, without comprehension. Then he realized the humor in it, and felt nothing except surprise. It had never occurred to him that Varzil the Good made jokes! And rather than putting him at ease, it just made his rage increase. How dare this man play games with him! "The hell you say," he roared, letting all his frustrations release in the words.

Varzil did not appear at all offended. Instead, the old man cleared his throat, and continued to speak in a dry voice. "Have you never wondered at the custom of *di catenas?* Why we encircle the wrists? Perhaps the substance of the ceremony has been lost through the years, or become only a means of signifying alliances."

In spite of himself, Mikhail was interested. His anger faded, and his lively curiosity pushed forward. "I've never given it much thought, Varzil. And, truthfully, I think shackling two people together is rather . . . well, barbaric." In truth, Mikhail had never given the matter much thought before he met Marguerida. She had changed him, with her probing questions and her knowledge of worlds other than Darkover. Everything in his life seemed divided by her presence.

"Yes, I can see that. But, in the beginning, it was more than a symbolic thing, for it joined the *laran* energies of two into one, made them stronger than they were alone, and allowed them to create a unique link that could not exist in any other fashion."

Mikhail stared at Varzil. He did not know of any *di catenas* marriages that were even remotely like that which the old man suggested. Neither his parents nor his Uncle Regis and Lady Linnea struck him as being the least bit unified in their mental powers. And this was what was meant, he decided. It was a remarkable idea, but he was not certain he was up to it.

Marguerida rose, and joined them. He could sense her mind sorting out what Varzil had said, using her sharp wits to grasp the concept, tear it apart, then restore it to its original integrity. That she could do that in seconds, where his own slower mind took what seemed like forever, was at once a source of pride and irritation. Her mind, he thought, was like a bright dart, and his own more a heavy hammer that had to beat at things before he could understand them.

"I see what you want, and it makes sense." Marguerida stood beside him, looking down at the figure on the couch. "But how? Do you have a priest or someone lurking in the stonework?"

Mikhail smiled. "We are not much for priests on Darkover, Marguerida. Unless you count the *cristoforos*. Any lord of the Comyn can perform the ceremony—my father could have latched you and Gabe together quite legally, if he had had the courage to have you gagged."

"Or drugged," she muttered.

"He doesn't have the imagination to think of either of those things. And even if he had, he probably wouldn't have done it, because it would have caused a lot of talk, and my father does not like people to talk about him." They forgot the old man on the couch for a moment, looking at each other and smiling about *Dom* Gabriel.

Then his cough brought them back to attention, "Do you know why the woman's bracelet is always larger than the man's?"

"No, Varzil, I don't. It is one of the many things on Darkover that everyone assumes I know, and therefore no one tells me the reasons for." Marguerida's voice was brusque with impatience.

"I don't know either," Mikhail admitted. He was amazed at her, thinking she would snap and snarl at Zandru himself. He knew she was not fearless, just too tired to care any longer. Then he realized that his sense of confusion was fading. He was afraid, but in a remote way. What was in that water? he wondered. His mind felt clearer, and even his hunger had vanished.

The idea of actually marrying his beloved sank into his mind, spreading slowly across it. It felt right and wrong at the same time. He puzzled over it before he realized that they were being rushed into it, and that their feelings were not part of it. They must marry, and now.

Before he could sort out the complicated emotions, Varzil continued. "The woman has the larger band because she bears the greater strength—the strength to bring children into the world. In a peculiar way, the wife is the greater person in the marriage, Margarethe, not the lesser."

"I see. And that is why, for centuries, you have locked women up, killed them with childbearing, and kept them in servitude." The ferocity in her voice made Mikhail cringe.

"There are no perfect systems, Margarethe." Varzil did not sound disturbed at her criticism.

"No, I don't suppose there are." She sounded both angry and sad.

"Let's get on with this, before I . . ." She turned a golden gaze on Mikhail, and her expression softened. "We are meant to be together, you know. We always were. But I can't help wishing for clean clothes, and a hot bath, and lots of flowers. And my father, I want my father to be here." He could see the sparkle of tears in her eyes.

Mikhail turned to her and pulled her against him. *Dearest, please do not be so sad! I know this is not what you might have wished for, but I do love you, with all my heart.*

I know, Mik, and I love you. But I still feel as if I am being stampeded. I never thought I had a romantic bone in my body, and now I seem to have a great many of them, all wishing for music and a lovely gown. You've probably never heard the Kotswold Processional, and there isn't an organ on the whole of Darkover anyhow. But, somewhere in the back of my mind, I have been wishing to hear it played, with the flutes for the groom, calling the bride forward, and the viols answering. It is very soft, at first, and then it swells, as the voices come together, join, and begin the central theme. At last there is only a single voice, the flute and viol indistinguishable.

It sounds wonderful! He was deeply moved by her longing, and he could hear the strains of the music playing in her memory. It was surprising, too, because he never would have suspected her of having such longings. She had never, he realized, revealed the womanly side of herself to him, except in dreams a few times. That vulnerable part of her she kept firmly hidden, buttressed against injury. He knew her strength, and her fear of Ashara, but he realized he did not know her soft side at all.

You should have had it all—the gown, the waiting maids, the music—everything.

It's all right. I am just very tired, and everything seems overwhelming. This place—there is something strange about it, and I feel rather woozy. That water I drank seems to have made me . . . sort of drunk!

Me, too!

Mikhail looked down at the old man on the couch. Varzil's eyes were closed, and his hand with the great ring lay on the covers, limp and worn. But the breath that rose and fell in his chest was strong and steady. "Very well—we agree, since it is clear that you called us here for this."

"It must seem very cold to you, that I dragged you through the centuries to fulfill my own needs—and, indeed, I have prepared for this event for years and years. But it is not a selfish thing, I swear, for the future of Darkover depends on this marriage. The power I will bequeath unto you will be necessary in time."

"We have no choice but to trust you, Varzil."

"Oh, Mikhalangelo . . . I will not fail you again!"

"Again?" The back of his neck bristled.

"He means that other Mikhalangelo—the one that Robard thought was dead. The one you look like, and the Margarethe I resemble—except her eyes were not so gold as mine."

"Yes, I do. If things had worked out, they would have married, as they wished."

"But they died, didn't they, Varzil?"

"They did." The expression on the tired old face was infinitely sad.

Mikhail looked from Marguerida to Varzil, and back again. "Do you mean to imply we have lived before?"

"No, not precisely. The souls you bear are your own, not those of other people. But . . . there is a template of a kind, in the overworld, for every soul that has ever existed, or will exist in time to come, and from eon to eon it brings forth a similar thing. I, with all my knowledge, cannot explain it, but only accept it."

Mikhail was immensely relieved. For reasons he could not put into words, he could not bear the thought of being the reincarnation of some strange man from the past. It made him feel like a poor copy, a blurred image of himself, instead of the man that he hoped he actually was.

"So how do we do this?" Marguerida was restless, full of impatience now, as if she were about to take a dose of nasty tasting medicine, and wanted to get it over with quickly. He could smell the pleasant scent of stew on her breath, and the earthy, musky, womanly scent of her body. Mikhail decided he rather liked her with tangled hair, a dirty face, and the smell of horse on her clothing.

The silent crone who had hovered in the background shuffled forward, carrying a small wooden box, ornately carved with figures. When she reached them, she opened it, and Mikhail saw two fine copper bracelets resting on the soft cloth that lined the box. The metal no longer shone, but had oxidized to a greenish tint.

"These were intended for those other people, weren't they?"

"Yes, Margarethe, they were. I oversaw the making of them myself, even though I knew at the time that it was unlikely they would ever be used. I sense that you are uneasy about wearing them. I can only tell you that the love that Mikhalangelo and Margarethe held for one another was very great, as great as that which you have for one another. They were full of promise, those two brave souls, a promise that was unfulfilled."

"It sounds like a sad story."

"Yes, parts of it are sad. But there is hope in it as well. And triumph." He fell silent, thinking. "The story is not over yet, and I will not tell you what you would like to know."

"I didn't imagine you would, Varzil."

"You are a very clever woman, Margarethe, very quick."

"Am I? I feel more like a puppet with every passing moment."

Varzil gave a deep sigh, and slowly sat up on his couch. The blankets slipped down, revealing his gray robe. Sitting up, they could see he was not a tall man, and his bones seemed very fragile beneath his garments.

He reached out and took the box from the old woman, and then just looked at the verdigrised bracelets in silence. He seemed lost in his own thoughts, as if he had forgotten their presence. Then he roused himself, straightening thin shoulders with an effort.

"Tell me, Varzil, were you going to give your ring to this Mikhalangelo?" Mikhail was not certain why that question popped into his mind, but it did, and he wanted to know the answer.

"No, I was not. I realized only after he was taken what I must do, and it has cost me greatly to bear the knowledge and the waiting."

"Waiting for what?"

"Waiting for you to destroy the Tower of Mirrors, Margarethe, for without that shadow matrix which rests in your flesh, this scheme would come to naught. You do not know yet what you possess, and I cannot tell you, except that it—not I—made time your plaything. And I know time, as much as any mortal can. More, it foiled Ashara's plans as well."

Marguerida laughed. "Well, I am all for foiling that bitch, in any time and any place, for what she did to me, and to all those other poor women she overshadowed and used. I think you have it wrong, though. I think that I am time's toy, not the other way around."

Varzil nodded. "Sometimes it is difficult to tell one end of the stick from the other. Now, let us begin. Remove your silken glove, Margarethe, and you, Mikhalangelo, take out your matrix."

With some reluctance, Mikhail reached under his tunic and pulled out his matrix stone. He saw, from the corner of his eye, Marquerida strip the mitt back, revealing the blue lines that ran from knuckle to wrist. In the dim light, they appeared darker and more powerful. He wondered if it was only his eyes, or whether her training at Arilinn and Neskaya had intensified her strength.

Mikhail withdrew his matrix from its wrappings, and looked at it. It was a modest stone, as befitted his modest *laran,* and he glanced at the ring sparkling on Varzil's hand.

This was insane. He knew that no one could touch another's star-stone, without risk of shock—sometimes fatal shock—to both parties. He was certain he was not strong enough to control the energies which coursed between the lambent facets of Varzil's extraordinary and dangerous jewel.

Mikhail took a long breath, forming a protest in his mind, thinking as quickly as he could. If he did as Varzil asked, he would surely die. What good would it do to marry Marguerida, if he perished in the deed?

Mikhail opened his mouth to speak, and found his throat parched again. He tried to swallow and could not. The blood pounded in his skull, and he wondered if he was going to pass out. But the weakness passed, and instead he felt a sudden, unexplained sense of strength coursing along his veins, as if he had slept for a week and eaten two dozen meals.

But though his body felt renewed, his heart quailed before the fear that swept through him, gnawing at him, tormenting him. He remembered how he had been enthralled for weeks by Emelda, and how the little hedge-witch had toyed with him. He had had to prevail on his sister to rescue him—the deep shame still rankled.

Mikhail took a mental step back, looking at his position with a kind of cold remoteness he had never known he possessed. Why should he trust this doddering ancient, or even his beloved—a half-trained woman with an enigmatic tool of power branded into her in the overworld? He had no answer, no certainty, only a pale hope which seemed to him a frail thing, unworthy of dependence.

Varzil was watching him, his eyes rheumy, but filled with compassion, as if he sensed the war that raged in Mikhail's soul. Of course—Varzil was of the Ridenow, and their Gift was that of empathy! He did not want that, or sympathy either! All he wished for was to be gone from this place and time, to be anywhere else, where his choices were not so dire, where it did not feel as if his very soul were being rent and riven.

Marguerida flexed her hand then, drawing his attention with the gesture, and he saw the lines on it flash with luminescence, as if lightning were playing across her pale skin. He glanced at her face and found her eyes unfocused, inward looking, and her mouth was twisted as if she held back some terrible sound. Small beads of sweat broke out under the tumble of curls on her brow, gleaming wetness glittering in the soft light that rose from her hand, casting flickering shadows across her prominent nose and tight-lipped mouth.

Mikhail realized that she was fighting her own demons, just as he

had been a moment before. The sight of her silent struggle was unnerving—he did not want to know what tormented her. But if she
could face it, then he must, too, to be worthy of her. No—to be worthy
of himself!

Children, attend me now!

Mikhail tried to resist the command, but could not. He felt his eyes
turn away from Marguerida, and come to rest on the calm face of the
old man. His features were somehow different, younger, smoother
and more defined, as if he had moved back in time.

Behind Varzil he saw the serving woman. She was standing on the
far side of the couch, and she had her hands on his shoulders. Mikhail
could almost feel the strength flowing from her into the old man, and
his face grew younger each second. There was something about the
way she was supporting Varzil that seemed very significant, something
he yearned to understand. He stared, and as he looked, the crone's
face blurred, then transformed. The woman grew fair and young, as
Varzil had, and a brightness shone from her flesh.

Mikhail had to drop his eyes then, for the radiance of the woman
was too great. It was not that his eyes could not bear the light, but that
his soul could not. And as he looked down, he grasped what he had
been struggling to understand. There was no shame or loss of manli-
ness in taking support from a woman—but it must never be taken for
granted or abused. It was a gift, one he had never imagined existed,
and the sense of it rocked him to the core.

Mikhail could feel the light of the other woman, filling the room,
and his knees bent without his volition. He felt himself kneel on the
cold stone floor, so consumed by awe he was certain his heart would
cease beating. He lifted his eyes to the uncanny brightness, and saw a
soft smile that swept away everything, all fear and doubt. He could
have basked in that gentle gaze until the end of time.

His hand was closed around his starstone, and he thought it a
tawdry thing, unworthy of the presence which held him in its grasp. He
was trembling all over. Distantly, Mikhail was aware of the emptiness
in the pit of his stomach, of the cold stones against his knees, and the
ache of muscles. But those mundane concerns seemed to belong to
another man, another time.

Then he felt Marguerida's right hand on his wrist, her cool, soft
fingers touching his flesh. His body ceased its dreadful rictus at her
touch, and he could sense her awe moving through him, and his
through her. It was a moment of joining more intimate than anything
he could ever have imagined.

She was kneeling beside him, and a quick glance at her face revealed a joy that reflected his own. Her eyes were bright with tears, and they trickled down her cheeks and dribbled onto the collar of her tunic. He could feel Marguerida grounding his rising emotions, supporting his burgeoning strength in an echo of the figure behind Varzil.

We are gathered to join this woman, Margarethe of Windhaven, and this man, Mikhal Raven of Ridenow, called the Angel of the Serrais, into one person, one soul, one mind, and one heart. We invoke the blessings of the gods upon this union. Margarethe, do you vow to honor this man in body and mind, all the days of your life?

Mikhail waited, for there was no response from Marguerida for what seemed like an age of the world. At the same time, he noticed that the form of ritual Varzil was using was one which he had never heard before, one which omitted words he was accustomed to. The names were wrong too, and he pondered that as well. Then he realized that in this time and place those were the only names that Varzil knew to call them. Or, perhaps, there was some more complex reason for concealing their identities.

I will honor him all the days of my life.

And you, Mikhal Raven of Ridenow, do you vow to serve this woman in body and mind, all the days of your life?

Serve her? That seemed very odd to him, the reverse of the marriage vows he recognized, and for a second he hesitated. And then, in a rush of profound realization, he knew that he wished nothing better than to serve this woman. The words did not matter, only the intention.

I vow to serve this woman, in body and mind, all the days of my life.

The act of answering provoked a deep sense of rightness in him, and he felt the sweet smile of Varzil's helper increase, so he seemed feather light for an instant. He felt Marguerida's fingers grip his wrist more tightly, and they were warm against his skin.

Varzil took up the larger metal bracelet from the box on his lap, and reached out and placed it on Marguerida's wrist. Then he repeated the procedure, and the cool weight of the circlet lay against Mikhail's skin, heavier than he had expected.

I, Varzil Ridenow, Lord of Hali, witness these oaths, and hold them binding for all time. They are married not only by words but by the sweet blood of the earth. They are joined in flesh and spirit, as was intended from the time before time. I swear that these people are one, melded, united and inseparable, until the world ends.

For a moment, Mikhail felt himself released, as if some thread that had held him captive were unleashed. He knew that Marguerida felt it also, and he turned his face toward hers, and met her lips as if he had never kissed a woman before. She tasted of stew, sweat, and an incredible, almost painful sweetness; he knew he would remember this moment till he drew his final breath.

Mikhal Raven of Ridenow, give me now your matrix stone. Fear not!

Mikhail unclenched his sweating hand slowly, wondering why he felt no fear. If Varzil touched his stone, the world might end for him. But it was as if he were a man ensorceled, and he moved as if in a dream.

His small starstone floated off his hand, a mote of brilliance even in the great light that rose from the smiling woman behind the great man. It moved quickly across the space that was between Mikhail and Varzil, speeding like an evening bug, and then dropped onto the enormous matrix still adorning the hand of the *laranzu*. With a flash it vanished from his sight, and he tensed, suddenly terrified in spite of Varzil's reassurance.

But there was no shock, no trauma. What Mikhail experienced was a momentary giddiness, then the sense of being within the stone itself. He swam in its shining facets, buffeted by unseen forces that seemed to pass through him like light. He felt pierced through and through, in every cell of both his body and that other portion of him which he had never really known he possessed, the inner flame of his very being.

When Mikhail looked at Varzil, he saw his own face staring back at him, his own blue eyes shining with an unearthly light, his golden curls falling loosely on his brow. It was shocking, more shocking than the loss of his matrix, and his mind tried to rebel, to deny.

The vision passed, however, and suddenly Varzil was himself again, old and fragile. *Now, Margarethe, take the ring from my hand and learn something of your own powers—the hand which is marked for this occasion!*

But that would kill you!

Quick, my girl! I cannot hold the energies in check much longer. Do as I say!

Warily, Marguerida extended her left hand, and Varzil tilted his, so the ring fell from his finger into her outstetched palm. She did not move, but let the shining ring rest on her hand, her eyes gleaming. Her face went stiff, then her entire body was rigid beside him. Where her right hand touched him, Mikhail could feel the energy coursing through her body, could sense new channels being pierced fiercely, brutally. It was a terrible thing, even at second hand, and he knew she could not have endured it but for the presence of that strange other woman, the woman who now seemed to be made of light. He could sense the shining woman shielding his beloved, protecting her.

Give the ring to your husband, Margarethe.

Gladly! It was a heartfelt response, and the eagerness of it gave him a sense of reality, of being grounded in an ordinary moment in the midst of an extraordinary event.

Gingerly, as if she were made of glass, Marguerida turned to Mikhail, holding the ring in her open palm as if it burned, and said, "Give me your finger, and be quick about it, beloved! Now!"

Mikhail held out his left hand, and she slipped the heavy ring onto his finger, touching only the metal, not the jewel itself. *With this ring, I thee wed, Mikhail Hastur!*

Then thunder rang in his mind, the room spun, and he felt himself fall into darkness.

28

Margaret Alton sat under the branches of an evergreen, the rain trickling down her face, soaking her shivering body, holding Mikhail's head on her lap. She had tried to keep him dry at first, but that was impossible. The wind, while not violent, was steady, and blew gusts of rain and sleet under the spreading branches, invading every fold of fabric, chilling her and leaving her sodden and almost miserable.

She peered out from under the tree. The horses were standing with their heads together, looking resigned. She knew she should get up and unsaddle them, but she was too tired. Margaret looked up at the branches of the tree overhead, trying to see if the crow was there. It had been earlier, but now it had disappeared. She let herself sigh and shifted her weight a little under the weight of Mikhail's head.

That she was not completely miserable startled her, and made her feel mildly perverse. She was cold, hungry, and exhausted. Mikhail was surely all of those, and unconscious as well. Any normal person, she felt, should have been in complete despair. But she was just too tired and numb for desperation.

She stroked the wet curls on Mikhail's brow with icy fingers, and considered her situation again. Upon reflection, Margaret decided she was too angry to be properly miserable—angry at Varzil, and his nameless female companion, at Mikhail for being dead to the world, and angry at herself for being so helpless. If only she had the strength to get him up on a horse!

For the tenth or maybe the hundredth time, Margaret went over the moments just after Mikhail had accepted the ring from her shaking fingers. It had all happened so quickly. One second he had been looking into her eyes, and the next he was sprawled on the floor. And then the floor had vanished, and the round building as well, and she had found herself kneeling on the ground, with rubble all around her. The pink grass had disappeared, replaced by rank weeds and the burned remains of some rafters and something that might once have been a plow. Rain had struck her face, shocking her back into the present. Somehow she had managed to drag the limp body of her husband under the tree before she ran out of energy. He was heavy, and she had sworn at him.

Only the weight of the ornate bracelet on her wrist assured her that she had actually experienced the otherworldly wedding ceremony. Margaret looked at Mikhail and saw the sparkle on his hand. It did not look like Varzil's ring, for it was not very large. It did not look like much at all—certainly nothing worth all this trouble. But as she watched, Margaret could see it changing shape. It expanded and shrank from moment to moment. What did that mean? And what was she going to do?

One of her professors had once said in a lecture "There are things which the intellect can never grasp, no matter how it tries." She had dutifully copied down these words on her crystal notepad, thinking them rather foolish. Remembering the words as the wind gusted across her face, sending stinging rain into her eyes, Margaret conceded that he was right, after all. No matter how hard she tried, there was no rational way to explain the events of the past night and day. She wished she could give up trying, but her weary brain refused to let go completely.

Part of her mind continued to observe Mikhail, and she was grateful that she had at least mastered basic monitoring at Neskaya. His heart rate was steady, his temperature low but not dangerously so. But where his mind was, the mind she had come to know and love during her tumultuous months on Darkover, there was only a swirling chaos. Varzil must have been mad to imagine that he could transfer his own matrix to Mikhail, and they had been insane to have agreed.

For the moment, all she could do was hope he recovered with all his wits, and that he did not get pneumonia. It seemed a vain hope, and despair began to nibble at her. She shut it away abruptly, sternly admonishing herself to remain calm. It was easier thought than done. She would get herself steady for a few minutes, but as soon as she began to relax, all the fears and worries leaped out at her again, gnawing at her mind like hungry rats.

Instead of dwelling on things she could not understand or manage, Margaret studied her matrixed hand. It felt different, and it looked unfamiliar, too. The lines were very faint now, instead of clearly visible as they had been before. It almost seemed as if they had sunk into her flesh. She had spent enough hours staring at the accursed thing to know every line and juncture. Yes, it had changed. The brief contact with Varzil's ring had done something—it was no longer recognizable as the keystone it had once been. Damn! She had only started to get accustomed to the thing, and now it was transformed.

Margaret frowned. Maybe it was for the best. She hoped the change might help her stay out of Ashara's awareness. But how was it different? Or perhaps the question was how was *she?* Cold as she was, with the soaked fabric of her hood pressing clammily against her face, she could not shake the conviction that the very core of her being had been altered.

She tried to remember the moment of contact between her hand and the ring. Margaret had no clear impression of it, but her muscles quivered with memory. She had been flooded with impressions, for only an instant. No, not impressions. Information! How had that transformed her matrix?

Deep within her, Margaret sensed a stirring of knowledge. It was very faint, vague and elusive. It had something to do with her hands and her voice. There was another piece—Dio! Her heart thumped. Could she actually heal her stepmother? Did she dare to hope? And, if she could do that, could she help Mikhail now?

A hot tear rolled down her cold face. No, she couldn't. Not now, not yet. She had to learn what she already knew. The information was clear, crystalline, perfect. And utterly frustrating! There was no way to get to it. She felt as if she had a vast treasure in a chest, and no key. If only she were not so damn cold!

Margaret grabbed that thought firmly. She had a flint in her belt pouch, and her small knife. Theoretically, she could start a fire. She had done it a few times on the trail with Rafaella. But there was nothing to burn! The timbers scattered around her were drenched. The tree sheltering her was no good either—green wood was hard to burn, even if she had dry tinder. Besides, she did not have a hatchet, and there was no other way she could think of to get the branches off.

As weary as she was, Margaret doubted she could pull off more than a twig.

There must be another way to get warm. Margaret knew there were disciplines in every human world for generating heat. Yogis on Terra had been using them for millennia, and from some of the stories she had heard about the *cristoforos* up at Nevarsin, they had developed them as well. Unfortunately, she had never studied any of them.

Heat was just energy, wasn't it? And *laran* was energy as well. So, if she was so clever, why couldn't she think of some way to generate heat with her matrix?

Margaret glared at her hand, wishing that she had paid more attention in her physical science classes. The mathematics of physics had not been difficult for her, for she had always thought that equations were rather musical, and had even wondered if one could not find a way to turn these elegant facts into song. But the practical side of the subject, the nature of gravity, nuclear fusion, and even electricity, had eluded her. She did not have the mind of an engineer, and she knew it.

At the same time, she realized, monitoring was merely the observance of the energy of a body. That was what Liriel had told her, and Istvana as well. But where did the energy to monitor come from? Was it in the starstones themselves, or did the monitor draw them from within? Because a good circle monitor, she knew, could regulate the energies of the others, keep them from injuring or totally exhausting themselves. It seemed a shame she had only learned the rudiments, and that she had not asked the right questions when she had the opportunity. If only Istvana were here—only she hadn't been born yet, and two time travelers were more than enough!

Where did heat come from? The sun, obviously, but that was no help. Darkover's bloody sun was hidden behind thick clouds now. How long had they been in that round house? It had not felt like a long while, but for all she knew, several days or even several weeks had passed without her being aware of it.

What else? Food. That was the main source of energy for humans. It was not perhaps the best thing to think about, because she was very hungry, and the gobbled stew she had eaten—if it had really existed— seemed to be long gone. Had there been clouds when they rode toward the place? She couldn't remember, even by flogging her tired brain. Well, it was almost always snowing or raining on Darkover, so likely there had been.

Briefly, she entertained the wonderful notion of somehow conjuring up a good meal out of thin air, and discarded it with regret. If she had been telekinetic, perhaps, but she was not, as far as she knew.

Istvana said that occasionally *laran* produced people who could move small objects, and that in the Ages of Chaos, it had been possible to use the enormous relay screens to actually transport people from place to place. Now, *there* was a bit of technology the Terranan would love to get their grubby hands on, wasn't it? It was fortunate that this was a lost art, she decided. Else there would have been Federation Marines on Regis Hastur's stoop, demanding he surrender it.

If she had no food, and the sun was out of reach, what else was there? She might as well try to reach the molten core of the planet.

This flippant idea flitted across her mind, then demanded her attention. Notions of heat and dryness flitted around in her skull like lightning bugs, promising something she could not quite grasp. Frustrated and angry again, Margaret made a fist and pounded the mud and rotting pine needles.

Margaret was too weary and too cold to continue her unproductive behavior for very long, and she gave it up reluctantly, wiping her hand across her soaked trousers. She made herself breathe slowly, and calmly, checked Mikhail once more, and returned to the problem.

The blood of earth. The words drifted though her mind, and she remembered that Varzil had used that phrase to describe the copper *catenas* bracelets. And copper, she remember from her physics classes, was an excellent conductor! Unfortunately, most of what she knew about conductors was musical. Really, for an educated woman, she was very ignorant!

Margaret gazed at the thick object encircling her right wrist, where her arm curved over Mikhail's shoulder. She smiled a little in spite of everything, seeing this irrevocable evidence of a real event, one that she had secretly yearned for, without ever admitting it to herself completely. They were married, one person not two, and if she regretted the absence of all the delightful parts of the celebration—the food—especially the food!—the music, the wedding gown she was sure that Aaron would have made for her—at least she had done the deed.

"Hell of a way to spend what should be the happiest day of my life," she growled.

Mikhail stirred a little at the sound of her voice, mumbled something unintelligible, then fell silent. "Wake up! Come on, Mik! You are going to miss the wedding night if you don't wake up!"

The wedding night. Margaret found herself shuddering. The years of Ashara's overshadowing rushed through her mind. She had never even kissed anyone until Mikhail had embraced her the previous summer, so powerful was the admonition to keep herself apart. She was almost glad for a moment that Mikhail was in no condition to consummate the marriage, then, suddenly, unreasonably, furious at him. "Wake up, damn you!" She jiggled his shoulder with her hand, trying to shake him enough to rouse him out of his stupor. Why couldn't she make up her mind one way or the other?

There was no response, and she sighed a little. Then she lifted her arm off his shoulder and stared at the bracelet. It was ornate, even more complicated in design than that which encircled the wrist of Lady Linnea. It appeared to be an elongated beast of some sort, biting its own hindparts. She held it closer to her face, trying to see what it was. Not a snake, she decided, though she knew that this animal was often depicted with its tail in its mouth. More like a panther or some other catlike creature.

The eyes of the beast glittered, and she now saw there were small starstones set into the metal, not only in the orbs, but miniscule ones spread along the curving tail, like fine, shining dust. It was a very beautiful thing, the verdigrised sheen gleaming with rain.

Margaret reached out with the fingers of her left hand and turned the bracelet slowly, looking at all the details for the first time. When she placed her thumb and forefinger around one side of it, she had the sensation of movement, as if it were alive at her touch. She snatched her fingers away, alarmed for a second. No, not that. The bracelet was reacting to the energy of her shadow matrix.

For a moment she was lost in the wonder of the thing, that an inert bit of metal and gem should respond to her touch. There was something very important in this, if she could only grasp it. *Copper is an excellent conductor* her weary mind reiterated. *I know that,* she mentally shouted at herself, *but what does it mean?*

Before she quite knew what she was doing, Margaret set her right hand down flat against the mud, and clasped her left around the bracelet so hard it made small indentations in her icy fingers. Nothing happened. Well, why should it? She cursed, but she did not draw her hand back. Margaret could sense that in the back of her mind there was something she was overlooking. What was it? A piece of music— hardly likely. Why was she thinking of music when what she wanted was warmth! It was not music, but something like that—an equation?

Rain gunneled over her face, making her blink, then shake her head vigorously, spattering drops from her tangled hair all around her. It was right on the tip of her tongue, on the edge of her mind. Something. What was an equation? A symbolic representation of . . . of an idea, a mathematical concept of how the universe worked. A=b, and e=mc squared, and all the rest of those economical statements of reality. And musical notation was equationlike, expressing the concept of melody.

For as long as she was taking the required physical science classes, she had kept a great many equations in her mind, until she passed the tests. There was one for fusion, she remembered, and another for fission, and even a rather complex one which described electricity. Margaret wondered what would happen if she could just remember that last one right this second. It did not seem like a very good idea to try while sitting in the middle of a puddle. If it worked at all, she would probably electrocute herself and Mikhail at the same time.

And she wanted heat, not electricity. Surely she could remember that one, if she tried hard enough. Unfortunately, she seemed unable to find the formula for heat in her disordered mind.

I am being too literal, she decided. *I am forgetting that all of this stuff is symbolic—it is not the equation that matters, but the concept! The equation is not the thing, but the idea of the thing. This stuff gave me a headache ten years ago, and it still does!*

Margaret twisted her head from side to side to release the tension in her neck, and flexed her shoulders. She returned to her deep breathing, focused her mind on the notion of warmth, and squeezed her matrixed hand around the bracelet. The critical portion of her mind informed her that she was a fool, that there was nothing she could do, that she was incompetent and was going to die of cold or hunger, and she struggled to silence that voice.

Time seemed to stand still, as if she were hovering on the edge of some precipice, unable to make the leap across the abyss. She felt as if there were glue around her, muffling her energy, her breath, everything. And then, without any perceptible alteration, Margaret felt herself move in that timeless space in her mind, slip between places which she would never be able to describe, and blunder into a sense of heat that was incredible.

Her body shuddered a little, flinched at the sudden feeling of warmth that raced along her flesh, and seemed to sear her to the bone. It only lasted a moment, but that was long enough! Then she snatched her matrixed hand away from the bracelet and let herself scream. The sound was startling, a shrill call that rang through the pouring rain, across the stony ground, charging into the air like brightness before it faded into silence. Both horses jerked their heads up, and regarded her nervously.

She looked at her hands, expecting to find them burned, but they seemed normal enough. Then she noticed that the bracelet on her arm was no longer green, but was its natural, shining copper color, as if her recent experiment had burned away the verdigris, and restored it to its original condition.

Margaret leaned back against the trunk of the tree, too tired for a moment to do anything except rest. Then she realized that her body was not only warm, but heated, as if she had a slight temperature, and that her clothes were almost dry. It was a very peculiar sensation, and she decided that she had been very lucky not to have torched herself, and Mik as well.

He was still resting on her lap, but his curls were dry, and his face seemed to have more color than a few minutes before. She stroked his hair gently, patted his cheek, and just gazed at him, her heart swelling with emotion. Her feelings had been confined for so long that she could barely stand to experience them. She needed to keep her wits about her, but it was hard.

Tenderness, it seemed, was a much more powerful feeling than she had ever imagined. What she felt as she coiled a golden curl around her finger and then ran it down the exquisite curve of Mikhail's ear was that, and much more. Margaret had never felt such peace, except in music. She decided to enjoy it while it lasted, knowing full well that feelings shifted and transformed between one breath and the next, that they were rarely constant. She would have liked to continue in this mood forever, but she was wise enough to know it could not last.

In a rush of wings, the great sea crow alighted on Mikhail's hip. It croaked a greeting. "Where the hell have you been?" she snarled. It stared at her with a beady red eye and cawed a response which left her still in the dark. At the same time, there was an air about the dratted bird. It looked quite smug, Margaret decided at last.

Then, through the steady patter of rain, Margaret heard the sound of hoofbeats, the jingle of bridles, and the creak of leather saddles. The noise made her mouth go dry with fear, and her heart thudded. What if it was Ashara!

She pulled Mikhail's still soggy cloak over him, hoping its brown coloring would hide him. The shadows of the branches fell across him. She yanked her hood up again, hiding the pale sheen of her skin, and tucked her hands away. The terror hammered in her blood, and she held her breath until her ears rang, and she felt dizzy and sick. She gasped for air. If only she could become invisible!

The crow betrayed her with a flap of wings and a greeting call, as it flew from beneath the tree and toward the sound of the oncoming riders. Margaret crouched over Mikhail's body, trying to shield him against she knew not what. For a moment she completely forgot she had any weapons, that she could defend herself. Then she remembered the bandits. The helplessness left her, replaced by the grim determination to defend her husband, or die trying.

Margaret held her breath again and heard the sound of several people dismounting, the squishy noise of boots in mud, and the rustle of wet cloaks. She heard a woman's voice, speaking to the crow, and listened as it replied. She went cold all over. She bit her lower lip while she clutched Mikhail's shoulders beneath his coverings.

The sound drew nearer, and after a minute, she could see several pair of trousered legs, and the dark red boots that came from the Dry Towns beneath them. There was mud on the boots, and splashes on the trousers, as if they had ridden hard.

A head bent down, a woman's round face peering beneath the branches, curious and cautious. As soon as Margaret saw the short-cropped hair, the plain face, and the well-worn sword belt that hung around the waist of the stranger, she knew that the woman was a Renunciate. The breath she had been holding released with a little gasp. The crow had not betrayed them, but had brought help.

Other faces joined the first, weathered ones, the skin roughened by sun and snow. Then the first woman smiled, showing several missing teeth, and she crouched down to bring herself to eye level with Margaret. "Greetings, *domna.*" She seemed to understand Margaret's wariness, for she made no move to draw closer.

"Greetings, and well met." She hoped they were, for she remembered that Rafaella had told her the Renunciates had been mercenary soldiers, for hire to the many kingdoms which had dotted the land before the formalization of the Compact.

"I am Damila n'ha Bethenyi. We were passing, and your fine bird flew onto the shoulder of our *breda,* Morall, and told her of your distress." She chuckled softly. "Nearly knocked her out of the saddle."

"He does that sometimes, but, *Mestra* Damila—*told her?*"

"Morall has the beast-speak *laran, domna.* May we assist you? You seem to be sitting in a puddle, and that cannot be comfortable."

"No, it isn't." She shifted the cloak away from Mikhail's face. "My husband is ill." It was the first time she had said the word aloud, and it felt very strange on her tongue.

His right hand slipped down, clenched into a fist, and she noticed that the great jewel was hidden, that only the metal of the band was visible on his finger. Margaret held back a shudder at the thought of Varzil's matrix touching Mikhail's flesh, then relaxed a little. It was no longer Varzil's stone, but some amazing conjunction between two matrices, one of which was keyed to Mikhail. That was why he was not dead, but only unconscious. And perhaps witless, but she did not dare think about that.

One of the other women laughed uproariously. "Well, we did not think you were trysting in the rain!" The rest of the group seemed to find this highly amusing, and Margaret was very surprised when she found herself laughing as well. The terror and despair which had gripped her faded away, leaving her only cold, hungry, and exhausted.

Two of the Renunciates crawled beneath the low branches of the tree, rolled Mikhail off her lap, wound his cloak about him, and dragged him out. As Margaret crept out stiffly from beneath the tree, another woman bent over him. She peeled back an eyelid and gave a grunt. "What ails him?" she asked.

"Matrix shock, I believe." How else could she describe what had occurred?

"I see." The answer seemed to satisfy the stranger, and Margaret felt relieved. "We must make a litter, and get him to shelter as quickly as possible. You there, Jonil, see to the cutting of some branches, the straightest you can find, and Karis, you tear up some blankets for bindings."

Margaret watched in a daze. She barely grasped what was going on around her, except that Mikhail was being taken care of. She wanted to help, but lacked the strength to move.

It was not until he had been hoisted onto a hastily constructed litter that she found herself able to stir. Margaret went over to Mikhail's unconscious form. She tucked both his hands down into the sides of the litter, then fussed with the arrangement of the blankets, to conceal her real purpose. He stirred and groaned a little at her touch, as if he were trying to climb out of whatever depths he had fallen into. She bent forward and kissed his cold cheek. "It will be all right, my love," she whispered.

Damila said, "We will go to the old El Haliene place."

Margaret jumped at the sound of that name. "Where?" She hardly wanted to meet any of Amalie's relatives, or anyone else just then.

"I see you don't know it—been abandoned for years, since Dom Padriac's father built the new keep. No one uses it except us Sisters."

"Thank you, *breda*." She used the inflection which meant "kinswoman," and prayed she had it right. That little word had more meanings than a cat had lives, and some of them were more intimate than others. "Is it very far?"

Damila looked surprised, and she peered at Margaret in the light rain. Apparently her use of the word was unexpected. "Oh, ten or eleven miles. The country is rough, but we know our way."

Margaret nodded. Then she drew herself onto the soaked leather of her saddle, shivered all over, and tried to prepare herself for a long, wet ride. The crow alighted on her pommel and settled into place. "You are a very fine fellow, a king of crows," she told it, "and I will see that you have a nice, fresh mouse or two for your supper, if I have to catch the things myself!"

One of the woman now mounted grinned. "He thanks you for the thought, but he would prefer some fish."

"Of course. How foolish of me." It was immensely reassuring to speak of nothing more remarkable than the antics of Mikhail's bird, and something taut within her released its grip. She took several deep breaths, let herself feel relieved, and twisted her neck back and forth to ease the tension.

Margaret looked around, trying to find any trace of the round stone house which had been there a few hours before. All she saw was weeds and a few stones, the remains of several burned timbers, and the broken glass of a long vanished window. There was no trace of the low wall they had crossed. It seemed to be just an empty bit of earth with a few trees growing in it. Another mystery she would probably never solve.

She forced her chilled hands around the reins, and prepared to follow her rescuers. Part of her was relieved, and the rest of her settled into worrying about Mikhail. Damila, apparently the leader of this band of women, drew her horse beside Margaret's. "It will be all right, *domna.*"

"Thank you for coming," she murmured, almost too tired to speak now. All she wanted was dry clothes and some food. And to have Mikhail safe. It seemed a great deal, at that moment. Margaret let her mind collapse into exhaustion, clucked the dun mare forward, and started after the women.

29

It was close to dusk when they rode into the ruins. Margaret was too cold and wet to do more than glance around at the stone buildings. There was a lonely and desolate air to the place, but the walls of the remaining structures seemed sound enough.

Margaret dismounted quickly, and her knees gave way, sending her sprawling into a puddle. She struggled to her feet. She was already so wet and muddy that it did not matter.

One of the Sisters led her mare away. At the same time, two others carried the litter through a dark doorway. Margaret hurried after them and nearly stumbled on the sodden hem of her cloak.

Margaret found herself standing just inside an immense kitchen, not unlike the one at Armida. There were two hearths, one on each side of the room, and each one large enough to roast an ox. Little slit-windows were set high on the walls, and as her eyes adjusted to the faint light coming through them, she saw a beehive-shaped oven against one wall. There was a long table in the middle of the room, its wood covered with dust, cracked here and there. Benches ran along both sides of it. It must have been a welcoming place once. Now it just seemed damp and gloomy.

There were high rafters overhead, and a continuous, soft noise from them. Margaret realized that the floor was covered in droppings, and she looked up and saw movement, flashes of white and gray, on the smoke-darkened beams. Pigeons or doves, she was not sure which.

Morall, the beast-speaker, followed her glance. She smacked her lips and said, "Supper!" Her thick eyebrows drew together, and she gazed fixedly at the rafters. A dozen or more birds flew down, and Margaret turned away, as Morall efficiently wrung their slender necks. She knew it was silly, but she preferred not to see her dinner alive before she ate it.

For several minutes, she stood just inside the doorway, out of the way of the bustling women, and did not move. The Sisters were going about their tasks briskly, and the pleasant smell of burning wood began to drive away the dank and musty smell of the old keep. They had put Mikhail on the floor, to the side of one fireplace, and taken away his drenched blankets. The woman who had examined him was tugging his boots off, and tucking dry covers over him.

Margaret finally noticed she was shivering. With a great effort, she removed her cloak and hung it on a peg on the wall. Her clothes were cold and clammy, and her hair dripped down her back. She pulled her leather gloves off, and pulled the butterfly clasp out of her hair. Somehow it had managed to remain on her head, which seemed a minor miracle under the circumstances. She shoved it into her pouch, and plucked out the hairpins that still clung to her fine curls. After she wrung as much water out of her hair as she could, she wound it up into a knot on the top of her head, and pinned it into place. She did not care if she was being immodest—she wasn't going to have wet hair on her neck!

The woman who was tending Mikhail came towards her. "You must get out of those wet clothes, *domna*. Come with me."

Dumbly, Margaret followed her to a small, cold chamber that smelled of long vanished meats and cheeses. She felt totally detached from the situation, as if she were dreaming. The woman opened a bundle of fabric and pulled out something long and white. She shook out the folds and smiled. "Get out of those things, *domna*. You will catch your death of cold." She spoke as one would to a child, and indeed, Margaret felt very much like one.

The effort to obey was almost too great. The buckle on her belt seemed a monstrous puzzle, and even the knots in her drawstrings were difficult. One by one, Margaret's garments came off, each sopping layer clinging to the one beneath. The yet unnamed woman was indifferent to Margaret's near nakedness, and she was just too tired to be self-conscious.

When she was down to her underdrawers, Margaret noticed she still had the silken mitt on her right hand. The palm was slightly muddy, and where the left one had vanished she could not remember. It did not seem to matter. It was too cold in the pantry to stand around, so she took the white gown the woman offered, and slipped it over her head. It was a thick woolen nightgown, clean smelling and soft. It fell in folds against her icy skin, caressing her. Then she leaned against the wall and tugged off her boots. They made a squelching noise, and she wiggled her toes in her hose. They were damp, but not wet, so she decided to keep them on for the present. The state of the floor in the kitchen was not inviting to bare feet.

Exhausted, she just leaned against the wall for a few minutes, breathing slowly, trying to adjust to being comparatively warm, dry, and out of the inclement weather. After a while, Margaret picked up her boots and the belt with its pouch, and went back into the kitchen.

Stocking-footed, Margaret went through the great room. She passed by the oven, a huge structure made of brick and tile, and was startled to find it was very hot. Its welcome warmth penetrated into her bones as she went by, and her cheeks began to feel almost hot.

After she had set her boots by the hearth, Margaret bent over Mikhail. His skin felt warm, and his color was better, but he remained unconscious. For a moment she considered trying to rouse him with her hand. Then she decided that would be very stupid. Mikhail needed time to heal from matrix shock, and she was too tired to do anything useful for him, no matter how much she wanted to.

But she needed something to keep herself busy, to keep her mind from fretting any more than it already was. Margaret spotted a broom leaning against the corner. She grabbled the handle and started sweeping. Her arm muscles protested, but she ignored them. The regular rhythm soothed her mind, and after a time her fears began to ease as well.

She worked her way down one side of the long table and across the end before her strength ran out. She collapsed on the end of the closest bench, and shook all over. In spite of the heat of the room, and her own exertions, she was cold all over. But it was more than that. All the things she had endured came together, overwhelming her completely. Tears spilled down her cheeks, and she choked back the sound of sobs, swallowing the terrible noises that welled in her throat.

Margaret did not know how long she sat there, crying silently. A pair of rough hands took the broom away at some point, and after a time she smelled something cooking. Her mouth watered. Food. She snuffled and tried to stop crying, but only managed to do so for a short time. Then it started all over again, leaving her feeling hollow with hunger and shame at her own weakness.

The woman who had given her the nightgown came over with a small crockery bowl. It was steaming and there was a faint smell of herbs as she handed it to Margaret. "You just drink this, and it will put the heart back in you soon enough, *chiya.*"

"Thank you," she whispered. Margaret let the bowl sit in her hands, feeling the blessed warmth creep into her fingers. She lifted it to her lips and sipped, expecting something nasty tasting and full of virtues. Instead, she got a pleasant mouthful of minty liquid, sweetened with honey. It slid down her throat like silk, and she could feel the heat of the drink enter her stomach and begin to ease her aching body. She had almost finished the stuff when she realized that she had drunk it before, on the trail with Rafaella on the trip to Neskaya. What had she called it—waytea? the main ingredient was bitterroot, a strong stimulant. Honey and mountain mint were added to make it drinkable, but it was still dreadful stuff.

The taste and the memory gave her a sense of connection to her friend. She wished Rafaella could be with her now, and wondered what the Renunciate would have made of these earlier members of her Order. Margaret was sure that Rafi would have enjoyed meeting Damila and the others, and hoped that someday she would be able to tell her about it.

The waytea jolted her mind, and Margaret began to quiver with alertness. She noticed everything at once, a state she knew was a combination of exhaustion and the stuff in her cup. She had a false sense of clarity, as anything she looked at seemed brighter than normal. While she waited for the sensation to diminish, she noticed that the table had been scrubbed clean, and a cloth was laid at the other end of it. She smelled roasting birds, herbs, spices, woodsmoke, and her own sweat in a pungent mixture. It was all rather overwhelming.

A woman was standing at the table across from her, pounding something in a large bowl, pulling it back and forth, kneading some kind of dough. She caught a whiff of soda from it, and smiled. A yeast bread would not be ready for hours, and her mouth was already watering in anticipation. Margaret watched the woman flip the dough out expertly onto a floured plate, and plunge her fingers into the gleaming mass. She formed it into round loaves and walked over to the oven, put her hand into the opening and nodded. Then she picked up a wooden object, a long handle with a flattened platform at the end, slipped it under the two loaves, and carried them to the oven. She shoved the thing into the opening, wiggled the handle, and withdrew it, leaving the shaped loaves behind.

The woman wiped her floury hands on the tops of her trousers. Then she hauled a heavy bag onto the table, and poured out a mass of onions, golden carrots, and the potatolike roots of which Margaret had become inordinately fond.

"Can I do anything to help?"

The Renunciate gave her a hard look for a moment. "Your hands steady enough to handle a knife?"

"I don't know, but let me try. I don't think I am up to peeling, but chopping seems almost possible."

That got a grin. "I am Jonil n'ha Elspeth, and I would be glad of a chopper. It will make the work go quicker. Not that I mind it, but it always reminds me of my poor mother, sitting by the fire, trying to make stew from one onion and some millet. She was always tired, and there was never quite enough to eat."

Jonil pulled two knives from her waist, handed the longer one across the table, and began expertly peeling the skins of the root vegetables. When she finished one, she shoved it over to Margaret, and Margaret cut it into quarters, then made smaller pieces. They worked in silence for a time, until there was quite a mound of cleaned and cut vegetables between them. Around them, the others were chatting quietly, laying out bedding, and turning the room from a deserted kitchen into a livable place. The smell of cooking pigeons mingled with the smoke, and the delightful scent of baking bread began to drift from the oven.

"When I joined the Sisters," Jonil said quietly, "I thought I would never have to cook again—because I wanted more than anything not to be like my poor mother." She gave a snort of laughter. "Can't imagine what I was thinking of, since Sisters have to eat like anyone else. I learned the sword, but I am not very clever with it, and so I have ended up doing all the things I wanted to get away from. But I almost always have enough to eat."

Margaret's eyes were watering from cutting onions, and she blinked away the tears. She was still very tired, but the waytea made it possible to ignore it. Then she took the cuff of the thick gown and wiped her eyes. She felt the heavy, cold touch of the bracelet brush her cheek. It gave her a start, for she had forgotten it, and she glanced down at the sparkling eyes of the beast for a second. "yes, enough to eat is surely one of life's pleasures."

"I never thought to be sitting at a table cutting up stew with a fine lady. We have had a few come to us, but most of them were all but useless in the kitchen."

The woman called Karis came up with a cauldron, set it on the table, and began filling it with the vegetables. She worked slowly, and Margaret did not need to be a telepath to know that both of these women were very curious about her, and about Mik, and were just too polite to pry openly. She realized she had not even told them her name, and that they had not asked it either.

She started to introduce herself, then stopped. What should she call herself? Margarethe of Windhaven, the woman she resembled closely enough to have fooled Robard MacDenis, was dead. She held back a shiver. She did not want to be anyone but herself, let alone a dead person. More, she had a deep certainty that she must speak with care. She was out of her own time, and the less she said, the better. What she needed was a nice, fairly innocuous name, something almost anonymous. She needed to be a Jane Doe or Mary Smith, and her tired brain was not cooperating.

At last she said, "I am called Marja . . . Leynier." There were Leyniers in her bloodline, but the falsehood made her tense a little. And retreating into the nickname she had not used in years felt a little peculiar as well.

"Marja—now that is one I never heard before," Jonil answered cheerfully. "Right pretty, like its bearer."

Margaret laughed at that. "Pretty! I feel like a drowned rat."

"You looked like one, at first, *domna.*" Both of the women chuckled at Joris' remark.

Karis picked up the cauldron and hauled it over to the fireplace. Margaret saw her add some water from a wooden bucket, then drop in some chucks of dried meat as well, and set it on a hook above the flames. Jonil glanced over her shoulder. "I better go see to the seasonings, or Karis will put in handful of pepperpods, and it will be too spicy to eat. She is a good woman, but she can't be trusted with flavor. If she were a singer, I'd say she was tone deaf." With that Jonil rose and walked over to the fireplace, leaving Margaret to stare at the pile of peelings.

There was an end of a carrot in the pile, and she picked it up and crunched it. It was tough and woody, but it still had a slight sweetness, and the taste of earth as well. Margaret chewed and chewed, until her jaw ached slightly, and finally swallowed.

Damila came and sat down across from her. She gave her close-cropped hair a finger combing. "Your husband seems to be just sleeping now, but I think he may throw a fever before the night is over.

Vanda is brewing up some feverwort, just in case. It is best drunk cold, so we need to make it up now." She paused, looked uncomfortable, and cleared her throat. "How did you end up . . . under that tree?"

"I am not sure," Margaret temporized. "Everything is very hazy."

"Well, how did he get matrix shock?"

"He touched something. . . ." That was true as far as it went, and Margaret decided not to elaborate. She tried to look stupid, and wished that Damila would stop asking questions. It crossed her mind that she had the capacity to compel the woman to leave her alone, and shuddered at the idea.

Fortunately, Damila appeared to think her shiver was perfectly normal. "What was it?"

"I think it was a trap-matrix, but I am not sure. It affected me as well. There was a blaze of light, and that is all I really remember." She felt her face pale, and was amazed that she could fib without blushing.

"Ah, well, that explains it. That Varzil Ridenow, the Lord of Hali, has been trying to find all of them, and destroy them, but there are so many, in old houses and other places. And his hunting days are over. He's been in the *rhu fead* for more than a month, lying in state, I suppose, though no one has come to see him. That's the rumor, anyhow. One of them. Another says he is already gone, and then there are those who insist he is in hiding, and not in the *rhu fead* at all. I don't know what to believe. All I am sure of is that the Compact is tottering like some old gaffer, on its last legs. That is good for us, because it means a lot of lords are looking for fighters, even women. As if we hadn't enough of that." Damila hesitated. "You are not telling me everything, are you?"

Margaret hardly heard her, because she was trying to remember what the *rhu fead* was. At last her weary brain coughed up the answer, and she recalled that this was the name of some sort of chapel, near Hali Tower, a place of power. That made a strange kind of sense, because Varzil had brought them to Hali. But why had they ended up going off to that imaginary house? She was not sure why, but it was very important, and she wished Mikhail was awake to question.

"No, I am not telling you everything, and I am sorry about that." She shrugged slightly. "I don't think you would believe me if I did."

Damila nodded. "You and the man, you are not from around here, are you?"

Margaret found herself laughing almost hysterically. Several of the Sisters turned and stared at her. "You could say that, Damila. You could definitely say that!" When she had managed to contain her merriment a little, she asked, "How did you know?"

"I've never seen clothes quite like yours before, and you speak oddly." She paused and frowned for a moment. "It is almost as if you were thinking in another tongue."

"I thank you for trusting me in spite of that. I have told you all that I dare." *I don't want to make some chance remark that will change the future, even though I can't think what that might be.*

Damila nodded gravely. "When I left home to join the Sisters, my father cursed me. He said that I was crazy, that I was a stupid girl who did not know her own mind. And I swore to myself that I would never assume that another woman did not know what she was about, even if it seemed to me to be silly or ill-considered. This is the first time I have ever had to remember that vow, but it seems that keeping to it is the best course. Where are you and your man going?"

Margaret gave a deep sigh. "I wish I knew."

Jonil was pulling the loaves out of the oven now, and the hot smell of fresh bread floated through the room. She used the long-handled platform to carry the golden mounds to the table. She set the loaves on a tray on the table, and walked away. It was all Margaret could do not to reach out and tear a piece off and stuff it into her mouth.

Wooden bowls and spoons were brought out, and some battered trenchers as well. Margaret and Damila got up and moved down the table, seating themselves across the board from one another. Small wooden cups were placed along the table cloth, and a birchwood ewer stood at the far end. The members of the band began to take their places, talking quietly and wiping their hands on their garments.

She saw Damila reached a work-corsened hand across the table. Margaret felt the woman on her other side reach for her left one. She snatched the left hand quickly. The unknown woman stared at her in shock.

"We must say the blessing, and we always . . ."

"What is it?" Damila's tone was curt and demanding.

Margaret flinched at the suspicion and hostility in the voice. Her left hand was bare, but she still wore the mitt on the right one. It smelled of the onions she had chopped, in a sorry state for such an elegant accessory. She was so tired she had forgotten everything, and nearly been stupid.

She stripped off the remaining glove, turned it wrong-side to, and pulled it over her left hand. When Margaret looked up, she found herself the object of eight pair of astonished and rather hostile eyes. She blushed all the way to the roots of her hair. What was she supposed to say?

The woman said, "Does my touch offend you, then?"

"No, certainly not. But if you had touched that hand unshielded, I do not know if you would have survived. I did it to protect you, not to offend you."

The beast-speaker, Morall, nodded in agreement. "There is a *laran*-brightness on her hand, very faint, but I remember noticing it when we came into the hall here. She did rightly, Dorys, so don't get your trousers in a twist. Now, let's say the blessing! I didn't wring those necks and pluck all those damn feathers to have the birds get cold and nasty while we debate the niceties."

Hands were joined, and Dorys placed her fingers in Margaret's very cautiously, a bit wide-eyed. *Oh, my! What a narrow escape! I might have been killed!*

Margaret caught the woman's fear, and tried to ignore the spill of thoughts around the table. She had almost learned to block out the continuous mental chatter that was the normal working of human minds, but it was more difficult when she was tired. She heard a fragment here and there—Vanda wondering if Mikhail would get a fever, Jonil thinking of the yeast bread she had started earlier—ordinary thoughts. But she could not completely ignore Damila's. The leader of the band was full of concerns, and very much wished she had not rescued them. She wanted to be rid of her unwelcome guests as quickly as possible.

Vanda began to speak. "For the gifts of this food, and this shelter, we thank the Goddess who guides and protects us. We thank the animals who gave us their meat, and the plants which gave us their sustenance. We thank the rain for giving us water, and the earth for supporting us, now and forever."

It was a simple blessing, like others Margaret had heard. But the sincerity of the women moved her deeply, and made her wish she had not had to deceive them. This was no empty rite, but something full of real meaning and genuine belief. She swallowed hard and blinked back tears.

Dorys withdrew her hand as soon as the words were done. While the platter of birds was passed down the table, Margaret wondered which Goddess they meant. Hadn't Rafi told her something about that? It was Avarra, the Dark Goddess, she remembered after a second of groping in her weary brain. She recalled the painting of that deity on the ceiling of the grand dining room in Comyn Castle, and that other figure, that of Evanda, the Lady of Spring and Light. With a slight start she realized that the image of Evanda was not unlike the shining woman who had supported Varzil during that incredible wedding ceremony.

A small bubble of hysteria rose in her throat, and she choked it back. Had she actually eaten rabbithorn stew and a slab of warm bread made by the hands of Evanda? It seemed too much for a moment. Then her mind balked. She refused to be upset by more speculations! The band circling her wrist was evidence of the event. Everything else was unimportant. If all the gods in the universe had been there, it would still be the same. Besides, there were enough *real* things to be worried about!

Breathing deeply, Margaret calmed herself. She watched Jonil tear a loaf of bread into chunks, strong hands pushing the warm mound apart. The sight steadied her, and she felt her mind quiet, and her emotions as well. She was still just herself, whether she was Margaret Alton or Marguerida Alton-Hastur, and she was very hungry. Nothing else was important at that moment.

Damila handed a piece of bread across the table to her, and soon the platter of birds arrived. She took one and pulled off a limb. It tasted dark, wild, and gamey. There was some spice on the skin, herbs and oil rubbed on it before cooking, a delicious taste she had not encountered before.

Margaret chewed and chewed, for the bird was tough, but the finest cuisine of Therdara wouldn't have tasted better to her. She was barely aware of the others at the table, so deep was she in the sensuous enjoyment of the food. She took a bite of bread and tasted the faint sour flavor of baking soda.

"Jonil, the bread is simply wonderful, and the bird is delicious!" The words popped out, and Margaret was surprised at how tired her voice sounded.

"Thank you, Marja." She smiled a little, and gestured around the table with a greasy hand. "My sisters are so used to my cooking that they sometimes forget to tell me if they like it."

This made two of the Renunciates redden beneath their weathered skins, and look down at their plates, as if embarrassed. But Morall just laughed. "No one tells me I did a good job getting the food, so why should we tell you it tastes good? You should just be pleased we don't complain."

"Oh, no, Mora. We would not dare complain, lest Joni put mock mint in the stew and make us sorry we ever opened our mouths to eat or speak." This was a woman about Margaret's own age, with pale hair and mischievous eyes.

"Would you do that?" Morall leaned forward to look down the board at Jonil.

"I might, if I were sufficiently annoyed. And there are worse things than mock mint." She added this rather darkly, but with a playful light in her eyes. "A bit of *densa* would have you jumping off your horse to shit every other minute."

Everyone laughed except Morall. She frowned for a second, then relaxed. "I'll remember that, if I find myself with the runs."

When the birds had been eaten, Jonil got up and brought the cauldron to the table. She served out stew into the wooden bowls. Margaret discovered with surprise that her stomach felt almost full, but she took some stew and ate it slowly. It tasted more familiar, like something Rafi had made on the trail, and she found herself wishing again for her dear friend. The carrots and onions had not been cooked so long as to turn to mush, and were still flavorful and a bit crunchy, and whatever meat had been added had a pleasant salty taste. She managed to finish most of the bowl before she had to stop eating.

With some cheese and slices of apple, the meal was complete. Everyone got up, their previous suspicion returning, and left her sitting on the bench. Margaret did not blame them a bit, though she felt rather sad. Karis brought a bucket and set it down on the table. She began to clear the dishes, and wash them in the bucket, singing quietly to herself as she worked.

Margaret listened to the song, trying to memorize it. The food had revived her to a degree, and it was almost reflexive. The language was archaic, but the melody not difficult. It had been composed in a minor key that gave it a wonderful, haunting quality. The lyrics told of two sisters, their love for one another, and their painful separation. She concentrated, trying to penetrate the tale, for it was one she had never heard before, either in song or story.

> " 'She asked the rush and reed
> Of beloved *breda Maris*
> On *Valeron's* swift banks.
> She asked the stone and seed
> Of treasured *breda Maris*
> On *Valeron's* high banks.
> She asked the water and weed
> And heard only
> To the Sea, To the Sea.' "

The verses rolled on and on, like the river and the sea themselves, with the seeker asking all and sundry, whether beast or bush, where Maris had gone. The song had an eerie rhythm, like the beat of waves against the shore at low tide, quiet and a little sad. Even as it started,

Margaret knew the tale would not have a happy conclusion. And as the final verse drew to a close, the unnamed sister threw herself into the rushing waters of the River Valeron, and drifted down to the cold sea of Dalereuth, calling for Maris and finding no answer. The refrain, *"Ahm Maree,"* "to the sea," playing as it did with the sound of the name Maris, gave Margaret shivers.

"That was very beautiful," she said quietly, in spite of herself.

"Huh? Oh, the song? I always sing it when I wash up—it suits the job."

"Yes, it does."

The bench under her seemed hard and unforgiving now the song was over, and her shoulders drooped. Her eyes itched with fatigue. She dragged herself to her feet, half staggered toward the fireplace, and flopped down next to Mikhail. Her stockings were disgustingly filthy but she did not have the energy to pull them off.

Margaret steeled herself. Then she monitored the unconscious form beside her. All his vitals seemed normal, but his mind remained unreachable. She felt despair rise in her throat, and swallowed it, commanding it to be gone. She was too tired to think now. Later, when she had slept, she would think of something.

Margaret rearranged the blankets, ignoring the horsy smell clinging to them. She snuggled down, feeling the pleasant heart of Mikhail's body next to hers, and scenting the distinctive odor of maleness she had occasionally caught when she hugged her father. Thinking of Lew made her wonder what was happening in Comyn Castle, but she was too tired to hold that thought.

She turned on her side and pillowed her head on Mikhail's shoulder. For a moment Margaret just rested there, feeling odd and utterly right at the same time. Then she put her right hand over his left arm, heard the bracelets clink as they met, and closed her eyes. *So this is what married life is like,* she thought, and smiled.

30

Mikhail woke abruptly, without any of the drowsy semi-sleep he normally enjoyed. One moment he was falling through some infinite space, the next he was staring up at darkened beams crowded with cooing pigeons. Where was he?

He turned his head carefully and found Marguerida beside him, snoring delicately in deep sleep. A jumble of images exploded in his mind: pink grass, a huge jewel, a shining woman and a man lying on a couch. Varzil the Good! He had actually come to the past and spoken with the ancient *tenerézu*. And something else. For a moment Mikhail groped for the elusive thought. Then he felt the weight of metal encircling his wrist and remembered. *We are married. At last! Mother will never forgive us!* Then the demands of his body interrupted his thoughts.

He sat up quickly, and his head swam. His bladder felt ready to burst, and he was ravenous. Mikhail dragged himself up to his feet, and staggered toward the door, loosening the drawstring on his trousers as he stumbled. He managed to make his way a few steps beyond the doorway, into a muddy rut, before he paused and relieved himself. Then he closed his pants and just stood there, swaying a bit, with cold water seeping up into his stockings. If only he could have found a dry patch! He leaned against a wall, breathing slowly, trying not to sit down in the puddle.

When his legs stopped trembling, he retraced his steps into the building. Where were they? It seemed to take forever, and he felt weak and terribly stupid. Once inside again, he realized they were in a huge kitchen, and not a very clean one at that. Why were they sleeping in a kitchen, and why did he faintly remember other people? There seemed to be no one there except Marguerida, still asleep. He must have dreamed it, surely.

Mikhail sank down on a bench along the table and found there was a loaf of bread sitting on the board. Beside it was some cheese, a few withered apples, some raisins, and two cooked birds. He stared at these for a long time, then reached out and took a bit of cheese. It was salty on his tongue, and he noticed for the first time that his mouth was parched. There was a wooden ewer on the table, and a small, round wooden cup. He tried to pour himself some water, but his hands were so tremulous that he got more on the table than into the wooden cup.

Mikhail drank, slowly and deeply, letting the sweet taste of clean water stay in his mouth for a moment before he swallowed. He thought he remembered his head being lifted, and someone dribbling some disgusting liquid into his mouth. When had that happened, and where had the bread come from, and the roasted birds? Surely Marguerida had not baked bread during. . . . was it one night or several? He was not sure, and that made him shiver.

A little revived by the water, his mind seemed to clear. He had a faint memory of many voices, all female, and a long, bumpy ride. He had not dreamed that, surely. But, where were those speakers? The flutter of wings overhead was the only sound in the room, except the faint crackling of the fire on the hearth. He could not really concentrate. Instead of worrying further, he pulled a leg off one of the birds and started eating. He alternated sips of water with the fowl, and slowly began to feel less hollow.

There was something he needed to remember, but it eluded him. It nagged at the back of his mind as he ate. After only one leg and a bit of the breast, he found he could eat no more, and poured himself another cup of water. Pigeon and cheese might not be the best choice, he thought, for his belly started to cramp suddenly. Was the water tainted?

Mikhail rose unsteadily and tottered back toward the bedding, his damp stockings making a nasty, squishing sound across the cold stones of the floor. The fire was only embers now, and he saw a few logs and sticks piled beside the hearth. Mikhail sank down beside it, and reached for a small branch. It took an enormous effort, but he managed to pull some of the sticks onto the coals. He watched the flames begin to lick at the wood. Then he began to feel incredibly cold. It must be because his feet were soaked. He wrestled off one sodden stocking, but the other one was beyond his dwindling strength. He just sat on the warm hearthstones, with a wet sock dangling from his fingers, too tired to move.

His eyelids seemed to weigh a great deal, and his head drooped onto his chest. He slipped into a light drowse, then snapped awake again. Mikhail stared into the flames. He groaned, and tried to roll a small log into the fireplace. The heat was wonderful, and he wanted more!

"Wha . . . ?"

The sound of a sleepy voice startled him, and his fingers lost their grip on the log. It rolled onto his unprotected foot. He roared at the pain, and heard the muffled sound of blankets being shoved aside. In a moment Marguerida was behind him, bending down, her face very white.

She gripped his shoulders, and Mikhail leaned back. He rested against her chest, feeling the warmth of her skin against his. What lovely breasts she had underneath that nightgown. A pity he did not have the strength to do more than lean against them. And why was her hair piled up on the top of her head in that provocative, wanton manner. Was she trying to drive him mad with the sight of her slender neck?

"What were you doing?" Her voice was sharp with concern.

"Piss," he muttered. His mind was muddled again, and speech seemed difficult.

"Oh, I see. You need to rest, Mik. Here, let me get you back to . . . where are the Sisters?" He sensed a stab of fright. Then she stiffened, and he knew she was forcing herself to remain calm.

Mikhail let her help him over to the pile of blankets. She laid him out, pulled the other sock off his foot, and covered him up, tucking the blankets around him. Then he watched her add some logs to the fire, and go to the table. Her movements had a remote quality, as if he were watching everything from some great distance. He struggled to penetrate the detachment enveloping him, but it was impossible.

He saw Marguerida look at the victuals on the board, frown, and shrug. Then she came back to him, knelt beside him, and stroked the hair off his face. "How do you feel?"

"Cold. Weak. Tired." The effort of those words seemed enormous.

"You won't feel cold much longer—your brow is pretty warm, and I think it is going to get hot in a little while. I hope they left some feverwort tea. I wish they had not left us . . . oh, Mik!"

"Who?"

"We were rescued by a band of Sword Sisters—at least I think that is what they were called—and they brought us here. I guess that Damila didn't think it was safe to remain with us. *Damn.*"

"Where?" His chest felt as if it were being crushed by an enormous weight now, and every joint in his body was hot, while his flesh was chilly.

"Where? Oh, where are we? They called it the old El Haliene place. Damila said it was abandoned, and that the Sisters use it for themselves. We camped here, and they made dinner, and . . . I suppose they crept off while we slept. Sensible, but I wish they hadn't. At least they left us some food."

"Ate."

"Yes, I saw that." She patted his hand in a kindly way, but he wished she had not, for his skin was so tender that even a gentle touch was painful. He flinched in spite of himself. "Well, we will just have to make the best of it. We have water—there must be a well in here somewhere, and I'll find it. And we have some food, so we won't starve."

Mikhail felt himself shudder all over then, and his back arched: muscle spasms raced along his body, leaving him writhing in agony, and he heard himself cry out. He tried to stifle the terrible sounds, but it was impossible. Distantly, he heard Marguerida give a sharp sound of distress, and curse.

The little food he had eaten tried to leap from his belly, and his mouth filled with bitterness. He felt two strong hands grip his shoulders and sit him up, so he did not choke, and mercifully, he did not spew either. He shook and shook, every joint screaming in agony, fire racing along his blood.

"Your hand," he managed to gasp.

Mikhail! What do you mean, my hand?

Spasms stop under one.

Huh? Oh, yes. Of course! I can see that your left arm is twitching less than your right. I wonder. . . .

He felt his body being shifted against hers, and then her left hand came down and rested on his chest. Even as he gasped for air, he felt a subtle change in his body, as if his heart were slowing down to something like normal. Vaguely he realized that Marguerida was using her own heartbeat to regularize his, that she was using her own matrix to rechannel his energy.

What was happening to him? Mikhail saw a blazing jewel in his mind again, and it all rushed back. He was wearing the matrix ring of Varzil Ridenow! He could even feel the metal of the band against his skin. And the gem itself was pressing upon his clenched palm. Matrix shock!

Mikhail forced his hand open. He could feel the sweat on his face as he struggled to extend his fingers. Then, his muscles still twitching terribly, he rolled the band around so the stone stood above his finger. It seemed to take forever, but he knew it had happened quickly.

He felt his lungs labor less now. His heart was steadying to a regular beat. Mikhail could hear Marguerida muttering to herself under her breath, moving her hand here and there. There was a small bloom of panic in her mind, held at bay by will and training, and an incredible determination.

It was a fine thing, an admirable one, and something within him tried to match it, to mingle with it, for its beauty and its strength. At the same time, part of him was aware that Marguerida was doing something very unorthodox, that she was using her *laran* in a way he had never before observed. No monitor or healer had ever done this. Was it one of Istvana's innovations?

The fire in his joints began to ease, and the spasms of his limbs faded away. He felt as if he were floating in a warm bath, a gentle sea that supported his body. It was like falling into a song. Energy lapped his sinews instead of torturing them.

What are you doing?

Hush!

Mikhail did as he was bid, trusting her more than he had ever trusted another person in his life. She had done this before, hadn't she—when he thought she was going to choke Varzil. It was too much, that memory. He was afraid to think. Madness seemed only a breath away, and he dared not let it overwhelm him. He must trust Marguerida, and nothing more. But, it was so hard to do that.

His tortured muscles begin to uncoil, going slack with exhaustion. Mikhail discovered he was too tired to think or feel at all. Nothing mattered now except rest.

Rest! A cold, merciless presence stirred in him. *Hide behind a woman's skirts? Let her do all the work?* The wonderful lethargy creeping along his limbs vanished, replaced by a fear and disgust that jolted him.

Mik! Stop fighting me!

The cry was far away, and he tried to ignore it. He did not want her help, her healing. He could not bear to owe her more than he already did. He was unworthy of her magnificence.

No, no—this was Marguerida! But . . . she was a woman, like Javanne, always intriguing, manipulating, and making him feel inadequate. If Marguerida helped him, saved him, he would be even less worthy. She would never let him forget how she had rescued him, would she? Of course not—women never relented. His mother never relented.

And she was so splendid, so wonderful. He was no match for her! No ring would ever make him her equal. It was a contest he could not win.

Mikhail looked into himself, and saw a twisted face stare back at him. It was the saddest face he had ever seen, a starved countenance. And yet it was his own familiar features looking at him, forlorn and hungry-eyed. He hated it, the weakness of it—what a disgusting fright! It would be better off dead.

Beneath his revulsion, from a place he never dreamed existed, came a tendril of pity. It was so small he barely noticed that it made a pocket of warmth in his coldness, a trail of heat in the ice of his soul. Poor thing, all alone in the dark. Poor Mikhail—not good enough to please his mother, to win her affection. Not good enough to step into Regis' shoes. And surely not good enough to wear the jewel on his hand.

Pain crushed his chest again, and his sad, dark twin lay across him, in a lover's pose. He could feel its hot, fetid breath against his cheeks. He wanted to struggle, to wriggle away from the weight of himself. He had been fighting this sorrowful monster for years, and never could he best it. He might as well give up and let it suck his breath away. He was too weary to go on fighting any longer.

The specter vanished then, and another face floated above his. It was an old man, dignified and wise. Eyes gazed at him, filled with great compassion, and that hurt him and angered him as well. He did not want pity—he knew what he was! But Varzil's blue eyes bored into him.

I am too flawed. I cannot bear this thing you have given me!

Mikhalangelo, we are all flawed. And you have the strength to wield the matrix, if you will only be a little kinder to yourself.

Kinder, Am I not weak enough without adding that? The words spat out of him, filled with selfhatred and rage.

The grave face smiled above him. *You hold yourself to a standard even a god would find daunting, my son. The merest imperfection in you seems magnified into a monstrous failure. Can you feel the weight of these things pressing against you?*

Yes!

Ten times the Wall around the World weighs on your heart. Mikhalangelo. It is not my little ring that oppresses you, but only your fear.

I want to die!

You will, but not this day. Let go! It is not treasure that you are clutching, but only a pack of rubbish.

Rubbish? That seemed a remarkable description for the misery he felt.

Small flaws magnified into great failings are the rubbish of the soul. Release your grip on this monster you have made of yourself. You are worthy of your Margarethe, but more, you are worthy of yourself!

Am I?

You will have to trust my judgment in the matter.

He struggled for what seemed a great time, but eventually he flagged. How great a toll it took to wrestle with himself. And how foolish it was.

Great washes of emotion flooded across him—light and dark, good and ill. He had never suspected he contained so many feelings, nor how powerful they were. They ran together, pooling, until he could no longer distinguish one from another. He let himself sink into that calming whirl of old, worn-out fears and desires, drowning his despair and hope at once. This was for the best.

He could feel his body fail, his heart ceasing to beat in his breast, his blood halting in his veins. Mikhail waited for death now, accepted it, mourned himself without self-consciousness. Soon it would be over. At least he would perish whole instead of in bits and pieces.

Dammit, Mik! Don't quit on me now! He felt a smart slap on his face, a stinging of flesh upon flesh. It was like having cold water pour into him, clear and bright and refreshing.

A fist thumped against his chest, and his heart jumped. His anguish receded, but the memory of it lingered like the taste of salt on his tongue. He was resting across Marguerida's lap, looking up at a very angry woman. There was a sheen of sweat on her forehead, and some of her fine hair had escaped from the pins, giving her a frenzied appearance. Her golden eyes were like small flames.

"Ouch," he said, rubbing his sternum. "That hurt."

"Good! If you ever try cardiac arrest on me again, I will pound you even harder!"

"I was not *trying* cardiac arrest," he mumbled, feeling injured and misunderstood. "You make it sound as if I did it on purpose."

Marguerida laughed shakily, and some of the high color left her face. "I suppose I did. You just scared ten years off me, and that . . . well, it makes me so angry!" A tear rose in one eye, and began to slip down her cheek unnoticed. "So far our married life has been terrible," she muttered.

Marguerida began to sob, and Mikhail wished he had the strength to comfort her. All he could manage was a feeble pat on the hand which rested on his chest and a few meaningless phrases. Something nagged at his disordered wits, and after a minute he said, "Our married life?"

The sobs choked to a halt in a sputter of coughing. Marguerida grabbed his wrist and drew his arm up, so he could see the circlet resting here. "You mean you don't remember promising to serve me all my days, you silly dolt!"

"Did I do that?" It was all very vague and fuzzy, but he did seem to remember some sort of promise. Still, *serve* her? "Why don't I remember—was I drunk?"

"All you had was water! Don't provoke me, Mikhail Hastur! I am stretched too thin to take it. Don't you remember *anything?* Varzil marrying us, and . . . and *Her?*"

"Her?"

Margaret seemed unusually hesitant to answer. "Evanda, I think."

He had a burst of memory, of a woman's face, beautiful and radiant, the smell of stone and stew, and a voice speaking. Mikhail remembered the weight of the bracelet when it was put upon his wrist, and Marguerida saying, "With this ring . . ." And then all reality had vanished, leaving him wandering in some lightless place.

"Oh, Mik, I was so frightened for you. Can't you remember?"

"It all seems very confused yet, but, yes, I certainly remember the woman." He paused and sighed a little, feeling his exhaustion, but also a kind of relaxed vigor, as if he had come a great distance in a short time. "Amos is not going to believe that story, I promise you."

"Amos?" Marguerida looked puzzled, then concerned, as if he were raving.

"Don't you remember our imaginary grandchild?"

"Oh, yes." She almost giggled with relief. "Humph! The way we have been going, we aren't going to have any children, let alone grandchildren." Then her face turned quite red, and her eyes shifted away. She held her shoulders uncomfortably, tense and frightened.

"Poor Marguerida. I don't remember clearly after you put that ring on my hand. I just fell off the edge of the world or something."

"I'm not completely sure. All I know is that the building vanished—I don't think it was ever there at all, Mik—and I found us sitting in the pouring rain. You were unconscious, so I managed to drag you under some trees. We were getting wetter and wetter, and I was almost out of my mind. So, being the wise and sensible person that I am, I decided to perform an experiment with heat exchange and I think I nearly crisped both of us. If I did not know it before, I now understand why a little knowledge is a dangerous thing."

"But how did we get here?"

"The crow did it."

"Huh?"

"No, it did not fly us here. It went and found some women, Sisters of the Sword. And they loaded you onto a litter, and we came to this place." She glanced around the shadowed kitchen and sighed. "I think they decided we were too dangerous to be around, because they sneaked off while we were sleeping. I don't know how they did it, but I was so tired that probably an entire army could have tromped through, and I would not have stirred. I assume they left our horses behind, in whatever serves for a stable in this ruin."

"I see. I am sorry that . . ."

"Don't be stupid! You couldn't help getting sick. It is just that I have been nearly out of my mind with worry, and I tend to take things very personally at times like this. It is not a very helpful trait, but I can't seem to shake it." She frowned a little. "Maybe it's in my genes, because the Old Man does it, too. Oh, how I wish he were here right now! Hell, I'd even be happy to see your father! Or your mother, or even Gisela Aldaran, and my councilor from University, who was a real pain." He could hear the fatigue in her voice, and knew she was holding herself together by will alone.

"Beloved, tell me what you just did to me. It wasn't like anything I ever felt before."

"It's hard to say, exactly, because I confess I was working completely intuitively, as if I were composing a piece of music." She paused, frowned and thought for a few seconds. "What I thought I was doing was giving you a good currying!"

"A what?"

"As with a horse—curry-combing. I just kept combing the knots and tangles in you out with my matrix. And there was something else, too." Marguerida went silent for a minute. "When I took Varzil's matrix to give you, there was an instant where it touched me. I learned something I have not sorted out yet, but I think I might be discovering how to heal. I've been learning all along how to use this accursed thing—when I killed the bandit and when I cleared Varzil's channels. But those were crude. . . . How do you feel?"

"Achy. Tired. But clean and clear, too. All I need is a week's sleep, lots of food, a bath, and some fresh clothing. I hate the way I feel, but the way I smell . . . ugh!"

"We are both good and stinky. And I will wager there is not a bath to be had in a hundred miles. And unless I can catch some more pigeons, all the food we have is there on the table."

Mikhail felt his eyes grow heavy, and found himself slipping into doze. "I haven't been a very good provider, so far, my *caria*. Forgive me." Then, within moments, he fell into a profound sleep.

Singing woke him. Mikhail went from dreaming to near waking slowly, and the rippling notes seemed to be part of both states. He lay very still and listened. Beneath the words he heard the steady brush of a broom across stones, the coo of the birds overhead, and the patter of soft rain outside. It was a seamless sound, all joining into the music.

Carefully, Mikhail sat up in the blankets. His body was warm but not feverish. The clammy dampness of his garments told him he had been sweating in his sleep. He looked around the kitchen, and found Marguerida across the room, wielding a broom. She had taken off the white nightgown, and was wearing only her chemise and a single petti-coat. Her hair was tied under a square of cloth, so the back of her neck was completely exposed. It was something no Darkovan woman would have done, and he was astounded by how erotic it was, and how strongly his body responded.

For a minute he watched her, seeing her content. Mikhail had never known Marguerida to be so composed. He supposed, after all they had been though, that sweeping the floor was a pleasant change. "What are you singing?" he asked quietly, so as not to startle her out of her mood.

"What? Oh, you are awake!" She turned toward him, smiling, her face flushed with work, and looked as beautiful as any woman he had ever seen. "It is just an old rowing song from Thetis, one they do to keep time for the oarsmen."

"It is very pretty. But why are you sweeping?" Mikhail gestured at the birds overhead. "It is just going to get messy again."

"As long as we are here, I'd like the place to be liveable," she replied a bit tartly. "While you slept, I located the well, found the remains of the pantry, and unearthed a good-sized pot that was over-looked. I have heated water, so you can have a wash."

"Good. I need it!"

"I already did, and it felt wonderful." She seemed to notice then that she was dressed immodestly, glanced down at herself, and shrugged. "I found more wood to burn, so we won't be cold."

"That's fine." Mikhail could sense the awkwardness that lay between them, the slight tension of two people who, while married, were not yet truly wed. He did not need to be telepathic to know that she was uncomfortable, but he was, too. No, not uncomfortable but shy.

Mikhail had not felt shy around any woman since he was in his teens. The emotion puzzled him now. Then he realized that this was not just any female, but the one woman in the world he loved, and that made a great deal of difference. This could not be some casual seduction. He was sure that the first time would be remembered by both of them, for as long as they lived. He had to be careful, and gentle, no matter how eager he felt, how desperately he wanted her.

He pushed aside his blankets, and went over to the hearth. There he found a metal pot with warm water in it, and something floating on the top. He sniffed cautiously, and smelled lavender and soap weed. Where had she found that?

Mikhail pulled off his noisome tunic and undershirt, loosened his pants and found there was a washcloth folded nearby, still damp from her use. As he began to clean himself, he marveled at Marguerida's enormous adaptability. He could not imagine Gisela Aldaran, or any other woman of his own class, sweeping floors or doing laundry. He knew, because she had told him, that she had lived in primitive conditions on several worlds. She said she had lived in huts, worn little besides feathers and flowers, eaten uncooked meat, and done things he found unimaginable. She had likely swept out those huts, too.

This was a dimension of Marguerida he had never considered before, and would not have regarded with as much respect if he had not spent those months at Halyn House, mucking out stables and hammering wooden pegs into drafty windows. A humble broom, he suspected, had never graced his mother's hands, nor those of Gisela. There were always servants to see to such matters, and he realized again how privileged he had been.

The warm, scented water laved his skin sweetly, and he felt much better, if a little hollow in the middle. The foul stink of his own sweat vanished. He would have liked some real soap, but that would have been asking for a great deal, and the soap weed did the trick, if a little crudely.

"I went out when the rain paused," Marguerida interrupted his musings, "and looked around. The horses are in a room I think was the buttery before. The Sisters left enough oats for them for a couple of days, and they will not want for water. So as soon as you feel up to riding, I think we can head off. Once we run out of food, we will have to go." She sounded worried and tired.

"Yes, I know." He finished his washing, took his undershirt and balled it up, and thrust it into the pot. He mushed it around, rubbing the fabric between his fingers, until it caught on the ring. Varzil probably never did his own laundry. This thought amused him as he unhitched the snag, pulled the soaking garment out of the water, and wrung it out as best he could. Then he hung it from a hook on one side of the fireplace, and heard it begin to drip on the warm stones. He saw that his stockings had been removed while he slept, washed and hung up to dry, with hers beside them. There was something very warming about it, this sense of being taken care of. And, for the first time, he did not resent it.

There was a wooden bucket standing near the hearth, and it was full. Mikhail emptied the pot on the floor of the kitchen, refilled it and set it to warm. It gave him an enormous pleasure to perform this simple task. If only everything else could be so easy. Satisfied, he turned and asked, "Where is our crow friend?"

"He was with the horses when I looked, and I think he is reducing the mouse population. I never knew crows hunted—but that is a very remarkable bird, all around." She stopped sweeping, leaned the broom against the long bench on one side of the table, and sat down suddenly, her face very pale.

"What's the matter?"

"Ashara! I can sense her. She is looking for something—not anything specific, I think. But I feel like someone just walked on my grave!"

Mikhail sat down beside her, and took her right hand in his left, so their bracelets chimed together. "I want to tell you I will protect you from her, but I really don't know if I can."

She shook her head, and pulled off the kerchief. Her cheeks had smudges of dirt on them, and she rubbed her face, making the situation worse. "I am not the child I was when she overshadowed me the first time, and now I have this," she said as she flexed her other hand. "The thing is, you see, that she could kill me, but I dare not kill her, because that would change everything. I've been thinking on it while I swept. We have to be like mice in the wainscoting, so she will not notice us."

Mikhail put his arm around her shoulder and drew her against him. "Wearing Varzil's ring, that is going to be a good trick. I feel as if I am about as subtle as a beacon."

"She isn't expecting you, Mikhail. And, besides, it isn't his any longer. It's part yours and part his—something new. I only wish I knew how long we needed to hide, and how we are going to do it."

He could smell her body, sweet with lavender, and feel the pulse of her blood beneath his fingers. "I may be able to answer that, though I suspect you will not like it. While I slept, I dreamed, and in the dream I had a chat with Varzil—at least that is what I remember. In about forty days, if I understood it right, we need to be at the *rhu fead*. Beyond that, things become somewhat vague."

"Forty days?" She sounded astounded. "Forty . . . What are we supposed to do in the meantime—twiddle our thumbs?" Her voice was shrill and he could feel her tremble against him. Her calm had fooled him. She was closer to breaking than he had guessed.

"Even Varzil cannot command the moons, my dearest." Mikhail regretted the words immediately.

"Damn the moons and damn Varzil! Ashara will find me before then, I just know it. And we can't hide out here for all that time. We will starve."

"No, we can't. And we will leave here soon." Mikhail paused, trying to find the right words to say now. "This is awkward, but I think she is looking for a maiden, not a woman, Marguerida." He waited to see if she understood his meaning.

"What? Oh, I see—you think we should . . . then I will be different! Mikhail Hastur that is about the least romantic thing I ever heard! Not that I expected roses and violins, but. . . ." Marguerida sputtered to a halt, her mouth pinched with vexation, but her eyes twinkled slightly.

He stroked the tangled curls off her brow and kissed her lightly. Then he began to pluck the hairpins from her hair. Silky red tresses slid across his hand. He had wanted to do this for months. "I cannot give you roses, but you already have my heart, Marguerida," he whispered. She was deeply frightened, but even so he could sense the stirrings of arousal in her. The smell of her and the feel of her soft skin beneath his hand was almost more than he could bear. But he knew he must go slowly. She would panic if he rushed her.

Marguerida giggled against his neck, the warmth of her breath tickling him. "That is a good beginning—go on."

"You are also the finest and bravest person I have ever known." She did not move, and he knew that he had not found the right words yet. "You are the most beautiful woman I have ever seen. I love the way your eyes glint in the firelight, and how your hair is never tidy. The moment I set eyes on you, Marguerida Alton, I wanted to rip off all your clothes, and have my way with you! The curve of your mouth makes my heart beat faster, and when you laugh, it rejoices, and when you weep, it breaks. I have wanted to do this for ages." He pushed aside the hair at the back of her neck, revealing the smooth skin that ran down toward her spine. Then he kissed her there, softly, the heat of her satin skin against his lips.

Mikhail could feel the tension in her body, the tightness of her limbs, the way she tried to hold herself away. At the same time he found an answering of flesh, a longing, sweet and tentative, but very real. He felt her left hand come to rest on his bare chest, the fingers brushing his skin lightly, as if she were afraid.

Marguerida seemed to realize what she was doing, for she snatched her hand away swiftly, pulled free of him, and looked at it. When she turned towards him, her eyes were very wide. She swallowed hard, and then placed her left palm against his chest, and he half expected to feel a jolt of energy hit his heart. There was nothing except a faint trickle of laran, like passing a veil, in the touch.

"You are the one person I can hold without danger to either of us." There was awe in her voice. "I never guessed that. I wonder . . ."

"Wonder later, my darling."

Marguerida put her arms around his neck then, and pressed her mouth against his, melting against his chest as if she had done it a thousand times before. They were both a little breathless when they drew apart, twined hands, and rose as one.

They slipped down on the rumpled blankets beside the fireplace, touching and kissing softly. Mikhail was nearly overcome by the harsh demands of his body, but he refused to hurry, much as he longed to. He brushed her breast with his lips, heard a little gasp, and sensed her tense with excitement. He kissed the line of her body, from breast to hip, and felt her trembling beneath his touch.

Then, in a burst of energy, all the passion which had been denied Margaret all of her life broke through some invisible barrier. It flooded his mind and body, warm and eager, uncertain and yearning. For the merest instant, there was resistence, and then abandon, beyond anything he dared to dream of.

31

Two mornings later, in a drizzling rain, they rode away from the deserted ruin, heading south. Even if they had not run out of food for themselves, there was no fodder left for the horses, and that had forced the decision. Mikhail was smiling, thinking of how Marguerida had grinned fiendishly as she said, "Love won't fill our bellies—no matter how often we try to make it."

Mikhail was still stunned by the way in which Marguerida had changed, once the first desperate, clumsy coupling was accomplished. The only word he could think of was wanton. He had never suspected her of having so much imagination and sheer naughtiness. And it was all his—if she did not wear him out first. She certainly had tried.

Still, he had not felt so well in years, as if his marriage to Marguerida had fulfilled some lack in him he had not known he possessed. Now, if he could only solve the problem of how they were going to survive until they could escape from the past, he would be completely happy. Mikhail had no clear plan, and this disturbed him. Indeed, he almost felt that he was being drawn along toward some invisible goal—that his destiny remained incomplete. He refused to let this suspicion dampen his spirits, but a dark bloom of worry began to grow in his mind.

Marguerida made a little sound of distress, distracting him from his silent musings. "What is it?"

She favored him with a glowing grin from beneath the shadow of her hood, and his heart leaped with delight. "I'm not sure. I feel a little strange—light-headed. And hungry and queasy at the same time. Maybe that last bird was a bit off, or the bread was getting moldy. It's nothing."

"I feel fine, so it probably is not the food. Are you coming down with something?" That seemed unlikely, since Mikhail knew that the Terranan inoculations she had had before coming to Darkover were damn-near miraculous.

"I don't think so. Mostly I am sore, Margaret blushed. "And my breasts are really tender."

Mikhail thought about her beautiful breasts and got aroused in spite of himself. It was not something that was very comfortable on horseback, and certainly he should have sated his lust by now. Had he been too rough with her? "I am sorry, *caria.*"

"I don't believe it was anything we did, dearest." She gave a little sigh, and looked very happy. "Well, perhaps we were a bit too enthusiastic. All I know is that I feel different than I ever have in my life. When I touched Varzil's ring, I could feel something change inside me. And when we loved, it changed again. I expect it will just take some time for my body to adjust, as it did when I first acquired my matrix pattern. I've been through a lot in the past few months, you know."

"You have indeed." There seemed to be nothing more to say. Mikhail wondered about his own body, aware that accepting Varzil's matrix had changed him in yet unknown ways. He wished there were someone to consult, for Marguerida did not know much more than he did. Perhaps the best idea would be to return to Hali Tower and see if Amalie El Haliene could be made to answer some hard questions. Then he shook his head—that did not feel right.

They rode on in silence for a short time, passing through another patch of barren earth, with dreadful, deformed plants the only living things to be seen. It was not the first time they had encountered this devastation, and was not likely to be the last, and Mikhail found himself sorrowing for the land, for his world and the destruction which his ancestors had wrought. He was amazed his world had survived the Ages of Chaos, glad that he had not lived in these times.

Ahead there was a stand of conifers and hardwoods, just beyond the blighted area. He wondered how it could be that one acre was ruined, but the next appeared healthy and sound. The rain muffled everything, and he found himself straining for the sound of birds.

It was too quiet! Despite his longing to be under the shelter of those trees, Mikhail suddenly felt a prickle of danger. He guided his horse to the left, circling the small grove, and Marguerida followed him without question.

He glanced down at the crow riding on his pommel. The great bird was hunched, its red eyes alert. Mikhail wished he had the *laran* to hear its avian thoughts, for he knew that the senses of the crow were better than his own.

Suddenly, eight armed men galloped out from the shelter of the trees, spurring their steeds and clearly intent on intercepting them. They were all garbed in gray, with shining gold trim, and they rode with military precision. He could see that they had helms of steel, as well as swords.

They drew up, surrounded Mikhail and Marguerida, and halted. Mikhail could see their faces, grim and expressionless. They did not speak, but just sat on their steeds, staring. And they all looked identical.

Mikhail—they are not human.

What?

They can't be—I can't read their minds. There is not a hint of the energy of a human brain.

What do you think they are?

Clones of some sort, perhaps. Or some kind of robots, except they are flesh and blood, not metal. I don't know.

Before he could continue the exchange, another man rode out from the trees, and the riders parted, letting him through. He was slender and pale and his eyes gleamed amber in the reddish-gray light that came through the clouds. Mikhail guessed his age at thirty, and by the fineness of his garments and the deference paid him, someone with authority.

The man reined in his horse, and just stared at them for a long, silent moment. He looked at their cloaks very hard, as if something about them bothered him. His thin mouth twisted a little. "Greetings," he said at last, without any inflection. There was something very cold in the single word, and Mikhail held back a shiver.

"Well met, *vai dom,*" he answered.

"I am Padriac El Haliene." He looked from one of them to the other, raised an eyebrow at the heavy bracelet on Marguerida's wrist. A puzzled look came into his haughty face, as if he had expected something, but not that. "Whence come you?"

"From the north." That was true as far as it went. Mikhail and Marguerida had discussed what, if anything, they should tell people, and tried to construct some story that would pass cursory examination. She had chosen to be Marja Leynier, and he had decided to use Danilo, the name he had been called when he was first Regis' heir, before Dani Hastur had been born. But Danilo who? He had not been able to choose a family name, no matter how he tried. It was as if some part of him resisted the name, or perhaps what he called himself was of greater importance than he had ever imagined.

Dom Padriac did not speak for a moment. Mikhail was sure he was listening to someone, not actually thinking. "Whose *leroni* are you?" The question was sharp, a bark which brooked no denial.

Mikhail hesitated, uncertain how to respond. He had not realized how very different the Ages of Chaos were until that moment, for the question was one that did not arise in his own time. The form of it implied possession, not allegiance, and he understood that the *laran* he had rendered him some sort of property. It was unimaginable, and he was angry and dismayed at the same time. But for the eight silent creatures that watched them with empty eyes, he would have liked to knock *Dom* Padriac out of the saddle and give him a thrashing.

Mik—he is the one who got Amalie's folk away from Hali—I am sure of it! And there is someone else . . .

"Whom do you serve?" *Dom* Padriac snapped when neither of them answered.

He remained silent, considering Marguerida's thought. Then he sensed a subtle pressure in his mind, and had the impulse to speak his name. It was revolting, and all too reminiscent of Emelda's presence. A truth-spell! Mikhail held back a shudder, trying to remain calm. That was a form of coercion almost unknown in his time, but he had heard about them while he was at Arilinn.

There was a bray, and a little donkey trotted out from beneath the shadows of the trees. A woman, whose legs almost brushed the wet ground, sat awkwardly on it. She rode up beside *Dom* Padriac and gave him a furious glance.

He returned it with glittering hatred. Dom Padriac lifted his riding quirt and snapped it across the little woman's shoulder. The heavy wool of her tunic softened the blow, but she tottered and nearly slipped from the side-saddle where she perched uneasily. "Incompetent bitch! Whose are they? Why can't you make them answer." The little *leronis* made no answer, but just looked miserable as the rain trickled down her round face.

"It matters not," she hissed. "They are strong enough to be useful in the work." She glanced at Mikhail, and her eyes widened a little. Then she shook her head, as if to dispel some perturbing thought. He could almost hear her mind refuse to believe what she saw.

Before he could make any sense out of the look, Marguerida interrupted. *Mik—I am having one of my damnable flashes again. Our fates are somehow entangled with that funny little lady, and with* Dom *Padriac as well. Just go along for the present.*

It is not as if we had a choice, is it? Mikhail felt he had not had many opportunities to choose since he had been called to ride to Hali in the middle of the night, and he had a stab of resentment.

No. These men—well, they are not men, precisely—would capture us. And the woman keeps trying to get into my mind, and yours as well. She's very curious about us, but too terrified of him to dare say anything.

I know.

Dom Padriac gave a little sniff, and a shrug. Then he said, "You will do my bidding without question. Is that understood?" He turned his horse away before either of them could reply, as if he expected to be obeyed instantly.

Resigned for the moment, Mikhail spurred his horse forward. Then he realized the crow had vanished, and wondered where it had gone. He glimpsed a dark shape in the trees as they rode past the copse, and a flash of white feathers. The bird could take care of itself, he decided, and only hoped he could do the same.

After two hours of riding, a structure came into view, a castle of such proportions that Mikhail marveled even as his heart sank. There was no fortress on the Darkover he knew to equal it. But what struck him most deeply was that he did not even know of the remains of such a place. True, he had never completely explored the lands of the Elhalyn Domain, but he was certain that if the ruins of this monstrous pile were to be found, he would have heard of it. Even hundreds of years of farmers scavenging the stones would not have erased it entirely.

This could only mean that it had been utterly destroyed, wiped out of memory and history. His heart sank as he looked at the two great towers rising about the high wall surrounding them. A strange sense of fatedness possessed him. He knew, down in his bones, without even a vestige of the Aldaran Gift, that he was part of the destruction of this place. The feeling was as inescapable as the fortress itself appeared to be. Had Varzil brought them all this way to have them die here?

He glanced at Marguerida. Her face was shadowed by the hood of her cloak, but what he could see of it was grim. Mikhail could sense her mind, narrowly focused. She was defending herself against the donkey-riding *leronis,* he decided, and something more. What? Trying to disguise her *laran,* as the ring he wore seemed able to hide itself.

Mikhail looked down at his hand, gloved and concealing the ring. He could sense the power that rested on his hand, but knew he had not the ability to use it. *Yet.* Each time he slept, Mikhail felt the ring, as if it had a voice and spoke to him. Each waking was confused, as if his mind had been crammed with information, too much to grasp quickly. It was unlike anything he had ever experienced before, frightening and invigorating at the same time. It would be years, he thought, before he would truly understand the nature of this inheritance. First he had to survive whatever lay behind those looming walls, and somehow get himself and Marguerida safely to the *rhu fead* at the right time. It was a daunting prospect, made worse by an empty stomach and damp clothing.

Mikhail forced his mind away from these overwhelming thoughts. Instead, he studied the keep. He saw the stern battlements of stone, and counted the men who stood on them. He noted how the gate was barred, and how many men it took to shift the enormous log which secured it. He might never need to know these things, but he was not sure he would have another chance to study the fortress which could easily be their prison.

Grooms darted out into the rain, real men, not eerie identical creatures like Padriac's riders. They were an unhealthy-looking lot, and nervous as well. Mikhail dismounted, and stepped over to help Marguerida down, but *Dom* Padriac was there before him, reaching out a soft hand toward her. Marguerida remained in her saddle, and looked down at *Dom* Padriac as if he had just crawled out from under a rock. Her expression was queenly, stern, and dignified. It reminded Mikhail of Javanne Hastur at her proudest, and he decided that his beloved could very well look after herself for the moment.

Mikhail slipped around the now gaping lord, and held up his hand. Marguerida grasped it and descended. Then she turned to *Dom* Padriac, her golden eyes aglitter with barely concealed fury. "I did not know that manners in the south were so crude. No one may touch me but my *husband!*"

Dom Padriac's pale face went completely white. His eyes grew large. His narrow mouth twisted, and it was clear he was not used to being spoken to in that way, especially by a woman. His hand gripped the riding quirt, and for a second Mikhail thought he was going to strike her, as he had the pitiful female on the donkey.

Then *Dom* Padriac loosened his hold, relaxed, and grinned without humor or warmth, his earlier assurance returning. "I can touch any-one I please," he began silkily. "I do not believe you understand that I now *own* you, and I can do anything I like . . ."

The portly *leronis* slipped off her mule, and scurried over, almost squealing with urgency. She plucked at *Dom* Padriac's sleeve. "Let her be!" she hissed. Her eyes were bulging, and the expression on her face was one of near terror.

"What!"

The outraged lord turned on her. Although she was trembling visibly, the tiny woman held her ground. "Please, lord—be careful. She is something I have never encountered before, some new *laran* they have bred in the north, no doubt." She had his complete atten-tion now. "And is it not said that only a fool makes enemies of his *leroni?*"

"Enemies?" *Dom* Padriac turned this over in his mind for a mo-ment. "Do they say that? I cannot remember hearing it before. But, perhaps you are right." Then he shook his head a little. *A pack of parasites, these* leroni. *They expect to be treated like princes, to have the best food and the warmest rooms. They have made us dependent on their foul sorceries. I would cheerfully kill all of them, down to the last one, if I could. And when I get hold of Hali Tower, and have done what I must, and driven the Hastur-kin out, I just might. We would be better off with-out them—even her!*

The thoughts came into Mikhail's mind like a whisper from the end of a long corridor, but there was no mistaking the intent. As Mikhail stood on the slimy cobbles, his previous sense of destiny re-turned again. He hoped it included the chance to kill this man.

The wind shifted, and he forgot everything as his belly tried to revolt. The green scum under his feet stank, but the smell came from somewhere else. It was disgusting. But more than that, it was *wrong,* not the unpleasant scent of moldering that was often found in stone-work, but something decidedly unhealthy. No wonder the grooms all looked unwell.

Mikhail was growing more puzzled by the second. The whole situa-tion was bizarre. *Dom* Padriac had never asked their names, for which he was grateful. They had been kidnapped and were being pressed into service to destroy Mikhail's own ancestors, if he had heard the thought rightly. Why? And how? He knew he had most of the pieces, but he could not put them together into a coherent picture.

The courtyard was shadowed by the two towers, and he could see other buildings as well. There was a small stone house with red doors on one side, and another that had the smell of a tannery wafting from it. Beside the stench from the cobbles, it was a pleasant, normal smell.

The door at the bottom of one of the towers opened then, and a woman emerged. She was young, in her late teens or early twenties, and her red hair glinted in the gray light of the day. There was a sprinkling of freckles over her pert nose, and her soft mouth was suited to smiling. But it was drawn taut, and her eyes were narrow and wary. "Oh, you found them!" She glanced at Mikhail, but her attention was all for Marguerida. She searched the face of his wife, and her dark gray eyes seemed to cloud at what she saw. A faint look of alarm passed over her face, and she glanced at the squat *leronis*. Mikhail saw something pass between the two women, a look of fear. They were afraid of Marguerida, he was certain. And more, they were afraid to tell their lord why.

Dom Padriac gave a brief nod. "Yes, I found them, just as you told me I would, sister. I trust you are satisfied now, because I have better things to do with my time than wait in the rain for *leroni*, however useful they might be."

"Of course you do, Padriac." Her voice was sweet, cozening, but there was tension in it. She sounded as if she were used to humoring the man, and Mikhail had the sense that he was stepping into a tangle, a thistle patch of conflict, between them. "Come along, you two. I can see you need a bath and some clean clothing, and a hot meal."

"They must begin working by morning," Padriac insisted. "We cannot wait any longer to start."

"Yes, brother. I do know what I am doing. We will have them in the screens and all will go according to your plan." In spite of these words, she did not sound at all sure. The tone of her voice, and the way she held her body spoke of fear and a deep desperation.

We seem to have jumped from the frying pan into the fire. Mik, I have a bad feeling about this.

Very aptly put, but I don't see anything we can do about it at present. I am not what she expected, nor what Dom Padriac did either.

I guessed as much. Let us hope that will keep them off-balance until we can find out what is going on. He intends some great wrong, and these women are helping him.

"Welcome to El Haliene Tower. Now come along" the woman said quietly, as if she assumed they would obey her immediately. "I am Amirya Haliene. I will show you to your quarters." She turned her back and started back across the cobblestones. After a moment, Mikhail and Marguerida followed her.

They entered a dim chamber, as spare as a barrack. Two torches flickered inadequate light around the room, and there were no hangings on the walls. It was cold and unwelcoming, and smelled nasty. Marguerida gave a little shudder and moved closer to her husband.

Mikhail could see a narrow stairwell rising from the back of the room, curving upward to the floors overhead. The damp smell of must was everywhere, and also the pungent scent of matrix screens. It was eerily still, but he could sense the presence of people nearby.

They followed her in silence. Again Mikhail was startled that she did not ask their names. He also wondered at the variance of hers—he had never heard Haliene before—and wondered if she were a full sister of Padriac, or something else. They were similar in appearance, but they could easily be half siblings.

Amirya led them behind the curving staircase, into a narrow corridor that ran toward the back of the building. It was dark and oppressive, and the stench of mold was everywhere. It was also very chilly, and Mikhail was glad of his cloak, even though it was rather damp from the rain. He felt Marguerida draw closer to him, slipping her hand over his elbow. The smell of lavender from their attempts at washing wafted across him, and he felt somewhat less anxious. As long as he had Marguerida, he decided, he was prepared to face anything.

The corridor had several doors along its length, and Amirya opened one. "This will be your room." she told Marguerida. "Yours will be at the other end of the hall."

"We are man and wife, and we do not sleep apart from one another," Mikhail almost snapped. He didn't want Marguerida separated from him by even one wall, let alone several.

Amirya just stared at him. Then she looked at his wrist, and saw the circlet on it, and frowned as she noticed the matching one on Marguerida's arm. "Married? But . . ."

"But what?"

"How can this be? This will ruin everything. I don't understand this—it was not what I foresaw at all! No wonder Padriac was . . . oh, damn!"

"What will it ruin?" Marguerida asked, her voice tense.

"Nothing. It does not matter. It will all be over soon."

"Stop speaking in riddles, Amirya." There was a hint of command in Marguerida's voice, enough to make the other woman stiffen slightly.

"We . . . my brother . . ." She paused, drew a deep breath, and began again. "I am the Keeper here, in El Haliene Tower, and I found you when I was seeking a means to destroy the King's Champion. I would not be Keeper if our cousin Amalie had not been so clever and escaped us. She should have let us into Hali when we came, and joined us, but she has no loyalty." *I am loyal to Padriac, and I will be rewarded. And I am glad that Amalie escaped, for if she was here, I should not be Keeper.*

"I have never heard of any El Haliene Tower," Mikhail answered slowly.

"I am not surprised, for we have been working in the greatest secrecy for over a year, creating the screens and preparing for . . . There has never been a Tower such as ours. It is even greater than Hali, I am sure."

"You do not sound sure, Amirya," Mikhail said. "You sound as if you were whistling past the graveyard. And are you not quite young to be a Keeper?"

To his surprise, Amirya grinned. "That is the best of it, for no one expects someone as young as I am to be able to handle the energies, so we were able to continue unsuspected. Well, almost. I think Varzil Ridenow had a hint or two, but he was too old and toothless to do anything about it."

At that moment, Mikhail had the sense of distant laughter. He knew that whatever Amirya had foreseen, Varzil's hand was in it. The old *laranzu* might be dying, or dead already, but toothless he was not.

He felt the ring tingle on his finger, and found his mouth stretching into a wolfish grin. Mikhail could sense something strong and dark stir within him, flexing like a great beast. He wanted to release it, but sensed he must restrain his impulse to destroy this place for another time. Still, the promise of it heartened him in a wonderful way.

Marguerida looked through the open door into the room. "I think we can manage in here. The bed is a little narrow, but neither of us is plump."

Amirya was shocked and upset. "You can't intend to . . . *accandir*—when you are working the screens! I insist . . ."

"You can insist all you like, *domna*. It will not make any difference to us." Then Marguerida smiled at Amirya. "Besides, we do our best work when we *accandir*. Don't we, *cario?*" She gave Mikhail a look that spoke volumes, all of them lusty. For a woman who had never known any man two days before, she had, after her initial uncertainty, taken to the whole thing with great and exhausting enthusiasm.

The woman peered at Marguerida, then at Mikhail. *"What* are you?"

"At the moment, we are two very tired people. There was mention of a bath, I believe." The coolness of Marguerida's voice was chilling, even to Mikhail who knew her so well.

"You keep shifting before my eyes—what are you!" The panic was unmistakable now.

I think you are better off not knowing. Mikhail sensed his wife shift to forced rapport, and felt the power within it, and the threat as well.

Shifting? What do you think she means, Marguerida?

I'm not sure, but I suspect that we are not anchored in this time, and to someone with Sight, it might appear that we move in and out of view.

Amirya's face looked haggard and uncertain. She bit her lip and clenched her hands into dainty fists, her freckles standing out in the dim light of the corridor. "I will make you tell! I dare not risk failing my brother. We will use truth spell, if we must."

"I do not think that would be wise of you," Marguerida replied. "And it might be fatal to any who tried. But that is your decision, Amirya, not mine. You had us brought here, and must suffer the consequences."

"What am I going to do?" It was the wail of a young woman stretched beyond her resources. "It isn't supposed to be like this! You are not what you seem, and if I tell Padriac that, there will be the devil to pay. If he does not get what he wants . . . I can't bear to think of it!"

"Perhaps you might consider, then, if giving your brother what he thinks he wants is such a good idea. Constructing a secret Tower, keeping *leroni* in unwilling servitude—none of that sounds very wise to me. This place reeks of darkness, and I believe you know it, Amirya. I think you know you are doing something wrong, and I think it gnaws at you."

"If only . . . if only I could be sure," she whispered, her slender body trembling.

"There is no way to be sure of anything except that the sun will rise in the morning, and there will be snow in winter. The rest is choice, and consequences. I know our fates are entwined for the present, and that you can change the outcome, if you really wish to. But keeping your brother happy may not be possible."

Tears sparkled in Amirya's dark eyes, glistened on her light-colored lashes, and then slid down her cheeks. "I am so afraid. I thought I was afraid before, but . . ."

"I know. We both know. But if we do not get some food soon, we are both going to drop in our tracks, and that will most assuredly displease your brother."

Mikhail knew that Marguerida was not using the voice of command now, but was somehow influencing the vulnerable girl all the same. He noticed that her left hand was making tiny movements against her body, and would have laughed aloud if he dared. She was doing some manner of healing on the wretched girl, calming her fears. And he knew enough of human nature to suspect that Amirya would promptly persuade herself that she had overreacted, or only imagined that she had seen them shifting in front of her eyes.

He watched some of the terrible tension drain away from Amirya's body. "Yes, of course. I will have a servant bring you a tray of food. The bathing chamber is the second door down—do not open any of the other doors! I do not want the others disturbed while they are resting. They need their strength. And I will see that some clean, dry clothing is brought."

Amirya turned and fled down the corridor, as if she wanted to put as much distance as possible between them. *I will keep them in their room—I dare not use them, not now. What am I going to do!*

Marguerida went into the narrow, gloomy chamber, took off her cloak and hung it on a peg, then sank onto the edge of the bed. Her shoulders drooped with exhaustion as Mikhail sat down beside her. "At least we are out of the rain," she muttered miserably.

The stillness seemed to grow, and Mikhail felt himself fall into a relaxed frame of mind. There was nothing he could do for the moment, and it was good to be in from the weather. Marguerida was right.

He felt his senses begin to tingle, as if they were spreading out from his body, like lines of light. It began slowly, and was so subtle that he barely noticed it until he encountered the presence of another person. It was not Marguerida, but a complete stranger, and a sick one at that. Where was he?

After a moment Mikhail knew the person he was sensing was two doors down the corridor. He got nothing else except the sense of some terrible fatigue and sickness—no personality. He could not even tell if the man was young or old.

He let his awareness expand and roam freely. He did not like what he found. All around them, there were exhausted people, all of them with *laran*, and many of them not only tired, but also injured in various ways. He sensed several burns, one person who hovered on the brink of madness, and someone who was very near to death. He wrenched himself away quickly.

Mikhail started. He had never been able to do that before, just reach out and observe. In theory it was not that different from monitoring a circle. The actuality was astonishing. He knew that he could explore the entire keep, from attic to cellar, easily and completely. But not just then. He would have to be cautious, he decided.

What was he becoming? The query rose in his mind, and the hairs on the back of his neck bristled. He turned to speak to Marguerida, and found she had slipped onto the thin pillow, and was asleep. He stared at her for a moment, seeing how her face relaxed in repose. He should sleep too, until food was brought. But he was not really tired. He wanted to know what he was turning into.

No, that was not the right question. What were *they* becoming was better. It had something to do with Marguerida, with the inexplicable way in which their energies had woven together during the bizarre wedding ceremony. Mikhail was fairly certain that while he had inherited Varzil's matrix, he had not absorbed that man's laran. At least there was no hint in any record he was aware of that it was possible to transfer laran powers from one person to another.

How much of Varzil's great knowledge was riding on his finger? And how was he going to discover its secrets? Or did he already know the secrets, but was unable to bring them into his mind? *I have my own shadow matrix now.*

Mikhail looked down at Marguerida's hand, covered in the worn silk mitt. Even through the fabric he could sense the lines that ran along her flesh, and could feel the resonance of them in his own body, and in the matrix he wore.

Yes, that was part of it. We really are two parts of a whole. The realization rocked him, but he knew it was true. He began to understand why the whole thing had depended on Marguerida, on her own unusual matrix. He felt a little dizzy as he tried to grasp the implications of the thing, and after a moment, he had to give it up. It was too much to contain in the mind. At the same time, he knew in his bones and sinews that he now possessed a greater power than he had ever imagined possible, let alone that he might be master of. No—not master. That might come in time. For the present, he was still himself, Mikhail Hastur, and he had a great deal to learn.

A shuffling sound came down the corridor, and then a servant appeared at the still open door of their room. It was a middle-aged man, carrying a heaped tray. Rich smells rose from it, and Mikhail could see two roasted fowl, a bowl of boiled grain, and most of a loaf of bread. There were a couple of rather soiled napkins, and wooden spoons as well.

The servant did not speak, but just thrust the tray toward Mikhail. He took it and put it down on the end of the bed, since the only table in the room was occupied by a pitcher and bowl for washing, and watched the fellow shuffle away. There was something disquieting about his behavior, but he could not imagine what.

"Wake up, sleepy head. There is food."

"Uhm?"

Marguerida roused, and peered at him owlishly for a second. She sniffed and grinned. "It smells good."

Mikhail put the tray between them and she drew a napkin over her lap, and reached for one of the birds. She tore it in two, then yanked the leg off the breast, and sank her teeth into it. A gobbet of fat ran down her chin, and she rubbed it aside with her wrist, hitting herself with the bracelet. Mikhail hardly noticed, being too involved with satisfying his own hunger. By the time he second servant appeared, carrying clothing, he was quite greasy, and did not really care. He was going to bathe as soon as he finished eating, and he was looking forward to that.

The servants came and went in complete silence, and he wondered if they had been ordered not to speak. It was puzzling, but he was still too hungry to think about it. Mikhail tore off a slab of bread and took a large bite. It tasted slightly wrong, and he made a face. There was something sour in it. Any other time he would have spat it out. Instead he chewed, swallowed, and wished there was some wine or beer to wash it down. He spent a moment thinking of the fine beer that *Mestra* Gavri brewed in her inn near Ardais Castle, in an old building that had not even been constructed yet, and then shrugged. He took one of the spoons and tried the boiled grain. It was overcooked, thick and pasty and without any particular flavor, and reminded him of the dreadful meals he had endured at Halyn House.

Marguerida had finished half her fowl, and tried the grain. She made a face. "The cook must be having an off day," she muttered.

Mikhail wiped his mouth on the back of his hand. "Or else the Elhalyns just never hire good ones. I wonder why the servants did not speak."

"Yes, I noticed that, too. I think they were compelled to silence— at least I felt something like that when the man brought the food. I think that strange woman who was with *Dom* Padriac is doing some things that would make Istvana furious, if she knew."

While you were taking a nap, I did a little exploring—all without leaving the room. There are leroni all around us, and they are in terrible shape. Something dreadful is going on in this place, and I wish I knew what it was.

Exploring without leaving the room?

A new trick I seem to have gotten with Varzil's ring.

Can you teach me? It sounds useful. Gah! This grain is disgusting.

Have you ever thought that the wonderful thing about telepathy is that you really can talk with your mouth full?

No, and if you make me choke with laughing, you will likely kill me. What do you make of all this, Marguerida?

No you can't teach me, or no you never thought of that?

You have thought of something, and you don't want to tell me what it is.

How did you know?

Because you always try to distract me from unpleasant things with your jokes, caria.

I suppose I do. A deplorable character flaw. Very well. I think that Dom *Padriac is trying to get fissionable materials.*

What! How did you leap to that idea?

Several things. I noticed just a bit of a glow on the stairs leading up from the entry, when we came in. It set me thinking. And I remembered that when I was trying to read the entire scriptorium at Arilinn, and driving the archivist nearly mad, I came across a few documents that suggested to me that at one point, low-yield atomic devices were used—during the time we are in now. Damn! My mind feels befuddled. One of the things that Varzil did was put a stop to that, but the knowledge still exists, and I think Dom *Padriac intends to use it.*

But why? Mikhail was aware that there were a few places on Darkover which still glowed in the night, and which were avoided by everyone. And his Terranan education had given him a rudimentary knowledge of physics. He was not surprised that Marguerida had a better grasp of it. What science he knew was that of the matrix, not of chemistry or physics as used by the Federation.

From the little that Amalie told us, I think he has some dispute with the Hasturs in Thendara. Now, Mik, if your foe was in a certain place, and you had the capacity to destroy that place, what would you do?

Mikhail was too stunned for a moment to reply. It went against everything he believed in. To strike an enemy from a distance was cowardly and dishonorable. But Marguerida was right. During the Ages of Chaos, before the making of the Compact, that was exactly how the small, warring kingdoms had behaved.

That is horrible! Surely if that had happened . . . there would be some record . . .

Mik, I don't pretend to understand it—but we know it did not happen, and perhaps the reason is that we were the ones to prevent it. But, right now, what we have to do is learn what is actually going on in this Tower, and then figure out what to do. The real question is whether our actions change the future, or preserve it.

He felt his heart sink. But he looked at her, her lower face greasy with fat, her hair tangled, and her golden eyes surrounded by dark circles of fatigue, and felt it lift again. He leaned across the tray between them and planted a messy kiss on her mouth. As long as Marguerida was with him, he was sure he could face anything.

Mikhail bit into his bread again, and felt his mouth pucker. Was the grain moldy or something? And why was he feeling woozy, with food in him? Weak and stupid. He spat it out. He rose and poured some water from the pitcher on the stand into his hand and cupped it into his mouth.

Marguerida was looking at him, her eyes unfocused. She looked down at the food for a moment. "I'll have her guts for garters!" She spoke in Terran, not *casta,* and Mikhail had to struggle to translate the words. "The food is drugged! Or poisoned." She made a gagging noise, staggered to her feet, and leaned over the bowl on the stand, retching and spewing.

Mikhail gripped her shoulders, supporting her. She was right, and he spent a futile moment being furious. Then he felt his hand warm beneath his ring, and he sensed a flow of well-being course along his body. Whatever had been in the bread, and perhaps the boiled grain, changed. He watched it transform, amazed and fascinated.

Marguerida stiffened in his grasp, and he knew she, too, was feeling the incredible sensation of being cleansed. And it was from him, not from her. He, too, could heal. For no reason he could bring to mind, this pleased Mikhail inordinately. She spat once more into the bowl, rinsed her mouth and face, and stood up, leaning against his shoulder. "Whatever you just did, I feel better."

"I do, too. And as for that woman's guts, you are going to have to share them with me!"

Marguerida laughed and slipped her arms around him. He could sense the roil of her emotions, and knew she was laughing to hold the other feelings at bay, the rage and helplessness. "Here we are, hungry enough to eat a bear, and the food is toxic. And stuck in a dreadful castle as well. Why am I not completely terrified?"

"I don't know, beloved, but I am glad that you are not. And if I can just discern how, I think I can do something about the food. The fowl is safe, and it is the bread and grain which have been poisoned. We will manage, somehow." Mikhail knew he should be afraid, and part of him was. Together they could solve the problem—not separately, but as one. As they were meant to be. And somehow they must survive.

32

"I wonder if Amirya is just going to let us sit here, eating our heads off and being bored until the end of the world," Marguerida complained on the fourth afternoon of their confinement.

"You didn't seem bored an hour ago," Mikhail replied, smiling at her.

"We can't spend the rest of our lives making love and sleeping, Mik!"

"I can think of worse fates, but you are right. It's amazing we haven't gotten on each other's nerves. This room seems to get smaller every time I look at it. But, while you were having a nap earlier, I did some more mapping. I am getting rather good at it."

"Find out anything useful, or were you just eavesdropping?"

Mikhail shifted on the narrow bed, trying to find a more comfortable position. He was sitting with his back against the wall, with his legs tucked up tailor fashion, and he ached for freedom. He had learned much during the enforced confinement, though he did not understand all of it yet. "I discovered there is a large cache of explosives on the other side of the Tower—in that stone building with the red door we saw when we arrived."

"How did you manage that? I still don't understand how you do this mapping trick—do you?"

"No, I don't. I assume it is a function of the matrix, and just accept it. All I know is that I can sort of feel spaces, which I could never do before, and sometimes I can sense what is in them. For instance, I know there is a proper banqueting hall in the other tower—very grand, if a little chilly. Dom Padriac spends a good bit of time there, dreaming of destroying Thendara, I suspect. I did not stay long, for fear my presence might be noticed."

"I am more interested in getting out of here."

"That won't be easy. This corridor we are on is locked at the end where it goes into the kitchens, from the other side. There is a cook and several servants, but none of them talk very much, so I haven't been able to pick up gossip. Still, there is an air of anticipation that I have noticed, a kind of general anxiety, so I think things are coming to a head. If we could somehow get through that door, and past the kitchen, the stables are about a hundred yards beyond. Then there is the gate, which we could not open between us."

"Oh, I don't know." Marguerida flexed her left hand and narrowed her eyes. "I think, if I could get to it, I might be able to do something."

Mikhail studied her. She slept a great deal, and was quiet for long periods, which was a difference that worried him at first. The Marguerida he knew was much more alert and active. Now she seemed dreamy much of the time. But he knew that she was doing some sort of work, for while she was sleeping, he got impressions from her mind that were very complex. Her contact with Varzil's matrix had clearly provoked changes in her that she needed time to integrate. He had the same problem, and had been glad that Amirya had ignored them, instead of putting them to work, as she had promised her brother she would.

"Yes, you probably could. If we could get there. Which we cannot at present." He shifted again. "I've tried to map the whole place, and the one area I can't penetrate is right over our heads. I can sense a lot of screens, but it is so well dampered that it makes the Crystal Chamber seem like a sieve. And I know that the people in the other rooms go up there, and that they are sick. I've never seen anything like it, Marguerida. They are wasting away."

On the second night, he had heard the shuffling of many feet outside his door. He had felt their illness, and the silence of their minds as well. They did not seem to know their own names, and there was none of the normal hum of thoughts that he expected. They did not speak either, which was even more disturbing.

He followed them with his mind, and was surprised when they all seemed to vanish completely a few minutes later. It was then he had discovered that the upper floors of the building were protected by telepathic shields that made it impossible to see beyond them. It was as if the upper stories were invisible, although he knew they were there.

"I know, and it makes me furious. They are drugged into submission, and I expect Amirya assumes we are as well. But I don't think the drugs are the cause of what ails them—there is some poison in this place and I am not sure we will not fall ill if we remain here much longer. A pity we can't just blast our way out of here."

"I know, but *laran* has its limits, even this." He looked down at the ring glittering on his hand, and wondered if he would live long enough to learn how to use it. He had already discovered how to map with it, to throw his senses afar. But the information he gathered was vague and shadowy, interesting but not immediately useful. He wanted action, and he wanted it soon.

There was a soft knock on the door, and it opened. One of the silent servants stood in the hall, and he gestured them to follow him. Mikhail stood up and discovered one of his feet had fallen asleep while he sat. Pins and needles danced in his toes as he bent down and pulled on a pair of soft slippers. They had been provided with comfortable woolen robes as well, and both had been happy to discard their filthy clothing.

"We are finally being summoned."

"I see that—and about time, too!"

The servant, white-faced, placed a finger to his lips, and shook his head, admonishing them to silence. The man was thin to the point of emaciation, and looked terrified. Mikhail ignored him. "How do you feel, my dearest?"

"Up to my neck in kittens. This place is oppressive. No matter how much I sleep, I don't seem to feel rested. I do not feel sick or anything. Actually, if I were to describe my condition, I would say I was very happy for no reason at all." Then she smiled at him. "Well, being married to you is reason enough."

Mikhail chuckled. "If you can feel happy in our present circumstances, *caria*, then you are even more amazing than I thought."

And we better shut up, before that fellow has a fit, Mik.

Fellow? Oh, I had quite forgotten him. You are right. And perhaps now we will discover exactly what is going on. Any flashes of the future?

None I would choose to dwell on—something with fire, and I don't like it one bit!

Fire! That does not sound very promising. I wish I knew why no one talks. I've never known servants who did not want to gossip. And this man's mind is vacant of anything except his immediate task. Mikhail could sense her unspoken anxiety. It must be hell to have flashes of the future with no means of being sure what they meant until it was too late.

Mik, if no one can talk, then they cannot collude. I suspect that without whatever form of repression is being used. Dom *Padriac would have a rebellion on his hands. And I think that Amirya has her hands full, trying to please him and also to complete this devilish work of theirs.*

But how can they work in the screens, then?

I think we are about to find out.

You seem awfully calm about this.

Do I? Well, I am not. But—don't you feel it?

What?

That everything is coming to a head, and soon?

No. All I can say with certainty is that I must be here, and do whatever must be done, whether I like it or not. I don't have any sense of time, just of purpose.

Of course! Now I understand something that has been nagging in my mind for days. I sense time, and you know what we must do. He could feel her burst of emotion, relief and pleasure at finally solving a problem, and something more for which he could find no description. *That is what Varzil meant when he said that we must become one out of two.*

The corridor was filling with men and women who moved like machines with slow, stiff gestures that were disturbing. Their faces were empty of any feeling, and Mikhail did not need telepathy to know that these poor wretches had no volition.

Mikhail felt his anger stir, then found Marguerida's hand on his arm, squeezing.

Try to look stupid, Mik, or we will end up back in that room.

What do you mean?

Amirya and Padriac keep these folk in thrall so they cannot sabotage the work. That's why she hasn't taken us up sooner—she wanted to be sure we had eaten enough drugged foot to be nice and docile.

Docile? You?

Its a good thing you thought to smuggle what we did not eat into the privy! I would have tried to hide it under the bed, and probably we would have some vermin for companions by now.

Very likely.

These poor people are like a bunch of zombies.

Zombies? I don't know that word.

Revenants, Mik. Walking dead, and from the look of them, dead is the operative word. I want to help them, to heal what ails them. My hand is itching to get to work, and it is very unpleasant! But we had better look meek and dumb, until we get into the upper part of the Tower. Come on—tonight is the night, I hope!

They went through a door, and began to climb a narrow stairwell. There was no sound except the shuffling of slippered feet on stone, and an occasional moan from one of the people. The woman ahead of Mikhail halted once, leaned against the wall, and gasped. Then she looked at him with dull but anguished eyes.

Marguerida leaned around him and looked at the woman sharply. Then she moved her left hand quickly, making a clawing motion in the air before the stranger. The woman jumped as if jolted, her eyes brightening a little. Something like a smile played across her wan lips, and she shook her head as if to clear it. Then she dropped back into a defeated posture and began to climb again. Only a slight vigor in her steps betrayed the change.

The pungent scent of ozone grew more apparent as they ascended. Mikhail glanced at his wife, but for once the nearness of many matrixes did not appear to be disturbing to her. Indeed, she had a look about her that suggested she was able to endure the environment as she never had at Arilinn.

Three floors up they came to an enormous chamber that gleamed with matrix screens, larger than anything Mikhail had ever seen. The room almost trembled with energy, and his first impression was of enormous power. On closer examination, Mikhail noticed that the screens were full of weaknesses, flaws in the crystal, and the sorts of misalignments that would have driven any technician to tears.

Amirya was waiting, standing in the center of the room, her lower lip gnawed raw, and her eyes narrowed to pinpricks. There were dark circles around those eyes, as if she had not slept in several days, and her hands were clenched. Her will seemed to be all that was keeping her from collapsing, and he had a moment of pity for her. Then he looked at the sick *leroni* waiting around her, their hands limp against their sides, and it vanished. He could almost smell her fear.

The west screen is malfunctioning again. Fix it!

Two of the benumbed *leroni* shuffled across the floor, dragging their feet. He could sense them resisting, in spite of their drugged minds. The woman Marguerida had helped on the stairs gave them a swift glance, and just the hint of a smile. He wondered if there was any way his wife could help the others in the same way, without Amirya becoming aware of it. A plan started to rise in his mind.

He watched the two, a man and the woman from the stairs, approach the screen. They both pulled on thick gauntlets, their movement clumsy. They looked at the screen, and then the woman did something he could not quite see. When she turned, she had a large matrix stone in her hands.

Amirya cursed in a hissing whisper, as if her control were ready to snap completely. *No, no! Fix it, I said!*

Domna, this crystal is cracked.

It was not cracked last night! Even in the mind, her words rang shrill, on the edge of hysteria. *We must finish the mining tonight!*

Domna, the crystal is ruined.

Amirya flew across and struck the woman across the face, screaming with frustration. Then the room was very quiet. The woman recovered a little, grew calmer. *Replace the crystal!*

Domna, we have nothing to use. There was a dullness in the reply, a lack of emotion, but Mikhail was certain that this was a ruse. Amirya was too harried and exhausted to notice that the woman was no longer completely helpless.

It looks as if these poor slaves have been doing a little sabotage of their own, Mik.

Yes, I think you are correct. And Amirya's problem is that in order to keep them working meekly, she has to keep them drugged, and drugged people make stupid mistakes. More, she doesn't have the experience to actually direct a circle—notice that the others are just standing around like dummies. She is on the edge of losing control—now, how we use that to advantage?

Poor Amirya. The expression on Marguerida's face was compassionate, but there was a light in her eyes that was cold and terrible. Mikhail hoped she would never turn that gaze on him, for it was terrifying, and more, there was something quite impersonal in it. He knew that she would do whatever she had to, and worry about the consequences later.

He decided that while Amirya was distracted, he should map out this chamber, and one he sensed beyond a closed door. These had been so well shielded that he had not been able to penetrate them during his earlier mental excursions, and he realized that if the poor Keeper had not been forced by circumstances to bring them up, he never would have had the opportunity at all. She was afraid of them, and would likely have let them molder in their room until it was too late.

I don't suppose you have any great ideas how to proceed. Can you see that stuff in the next room?

What stuff? Oh, that. I can only see it through you, but it looks like some low-grade uranium, I think. Well, something radioactive anyhow. I have no idea if there is uranium on Darkover. Do you? No wonder Amalie was having fits. This is bad, very bad, because there is no safe way to get rid of it that I know of. I am not even close to being a nuclear engineer, Mik.

Can't it be . . . changed?

Changed? Hmm. In theory, any element can be transformed into something else, but the amount of energy it takes is beyond human reach. I seem to remember something about being able to turn lead into gold, which was the dream of the alchemists, long ago, with nuclear materials. Which does not help at all. I can't work at subatomic levels—can you?

I might, if I had a dozen years to study my matrix.

If we had a rocket, we could send it into the sun. Mikhail knew Marguerida was trying to keep her own spirits up, but he could feel the sense of despair that was beginning to eat at her. She was frightened of the glowing stuff in the other chamber, and he was almost glad that his ignorance kept him from sharing her fear completely.

And if we had wings, we could fly away!

They both fell silent, watching the miserable *leroni* perform tasks with sullen clumsiness. Their minds might be overshadowed, but something of their wills remained, or they would not be able to work at all, Mikhail realized. Amirya had to leave them enough volition to function, and he thought that keeping that balance was taxing her to the utmost.

The man and woman at the west screen had put down the damaged crystal, and were lifting another one from a box. The man grunted, shifted his weight abruptly, and the large stone fell to the floor, shattering into several large chunks. Then the weary man looked up, glanced at Mikhail, and he saw a momentary flash in the sad eyes, a gleam of rebellion. It was gone almost as quickly as it had appeared, and he looked down at the ruined stone, seeming surprised.

The Keeper turned and screeched. Mikhail moved across the chamber, his legs carrying him without any conscious thought. He reached Amirya, and balled his fist. Then he brought it up in a swift motion, and caught her chin against his knuckles.

Amirya staggered for a second, then went down in a heap of garments. Mikhail stood over her unconscious form, struggling with conflicting feelings. He experienced a profound satisfaction. She had not been expecting a physical assault, only those of *laran*. And she had assumed him drugged into servility. He shook his hand hard. It had hurt!

The atmosphere in the room shifted. The *leroni* stirred, restless and bewildered. Their dull eyes regarded Mikhail, and one grizzled fellow started into a slow grin. "Now, why did none of us think of that?" he asked in a gruff voice.

One woman collapsed, and another started to vomit. The man who had spoken shook himself, as if trying to rise above the drugs in his body, to free himself of them. But the others just stood, helpless and exhausted. And from their silence, he suspected they were afraid of him and Marguerida, too.

Marguerida—we have to get them functioning.

Yes, we must. You take that man that dropped the crystal, and I'll start on the woman.

Mikhail stepped over the unconscious Keeper, and walked over to the man beside the screen. He was a little afraid, for while he had learned how to clear Marguerida, he had never done any healing on another person. She had her own matrix to protect her, and he was concerned that he might kill the man with intended kindness. Still, it had to be done, and quickly.

He lifted his hand slowly, and felt warmth begin to pulse along his muscles. Marguerida had told him as well as she could how it felt to clear him back in the deserted kitchen, and he could only hope he had understood her. A flush of well-being coursed along his veins, and he felt as if he glowed. Then he extended his hand and tried to perceive the man's own distinct energy, tried to mesh with it. It was very difficult, and he could feel sweat popping out on his forehead. He did not know the man as he knew his wife.

All his awareness narrowed to a single point, and he channeled energy through it. It felt peculiar, and he wanted to pull away. It was intimate, more so than working in a circle, and with a complete stranger, it aroused something distasteful in him. Then he realized it was too much like sex for his own liking. Mikhail had never been with a male, and had never wished to be.

Then he felt a surge from himself, and the man gasped. His pale face went rosy, and he gave Mikhail a look that spoke volumes. He must have felt the same way—it was not rape, but close enough to it to be embarrassing.

"Whoever you are, thank you. I am Davil Syrtis."

"What should we do about *her*," asked the woman Marguerida had helped. "I'd like to break her neck," she added viciously, "but killing is almost too good for her."

"Now, Betha—hasn't there been enough killing?"

"She let my sister Clarinda die of burns," Betha replied, baring her teeth. "And she kept us here, pulling up that dreadful yellowstone, and did not care if we lived or died. She is a monster."

"Amirya is a problem, but not the greatest one." It was the gruff man who had spoken before. Marguerida was just stepping away from him, and had apparently done some quick work. "We are trapped here, and we have to escape. And we cannot leave the yellowstone just sitting in there—because it is too dangerous." He looked at Mikhail, then at Marguerida. "I hope you have not gotten us out of the cook-pot and into the fire, strangers."

The woman called Betha feebly chuckled. "Don't mind Marius—he always looks on the dark side. But, what are we going to do?" She put a hand to her forehead. "My mind feels as if it was stuffed with Dry Town cotton, and not the finest sort either! Ever since they dragged us here from Hali, they have been giving us something filthy. Some *aphrosone,* and something else, too. But she found out we could not really work with it—it made us too stupid to be useful! So there has been less of it, but I still feel . . . feeble-minded!" There was no mistaking the outrage in her voice, and the way in which she looked at the unconscious Keeper did not bode well for Amirya.

Mikhail hesitated now, still discomforted by his healing of Davil. These folk were looking to him and Marguerida for rescue, and they did not have a plan. He felt the stirring of his doubting self, his un-loved shadow, so full of despair. Would he ever be free of his fears? What could they do? They were both younger than several of the men, and most of the women. They were out of place and out of time, and both now had powers they had not learned to use completely. But they must not fail these people. Somehow, they had to think of a way to save them and themselves as well.

Mikhail forced himself to focus. He started checking off on his fingers. "We have to neutralize Amirya, destroy the screens completely, and get rid of that yellowstone. And escape from here." He added the last, but he despaired of reaching that stage.

Marius cackled. "We can hardly stand up unassisted. She has kept us weak, even though she needed us to be strong enough to work."

"What manner of *laran* is this?" Davil asked. "Are you a healer or an angel?"

Before Mikhail could think of a reply, he noticed the flutter of Amirya's eyelids. Her hand moved toward the starstone dangling between her breasts. The gesture was one he had seen before, and Mikhail had a sense of his own fate so strong it nearly made him sick. He had prepared for this moment without ever guessing it. If he had never met Emelda, he could not do what he must.

Mikhail swallowed his revulsion as he reached out and took the leather thong in his fingers. For a second Amirya's eyes met his, pleading, demanding. There was a brief struggle of wills as his hand closed around the narrow leather and pity warred with fury within him. She was very young and foolish, but he could not let that stop him. Then he yanked the lace sharply, and felt it give between his fingers.

Amirya gave a thin cry, a wailing note of despair, and slipped back to the floor. Her eyes rolled back in her head, showing the whites, and then her entire body began to convulse. Sickened by what he had done, Mikhail could only stand over her, the matrix dangling from his hand, hating himself and knowing he had had no choice.

"Why do you weep for that creature?" Davil's question brought him back, and to his surprise, he found that tears were running down his face.

"I don't know," Mikhail replied, wiping away the wetness with his sleeve. And he did not, for his feelings were almost overwhelming. He had to get himself calmed down, and quickly. Later, when they were away from this hateful place, he would curse himself and Varzil and fate. But not now.

"It is no worse than she has done to us," Marius muttered bitterly.

Betha had turned toward one of the working screens, while Marguerida continued her way around the circle of workers, clearing their drug-drenched cells. Mikhail watched Betha, who was probably a mechanic, study the screen knowledgeably. Then she began to displace the crystals, working with care, the thick gloves impeding her efforts. One of the men who had not spoken yet joined her after Marguerida had done her work, and between them they had the screen disabled quite quickly.

Mikhail was still extremely upset, and he felt remote and distant from the movements of people around him. He tried to bring himself back to the task at hand, knowing that what he had done to Amirya was actually the easiest item on his list, and dismantling the screens, in the hands of competent technicians, was not very difficult. But the hard parts lay ahead, and he almost despaired.

What could he do about the yellowstone? And how were they going to escape this dreadful place? Ten exhausted *leroni* were no match for the barrack full of armsmen he had discovered in his mental wanderings, even with Marguerida's restorative abilities.

He shook himself, forcing his fears down in his mind. These people were looking to him for leadership, and he was sure none of them guessed how inadequate he was for the task. Mikhail realized he must risk it, that he must be cunning as he had never been in his life. *Laran* was all very well and good, but this needed something more—like a hundred mounted men attacking the keep. He laughed at himself a little.

"That room beyond—I can sense yellowstone in it. How is it contained?"

Mikhail found Davil looking at him with interest. "There are screens in it, holding the stone in place, but it still leaks, and we have lost several people from the poison of it. No one, not even the woman," he said gesturing toward Amirya, "can enter it without hazard, and we all feared the day when it will exceed the power of the screens to hold it safely."

"So you worked from this room to draw the stuff from the earth?"

"Exactly."

Marguerida, will fire destroy . . . whatever it is?

Hardly. I suspect it must be low-grade uranium, which is a yellow ore, if I remember correctly. I suppose we ought to be grateful it is not radioactive cobalt, which is even nastier. I am stunned that anyone would think they could play with this stuff safely.

Yes. What about compressing it?

Bad idea. The only thought I can come up with is reinforcing the stasis field that already surrounds it—and I have no clue as to how one might do that. I mean, when they put Dio into stasis, Uncle Jeff tried to explain the process to me, but I confess I did not really grasp the concept. Like so much about laran, there was a great deal I did not understand.

I wish we could just send it back where it came from.

We should have thought about that before they started dismantling the screens.

Damn!

Marguerida had finished her work now, and looked rather pleased with herself. She had a slight sheen on her brow, and her curls were damp against her pale skin. He watched her sit down on a low bench close to the wall and draw her mitt back on, apparently unaware of the uneasy glances she was getting from the people she had just aided.

She went into the trance state he was now familiar with, her face empty of all expression, her eyes hooded. What she saw when she entered this state of mind he could only guess, but he trusted her to know what she was doing. And he felt himself become calm as he watched her, his own roiling emotions flowing away.

After perhaps a minute she straightened her back, and the empty look vanished. Her gaze was lucid and golden. *It's about time!*

It's about time you figured out the answer?

No. Time is the answer.

I don't understand—if time is the answer, what is the question?

Sorry, Mik. I don't mean to be obscure, but this is very hard to explain. I don't have the vocabulary, and neither do you. All I can say is that we have to think of a way to remove that yellowstone from this present—and where or when it will go I cannot think.

You are not making a whole lot of sense, caria.

I know. It is something to do with the nature of my shadow matrix. In a sense, this pattern is neither here nor there. I mean, it is part of the overworld and part of the material world at the same time. And Varzil said time is something I can. . . . manipulate. I wish I had been able to manipulate more time with him! But if his words mean anything, and they must, then my peculiar ability is to be able to fiddle with time.

That's a big assumption, caria.

Yes, it is, and I would not be making it, if I had not done the healings I have.

Now I am really lost—what does the healing have to do with time.

Everything! Damn, this is difficult! It is not just clearing channels— that is the mechanical part. The real healing comes from the memory of wellness, for getting the body back into a time when it was fit.

Mikhail weighed this idea. He remembered how Marguerida had helped him through the matrix shock, and realized that it was almost exactly as she had just said. He just could not see how this had anything to do with the problem of disposing of the filthy stuff in the adjoining chamber.

"Is there, nearby, a Forbidden Place?" Looks of incomprehension met Marguerida's question for a moment. Then Davil nodded slowly.

"To the west, about ten miles, I would guess, there is an old glow, where one dares not go. It is a small one, and there are things growing around the edges of it that are very strange."

"Ten miles." Marguerida looked very thoughtful. Then she shook her head. *I wish I had been able to pay better attention to my matrix mechanics class at Arilinn. Or that I was telekinetic—not that I want more* laran, *but it would be useful.*

Mikhail watched her, admiring her steadiness. The room grew very quiet, as if the *leroni* knew that something was going on that demanded silence. He waited for her to continue.

Suddenly he felt as if someone had grabbed the back of his neck and thrust his head downward. Mikhail stared at the ring glittering on his finger. It danced before his eyes, shifting and changing, the facets shrinking and growing. At one moment, his own smaller matrix was a shadow within the greater one, and then they seemed to change places, and Varzil's was the nearly invisible portion. The effect was dazzing, and his mind quailed. He seemed to lose all sense of himself, of the present, and was lost in the contemplation of the object.

What did he know about Varzil's stone? Mikhail racked his brains. He knew it had been used by a great empath to heal Lake Hali. Those two elements seemed critical, but he could not make any immediate sense out of it. Empathy was the Ridenow Gift, and he did not possess it. But that ring had sat on Varzil's hand for most of a century, and perhaps it contained the memory of the *laranzu's* gift.

Memory—Marguerida had said something—ah, the memory of wellness! That was too poetic for him, too magical. Perhaps he was too literal to grasp the implications of it. Yet he had, and quickly.

Time and space and memory. The words belled in his mind, tolling deeply, evoking impressions. He tried to keep a grip on himself, to escape slipping away into the rush of images that passed through his consciousness. If only he could grasp something firmly.

Through time and *space*. Mikhail drew a deep breath. He sensed quickening in his tortured mind, a coalescence of elements, like a picture that was beyond any verbal expression. He stared at the image in his mind, trying to hold it, to force it into his memory. It shimmered, moving around, but at last he felt a certain solidification in it. The sight left him almost faint, for it was an awesome construct. And he had no idea what to do with it, now he had it.

Mikhail lifted his head, and the image remained before his eyes. He stretched his awareness, as he had done in mapping the Tower, toward the room beyond. The shields which had frustrated him earlier now seemed transparent. The stasis which contained the ore was becoming unstable, and, if he did nothing, would fail. But what should he do?

He withdrew his attention. Was there some way to turn the field backward in time, to make it return to a moment when it had contained nothing except space? It did not seem plausible, but his intuition leaped ahead, embracing the idea.

"Marguerida, can you think of some way to move that room—the whole thing—backward in time?"

Mikhail found himself the center of ten pairs of eyes, as the rest of the *leroni* stared at him. It was clear from their expression that they thought he was mad. He was not certain they were wrong. But the sense of sureness persisted, in spite of his doubts. He had to follow his path, let the matrix guide him, and keep his fears from corrupting his purpose.

No, Mik, I can't. Even if we had ten teleports, I don't think it would be possible. Wait! Forget about the damn uranium, and think about the stasis field—about the screens themselves.

The screens? The ones in there are starting to degrade, and will collapse soon, no matter what we do.

Listen to me. Stop worrying about the ore! Matrixes have a temporal function, one that no one has ever explored, unless it was Varzil himself. They must. The larger the matrix, the more time it can contain. That is how Ashara managed to continue on all those centuries—because she found some way to shift in time, and her Tower in the overworld was part of it.

What are you suggesting?

Can we regress those screens—take the time out of them?

Take them out of time . . . ?

No—take the time out of them!

Mikhail was dumbfounded. The image that had formed in his mind returned, and he understood it. The power of it was enormous. He had no idea how to direct it. Then the terror abated, as if someone was drawing it away from him. He could not do it alone, or even with only Marguerida. He would have to depend on the abilities of ten strangers, all of them worn and weary from their imprisonment. How could he direct them, or himself? It was too much to ask of him.

Mikhail clenched his hands, then released them. Cold sweat trickled down his sides. Then he braced himself, took several deep breaths and said, "We will have to create a circle for this, and you will have to trust me. I have never functioned as a Keeper before, but I will have to." Then a smile stretched his mouth. All the knowledge he needed was gleaming on his finger, and all he need do was surrender his will to it.

Davil gave him a hard look. "You have already shown yourself to be able—though we do not even know your name. What do you wish to accomplish?"

"I want to degrade the stasis in the next room, make it go backward, if you will."

"Only Varzil," Marius began, "could do such a thing."

"How do you know that?"

"I was with him when he restored the lake."

"Good." Mikhail was heartened by this, even if Marius looked very dubious. "Can you tell me precisely what he did?"

"No. He understands time, and he . . . well, it is hard to say." The older man gnawed his lower lip for a moment. "He turned it backward, it seemed to me. Ah, now I see what you mean. You think if you can turn that room backward . . . yes, that might even work. Or we could all get killed trying it."

"That is always a possibility," Mikhail admitted, facing the fear that ate at him. "It is that or leave that stuff here, for *Dom* Padriac to use, or try to use."

"I don't think he can do much without his sister, but there is a chance he might find another to do his bidding." Marius glared at the woman on the floor. The rise and fall of her breast showed she was alive, but only barely. Then he raised his shadowed eyes to Mikhail. "But, before we begin, who are you? You have called her Marguerida, but *who* are you?" The older man looked stubborn.

Mikhail was aghast. He had not realized he spoke her name. He felt his belly clench again, and realized that he stood at some sort of crux in time, in history as it would be remembered if any of the *leroni* survived. If only he had a clue to what to call himself now. All the names he had tried with Marguerida seemed wrong. It had to be something that sounded right, but it could not be the name of a person who had lived in that time.

He started to open his mouth, and was suddenly caught in a fragment of memory, of the words of his dream. Mikhalangelo, Varzil had called him. That man was dead. And a part of history, "Call me Angelo," he said at last.

Marguerida's eyes widened, and he saw her throat twitch with swallowed laughter. *Really, Mik! How could you?*

Well, I am one of the Lanart Angels, my darling.

Lanart devils is more like.

"Very well," Marius said cautiously, as if he knew he was being lied to, but decided it was not worth pursuing.

The *leroni* began to settle into a circle, their training asserting itself in spite of their fatigue and the questions which troubled their minds. Mikhail watched them arrange themselves, and was deeply moved by their courage and willingness to accept his leadership. And he could not help but wonder what they would remember afterward, and what they would say. There was, to his limited knowledge, no Angelo mentioned in history, nor any Marguerida either. But so many records had been destroyed, there might well have been a dozen.

The courage and trust of the *leroni* heartened Mikhail. He could feel his own doubts begin to fall aside as the room grew quiet. He hoped he would not falter, that he could trust his own intuition as they were trusting him, and bring all of them out of this dangerous situation without harm.

Mikhail stood very still. He could sense the people around him bringing their various energies into focus, and, without any direction, he knew Marguerida had posted herself to monitor the circle. It was the best possible use of her powers, and he relaxed slightly.

Then he stared into his matrix. He felt himself draw their powers together in a network. Mikhail started to strain to order the energies, and encountered immediate resistance. Was he wrong? It had been easier and clearer a few moments before. Then he realized that he must let his will step back, and allow the knowledge within his matrix to guide him. He was only a vessel, a vehicle to harness minds and spirits to a single purpose. The sensation was one of great power, but with it a tremendous humility, an awe at what he was about to do.

The circle ceased to be individuals as the power increased. He could sense Marguerida, moving from person to person, balancing the energy, keeping everyone focused. The image he had seen earlier began to reform in his mind. It seemed a field of sparks, little motes of brilliance in darkness. It wavered, then solidified again.

Mikhail bent everything he possessed into holding that image steady, knowing that this was his task. He forgot about everything except the pattern of lights.

His sense shifted, and he knew that something was about to happen. Time flowered, blossoming in his cells. He peered at the pattern in his mind. All the little twinkles seemed identical, but he knew that one held the key. He stared at each light in turn, until he felt as if his eyes were dazzled.

A sickening terror gripped him. He was not strong enough, he was not ready for this! He was not skilled enough even to guide himself. The image shivered in his mind's eye, and he forced his will back again. Let the matrix do the work, he tried to tell himself.

Breath faltered, then heart. Mikhail could feel his body start to die. Then he was steadied, and air once more flowed into his lungs. His heart pounded as he drove himself back into the pattern. There it was! It was just a dart of light, identical to all the others, and yet he knew it was what he sought.

Mikhail stared at that spark. The others began to fade as he looked, and he waited, knowing that he must, without knowing why. All the dazzling bits had paled into insignificance except the one. Eternity encompassed him, and the matrix held him unmoving within it.

What now? Mikhail waited in an endless moment. Then, with a delicacy that seemed impossible, he reached out and gave it the tiniest push.

The spark trembled, then seemed to move very fast, speeding away from his view into nothingness. He heard a terrible roar, the sound of stones cracking. Someone screamed. And his body was his again, and it was he who was howling, great raw sounds pouring from his mouth. Mikhail slipped to the cold floor, almost insensate.

His body felt like ice, and his head throbbed. Then he heard a familiar voice crow with jubilation. *"You did it!"*

33

A chaos of voices surrounded him. Mikhail wanted to tell them to be quiet, but his throat hurt terribly, and his tongue felt too large for his mouth. All he managed was a feeble moan of protest.

Marguerida bent over him, her eyes enormous. Then her hand moved over his body, sweeping away some of the anguish in his muscles. He felt firm hands on his shoulders, supporting him not very gently. Mikhail looked behind him and found Davil. "Did it work?" His voice croaked like a crow.

"Yes, but don't ask me how. It was the most remarkable . . ."

"We have to get out of this place right now," one of the other announced. "The stasis chamber exploded—it is sure to collapse any moment, and that will bring the roof down. We will have guards here in a flash and that bitch of *Dom* Padriac's as well.

As Davil and Jonathan helped Mikhail to his feet, he heard Marguerida ask, "Who?"

"Leonora, the *dom's leronis.*"

"Damn. I had forgotten all about her—we need a distraction."

"There is something I can do," Betha said grimly, her eyes narrowing to slits. "Even though it goes against the grain, and I swore I would never do this again." She looked troubled, uncertain, but determined all the same.

Everything was happening too quickly, and Mikhail knew that his part was over for now. Still, he wanted to hold on, to help in some way. What an idiot he was—he could hardly stand on his own two feet! Mikhail watched Betha look down at her matrix stone and focus. She shuddered all over, and there was a deep sound somewhere in the keep, a booming noise that shook the stones around them.

What the . . . ?

Betha's a firestarter, Angelo, but I do fear she has overdone it a bit.

Davil was supporting Mikhail, who swallowed hard and winced at the pain of just standing. This was a very rare *laran,* and one to be feared, for it often consumed its creators. He had never actually encountered anyone who possessed it, and he glanced at Betha with unease.

Everyone started for the stairwell. Marguerida slipped her shoulder under Mikhail's arm and Davil released his hold as the sound of explosions continued. Mikhail kept one hand on the wall of the stairs and the other around his wife. Despite Marguerida's efforts, he still felt disoriented. He was afraid that they were going get burned alive.

At the bottom of the stairs, they could hear shouts and the dreaded crackle of a fire raging. It seemed to be on the other side of the entry door, so they turned down the corridor. There was another boom, and the stones around them shook. Then there was a cracking noise, and the ceiling above them began to tremble. With Davil supporting Mikhail's other side, they raced along the corridor past their rooms as the ceiling began to collapse behind them, great and small blocks of masonry tumbling down on all sides.

The door at the end of the corridor was closed, and Mikhail knew it was barred from the opposite side. Marius pulled at the knob, his face twisting with frustration. Now they were all crowded together, trying to escape the falling debris. There were screams, and shouts. A rafter crashed down, catching one of the men on the shoulder.

Marius was white and panicky now, and Mikhail could see him scrabble at the wood of the door, clawing it with his long fingers. It was futile. The door had been solidly built, intended to keep people in or out. Marguerida leaned against him, and he could sense her mind racing. She narrowed her eyes to slits, her expression grim. Then he heard the bar pulled back.

The door swung back. One of the silent servants stared at them. He did not try to stand in their way, but just remained there, looking dull-witted. He glanced at Marguerida. She must have used the Alton

Gift to compel the man to open the door. Then there was the sound of another explosion, and no more time to think. They raced through the next corridor, and the man who had opened the door followed behind them.

The huge kitchen was almost deserted. One of the servants rose from the hearth, looking very puzzled. The whole building was quaking around them.

One of the *leroni* urged the servant ahead with little shooing gestures. They started for the door of the kitchen. Mikhail knew, from his explorations of the past few days, that it opened into a small courtyard that backed on the stables. They entered the space, into a world of flickering orange light and billows of black smoke. Sparks filled the air, and he could hear the voices of men shouting for water. The smoke made his lungs ache, and horses neighed frantically. There was another smell, an acrid stench he recognized. Explosives! That bone-rattling boom a few minutes before must have been the armory going up.

They rushed into the stable, and everyone pulled open stall doors as they fled down the length of it. The horses were frantic, but the presence of humans seemed to calm them a little, and only a few reared dangerously. It was a frightening experience, but he was strengthened by adrenalin and when he found his big gelding, he grabbed the hackamore on his muzzle, and dragged the large animal along with him.

Mikhail looked for Marguerida then, and found her on his heels, her face white and strained. With a quick movement, he pulled himself onto the horse, then leaned down and helped her up behind him. Then he bent low over the horse's long neck, and the steed bolted toward the far end of the stable.

Exiting the barn into the yard where they had arrived, they were surrounded by terrified, hysterical animals, guards in various states of undress, and some of the *leroni*. A few had managed to duplicate Mikhail's feat and were mounted, and he could see Marius and Betha pulled up behind him. But it was too chaotic for him to count people, and he kneed his horse through two staring guards, who only jumped aside at the last second.

Beside him, a horse reared and struck out at one of the men, screaming with panic. He pulled the gelding aside, cursing the clumsiness of the hackamore, and risked a glance over his shoulder. Marguerida was clinging to him, holding him tightly around the waist, her huge eyes reflecting the orange lights of flames. What remained of the top floor of the Tower blew at that moment, releasing the energy remaining in the matrix screens in a blast that shook the earth and nearly knocked them both off the animal.

The shock wave sucked the air from their lungs, and then it struck the second tower. There was a great thunder of falling stonework, and the ground trembled beneath the horse. Mikhail's only thought was to escape while they could. He headed toward the high wall that surrounded the keep, aware of the *leroni* around him, but so focused on the task of keeping his horse steady that he was not certain everyone had escaped.

Several figures ran toward him, and he caught the flash of swords in the ruddy glow of the fire. He saw the slender face of *Dom* Padriac among them, his features twisted with rage. He ran straight at Mikhail's horse, clearly intending to skewer the animal, and Mikhail barely managed to pull the horse aside before he did.

Dom Padriac turned gracefully, and Mikhail yanked at the horse's mouth, trying to escape the sweep of the sword. He felt the tip of it whisper past his soft slippers, and wished he were not weaponless. With two riders, the gelding lacked the power to move quickly, and he knew that the unmounted man actually had a small advantage.

Davil seemed to appear from nowhere and charged toward their attacker. He lifted something oblong and brought it down on *Dom* Padriac's skull, a glancing blow. Mikhail saw it was a rolling pin, from the kitchen. How ignominious, he thought, elated.

Dom Padriac staggered, and his knees buckled slightly. Then he shook his head, regripped his sword more firmly, and headed toward Mikhail again, shouting something he as he did. In the roar of the fire, and the screaming of the animals, his words were lost.

There was a rush of wind past Mikhail's head, and something dark flew into *Dom* Padriac's face. In the flare of the fire, Mikhail saw the sea crow dig its talons into the proud face, then pierce an eye with its sharp beak. *Dom* Padriac's words turned to incoherent shrieks, and he clawed at the crow with his free hand, then brought his sword up in a sweep of metal. It caught the great sea crow across the rise of its wings, and even in the poor light, Mikhail could see a line of blood appear on the black feathers.

The crow fluttered, struggling. He heard a rough caw, and saw the great talons sink into the throat of *Dom* Padriac El Haliene, piercing the flesh. Blood spurted out, gushing over the dying bird. For a moment, *Dom* Padriac remained standing. His hand closed around the crow and pulled it free, dropping it onto the now blood-slicked stones at his feet. He stared at Mikhail and Marguerida from his remaining eye, gurgled, and fell headlong beside the dead bird.

Mikhail felt heartsick at the loss of his avian friend. He forced himself to pay attention to the men milling nearby, to the *leroni* who were grouping themselves around him, like some honor guard. He turned the gelding toward the gate again, and saw the guards hesitate at the sight of their dead liege.

Then there was another rumble of collapsing masonry, and the fire seemed to enlarge and consume the remaining floors. One man, more clearheaded than the rest, turned to his fellows and said, "Let's get out of this accursed placed. Open the gates!"

"But, Raol," another protested.

"The *dom* is dead—we are finished here! Do you want to die, Fredrik?"

Several of the men did not wait to hear his answer, but ran to the huge gate and began to slip back the great wooden bar. They pulled the gate back with ropes, and pushed through it without a backward glance. Mikhail breathed a lungful of smoky air, and then kneed the gelding. He coughed a little as he went beneath the arch of the gate, and into the flickering darkness.

The night was cloudcast, and a little chilly, but Mikhail decided he had never seen a lovelier night. Wearing only a woolen robe intended for indoors, cloakless, he could feel the pleasant warmth of Marguerida's body pressed against him. He could almost make out the heavy scent of trees, as he started to urge the horse forward, with the others around him. There was a silence between them, as the sounds of destruction continued.

They rode for several minutes, and Mikhail had no idea which direction they were going. He was very tired now, and sad as well. The crow was dead. It had saved him for the last time. Depression began to eat away at his earlier elation. Then he felt Marguerida's grip tighten on his flat stomach.

Mik—there is someone following us.

Friend or foe?

I think it is that little woman—Leonora?—and she is very angry. They are not very far behind either.

Just then Davil spoke. "We are being pursued. It looks as if the old woman managed to save her blasted riders. They would follow her into hell itself. She always was a tough one." There was a kind of grudging admiration in the words.

"Who is she?" Marguerida asked.

"The *dom*'s mother, *Domna* Leonora. She was too old to become a Keeper when the Lord of Hali organized his Tower, too old and already a mother as well. But ambitious nonetheless, they say."

"We are no match for armed men," Marius complained. There was an undertone of fear in his voice, as if he kept his terror at bay by will alone.

"No, we aren't," Mikhail agreed. "But she must be mad if she thinks she can . . ."

"Crazy and cunning, *Dom* Angelo. My father always said it would have been better if she had been a man, not a woman, and he should know, being her younger brother and all." Davil gave a slight shrug in the dimness. "She was a wild girl, and grew into a strange woman, he said. Full of hatred, because my grandfather married her off to *Dom* Rakhal El Haliene, who was mean and passed his meanness on to his son."

What should he do? Mikhail felt the exhaustion of the past few hours envelop him. He was too weary and sad for this. He tried to summon up some energy, but felt only his own emptiness. He needed rest, and a place to hide himself and Marguerida.

Go to the Lake, my son.

The Lake?

Hali will conceal you.

The command rang in his mind firm and comforting. He could not imagine how Lake Hali might conceal him, but he did not question the voice in his mind. Instead, Mikhail felt a vast relief that he did not have to make any decision at all for the present.

Mikhail cleared his still raw throat. "I think it best if we split up. They will have a harder time if they are trying to follow several parties instead of one."

Davil was looking at Mikhail. "That will be fine for us, but she is looking for you, Angelo."

"Then we will just have to trust she will not catch us. She will regret it if she does."

"No doubt." Davil hesitated. "Very well. We will split up—I will take some of us to the north, and Marius can take the others to the south. Which group will you join?"

"Neither, Davil. Here we part ways forever. I have been honored to have met all of you, but I have another path which I must follow." He spoke with more confidence than he felt.

Davil looked a little sad, and so did several of the other *leroni*. But he nodded, accepting the decision. "Fare thee well, Angelo—or whoever you may be! You are well-named!" Then he flashed a grin in the darkness, his white teeth gleaming, and began to reorganize the *leroni* into two groups.

Mikhail kneed the gelding ahead. He had his bearings now, and he could just see the faintest glimmer of the rising sun on the horizon, coloring the clouds a delicate pink. A soft rain started to fall, and as they rode away, the wind rose a bit. The rain began to soak their robes, and he shivered. The pink dawn was all gray now.

Mikhail felt Marguerida's head rest against his back, her fingers laced around his middle. He could feel her healing shadow matrix lapping though him, refreshing and invigorating. The horse was moving at a decent pace, considering the weight of two riders, and he knew he could not force the animal to go any faster. He breathed the clean air and waited for the sound of hoofbeats behind him.

The bloody sun had just edged above the distant horizon when he finally heard them, and he could see the banks of the lake ahead of him, cloaked in rosy mist. It was not far, but he urged the tired horse on, and saw the mist creeping toward him. The gelding gave a grunt, then moved into a laboring canter. The noise of several horses drew nearer and nearer.

"There they are! Get them!" It was the shrill voice of a woman.

The gelding stumbled and went down. Mikhail rolled free with Marguerida still clinging to him, then stumbled to his feet as he saw the first of the riders racing toward him. It was one of the identical constructs who had captured them, silent and utterly expressionless.

Mikhail pulled Marguerida to her feet, and they stood together a moment. Then she pushed herself free, swallowed hard, and gave an eerie vocalization that made his blood run cold. The oncoming horse jerked and reared, dumping its rider on the ground and then dashed away into the few trees that grew near the lake.

Two more riders appeared, and then they saw Leonora, clutching the pommel of a saddle, riding astride and looking both determined and frightened. She had smuts of ash all over her round face, and her hair was draggled. Her eyes were huge, and her mouth a maw of fury.

Marguerida repeated her strange call, and the closest horses balked. One threw its rider overhead, and the other reared and sent the man slamming into the high back of the saddle. The horse that *Domna* Leonora was riding screamed and twisted its head, as if something was hurting it.

The woman pulled herself off the horse, dropped to the ground with a soft thump, and flew at them, her hands before her. Mikhail could sense the force of her personality, even at the distance separating them. Something tried to seize his mind, but it was like the buzzing of a gnat.

Marguerida stiffened beside him. He sensed that they were engaged in a silent battle of wills. It took him an instant to realize that he was watching two women with the Alton Gift of forced rapport come head to head.

Domna Leonora halted, looking startled. She gave a little huff, and squared her drooping shoulders, then closed her eyes. At the same moment, he saw a slow smile spread across Marguerida's face, and he had the oddest feeling that she was actually enjoying herself. Her golden eyes sparkled in the early morning light.

Then *Domna* Leonora staggered, and went down on her bottom, into a small puddle behind her. Her eyes snapped open and one of the armsmen urged his horse forward. His face was so blank that Mikhail could not guess what he expected to do.

"Come on—run!"

Marguerida's voice snapped him out of contemplation, and he felt her hand clasp his. He turned and bent his stiff and tired legs, then started to run. She was beside him, panting but keeping pace. Behind them he could hear Leonora screaming with fury.

The mist of the lake coiled around them, tendrils of moisture like soft fingers, touching his already wet skin as they crossed some invisible boundary. Lake Hali embraced them, drew them into her depths, into silence and stillness, and an utter emptiness.

He floated, floated. He had come a great distance, so great he could not remember where he began. Nothing existed here. Not even himself—nameless and placeless.

There was only a vast longing. It stung him, and a mote of something seemed to stir in the nothingness. What was it? He longed for light or darkness—anything but this void. The spark expanded, but it could not divide the endless emptiness.

A heat passed through him. If he could just hold it, name it. . . . Anger? The word was without meaning there. It belonged in another place. He belonged in another place. But where? The heat passed, and he floated in the void, waiting for release, empty within. It was so still. So still. . . .

Was that a sound? He tried to sense it, but it was gone. A tremor ruffled his emptiness, a presence penetrated it, piercing him through and through.

The void released its hold, and fury ripped across it. There was a voice speaking, a deep rumble. He listened without hearing, feeling words that lacked meaning cover him, smother him.

There is nothing here, not even . . . who am I? Alone. No time, no place, no one else . . . alone. But there should be someone, or some-

thing, if only . . . remember. Time and space and memory. No meaning.

Shifting, something is shifted. Movement changes—no, not that. What? Ah, yes. Feeling stuff. A word—gone, all gone. Need to catch . . . Catch? Grab? Seize? Clutch? What are those? What am I?

Better, now. Stay hot! Burn! Flames! Surge to . . . where? What? No where to go. Only here, meaningless here. Drifting beyond meaning. I WANT—

Spinning in emptiness, no direction, no point, hopeless, loss, FEAR! Clenching fear! Hold, hold! Cold fear brings brightness! Slipping away. So hard. Running out of time! What is time? Where is time? Wrongness? Rightness?

Where am I? Where is . . . Other? Other? What is that? Missing piece . . . of what? Self? Self is Other? Nothing but sparkles, motes of nothing.

GIVE IT BACK! Give me back myself!

Alone, alone, alone. Heat gone, cold gone. Sparkles gone. Calling to sparkles. Silence.

What's that? The silence stirs. Where? Terrible noise—find terrible noise! Seek! Seize!

Mikhail felt himself wrenched into air, cold and clammy, and found a hand in his, holding so tight it ground something into his finger. It was painful. Something was squeezing his hand, and something else was hauling at his collar! Someone was trying to kill him!

He gasped and began to struggle feebly. Then he felt himself pull away, and there was a rock in his hand. He closed his fingers around it and started to lift it, but there was no strength in his arms. He tried to twist free, but he was too weak.

"Dammit, Mik!" Something gripped his shoulders and shook him hard. His teeth chattered.

"Ouch! Stop that!" He peered out. There was nothing except a blur at first. Then he saw Marguerida, and everything flooded back. It was an overwhelming rush of memory and emotion, and he retched weakly. Her breath was warm against his cheek, and her hand on his shoulder tingled.

"Hurry!" She dragged him upright, on legs that felt like straws.

"Hurry?"

"Did you leave your brains in the bedamned lake?" She was furious with him, and he could not understand why. There was too much in his head, and all of it was jumbled together.

"What happened?"

"Damned if I know, and we don't have time to discuss it now. Get a grip on yourself! I can't carry you, and we have to hurry!"

"Why?" He knew she must be right, but he still felt dazed.

Then he heard voices, men speaking quietly, and the soft whicker of horses. They were not in sight, but close enough. Too close. Hadn't they escaped?

Then the fear came back, so strong it nearly drove him to his knees. Mikhail shivered, trembled, and wanted to weep. *She* was going to catch him! No! He felt a power rush into his limbs, a combination of terror and will. His hand was trembling beneath the ring. He felt a surge from it, bracing. His feet began to move, his legs following, and then suddenly he was dashing across pink grass, toward a gleaming building that stood at the top of a small rise.

He heard himself pant, and felt Marguerida beside him. Mikhail knew his legs were moving, but he had a distinct sense that something else supported him. It was very strong, the presence within him, and he moved quickly.

"There they are! Get them!" It was a woman's voice, sharp and authoritative, and the sound of it nearly made him stumble. He heard Marguerida gasp and cry out.

Hoofbeats thundered, making the earth beneath his feet tremble, and he reached toward the unseen source of his strength. It seemed to pull him along, wrenching at his heart, dragging him forward even as his terror made him want to hesitate.

They came to the white building just as the horsemen were within a few strides of reaching them. Mikhail glanced quickly behind him, saw the men and the woman with them, a small, middle-aged woman with a fixed expression. Their eyes met for only an instant, but it was enough to make his laboring heart skip a beat. Ashara Alton, the creature he had only glimpsed in the overworld, in the flesh. His throat went dry.

Mikhail dragged Marguerida's hand against his chest, and pushed her ahead of him. The building appeared to be quite solid, and he could not see any entrance, but he felt the pull of something, leading him to the right. He shoved the small of her back, urging Marguerida forward, then moved to protect her with his body.

They raced along the round walls, the horses coming nearer. His heart pounded against his ribs, and cold sweat poured from his face. He could smell the heated flesh of the animals. They were not going to make it!

Something boiled up in him at that moment, a sense of fury and outrage. Mikhail turned around, and found one horseman almost upon him. There were more, crowding at them. He roared with rage, lifted his hand without thinking, and released all his pent-up anger in a gesture. It seemed to flow out of his heart and into his hand.

A sheet of brightness rose in front of the riders, and the animals reared and struck at it. He could hear the screams of the horses, and could see men falling from their mounts. There was a smell like lightning, then the stink of singed grass.

Only two riders remained, the woman and one man. The man took one glance, and turned his horse aside. But the woman remained, glaring with frustration as the barrier flared in the darkness. She made a fist and raised it. "I will not let you destroy me!"

Mikhail turned quickly, found Marguerida staring at the woman, frozen with terror. Her face was completely white, and her eyes were empty. Mikhail pulled at her arm, and when she did not move, he threw her over his shoulder. She lay there limply.

Ahead he could feel the veil of the *rhu fead* only a few steps away. And above him, he sensed the four moons conjoining. How? They had not been here long enough . . . how long had they been immersed in the strange waters of Lake Hali? Not now, he scolded himself! Light as she was, Marguerida was a burden, and he forced his feet to move, almost stumbling. He could hear the scream of Ashara behind him, but he concentrated on reaching the portal that promised escape.

The veil shimmered, and Mikhail plunged through it.

34

Cold struck him like a fist, and icy snow stung his face. The indoor robe Mikhail still wore could not keep out the wind. In the darkness he could just make out Marguerida. She was sitting in a drift a few feet away, looking stunned.

Mikhail dragged Marguerida to her feet. She stumbled up, then bent over and vomited in the snow. "I hate time travel," she hissed through chattering teeth."

"Come on. We have to find some shelter."

"Where?"

"If we are back where we began, there will be an inn near the ruins of the Tower." Mikhail hoped his assumption was correct, because he did not know what he would do if they had ended up in another time or another place. He just hugged Marguerida against him and started walking, keeping the wind to his back.

In just a few minutes the soft slippers he was wearing were coated with ice, and he was colder than he had ever been in his life. His breath came in short gasps, and it was all he could do to keep moving. Marguerida pressed against him, silent in her misery, keeping pace by will alone. It was impossible to speak in the cold, but he heard her thoughts.

Do you know where we are going? Or have any idea where we are? You want the truth? No. I am assuming that the storm we dropped into is from the Hellers, which is usual in winter, so keeping our backs to it will keep us heading south toward Thendara.

We need help Mik. Dressed as we are, we can't go too much farther before we get hyperthermia. After all we've been through, we can't end up freezing to death—we just can't!

For a moment he felt powerless. She was right, but he had no idea how to summon help when he did not even know where they were. But he did have Varzil's matrix. All he needed to do was use it.

Before he could put this thought into action, he felt Marguerida's body tense against his, straining as if she were reaching for something.

What are you doing?

I know there is someone nearby. I just hope it is a telepath. HELP. HELP!!!

CHIYA! There was no mistaking Lew Alton's mental voice, even in the howling of the wind. *Where are you?*

How should I know—I can't see three feet in front of my face! I am lost in the snow and freezing to death. Marguerida's flare of temper was heartening. But how was anyone going to find them in this swirling whiteness? They had to keep moving until they were rescued, even though all he wanted to do was collapse. Every step was agony now, the cold seemed to consume them. They were so close, but he knew they could easily die before they were found. He ignored the familiar sense of despair, and tried to think of some solution.

The ring! Mikhail unclenched his hand painfully. He stopped trudging and closed his eyes, focusing on the matrix. After making contact with the starstone, he felt himself shift into it. The wind seemed to vanish, and the cold as well. He felt Marguerida press closer, and sensed her immediate and unquestioning understanding. He knew they were standing in a globe of energy which kept the elements at bay, and shone like a beacon in the night. Now, if he could only sustain it long enough for them to be found.

Then Marguerida raised her left hand, and Mikhail felt his fatigue begin to drop away. Their shadow matrices mingled, meshing perfectly, and they stood warm and secure within a pillar of blue fire.

How long can we keep this up?

A long time, Mik.

Are you sure?

No, of course I am not sure! But I don't feel as if I'm consuming my energies, nor yours either.

"By Aldones! What is that!" The sound of a man's voice came

from the whiteness, and then the complaint of a horse. Mikhail released his concentration, and stepped back into bitter cold and blowing snow. There were half a dozen figures riding toward them. In a minute they were surrounded, sheltered by the body of the horses. Lew Alton dismounted stiffly.

He did not speak, but only pulled Marguerida into the folds of his enormous cloak. As one of the Guardsmen handed Mikhail a cape, he wondered how Lew had gotten there, and how long he had been searching.

Lew Alton reached out and drew Mikhail against him. The older man pressed his lips against his daughter's cheek, muttering incomprehensibly. Mikhail caught murmured words of endearment, and then, to his astonishment, he felt Lew kiss his face as well. There was a trickle of wetness on the bearded mouth that touched him, and he realized that Lew was crying.

"I have been nearly out of my mind. We've been looking for you for hours!"

"Hours?"

"Can we have this tearful reunion indoors? I am getting frostbite!" Marguerida's voice was brusque, but the wind muffled the sound of it.

"Quite right, daughter!" Lew turned, and a Guardsman dismounted. Mikhail saw that he was leading their horses, his bay and Marguerida's Dorilys. Another of the riders was untying the blanket that lay behind his saddle. He handed it down, and Mikhail draped it around Marguerida. She clutched it closely.

In a moment, they were mounted, and trotting away from the ruins of Hali Tower. Despite the cape, Mikhail was still very chilled, and it took all his endurance to stay in the saddle. He could tell that Marguerida was having the same trouble, for she was trying to keep the blanket around her while guiding her horse. Finally, one of the men reached out, took the reins from her trembling hands, and led Dorilys.

Just when he was sure he could not go any farther, he saw the lights of the inn gleaming faintly in the whiteness. There was a red light in the east, and he realized it was almost dawn. Had Midwinter Night just ended? Had merely one night passed in their own time while they had spent days in the Ages of Chaos? Mikhail felt a peculiar sense of disorientation. Lew Alton had said "hours."

The door of the inn opened, and welcoming light poured out onto the trampled snow in the courtyard. Mikhail managed to get off Charger, but his knees buckled under him. Two Guardsmen grabbed his elbows and half carried him inside. Lew had already gotten Marguerida off her horse and carried her into the blessed shelter.

The warmth of the inn touched his icy cheeks. He could smell woodsmoke and cooking cereal. His mouth watered. Then he shivered all over, for his robe was soaked with melted snow. He was so tired.

At the same time, he felt remote from the present, as if part of him were still in the past. He tried to push the feeling away, but he could not shake the idea that a lifetime had passed for him—another life in another world. He glanced down at the ring on his trembling hand and sighed. It was going to take a long time to sort everything out.

The Guardsmen helped Mikhail into the common room of the inn, half dragging, half carrying him toward the roaring fire, and set him down in a large chair. Incuriously, he watched Lew set Marguerida down into a chair a few feet away. Her hand dangled over the arm of the chair, the now bright metal of the *catenas* bracelet shining in the firelight.

"Let's get them out of these wet clothes! Samel!" Lew shouted as he stood up, his face a little ruddy in the firelight. "We want dry clothing—now!" The innkeeper nodded, and hurried off. He returned almost immediately with some of the servants from the inn.

Mikhail felt himself being hauled to his feet, as the sopping indoor gown was dragged over his head. From the muffled protests across the room, he knew that Marguerida was being stripped of her wet garments as well. He heard some scandalized squawks from Samel's wife, and then Lew telling her "Modesty be damned!"

Mikhail collapsed back into the chair, relieved that someone else was in charge. When a thick mug was thrust into his limp hand, Mikhail lifted it to his mouth and drank. It was hot cider, so sweet it made his teeth ache, with something else, a dark underflavor concealed in the sweetness. He felt a jolt of energy course through his body, and knew it was bladderwort, a powerful stimulant. His body was screaming for sleep, which would be almost impossible now, but he knew it would help him resist the effects of the cold.

Warmth seeped into his body. Remoteness and exhaustion faded as the bladderwort entered his bloodstream. Now, if he just had the strength to pull off his icy slippers!

But before he could rouse himself to movement, Lew knelt in front of him and pull off his footwear. Mikhail was shocked and oddly touched. This was no task for a lord of the Domains, and yet it seemed right to him. His father-in-law—the term rocked his mind for a moment—never had been one to respect convention.

Mikhail looked over at his wife. She was wearing a thick blue robe now; her face was very white and she was shivering. One of the servants had a towel and was trying to dry her tangled hair with it. His beloved gave a little yelp of pain and pushed the woman away with a weak gesture.

The bladderwort continued to do its work, and he almost wished it would not. He felt acutely sensitive—as if he could feel every single thread in the robe he was wearing. The light of the fire which had been so pleasant a few minutes before now seemed eye-searing. He blinked away tears. It began to feel as if fire-ants were racing around his body, both within and without, the sensation of invisible feet and clicking mandibles almost real. He would gladly have jumped out of his skin.

The feeling lasted for only a minute, then faded away. His cheeks felt hot, and he had a blinding headache. He rubbed his brow with a trembling hand, and felt the pain lessen immediately. Without thinking he had used the ringed hand. How was he going to live with this thing? How had Varzil managed? He sighed as the tense muscles in his neck started to relax.

A grizzled head penetrated his field of view, and a spoon moved toward his mouth. The innkeeper grinned at him, and Mikhail opened his mouth, feeling quite childlike, and found mealmush on his tongue. It was something they fed the very young, after weaning, and the very ill or old. It was thick and not very pleasant, but he swallowed it, and let Samel continue to feed him, as Lew was feeding Marguerida.

After a while, he shook his head. "I can't eat any more right now, Samel. Thank you."

"Very good, *vai dom*. You just give a holler—well, a croak, then— if you want more."

"What I want now is some plain tea, the mint sort, with some honey. My throat feels terrible." It did, but he was not surprised he had not noticed it earlier.

"Surely, surely." Samel bustled off, and in a few minutes, someone handed him another mug, mountain mint sweetened with the famous honey of Hali. Mikhail gulped down half of the mug, and felt his body accept it with greed.

He looked up, and found Lew Alton sitting by the hearth a few feet away, watching him intently. Then he realized that Lew was not really looking at him, but at the ring which sparkled on his hand. Mikhail followed the gaze.

The object on his finger shifted in the light, growing larger and smaller, almost pulsing. It was never the same from one second to the next. Mikhail looked at it, felt his awareness fall into the corruscating facets of the jewel, and then withdraw. He could sense that it contained a vast amount of information. Each time he looked at it, he seemed to learn something in a burst of energy. He shook his head and lifted his eyes. He was too tired right now. It would take him years to understand the strange gem. No, decades.

Mikhail shook his head, trying to clear his mind. He frowned. Something had happened to him while he was in the lake—and he and Marguerida must have been in it for a long time. He had had no sense of time passing, but he remembered that the moons were not supposed to conjoin for forty days after the dream in the deserted kitchen. If he counted the two days there, and the four they had spent captive, that left thirty-four unaccounted for. And there had been a voice, he thought, instructing him, while he floated in that peculiar place.

"Fascinating," Lew commented, interrupting his thoughts. Then he quirked an eyebrow and waited for Mikhail to speak. When he did not, Lew added, "I have seen some remarkable things in my life, including the Sharra Matrix, but nothing quite like that."

"No. It is unique. I do not feel entirely worthy to wear this, but I do not have any choice." The tea had soothed his throat, and he no longer sounded like a crow. The crow! All the grief he had not had time to experience welled up in his chest, then sank away. He was still too weary, numb, and confused for it.

"No choice?" Lew sounded amused, as if he knew that condition very well.

Mikhail forced himself to respond to this playful tone, letting his sadness diminish. "You could say that I freely accepted my destiny, and am now having a bit of regret."

Lew roared his wonderful laugh. "I think I know how you feel, Mikhail."

"I'm glad someone does, because I am not entirely sure I know how I feel. Glad to be here, sad, bewildered—those are some of the more obvious ones. Were it not for the ring, and this," he added, lifting his left arm a little so the bracelet showed, "I might be able to convince myself I had dreamed the entire episode. I hope you do not mind, Lew—but it really does not matter a bit if you do."

"Mind? That you have managed to accomplish what I could not? No, I do not mind, though I am curious about how you came by those bracelets. The design is ancient, and I also wonder who performed the marriage."

"Would you believe Varzil the Good did? In the Ages of Chaos?"

Lew had just taken a swallow from his mug when Mikhail spoke.

His eyes bulged, and he choked. He coughed for a few seconds, then glared at Mikhail. "No, I would not!"

"I did not think you would," Mikhail replied, with a deep sense of satisfaction at Lew's astonishment. It was such a clear emotion, free of ambiguity, almost refreshing.

"And Evanda, I think," Marguerida added. "She was the witness, and she made some excellent stew that I ate. A pity Mik did not have a chance to sample it, for how often can one boast to have eaten the food of the gods." She laughed weakly.

Lew looked confused and slightly angry. "If I did not know the two of you so well, I would think you were making the entire thing up to irritate me. *Varzil? Evanda?*"

"Well, I cannot be absolutely sure it was she, but she looked very much like that painting on the ceiling in the grand dining room at Comyn Castle, after she stopped disguising herself as an old woman, except her hair was brighter and her eyes were . . . indescribable." Marguerida sighed. "And, truly, seeing her was not the most remarkable thing that happened, was it, *cario?*"

"After she stopped . . . *chiya!* Can you at least try to start at the beginning, for the sake of my aging wits?" *They both appear to be well enough, but they are so different. I want to believe them, but it is so incredible, and* Dom *Gabriel is not going to swallow any tales of Varzil. They have both lost considerable weight in what has only been a few hours, and . . . damn!*

Marguerida looked toward Mikhail, their eyes meeting. He felt her tiredness and her passion, her steadfastness, and something more. It was a change he had noticed earlier, but the rush of events had kept him from realizing the meaning of it. She had seemed different, more calm, and she had a glow which he saw she still possessed. Reflexively, he swept her with a rapid monitoring, feeling his hand warm beneath the great stone.

My darling—you are pregnant!

Am I? Is that why I feel so peculiar?

But, how . . . ?

We did make love for days and days, you know. And I have heard rumors that this activity often leads to children. I have been so tired and so busy that I did not take a good look at myself, but now I see. Yes, I see Domenic Alton-Hastur *quite clearly. Very healthy, and large for being only a week old.*

Mikhail was overwhelmed. He could not speak for the feelings that rose in his chest. He tottered up on unsteady legs, went over to her chair, and bent down. He brushed the tangled curls away from her forehead and kissed her brow. The sense of quiet bliss that radiated from her was beyond magnificent. He wanted to bask in it forever.

Marguerida just nestled her head against his chest, rubbing his sternum, and smiled. *He seems none the worse for having been witness to our strange adventures. I never thought I would be grateful for having some of the Aldaran Gift, Mik, but just now I am, for I know that our son will be fine. Domenic Gabriel-Lewis Alton-Hastur will be a son to be proud of.*

With all that piled on him, I will be surprised if he isn't a real handful. Thank you, my dearest. And he is likely about forty days old, not seven or eight.

What an odd thing to say, Mik.

We were in Lake Hali for longer than you think, Marguerida.

Ah—that explains it. She did not seem surprised. *Time is such a mystery, even to me, who supposedly can play with it.*

Lew cleared his throat softly, bringing Mikhail back to the present. He turned, slipped his hand off Marguerida's shoulder, and stumbled back to his chair, happy and exhausted. He saw his wife lean back, resting her head contentedly against the soft upholstery, with a slight smile playing across her lips. She had never seemed more beautiful, even with deep circles beneath her golden eyes, and her hair a mass of wild curls and snarls.

Settling back into the chair, and reclaiming the now tepid mug of mint tea, Mikhail grinned at Lew Alton. He stretched his legs out toward the fire, leaned his head back, and said, "We will make you a grandfather in about eight months—close to Midsummer, I believe. I hope you are pleased."

"Pleased! Of course I am delighted! But—eight months? I do wish you will tell me what the hell is going on!" The expression on Lew's scarred face was stunned, pleased and more than a little confused, as if he could not take in everything at once.

"We had a strange shared dream, months ago. Everything followed from that."

The tale unfolded, with Marguerida telling the part about the Sisters of the Sword, or adding bits and pieces when he faltered. Lew listened without comment or question, his brow furrowed with concentration. Every once in a while he opened his mouth to ask something, but thought better of it. After a time, the tale was complete. It sounded no more believable for being told in a somewhat orderly fashion, and Mikhail was left empty when they stopped at last.

"That is, without a doubt, the most preposterous recitation I have ever heard!" Lew said when Mikhail fell silent. "No one is going to believe you. I can hardly believe you myself, and I am a sympathetic listener."

Mikhail held out his hand. "This should convince anyone who matters." The ring sparkled in the firelight.

"Perhaps. But some people, like your mother, are going to be very difficult, Mikhail." Lew sighed and then grinned wickedly. "On the other hand, Regis is going to be very pleased."

"Is he? Why?"

"Well, in the first place, you are safe and sound—though many people are going to question the latter—and in the second you have rescued him from having to accept *Dom* Damon Aldaran's terms for joining the Comyn Council. Gisela will be very angry, and it may even ruin Regis' plan to get the Aldarans to the Council table. I cannot see the future. We will just have to wait and see how things work out. But it will certainly be interesting." Lew seemed to look forward to that.

Marguerida gave an enormous yawn. "I am so sleepy . . . can I go to bed now?"

"Forgive me. I should have had you in bed an hour ago—but I could not let my curiosity wait until morning."

"It is morning already," she murmured. "And there is something you have not told us, something very important." Marguerida forced her eyes wider.

"True. I was going to wait for a better time, when you were less tired." Lew looked very uncomfortable. "You see, that calling in the ballroom had some terrible consequences. Several people went into shock, and two died." He paused again, looking at Mikhail with sorrowful eyes. "One was young Emun."

"Oh, no!" Mikhail felt the tears rise in his eyes, and streak down his cheeks. His heart ached—he was responsible! At last he understood how Marguerida must have felt about Domenic Alar's accident. He glanced at her through his tears, and saw the pain in her face.

Lew shook his head. "All that he had been through at Halyn House had weakened him, I believe, and he could not survive the experience. Mikhail, you are not to blame."

"So, I will be the Elhalyn king after all." Mikhail's words were rough bitter.

"No, I think not." Lew looked at them. "*That* is going to change everything." He pointed at Mikhail's hand, shook his head, and looked grave and worried. "It is going to be a real mess, you know."

Mikhail looked at his new father-in-law stupidly. Then he glanced down at his ring, and the ramifications of the matrix he now bore began to penetrate his weary mind. He had not thought about it before, being much too busy just trying to keep alive. How could he have failed to consider how much possessing this artifact might shift the balance of power on Darkover? It was all very well for Varzil the Good to have wanted to get his matrix away from Ashara Alton, into a future where she no longer existed, but the long dead *tenerézu* could not have foreseen the problems it would cause.

Marguerida scowled as she grasped the implications. "Yes, and everyone will shout and pound on the tables, and slam doors, and have a wonderful time yelling themselves blue in the face!"

The elation he had felt half an hour before, finding out that he would be a father, dissolved. Mikhail was overwhelmed with a sense of unworthiness. Was he really now the most powerful man on Darkover? It was almost too much to bear. He wanted to pull the hateful thing off his hand and cast it into the fire on the hearth. The ring did not belong in the time he lived in. It was a relic of another era, a terrible past that Mikhail did not wish to see reborn.

Mikhail shuddered all over. His eyes burned. If only he could sleep, and forget everything. He did not want this power, did he? Then he felt a bit of laughter bubble in his chest. What did he imagine—that now he could wave his hand and make miracles? What a fool he was, to be sure!

"I won't let it change things," he muttered to Lew.

"You . . . what?" Lew gave a sharp bark of bitter laughter. "I admire your sentiments, son, but now is not the time to discuss this. Off to bed with the two of you. I cannot wait to see Regis' face when you tell him your tale—but I will have to forego that pleasure for a while."

"Regis' face—think of Aunt Javanne's!"

"True, Marguerida, true. She will be fit to be tied. As if she isn't already, with the two of you dashing off in the middle of the night! Well, my life is going to be more exciting than I thought." Lew seemed oddly pleased by the prospect.

"Father . . . I know what to do for Dio now." Marguerida's voice was heavy with drowsiness, her chin slipping towards her chest. "I cannot cure her, but I can give her more time," she whispered. "More time." Then her eyes closed.

Lew Alton stared at his daughter, his scarred face undergoing a transformation, from solemn to stunned, then widening into disbelief and hope. He stood up, and for a moment it seemed that he would try to shake her awake. Instead, he shifted her limp body around, lifted her up, and started toward the stairs that led to the upper story of the inn. Her head rested against his shoulder, and Mikhail had a stab of jealousy that he was too tired to sustain. "Do you think she knows what she is talking about, Mik?"

Mikhail staggered to his feet. "I have an inkling, yes. She can heal with that hand of hers, or cause harm. She means what she says, Uncle Lew."

"That she does. Now, to bed with the pair of you!" *I have my child back, and perhaps my Diotima as well. It is all too much. Thank the gods for this miracle.*

Three mornings later, a large carriage creaked into the innyard, accompanied by several Guardsmen. Mikhail was in the taproom, and he heard the ruckus in a vague way. He was still very tired, and had spent his days doing little besides eating and sleeping. Marguerida was upstairs still, fighting a cold.

He stood up slowly, feeling ancient for a man of twenty-eight, and started toward the door. They were going back to Thendara, but he was not entirely eager to get there. If he had had a choice, he would have stayed at the inn with his wife until they were completely recovered, avoiding the intrigues he knew would ensue. He resigned himself to the uproar that awaited them, shrugging away his anxiety with difficulty.

Mikhail heard a slight scuffle behind him, and turned and found Marguerida walking down the stairs. Her nose was red from her cold, but her hair was brushed to a glossy sheen, and she was wearing a brown wool dress that had belonged to the innkeeper's daughter. She smiled at him, snuffled slightly, and coughed. "I wish I had pneumonia," she muttered.

"Why would you want that, *caria?*"

"They can cure pneumonia," she answered darkly, then glared at him when he laughed. "The only thing I can think of is that if Gisela gives me any trouble, I can just sneeze on her."

"Surely you would prefer to give her something more potent than a cold."

Marguerida slipped her arm into his. "Not really. I am not really feeling vengeful—just a wee bit petty this morning."

"Well, you look wonderful, despite having a very red nose."

"I don't feel wonderful."

The door of the inn opened, and Liriel, cloaked and muffled, swept into the entry. She pushed the hood back from her shining red hair, and started to remove her gloves. Marguerida released her hold on Mikhail's arm and almost ran across the remaining space toward his sister. She started to hug Liriel, then remembered her cold, and stopped, looking frustrated.

Liriel unhooked the clasp of her cloak and slipped it off her wide shoulders. She draped it over her arm, and swept her free arm around Marguerida's waist, planting a light kiss on her cheek. For a moment they stood facing him, two tall women, each splendid in a distinct way. Then Liriel released his wife, and embraced him.

"Mother thinks she should have drowned you at birth, *bredu,*" she said, smiling cheerfully. "And I might agree, if I were not so very happy to see you!"

"This is a pleasant surprise, Liri. I did not expect you to come with the carriage."

"Uncle Lew asked me to come, and I was glad enough to do it, though I am beginning to have a real aversion to all manner of wheeled vehicles. But I had no choice. At least the way from Thendara is easier in this direction than to the west. You do not appear to be any worse for your adventures—did you really travel into the past?"

"We really did, though we do not expect anyone to believe us."

"Good, because they will be difficult to convince. Both Father and Mother are sure that the two of you just dashed away to irritate them, and, truthfully, Uncle Regis feels almost the same way. If it had not been for that voice at the ball, everyone would think . . . no matter. You are both safe, and that is the only important thing, isn't it?"

"It is, as far as I am concerned, but I do not expect anyone to see things my way. I am very glad you came, Liri. But why?"

"Mik—she came because of me, you idiot," Marguerida interjected. She gave her still flat belly a pat. "She has come to check on little Domenic, of course. You've seen how Father is! He's nearly driven me mad, fussing over me, and he knew I would not want a stranger to assess my delicate condition." She gave a wicked grin. "You would think he was having this child!"

"Now, daughter," Lew's voice boomed out from beside the stairs. "I am only being careful."

"You are behaving like an old hen!"

Lew gave a shrug. "An old rooster, surely. And how *are* things in Thendara, Liriel?"

"Monstrous! I was so glad to escape, I nearly wept! We have managed to keep most of your adventures from becoming public—so far. No one knows you are married yet, except Regis and Linnea, Danilo Syrtis-Ardais, and our parents. But that is enough, for Mother is spitting mad, and Father is trying to think of some way to undo what has been done."

"And Uncle Regis?"

Liriel looked thoughtful. "He is being very . . . opaque."

"What about the Aldarans?" Marguerida asked this question.

"*Dom* Damon has withdrawn to his apartments, to drink a great deal no doubt, and Gisela has been enjoying frequent bouts of temper." An odd look passed across her face. "She has been sharing them with our brother Rafael," she added mysteriously.

See! I told you so, Mik!

You did, but it is not kind to remind me of it. Are you always going to be right? Fifty or sixty years of marriage to a woman who is always right could get a little tiresome.

Then I shall just have to try to be wrong at least once a week. I can't have you getting annoyed with me!

Never, not in a million years, caria.

If Liriel noticed this rapid byplay, she gave no indication. She went on with her descriptions. "Robert Aldaran has been a voice of reason, which has given me a very high opinion of him. Of course, when Robert hears the details of your adventures, he may change his ways. If I were to be entirely candid, I would say that everyone is having a fine time being upset—everyone except Ariel, who is resting nicely after the arrival of Alanna. No one is in the least bored, I assure you!" Liriel smiled broadly, her eyes alight with humor.

"I am not surprised," Lew commented. "We are a very passionate family."

"Mother is sure this is all your fault, Uncle Lew. She has hinted darkly at some Terranan plot, that the voice was only some manner of technology, and all of it done in order to whisk Mik and Marguerida away."

"My . . . my fault! Of all the . . . Terranan plot?" Lew sputtered to a halt, and a look of interest began to play across his face. "I had not given Javanne credit for so much imagination."

Marguerida slipped her arm through his and smiled. "There, there, Father. Don't take it too much to heart. We will get everything straightened out eventually."

Lew gave his daughter a strange look. "You seem to be very serene, daughter. It's almost . . . unnatural. I expected you to be more emotional, now that you are about to be a mother. But, tell me, just how do you imagine we are going to straighten things out?"

Marguerida merely shrugged, looking beatific until she erupted into a brief fit of coughing, while everyone laughed.

Lew lifted his proud head toward the rafters. "Women! I will never understand them, and the gods know I have tried!" Then he smiled at Marguerida, his face lighting up. "But if you can give my Diotima back to me, child, I shall be eternally in your debt."

"I will, Father, I will," Marguerida promised.

35

Mikhail and Marguerida had come back to Thendara a tenday after Midwinter to a chilly reception. Things had not improved appreciably during the ensuing week, when they had recounted their adventures several times to Regis, to *Dom* Gabriel and Lady Javanne, and to Danilo Syrtis-Ardais. Everyone else had been kept in the dark, except for the undeniable fact that they were now husband and wife. This had led to several harrowing encounters with Gisela Aldaran, which Mikhail wanted to forget.

The problem, he thought, was that there was just too many strong personalities residing in Comyn Castle, all of them bent on having their way, no matter what. Mikhail, somewhat refreshed after the quiet time at Samel's inn, was inclined to be amused, but his wife's nerves were strained to the limit by the constant expressions of temper and ill-feeling.

There was little, actually, to be happy about, other than that they were now safe. Javanne had at first refused to speak to Mikhail, but when she began, she would not stop. She pleaded, raged, cajoled, and snapped. It was as if the pent-up bitterness of a lifetime was spewing out, vicious and furious. She blamed Marguerida for leading him

⸺ ¡ray—at least this was the most frequent of her embarrassing pronouncements.

Even the matter of where they should rest their heads had been argued over. His mother, insisting that the marriage was not valid, had wanted her son to continue to reside in the family suite, and Marguerida in the Alton apartment. It was a silly thing, a minor squabble, but Mikhail had put an end to it by announcing he was still Elhalyn Regent, and would take his wife to that part of Comyn Castle. This pleased no one except Miralys and Valenta, both deeply distressed by the death of their brother. The young women were tearful, and clung to him in a way that touched him profoundly.

Now he was sitting in Regis' shabby study, waiting to hear why he had been summoned. His uncle had called the meeting without any warning, and he had no idea what he wanted. The air in the normally pleasant room was charged with unspoken emotions, and he anticipated the worst.

Javanne, he thought, looked pinched and old for the first time in his memory. There was a glitter in her eyes, an expression of near hatred, whenever she looked at him or Marguerida, that almost seemed to belong to another person. This saddened him more than anything else. He wanted to be reconciled with her, for he knew now how truly he loved and respected this woman, but Mikhail suspected that in her present temper, it was an impossible hope.

Lew had been right—his gift from Varzil changed everything. Not for the better either, he concluded grimly, looking at the faces of both his parents. Javanne was seething, and *Dom* Gabriel looked like a man driven to the brink. He felt a curious empathy for his father, an emotion he had never felt before. Mikhail had never imagined how difficult it must have been to be married to Javanne all these years. He had long regarded *Dom* Gabriel as a rather dull fellow, but now, as if he were seeing him in a completely new light, he recognized him to be a person who was both more intelligent and more courageous than he had ever believed.

Regis was sitting behind his desk, drumming his fingers against the wood. The strain of the past days showed in his face as well. Beneath the white hair, his brow was lined, and his eyes looked tired. Regis, who rarely raised his voice, had shouted a number of times in Mikhail's hearing, and he knew that his patience must be worn thin. Lady Linnea was beside him, looking as cross as Mikhail had ever seen her. Then she glanced at Mikhail, and a shadow of a smile graced her mobile mouth.

Lew Alton came into the room and took a seat beside Mikhail. He appeared untroubled, and Mikhail took heart from his expression. Marguerida, who was sitting on Mikhail's other side, leaned forward to share a long look with her father, then relaxed back into her chair. Mikhail wondered what had passed between them in that moment. Then he looked at Danilo Syrtis-Ardais, aloof and unperturbed, standing behind Regis' chair. Of all the people in the room, he alone appeared unconcerned. Indeed, there was a slight sparkle in his pale eyes, as if he knew something pleasant, some secret he was enjoying.

Mikhail realized that something was going to be decided at last, and he felt a relief in that. And at least there were no Aldarans present, only family. He would be pleased if he never had to see any member of the Aldaran clan again, except Robert, who was behaving like the sensible man that he was. He silently blessed him, and his own brother Rafael as well. If Rafael had not kept Gisela company, he was sure she would have gone after either him or Marguerida with a knife.

Javanne Hastur cleared her throat and began to speak. "I have hit upon a solution to this whole nonsense, and I am only surprised no one else has thought of it sooner. Have this farce of a marriage annulled immediately. It is clear to me that if Marguerida is really almost two months pregnant, as Liriel has assured me she is, then Mikhail cannot be the father. She did not arrive in Thendara until just before Midwinter! That makes the marriage invalid—as if it were not already, since neither I nor Gabriel gave our permission." She glared at Lew, as if she suspected he had been behind the whole thing. He returned her look so solemnly that Mikhail almost chuckled. His father-in-law had turned out to be a valuable ally, and a good friend as well.

Regis looked wearily at his sister. "Don't be a fool! You are the only person who has heard the tale who insists it is a fable, that Mikhail and Marguerida are not telling the truth as they experienced it."

"Then I am the only one who realizes that she somehow arranged all this—perhaps with the help of Rafe Scott!" Javanne's voice was shrill, and there were blotches of red on her cheeks. Mikhail could see her hands curl into claws, and tremble.

"Please, my dear," *Dom* Gabriel began, trying unsuccessfully to calm her.

"I will not be silenced! You may be beguiled by this incredible story, but I am not! Marguerida is too ambitious to be . . ."

"I think you speak of your own ambitions, not Marguerida's, Javanne," Regis said quietly.

His sister responded with a look that should have turned him to stone. "Can't you see that she has Mikhail wrapped around her finger, and that she must not be allowed to rule through him!"

"Mother, stop it! You insult me as well as my wife. The Elhalyn kingship has no real power, so even if I were the spineless weakling you are making me out to be, it would not matter." Mikhail was surprised by the bitterness in his voice, then ashamed at himself. He should have more control.

Javanne turned on him, almost spitting in her fury. "You cannot sit there with that *thing* on your hand and pretend you expect to sit complacently on the Elhalyn throne. Regis must declare you his final heir, and you must be guided by wise council to succeed him." Her rage vanished and she gave a half smirk, as if she had settled the matter to her own satisfaction, and assumed that everyone would agree to it.

Everyone was aghast, then acutely embarrassed. The mask had fallen away at last, and Javanne Hastur's scheme to govern Darkover through her son lay revealed. Mikhail shook his head. "I have never been guided by you before, Mother. Surely you cannot imagine I will be now or in the future."

"You would have been, if Marguerida had not seduced you."

This was too much, and his wife began to laugh, and then guffawed until huge tears rolled down her cheeks. Six people looked at her in astonishment, while Mikhail had to struggle to keep himself from joining in her merriment. When she finally got herself in hand, Marguerida wiped her streaming eyes with the edge of her sleeve and said, "Forgive me, Aunt. I have never seduced anyone in my life, and the words struck me . . . oh, dear." She went off into a fresh stream of giggles, while Javanne simmered in her chair.

"You don't think much of me, do you, Mother?"

"Of course I do—you are my son!"

"But you do not think I am fit to rule anything without your guidance."

Javanne's expression hardened and her eyes had a dangerous sparkle. "I know what needs to be done, unlike the rest of you."

"You have waited years for the opportunity to become the power behind the throne, haven't you, Mother? You failed with your brother, but imagined you might succeed with me. That is why you have held Regis to his oath, and kept him from giving Dani his rightful inheritance. And when Marguerida appeared, all your intrigues were ruined. I am sorry, truly I am." Nothing he said seemed to reach her.

"Mikhail, that is more insightful than anything I have heard you say before," Regis said before Javanne could reply.

"Yes, I suppose it is." He lifted his hand, gloved now, like his wife's, to avoid inadvertent contact. "Varzil was a Ridenow and an empath, and I seem to have learned something of that from wearing this. Not that one really needs any Gift to recognize my mother's thwarted ambitions." He caught the stricken look in his uncle's eyes. "No, the ring has not made me kinder. Sorry, Uncle, but too much has happened to me."

"Yes, it has. I had my moment, when I bore the Sword of Aldones, but it was only that—a moment. I surrendered my burden, but you cannot put yours aside, ever. I know you will not challenge me, for you are too honorable for that, no matter what my sister may hope. But we must settle the matter, because there are others, right here in the Castle, who would intrigue to embroil you in some rebellion or another. I cannot assume that you would be wise enough to resist them." Regis shook his head. "That is not a reflection on your character, Mikhail, just an understanding of human nature."

"I did not ask to receive this matrix, but I think we all have to accept that I have it, now and forever. I can hardly toss it aside, can I?" Mikhail let his shoulders sag a little. Then he looked around the room and realized that the immediate future of Darkover was going to be decided by the people in this room. For a moment, he felt very young and out of his depth. The emotion passed, and a certain calm descended on him. Whatever the outcome, he would endure it, even though it likely meant occupying the Elhalyn throne for the rest of his days.

"That is the most sensible thing I have heard since I came into this room," *Dom* Gabriel growled. "Stop your demons, woman! You are plaguing us all."

Javanne flinched, and her face looked ancient. Then she stiffened, and her skin reddened as her eyes narrowed. Emotions seemed to play across her body, frustration and anger and a deep sorrow that moved Mikhail. He could not help feeling sorry for her, even though he knew that she would become even angrier if he offered her his pity. She was completely lost in her own feelings, and instead of using the intelligence he knew she possessed, she could only rage helplessly.

Marguerida, who had been playing with her bracelet, turning the cat-shape around on her wrist, looked up. "You are acting like a spoiled child, Aunt Javanne, and it does not suit you. Yes, I know I should not say that. But ever since Midsummer you have been scheming and plotting. Is that why you sent Mikhail off to Halyn House, Regis? To get him out of Javanne's sight?"

"You have me there, Marguerida. That was indeed part of the

reason. Danilo tried to persuade me not to, but I did not listen. I needed time to try to reclaim the Aldarans, and to get the Comyn Council functioning again. I was wrong, and Danilo was right." He glanced at his paxman, and was answered by a slight smile and a nod of acknowledgment. "Of course, I had no idea you two were going to dash off into the past and come back with something that would make matters worse."

"How worse, Uncle?"

"I can hardly deny you my throne, not while you are wearing that. And that leaves my own son in a bitter position." He looked at Linnea. "The balance of power which I have struggled to preserve is undone. Even if you had not received that matrix, your marriage to Marguerida would still have made things difficult—but the two together is nearly impossible to resolve without someone being very disappointed."

Danilo Syrtis-Ardais cleared his throat, and everyone looked at him. His pale eyes were gleaming with something like mischief, and Mikhail wondered what the joke was. From Regis' expression, he was just as puzzled as Mikhail.

Having gotten everyone's attention, Danilo began to speak. "Has everyone had their fill of recriminations and complaints? Are we agreed that the most immediate problem is the succession of both of the Hastur and the Elhalyn Domains? Or are we going to fight among ourselves until the Terranan realize our instability? They have been waiting for years for the opportunity to seize our planet, you know."

"Fine words, but how do you propose to manage things—which it is not your place to do in any case!" Javanne snarled at him, looking for some target for her ire.

"I do not intend to manage anything but myself," Danilo answered dryly, "a course I recommend to others. I am no kingmaker, nor have I any ambitions to become one. But, here are the facts, unpleasant as they might be. Mikhail is an adult, trained to govern, and he now is the possessor of a tool which gives him enormous power. He is also Regis' first heir."

"But . . ." Javanne began.

Danilo lifted his hand, a graceful gesture that did not conceal the strength in it. "Please, allow me to finish, Lady Javanne. We have a problem—that we have two heirs to one position. And, my dear Javanne, you cannot have it both ways. You cannot insist that Regis abide by his oath while at the same time resisting Mikhail's legitimate claims. The succession is a family problem, but it is also a problem for the world we live on. And we must set aside our prejudices and look at it in that way."

"And just what do you propose, then?" Lew Alton asked the question that was in everyone's mind, and Mikhail looked at him gratefully.

"In truth, this is not my proposal, but that of another." Danilo gave a mild chuckle, and it was quite clear that he was enjoying himself enormously. He strode across the room, and opened the door.

Dani Hastur, his face white with tension, stepped into the room, tugging down the hem of his tunic. There were beads of sweat on his brow, and his eyes squinted with anxiety. Still, he looked resolute, the small chin he had inherited from his mother set as firmly as was possible. He paused, bowed to his father, then to the rest of the amazed assembly.

"Go ahead Dani. Tell them your idea." Danilo's voice was brimming with suppressed laughter but also pride.

"Yes, sir." He stood there, silent and uncomfortable, swallowing hard. At last he burst out. "Father—I do not want to be the next Hastur!"

"What!" Regis half rose in his chair, then sank back, stunned.

"I don't want to succeed you. I could never do the job! Even if cousin Mikhail did not exist, I could not take on the responsibility."

"But, son—you are young and . . ."

"No! I have lived in dread for years that you might die and I would end up trying to step into your shoes. I was glad that you never made me your heir! I am unsuited, by my own character, to become the Hastur of Hastur."

"Dani," Lady Linnea began gently, "come and sit down beside me. This is very brave of you, but you are too young to realize what you are saying!"

"Too young to know myself, you mean." The misery in his voice was unmistakable, and Mikhail felt his heart sink. Dani slipped into a chair. "But I do know who I am. I have no skill for rulership, and Mikhail does. Oh, you have done your best to train me, Father, but it is like teaching a horse to dance the *pafan*. The will might be there, but the ability is lacking."

This made everyone except Javanne laugh, in spite of the tension in the room. The paxman handed Danilo Hastur a glass of wine, hiding a smile and trying to appear grave. The young man took a gulp, and his face reddened as some spilled down the sides of his mouth.

"Go ahead, Dani. Tell them what you came to me about yesterday morning." Danilo Ardais' voice was soft and calm, and his young namesake seemed to relax as the paxman spoke.

"In terms of blood," Dani started haltingly, "Mikhail and I are equal in our claims to the Elhalyn Domain. Each of us has Alanna Elhalyn for a grandmother, as do all of Aunt Javanne's children. What I think would be good would be that I . . ." His young voice faltered, and his blue eyes shifted from side to side, like a trapped thing.

"What, son?" Regis spoke very gently, as if he was aware that he must not make his son any more frightened than he was already.

Dani gave his father a quick look, then stared straight ahead, so that his eyes met Mikhail's. "This is my idea." He drew a shaking breath. "I propose I should marry Miralys Elhalyn as soon as she is of age, and be the Elhalyn king, and that our sons will follow me." When no one spoke, all the color drained out of his face, and he looked around frantically. He did not appear to realize that everyone except Danilo Ardais was too stunned to react. After several seconds, he plunged ahead. "I am, as far as I know, sane and hearty—if somewhat more interested in verse than governance. My friend Emun is dead, and his brothers can never take the throne. And Mira loves me—don't tell me we are too young to know our minds! We suit one another. You, Aunt Javanne, were not much older than she is when you married *Dom* Gabriel!"

"I have no objections to you marrying Miralys," Javanne answered slowly, her mind clearly working furiously. "But I do not think you realize what you are giving up." Mikhail sensed that she was considering the possibilities of changing her direction, of insisting that young Dani be made Regis' successor, with the idea of manipulating the young man to her own ends. It was an idea that had not occurred to him before, nor, he suspected, to his formidible mother.

"But I do! I am giving up a lot of headaches and heartaches that I never wanted to begin with! Father is a prisoner here. He has not been out of Thendara in years, and he almost never leaves Comyn Castle. He rarely has a moment to think of anything but Darkover. Who would want that?"

"Out of the mouths of babes," Lew muttered. He noticed Javanne glaring at him, and returned the look. "This is an elegant solution, Regis—if somewhat unorthodox. Dani's vigor will restore the Elhalyn line, and . . ."

"And your mad Terranan daughter will be able to do just as she likes," snarled Javanne.

"I would never do anything that would endanger Darkover, Aunt." Mikhail could sense that his wife was holding her frayed temper in with an effort, trying to remain calm in spite of considerable provocation.

"Oh, I am sure you believe that. But you are not to be trusted, and neither is my son! You have proved that by running off into the night and. . . ."

"Mother, you are obsessed. You have lost all perspective." Mikhail felt his face flame. "Regis is hardly in his dotage!"

"Why, thank you, Mikhail," his uncle answered wryly. "I was hoping someone would notice that. And, of course, that is not the real problem, is it?"

"I don't understand," Mikhail answered.

"The question is really how I am going to continue to rule Darkover while you are the most powerful man on the planet?" He shook his head, making his white hair slip down onto his forehead, and looked both amused and weary. "You don't see it, do you, Mikhail? No, you would not. Now you are a threat to me, as you were not before. And I must wonder if you will have the patience to wait for me to die naturally."

"Uncle!" Mikhail was stunned and hurt. It took all he could to keep from shouting in rage at being misjudged like this. How could anyone doubt his loyalty? He forced his feelings aside with an effort. "The Hasturs are a long-lived family, and I fully expect you to go on for another half century."

"And just what do you plan to do in the meanwhile?" Regis' eyes bored into him.

"Raise my son, and any other children that we have. Learn and study. This gift of Varzil's will take me decades to understand." As he spoke the words, Mikhail realized they were true. He had a task that was important, to understand the powers that had been thrust on him so suddenly, and it occurred to him that with what he had learned already, he could change the face of matrix science. He almost laughed. Now that he could become the ruler he had imagined when he was a young man, he no longer needed or wanted the job. Worse, it was unlikely that he would be able to convince anyone that he meant what he was saying.

"You really believe what you are saying, don't you? What if I suggested you retire to some remote place—Dalereuth, perhaps. It is near the sea, and Marguerida might like that." There was a sly look on Regis' face now, and Mikhail had a fresh understanding of how his uncle had managed Darkover for the past two decades.

At the same time, he quietly simmered with resentment. Two could play at this game! "Or I could leave Darkover completely. I have always wanted to travel, and Marguerida would just love to go back to University and complete some of her work. Perhaps I might take Herm Aldaran's vacant place in the lower house of Federation senate."

The expression on his uncle's face was shocked and dismayed, as if he had not anticipated this possibility. Then Mikhail realized that Regis was improvising again, and had no serious intention of exiling them to Dalereuth or anywhere else. He was testing Mikhail, and if he did not like it, at least he could understand the logic of it. And, he knew instantly, he would never be allowed to leave Darkover while he wore Varzil's ring.

Regis stared at his nephew, his face a study in conflicting emotions. Mikhail glared back and waited until Regis dropped his eyes, looking a little uncomfortable.

Regis and Danilo Syrtis-Ardais exchanged a look and an unspoken communication. The silence in the room was almost unbearable, and the rising of the winds outside the great castle seemed to reflect the strained emotions within. At last he turned away from Danilo, and looked around the room. His eyes came to rest on Dani's anxious face. "My son's idea—which has taken me completely by surprise—is not without merit. Not to mention a generosity of spirit which I wish were more general, especially in this room!"

Dani blushed at this praise, and Mikhail smiled at his young cousin. Beside him, Marguerida stirred again, and sat up a little straighter in her chair. Her face was calm, queenly and certain, and Mikhail suspected that she had just had another of her precognitive flashes. He laced his fingers into hers, so the metal of their bracelets touched and rang, a sweet sound in the room.

"You trained Mikhail to succeed you, Regis," Marguerida began. "But now you are beginning to fear him. That is natural, I suppose. But if you let that fear rule you, then the thing you fear will almost destroy all that you have struggled to create. You have a wonderful opportunity to continue your work, with Mikhail supporting you! The question is, are you going to take it, or refuse it?"

"You see! Marguerida is already intriguing to bring my son into power!" Javanne glared at Lew Alton. "She is so much your child, storm crow!"

"Thank you, Javanne," Lew snapped. "She is, indeed, and I am damned proud of her."

"You told me once that the man who had Marguerida for a wife would have a wise counselor, Mikhail, and you were right." Regis gave a sigh and looked tenderly at Lady Linnea. "Thank you, Marguerida.

You have stated my problem all too clearly. You have a real gift for cutting through the clutter and going to the heart of the matter."

"You are welcome. Please believe me when I say that I have only the best interests of Darkover in mind, Regis. If my father is right, and I think he is, the Federation is going to become a larger problem than it ever has been before, and we have to be united to face it. Your policies have been wise. But the future will demand a strong leader, and if Mikhail is not the right man for the job, then who is?"

"Who indeed," Regis answered. He looked at his son. "You have been very brave to think of this, Dani, but why did you not come to me with your idea?" He sounded a little hurt.

"I . . . couldn't! You are too busy with important things!"

"Too busy?" Regis was stricken. He looked at his paxman again. "Let that be a lesson to you, Mikhail, not to let running a planet get in the way of talking to your children. I am glad you could confide in Danilo, my son."

"Oh, I can always talk to him," Dani answered, looking very young now. "He has time for me, you see, and you do not. I have always known that."

"I see. In the future, I shall try to do better. I promise you that, Dani." There was so much regret in Regis' voice that Mikhail had to hold back a shiver.

"I take it then that you intend to name Mikhail your successor, and allow your son to become the Elhalyn king," Javanne snarled.

"That is what you have always wished for, isn't it?" Brother and sister gazed at one another, and Javanne dropped her eyes first.

"Yes," the older woman whispered. Then her indomitable spirit asserted itself. "And I will live to see you regret this day! I will urge the other Domains to . . ."

"You will do nothing of the sort!" Dom Gabriel snapped. "You will keep quiet, Javanne. Control yourself for once."

Lady Javanne Hastur rose to her feet, swept the gathering with a venomous look, and left the room, slamming the door behind her. After a moment, Dom Gabriel went after her, his face red with anger, and his shoulders hunched.

"She is going to make trouble, you know," Lew commented.

Regis chuckled. "My dear sister was born to trouble, I think. Now, we must decide how to proceed from here. I am open to suggestions."

No one spoke immediately. The room grew very still again, but the tension that had existed before was gone. Several minutes passed in silence, and young Dani squirmed a little in his chair.

Finally, Mikhail looked at his wife, and realized that everyone had been so busy trying to determine his future, they had not given any thought to hers, as if she had ceased to matter now. This irked him, and gave him an idea as well. "I think that when the weather is better, Marguerida and I should return to Neskaya and work with Istvana Ridenow." He saw the light in her eyes and knew this idea appealed to her.

Regis shook his head. "Neskaya is too far, and Marguerida is not going to dash about while she is pregnant. My son was right—if you are my heir, you must remain in Thendara, or go no further away than Arilinn. You will be a prisoner of a sort, as I have been. But I think that you are right that Istvana is the right *leronis* to guide you. I will ask her to come here. There was a Tower here, once, and there might be again." He smiled at Marguerida. "Yes, I know you have no happy memories of that, but we can make a new beginning—this is a new beginning for all of us, even me!"

"Yes, it can be, if we have the strength to dare it." Her voice rose slightly, as if she were challenging Regis Hastur in some way Mikhail could not grasp. It was only a moment, but he saw how his uncle's eyes met Marguerida's, and knew that some unspoken agreement had passed between them. "Now, what of the Alton Domain?" She glanced at her father, then at Regis. "I think it would be best if I resigned my claim in favor of either my Uncle Gabriel, or one of his other sons. If you do not mind terribly, Father."

"That is a very sensible choice, since I do not want it, and *Dom* Gabriel does," Lew answered. "But I want a seat on the Comyn Council. I will *not* be a power behind the throne, either to Regis or my son-in-law! I want everyone to be able to see me, and know what I am up to. Anything else would be suspect."

"Very well—that settles it. *Dom* Gabriel will continue to hold the Alton Domain," Regis said as the door opened and the man himself stepped back into the study. The look on *Dom* Gabriel's face made Mikhail want to shout with pleasure when he heard what was being said. His weathered features looked ten years younger. "And his sons will succeed him."

"That will teach me to leave the room and run after my poor wife," *Dom* Gabriel growled, his voice rough with emotions. "Javanne is frantic. I have never seen her like this, and I fear for her mind. I tried . . . but there was nothing I could do, except order a sleeping draught administered." He looked sad and worried, but pleased at the same time. "Lew, do you agree to this?"

"Completely, cousin. You have been master of the Domain for

decades, and it would be silly to change that. If it is not broken, why fix it?"

Gabriel sighed and smiled, entirely transforming his face. "There will always be a welcome for you at Armida, Lew."

"That is all I would ask for."

Dom Gabriel gazed at his son. He cleared his throat a few times, looking very uncomfortable, and finally managed to speak. "I have never understood you. You are a mystery to me, Mikhail, and I do not like mysteries. But I see that I have long misjudged you, and I confess it. Because you are unlike me, I mistrusted you."

"Father!"

"Don't interrupt! This is hard enough to say. I could not see your qualities because I was too mule-headed! You are a loyal man, and a loyal son—it has taken your mother's folly to let me realize this. I can only hope you can forgive an old man for being a fool."

Mikhail stood up and embraced his father as he had not done in years. "There is nothing to forgive." He felt Dom Gabriel's ragged breath against his cheeks, and knew the older man was holding back tears with difficulty. "I did not understand you either!"

"We shall just have to try harder in the future, then." Gabriel gave a shuddering sigh and released his hold on his son. He moved to Marguerida and extended his hand. "And you, daughter, whom I have never welcomed into the family—can you forgive me, too?"

Marguerida ignored the hand and stood up quickly. She hugged her uncle fiercely, tears sparkling in her eyes. Then she planted a kiss on the weathered cheek. "You are the kindest man in the world! Thank you!"

"After what I did last summer, I hardly . . ."

"Oh, no! That is the past, Uncle. Let it go! I already have!"

Mikhail felt his heart swell. He had feared that he would never be on easy terms with his father, and that the man would never accept Marguerida as his daughter-in-law. Now he realized that much of Dom Gabriel's opposition had been because of Javanne, and that, perhaps, with an effort on both sides, he could be a real son to the older man.

"If only all our problems were so easily remedied," Regis commented, clearly moved but holding his feelings in check. "Like the Aldarans." Everyone in the room groaned, except for young Dani. "But, for today, I think we have done enough. I, for one, would like some peace and quiet. And some time to get to know my amazing child," he added, gazing fondly at his son.

Danilo Hastur's face lit up. His eyes brightened with unshed tears and he blinked them away quickly. Then he grinned at his father and mother, his usually serious expression vanishing.

"Peace and quiet, Regis?" Gabriel shook his head. "You will have to move to another world, for I do not think you will find it on Darkover."

While everyone laughed at this, Mikhail felt himself uncoil, the tension he had endured fading away. His heart was full as he took Marguerida's bare hand in his. He had the position he had stopped wanting months before, and he would, he knew, spend the rest of his life learning to use his matrix, and helping Regis keep Darkover safe. But he was reconciled with his father, at least until the next meeting of the Comyn Council, where they were probably going to butt heads. That little was more than he had ever hoped for. And he had Marguerida beside him, and soon they would have a son to rear. At that moment, life seemed as close to perfection as anyone could desire.

EPILOGUE

Lew Alton watched his daughter walk into the chamber where Diotima Ridenow lay surrounded by a stasis field. She moved gracefully, despite the just visible prominence of her belly. There was an assurance about her that seemed to increase each day. The unhappy young woman whom he had taken away from Arilinn months before was gone, forever he suspected. If the presence of the screens overhead disturbed her, she did not show it. Mikhail Hastur was beside her, looking serious. He could sense their charged emotions, the intensity and the harmony as well.

He was so grateful to have her back. He had never told her how terrified he had been at Midwinter. That she was not only returned to him but married and with child as well seemed nothing short of a miracle. And now she proposed to perform another, to restore his dear Diotima to a semblance of health. How could any man be so fortunate? Lew was almost afraid to think about it, for fear that something might go amiss.

Marguerida had assured him that she was in no danger doing the healing she planned, but he was not sure he believed her. She had only said that she knew what she was doing, and that she could give Dio more time. How was a mystery and would remain so. He wanted Dio back so much!

His little Marja was going to make him a grandfather before he had really gotten comfortable with being a father. What manner of child would this Domenic Alton-Hastur be? Well, if he followed the family tradition, he would probably be a real scamp, and turn Marguerida's fine hair gray. It was a happy prospect.

Lew walked into the chamber behind his only child, and watched her. She bent over the coffinlike apparatus for a few seconds, as the song from her recorder rose to a climax. He recognized it—a Thetan love ballad that broke his heart every time he heard it. Then she reached over to turn off the machine, and silence filled the room.

The sudden silence was eerie, and he could see that the others, Liriel and Jeff Kerwin, were also disturbed by the cessation of the music, so many months had the chamber rung with Marguerida's voice. The very stones of Arilinn had probably absorbed all those melodies—a fancy that pleased him more than a little.

Marguerida nodded at Jeff. The old Keeper hesitated for a long moment, then released the field, and the flickering light that had surrounded Dio for months vanished. Marguerida moved her hand across the body that rested there, seeming to be only asleep. Diotima looked worn and thin and older than her years. Her pale hair, once so lustrous, looked brittle and dry, and her fair, delicate skin lacked the suppleness Lew knew so well. He let his heart clench, let his fear consume him for a moment. How could he bear it if Marguerida failed and Dio died?

For several minutes nothing happened. Marguerida continued to examine Dio's form with her matrixed hand, occasionally looking to Mikhail in unverbalized consultation. He glanced at Liriel, who was monitoring his daughter, and Dio as well, and told himself that no harm could come to either of them. That was the theory, in any case. The only problem, Lew thought, was that he had never been much on theory.

If only he could do something! Lew's impatience was like a furious itching, as if his skin were on fire. What was taking so long? What was Marguerida *doing?* Why had he ever agreed to let her attempt this?

He watched his daughter hold her hand over Dio's chest, and saw the faint lines on her hand begin to brighten and then glow. Lew could see the shape of the shadow matrix clearly now. Then light began to pulse around her, until she was a shimmering figure in the dim light of the room. What? Then he saw that Mikhail was using his own powers to protect and support her. The two of them were working as one, and from the glimpse he had of Liriel's face, something quite remarkable was happening.

The illumination diminished as Marguerida stood upright, her face calm. She smiled at him reassuringly. Then Dio's eyelids fluttered, and he forgot everything else. He darted to the receptacle, his boots ringing a sharp tattoo on the stone floor.

Lew Alton bent over his wife, and watched her give a familiar feline yawn. She blinked a few times, and began to stretch her arms and legs sensuously, comfortably.

Dio opened her eyes and stared at him for a second, as if she did not know who he was. Then her luminous smile appeared, and she reached for his hand. Lew's heart thudded in his chest, and he could barely breathe for the joy that possessed him.

Lew closed his hand around hers, feeling the papery skin, and the blood pulsing beneath it. She swallowed and made a little face, as if she tasted something unpleasant. Then she whispered, her eyes round with wonder, "Oh, Lew! There was . . . such music!"